THE
ART
OF THE
STORY

THE
ART
OF THE
STORY

An International Anthology of
Contemporary Short Stories

edited by

DANIEL HALPERN

VIKING

VIKING
Published by the Penguin Group
Penguin Putnam Inc., 375 Hudson Street,
New York, New York 10014, U.S.A.
Penguin Books Ltd, 27 Wrights Lane, London W8 5TZ, England
Penguin Books Australia Ltd, Ringwood, Victoria, Australia
Penguin Books Canada Ltd, 10 Alcorn Avenue,
Toronto, Ontario, Canada M4V 3B2
Penguin Books (N.Z.) Ltd, 182–190 Wairau Road,
Auckland 10, New Zealand

Penguin Books Ltd, Registered Offices:
Harmondsworth, Middlesex, England

First published in 1999 by Viking Penguin,
a member of Penguin Putnam Inc.

1 3 5 7 9 10 8 6 4 2

PUBLISHER'S NOTE
These selections are works of fiction. Names, characters, places, and incidents either are
the product of the authors' imagination or are used fictitiously, and any resemblance
to actual persons, living or dead, business establishments, events, or locales is entirely
coincidental.

LIBRARY OF CONGRESS CATALOGING IN PUBLICATION DATA
The art of the story / edited by Daniel Halpern.
p.   cm.
ISBN 0-670-88761-7
1. Short stories.   2. Fiction—20th century.   I. Halpern, Daniel, date.
PN6120.2.A74   1999
808.83'01—dc21   99-13816

This book is printed on acid-free paper.
(∞)

Printed in the United States of America
Set in New Caledonia

for

LEA SIMONDS & STEPHEN GRAHAM
who believe in the art

Unlike the novel, a short story may be,
for all purposes, essential.

—*JORGE LUIS BORGES*

ACKNOWLEDGMENTS

In such an undertaking there are always many people to thank—without whose help many doors would have remained closed. To that end, I would like to thank for their generous involvement with this anthology: Aron Aji, Antonella Antonelli, Nicole Aragi, Maarten Asscher, Laurence Badot, Russell Banks, Lee Brackstone, Sam Boyce, Liz Calder, David Chestnut, Faith Hampton Childs, Andrej Codrescu, Andrew Coffey, Arnulf Conradi, Caroline Dawnay, Rikki Ducornet, Maria Enberg, Anne-Louise Fischer, Gary Fisketjon, Richard Ford, Carlos Fuentes, Jonathan Galassi, Georgia Garrett, Per Gedin, Ann Godoff, Harriet Goldman, Elise Simon Goodman, Gloria Goodman, Nadine Gordimer, Nan Graham, Jaco Groot, Petra Christina Hardt, Sloan Harris, Gerald Howard, Amy Hundley, Bruce Hunter, Victoria Hutchinson, Carol Janeway, Derek Johns, Diane Johnson, Philip Gwyn Jones, Patricia Kavanagh, Karen Kennerly, Caradoc King, Ursula Kohler, Ruth Lanna, Rika Lesser, Julian Loose, Sarah MacLachlan, Koukla MacLehose, Agneta Markas, Maria Massie, Peter Matson, Peg McColl, Fiona McCrae, Laura McDowell, Bruce R. McPherson, David Miller, Ravi Mirchandani, Susan Moldow, Geoff Mulligan, Michael Naumann, Joyce Carol Oates, Griselda Ohannessian, Tony Peake, Nicholas Pearson, Maggie Phillips, Tina Pohlman, Alexandra Pringle, Clare Reihill, Johannes Riis, Karen Rinaldi, Ray A. Roberts, Robin Robertson, Elisabeth Ruge, Heather Schroder, Dick Seaver, Andre Shiffrin, Elisabeth Sifton, Francesca Sintini, Susan Sontag, Jean Stein, Peter Straus, Robin Straus, Toru Tamaki, Amanda Urban, Harriet Wasserman, Phyllis Wender, Drenka Willen, Jeanne Wilmot, Octavia Wiseman, George Witte, and Bob Wyatt.

In particular, I want to thank Leigh Anne Couch, who helped in every imaginable way from the very start of this project, as well as Richard Abate, without whose tireless—and endless!—work this volume would have remained merely a good idea. And a special acknowledgment goes to Jean Stein's vision of *Grand Street*, which consistently publishes literature in translation and whose back issues proved an invaluable source of lesser-known international authors.

No anthology is complete without a heartfelt thanks to the in-house editors, for their patience, supportive interest, and input: Kathryn Court and Laurie Walsh, who worked with delicate touch and firm insight—and who believed from the start in the necessity of such a collection.

CONTENTS

PREFACE

It's been fifteen years since I began compiling *The Art of the Tale*, the predecessor to this collection of international short stories. That anthology included stories published after 1945, by writers born in the twentieth century (all but twelve before 1938, the cutoff for this book), with the exceptions of Jorge Luis Borges, Isak Dinesen, Yasunari Kawabata, and Vladimir Nabokov, each born within five years of this century. It was my goal then, as it is now, at the end of the twentieth century, to take a look at what writers are doing with the short story around the world.

When I queried the writers from the previous collection, the major influence, by a very large margin, were the stories of Anton Chekhov. The model for the *contemporary* story—at least for those included here—is different in a number of ways, as I think will be evident. Reading through the stories again, I find the work very much in sync with contemporary themes and modes of expression. These are stories sensitive to the moves of a popular culture that imprints with vigor something more current, more "of the moment" culturally, stories less in "the classical mode" and more *reactive* to the media in all its venues. These younger writers have distanced themselves—sometimes subtly, sometimes less so—from the influential writers practicing during the first two or three decades of the twentieth century, not to mention nineteenth-century models. This was not the case for the majority of writers, now over age sixty-five, from *The Art of the Tale*, who seem clearly to have emerged via their literary inheritance.

I began the current enterprise by considering well over three hundred writers born after 1932, relying heavily on a network of writers, editors, agents, and friends to suggest stories that might have escaped my attention. Unlike reading for the first anthology, where the established masters—Jorge Luis Borges, Paul Bowles, Italo Calvino, Flannery O'Connor, Vladimir Nabokov, R. K. Narayan, Isaac Bashevis Singer, William Trevor, John Updike, and Eudora Welty, to name a small handful of the worthy—were givens, I thought, foolishly perhaps, that finding as many as *fifty* writers from around the world who had produced some kind of accomplished body of work would be more difficult. So I initially set the birth date for inclusion at 1933. I was soon overwhelmed by the number of truly outstanding *contemporary* international practitioners of the short story, and in order to make sense of the selection—and at the same time produce a book under a thousand pages—I reluctantly raised the date for inclusion to writers born *after* 1937—that is, writers born between 1938 and 1970, the generation just overlapping the youngest writers in *The Art of the Tale*. Those cut by changing the date from 1933 to 1938 are central to the continuum, as I imagine it, staked out by these two anthologies and I would like to indulge myself by listing this group of writers here—after all, anthologies are very much about *lists*—while lamenting their absence from these pages: Jurek Becker (1937); Andrei Bitov (1937); A. S. Byatt (1936); Don DeLillo (1936); Anita Desai (1937); Andre Dubus (1936–1999); Gail Godwin (1937); Lars Gustafsson (1936); Jim Harrison (1937); Bessie Head (1937–1986); Danilo Kiš (1935–1989); Onat Kutlar (1936); José Luandino Vieira (1936); Vladimir Makanin (1937); David Malouf (1934); Norman Manea (1936); John McGahern (1934); Cees Nooteboom (1933); Kenzaburo Ōe (1934); E. Annie Proulx (1935); Thomas Pynchon (1937); Moacyr Scliar (1937); Carol Shields (1935); Robert Stone (1937); Soren Titel (1935); Göran Tunstrom (1937); Mario Vargas Llosa (1936).

And then there is the even more lamentable list of writers whose work I know and respect and *would* have included, were space not the restrictive issue. Although tempted, I'm not going to list these writers.

It's an imperfect world, and the world such an anthology can circumscribe and delineate is a world *confined,* at best. In gathering together this particular selection of international stories, I was able to locate writing that does not easily find its way into the hands of the general reader—especially the reader confined to English. These stories wander through a variety of modes, written by a group of disparate writers, schematizing their worlds in ways quite distant from each other.

Thirty-five countries are represented in *The Art of the Story*; there were twenty-six in *The Art of the Tale*. It drums the obvious to suggest that my goal was to represent each writer with the best story I could find, sometimes from a limited group of stories, given the vicissitudes of translation—ours being a country that does not happily support much in the way of translated literature. Of course, this was *the* issue with writers of other languages, as I was able to consider only work already translated into English.

I hope this new collection illustrates the depth and range and *health* of the short story, even though it is not currently the most fashionable genre among publishers—certainly we're not in a period any way similar to that initiated by the "sudden" discovery (we're also slow to recognize genius in our midst) of Raymond Carver's work, back in the late seventies. Notwithstanding what has already been said regarding influences, inherent throughout *The Art of the Story* is the quietly acknowledged art of the great practitioners of this genre, even if these younger writers feel less obligated to acknowledge that debt in any but the most oblique ways. Vulnerable to the dictates of what's here and now, they respond more readily to their own cultures than to any inherited literary tradition. There seems to be an investigative nature to the fiction of these stories written so close to the end of this century, a tendency, especially among writers from emerging nations, to use the story as a means of orientation, to restate for themselves their position—politically, socially, and artistically—as if for these writers there is radically less separation between reality and the imagination. It is by way of the short story that writers are able to define the world in which they find themselves, wherever (and whatever) that turns out to be.

The fiction you are about to read in these pages configures the extremes of human nature. The stories are narratives well told: documents of our condition, seemingly limitless in their array of setting, tone, dialogue, and method of storytelling. It is via this ancient genre that the human spirit finds voice in its many tongues.

—DANIEL HALPERN

THE
ART
OF THE
STORY

Ama Ata Aidoo

A Gift from Somewhere

(GHANA)

The Mallam had been to the village once. A long time ago. A long time ago, he had come to do these parts with Ahmadu. That had been his first time. He did not remember what had actually happened except that Ahmadu had died one night during the trip. Allah, the things that can happen to us in our exile and wanderings!

Now the village was quiet. But these people. How can they leave their villages so empty every day like this? Any time you come to a village in these parts in the afternoon, you only find the too young, the too old, the maimed and the dying, or else goats and chickens, never men and women. They don't have any cause for alarm. There is no fighting here, no marauding.

He entered several compounds which were completely deserted. Then he came to this one and saw the woman. Pointing to her stomach, he said, "Mami Fanti, there is something there." The woman started shivering. He was embarrassed.

Something told him that there was nothing wrong with the woman herself. Perhaps there was a baby? Oh Allah, one always has to make such violent guesses. He looked round for a stool. When he saw one lying by the wall, he ran to pick it up. He returned with it to where the woman was sitting, placed it right opposite her, and sat down.

Then he said, "Mami, by Allah, by his holy prophet Mohamet, let your heart rest quiet in your breast. This little one, this child, he will live . . ."

And she lifted her head which until then was so bent her chin touched her breasts, and raised her eyes to the face of the Mallam for the first time, and asked, "Papa Kramo, is that true?"

"Ah Mami Fanti," the Mallam rejoined. "Mm . . . mm," shaking awhile the forefinger of his right hand. This movement, accompanied simultaneously as it was by his turbanned head and face, made him look very knowing indeed.

"Mm . . . mm, and why must you yourself be asking me if it is true? Have I myself lied to you before, eh Mami Fanti?"

"Hmmmm. . . ." sighed she of the anxious heart. "It is just that I cannot find it possible to believe that he will live. That is why I asked you that."

His eyes glittered with the pleasure of his first victory and her heart did a little somersault.

"Mami Fanti, I myself, me, I am telling you. The little one, he will live. Now today he may not look good, perhaps not today. Perhaps even after eight days he will not be good but I tell you, Mami, one moon, he will be good . . . good . . . good," and he drew up his arms, bent them, contracted his shoulders and shook up the upper part of his body to indicate how well and strong he thought the child would be. It was a beautiful sight and for an instant a smile passed over her face. But the smile was not able to stay. It was chased away by the anxiety that seemed to have come to occupy her face forever.

"Papa Kramo, if you say that, I believe you. But you will give me something to protect him from the witches?"

"Mami Fanti, you yourself you are in too much hurry, and why? Have I got up to go?"

She shook her head and said "No" with a voice that quaked with fear.

"Aha . . . so you yourself you must be patient. I myself will do everything . . . everything. . . . Allah is present and Mohamet his holy prophet is here too. I will do everything for you. You hear?"

She breathed deeply and loudly in reply.

"Now bring to me the child." She stood up, and unwound the other cloth with which she had so far covered up her bruised soul and tied it around her waist. She turned in her step and knocked over the stool. The clanging noise did not attract her attention in the least. Slowly, she walked towards the door. The Mallam's eyes followed her while his left hand groped through the folds of his boubou in search of his last piece of cola. Then he remembered that his sack was still on his shoulder. He removed it, placed it on the floor and now with both his hands free, he fished out the cola. He popped it into his mouth and his tongue received the bitter piece of fruit with the eagerness of a lover.

The stillness of the afternoon was yet to be broken. In the hearth, a piece of coal yielded its tiny ash to the naughty breeze, blinked with its last spark and folded itself up in death. Above, a lonely cloud passed over the Mallam's turban, on its way to join camp in the south. And as if the Mallam had felt the motion of the cloud, he looked up and scanned the sky.

Perhaps it shall rain tonight? I must hurry up with this woman so that I can reach the next village before nightfall.

"Papa Kramo-e-e—!"

This single cry pierced through the dark interior of the room in which the child was lying, hit the aluminium utensils in the outer room, gathered itself together, cut through the silence of that noon, and echoed in the several corners of the village. The Mallam sprang up. "What is it, Mami Fanti?" And the two collided at the door to her rooms. But neither of them saw how she managed to throw the baby on him and how he came to himself sufficiently to catch it. But the world is a wonderful place and such things happen in it daily. The Mallam caught the baby before it fell.

"Look, look, Papa Kramo, look! Look and see if this baby is not dead. See if this baby too is not dead. Just look—o—o Papa Kramo, look!" And she started running up and down, jumping, wringing her hands and undoing the threads in her hair. Was she immediately mad? Perhaps. The only way to tell that a possessed woman of this kind is not completely out of her senses is that she does not unclothe herself to nakedness. The Mallam was bewildered.

"Mami Fanti, *hei*, Mami Fanti," he called unheeded. Then he looked down at the child in his arms.

Allah, tch, tch, tch. Now, O holy Allah. Now only you can rescue me from this trouble, since my steps found this house guided by the Prophet, but Allah, this baby is dead.

And he looked down again at it to confirm his suspicion.

Allah, the child is breathing but what kind of breath is this? I must hurry up and leave. Ah . . . what a bad day this is. But I will surely not want the baby to grow still in my arms! At all . . . for that will be bad luck, big bad luck. . . . And now where is its mother? This is not good. I am so hungry now. I thought at least I was going to earn some four pennies so I could eat. I do not like to go without food when it is not Ramaddan. Now look—and I can almost count its ribs! One, two, three, four, five. . . . And Ah . . . llah, it is pale. I could swear this is a Fulani child only its face does not show that it is. If this is the pallor of sickness . . . O Mohamet! Now I must think up something quickly to comfort the mother with.

"*Hei* Mami Fanti, Mami Fanti!"

"Papaa!"

"Come."

She danced in from the doorway still wringing her hands and sucking in the air through her mouth like one who had swallowed a mouthful of scalding-hot porridge.

"It is dead, is it not?" she asked with the courtesy of the insane.

"Mami, sit down."

She sat.

"Mami, what is it yourself you are doing? Yourself you make plenty noise. It is not good. Eh, what is it for yourself you do that?"

Not knowing how to answer the questions, she kept quiet. "Yourself, look well." She craned her neck as though she were looking for an object in a distance. She saw his breath flutter.

"Yourself you see he is not dead?"

"Yes," she replied without conviction. It was too faint a breath to build any hopes on, but she did not say this to the Mallam.

"Now listen Mami," he said, and he proceeded to spit on the child: once on his forehead and then on his navel. Then he spat into his right palm and with this spittle started massaging the child very hard on his joints, the neck, shoulder blades, ankles and wrists. You could see he was straining himself very hard. You would have thought the child's skin would peel off any time. And the woman could not bear to look on.

If the child had any life in him, surely, he could have yelled at least once more? She sank her chin deeper into her breast.

"Now Mami, I myself say, you yourself, you must listen."

"Papa, I am listening."

"Mami, I myself say, this child will live. Now himself he is too small. Yourself you must not eat meat. You must not eat fish from the sea, Friday, Sunday. You hear?" She nodded in reply. "He himself, if he is about ten years," and he counted ten by flicking the five fingers of his left hand twice over, "if he is about ten, tell him he must not eat meat and fish from the sea, Friday, Sunday. If he himself he does not eat, you Mami Fanti, you can eat. You hear?"

She nodded again.

"Now, the child he will live, yourself you must stop weeping. If you do that it is not good. Now you have the blue dye for washing?"

"Yes," she murmured.

"And a piece of white cloth?"

"Yes, but it is not big. Just about a yard and a quarter."

"That does not matter. Yourself, find those things for me and I will do something and your child he shall be good."

She did not say anything.

"Did you yourself hear me, Mami Fanti?"

"Yes."

"Now take the child, put him in the room. Come back, go and find all the things."

She took the thing which might once have been a human child but now was certainly looking like something else and went back with it to the room.

And she was thinking.

Who does the Mallam think he is deceiving? This is the third child to die. The others never looked half this sick. No! In fact the last one was fat. . . . I had been playing with it. After the evening meal I had laid him down on the mat to go and take a quick bath. Nothing strange in that. When I returned to the house later, I powdered myself and finished up the last bits of my toilet. . . . When I eventually went in to pick up my baby, he was dead.

. . . O my Lord, my Mighty God, who does the Mallam think he is deceiving?

And he was thinking.

Ah . . . llah just look, I cannot remain here. It will be bad of me to ask the woman for so much as a penny when I know this child will die. Ah . . . llah, look, the day has come a long way and I have still not eaten.

He rose up, picked up his bag from the ground and with a quietness and swiftness of which only a nomad is capable, he vanished from the house. When the woman had laid the child down, she returned to the courtyard.

"Papa Kramo, Papa Kramo," she called. A goat who had been lying nearby chewing the cud got up and went out quietly too.

"Kramo, Kramo," only her own voice echoed in her brain. She sat down again on the stool. If she was surprised at all, it was only at the neatness of his escape. So he too had seen death.

Should any of my friends hear me moaning, they will say I am behaving like one who has not lost a baby before, like a fresh bride who sees her first baby dying. Now all I must do is to try and prepare myself for another pregnancy, for it seems this is the reason why I was created . . . to be pregnant for nine of the twelve months of every year. . . . Or is there a way out of it at all? And where does this road lie? I shall have to get used to it. . . . It is the pattern set for my life. For the moment, I must be quiet until the mothers come back in the evening to bury him.

Then rewrapping the other cloth around her shoulders, she put her chin in her breast and she sat, as though the Mallam had never been there.

But do you know, this child did not die. It is wonderful but this child did not die. Mmm. . . . This strange world always has something to surprise us with . . . Kweku Nyamekye. Somehow, he did not die. To his day name Kweku, I have added Nyamekye. Kweku Nyamekye. For, was he not a gift from God through the Mallam of the Bound Mouth? And he, the Mallam of the Bound Mouth, had not taken from me a penny, not a single penny that ever bore a hole. And the way he had vanished! Or it was perhaps the god who yielded me to my mother who came to my aid at last? As he had promised her he would? I remember Maame telling me that when I was only a baby, the god of Mbemu from whom I came had promised never to desert me and that he would come to me once in my life when I needed him most. And was it not him who had come in the person of the Mallam? . . . But was it not strange, the way he disappeared without asking for a penny? He had not even waited for me to buy the things he had prescribed. He was going to make a charm. It is good that he did not, for how can a scholar go through life wearing something like that? Looking at the others of the Bound Mouth, sometimes you can spot familiar faces, but my Mallam has never been here again.

Nyamekye, hmm, and after him I have not lost any more children. Let me touch wood. In this world, it is true, there is always something somewhere, covered with leaves. Nyamekye lived. I thought his breathing would have stopped, by the time the old women returned in the evening. But it did not. Towards nightfall his colour changed completely. He did not feel so hot. His breathing improved and from then, he grew stronger every day. But if ever I come upon the Mallam, I will just fall down before him, wipe his tired feet with a silk kente, and then spread it before him and ask him to walk on it. If I do not do that then no one should call me Abena Gyaawa again.

When he started recovering, I took up the taboo as the Mallam had instructed. He is now going to be eleven years old I think. Eleven years, and I have never, since I took it up, missed observing it any Friday or Sunday. Not once. Sometimes I wonder why he chose these two days and not others. If my eyes had not been scattered about me that afternoon, I would have asked him to explain the reason behind this choice to me. And now I shall never know.

Yes, eleven years. But it has been difficult. Oh, it is true I do not think that I am one of these women with a sweet tooth for fish and meats. But if you say that you are going to eat soup, then it is soup you are going to eat. Perhaps no meat or fish may actually hit your teeth but how can you say any broth has soul when it does not contain anything at all? It is true that like everyone else, I liked kontomire. But like everyone else too, I ate it only when my throat ached for it or when I was on the farm. But since I took up the taboo, I have had to eat it at least twice two days of the week, Sunday and Friday. I have come to hate its deep-green look. My only relief came with the season of snails and mushrooms. But everyone knows that these days they are getting rarer because it does not rain as often as it used to. Then after about five years of this strict observance, someone who knew about these things advised me. He said that since the Mallam had mentioned the sea, at least I could eat freshwater fish or prawns and crabs. I did not like the idea of eating fish at all. Who can tell which minnow has paid a visit to the ocean? So I began eating freshwater prawns and crabs—but of course, only when I could get them. Normally, you do not get these things unless you have a grown-up son who would go trapping in the river for you.

But I do not mind these difficulties. If the Mallam came back to tell me that I must stop eating fish and meat altogether so that Nyamekye and the others would live, I would do it. I would. After all, he had told me that I could explain the taboo to Nyamekye when he was old enough to understand, so he could take it up himself. But I have not done it and I do not think I shall ever do it. How can a schoolboy, and who knows, one day he may become a real scholar, how can he go through life dragging this type of taboo along with him? I have never heard any scholar doing it, and my son is not going to be first to do it. No. I myself will go on observing it until I die. For, how could I have gone on living with my two empty hands?—I swear by everything, I do not understand people who complain that I am spoiling them, especially him. And anyway, is it any business of theirs? Even if I daily anointed them with shea-butter and placed them in the sun, whom would I hurt? Who else should be concerned apart from me?

But the person whose misunderstanding hurts me is their father. I do not know what to do. Something tells me it's his people and his wives who prevent him from having good thoughts about me and mine. I was his first wife and if you knew how at the outset of our lives, death haunted us, hmmm. Neither of us had a head to think in. And if things were what they should be, should he be behaving in this way? In fact, I swear by everything, he hates Nyamekye. Or how could what happened last week have happened?

It was a Friday and they had not gone to school. It was a holiday for them. I do not know what this one was for but it was one of those days they do not go. When the time came for us to leave for the farm, I showed him where food was and asked him to look after himself and his younger brother and sisters. Well my tongue was still moving when his father came in with his face shut down, the way it is when he is angry. He came up to us and asked "*Hei*, Nyamekye, are you not following your mother to the farm?" Oh, I was hurt. Is this the way to talk to a ten-year-old child? If he had been any other father, he would have said, "Nyamekye, since you are not going to school today, pick up your knife and come with me to the farm."

Would that not have been beautiful?

"Nyamekye, are you not following your mother to the farm?" As if I am the boy's only parent. But he is stuck with this habit, especially where I and my little ones are concerned.

"Gyaawa, your child is crying. . . . Gyaawa, your child is going to fall off the terrace if you do not pay more attention to him. . . . Gyaawa, your child this, and your child that!"

Anyway, that morning I was hurt and when I opened up my mouth, all the words which came to my lips were, "I thought this boy was going to be a scholar and not a farm-goer. What was the use in sending him to school if I knew he was going to follow me to the farm?"

This had made him more angry. "I did not know that if you go to school, your skin must not touch a leaf!"

I did not say anything. What had I to say? We went to the farm leaving Nyamekye with the children. I returned home earlier than his father did. Nyamekye was not in the house. I asked his brother and sisters if they knew where he had gone. But they had not seen him since they finished eating earlier in the afternoon. When he had not come home by five o'clock, I started getting worried. Then his father too returned from the farm. He learned immediately that he was missing. He clouded up. After he had had his bath, he went to sit in his chair, dark as a rainy sky. Then he got up to go by the chicken coop. I did not know that he was going to fetch a cane. Just as he was sitting in the chair again, Nyamekye appeared.

"*Hei*, Kweku Nyamekye, come here."

Nyamekye was holding the little bucket and I knew where he had been to. He moved slowly up to his father.

"Papa, I went to the river to visit my trap, because today is Friday."

"Have I asked you for anything? And your traps! Is that what you go to school to learn?"

And then he pulled out the cane and fell on the child. The bucket dropped and a few little prawns fell out. Something tells me it was the sight of those prawns which finished his father. He poured those blows on him as though he were made of wood. I had made up my mind never to interfere in any manner he chose to punish the children, for after all, they are his too. But this time I thought he was going too far. I rushed out to rescue Nyamekye and then it came, wham! The sharpest blow I have ever received in my life caught me on the inside of my arm. Blood gushed out. When he saw what had happened, he was ashamed. He went away into his room. That evening he did not eat the fufu I served him.

Slowly, I picked up the bucket and the prawns. Nyamekye followed me to my room where I wept.

The scar healed quickly but the scar is of the type which rises so anyone can see it. Nyamekye's father's attitude has changed towards us. He is worse. He is angry all the time. He is angry with shame.

But I do not even care. I have my little ones. And I am sure someone is wishing she were me. I have Nyamekye. And for this, I do not even know whom to thank.

Do I thank you, O Mallam of the Bound Mouth?

Or you, Nana Mbemu, since I think you came in the person of the Mallam?

Or Mighty Jehovah-after-whom-there-is-none-other, to you alone should I give my thanks?

But why should I let this worry me? I thank you all. Oh, I thank you all. And you, our ancestral spirits, if you are looking after me, then look after the Mallam too. Remember him at meals, for he is a kinsman.

And as for this scar, I am glad it is not on Nyamekye. Any time I see it I only recall one afternoon when I sat with my chin in my breast before a Mallam came in, and after a Mallam went out.

Hanan Al-Shaykh

The Keeper of the Virgins

(LEBANON)

One of the women wondered aloud if he was a dwarf in every way. The other women sitting at the intersection burst out laughing. Even though they prayed to God to forgive them, their laughter grew louder before the dwarf was out of sight.

They had grown used to seeing him every morning shortly after they set to work, bending over the hibiscus bushes to gather the wine-colored blossoms. He would go by with a confident step, heading for the convent, where the pure ones lived, books and magazines tucked under his arm, a cloth bundle containing his food for the day held firmly in his hand. He was content to greet the hibiscus pickers as he passed, although they welcomed him enthusiastically and offered him a glass of tea or some warm bread. He knew it was because he was a dwarf and they felt sorry for him, but he had a great sense of his own importance. Besides keeping up with the politics of his own country and the Arab world in general, he had broadened his interests to take in the whole planet. He studied thoroughly and remembered everything he learned, delved into dictionaries, read novels, both translated and local, and underlined passages in pencil when the subject matter appealed to him or he liked the sound of the words. He wrote poetry and prose, and sent it to newspapers and magazines, even though not a single line of it had ever been published; and he had been going to the convent and waiting by the main gates in its outer wall for a year or more.

He would sit in the generous shade of a sycamore tree or lie on a blanket he had brought with him beneath its spreading branches, staring at the convent walls. He had learned the shape of their dusty red stones by heart; their uneven surfaces and the way they were arranged reminded him of a tray of the vermicelli pastries called *kunafa*. He spent these long stretches of time either reading, sometimes to himself and sometimes out loud, or building a fire with a few sticks to make tea, or waiting for the hoopoe, which appeared out of nowhere from the direction of the trees and the water or from the bare, stony desert. Every now and then he would stare hard at the iron gates of the convent, hearing some kind of a commotion on the other side. But he was convinced that it was a figment of his imagination because the place was always calm and still again at once, as if there had been no interruption.

But as the days went by he discovered from one of the men building the nearby tombs, who sat and chatted with him for a while each evening, that the noise he heard was real enough, as the nuns used to sweep the convent yard every now and then. This ruined his concentration for some considerable length of time: he could not read with such enthusiasm, or savor a choice sentence or the hot sweetness of a glass of tea or the food he brought with him. He became entirely focused on the iron gates, as if by staring at them he could melt them and make them collapse before his eyes.

During his first few weeks of frequenting the monastery, he had tried to have a conversation with the nuns to persuade them to open the gate, but each time his request had been refused in dumb silence. He had asked if he could sweep the yard for nothing, worship in the church, confess, but still he met with no response from behind the closed gates. Gradually he became convinced that everybody had joined forces to concoct a lie about the existence of this convent, because he was a dwarf, and he knew very well what people thought about dwarves. They were all lying to him: the tomb builders, the hibiscus women, his family, the wind, which must have cooperated with them by making some noise behind the abandoned gates; Georgette's mother, who had lamented long and loud because her daughter had joined the pure ones and their door had closed behind her, never to open again.

Georgette's family must be hiding the truth. Georgette must have gone mad and been locked away, for just before the rumor went around that she had entered the convent, she would only leave the house to walk over thorns until her feet bled.

The dwarf became convinced that many people profited from his visits to the convent. His mother regularly rose at dawn to get his food ready, as if he had a job to go to. His younger brother must have heaved a sigh of relief at this new routine of his, for however much he might love the dwarf, he had to be forced to let him participate in his nights out with his friends. They all used to sit in the dwarf's presence as if they were on eggs, wary of any joke or chance phrase that might offend him or hurt his feelings. Still, he couldn't remember his brother ever praising him for his determination when he saw him preparing to go to the convent, nor even the hibiscus women, who must have relished the chance to invent hilarious, irreverent stories about him. And what did the tomb builders think of him? He couldn't bear to let these thoughts torment him anymore, and hurried resolutely to bang on the gates with his giant hands. As usual, he asked for Georgette. He wanted to see her, to thank her for the affection she had heaped on him. Time stood still and he felt as if all the power in his body was in his huge, solid fist with its wide-apart fingers. As he was about to start hammering on the gates again, he heard a soft voice whispering to him that Georgette said hello but seeing her was out of the question.

From that moment on he began to have a fixation about the convent. The iron gates, bolted and barred, had an obsessive hold over him. Georgette's mother had wailed that she would never see her daughter again even when she died. How did they exist in there for all those years without being tempted to step over the threshold for a moment?

The gates, unmoved by his devotion to them, had opened a few times when he was not there; he had discovered their treachery by looking for evidence each morning, and had found tire tracks made by cars, trucks and mule-drawn carts. He brought his face close to the ground to find out whether the gates had been opened wide or only on one side, biting his lip in remorse because he had missed a chance to see the pure ones as they opened the gates and took the things and paid for them. Where did they get the money from?

As time passed, the dwarf grew ever more obsessed with the convent and its inhabitants. He no longer tried to explain it, and those who saw him waiting regularly at the gates ceased to worry about him. No doubt they told themselves that it was something to do with the way dwarves looked at things, and their different mentality.

Then one night the dwarf failed to return home. His mother wept loudly, blaming herself for not stopping his visits to the convent before. She was sure that a wild animal had blocked his path and eaten him in one mouthful. His brother suspected that a group of acrobats had kidnapped him and taken him to the city to train him to work in the circus.

He set off for the convent at high speed. He passed the hibiscus gatherers and they directed him to it. One of them winked at him, so he thought better of asking if they had seen the dwarf. The moment he stood before the gates he was seized by a violent sense of apprehension. One last grain of hope had remained, but there was no sign of the dwarf, only the tree and the blanket that he had hung over a branch and the stone where he used to sit; a few empty soap-powder cartons, which had been blown up against the walls; and crushed and broken coffins, some lined with black material and emblazoned with white crosses. The wind whistled and in the distance he could see the builders at work on new tombs. He shouted his brother's name and was answered by silence. He began to blame himself. He had known that his brother was running away from reality by taking refuge at the convent, making everyone think that he was strong enough to do the daily round-trip on foot, about four hours in all, so that he could come home proud of having had some adventures.

Adventures? The roads were always the same: deserted, except for stretches of date palms, canals and the sounds of frogs croaking and an occasional donkey braying.

The brother stumbled hurriedly over the remains of human bones and crumbling skulls and entered a burial chamber with no roof or doors. He read on its whitewashed walls, "Remember, O Lord, your obedient servant"; "Remember, O Lord, your erring servant"; "Remember, O Lord, your righteous servant, your repentant servant." Suddenly he burst into tears, mortified that deep down inside he had blessed his brother's daily visits to the convent. He had not wanted it to be known that he was the dwarf's brother, that he lived under the same roof as the dwarf. He rushed outside and over to the tomb builders. One of them was painting a tomb a reddish-brown color and he asked him if he had seen the dwarf. The man pointed toward the convent. He turned and ran back and pounded on the iron gates, calling out the dwarf's name. To his astonishment he heard his voice: "Yes?"

"Thank God you're safe," he said, crying tears of joy. "Come on, let's go home, or your mother will do herself mischief."

"Don't worry," replied the dwarf. "Tell her that I've become the nuns' watchman. I'm happy. Don't worry."

The dwarf had only gained access to the convent by jumping in. Not by bouncing in off a springy bedstead, an idea he had quickly banished from his mind, nor by piling the wrecked coffins one on top of another. Instead he had jumped onto the shoulders of the Lord Bishop, who had come from the city to pay his annual visit to the convent with several crates of luggage. The dwarf had planned for this moment for a long time during his vigils by the gate. He didn't know where he had found the courage, agility and speed of thought that had enabled him to leap out as soon as he heard the car engine and alight on the hood before it stopped, like a winged insect, then jump on the Lord Bishop and relieve him of one of the crates and rush off with it, his heart beating with almost unbearable ferocity. He hurried disbelievingly through the open gates into the courtyard. To force himself to take in what was happening, he stood stock-still at the gates once they had been closed again, seeing them from the inside for the first time. He was certain that they would be opened again shortly and he would be hurled back outside. But things no longer hinged on him. It was as if he had disappeared from sight. The nuns began to gather around in their white habits and crowns of artificial flowers, bowing their heads before the Lord Bishop, who looked like a big black bird, and bending over to kiss his hand.

They were like brides, some of them extremely young and pretty. As they stood in line, their heads drooping bashfully, they resembled a row of beautiful narcissus. For a few moments the dwarf felt embarrassed and scared. He tried to suppress his breathing, which had suddenly become audible. Then he found the Lord Bishop was looking at him. "Is this the one?" he was asking.

One of them, the senior nun, answered him humbly, but with affection, "Yes, My Lord."

Turning back to him the bishop said, "The nuns have told me about you. You have been blessed. You will watch over them."

The dwarf felt awkward in the bishop's presence. He didn't know how to answer him. He had been immensely curious to see what was behind the gates; it was like the time he split a battery in two to see what was inside it. And now the bishop was offering him a job as a handyman to the pure ones, and he found himself agreeing to stay in the convent and oversee the cultivation of the fruit and vegetables, without giving the matter more than a moment's thought.

He hadn't imagined the convent would be like this. It bore no relation to its outer walls and to the countryside around it, which was all sand, and the color of sand. The dwarf developed an attachment to the colors in the convent in his early days there. Some of them he was seeing for the first time, sculpted on the walls, or in paintings of animals, bats, angels, flowers, and women holding drums and wearing ornate brocade dresses, flying through the skies or in boats on the sea, with lances and daggers and swords in the background. Then gradually his eyes grew accustomed to the darkness, and he began to see clearly and especially to notice how the nuns lit up the place in their white clothes.

A week went by and the dwarf still hadn't guessed which was Georgette, because they all looked the same. Humbly, they took turns to kneel and pray before the statue of the crucified Christ until their eyes were almost as big as goose eggs. They didn't leave the statue alone day or night, massaging its feet with rose water, putting compresses soaked with oil and perfume on the nails of the crucifix, lighting candles, burning incense, and raising their voices in sweet, sorrowful chanting. They dedicated themselves to their love so whole-heartedly that he once had the feeling that all they did was hover in the air awaiting their turn to cling to the figure on the cross for a few moments before going back to their places. He didn't know why, on a certain day, they brought in a doll and dipped it in water, praying all the time, then rubbed it with col-ored stones that gave off an enticing fragrance, dried it with an embroidered cloth and dressed it in white baby clothes, which they had taken from a cloth bag studded with precious stones and tied with ropes of pearls.

They were eaten up heart and soul with their love for Christ. This was true love, the like of which he had never found in any novel, translated or other-wise. Never before had he encountered such passion and devotion. Was this what they called sacrifice? The dwarf checked himself. Of course. They had sacrificed the world and their families for the sake of this love, or for the sake of competing for this love. Closing his eyes, he decided to respond to their love, to help them realize that Christ knew about them and the way they showed their love for him. Moreover, Christ had sent the dwarf as a messen-ger to them. Wasn't that what the old nun had said? He would help those who were waiting their turn to love Christ by doing their embroidery with them, or by changing the linen in the church. He would snatch the washing out of the boiling water to save them from having to do it. He would have liked to hang it up to dry in the scorching sun, but he wasn't tall enough to reach the washing line. He would light the coals and fan them until they were glowing embers and load them into the flatiron. He would plant flowers and pick them for the garlands they wore on their heads, so that they didn't have to use artificial flowers. He would feed the hens with grain day and night until they were bursting with health and well-being and laid the choicest eggs in the country. He'd polish the nuns' shoes until they could see their faces in them. He'd make their mud-brick beds for them and be close to their sheets—for Christ must smell that they were clean.

At this the dwarf halted his flow of enthusiasm and supressed the leap in his heart, as he did every time he heard the rustle of their bare feet on the cool-ness of the earth floor. He closed his eyes firmly as if this also closed his ears and steadied his heartbeat, which broke away from its usual rhythm at these unpredictable thoughts.

After a few months the dwarf found that he had become quite used to these expectant brides of Christ as they moved around him holding whispered conversations, sighing gently, smiling at him, and not concealing their bad moods in his presence. It was as if he had become one of them, and what was more he had pledged himself to the virgins, swearing that nothing would separate him from them but death. When he died he would put their love to the test. They would either return him to his family or put him in the burial chamber, where he had gone one day with the senior nun to help her sweep the floor. He wouldn't have been able to see anything, but the old woman had lit a little candle and held it up to a casket on a high wooden shelf and raised the lid. He gasped in fright at the sight of a bony frame. The ribs were plainly visible and some flesh still clung around the hands. He heard the old nun's voice whispering, "You shouldn't be frightened. You were sent to us by the Lord."

And so it was. The dwarf only looked at the iron gates occasionally, when he heard his mother's cough and knew that she still had not lost hope. At first this caused him pain, especially when he pictured her sitting on the stone where he had sat. He heard his brother calling him day after day, banging on the gates, urging him to come home. But the dwarf followed instructions, did not reply and turned back to his work. He was growing used to this obligatory link being severed, so that he could concentrate on what he wanted and not let the vibrations from the trivia of the outside world intrude and confuse him. However, when he pictured his mother and his brother taking turns to sit on the stone, he couldn't help thinking of the hoopoe and wondering whether it came to them as it used to come to him, from the direction of the green trees and the canal, or from the barren land, looking for bread crumbs.

Translated from the Arabic by Catherine Cobham

Julia Alvarez

Amor Divino

(UNITED STATES)

The tiny great-granddaughter wants to visit Papito and give him today's kisses. She keeps tugging at Yolanda's hand. "Let's go comb his hair," she pleads. "Let's go give him a drink of water." She thinks of the doddering old man in his wheelchair as a human-size doll she can play with, but since she's not allowed over to the little house by herself, she has to get her aunt to take her.

Papito lives with a crew of around-the-clock maids who have been taught CPR by one of the aunts and pronounced nurses. In their starched uniforms and white oxfords, they look the part, but turn your back on them, and they are cooking sweet beans in the kitchen or watching soaps on the old man's TV or reading the paper that is still delivered every day as if Don Edmundo were not blind, and almost deaf, and completely out of it. Every time Yolanda crosses over, there's a scramble to posts. It gives her a charge to think of her old grandfather, the big man in his time, now surrounded by native women rolling their hair in his presence and singing merengues out loud.

Yolanda has been going over there often, and not just at the great-granddaughter's request. She has come down for one of those quickie divorces you can get in twenty-four hours, but some major battles have been fought long distance over the telephone. There is no privacy at any of the other houses, and so often during this trip, Yolanda has come to have her shouting matches in Papito's house. The one phone is in the day room where the old man sits dozing in front of the television. The maids turn down the volume out of courtesy to the doña on the phone, but they keep watching their TV soap or glance surreptitiously at the live soap of Yolanda arguing in English with her soon to be ex-husband.

"I did not say that. What a jerky thing to say!" Yolanda accuses him. She has reached John at his office in San Francisco where he prefers not to be called for disagreeable things. "It doesn't have to be disagreeable. It's you who are so damn —" Yolanda stops herself. There are limits in front of other people.

The appliances in her grandfather's house have not been updated for twenty years—since he and her grandmother took sick and left the big house for this handy little one at the edge of the compound. The black rotary phone sits like the judge in his black robes at the palace of justice where she spent the afternoon. Before the divorce can be finalized, another affidavit is required from Yolanda's husband renouncing all rights accruing to the de la Torre or García name in perpetuity. This is a precaution that Yolanda's uncle lawyer has taken in case this man is some sort of scoundrel. Who knows, they all liked him well enough, but here's their childless niece divorcing him within five years of the marriage. The only reason for a woman to do such a thing is if the man has proven that he is not a man. Can't deliver the goods. And they have heard things about San Francisco. Anyhow, the paper must be signed for the safety of the clan.

"I don't want your fucking money!" John is saying. His British accent makes the expletive all the more shocking, as if he has had to stoop much more than an American to use such language.

"I don't have any money." They both know she is as poor as a church mouse now that she has left him, but there is a supposed share in some family fortune that will come to her in the future if all the right people die off. "In fact, I don't give a damn about their damn money. But it's a requirement of the laws in this country."

"Laws—ee-God! What laws?! The place is a zoo. Shall I remind you, my dear, that there was a coup the day we were married."

"I'll ask you please not to name-call my native land, if you don't mind." This is ridiculous, Yolanda is thinking. What have we come to?

And of course, he is right but she does not want to be reminded. The tanks rolled out onto the streets the morning of the wedding, trapping them in the compound with the twenty-pound wedding cake across town at the baker's and the flowers wilting in the national cathedral. So as not to disappoint the bride and groom, an uncle persuaded a General friend to come out of one of the army tanks and marry them under martial law in the orchid garden in back of the grandfather's house. The grandfather, who still had his wits about him, gave Yolanda away since her father was stranded at the airport. But the grandmother was not as cooperative. She sat by, looking grim in a pink chiffon gown held together with safety pins hidden by the shawl draped over the back of the wheelchair. She threw her handful of rice out of turn and petted Yolanda as she was saying, *si*, she was taking John Merriweather, the third, to be her lawful husband. Before the year was out, the grandmother would be dead.

Yolanda still kicks herself on her bad planning. She missed out on a big church wedding, pew on pew of uncles, aunts, cousins, a momentous sense of adding a new branch to the family tree. Only a totally Americanized Dominican would plan her wedding the day after elections! Invariably there is a coup or revolt or some sort of incident. But then, why hadn't her family advised her differently? She can guess why. They had been so relieved that the crazy Yolanda was finally going to settle down with a decent man that they were not about to suggest any delays.

"I don't wish to continue this conversation," John is saying. "I've already told you I want an American divorce. I don't trust any manifestos, declarations, or documents from there."

She remembers, in fact, that when they got back to the States, John insisted on a civil ceremony in case the martial one hadn't been legal. "It's all your fault, you know. If you hadn't married us twice, we could just tear up our Dominican license and call it a day."

There is a pained silence at the other end. Of course, it would never have been that easy to part. "Hardly," is all he says, and her heart goes out to him. But then, more dogmatically, the John she finds so impossible to love concludes, "This has gone on long enough. My answer is no. N.O." The simple word spelled out, just like her mother used to do, insulting not just her will but her intelligence.

"Why can't you just sign the goddamn paper?" She is close to tears with frustration, with wanting him against all the hard evidence of years of not agreeing on anything. "Why do you have to make it so hard for me! Damn you, damn you!"

She sees the grandfather's head jerk up. Maybe he is not so deaf. He has heard something and his face is a mask of pain. *"Ay, ay, ay!"* he calls out.

She lays the receiver carefully on its cradle, almost as if to prove to the maids that she is in control of the situation. But of course, she is sobbing, and now, not just because of the distressing call with John, but because she has upset the grandfather.

She goes to him, puts her head on his lap. "It's okay, Papito, it's okay." If he could only comfort her, but what can this drooling, bleary-eyed old man offer her but the terrible image of what lies ahead? His hand goes up as if he were about to smooth the wrinkles from her forehead, but in fact, he is reaching for the handkerchief in his right pocket. The lieutenant, it is called. The one in his left pocket is called the lady. "Why?" Yolanda has asked Milagros, the oldest and most responsible of the nurses.

"Just Don Edmundo's way to be romántico, I suppose."

"Ay Dios, ay Dios mío." He is dabbing at the phlegm in his eyes. Is he crying, Yolanda wonders. Perhaps the violent arguments over the phone have reminded him of his own losses. "In some ways, God is kind," one aunt has noted about Papito's senility. "At least, he doesn't know Mamita is gone." But Yolanda is sure that the old man yearns for his young bride, his beautiful wife, all the faces of a great love that is legendary in the family.

"Papito," she has to shout so he hears perhaps a semblance of her voice. He nods violently up and down like a horse being reined. "Papito, it's me, Yolanda!"

"Yolanda," Milagros confirms. "Yolanda, your granddaughter, the poetess, the daughter of your daughter, Laura, the nervous one. Yolanda, who married the Englishman."

Yolanda winces, still it will not do to try to update the complicated family tree that's hard enough for even a sound memory to keep straight. So many names are repeated generation to generation: Yolanda, for instance, shares her name with two cousins and now three little nieces—all of them named after the grandmother, Yolanda Laura María. To help the grandfather out, everyone in the family has had to be reduced to an appropriate epithet. Yolanda, the poet. Carmencita, who plays the flute. Mundín with the freckles. But in the last year, many of those names and epithets have been washed away, and only with constant repetition does the grandfather sometimes dimly recall the person in question. Suddenly, his face will light up, his nods become measured, intelligent. Yes, yes, of course he remembers. But there is no such recognition at the moment.

"He is tired," Milagros apologizes for him. "He did not sleep well last night."

"Why?" Yolanda turns to the grandfather, "Eh, Papito? Why didn't you sleep well?" It seems rude not to include him in a discussion of his tedious days and nights.

"He wakes up and wants me to speak to him in English. And what can I do, Doña Yolanda? I don't know how to speak in English. So, he gets very upset and what Don Edmundo never did in his whole life, he loses his temper. He calls me names." She shakes her head.

"He doesn't mean it, Milagros, you know he doesn't mean it."

But the older woman is tearful. She has been with the family forever, and she has a grievance. "What he never did in his whole life, Don Edmundo, he calls me a slut."

"Ay, Milagros, I'm sorry." Yolanda squeezes the woman's shoulder. "Next time, wake me up, please. I'll speak to him in English."

She takes her grandfather's hand. The skin is cool and moist and does not feel fully human. She wonders if he is lonely, if that is why he—like she—is not sleeping well. Maybe he is missing the grandmother. She knew English. She would have been able to oblige him in that as well as in other things.

"Papito, want to speak English?" Yolanda asks him now. Maybe he can get this odd craving out of his system before nightfall. "My name is Yolanda. I'm your granddaughter. Yolanda, the poet."

He stops his drastic nods and listens attentively. "Sí, sí, sí," he says finally in Spanish. There is strength in his old hand now. "Yolanda, la poetisa, sí, sí, sí."

She feels a surge of joy. She has made contact with the old man. Damn John and the whole sorry mess they are in!

"Shall I recite for you?" Yolanda does not wait for an answer. That was always her part—why she got the poet epithet. She begins his favorite one:

> Amor, divino tesoro
> Ya te vas para no volver . . .

The cook comes out of the kitchen; the young, sassy cleaning maid is leaning against the door of the bedroom. "Echale, Doña Yolanda," she says. "What pretty sentiments."

As a child, she would be marched out in front of the grandparents and their company, in a dress she was only willing to put on for the occasion, tomboy that she was, to recite bits of poems that the grandfather had taught her. Of course, only later, when she studied literature, did she find out that many of these poems were grossly misquoted. The old man never had much of a memory, even as a young man. That's why he entrusted his poetry to his granddaughter. His favorite, for instance, the one she has just recited, should really be addressed to Youth, divine treasure. But the grandfather mixed up Youth with Love, so it is *Amor, divino tesoro,* that is now leaving, never to return.

"You like that one, don't you, Papito?" she asks him now.

"*Amor, divino tesoro,*" he begins, but his memory can't take him any further than that.

Still, it is an achievement that will be bruited about the compound for the next week. Yolanda has gotten the old man to recite poetry. What is discussed in quieter tones is the problem with the papers that have not arrived from San Francisco. The divorce can't go through until all the forms have been signed—and it's not just the release on property that hasn't been returned, but the no-contest form, the proxy form for the court's lawyer representing the husband, the proof of British citizenship. Perhaps the Englishman doesn't really want a divorce, for why wouldn't he cooperate in this effortless proce- dure that won't cost him anything? Is she sure this divorce is mutual or has she flown off the handle again as she used to when she was a child? "I am very sure," Yolanda is willing to swear on any of their rosaries. She puts as much certainty in her voice as she can muster. "It's over. We don't love each other anymore."

The aunts shake their heads sadly. "But is that any reason to divorce? Love, after all, comes and goes in a marriage."

And the days come and go, and the papers do not come. Yolanda is deter- mined not to call John again. Instead, she writes him an express letter. *Please, for the love of what we had, let's just get this over and done with. You know what will happen if I come back and we go through a divorce there. We will end up hating each other.*

Or worse, she thinks. We will end up back together again, making a go of it. Miserable but married, like so many of these aunts, she thinks. Or like— though no one is supposed to remember what happened since it has all been plastered over with the legend of their great love—like her grandfather in his last few years with the grandmother.

They were a great match—the family was so pleased—the wayward niece, her head filled with crazy ideas—what came of sending the girls away to American schools!—and the young dapper businessman with his head screwed on right, newly arrived in the States from Britain. "With titles," Yolanda's mother raised her eyebrows significantly.

"It's not titles, Mami, he has a number after his name. The English are more efficient than we are if they're going to keep repeating a name genera- tion to generation."

Still, it was titles for the mother, titles in the British accent, titles in the way John was so reasonable and could talk her high-strung daughter into settling down, cutting her hair, dressing in outfits, eating meals instead of just snacks out of boxes and cans. He would provide the solidity, and she would be the breath of fresh air, breezes blowing in from the garden, the piano in the parlor, the sweetness and light of the union. All well and good, Yolanda thinks, but that's not what happened in the marriage.

If Yolanda were to pick the painting that best represents her struggles with John, it would be a Chagall they once saw together when they were visiting her parents in New York. The young woman was flying up into the sky and the groom was holding her by the ankles, trying to pull her back down. Or was he hoping to be lifted up into that starry sky? She had put the question to John as they stood in front of the painting. What did he think was going on?

"It's a painting, not a bloody psychological test," he had mocked, his hand at her back, ready to escort her to the next painting. Personal questions embarrassed him, particularly personal questions asked in public places.

But she had dug her heels in and persisted. "Ah, come on. What do you think—is he going up or is she coming down."

"Joe-land-er," he chided. He never could get her name right. "That's enough, really."

"But why can't you play with me? Why can't you just guess what you think is going on between them?" Her voice had that teary, antagonistic tone. Now people were looking.

"They're headed for a big fight, if you ask me," he had hissed at her. And then, turning abruptly, he had proceeded to the next painting by himself. She could see it was another Chagall, the girl completely airborne by now. She could not make out what the man was doing from her vantage point. Stubbornly, she stood in front of her own painting, arms folded, and waited until he had left the room before bursting into tears. They were always having these silly fights. They could never agree on anything.

But still they clung to each other. For three years they had lived together on and off—John putting up with all the travesty of pretending he had his own apartment, since her family would have disowned her if she had told them she was shacking up with a man. But San Francisco was across the country from New York and almost across the world from the Island, and the red phone was always answered by Yolanda. Finally, they had decided either to tie the knot or make a clean break of it since they were getting on in years and both imagined they wanted a family. That would have been the moment, Yolanda sees it now, to take stock and cut the cord. But instead they had married.

And now in the warm safety of the compound, she can see why she made the choice she did: she was marrying her family! After all her mistakes and craziness, the way back home was through a man who would fit into the clan—instead of the hippie boyfriends who lectured her uncles about multinational corporations and the military industrial complex. John golfed with the cousins and took long rides in the countryside with the grandfather, plotting the location for a plant they were going to build to manufacture again the old family tiles the grandfather's sons had already ruled were no longer cost-efficient to produce. But John had calculated a way to make them cheaply. She loved that about him—John would always find a way. And the old grandfather had come to life again—the forgetfulness seemingly put aside except for brief spells that were chalked off as the bad memory of old age. He loved those drives in the country with John. "My two favorite men," Yolanda had laughed.

But she knew that mostly the grandfather was wanting to get out of the house to avoid the grandmother. She was on the warpath those last years. He had tricked her. He had brought her to live in the compound when she had wanted to spend her old age spreading her wings in the apartment she had talked him into buying in New York. There, she could drink and gamble and eat what she wanted to her heart's content. Here, everything she did was monitored by members of the family and the small watchful army of nursemaids.

Daily, one could hear her howls of fury coming from the little house, her voice yelling vulgarities at him, and the old man pleading, "Yolanda, please, I beg of you. Yolanda, try to control yourself, please, for the love of God."

Not for the love of God and not for the great love there had been between them would the grandmother put aside her anger toward him. One time she accused him of sleeping with his nurse and cut up his bedsheets with a butter knife. "I'm an eighty-year-old with one foot in the grave," the grandfather reasoned with her. "You've still got your pistol, don't you?" the grandmother snapped, grabbing for his crotch. On another occasion—though it was hotly debated whether or not the grandmother knew what she was doing—she had put rat poison in his food because he would not let her send the chauffeur for a bottle of rum. Thank God the cook had caught her or it would have been the grandfather preceding the grandmother to the grave.

John had tried to intervene, but the grandmother had looked him squarely in the eye: "You're not the first cock in the barnyard, you hear me! And you're not going to be the last."

John had been insulted, but Yolanda had laughed. "How the hell has she figured my life out?" she wondered. All the stories of Yolanda's and her sisters' misadventures had been kept from the old people. Sometimes, catching that wild look in the gray eyes, Yolanda could see why she had been named after her grandmother. She, too, had that crazy yearning to let loose and fly up beyond the reach of her husband, her bossy children, the vigilante nursemaids, the little house, the doll-size life. No wonder she had pelted Yolanda with rice just before the exchange of vows at the wedding. The old woman had foreseen that the rather formal, young Englishman was not suited for her granddaughter who had her naughty blood coursing through her veins.

"Not yet," the aunts had said, holding her fist closed so she wouldn't throw any more rice. When the ceremony was over, they let her hand go. "Now, Mamita, now it's time."

"It's too late," the grandmother had said glumly and thrown the rice in spite at the General.

Yolanda crosses over to the grandfather's house, this time legitimately to visit the old man. The great-granddaughter skips at her side, little Yolanda, the seventh, or whatever number Yolanda they are up to by now in the family. "We might not be able to stay long," Yolanda prepares the child. Papito has not been feeling well. He seems even more lost than usual in the coils of his memory. The nurses have to remind him to chew the food in his mouth, and then, of course, to swallow it.

Little Yolanda has brought her beach pail along, for she means to wash Papito's feet. "Maybe I will just wipe his mouth with the lieutenant," she tells herself, then looks up at her aunt to see if that will be all right.

Yolanda has to smile. If she and John had gotten along, they could have had a little treasure of a girl like this. Yolanda, the eighth, combing their hair and wiping their drooling mouths in old age. There are pluses to keeping an alliance going. Love is not the only lovely outcome of a marriage.

Already from this distance, Yolanda can hear the commotion of Milagros waking the grandfather from his nap. "*Buenas tardes,* Don Edmundo. I said, BUENAS TARDES. Yes, it's afternoon, it's quarter to four. Yes, QUARTER TO FOUR, in the afternoon, yes. Don Edmundo. Your name is Don Edmundo, no I'm sure it's Edmundo, after your father Edmundo Antonio, yes."

Yolanda looks down at the great-granddaughter. Maybe they should cancel this visit. But the little girl is swinging her beach pail, ready to wash the old man's feet and play with the handkerchiefs in his pockets. She seems unaffected by the shouting. After all, she too sometimes has to be reminded that it's bedtime, that she must chew her sweet plantain instead of gulping it down.

As they approach the house, servants begin to pour out of the different entrances: the chauffeur who was using the phone, the maids from the aunts' houses who come over here to wash their hair at the spare shower, the gardener taking lottery bets. "It's just us!" Yolanda feels like calling out.

Inside, Milagros is still trying to convince Papito that his name is Edmundo and that yes, he did marry. But the grandfather protests angrily. How can he have been married when he is just a boy in short pants, when they only recently put his mother in the ground? Milagros looks over at Yolanda and mouths, "He is misremembering Doña Yolanda's death."

"Let it be," Yolanda advises. What does it matter? The gossamer web of births and marriages, the fragile filaments of vows and hopes and fears that connect them into a family have already been torn from his memory. Let him be a little boy. A playmate for his great-granddaughter.

Little Yolanda meanwhile has climbed up on her great-grandfather's lap and tugged the handkerchief out of his left pocket. "Papito, here is the lady. She wants to wipe your mouth."

Yolanda feels her heart is being held in place by such a thin, frayed filament, she is sure if she takes a breath, her heart will smash against her ribs. She keeps eyeing the phone, hunched on the sideboard. With this scene playing all around her, anything can be endured, anything. She feels like calling John and saying, okay, don't send the papers, I'm coming home.

The phone rings, smashing her heart's vision so she feels a hollow in her chest. But she cannot let herself be fooled by pity into cowardly choices. The phone rings again, and it is the great-granddaughter who scrambles off the old man's lap and answers it. Yolanda supposes it is the chauffeur's party calling back, thinking the coast is clear.

But the great-granddaughter hands the phone to Yolanda. "It's somebody talking funny," she says, making a face.

It is John. He just called her at her aunt's and was told Yolanda was over at her grandfather's house. "How is the old fellow? Is he well enough that I can say hello?"

Tears spring to Yolanda's eyes. "Not at all. Ay, John, he doesn't even know who he is."

"What a pity," he says quietly, and she knows he is genuinely sad to hear the news.

"Look, John," she begins. "I'm sorry about the other day —"

"I'm sorry as well. That's why I'm calling. You're right, I'm being silly. I've sent the papers. They should be there by Tuesday."

"Thank you, thank you," she sobs, for how can she be truly grateful to him for agreeing to become an absence in her life? And yet, she must not turn back now. With that strong will that so often clashed with his, she forces herself to engrave it in her memory. John Merriweather, the third, 1975-1983, the years he was part of her family.

That night she lies awake, remembering other nights from her childhood in a bed not unlike this one, in this very compound, with these very night sounds, the cicadas, the radio going in one of the bedrooms, a child crying out, the tired voices of the servants coming from the back of the house. She wants to keep her memory busy so she will not think of his body tucked in the hollow her body makes, his breath in her hair. Momentarily, she wishes for that blessed blank in the grandfather's head—not to feel the pain of what is gone, never to return. But no! That would be cowardice, to erase the touch of a hand, the look on a face, the lilt of a voice, to tear the web that continues to spin itself, generation to generation, true love to true love. She thinks of the great-granddaughter, the gray eyes, the curl in her hair, so familiar. And then, in lieu of counting sheep, she begins the long roll call of all the living members of the family.

She must have dozed off, for the next thing she knows Milagros is shaking her awake. "Doña Yolanda, begging your pardon."

"What? What?" She has a heartbreaking moment of thinking she has lost the other man in her life all in one day.

"Don Edmundo is worked up. He wants to speak in English. You said I should wake you."

In a second she is out of her bed and in her robe and hurrying across the dark compound grounds with Milagros. The night watchman leads with his flashlight, beaming a faint path on the old-tile stepping-stones in the garden.

In the bedroom, all is quiet now. The little night lamp glows so peacefully that Yolanda wonders if she hasn't stepped into the wrong room in the compound. Maybe she has been misled into a child's bedroom? The grandfather lies tucked in his bed, his hands folded at his waist, his mouth hanging open, his milky eyes gazing up at the ceiling.

"He quiets down in spells," Milagros explains. "He will start up again, you will see."

Yolanda sits down on the edge of the bed and takes his old hands in hers. She can feel his chest moving, up and down. "It's okay now," she tells the nurse. "Go get some sleep. I'll talk to him." She wants this moment with the grandfather, no one watching, no one repeating in a loud voice what she wants to say to him.

"Good night then, and forgive the molestation."

"Not at all, Milagros, not at all."

"Papito," she whispers when the door closes. "I'm here. It's me, Yolanda."

His face comes fully awake, a smile suffuses his features. He places Yolanda's hands inside his pajama top above where his heart should be and pulls her down to him. His sour-smelling, toothless mouth rains her with kisses. "Oh yes, oh yes," he is saying in English. "Let's not fight, let's not fight," he pleads.

Yolanda lets herself be kissed. She kisses his hands, she kisses his forehead.

"Now it's all fixed between us, now it's all fixed."

"Yes, yes," she agrees with him. And for a moment it is she in a gown so white and puffy, she could be floating above the ground, down the long aisle of the national cathedral, toward her handsome groom, the five bright-eyed children, the big house in the Island, the apartment in New York, the six new Yolandas, the happy face of the future. Yes, for a moment, she, too, has found love's divine treasure buried deep in her grandfather's memory.

Martin Amis

The Immortals

(ENGLAND)

It's quite a prospect. Soon the people will all be gone and I will be alone forever. The human beings around here are in very bad shape, what with the solar radiation, the immunity problem, the rat-and-roach diet, and so on. They
are the last; but they can't last (though try telling *them* that). Here they come
again, staggering out to watch the hell of sunset. They all suffer from diseases
and delusions. They all believe that they are . . . But let the poor bastards be.
Now I feel free to bare my secret.

I am the Immortal.

Already I have been around for an incredibly long time. If time is money, then
I am the last of the big spenders. And you know, when you've been around for
as long as I have, the diurnal scale, this twenty-four-hour number, can really
start to get you down. I tried for a grander scheme of things. And I had my
successes. I once stayed awake for seven years on end. Not even a nap. Boy,
was I bushed. On the other hand, when I was ill in Mongolia that time, I
sacked out for a whole decade. At a loose end, cooling my heels in a Saharan
oasis, for eighteen months I picked my nose. On one occasion—when there
was nobody around—I teased out a lone handjob for an entire summer. Even
the unchanging crocodiles envied my baths in the timeless, in the time-
mottled rivers. Frankly, there wasn't much else to do. But in the end I ceased
these experiments and tamely joined the night-day shuttle. I seemed to need
my sleep. I seemed to need to do the things that people seemed to need to do.
Clip my nails. Report to the can and the shaving basin. Get a haircut. All these
distractions. No wonder I never got anything done.

I was born, or I appeared or materialized or beamed down, near the city of
Kampala, Uganda, in Africa. Of course, Kampala wasn't there yet, and neither
was Uganda. Neither was Africa, come to think of it, because in those days the
land masses were all conjoined. (I had to wait until the twentieth century to
check a lot of this stuff out.) I think I must have been a dud god or something;
conceivably I came from another planet which ticked to a different clock.
Anyway I never amounted to much. My life, though long, has been largely
feckless. I had to hold my horses for quite a while before there were any

human beings to hang out with. The world was still cooling. I sat through geology, waiting for biology. I used to croon over those little warm ponds where
space-seeded life began. Yes, I was there, cheering you on from the touchline.
For my instincts were gregarious, and I felt terribly lonely. And hungry.

Then plants showed up, which made a nice change, and certain crude lines
of animal. After a while I twigged and went carnivorous. Partly out of self-
defense I became a prodigious hunter. (It was hardly a matter of survival, but
nobody likes being sniffed and clawed and chomped at the whole time.) There
wasn't an animal they could dream up that I couldn't kill. I kept pets, too. It
was a healthy kind of outdoors life, I suppose, but not very stimulating. I
yearned for . . . for reciprocation. If I thought the Permian age was the pits it
was only because I hadn't yet lived through the Triassic. I can't tell you how
dull it all was. And then, before I knew it—this would have been about
6,000,000 B.C.—the first (unofficial) Ice Age, and we all had to start again,
more or less from scratch. The Ice Ages, I admit, were considerable blows to
my morale. You could tell when one was coming: there'd be some kind of cosmic lightshow, then, more often than not, a shitstorm of moronic impacts;
then dust, and pretty sunsets; then darkness. They happened regularly, every
seventy thousand years, on the dot. You could set your watch by them. The
first Ice Age took out the dinosaurs, or so the theory goes. I know different.
They could have made it, if they'd tightened their belts and behaved sensi-
bly. The tropics were a little stifling and gloomy, true, but perfectly habitable.
No, the dinosaurs had it coming: a very bad crowd. Those lost-world adventure movies got the dinosaurs dead right. Incredibly stupid, incredibly
touchy—and incredibly *big*. And always brawling. The place was like a whaling yard. I was onto fire by then, of course, and so I ate well. It was burgers
every night.

The first batch of ape-people were just a big drag as far as I was concerned.
I was pleased to see them, in a way, but mostly they were just a hassle. All that
evolution—and for this? It was a coon's age before they ever amounted to anything, and even then they were still shockingly grasping and paranoid. With
my little house, my fur suits, my clean-shaven look, and my barbecues, I stood
out. Occasionally I became the object of hatred, or worship. But even the
friendly ones were no use to me. *Ugh. Ich. Akk.* What kind of conversation do
you call that? And when at last they improved, and I made a few pals and
started having relationships with the women, along came a horrible discovery.
I thought they would be different, but they weren't. They all got old and died,
like my pets.

As they are dying now. They are dying all about me.

At first, around here, we were pleased when the world started getting
warmer. We were pleased when things started brightening up again. Winter is
always depressing—but nuclear winter is somehow especially grim. Even I
had wearied of a night that lasted thirteen years (and New Zealand, I find, is
pretty dead at the best of times). For a while, sunbathing was all the rage. But

then it went too far in the other direction. It just kept on getting hotter—or rather there was a change in the nature of the heat. It didn't feel like sunlight. It felt more like gas or liquid: it felt like rain, very thin, very hot. And buildings don't seem to hold it off properly, even buildings with roofs. People stopped being sun-worshipers and started being moon-worshipers. Life became nightlife. They're fairly cheerful, considering—sorrier for others than they are for themselves. I suppose it's lucky they can't tell what's really coming down.

The poor mortals, I grieve for them. There's just nothing they can do about that molten fiend up there in the middle of sky. They faced the anger, then they faced the cold; and now they're being nuked all over again. Now they're being renuked, doublenuked—by the slow reactor of the sun.

Apocalypse happened in the year A.D. 2045. When I was sure it was coming I headed straight for the action: Tokyo. I'll come right out and say that I was pretty much ready to quit. Not that I was particularly depressed or anything. I certainly wasn't as depressed as I am now. In fact I had recently emerged from a five-year hangover and, for me, the future looked bright. But the planet was in desperate shape by then and I wanted no part of it anymore. I wanted out. Nothing else had ever managed to kill me, and I reckoned that a direct hit from a nuke was my only chance. I'm cosmic—in time—but so are nukes: in power. If a nuke hasn't the heft to blow me away (I said to myself), well, nothing else will. I had one serious misgiving. The deployment fashion at that time was for carpet detonations in the hundred-kiloton range. Personally I would have liked something a little bigger, say a megaton at least. I missed the boat. I should have grabbed my chance in the days of atmospheric tests. I always used to kick myself about that sixty-meg sonofabitch the Soviets tried out in Siberia. Sixty million tons of TNT: surely not even I would have walked away from that. . . .

I leased a top-floor room at the Century Inn near Tokyo Tower, bang in the middle of town. I wanted to take this one right on the nose. At the hotel they seemed to be glad of my custom. Business was far from brisk. Everybody knew it would start ending here: it started ending here a century ago. And by this time cities everywhere were all dying anyway. . . . I had my money on an airburst, at night. I bribed the floor guard and he gave me access to the roof: the final sleepout. The city writhed in mortal fear. Me, I writhed in mortal hope. If that sounds selfish, well, then I apologize. But who to? When I heard the sirens and the air-whine I sprang to my feet and stood there, nude, on tiptoe, with my arms outstretched. And then it came, like the universe being unzipped.

First off, I must have taken a lot of prompt radiation, which caused major headaches later on. At the time I thought I was being tickled to death by Dionysus. Simultaneously also I was zapped by the electromagnetic pulse and the thermal rush. The EMP you don't have to worry about. Take it from me, it's the least of your difficulties. But the heat is something else. These are the kind of temperatures that turn a human being into a wall-shadow. Even I took a bit of a shriveling. Although I can joke about it now (it ain't half hot, Mum; phew, what a scorcher!), it really was rather alarming at the time. I couldn't breathe and I blacked out—another first: I didn't die but at least I fainted. For quite a while, too, because when I woke up everything had gone. I'd slept right through the blast, the conflagration, the whole death typhoon. Physically I felt fine. Physically I was, as they say, in great shape. I was entirely purged of that hangover. But in every other sense I felt unusually low. Yes, I was defi- nitely depressed. I still am. Oh, I act cheerful, I put on a brave face; but often I think that this depression will never end—will see me through until the end of time. I can't think of anything that's really very likely to cheer me up. Soon the people will all be gone and I will be alone forever.

They are sand people, dust people, people of dust. I'm fond of them, of course, but—they're not much company. They are deeply sick and deeply crazy. As they diminish, as they ebb and fade, they seem to get big ideas about themselves. Between you and me, I don't feel too hot either. I look good, I look like my old self; but I've definitely felt better. My deal with diseases, inci- dentally, is as follows: I get them, and they hurt and everything, yet they never prove fatal. They move on, or I adapt. To give you a comparatively recent ex- ample, I've had AIDS for seventy-three years. Just can't seem to shake it.

An hour before dawn and the stars still shine with their new, their pointed brightness. Now the human beings are all going inside. Some will fall into a trembling sleep. Others will gather by the polluted well and talk their bullshit all day long. I will remain outside for a little while, alone, under the immortal calendar of the sky.

Classical antiquity was interesting (I suppose I'm jumping on ahead here, but you're not missing much). It was in Caligulan Rome that I realized I had a drink problem. I began spending more and more of my time in the Middle East, where there was always something happening. I got the hang of the eco- nomic masterforces and flourished as a Mediterranean trader. For me, the long hauls out to the Indies and back were no big deal. I did good but not great, and by the eleventh century I'd popped up again in Central Europe. In retrospect that now looks like a mistake. Know what my favorite period was? Yes: the Renaissance. You really came good. To tell you the truth, you aston- ished me. I'd just yawned my way through five hundred years of disease, reli- gion, and zero talent. The food was terrible. Nobody looked good. The arts and crafts stank. Then—pow! And all at once like that, too. I was in Oslo when I heard what was happening. I dropped everything and was on the next boat to Italy, terrified I'd miss it. Oh, it was heaven. Those guys, when they painted a wall or a ceiling or whatever—it stayed painted. We were *living* in a master- piece over there. At the same time, there was something ominous about it, from my point of view. I could see that, in every sense, you were capable of anything. . . . And after the Renaissance what do I get? Rationalism and the industrial revolution. Growth, progress, the whole petrochemical stampede.

Just as I was thinking that no century could possibly be dumber than the nineteenth, along comes the twentieth. I swear, the entire planet seemed to be staging some kind of stupidity contest. I could tell then how the human story would end. Anybody could. Just the one outcome.

My suicide bids date back to the Middle Ages. I was forever throwing myself off mountains and stuff. Boulder overcoats and so on. They never worked. Christ, I've been hit by lightning more times than I care to remember, and lived to tell the tale. (I once copped a meteorite full in the face; I had quite a job crawling out from under it, and felt off-color all afternoon.) And this was on top of fighting in innumerable wars. Soldiering was my passion for millennia—you saw the world—but I started to go off it at the beginning of the fifteenth century. I who had fought with Alexander, with the great Khans, suddenly found myself in a little huddle of retching tramps; across the way was another little huddle of retching tramps. That was Agincourt. By Passchendaele war and I were through. All the improvisation—all the know-how and make-do—seemed to have gone out of it. It was just death, pure and simple. And my experiences in the nuclear theater have done nothing to restore the lost romance. . . . Mind you, I was slowly losing interest in everything. Generally I was becoming more reclusive and neurotic. And of course there was the booze. In fact, halfway through the twentieth century my drink problem got right out of hand. I went on a bender that lasted for ninety-five years. From 1945 to 2039—I was smashed. A metropolitan nomad, I lived by selling off my past, by selling off history: Phoenician knickknacks, Hebrew scrolls, campaign loot—some of it was worth a bomb. I fell apart. I completely lost my self-respect. I was like the passenger on the crippled airplane, with the duty-free upended over my mouth, trying to find the state where nothing matters. This was how the whole world seemed to be behaving. And you cannot find this state. Because it doesn't exist. Because things do matter. Even here.

Tokyo after the nuclear attack was not a pretty sight. An oily black cake with little brocades of fire. My life has been crammed with death—death is my life—but this was a new wrinkle. Everything had gone. Nothing was happening. The only light and activity came from the plasma-beams and nukelets that were still being fired off by some spluttering satellite or rogue submarine. What are they *doing*, I asked myself, shooting up the graveyard like this? Don't ask me how I made it all the way down here to New Zealand. It is a long story. It was a long journey. In the old days, of course, I could have walked it. I had no plans. Really I just followed the trail of life.

I rafted my way to the mainland and there was nothing there either. Everything was dead. (To be fair, a lot of it had been dead already.) Occasionally, as I groped my way south, I'd see a patch of lichen or a warped mushroom, and later a one-legged cockroach or an eyeless rat or something, and that lifted my spirits for a while. It was a good eighteen months before I came across any human beings worth the name—down in Thailand. A small fishing community sheltered by a cusp in the coastal mountains and by freak wind conditions (freak wind conditions being the only kind of wind conditions there were at that time). The people were in a bad way, naturally, but still hauling odds and ends out of the sea—you wouldn't call them fish exactly. I begged for a boat and they wouldn't give me one, which was understandable. I didn't want to argue about it, so I just hung around until they all died. That didn't take too long. I had about a four-year wait, if I remember correctly. Then I loaded up and pushed off and didn't care where the hell the winds took me. I just pushed off into the dying sea, hoping for life.

And I found it, too, after a fashion, down here among the dust people. The last. I'd better make the most of these human beings, because they're the only human beings I've got left. I mourn their passing. What is it to want others, to want others to be?

Once, finding myself in ancient China with plenty of cash and a century to kill, I bought a baby elephant and raised her from infant to invalid. I called her Babalaya. She lived for a hundred and thirteen years and we had time to get to know each other quite well. The larky way she tossed her head about. Her funny figure: all that bulk, and no ass (from the rear she looked like a navvy, slumped over the bar in a Dublin pub). Babalaya—only woman I ever cared a damn about. . . . No, that's not true. I don't know why I say that. But long-term relationships have always been difficult for me and I've tended to steer clear of them. I've only been married three or four thousand times—I'm not the kind to keep lists—and I shouldn't think my kids are even up there in the five figures. I had gay periods, too. I'm sure, though, that you can see the problem. I am used to watching mountains strain into the sky, or deltas forming. When they say that the Atlantic or whatever is sinking by half an inch a century, I *notice* these things. There I am, shacked up with some little honey. I blink—and she's a boiler. While I remained stranded in my faultless noon, time seemed to be scribbling all over everybody right in front of my eyes: they would shrink, broaden, unravel. I didn't mind that much, but the women couldn't handle it at all. I drove those broads crazy. "We've been together for twenty years," they'd say: "How come I look like shit and you don't?" Besides, it wasn't smart to hang around too long in any one place. Twenty years was pushing it. And I did push it, many, many times, on account of the kids. Apart from that I just had flings. You think one-night stands are pretty unsatisfactory? Imagine what I think of them. For me, twenty years is a one-night stand. No, not even. For me, twenty years is a knee-trembler. . . . And there were unpleasant complications. For instance, I once saw a granddaughter of mine coughing and limping her way through the Jerusalem *soukh*. I recognized her because she recognized me; she let out a harsh yell, pointing a finger which itself bore a ring I'd given her when she was little. And now she was little all over again. I'm sorry to say that I committed incest pretty regularly in the very early days. There was no way around incest, back then. It wasn't just me: everyone was into it. A million times I have been bereaved, and then another million. What pain I have known, what megatons of pain. I miss them all—how I miss them. I miss my Babalaya. But you'll understand that relationships of every kind are bound to be fairly strained (there will be tensions) when one party is mortal and the other is not.

The only celebrity I ever knew at all well was Ben Jonson, in London at that time, after my return from Italy. Ben and I were drinking buddies. He was boisterous in his cups, and soppy too, sometimes; and of course he was very blue about the whole Shakespeare thing. Ben used to sit through that guy's stuff in tears. I saw Shakespeare once or twice, in the street. We never met, but our eyes did. I always had the feeling that he and I might have hit it off. I thought the world of Shakespeare. And I bet I could have given him some good material.

Soon the people will all be gone and I will be alone forever. Even Shakespeare will be gone—or not quite, because his lines will live in this old head of mine. I will have the companionship of memory. I will have the companionship of dreams. I just won't have any people. It's true that I had those empty years before the human beings arrived, so I'm used to solitude. But this will be different, with nobody to look forward to at the end of it.

There is no weather now. Days are just a mask of fire—and the night sky I've always found a little samey. Before, in the early emptiness, there were pets, there were plants, there were nature rambles. Well, there's nothing much to ramble in now. I *saw* what you were doing to the place. What was the matter? Was it too *nice* for you or something? Jesus Christ, you were only here for about ten minutes. And look what you did.

Grouped around the poisoned well, the people yawn and mumble. They are the last. They have tried having kids—I have tried having kids—but it doesn't work out. The babies that make it to term don't look at all good, and they can't seem to work up any immunity. There's not much immunity around as it is. Everybody's low.

They are the last and they are insane. They suffer from a mass delusion. Really, it's the craziest thing. They all believe that they are—that they are eternal, that they are immortal. And they didn't get the idea from me. I've kept my mouth shut, as always, out of settled habit. I've been discreet. I'm not one of those wellside bores who babble on about how they knew Tutankhamen and scored with the Queen of Sheba or Marie Antoinette. They think that they will live forever. The poor bastards, if they only knew.

I have a delusion also, sometimes. Sometimes I have this weird idea that I am just a second-rate New Zealand schoolmaster who never did anything or went anywhere and is now painfully and noisily dying of solar radiation along with everybody else. It's strange how palpable it is, this fake past, and how human: I feel I can almost reach out and touch it. There was a woman, and a child. One woman. One child. . . . But I soon snap out of it. I soon pull myself together. I soon face up to the tragic fact that there will be no ending for me, even after the sun dies (which should at least be quite spectacular). I am the Immortal.

Recently I have started staying out in the daylight. Ah, what the hell. And so, I notice, have the human beings. We wail and dance and shake our heads.

We crackle with cancers, we fizz with synergisms, under the furious and bird-less sky. Shyly we peer at the heaven-filling target of the sun. Of course, I can take it, but this is suicide for the human beings. Wait, I want to say. Not yet. Be careful—you'll hurt yourselves. Please. Please try and stay a little longer.

Soon you will all be gone and I will be alone forever.

I . . . I am the Immortal.

Reinaldo Arenas

The Glass Tower

(C U B A)

Ever since he had arrived in Miami, after the veritable odyssey of escaping his native country, noted Cuban author Alfredo Fuentes had not written a single line.

For some reason, since the day he arrived—and it had already been five years—he had found himself accepting all kinds of invitations to speak at conferences, to participate in cultural events or intellectual gatherings, and to attend literary cocktail and dinner parties where he was inevitably the guest of honor and, therefore, never given any time to eat, much less to think about his novel—or perhaps story—the one he had been carrying around in his head for years, and whose characters, Berta, Nicolás, Delfín, Daniel, and Olga, constantly vied for his attention, urging him to deal with their respective predicaments.

Berta's moral integrity, Nicolás's firm stance against mediocrity, Delfín's keen intelligence, Daniel's solitary spirit, and Olga's sweet and quiet wisdom not only clamored for the attention that he was unable to offer, they also reproached him constantly, Alfredo felt, because of the time he was spending with other people.

Most regrettable of all was that Alfredo hated those gatherings, but was incapable of refusing a gracious invitation (and what invitation isn't gracious?). He always accepted. Once there, he would be so brilliant and charming that he had earned a reputation, particularly among local writers, as a frivolous man who was something of a show-off.

On the other hand, if he were to turn down invitations to such gatherings at this point, everyone (including those who were critical of his excessive talkativeness) would consider it evidence of inferior breeding, selfishness, even a false sense of superiority. Thus, Alfredo found himself caught in an intricate web: he was well aware that if he continued to accept the endless flow of invitations, he would never write another word, and if he didn't, his prestige as a writer would soon fade into oblivion.

But it was also true that Alfredo Fuentes, rather than being at the center of those obliging crowds, would have much preferred to be alone in his small apartment—that is, alone with Olga, Delfín, Berta, Nicolás, and Daniel.

So pressing were his characters' appeals and so eager was he to respond that just a few hours earlier he had vowed to suspend all social activities and devote himself entirely to his novel—or story, since he didn't yet know exactly where all this might lead him.

Yes, tomorrow he was definitely going to resume his solitary and mysterious occupation. Tomorrow, because tonight it would be practically impossible for him not to attend the large party being given in his honor by the grande dame of the Cuban literary circles in Miami, Señora Gladys Pérez Campo, whom H. Puntilla had nicknamed, for better or for worse, "the Haydée Santamaría of the exile community."*

This event, however, was not merely cultural, but also had a practical purpose. Gladys had promised the writer that she would lay the foundation, that very evening, of a publishing house that would print the manuscripts that he had, at great risk, smuggled out of Cuba. Alfredo, incidentally, didn't have a penny to his name and this, of course, could give him a tremendous financial boost, as well as help to promote the works of other important but still unknown writers less fortunate than Alfredo, who already had five books to his credit.

"The publishing project will be a success," Gladys had assured him on the phone. "The most prominent people in Miami will support you. They will all be here tonight. I am expecting you at nine, without fail."

At five to nine, Alfredo crossed the vast, manicured garden toward the main door of the Pérez Campo mansion. The scent of flowers swept over him in waves, and he could hear pleasant melodies emanating from the top floor of the residence. As he listened to the music, Alfredo placed his hand against the outside wall of the house, and the stillness of the night conspired with the garden and the thickness of the wall to give him a sense of security, of peace almost, that he had not experienced for many years, too many years. . . . Alfredo would have preferred to remain there, outside the house, alone with his characters, listening to the music from far away. But, always keeping in mind the solid publishing project that would perhaps one day allow him to own a mansion like this one and that could also mean the future salvation of Olga, Daniel, Delfín, Berta, and Nicolás, he rang the doorbell.

Before one of the maids (hired specially for the reception) could open the door, an enormous Saint Bernard belonging to the Pérez Campos lunged toward him and began licking his face. This display of familiarity from the huge dog (which answered to the name of Narcisa) encouraged similar shows of affection from the other dogs, six Chihuahuas who welcomed Alfredo with a chorus of piercing barks. Fortunately, Gladys herself came to the rescue of her guest of honor.

Fashionably attired—although rather inappropriately for the climate—in an ankle-length skirt, boa, gloves, and a large hat, the hostess took Alfredo's arm and led him to the most select circle of guests, those who would also be

---

*Haydée Santamaría was the director of the government publishing house, La Casa de las Américas, that decided which books would be published in Cuba.

most interested in the publishing venture. Gladys, at once solemn and festive, introduced him to the president of one of the city's most important banks (in his imagination Alfredo saw Berta making a face in disgust); to the executive vice president of the *Florida Herald*, the most influential newspaper in Miami ("A horrible, anti-Cuban paper," he heard Nicolás's voice saying from a distance); to the governor's personal assistant; and to an award-winning lady poet ("A couple of serious bitches," Delfín's sarcastic voice piped in loud and clear). The introductions continued: a distinguished minister, who was a famous theology professor as well as the leader of the so-called Reunification of Cuban Families. ("What are you doing with these awful people?" Daniel shouted desperately from far away, causing Alfredo to trip just as he reached out for a famous opera singer's hand and fell instead directly into the diva's ample bosom.) Gladys continued with her introductions as if nothing had happened: a famous woman pianist, two guitarists, several professors, and finally (here Gladys assumed a regal bearing), the Countess of Villalta. Born in the province of Pinar del Río, she was an elderly woman, no longer in possession of lands and villas, but still holding fast to her splendid title of nobility.

As he was on the point of bowing discreetly before the countess, Alfredo sensed that the characters of his budding opus were again urgently demanding his attention. And so, as he kissed the lady's hand, he decided to search for the pen and paper that he always carried in his pocket, in the hope of being able to jot down a few notes. But the countess misconstrued his intentions.

"I certainly appreciate your giving me your address," said the lady, "but, as I am sure you will understand, this is just not the right moment. I do promise to send you my card."

And with that, the countess turned to the award-winning poetess, who had witnessed the scene and, apparently trying to help Alfredo, offered a suggestion. "Now that you've almost finished writing your address, why don't you give it to me? I do want to send you my latest book."

And instead of taking the notes his characters demanded (by now Olga was moaning and Berta screaming), Alfredo had no choice but to write his address on the piece of paper.

Trays brimming with assorted cheeses, hors d'oeuvres, pastries, and drinks were being passed around. Trays that, amid new greetings and inquiries, Alfredo saw approach and then disappear without ever having a chance to sample from them.

At midnight Gladys announced that, in order to make the gathering more intimate, they would all move to the glass tower. This elicited a very pleased *Aaah!* from the guests (even the countess joined in), and, led by their fashionable hostess, they set off immediately.

The glass tower, circular and transparent, rose at one side of the house like a gigantic chimney. While the guests climbed laboriously up the spiral staircase (except the countess, who was transported in a chair designed especially for this purpose), Alfredo again heard his characters' urgent cries. Imprisoned in Holguín, deep in the Cuban countryside, Delfín begged not to be forsaken; from New York, Daniel's groans sounded aggravated and menacing; from a small French village, Olga, sweet Olga with her pages still blank, looked at him with a combination of reproach and melancholy in her eyes; meanwhile Nicolás and Berta, right there in Miami, angrily demanded immediate participation in the narrative that he had still not begun. To appease them momentarily, Alfredo tried to raise his hand in a gesture of understanding, but, as he did this, he accidentally tousled the pianist's elaborate coiffure, and she in turn gave him an even more hateful look than Berta's.

By now they had all reached the glass tower. Alfredo was expecting the real conversation to begin at any moment; that is, they would finally start talking about the publishing plans and the first authors to be published. But just then, Gladys (who had changed into an even more sumptuous gown without anyone noticing) gestured with an elegant wave of her hand for the musicians to start playing. Soon the bank president was dancing with the wife of the executive vice president of the *Florida Herald*, who, in turn, began dancing with the governor's assistant. A college professor deftly whirled around the room in the strong arms of the opera singer, outclassed only by the celebrated poetess, who was now performing a prize-winning solo. Between the clicking of her heels and the frenetic undulations of her hips and shoulders, she careened over to Alfredo, who had no recourse other than to join the dance.

When the music ended, Alfredo thought that the time had finally come to discuss the central issue of the gathering. But at another signal from Gladys, the orchestra struck up a dance number from Spain. And even the most reverend minister, in the arms of the old countess, dared to venture a few parsimonious steps. As the dancing continued and the opera singer began to show off her high notes, Alfredo was sure he could hear quite distinctly the voices of his characters, now at very close range. Without interrupting his dance, he passed close by the glass wall and looked out into the garden, where he saw Olga, quivering desperately among the geraniums, begging to be rescued with silent gestures; farther away, by the perfectly trimmed ficus trees, Daniel was sobbing. At that moment, as the diva's notes reached a crescendo, Alfredo felt that he could no longer excuse his own indolence and, still dancing, he grabbed a napkin in flight and began desperately to scribble some notes.

"What kind of a dance is this?" interrupted the executive vice president of the *Florida Herald*. "Do you also keep a record of your dance steps?"

Alfredo didn't know what to say. On top of it all, the pianist's stare, suspicious and alert, made him feel even more vulnerable. Wiping his brow with the napkin, he lowered his eyes in embarrassment and tried to pull himself together, but when he looked up again, there they were, Nicolás, Berta, and Delfín, already pressing against the glass walls of the tower. Yes, they had gathered here from different places to pound on the windowpanes and demand that Alfredo admit them (infuse them with life) into the pages of the novel—or story—that he had not even begun to write.

The six Chihuahuas began barking excitedly, and Alfredo thought that they too had seen his characters. Fortunately, however, their barking was just one of Gladys's bright ideas (or "exquisite touches," as the countess called them) to entertain her guests. And entertain them she did when, following her steps and the beat of the orchestra drums, the Chihuahuas surrounded the Saint Bernard, Narcisa, and, standing on their hind legs, imitated complicated dance steps with Narcisa herself as the central figure. For a moment, Alfredo was sure he saw a sadness in the eyes of the huge Saint Bernard, as the dog looked over at him. Finally, the audience burst into applause, and the orchestra shifted to the soft rhythms of a Cuban *danzón*.

Berta, Nicolás, and Delfín were now pounding even harder on the windows, while Alfredo, becoming more and more exasperated, whirled around in the arms of the award-winning poetess, Señora Clara del Prado (haven't we mentioned her by name yet?), who at that moment was confessing to the writer how difficult it was to get a book of poetry published.

"I know exactly what you mean," Alfredo agreed mechanically, distracted by his characters, who were now struggling on the other side of the glass like huge insects drawn to a hermetically sealed streetlamp.

"You couldn't possibly understand," he heard the poet's voice counter.

"Why not?"

By then, out in the garden, Daniel and Olga had begun sobbing in unison.

"Because you are a novelist and novels always sell more than poems, especially when the author is famous like you. . . ."

"Don't make me laugh."

By now Daniel's and Olga's sobs were no longer sobs at all but agonized screams that ended in a single, unanimous plea for help.

"Rescue us! Rescue us!"

"Come on," urged the celebrated poetess, "stop acting so modest and tell me, just between you and me, how much do you get a year in royalties?"

And as if the screams coming from the garden weren't enough to drive anyone out of his mind, Nicolás and Berta were now trying to break through the glass walls of the tower, with Delfín's enthusiastic encouragement.

"Royalties? Don't make me laugh. Don't you know that there's no copyright law in Cuba? All my books were published in other countries while I was still in Cuba."

"Rescue us, or we'll break down the door!" This was, without a doubt, Berta's infuriated voice.

"They're all thieves, I know that. But other countries don't have to abide by Cuban law."

With their bare hands and then their feet, Berta and Nicolás were beating on the glass wall, while the screams coming from the garden grew louder and louder.

"Other countries will adopt any law that allows them to plunder with impunity," Alfredo asserted clearly, ready to abandon the poetess in order to save his characters, who seemed, strangely enough, to be gasping for air, although out in the open.

"So how are you planning to get funding for the great publishing house?" inquired the award-winning poetess with an ingratiating twinkle, before adding in a conspiratorial tone: "Oh, come on, I'm not going to ask you for a loan. I only want to publish a little volume of mine. . . ."

Somehow—Alfredo could not figure out exactly how—Berta had managed to slip one hand through the glass and, right in front of her astonished creator, turned the lock and opened one of the tower windows.

"Look, lady," Alfredo said curtly, "the fact is I don't have any money. As far as the publishing house is concerned, I am here to find out how everyone here plans on establishing it and whether I can get my books published, too."

"We've all been told that you are going to be the backer."

At that moment, Delfín slid down the tower and was now hanging dangerously by his fingers from the edge of the open window.

"Watch out!" Alfredo screamed, looking toward the window and trying to avert his character's fall.

"I thought we poets were the only crazy ones," said the lady poet, staring intently at Alfredo, "but now I see that novelists are too—perhaps twice as crazy."

"Three times as crazy!" proclaimed Alfredo, running to Delfín's aid at the window, just as Berta González and Nicolás Landrove entered the room.

Alfredo felt embarrassed to have Nicolás, Berta, and Delfín Prats (whose life he had just saved) see him surrounded by all these people instead of being at work with them; therefore, feeling more and more under pressure to remove himself and his characters from the scene, he decided to say good-bye to his hostess and to the rest of the guests instead of waiting for the famous discussion to begin. Followed by Narcisa, who was now intent on sniffing his leg, he walked over to them.

But a strange tension permeated the tower. Suddenly nobody was paying any attention to Alfredo. Worse, he seemed to have become invisible. In her tinkling tones, the award-winning poetess had just communicated something to Gladys and her friends, and they all made faces as if surprised or offended. Alfredo did not need a writer's observational skills to realize that they were talking about him, and not favorably.

"He'd better leave!" he heard Gladys Pérez Campo mutter in a low, indignant voice.

But even if he understood (albeit with some measure of surprise) that those words referred to him, Alfredo felt so confused that he was not able to absorb them. Besides, the words had not been spoken directly to him, although they were certainly intended for his ears. Gladys's good manners and social standing would not allow her to make a public scene, much less force one of her guests to leave. Therefore, still with the intention of rescuing his characters (who were now, for their part, completely ignoring him), Alfredo pretended not to have noticed and tried to blend in with the conversation. But the countess gave him a look of such withering scorn that the confused writer took refuge in a corner and lit a cigarette. But wouldn't it be a sign of very poor breeding to leave without saying good-bye to the host and the other guests?

On top of everything else, right at that moment Delfín Prats opened the door to the spiral staircase, and Daniel Fernández and Olga Neshein came in. Holding hands and not even looking at Alfredo, they joined Nicolás Landrove and Berta González del Valle, both of whom had already had a few drinks and were well on their way to getting drunk. Once again Alfredo felt Narcisa's tail brushing against his legs.

The five characters of his story (by now, at least, he knew that these people were worth only a story) took great pleasure in walking around the room, eyeing everything with a mixture of curiosity and calculation. Alfredo concentrated all his energy on trying to make them leave. But they just would not obey. On the contrary, they mingled with the most prominent of the guests, the true elite, introducing themselves to one another, bowing and curtseying and exchanging pleasantries.

From the corner where he was hidden behind a huge tropical palm and obscured by the smoke from his cigarette, Alfredo carefully observed his five characters and discovered that none was dressed as he had decided. Olga, supposedly shy and sweet, had arrived wearing too much makeup and a tight miniskirt; she was gesticulating wildly, making faces and laughing too hard at a joke that the director of Reunification of Cuban Families had just told her. Meanwhile, Berta and Nicolás, the paragons of "unshakable integrity" according to Alfredo's vision of them, were kowtowing outrageously to the governor's assistant. At one point, Alfredo even thought he overheard them asking for a small business loan to open a pizzeria in the center of the city. For his part, Daniel ("the introverted, solitary one") had already introduced himself as Daniel Fernández Trujillo and was telling the award-winning poetess such off-color stories that the old countess had discreetly moved to another seat. But insolence seemed to have met its master in the talented Delfín Prats Pupo. While downing a beer (his fifth? his seventh?) straight from the bottle, he mocked his creator, that is, Alfredo Fuentes, in a manner that was not only grotesque, but also almost obscene and ruthless. With diabolical skill, Delfín Prats Pupo imitated Alfredo, exaggerating all of the writer's tics, gestures, and idiosyncrasies, including his manner of speaking, walking, and even breathing. Only then did Alfredo realize that he sometimes stammered, that he walked with his stomach thrust forward, and that he was bug-eyed. And as he watched his favorite character mock him, he also had to endure more face-licking from the passionate Saint Bernard.

"The worst thing of all is that for all his pretensions and ridiculous posturing as a brilliant author, he has no talent whatsoever and can't even write without making spelling mistakes. He often misspells my first family name and writes it without the *t*," concluded Delfín Prats Pupo, so as not to leave any doubt on the matter.

And everyone laughed, again producing a strange sound like the tinkling of wine glasses.

Increasingly nervous, Alfredo lit another cigarette, which he quickly dropped on the floor when Delfín Prats Pupo, mimicking his every gesture, began to light one too.

"Sir, would you please pick up that butt?" one of the nearest servants reprimanded him. "Or are you trying to burn the carpet?"

Alfredo bent down to do as he was told, and, while in that position, verified that the peculiar tinkling sound was produced by the tittering voices of the guests as they whispered, glancing at him with contempt. He brusquely extricated himself from the Saint Bernard's legs, as the dog howled pitifully, and approached the guests to try to figure out what was going on. But as soon as he joined the group, the governor's assistant, without looking at him, announced her immediate departure.

Suddenly, as if propelled by a spring, the guests decided it was time to leave. The countess was carried away in her imposing chair, while most of the guests kissed her hand, which was now transparent (at least to Alfredo). The famous opera singer was also leaving, on the (truly transparent) arm of the bank president. The minister turned to go while keeping up a lively conversation with the pianist, whose face was becoming more and more shiny and brilliant. When the award-winning lady poet left with Daniel Fernández Trujillo's arm around her waist, Alfredo saw the young man's hand sink effortlessly into her translucent body (although Daniel Fernández Trujillo's hand soon became invisible as well, and both figures fused into one). The black musicians were also leaving, led by Delfín Prats Pupo, who jumped around among them cheerfully, producing the familiar tinkling sound, while mimicking the gestures of the writer, who could do nothing to stop him. Olga Neshein de Leviant left with a mathematics professor, their hands entwined. In the midst of this stampede, Berta González del Valle stuffed her handbag with French cheeses, and Nicolás Landrove Felipe carted away the candy, both of them oblivious to Alfredo's signals and the protests of the hostess, Gladys Pérez Campo, who, on her way out in the company of her Chihuahuas, threatened to call the police. But her voice faded away into an imperceptible tinkling.

Within a few minutes, the hostess, the guests, and even the hired staff had disappeared, along with the characters of the story, and Alfredo found himself alone in the huge mansion. Disconcerted, he was getting ready to leave when the thunder of trucks and cranes reverberated through the building.

Suddenly the foundations of the house began to move and the roof disappeared; the carpets rolled up automatically; the windowpanes, freed from their casements, flew through the air; the doors left their frames; the paintings came off the walls; and the walls, moving at an unbelievable speed, vanished, along with everything else, into a huge truck. As everything disassembled and packed itself (the whole garden with its plastic trees, walls, and air fresheners was already moving out), Alfredo saw that the mansion had been nothing more than an enormous prefabricated cardboard set that could be installed and dismantled quickly, and that one could rent for a few days or even a few hours, according to the ad on the side of the large truck in which everything was being carted away.

In a flash, the site where the imposing mansion had stood became nothing but a dusty embankment. Standing at the center, still perplexed, Alfredo could not find (it no longer existed) the path that would take him back to the city. He walked around aimlessly, thinking about the story he had never written. But an enthusiastic bark pulled him out of his meditation.

Exasperated, Alfredo began running, but the Saint Bernard, evidently more athletic than the writer, caught up with him quickly, knocked him down and began licking his face. An unexpected joy came over Alfredo when he realized that her tongue was indeed real. He pulled himself together and got up. Caressing Narcisa—who followed him faithfully—he abandoned the site.

Translated from the Spanish by Dolores M. Koch

Margaret Atwood

Wilderness Tips

(C A N A D A)

Prue has folded two red bandanna handkerchiefs into triangles and tied them together at one set of corners. The second set of corners is tied behind her back, the third around her neck. She's wrapped another bandanna, a blue one, around her head and made a little reef knot at the front. Now she's strutting the length of the dock, in her improvised halter top and her wide-legged white shorts, her sunglasses with the white plastic frames, her platform sandals.

"It's the forties look," she says to George, hand on her hip, doing a pirouette. "Rosie the Riveter. From the war. Remember her?"

George, whose name is not really George, does not remember. He spent the forties rooting through garbage heaps and begging, and doing other things unsuitable for a child. He has a dim memory of some film star posed on a calendar tattering on a latrine wall. Maybe this is the one Prue means. He remembers for an instant his intense resentment of the bright, ignorant smile, the well-fed body. A couple of buddies had helped him take her apart with the rusty blade from a kitchen knife they'd found somewhere in the rubble. He does not consider telling any of this to Prue.

George is sitting in a green-and-white striped canvas deck chair, reading *The Financial Post* and drinking Scotch. The ashtray beside him overflows with butts: many women have tried to cure him of smoking; many have failed. He looks up at Prue from behind his paper and smiles his foxy smile. This is a smile he does with the cigarette held right in the center of his mouth: on either side of it his lips curl back, revealing teeth. He has long canines, miraculously still his.

"You weren't born then," he says. This isn't true, but he never misses the chance to bestow a compliment when there's one just lying around. What does it cost? Not a cent, which is something the men in this country have never figured out. Prue's tanned midriff is on a level with his face; it's still firm, still flexible and lithe. At that age his mother had gone soft—loose-fleshed and velvety, like an aging plum. These days they eat a lot of vegetables, they work out, they last longer.

Prue lowers the sunglasses to the end of her nose and looks at him over the plastic rims. "George, you are totally shameless," she says. "You always were." She gives him an innocent smile, a mischievous smile, a smile with a twist of real evil in it. It's a smile that wavers like a gasoline slick on water, shining, changing tone.

This smile of Prue's was the first interesting thing George stumbled over when he hit Toronto, back in the late fifties. It was at a party thrown by a real-estate developer with Eastern European connections. He'd been invited because refugees from Hungary were considered noteworthy back then, right after the uprising. At that time he was young, thin as a snake, with a dangerous-looking scar over one eye and a few bizarre stories. A collectible. Prue had been there in an off-the-shoulder black dress. She'd raised her glass to him, looked over the rim, hoisted the smile like a flag.

The smile is still an invitation, but it's not something George will follow up on—not here, not now. Later, in the city, perhaps. But this lake, this peninsula, Wacousta Lodge itself, are his refuge, his monastery, his sacred ground. Here he will perform no violations.

"Why is it you cannot bear to accept a gift?" says George. Smoke blows into his eyes; he squints. "If I were younger, I would kneel. I would kiss both your hands. Believe me."

Prue, who has known him to do these things back in more impetuous times, turns on her heel. "It's lunchtime," she says. "That's what I came to tell you." She has heard refusal.

George watches her white shorts and her still shapely thighs (with, however, their faint stippling of dimpled fat) going wink, wink, wink through the clear sunlight, past the boathouse, along the stone path, up the hill to the house. From up there a bell is ringing: the lunch bell. For once in her life, Prue is telling the truth.

George takes one more look at the paper. Quebec is talking Separatism; there are Mohawks behind the barricades near Montreal, and people are throwing stones at them; word is the country is falling apart. George is not worried: he's been in countries that were falling apart before. There can be opportunities. As for the fuss people here make about language, he doesn't understand it. What's a second language, or a third, or a fourth? George himself speaks five, if you count Russian, which he would prefer not to. As for the stone-throwing, it's typical. Not bombs, not bullets: just stones. Even the uproar here is muted.

He scratches his belly under the loose shirt he wears; he's been gaining a little too much around the middle. Then he stubs out his cigarette, downs the heel of his Scotch, and hauls himself out of his deck chair. Carefully, he folds the chair and places it inside the boathouse: a wind could come up, the chair could be sent sailing into the lake. He treats the possessions and rituals of Wacousta Lodge with a tenderness, a reverence, that would baffle those who know him only in the city. Despite what some would call his unorthodox business practices, he is in some ways a conservative man; he loves traditions. They are thin on the ground in this country, but he knows one when he sees one, and does it homage. The deck chairs here are like the escutcheons elsewhere.

As he walks up the hill, more slowly than he used to, he hears the sound of wood being split behind the kitchen wing. He hears a truck on the highway that runs along the side of the lake; he hears wind in the white pines. He hears a loon. He remembers the first time he heard one, and hugs himself. He has done well.

Wacousta Lodge is a large, oblong, one-story structure with board-and-batten walls stained a dark reddish brown. It was built in the first years of the century by the family's great-grandfather, who made a bundle on the railways. He included a maid's room and a cook's room at the back, although no maid or cook had ever been induced to stay in them, not to George's knowledge, certainly not in recent years. The great-grandfather's craggy, walrus-whiskered face, frowning above the constriction of a stiff collar, hangs oval-framed in the washroom, which is equipped only with a sink and a ewer. George can remember a zinc bathtub, but it's been retired. Baths take place in the lake. For the rest, there's an outhouse, placed discreetly behind a clump of spruce.

What a lot of naked and semi-naked bodies the old man must have seen over the years, thinks George, lathering his hands, and how he must have disapproved of them. At least the old boy isn't condemned to the outhouse: that would be too much for him. George makes a small, superstitious, oddly Japanese bow towards the great-grandfather as he goes out the door. He always does this. The presence of this scowling ancestral totem is one of the reasons he behaves himself, more or less, up here.

The table for lunch is set on the wide, screened-in veranda at the front of the house, overlooking the lake. Prue is not sitting at it, but her two sisters are: dry-faced Pamela, the eldest, and soft Portia, the youngest of the three and George's own wife. There is also Roland, the brother, large, rounded, and balding. George, who is not all that fond of men on purely social occasions because there are few ways he can manipulate them, gives Roland a polite nod and turns the full force of his vulpine smile upon the two women. Pamela, who distrusts him, sits up straight and pretends not to notice. Portia smiles at him, a wistful, vague smile, as if he were a cloud. Roland ignores him, though not on purpose, because Roland has the inner life of a tree, or possibly of a stump. George can never tell what Roland is thinking, or even if he is thinking at all.

"Isn't the weather marvelous?" George says to Pamela. He has learned over the years that the weather is the proper opening topic here for any conversation at all. Pamela is too well brought up to refuse an answer to a direct question.

"If you like postcards," she says. "At least it's not snowing." Pamela has recently been appointed a Dean of Women, a title George has not yet figured out completely. The Oxford dictionary has informed him that a dean might be the head of ten monks in a monastery, or "as tr. med. L. *decanus,* applied to the *teoðing-ealdor,* the headman of a *tenmannetale.*" Much of what Pamela says sounds more or less like this: incomprehensible, though it might turn out to have a meaning if studied.

George would like to go to bed with Pamela, not because she is beautiful— she is much too rectilinear and slab-shaped for his tastes, she has no bottom at all, and her hair is the color of dried grass—but because he has never done it. Also, he wants to know what she would say. His interest in her is anthropologi- cal. Or perhaps geological: she would have to be scaled, like a glacier.

"Did you have a nice read?" says Portia. "I hope you didn't get sunburned. Is there any news?"

"If you can call it news," says Pamela. "That paper's a week old. Why is 'news' plural? Why don't we say 'olds'?"

"George likes old stuff," says Prue, coming in with a platter of food. She's put on a man's white shirt over her kerchief arrangement but hasn't done it up. "Lucky for us ladies, eh? Gobble up, everyone. It's yummy cheese-and- chutney sandwiches and yummy sardines. George? Beer or acid rain?"

George drinks a beer, and eats and smiles, eats and smiles, while the family talks around him—all but Roland, who absorbs his nutriments in silence, gaz- ing out at the lake through the trees, his eyes immobile. George sometimes thinks Roland can change color slightly to blend in with his backgrounds; un- like George himself, who is doomed to stand out.

Pamela is complaining again about the stuffed birds. There are three of them, kept under glass bells in the living room: a duck, a loon, a grouse. These were the bright ideas of the grandfather, meant to go with the generally lodge- like décor: the mangy bearskin rug, complete with claws and head; the minia- ture birchbark canoe on the mantelpiece; the snowshoes, cracked and drying, crossed above the fireplace; the Hudson's Bay blanket nailed to the wall and beset by moths. Pamela is sure the stuffed birds will get moths too.

"They're probably a sea of maggots, inside," she says, and George tries to picture what a sea of maggots would look like. It's her metaphoric leaps, her tangled verbal stringworks, that confuse him.

"They're hermetically sealed," says Prue. "You know: nothing goes in, noth- ing comes out. Like nuns."

"Don't be revolting," says Pamela. "We should check them for frass."

"Who, the nuns?" says Prue.

"What is frass?" says George.

"Maggot excrement," says Pamela, not looking at him. "We could have them freeze-dried."

"Would it work?" says Prue.

Prue, who in the city is the first with trends—the first white kitchen, the first set of giant shoulder pads, the first leather pants suit have been hers over the years—is here as resistant to change as the rest of them. She wants every- thing on this peninsula to stay exactly the way it always has been. And it does, though with a gradual decline into shabbiness. George doesn't mind the shabbiness, however. Wacousta Lodge is a little slice of the past, an alien past. He feels privileged.

A motorboat goes by, one of the plastic-hulled, high-speed kind, far too close. Even Roland flinches. The wake jostles the dock.

"I hate those," says Portia, who hasn't shown much interest in the stuffed-bird question. "Another sandwich, dear?"

"It was so lovely and quiet here during the war," says Pamela. "You should have been here, George." She says this accusingly, as if it's his fault he wasn't. "Hardly any motorboats, because of the gas rationing. More canoes. Of course, the road wasn't built then, there was only the train. I wonder why we say 'train of thought' but never 'car of thought'?"

"And rowboats," says Prue. "I think all those motorboat people should be taken out and shot. At least the ones who go too fast." Prue herself drives like a maniac, but only on land.

George, who has seen many people taken out and shot, though not for driving motorboats, smiles, and helps himself to a sardine. He once shot three men himself, though only two of them were strictly necessary. The third was a precaution. He still feels uneasy about that, about the possibly harmless one with his too-innocent informer's eyes, his shirtfront dappled with blood. But there would be little point in mentioning that, at lunch or at any other time. George has no desire to be startling.

It was Prue who brought him north, brought him here, during their affair, the first one. (How many affairs have there been? Can they be separated, or are they really one long affair, with interruptions, like a string of sausages? The interruptions were Prue's marriages, which never lasted long, possibly because she was monogamous during them. He would know when a marriage was nearing its end: the phone at his office would ring and it would be Prue, saying, "George. I can't do it. I've been so good, but I just can't go on. He comes into the bathroom when I'm flossing my teeth. I long to be in an elevator with you, stuck between floors. Tell me something *filthy*. I hate love, don't you?")

His first time here he was led in chains, trailed in Prue's wake, like a barbarian in a Roman triumph. A definite capture, also a deliberate outrage. He was supposed to alarm Prue's family, and he did, though not on purpose. His English was not good, his hair was too glossy, his shoes too pointed, his clothes too sharply pressed. He wore dark glasses, kissed hands. The mother was alive then, though not the father; so there were four women ranged against him, with no help at all from the impenetrable Roland.

"Mother, this is George," said Prue, on the dock where they were all sitting in their ancestral deck chairs, the daughters in bathing suits with shirts over them, the mother in striped pastels. "It's not his real name, but it's easier to pronounce. He's come up here to see wild animals."

George leaned over to kiss the mother's sun-freckled hand, and his dark glasses fell off into the lake. The mother made cooing sounds of distress, Prue laughed at him, Roland ignored him, Pamela turned away in irritation. But Portia—lovely, small-boned Portia, with her velvet eyes—took off her shirt without a word and dove into the lake. She retrieved his dark glasses for him, smiling diffidently, handing them up to him out of the water, her wet hair dripping down over her small breasts like a water nymph's on an Art Nouveau fountain, and he knew then that she was the one he would marry. A woman of courtesy and tact and few words, who would be kind to him, who would cover up for him; who would pick up the things he had dropped.

In the afternoon, Prue took him for a paddle in one of the leaking canvas-covered canoes from the boathouse. He sat in the front, jabbing ineptly at the water with his paddle, thinking about how he would get Portia to marry him. Prue landed them on a rocky point, led him up among the trees. She wanted him to make his usual rakish, violent, outlandish brand of love to her on the reindeer moss and pine needles; she wanted to break some family taboo. Sacrilege was what she had in mind: that was as clear to him as if he'd read it. But George already had his plan of attack worked out, so he put her off. He didn't want to desecrate Wacousta Lodge: he wanted to marry it.

That evening at dinner he neglected all three of the daughters in favor of the mother: the mother was the guardian; the mother was the key. Despite his limping vocabulary he could be devastatingly charming, as Prue had announced to everyone while they ate their chicken-noodle soup.

"Wacousta Lodge," he said to the mother, bending his scar and his glinting marauder's eyes towards her in the light from the kerosene lamp. "That is so romantic. It is the name of an Indian tribe?"

Prue laughed. "It's named after some stupid book," she said. "Great-grandfather liked it because it was written by a general."

"A major," said Pamela severely. "In the nineteenth century. Major Richardson."

"Ah?" said George, adding this item to his already growing cache of local traditions. So there were books here, and houses named after them! Most people were touchy on the subject of their books; it would be as well to show some interest. Anyway, he *was* interested. But when he asked about the subject of this book it turned out that none of the women had read it.

"I've read it," said Roland, unexpectedly.

"Ah?" said George.

"It's about war."

"It's on the bookshelf in the living room," the mother said indifferently. "After dinner you can have a look, if you're all that fascinated."

It was the mother (Prue explained) who had been guilty of the daughters' alliterative names. She was a whimsical woman, though not sadistic; it was simply an age when parents did that—named their children to match, as if they'd come out of an alphabet book. The bear, the bumblebee, the bunny. Mary and Marjorie Murchison. David and Darlene Daly. Nobody did that anymore. Of course, the mother hadn't stopped at the names themselves but had converted them into nicknames: Pam, Prue, Porsh. Prue's is the only nickname that has stuck. Pamela is now too dignified for hers, and Portia says it's already bad enough, being confused with a car, and why can't she be just an initial?

Roland had been left out of the set, at the insistence of the father. It was Prue's opinion that he had always resented it. "How can you tell?" George asked her, running his tongue around her navel as she lay in her half-slip on the Chinese carpet in his office, smoking a cigarette and surrounded by sheets of paper that had been knocked off the desk during the initial skirmish. She'd made sure the door was unlocked: she liked to run the risk of intrusion, preferably by George's secretary, whom she suspected of being the competition. Which secretary, and when was that? The spilled papers were part of a take-over plan—the Adams group. This is how George keeps track of the various episodes with Prue: by remembering what other skulduggery he was up to at the time. He'd made his money quickly, and then he'd made more. It had been much easier than he'd thought; it had been like spearing fish by lamplight. These people were lax and trusting, and easily embarrassed by a hint of their own intolerance or lack of hospitality to strangers. They weren't ready for him. He'd been as happy as a missionary among the Hawaiians. A hint of opposition and he'd thicken his accent and refer darkly to Communist atrocities. Seize the moral high ground, then grab what you can get.

After that first dinner, they'd all gone into the living room, carrying their cups of coffee. There were kerosene lamps in there, too—old ones, with globe shades. Prue took George flagrantly by the hand and led him over to the bookcase, which was topped with a collection of clam shells and pieces of driftwood from the girls' childhoods. "Here it is," she said. "Read it and weep." She went to refill his coffee. George opened the book, an old edition that had, as he'd hoped, a frontispiece of an angry-looking warrior with tomahawk and paint. Then he scanned the shelves. *From Sea to Sea. Wild Animals I Have Known. The Collected Poems of Robert Service. Our Empire Story. Wilderness Tips.*

"Wilderness Tips" puzzled him. "Wilderness" he knew, but "tips"? He was not immediately sure whether this word was a verb or a noun. There were asparagus tips, as he knew from menus, and when he was getting into the canoe that afternoon in his slippery leather-soled city shoes Prue had said, "Be careful, it tips." Perhaps it was another sort of tip, as in the "Handy Tips for Happy Homemakers" columns in the women's magazines he had taken to reading in order to improve his English—the vocabularies were fairly simple and there were pictures, which was a big help.

When he opened the book he saw he'd guessed right. *Wilderness Tips* was dated 1905. There was a photo of the author in a plaid wool jacket and a felt hat, smoking a pipe and paddling a canoe, against a backdrop that was more or less what you could see out the window: water, islands, rocks, trees. The book itself told how to do useful things, like snaring small animals and eating them—something George himself had done, though not in forests—or lighting a fire in a rainstorm. These instructions were interspersed with lyrical passages about the joys of independence and the open air, and descriptions of fish-catching and sunsets. George took the book over to a chair near one of the globed lamps; he wanted to read about skinning knives, but Prue came back with his coffee, and Portia offered him a chocolate, and he did not want to run the risk of displeasing either of them, not at this early stage. That could come later.

Now George again walks into the living room, again carrying a cup of coffee. By this time he's read all of the books in the great-grandfather's collection. He's the only one who has.

Prue follows him in. The women take it in turns to clear and do the dishes, and it isn't her turn. Roland's job is the wood-splitting. There was an attempt once to press George into service with a tea towel, but he jovially broke three wineglasses, exclaiming over his own clumsiness, and since then he has been left in peace.

"You want more coffee?" Prue says. She stands close to him, proffering the open shirt, the two bandannas. George isn't sure he wants to start anything again, but he sets his coffee down on the top of the bookcase and puts his hand on her hip. He wants to check out his options, make sure he's still welcome. Prue sighs—a long sigh of desire or exasperation, or both.

"Oh, George," she says. "What should I do with you?"

"Whatever you like," says George, moving his mouth close to her ear. "I am merely a lump of clay in your hands." Her earlobe holds a tiny silver earring in the form of a shell. He represses an impulse to nibble.

"Curious George," she says, using one of her old nicknames for him. "You used to have the eyes of a young goat. Lecher eyes."

And now I'm an old goat, thinks George. He can't resist, he wants to be young again; he runs his hand up under her shirt.

"Later," Prue says triumphantly. She steps back from him and aims her wavering smile, and George upsets his cup of coffee with his elbow.

"*Fene egye meg,*" he says, and Prue laughs. She knows the meaning of these swear-words, and worse ones, too.

"Clumsy bugger," she says. "I'll get a sponge."

George lights a cigarette and awaits her return. But it is Pamela who appears, frowning, in the doorway, with a deteriorating scrub cloth and a metal bowl. Trust Prue to have found some other urgent thing to do. She is probably in the outhouse, leafing through a magazine and plotting, deciding when and where she will next entice him.

"So, George, you've made a mess," says Pamela, as if he were a puppy. If she had a rolled-up newspaper, thinks George, she'd give me a swat on the nose.

"It's true, I'm an oaf," says George amiably. "But you've always known that."

Pamela gets down on her knees and begins to wipe. "If the plural of 'loaf' is 'loaves,' what's the plural of 'oaf'?" she says. "Why isn't it 'oaves'?" George realizes that a good deal of what she says is directed not to him or to any other listener but simply to herself. Is that because she thinks no one can hear her?

He finds the sight of her down on her knees suggestive—stirring, even. He catches a whiff of her: soap flakes, a tinge of something sweet. Hand lotion? She has a graceful neck and throat. He wonders if she's ever had a lover, and, if so, what he was like. An insensitive man, lacking in skill. An oaf.

"George, you smoke like a furnace," she says, without turning around. "You really should stop, or it'll kill you."

George considers the ambiguity of the phrase. "Smoking like a furnace." He sees himself as a dragon, fumes and red flames pouring out of his ravenous maw. Is this really her version of him? "That would make you happy," he says, deciding on impulse to try a frontal attack. "You'd love to see me six feet underground. You've never liked me."

Pamela stops wiping and looks at him over her shoulder. Then she stands up and wrings the dirty cloth out into the bowl. "That's juvenile," she says calmly, "and unworthy of you. You need more exercise. This afternoon I'll take you canoeing."

"You know I'm hopeless at that," says George truthfully. "I always crash into rocks. I never see them."

"Geology is destiny," says Pamela, as if to herself. She scowls at the stuffed loon in its glass bell. She is thinking. "Yes," she says at last. "This lake is full of hidden rocks. It can be dangerous. But I'll take care of you."

Is she flirting with him? Can a crag flirt? George can hardly believe it, but he smiles at her, holding the cigarette in the center of his mouth, showing his canines, and for the first time in their lives Pamela smiles back at him. Her mouth is quite different when the corners turn up; it's as if he were seeing her upside down. He's surprised by the loveliness of her smile. It's not a knowing smile, like Prue's, or saintly, like Portia's. It's the smile of an imp, of a mischievous child, mixed in with something he'd never expected to find in her. A generosity, a carelessness, a largesse. She has something she wishes to give him. What could it be?

After lunch and a pause for digestion, Roland goes back to his chopping, beside the woodshed out behind the kitchen. He's splitting birch—a dying tree he cut down a year ago. The beavers had made a start on it, but changed their minds. White birch don't live long anyway. He'd used the chain saw, slicing the trunk neatly into lengths, the blade going through the wood like a knife through butter, the noise blotting out all other noises—the wind and waves, the whining of the trucks from the highway across the lake. He dislikes machine noises, but they're easier to tolerate when you're making them yourself, when you can control them. Like gunshot.

Not that Roland shoots. He used to: he used to go out for a deer in season, but now it's unsafe, there are too many other men doing it—Italians and who knows what—who'll shoot at anything moving. In any case, he's lost the taste for the end result, the antlered carcasses strapped to the fronts of cars like grotesque hood ornaments, the splendid, murdered heads peering dull-eyed from the tops of mini-vans. He can see the point of venison, of killing to eat, but to have a cut-off head on your wall? What does it prove, except that a deer can't pull a trigger?

He never talks about these feelings. He knows they would be held against him at his place of work, which he hates. His job is managing money for other people. He knows he is not a success, not by his great-grandfather's standards. The old man sneers at him every morning from that rosewood frame in the washroom, while he is shaving. They both know the same thing: if Roland were a success he'd be out pillaging, not counting the beans. He'd have some gray, inoffensive, discontented man counting the beans for him. A regiment of them. A regiment of men like himself.

He lifts a chunk of birch, stands it on end on the chopping block, swings the axe. A clean split, but he's out of practice. Tomorrow he will have blisters. In a while he'll stop, stoop and pile, stoop and pile. There's already enough wood, but he likes doing this. It's one of the few things he does like. He feels alive only up here.

Yesterday, he drove up from the center of the city, past the warehouses and factories and shining glass towers, which have gone up, it seems, overnight; past the subdivisions he could swear weren't there last year, last month. Acres of treelessness, of new townhouses with little pointed roofs—like tents, like an invasion. The tents of the Goths and the Vandals. The tents of the Huns and the Magyars. The tents of George.

Down comes his axe on the head of George, which splits in two. If Roland had known George would be here this weekend, he wouldn't have come. Damn Prue and her silly bandannas and her open shirt, her middle-aged breasts offered like hot, freckled muffins along with the sardines and cheese, George sliding his oily eyes all over her, with Portia pretending not to notice. Damn George and his shady deals and his pay-offs to town councillors; damn George and his millions, and his spurious, excessive charm. George should stay in the city where he belongs. He's hard to take even there, but at least Roland can keep out of his way. Here at Wacousta Lodge he's intolerable, strutting around as if he owned the place. Not yet. Probably he'll wait for them all to croak, and then turn it into a lucrative retirement home for the rich Japanese. He'll sell them Nature, at a huge margin. That's the kind of thing George would do.

Roland knew the man was a lizard the first time he saw him. Why did Portia marry him? She could have married somebody decent, leaving George to Prue, who'd dredged him up from God knows where and was flaunting him around like a prize fish. Prue deserved him; Portia didn't. But why did Prue give him up without a struggle? That wasn't like her. It's as if there had been some negotiation, some invisible deal between them. Portia got George, but what did she trade for him? What did she have to give up?

Portia has always been his favorite sister. She was the youngest, the baby. Prue, who was the next youngest, used to tease her savagely, though Portia was remarkably slow to cry. Instead, she would just look, as if she couldn't quite figure out what Prue was doing to her or why. Then she would go off by herself. Or else Roland would come to her defense and there would be a fight, and Roland would be accused of picking on his sister and be told he shouldn't behave that way because he was a boy. He doesn't remember what part Pamela used to take in all this. Pamela was older than the rest of them and had her own agenda, which did not appear to include anyone else at all. Pamela read at the dinner table and went off by herself in the canoe. Pamela was allowed.

In the city they were in different schools or different grades; the house was large and they had their own pathways through it, their own lairs. It was only here that the territories overlapped. Wacousta Lodge, which looks so peaceful, is for Roland the repository of the family wars.

How old had he been—nine? ten?—the time he almost killed Prue? It was the summer he wanted to be an Indian, because of *Wilderness Tips*. He used to sneak that book off the shelf and take it outside, behind the woodshed, and turn and re-turn the pages. *Wilderness Tips* told you how to survive by yourself in the woods—a thing he longed to do. How to build shelters, make clothing from skins, find edible plants. There were diagrams too, and pen-and-ink drawings—of animal tracks, of leaves and seeds. Descriptions of different kinds of animal droppings. He remembers the first time he found some bear scat, fresh and reeking, and purple with blueberries. It scared the hell out of him.

There was a lot about the Indians, about how noble they were, how brave, faithful, clean, reverent, hospitable, and honorable. (Even these words sound outmoded now, archaic. When was the last time Roland heard anyone praised for being *honorable*?) They attacked only in self-defense, to keep their land from being stolen. They walked differently too. There was a diagram, on page 208, of footprints, an Indian's and a white man's: the white wore hobnailed boots, and his toes pointed outward; the Indian wore moccasins, and his feet went straight ahead. Roland has been conscious of his feet ever since. He still turns his toes in slightly, to counteract what he feels must be a genetically programmed waddle.

That summer he ran around with a tea towel tucked into the front of his bathing suit for a loincloth and decorated his face with charcoal from the fireplace, alternating with red paint swiped from Prue's paintbox. He lurked outside windows, listening in. Trying to make smoke signals, he set fire to a small patch of undergrowth down near the boathouse, but put it out before he was caught. He lashed an oblong stone to a stick handle with a leather lace borrowed from one of his father's boots; his father was alive then. He snuck up on Prue, who was reading comic books on the dock, dangling her legs in the water.

He had his stone axe. He could have brained her. She was not Prue, of course: she was Custer, she was treachery, she was the enemy. He went as far as raising the axe, watching the convincing silhouette his shadow made on the dock. The stone fell off, onto his bare foot. He shouted with pain. Prue turned around, saw him there, guessed in an instant what he was doing, and laughed herself silly. That was when he'd almost killed her. The other thing, the stone axe, had just been a game.

The whole thing had just been a game, but it wounded him to let go of it. He'd wanted so badly to believe in that kind of Indian, the kind in the book. He'd needed them to exist.

Driving up yesterday, he'd passed a group of actual Indians, three of them, at a blueberry stand. They were wearing jeans and T-shirts and running shoes, the same as everybody else. One of them had a transistor radio. A neat maroon mini-van was parked beside the stand. So what did he expect from them, feathers? All that was gone, lost, ruined, years and years before he was born.

He knows this is nonsense. He's a bean counter, after all; he deals in the hard currency of reality. How can you lose something that was never yours in the first place? (But you can, because *Wilderness Tips* was his once, and he's lost it. He opened the book today, before lunch, after forty years. There was the innocent, fusty vocabulary that had once inspired him: Manhood with a capital M, courage, honor. The Spirit of the Wild. It was naive, pompous, ridiculous. It was dust.)

Roland chops with his axe. The sound goes out through the trees, across the small inlet to the left of him, bounces off a high ridge of rock, making a faint echo. It's an old sound, a sound left over.

Portia lies on her bed, listening to the sound of Roland chopping wood, having her nap. She has her nap the way she always has, without sleeping. The nap was enforced on her once, by her mother. Now she just does it. When she was little she used to lie here—tucked safely away from Prue—in her parents' room, in her parents' double bed, which is now hers and George's. She would think about all kinds of things; she would see faces and animal shapes in the knots of the pine ceiling and make up stories about them.

Now the only stories she ever makes up are about George. They are probably even more unrealistic than the stories he makes up about himself, but she has no way of really knowing. There are those who lie by instinct and those who don't, and the ones who don't are at the mercy of the ones who do.

Prue, for instance, is a blithe liar. She always has been; she enjoys it. When they were children she'd say, "Look, there's a big snot coming out of your nose," and Portia would run to the washroom mirror. Nothing was there, but Prue's saying it made it somehow true, and Portia would scrub and scrub, trying to wash away invisible dirt, while Prue doubled over with laughter. "Don't believe her," Pamela would say. "Don't be such a sucker." (One of her chief words then—she used it for lollipops, for fish, for mouths.) But sometimes the things Prue said were true, so how could you ever know?

George is the same way. He gazes into her eyes and lies with such tenderness, such heartfelt feeling, such implicit sadness at her want of faith in him, that she can't question him. To question him would turn her cynical and hard. She would rather be kissed; she would rather be cherished. She would rather believe.

She knew about George and Prue at the beginning, of course. It was Prue who brought him up here first. But after a while George swore to her that the thing with Prue hadn't been serious, and, anyway, it was over; and Prue herself seemed not to care. She'd already had George, she implied; he was used, like a dress. If Portia wanted him next it was nothing to her. "Help yourself," she said. "God knows there's enough of George to go around."

Portia wanted to do things the way Prue did; she wanted to get her hands dirty. Something intense, followed by careless dismissal. But she was too young; she didn't have the knack. She'd come up out of the lake and handed George's dark glasses to him, and he'd looked at her in the wrong way: with reverence, not with passion—a clear gaze with no smut in it. After dinner that evening he'd said, with meticulous politeness, "Everything here is so new to me. I like you to be my guide, to your wonderful country."

"Me?" Portia said. "I don't know. What about Prue?" She was already feeling guilty.

"Prue does not understand obligations," he said (which was true enough, she didn't, and this insight of George's was impressive). "You understand them, however. I am the guest; you are the host."

"Hostess," said Pamela, who had not seemed to be listening. "A 'host' is male, like 'mine host' in an inn, or else it's the wafer you eat at Communion. Or the caterpillar that all the parasites lay their eggs on."

"You have a very intellectual sister, I think," said George, smiling, as if this quality in Pamela were a curiosity, or perhaps a deformity. Pamela shot him a look of pure resentment, and ever since that time she has not made any effort with him. He might as well be a bump on a log as far as she's concerned.

But Portia doesn't mind Pamela's indifference; rather, she cherishes it. Once she wanted to be more like Prue, but now it's Pamela. Pamela, considered so eccentric and odd and plain in the fifties, now seems to be the only one of them who got it right. Freedom isn't having a lot of men, not if you think you have to. Pamela does what she wants, nothing more and nothing less.

It's a good thing there's one woman in the universe who can take George or leave him alone. Portia wishes she herself could be so cool. Even after thirty-two years, she's still caught in the breathlessness, the airlessness of love. It's no different from the first night, when he'd bent to kiss her (down by the boathouse, after an evening paddle) and she'd stood there like a deer in the glare of headlights, paralyzed, while something huge and unstoppable bore down on her, waiting for the scream of brakes, the shock of collision. But it wasn't that kind of kiss: it wasn't sex George wanted out of her. He'd wanted the other thing—the wifely white cotton blouses, the bassinets. He's sad they never had children.

He was such a beautiful man then. There were a lot of beautiful men, but the others seemed blank, unwritten on, compared to him. He's the only one she's ever wanted. She can't have him, though, because nobody can. George has himself, and he won't let go.

This is what drives Prue on: she wants to get hold of him finally, open him up, wring some sort of concession out of him. He's the only person in her life she's never been able to bully or ignore or deceive or reduce. Portia can always tell when Prue's back on the attack: there are telltale signs; there are phone calls with no voice attached; there are flights of sincere, melancholy lying from George—a dead giveaway. He knows she knows; he treasures her for saying nothing; she allows herself to be treasured.

There's nothing going on now, though. Not at the moment, not up here, not at Wacousta Lodge. Prue wouldn't dare, and neither would George. He knows where she draws the line; he knows the price of her silence.

Portia looks at her watch: her nap is over. As usual, it has not been restful. She gets up, goes into the washroom, splashes her face. She applies cream lightly, massaging it in around her fallen eyes. The question at this age is what kind of dog you will shortly resemble. She will be a beagle, Prue a terrier. Pamela will be an Afghan, or something equally unearthly.

Her great-grandfather watches her in the mirror, disapproving of her as he always has, although he was dead long before she was born. "I did the best I could," she tells him. "I married a man like you. A robber king." She will never admit to him or to anyone else that this might possibly have been a mistake. (Why does her father never figure in her inner life? Because he wasn't there, not even as a picture. He was at the office. Even in the summers—especially in the summers—he was an absence.)

Outside the window, Roland has stopped chopping and is sitting on the chopping block, his arms on his knees, his big hands dangling, staring off into the trees. He is her favorite; he was the one who always came to her defense. That stopped when she married George. Faced with Prue, Roland had been effective, but George baffled him. No wonder. It's Portia's love that protects George, walls him around. Portia's stupid love.

Where is George? Portia wanders the house, looking for him. Usually at this time of day he'd be in the living room, extended on the couch, dozing; but he isn't there. She looks around the empty room. Everything is as usual: the snowshoes on the wall, the birchbark canoe she always longed to play with but couldn't because it was a souvenir, the rug made out of a bearskin, dull-haired and shedding. That bear was a friend once, it even had a name, but she's forgotten it. On the bookcase there's an empty coffee cup. That's a slip, an oversight; it shouldn't be there. She has the first stirrings of the feeling she gets when she knows George is with Prue, a numbness that begins at the base of the spine. But no, Prue is in the hammock on the screened veranda, reading a magazine. There can't be two of her.

"Where's George?" Portia asks, knowing she shouldn't.

"How the hell should I know?" says Prue. Her tone is peevish, as if she's wondering the same thing. "What's the matter—he slipped his leash? Funny, there's no bimbo secretaries up here." In the sunlight she has a disorderly look: her too-orange lipstick is threading into the tiny wrinkles around her mouth; her bangs are brazen; things are going askew.

"There's no need to be nasty," says Portia. This is what their mother used to say to Prue, over the body of some dismembered doll, some razed sandbox village, a bottle of purloined nail polish hurled against the wall; and Prue never had an answer then. But now their mother isn't here to say it.

"There *is*," says Prue with vehemence. "There is a need."

Ordinarily, Portia would just walk away, pretending she hadn't heard. Now she says, "Why?"

"Because you always had the best of everything," says Prue.

Portia is astounded. Surely she is the mute one, the shadow; hasn't she always played wallflower to Prue's frantic dancer? "What?" she says. "What did I always have?"

"You've always been too good for words," says Prue with rancor. "Why do you stay with him, anyway? Is it the money?"

"He didn't have a bean when I married him," says Portia mildly. She's wondering whether or not she hates Prue. She isn't sure what real hatred would feel like. Anyway, Prue is losing that taut, mischievous body she's done such damage with, and, now that's going, what will she have left? In the way of weapons, that is.

"When *he* married *you*, you mean," says Prue. "When Mother married you off. You just stood there and let the two of them do it, like the little suck you were."

Portia wonders if this is true. She wishes she could go back a few decades, grow up again. The first time, she missed something; she missed a stage, or some vital information other people seemed to have. This time she would make different choices. She would be less obedient; she would not ask for permission. She would be less obedient; she would not ask for permission. She would not say "I do" but "I am."

"Why didn't you ever fight back?" says Prue. She sounds genuinely aggrieved.

Portia can see down the path to the lake, to the dock. There's a canvas deck chair down there with nobody in it. George's newspaper, tucked underneath, is fluttering: there's a wind coming up. George must have forgotten to put his chair away. It's unlike him.

"Just a minute," she says to Prue, as if they're going to take a short break in this conversation they've been having in different ways for fifty years now. She goes out the screen door and down the path. Where has George got to? Probably the outhouse. But his canvas chair is rippling like a sail.

She stoops to fold up the chair, and hears. There's someone in the boathouse; there's a scuffling, a breathing. A porcupine, eating salt off the oar handles? Not in broad daylight. No, there's a voice. The water glitters, the small waves slap against the dock. It can't be Prue; Prue is up on the veranda. It sounds like her mother, like her mother opening birthday presents—that soft crescendo of surprise and almost pained wonder. Oh. Oh. *Oh*. Of course, you can't tell what age a person is, in the dark.

Portia folds the chair, props it gently against the wall of the boathouse. She goes up the path, carrying the paper. No sense in having it blow all over the lake. No sense in having the clear waves dirtied with stale news, with soggy human grief. Desire and greed and terrible disappointments, even in the financial pages. Though you had to read between the lines.

She doesn't want to go into the house. She skirts around behind the kitchen, avoiding the woodshed where she can hear the *chock, chock* of Roland piling wood, goes back along the path that leads to the small, sandy bay where they all swam as children, before they were old enough to dive in off the dock. She lies down on the ground there and goes to sleep. When she wakes up there are pine needles sticking to her cheek and she has a headache. The sun is low in the sky; the wind has fallen; there are no more waves. A dead flat calm. She takes off her clothes, not bothering even to listen for motorboats. They go so fast anyway she'd just be a blur.

She wades into the lake, slipping into the water as if between the layers of a mirror: the glass layer, the silver layer. She meets the doubles of her own legs, her own arms, going down. She floats with only her head above water. She is herself at fifteen, herself at twelve, herself at nine, at six. On the shore, attached to their familiar reflections, are the same rock, the same white stump that have always been there. The cold hush of the lake is like a long breathing-out of relief. It's safe to be this age, to know that the stump is her stump, the rock is hers, that nothing will ever change.

There's a bell, ringing faintly from the distant house. The dinner bell. It's Pamela's turn to cook. What will they have? A strange concoction. Pamela has her own ideas about food.

The bell rings again, and Portia knows that something bad is about to happen. She could avoid it; she could swim out further, let go, and sink.

She looks at the shore, at the water line, where the lake ends. It's no longer horizontal: it seems to be on a slant, as if there'd been a slippage in the bedrock; as if the trees, the granite outcrops, Wacousta Lodge, the peninsula, the whole mainland were sliding gradually down, submerging. She thinks of a boat—a huge boat, a passenger liner—tilting, descending, with the lights still on, the music still playing, the people talking on and on, still not aware of the disaster that has already overcome them. She sees herself running naked through the ballroom—an absurd, disturbing figure with dripping hair and flailing arms, screaming at them, "Don't you see? It's coming apart, everything's coming apart, you're sinking. You're finished, you're over, you're dead!"

She would be invisible, of course. No one would hear her. And nothing has happened, really, that hasn't happened before.

Toni Cade Bambara

Gorilla, My Love

That was the year Hunca Bubba changed his name. Not a change up, but a change back, since Jefferson Winston Vale was the name in the first place. Which was news to me cause he'd been my Hunca Bubba my whole lifetime, since I couldn't manage Uncle to save my life. So far as I was concerned it was a change completely to somethin soundin very geographical weatherlike to me, like somethin you'd find in a almanac. Or somethin you'd run across when you sittin in the navigator seat with a wet thumb on the map crinkly in your lap, watchin the roads and signs so when Granddaddy Vale say "Which way, Scout," you got sense enough to say take the next exit or take a left or whatever it is. Not that Scout's my name. Just the name Granddaddy call whoever sittin in the navigator seat. Which is usually me cause I don't feature sittin in the back with the pecans. Now, you figure pecans all right to be sittin with. If you thinks so, that's your business. But they dusty sometime and make you cough. And they got a way of slidin around and dippin down sudden, like maybe a rat in the buckets. So if you scary like me, you sleep with the lights on and blame it on Baby Jason and, so as not to waste good electric, you study the maps. And that's how come I'm in the navigator seat most times and get to be called Scout.

So Hunca Bubba in the back with the pecans and Baby Jason, and he in love. And we got to hear all this stuff about this woman he in love with and all. Which really ain't enough to keep the mind alive, though Baby Jason got no better sense than to give his undivided attention and keep grabbin at the photograph which is just a picture of some skinny woman in a countrified dress with her hand shot up to her face like she shame fore cameras. But there's a movie house in the background which I ax about. Cause I am a movie freak from way back, even though it do get me in trouble sometime.

Like when me and Big Brood and Baby Jason was on our own last Easter and couldn't go to the Dorset cause we'd seen all the Three Stooges they was. And the RKO Hamilton was closed readying up for the Easter Pageant that night. And the West End, the Regun and the Sunset was too far, less we had grownups with us which we didn't. So we walk up Amsterdam Avenue to the Washington and *Gorilla, My Love* playin, they say, which suit me just fine, though the "my love" part kinda drag Big Brood some. As for Baby Jason, shoot, like Granddaddy say, he'd follow me into the fiery furnace if I say come on. So we go in and get three bags of Havmore potato chips which not only are the best potato chips but the best bags for blowin up and bustin real loud so the matron come trottin down the aisle with her chunky self, flashin that flashlight dead in your eye so you can give her some lip, and if she answer back and you already finish seein the show anyway, why then you just turn the place out. Which I love to do, no lie. With Baby Jason kickin at the seat in front, egging me on, and Big Brood mumblin bout what fiercesome things we goin do. Which means me. Like when the big boys come up on us talkin bout Lemme a nickel. It's me that hide the money. Or when the bad boys in the park take Big Brood's Spaudeen way from him. It's me that jump on they back and fight awhile. And it's me that turns out the show if the matron get too salty.

So the movie come on and right away it's this churchy music and clearly not about no gorilla. Bout Jesus. And I am ready to kill, not cause I got anything gainst Jesus. Just that when you fixed to watch a gorilla picture you don't wanna get messed around with Sunday School stuff. So I am mad. Besides, we see this raggedy old brown film *King of Kings* every year and enough's enough. Grownups figure they can treat you just anyhow. Which burns me up. There I am, my feet up and my Havmore potato chips really salty and crispy and two jawbreakers in my lap and the money safe in my shoe from the big boys, and here comes this Jesus stuff. So we all go wild. Yellin, booin, stompin and carryin on. Really to wake the man in the booth up there who musta went to sleep and put on the wrong reels. But no, cause he holler down to shut up and then he turn the sound up so we really gotta holler like crazy to even hear ourselves good. And the matron ropes off the children section and flashes her light all over the place and we yell some more and some kids slip under the rope and run up and down the aisle just to show it take more than some dusty ole velvet rope to tie us down. And I'm flingin the kid in front of me's popcorn. And Baby Jason kickin seats. And it's really somethin. Then here come the big and bad matron, the one they let out in case of emergency. And she totin that flashlight like she gonna use it on somebody. This here the colored matron Brandy and her friends call Thunderbuns. She do not play. She do not smile. So we shut up and watch the simple ass picture.

Which is not so simple as it is stupid. Cause I realize that just about anybody in my family is better than this god they always talkin about. My daddy wouldn't stand for nobody treatin any of us that way. My mama specially. And I can just see it now, Big Brood up there on the cross talkin bout Forgive them Daddy cause they don't know what they doin. And my Mama say Get on down from there you big fool, whatcha think this is, playtime? And my Daddy yellin to Granddaddy to get him a ladder cause Big Brood actin the fool, his mother side of the family showin up. And my mama and her sister Daisy jumpin on them Romans beatin them with they pocketbooks. And Hunca Bubba tellin them folks on they knees they better get out the way and go get some help or they goin to get trampled on. And Granddaddy Vale sayin Leave the boy alone, if that's what he wants to do with his life we ain't got nothin to say about it. Then Aunt Daisy givin him a taste of that pocketbook, fussin bout what a damn fool old man Granddaddy is. Then everybody jumpin in his chest like the time Uncle Clayton went in the army and come back with only one leg and Granddaddy say somethin stupid about that's life. And by this time Big Brood off the cross and in the park playin handball or skully or somethin. And the family in the kitchen throwin dishes at each other, screamin bout if you hadn't done this I wouldn't had to do that. And me in the parlor trying to do my arithmetic yellin Shut it off.

Which is what I was yellin all by myself which make me a sittin target for Thunderbuns. But when I yell We want our money back, that gets everybody in chorus. And the movie windin up with this heavenly cloud music and the smart-ass up there in his hole in the wall turns up the sound again to drown us out. Then there comes Bugs Bunny which we already seen so we know we been had. No gorilla my nuthin. And Big Brood say Awwww sheeet, we goin to see the manager and get our money back. And I know from this we business. So I brush the potato chips out of my hair which is where Baby Jason like to put em, and I march myself up the aisle to deal with the manager who is a crook in the first place for lyin out there sayin *Gorilla, My Love* playin. And I never did like the man cause he oily and pasty at the same time like the bad guy in the serial, the one that got a hideout behind a push-button bookcase and play "Moonlight Sonata" with gloves on. I knock on the door and I am furious. And I am alone, too. Cause Big Brood suddenly got to go so bad even though my mama told us bout goin in them nasty bathrooms. And I hear him sigh like he disgusted when he get to the door and see only a little kid there. And now I'm really furious cause I get so tired grownups messin over kids just cause they little and can't take em to court. What is it, he say to me like I lost my mittens or wet on myself or am somebody's retarded child. When in reality I am the smartest kid P.S. 186 ever had in its whole lifetime and you can ax anybody. Even them teachers that don't like me cause I won't sing them Southern songs or back off when they tell me my questions are out of order. And cause my Mama come up there in a minute when them teachers start playin the dozens behind colored folks. She stalk in with her hat pulled down bad and that Persian lamb coat draped back over one hip on account of she got her fist planted there so she can talk that talk which gets us all hypnotized, and teacher be comin undone cause she know this could be her job and her behind cause Mama got pull with the Board and bad by her own self anyhow.

So I kick the door open wider and just walk right by him and sit down and tell the man about himself and that I want my money back and that goes for Baby Jason and Big Brood too. And he still trying to shuffle me out the door even though I'm sittin which shows him for the fool he is. Just like them teachers do fore they realize Mama like a stone on that spot and ain't backin up. So he ain't gettin up off the money. So I was forced to leave, takin the matches from under his ashtray, and set a fire under the candy stand, which closed the raggedy ole Washington down for a week. My Daddy had the suspect it was me cause Big Brood got a big mouth. But I explained right quick what the whole thing was about and I figured it was even-steven. Cause if you say Gorilla, My Love, you suppose to mean it. Just like when you say you goin to give me a party on my birthday, you gotta mean it. And if you say me and Baby Jason can go South pecan haulin with Granddaddy Vale, you better not be comin up with no stuff about the weather look uncertain or did you mop the bathroom or any other trickified business. I mean even gangsters in the movies say My word is my bond. So don't nobody get away with nothin far as I'm concerned. So Daddy put his belt back on. Cause that's the way I was raised. Like my Mama say in one of them situations when I won't back down, Okay Badbird, you right. Your point is well-taken. Not that Badbird my name, just what she say when she tired arguin and know I'm right. And Aunt Jo, who is the hardest head in the family and worse even than Aunt Daisy, she say, You absolutely right Miss Muffin, which also ain't my real name but the name she gave me one time when I got some medicine shot in my behind and wouldn't get up off her pillows for nothin. And even Granddaddy Vale—who got no memory to speak of, so sometime you can just plain lie to him, if you want to be like that—he say, Well if that's what I said, then that's it. But this name business was different they said. It wasn't like Hunca Bubba had gone back on his word or anything. Just that he was thinkin bout gettin married and was usin his real name now. Which ain't the way I saw it at all.

So there I am in the navigator seat. And I turn to him and just plain ole ax him. I mean I come right on out with it. No sense goin all around that barn the old folks talk about. And like my mama say, Hazel—which is my real name and what she remembers to call me when she bein serious—when you got somethin on your mind, speak up and let the chips fall where they may. And if anybody don't like it, tell em to come see your mama. And Daddy look up from the paper and say, You hear your mama good, Hazel. And tell em to come see me first. Like that. That's how I was raised.

So I turn clear round in the navigator seat and say, "Look here, Hunca Bubba or Jefferson Windsong Vale or whatever your name is, you gonna marry this girl?"

"Sure am," he say, all grins.

And I say, "Member that time you was baby-sittin me when we lived at four-o-nine and there was this big snow and Mama and Daddy got held up in the country so you had to stay for two days?"

And he say, "Sure do."

"Well. You remember how you told me I was the cutest thing that ever walked the earth?"

"Oh, you were real cute when you were little," he say, which is suppose to be funny. I am not laughin.

"Well. You remember what you said?"

And Granddaddy Vale squintin over the wheel and axin Which way, Scout. But Scout is busy and don't care if we all get lost for days.

"Watcha mean, Peaches?"

"My name is Hazel. And what I mean is you said you were going to marry *me* when I grew up. You were going to wait. That's what I mean, my dear Uncle Jefferson." And he don't say nuthin. Just look at me real strange like he never saw me before in life. Like he lost in some weird town in the middle of night and lookin for directions and there's no one to ask. Like it was me that messed up the maps and turned the road posts round. "Well, you said it, didn't you?" And Baby Jason lookin back and forth like we playin ping-pong. Only I ain't playin. I'm hurtin and I can hear that I am screamin. And Granddaddy Vale mumblin how we never gonna get to where we goin if I don't turn around and take my navigator job serious.

"Well, for cryin out loud, Hazel, you just a little girl. And I was just teasin."

" 'And I was just teasin,' " I say back just how he said it so he can hear what a terrible thing it is. Then I don't say nuthin. And he don't say nuthin. And Baby Jason don't say nuthin nohow. Then Granddaddy Vale speak up. "Look here, Precious, it was Hunca Bubba what told you them things. This here, Jefferson Winston Vale." And Hunca Bubba say, "That's right. That was somebody else. I'm a new somebody."

"You a lyin dawg," I say, when I meant to say treacherous dog, but just couldn't get hold of the word. It slipped away from me. And I'm crying and crumplin down in the seat and just don't care. And Granddaddy say to hush and steps on the gas. And I'm losin my bearins and don't even know where to look on the map cause I can't see for cryin. And Baby Jason cryin too. Cause he is my blood brother and understands that we must stick together or be forever lost, what with grownups playin change-up and turnin you round every which way so bad. And don't even say they sorry.

Russell Banks

My Mother's Memoirs, My Father's Lie, and Other True Stories

(UNITED STATES)

My mother tells me stories about her past, and I don't believe them, I interpret them.

She told me she had the female lead in the Catamount High School senior play and Sonny Tufts had the male lead. She claimed that he asked her to the cast party, but by then she was in love with my father, a stagehand for the play, so she turned down the boy who became a famous movie actor and went to the cast party with the boy who became a New Hampshire carpenter.

She also told me that she knew the principals in Grace Metalious's novel *Peyton Place.* The same night the girl in the book murdered her father, she went afterwards to a Christmas party given by my mother and father in Catamount. "The girl acted strange," my mother said. "Kind of like she was on drugs or something, you know? And the boy she was with, one of the Goldens. He just got drunk and depressed, and then they left. The next day we heard about the police finding the girl's father in the manure pile. . . ."

"Manure pile?"

"She buried him there. And your father told me to keep quiet, not to tell a soul they were at our party on Christmas Eve. That's why our party isn't in the book or the movie they made of it," she explained.

She also insists, in the face of my repeated denials, that she once saw me being interviewed on television by Dan Rather.

I remembered these three stories recently when, while pawing through a pile of old newspaper clippings, I came upon the obituary of Sonny Tufts. Since my adolescence, I have read two and sometimes three newspapers a day, and frequently I clip an article that for obscure or soon forgotten reasons attracts me; then I toss the clipping into a desk drawer, and every once in a while, without scheduling it, I am moved to read through the clippings and throw them out. It's an experience that fills me with a strange sadness, a kind of grief for my lost self, as if I were reading and throwing out old diaries.

But it's my mother I was speaking of. She grew up poor and beautiful in a New England mill town, Catamount, New Hampshire, the youngest of the five children of a machinist whose wife died ("choked to death on a porkchop bone"—another of her stories) when my mother was nineteen. She was invited the same year, 1933, to the Chicago World's Fair to compete in a beauty pageant but didn't accept the invitation, though she claims my father went to the fair and played his clarinet in a National Guard marching band. Her father, she said, made her stay in Catamount that summer, selling dresses for Grover Cronin's Department Store on River Street. If her mother had not died that year, she would have been able to go to the fair. "And who knows," she joked, "you might've ended up the son of Miss Chicago World's Fair of 1933."

To tell the truth, I don't know very much about my mother's life before 1940, the year I was born and started gathering material for my own stories. Like most people, I pay scant attention to the stories I'm told about lives and events that precede the remarkable event of my own birth. We all seem to tell and hear our own memoirs. It's the same with my children. I watch their adolescent eyes glaze over, their attention drift on to secret plans for the evening and weekend, as I point out the tenement on Perley Street in Catamount where I spent my childhood. Soon it will be too late, I want to say. Soon I, too, will be living in exile, retired from the cold like my mother in San Diego, alone in a drab apartment in a project by the bay, collecting social security and wondering if I'll have enough money at the end of the month for a haircut. Soon all you'll have of me will be your memories of my stories.

Everyone knows that the death of a parent is a terrible thing. But because our parents usually have not been a part of our daily lives for years, most of us do not miss them when they die. When my father died, even though I had been seeing him frequently and talking with him on the phone almost every week, I did not miss him. Yet his death was for me a terrible thing and goes on being a terrible thing now, five years later. My father, a depressed, cynical alcoholic, did not tell stories, but even if he had told stories—about his childhood in Nova Scotia, about beating out Sonny Tufts in the courtship of my mother, about playing the clarinet at the Chicago World's Fair—I would not have listened. No doubt, in his cynicism and despair of ever being loved, he knew that.

The only story my father told me that I listened to closely, visualized, and have remembered, he told me a few months before he died. It was the story of how he came to name me Earl. Naturally, as a child I asked, and he simply shrugged and said he happened to like the name. My mother corroborated the shrug. But one Sunday morning the winter before he died, three years before he planned to retire and move to a trailer down south, I was sitting across from my father in his kitchen, watching him drink tumblers of Canadian Club and ginger ale, and he wagged a finger in my face and told me that I did not know who I was named after.

"I thought no one," I said.

"When I was a kid," he said, "my parents tried to get rid of me in the summers. They used to send me to stay with my uncle Earl up on Cape Breton. He was a bachelor and kind of a hermit, and he stayed drunk most of the time.

But he played the fiddle, the violin. And he loved me. He was quite a character. But then, when I was about twelve, I was old enough to spend my summers working, so they kept me down in Halifax after that. And I never saw Uncle Earl again."

He paused and sipped at his drink. He was wearing his striped pajamas and maroon bathrobe and carpet slippers and was chain-smoking Parliaments. His wife (his second—my mother divorced him when I was twelve, because of his drinking and what went with it) had gone to the market as soon as I arrived, as if afraid to leave him without someone else in the house. "He died a few years later," my father said. "Fell into a snowbank, I heard. Passed out. Froze to death."

I listened to the story and have remembered it today because I thought it was about *me,* my name, Earl. My father told it, of course, because it was about *him,* and because for an instant that cold February morning he dared to hope that his oldest son would love him.

At this moment, as I say this, I do love him, but it's too late for the saying to make either of us happy. That is why I say the death of a parent is a terrible thing.

After my father died, I asked his sister Ethel about poor old Uncle Earl. She said she never heard of the man. The unofficial family archivist and only a few years younger than my father, she surely would have known of him, would have known how my father spent his summers, would have known of the man he loved enough to name his firstborn son after.

The story simply was not true. My father had made it up.

Just as my mother's story about Sonny Tufts is not true. Yesterday, when I happened to come across the article about Sonny Tufts from the *Boston Globe,* dated June 8, 1970, and written by the late George Frazier, I wouldn't have bothered to reread it if the week before I had not been joking about Sonny Tufts with a friend, a woman who lives in Boston and whose mother died this past summer. My friend's mother's death, like my father's, was caused by acute alcoholism and had been going on for years. What most suicides accomplish in minutes, my father and my friend's mother took decades to do.

The death of my friend's mother reminded me of the consequences of the death of my father and of my mother's continuing to live. And then our chic joke about the 1940s film star ("Whatever happened to Sonny Tufts?"), a joke about our own aging, reminded me of my mother's story about the senior play in 1932, so that when I saw Frazier's obituary for Tufts, entitled "Death of a Bonesman" (Tufts had gone to Yale and been tapped for Skull and Bones), instead of tossing it back in the drawer or into the wastebasket, I read it through to the end, as if searching for a reference to my mother's having brushed him off. Instead, I learned that Bowen Charlton Tufts III, scion of an old Boston banking family, had prepped for Yale at Exeter. So that his closest connection to the daughter of a machinist in Catamount, and to me, was probably through his father's bank's ownership of the mill where the machinist ran a lathe.

I had never believed the story anyhow, but now I had proof that she made it up. Just as the fact that I have never been interviewed by Dan Rather is proof that my mother never saw me on television in her one-room apartment in San Diego being interviewed by Dan Rather. By the time she got her friend down the hall to come and see her son on TV, Dan had gone on to some depressing stuff about the Middle East.

As for Grace Metalious's characters from *Peyton Place* showing up at a Christmas party in my parents' house in Catamount, I never believed that, either. *Peyton Place* indeed based on a true story about a young woman's murder of her father in Gilmanton, New Hampshire, a village some twenty-five miles from Catamount, but in the middle 1940s people simply did not drive twenty-five miles over snow-covered back roads on a winter night to go to a party given by strangers.

I said that to my mother. She had just finished telling me, for the hundredth time, it seemed, that someday, based on my own experiences as a child and now as an adult in New Hampshire, I should be able to write another *Peyton Place*. This was barely two months ago, and I was visiting her in San Diego, an extension of a business trip to Los Angeles, and I was seated rather uncomfortably in her one-room apartment. She is a tiny, wrenlike woman with few possessions, most of which seem miniaturized, designed to fit her small body and the close confines of her room, so that when I visit her I feel huge and oafish. I lower my voice and move with great care.

She was ironing her sheets, while I sat on the unmade sofa bed, unmade because I had just turned the mattress for her, a chore she saves for when I or my younger brother, the only large-sized people in her life now, visits her from the East. "But we *weren't* strangers to them," my mother chirped. "Your father knew the Golden boy somehow. Probably one of his local drinking friends," she said. "Anyhow, that's why your father wouldn't let me tell anyone, after the story came out in the papers, about the murder and the incest and all. . . ."

"Incest? What incest?"

"You know, the father who got killed, killed and buried in the manure pile by his own daughter because he'd been committing incest with her. Didn't you read the book?"

"No."

"Well, your father, he was afraid we'd get involved somehow. So I couldn't tell anyone about it until after the book got famous. You know, whenever I tell people out here that back in New Hampshire in the forties I knew the girl who killed her father in *Peyton Place*, they won't believe me. Well, not exactly *knew*, her, but you know. . . ."

There's always someone famous in her stories, I thought. Dan Rather, Sonny Tufts, Grace Metalious (though my mother can never remember her name, only the name of the book she wrote). It's as if she hopes you will love her more easily if she is associated somehow with fame.

When you know a story isn't true, you think you don't have to listen to it. What you think you're supposed to do is interpret, as I was doing that morning in my mother's room, converting her story into a clue to her psychology, which in turn would lead me to compare it to my own psychology and, with relief, disapprove. (*My* stories don't have famous people in them.) I did the same thing with my father's drunken fiddler, Uncle Earl, once I learned he didn't exist. I used the story as a clue to help unravel the puzzle of my father's dreadful psychology, hoping no doubt to unravel the puzzle of my own.

One of the most difficult things to say to another person is I hope you will love me. Yet that is what we all want to say to one another—to our children, to our parents and mates, to our friends and even to strangers.

Perhaps especially to strangers. My friend in Boston, who joked with me about Sonny Tufts as an interlude in the story of her mother's awful dying, was showing me her hope that I would love her, even when the story itself was about her mother's lifelong refusal to love her and, with the woman's death, the absolute removal of any possibility of that love. I have, at least, my father's story of how I got my name, and though it's too late for me now to give him what, for a glimmering moment, he hoped and asked for, by remembering his story I have understood a little more usefully the telling of my own.

By remembering, as if writing my memoirs, what the stories of others have reminded me of, what they have literally brought to my mind, I have learned how my own stories function in the world, whether I tell them to my mother, to my wife, to my children, to my friends or, especially, to strangers. And to complete the circle, I have learned a little more usefully how to listen to the stories of others, whether they are true or not.

As I was leaving my mother that morning to drive back to Los Angeles and then fly home to New Hampshire, where my brother and sister and all my mother's grandchildren live and where all but the last few years of my mother's past was lived, she told me a new story. We stood in the shade of palm trees in the parking lot outside her glass-and-metal building for a few minutes, and she said to me in a concerned way, "You know that restaurant, the Pancake House, where you took me for breakfast this morning?"

I said yes and checked the time and flipped my suitcase into the back seat of the rented car.

"Well, I always have breakfast there on Wednesdays, it's on the way to where I baby-sit on Wednesdays, and this week something funny happened there. I sat alone way in the back, where they have that long, curving booth, and I didn't notice until I was halfway through my breakfast that at the far end of the booth a man was sitting there. He was maybe your age, a young man, but dirty and shabby. Especially dirty, and so I just looked away and went on eating my eggs and toast.

"But then I noticed he was looking at me, as if he knew me and didn't quite dare talk to me. I smiled, because maybe I did know him, I know just about everybody in the neighborhood now. But he was a stranger. And dirty. And I could see that he had been drinking for days.

"So I smiled and said to him, 'You want help, mister, don't you?' He needed a shave, and his clothes were filthy and all ripped, and his hair was a mess. You know the type. But something pathetic about his eyes made me want to talk to him. But honestly, Earl, I couldn't. I just couldn't. He was so dirty and all.

"Anyhow, when I spoke to him, just that little bit, he sort of came out of his daze and sat up straight for a second, like he was afraid I was going to complain to the manager and have him thrown out of the restaurant. 'What did you say to me?' he asked. His voice was weak but he was trying to make it sound strong, so it came out kind of loud and broken. 'Nothing,' I said, and I turned away from him and quickly finished my breakfast and left.

"That afternoon, when I was walking back home from my baby-sitting job, I went into the restaurant to see if he was there, but he wasn't. And the next morning, Thursday, I walked all the way over there to check again, even though I never eat breakfast at the Pancake House on Thursdays, but he was gone then too. And then yesterday, Friday, I went back a third time. But he was gone." She lapsed into a thoughtful silence and looked at her hands.

"Was he there this morning?" I asked, thinking coincidence was somehow the point of the story.

"No," she said. "But I didn't expect him to be there this morning. I'd stopped looking for him by yesterday."

"Well, why'd you tell me the story, then? What's it about?"

"About? Why, I don't know. Nothing, I guess. I just felt sorry for the man, and then because I was afraid, I shut up and left him alone." She was still studying her tiny hands.

"That's natural," I said. "You shouldn't feel guilty for that," I said, and I put my arms around her.

She turned her face into my shoulder. "I know, I know. But still . . ." Her blue eyes filled, her son was leaving again, gone for another six months or a year, and who would she tell her stories to while he was gone? Who would listen?

Nicola Barker

G-String

(ENGLAND)

Ever fallen out with somebody simply because they agreed with you? Well, this is exactly what happened to Gillian and her pudgy but reliable long-term date, Mr. Kip.

They lived separately in Canvey Island. Mr. Kip ran a small but flourishing insurance business there. Gillian worked for a car-hire firm in Grays Thurrock. She commuted daily.

Mr. Kip—he liked to be called that, an affectation, if you will—was an ardent admirer of the great actress Katharine Hepburn. She was skinny and she was elegant and she was sparky and she was intelligent. Everything a girl should be. She was *old* now, too, Gillian couldn't help thinking, but naturally she didn't want to appear a spoilsport so she kept her lips sealed.

Gillian was thirty-four, a nervous size sixteen, had no cheekbones to speak of and hair which she tried to perm. God knows she tried. She was the goddess of frizz. She frizzed but she did not fizz. She was not fizzy like Katharine. At least, that's what Mr. Kip told her.

Bloody typical, isn't it? When a man chooses to date a woman, long term, who resembles his purported heroine in no way whatsoever? Is it safe? Is it cruel? Is it downright simple-minded?

Gillian did her weekly shopping in Southend. They had everything you needed there. Of course there was the odd exception: fishing tackle, seaside mementos, insurance, underwear. These items she never failed to purchase in Canvey Island itself, just to support local industry.

A big night out was on the cards. Mr. Kip kept telling her how big it would be. A local Rotary Club do, and Gillian was to be Mr. Kip's special partner, he was to escort her, in style. He was even taking the cloth off his beloved old Aston Martin for the night to drive them there and back. And he'd never deigned to do that before. Previously he'd only ever taken her places in his H-reg Citroën BX.

Mr. Kip told Gillian that she was to buy a new frock for this special occasion. Something, he imagined, like that glorious dress Katharine Hepburn wore during the bar scene in her triumph, *Bringing Up Baby*.

Dutifully, Gillian bought an expensive dress in white chiffon which didn't at all suit her. Jeanie—twenty-one with doe eyes, sunbed-brown and weighing in at ninety pounds—told Gillian that the dress made her look like an egg-box. All lumpy-humpy. It was her underwear, Jeanie informed her—If only! Gillian thought—apparently it was much too visible under the dress's thin fabric. Jeanie and Gillian were conferring in The Lace Bouquet, the lingerie shop on Canvey High Street where Jeanie worked.

"I tell you what," Jeanie offered, "all in one lace bodysuit, right? Stretchy stuff. No bra. No knickers. It'll hold you in an' everything." Jeanie held up the prospective item. Bodysuits, Gillian just *knew*, would not be Mr. Kip's idea of sophisticated. She shook her head. She looked down at her breasts. "I think I'll need proper support," she said, grimacing.

Jeanie screwed up her eyes and chewed at the tip of her thumb. "Bra and pants, huh?"

"I think so."

Although keen not to incur Jeanie's wrath, Gillian picked out the kind of bra she always wore, in bright, new white, and a pair of matching briefs.

Jeanie ignored the bra. It was functional. Fair enough. But the briefs she held aloft and proclaimed, "Passion killers."

"They're tangas," Gillian said, defensively, proud of knowing the modern technical term for the cut-away pant. "They're brief briefs."

Jeanie snorted. "No one wears these things any more, Gillian. There's enough material here to launch a sailboat."

Jeanie picked up something that resembled an obscenely elongated garter and proffered it to Gillian. Gillian took hold of the scrap.

"What's this?"

"G-string."

"My God, girls wear these in Dave Lee Roth videos."

"Who's that?" Jeanie asked, sucking in her cheeks, insouciant.

"They aren't practical," Gillian said.

Jeanie's eyes narrowed. "These are truly modern knickers," she said. "These are what *everyone* wears now. And I'll tell you for why. No visible pantie line!"

Gillian didn't dare inform her that material was the whole point of a pantie. Wasn't it?

"Oh hell, Gillian thought, shifting on Mr. Kip's Aston Martin's leather seats, "maybe I should've worn it in for a few days first." It felt like her G-string was making headway from between her buttocks up into her throat. She felt like a leg of lamb, trussed up with cheese wire. Now she knew how a horse felt when offered a new bit and bridle for the first time.

"Wearing hairspray?" Mr. Kip asked, out of the blue.

"What?"

"If you are," he said, ever careful, "then don't lean your head back on to the seat. It's real leather and you may leave a stain."

Gillian bit her lip and stopped wriggling.

"Hope it doesn't rain," Mr. Kip added, keeping his hand on the gearstick in a very male way, "the wipers aren't quite one hundred per cent."

Oh, the G-string was a modern thing, but it looked so horrid! Gillian wanted to be a modern girl but when she espied her rear-end engulfing the slither of string like a piece of dental floss entering the gap between two great white molars, her heart sank down into her strappy sandals. It tormented her. Like the pain of an old bunion, it quite took off her social edge.

When Mr. Kip didn't remark favourably on her new dress; when, in fact, he drew a comparison between Gillian and the cone-shaped upstanding white napkins on the fancily made-up Rotary tables, she almost didn't try to smile. He drank claret. He smoked a cigar and tipped ash on her. He didn't introduce her to any of his Rotary friends. Normally, Gillian might have grimaced on through. But tonight she was a modern girl in torment and this kind of behaviour quite simply would not do.

Of course she didn't actually *say* anything. Mr. Kip finally noticed Gillian's distress during liqueurs.

"What's got into you?"

"Headache," Gillian grumbled, fighting to keep her hands on her lap.

Two hours later, Mr. Kip deigned to drive them home. It was raining. Gillian fastened her seatbelt. Mr. Kip switched on the windscreen wipers. They drove in silence. Then all of a sudden, *wheeeuwoing!* One of the wipers flew off the windscreen and into a ditch. Mr. Kip stopped the car. He reversed. He clambered out to look for the wiper, but because he wore glasses, drops of rain impaired his vision.

It was a quiet road. What the hell. Mr. Kip told Gillian to get out and look for it.

"In my white dress?" Gillian asked, quite taken aback.

Fifteen minutes later, damp, mussed, muddy, Gillian finally located the wiper. Mr. Kip fixed it back on, but when he turned the relevant switch on the dash, neither of the wipers moved. He cursed like crazy.

"Well, that's that," he said, and glared at Gillian like it was her fault completely. They sat and sat. It kept right on raining.

Finally Gillian couldn't stand it a minute longer. "Give me your tie," she ordered. Mr. Kip grumbled but did as she'd asked. Gillian clambered out of the car and attached the tie to one of the wipers.

"Ok," she said, trailing the rest of the tie in through Mr. Kip's window. "Now we need something else. Are you wearing a belt?"

Mr. Kip shook his head.

"Something long and thin," Gillian said, "like a rope."

Mr. Kip couldn't think of anything.

"Shut your eyes," Gillian said. Mr. Kip shut his eyes, but after a moment, naturally, he peeped.

And what a sight! Gillian laboriously freeing herself from some panties which looked as bare and sparse and confoundedly stringy as a pirate's eye patch.

"Good gracious!" Mr. Kip exclaimed. "You could at least have worn some French knickers or cami-knickers or something proper. Those are preposterous!"

Gillian turned on him. "I've really had it with you, Colin," she snarled, "with your silly, affected, old-fashioned car and clothes and *everything.*"

From her bag Gillian drew out her Swiss Army Knife and applied it with gusto to the plentiful elastic on her G-string. Then she tied one end to the second wiper and pulled the rest around and through her window. "Right," she said, "start up the engine."

Colin Kip did as he was told. Gillian manipulated the wipers manually; left, right, left, right. All superior and rhythmical and practical and dour-faced.

Mr. Kip was very impressed. He couldn't help himself. After several minutes of driving in silence he took his hand off the gearstick and slid it on to Gillian's lap.

"Watch it," Gillian said harshly. "Don't you dare provoke me, Colin. I haven't put my Swiss Army Knife away yet."

She felt the pressure of his hand leave her thigh. She was knickerless. She was victorious. She was a truly modern female.

Julian Barnes

Evermore

(ENGLAND)

All the time she carried them with her, in a bag knotted at the neck. She had bayoneted the polythene with a fork, so that condensation would not gather and begin to rot the frail card. She knew what happened when you covered seedlings in a flower-pot: damp came from nowhere to make its sudden climate. This had to be avoided. There had been so much wet back then, so much rain, churned mud and drowned horses. She did not mind it for herself. She minded it for them still, for all of them, back then.

There were three postcards, the last he had sent. The earlier ones had been divided up, lost perhaps, but she had the last of them, his final evidence. On the day itself, she would unknot the bag and trace her eyes over the jerky pencilled address, the formal signature (initials and surname only), the obedient crossings-out. For many years she had ached at what the cards did not say; but nowadays she found something in their official impassivity which seemed proper, even if not consoling.

Of course she did not need actually to look at them, any more than she needed the photograph to recall his dark eyes, sticky-out ears, and the jaunty smile which agreed that the fun would be all over by Christmas. At any moment she could bring the three pieces of buff field-service card exactly to mind. The dates: Dec. 24, Jan. 11, Jan. 17, written in his own hand, and confirmed by the postmark which added the years: 16, 17, 17. "NOTHING is to be written on this side except the date and signature of the sender. Sentences not required may be erased. If anything else is added the postcard will be destroyed." And then the brutal choices.

```
I am quite well
I have been admitted into hospital
     ⎧ sick    ⎫ and am going on well
   — ⎩ wounded ⎭ and hope to be discharged soon
I am being sent down to the base
                      ⎧ letter dated . . . . . .
I have received your  ⎨ telegram . . . . . . . .
                      ⎩ parcel . . . . . . . . . .
```

```
Letter follows at first opportunity
I have received no letter from you
 ⎧Lately
 ⎨
 ⎩For a long time.
```

He was quite well on each occasion. He had never been admitted into hospital. He was not being sent down to the base. He had received a letter of a
certain date. A letter would follow at the first opportunity. He had not received no letter. All done with thick pencilled crossing-out and a single date.
Then, beside the instruction <u>Signature only,</u> the last signal from her brother.
S. Moss. A large looping S with a circling full stop after it. Then Moss written
without lifting from the card what she always imagined as a stub of pencil-end
studiously licked.

On the other side, their mother's name—Mrs. Moss, with a grand M and a
short stabbing line beneath the *rs*—then the address. Another warning down
the edge, this time in smaller letters. "The address only to be written on this
side. If anything else is added, the postcard will be destroyed." But across the
top of her second card, Sammy had written something, and it had not been
destroyed. A neat line of ink without the rough loopiness of his pencilled signature: "<u>50 yds</u> from the Germans. Posted from Trench." In fifty years, one for
each underlined yard, she had not come up with the answer. Why had he written it, why in ink, why had they allowed it? Sam was a cautious and responsible boy, especially towards their mother, and he would not have risked a
worrying silence. But he had undeniably written these words. And in ink, too.
Was it code for something else? A premonition of death? Except that Sam was
not the sort to have premonitions. Perhaps it was simply excitement, a desire
to impress. Look how close we are. <u>50 yds</u> from the Germans. Posted from
Trench.

She was glad he was at Cabaret Rouge, with his own headstone. Found and
identified. Given known and honoured burial. She had a horror of Thiepval,
one which failed to diminish in spite of her dutiful yearly visits. Thiepval's lost
souls. You had to make the right preparation for them, for their lostness. So
she always began elsewhere, at Caterpillar Valley, Thistle Dump, Quarry,
Blighty Valley, Ulster Tower, Herbécourt.

No Morning Dawns
No Night Returns
But What We Think of Thee

That was at Herbécourt, a walled enclosure in the middle of fields, room for a
couple of hundred, most of them Australian, but this was a British lad, the one
who owned this inscription. Was it a vice to have become such a connoisseur
of grief? Yet it was true, she had her favourite cemeteries. Like Blighty Valley
and Thistle Dump, both half-hidden from the road in a fold of valley; or
Quarry, a graveyard looking as if it had been abandoned by its village; or Devonshire, that tiny, private patch for the Devonshires who died on the first day

of the Somme, who fought to hold that ridge and held it still. You followed signposts in British racing green, then walked across fields guarded by wooden martyred Christs to these sanctuaries of orderliness, where everything was accounted for. Headstones were lined up like dominoes on edge; beneath them, their owners were present and correct, listed, tended. Creamy altars proclaimed that THEIR NAME LIVETH FOR EVERMORE. And so it did, on the graves, in the books, in hearts, in memories.

Each year she wondered if this would be her last visit. Her life no longer offered up to her the confident plausibility of two decades more, one decade, five years. Instead, it was now renewed on an annual basis, like her driving licence. Every April Dr. Holling had to certify her fit for another twelve months behind the wheel. Perhaps she and the Morris would go kaput on the same day.

Before, it had been the boat train, the express to Amiens, a local stopper, a bus or two. Since she had acquired the Morris, she had in theory become freer; and yet her routine remained almost immutable. She would drive to Dover and take a night ferry, riding the Channel in the blackout alongside burly lorry-drivers. It saved money, and meant she was always in France for daybreak. No Morning Dawns . . . He must have seen each daybreak and wondered if that was the date they would put on his stone . . . Then she would follow the N43 to St-Omer, to Aire and Lillers, where she usually took a croissant and *thé à l'anglaise.* From Lillers the N43 continued to Béthune, but she flinched from it: south of Béthune was the D937 to Arras, and there, on a straight stretch where the road did a reminding elbow, was Brigadier Sir Frank Higginson's domed portico. You should not drive past it, even if you intended to return. She had done that once, early in her ownership of the Morris, skirted Cabaret Rouge in second gear, and it had seemed the grossest discourtesy to Sammy and those who lay beside him: no, it's not your turn yet, just you wait and we'll be along. No, that was what the other motorists did.

So instead she would cut south from Lillers and come into Arras with the D341. From there, in that thinned triangle whose southern points were Albert and Péronne, she would begin her solemn and necessary tour of the woods and fields in which, so many decades before, the British Army had counterattacked to relieve the pressure on the French at Verdun. That had been the start of it, anyway. No doubt scholars were by now having second thoughts, but that was what they were for; she herself no longer had arguments to deploy or positions to hold. She valued only what she had experienced at the time: an outline of strategy, the conviction of gallantry, and the facts of mourning.

At first, back then, the commonality of grief had helped: wives, mothers, comrades, an array of brass hats, and a bugler amid gassy morning mist which the feeble November sun had failed to burn away. Later, remembering Sam had changed: it became work, continuity; instead of anguish and glory, there was fierce unreasonableness, both about his death and her commemoration of it. During this period, she was hungry for the solitude and the voluptuous selfishness of grief: her Sam, her loss, her mourning, and nobody else's similar.

She admitted as much: there was no shame to it. But now, after half a century, her feelings had simply become part of her. Her grief was a calliper, necessary and supporting; she could not imagine walking without it.

When she had finished with Herbécourt and Devonshire, Thistle Dump and Caterpillar Valley, she would come, always with trepidation, to the great red-brick memorial at Thiepval. An arch of triumph, yes, but of what kind, she wondered: the triumph over death, or the triumph *of* death? "Here are recorded names of officers and men of the British armies who fell on the Somme battlefields July 1915–February 1918 but to whom the fortune of war denied the known and honoured burial given to their comrades in death." Thiepval Ridge, Pozières Wood, Albert, Morval, Ginchy, Guillemont, Ancre, Ancre Heights, High Wood, Delville Wood, Bapaume, Bazentin Ridge, Miraumont, Transloy Ridges, Flers-Courcelette. Battle after battle, each accorded its stone laurel wreath, its section of wall: name after name after name, the Missing of the Somme, the official graffiti of death. This monument by Sir Edwin Lutyens revolted her, it always had. She could not bear the thought of these lost men, exploded into unrecognisable pieces, engulfed in the mudfields, one moment fully there with pack and gaiters, baccy and rations, with their memories and their hopes, their past and their future, crammed into them, and the next moment only a shred of khaki or a sliver of shin-bone to prove they had ever existed. Or worse: some of these names had first been given known and honoured burial, their allotment of ground with their name above it, only for some new battle with its heedless artillery to tear up the temporary graveyard and bring a second, final extermination. Yet each of those scraps of uniform and flesh—whether newly killed or richly decomposed— had been brought back here and reorganised, conscripted into the eternal regiment of the missing, kitted out and made to dress by the right. Something about the way they had vanished and the way they were now reclaimed was more than she could bear: as if an army which had thrown them away so lightly now chose to own them again so gravely. She was not sure whether this was the case. She claimed no understanding of military matters. All she claimed was an understanding of grief.

Her wariness of Thiepval always made her read it with a sceptical, a proof-reader's eye. She noticed, for instance, that the French translation of the English inscription listed—as the English one did not—the exact number of the Missing. 73,367. That was another reason she did not care to be here, standing in the middle of the arch looking down over the puny Anglo-French cemetery (French crosses to the left, British stones to the right) while the wind drew tears from an averting eye. 73,367: beyond a certain point, the numbers became uncountable and diminishing in effect. The more dead, the less proportionate the pain. 73,367: even she, with all her expertise in grief, could not imagine that.

Perhaps the British realised that the number of the Missing might continue to grow through the years, that no fixed total could be true; perhaps it was not shame, but a kind of sensible poetry which made them decline to specify a figure. And they were right: the numbers had indeed changed. The arch was inaugurated in 1932 by the Prince of Wales, and all the names of all the Missing had been carved upon its surfaces, but still, here and there, out of their proper place, hauled back tardily from oblivion, were a few soldiers enlisted only under the heading of Addenda. She knew all their names by now: Dodds T., Northumberland Fusiliers; Malcolm H. W., The Cameronians; Lennox F. J., Royal Irish Rifles; Lovell F. H. B., Royal Warwickshire Regiment; Orr R., Royal Inniskillins; Forbes R., Cameron Highlanders; Roberts J., Middlesex Regiment; Moxham A., Wiltshire Regiment; Humphries F. J., Middlesex Regiment; Hughes H. W., Worcestershire Regiment; Bateman W. T., Northamptonshire Regiment; Tarling E., The Cameronians; Richards W., Royal Field Artillery; Rollins S., East Lancashire Regiment; Byrne L., Royal Irish Rifles; Gale E. O., East Yorkshire Regiment; Walters J., Royal Fusiliers; Argar D., Royal Field Artillery. No Morning Dawns, No Night Returns . . .

She felt closest to Rollins S., since he was an East Lancashire; she would always smile at the initials inflicted upon Private Lovell; but it was Malcolm H. W. who used to intrigue her most. Malcolm H. W., or, to give him his full inscription: "Malcolm H. W. The Cameronians (Sco. Rif.) served as Wilson H." An addendum and a corrigendum all in one. When she had first discovered him, it had pleased her to imagine his story. Was he under age? Did he falsify his name to escape home, to run away from some girl? Was he wanted for a crime, like those fellows who joined the French Foreign Legion? She did not really want an answer, but she liked to dream a little about this man who had first been deprived of his identity and then of his life. These accumulations of loss seemed to exalt him; for a while, faceless and iconic, he had threatened to rival Sammy and Denis as an emblem of the war. In later years she turned against such fancifulness. There was no mystery really. Private H. W. Malcolm becomes H. Wilson. No doubt he was in truth H. Wilson Malcolm, and when he volunteered they wrote the wrong name in the wrong column; then they were unable to change it. That would make sense: man is only a clerical error corrected by death.

She had never cared for the main inscription over the central arch:

AUX ARMEES

FRANCAISE ET

BRITANNIQUE

L'EMPIRE

BRITANNIQUE

RECON-

NAISSANT

Each line was centred, which was correct, but there was altogether too much white space beneath the inscription. She would have inserted "less #" on the galley-proof. And each year she disliked more and more the line-break in the word *reconnaissant*. There were different schools of thought about this—she had argued with her superiors over the years—but she insisted that breaking a word in the middle of a doubled consonant was a nonsense. You broke a word where the word itself was perforated. Look what this military, architectural or sculptural nincompoop had produced: a fracture which left a separate word, *naissant,* by mistake. *Naissant* had nothing to do with *reconnaissant,* nothing at all; worse, it introduced the notion of birth on to this monument to death. She had written to the War Graves Commission about it, many years ago, and had been assured that the proper procedures had been followed. They told *her* that!

Nor was she content with EVERMORE. Their name liveth for evermore: here at Thiepval, also at Cabaret Rouge, Caterpillar Valley, Combles Communal Cemetery Extension, and all the larger memorials. It was of course the correct form, or at least the more regular form; but something in her preferred to see it as two words. EVER MORE: it seemed more weighty like this, with an equal bell-toll on each half. In any case, she had a quarrel with the Dictionary about *evermore.* "Always, at all times, constantly, continually." Yes, it could mean this in the ubiquitous inscription. But she preferred sense 1: "For all future time." Their name liveth for all future time. No morning dawns, no night returns, but what we think of thee. This is what the inscription meant. But the Dictionary had marked sense 1 as *"Obs. exc. arch."* Obsolete except archaic. No, oh certainly not, no. And not with a last quotation as recent as 1854. She would have spoken to Mr. Rothwell about this, or at least pencilled a looping note on the galley-proof; but this entry was not being revised, and the letter E had passed over her desk without an opportunity to make the adjustment.

EVERMORE. She wondered if there was such a thing as collective memory, something more than the sum of individual memories. If so, was it merely coterminous, yet in some way richer; or did it last longer? She wondered if those too young to have original knowledge could be given memory, could have it grafted on. She thought of this especially at Thiepval. Though she hated the place, when she saw young families trailing across the grass towards the red-brick *arc-de-triomphe* it also roused in her a wary hopefulness. Christian cathedrals could inspire religious faith by their vast assertiveness; why then should not Lutyens' memorial provoke some response equally beyond the rational? That reluctant child, whining about the strange food its mother produced from plastic boxes, might receive memory here. Such an edifice assured the newest eye of the pre-existence of the profoundest emotions. Grief and awe lived here; they could be breathed, absorbed. And if so, then this child might in turn bring its child, and so on, from generation to generation, EVERMORE. Not just to count the Missing, but to understand what those from whom they had gone missing knew, and to feel her loss afresh.

Perhaps this was one reason she had married Denis. Of course she should never have done so. And in a way she never had, for there had been no carnal connection: she unwilling, he incapable. It had lasted two years and his uncomprehending eyes when she delivered him back were impossible to forget. All she could say in her defence was that it was the only time she had behaved with such pure selfishness: she had married him for her own reasons, and discarded him for her own reasons. Some might say that the rest of her life had been selfish too, devoted as it was entirely to her own commemorations; but this was a selfishness that hurt nobody else.

Poor Denis. He was still handsome when he came back, though his hair grew white on one side and he dribbled. When the fits came on she knelt on his chest and held his tongue down with a stub of pencil. Every night he roamed restlessly through his sleep, muttered and roared, fell silent for a while, and then with parade-ground precision would shout *Hip! hip! hip!* When she woke him, he could never remember what had been happening. He had guilt and pain, but no specific memory of what he felt guilty about. She knew: Denis had been hit by shrapnel and taken back down the line to hospital without a farewell to his best pal Jewy Moss, leaving Sammy to be killed during the next day's Hun bombardment. After two years of this marriage, two years of watching Denis vigorously brush his patch of white hair to make it go away, she had returned him to his sisters. From now on, she told them, they should look after Denis and she would look after Sam. The sisters had gazed at her in silent astonishment. Behind them, in the hall, Denis, his chin wet and his brown eyes uncomprehending, stood with an awkward patience which implied that this latest event was nothing special in itself, merely one of a number of things he failed to grasp, and that there would surely be much more to come, all down the rest of his life, which would also escape him.

She had taken the job on the Dictionary a month later. She worked alone in a damp basement, at a desk across which curled long sheets of galley-proof. Condensation beaded the window. She was armed with a brass table-lamp and a pencil which she sharpened until it was too short to fit in the hand. Her script was large and loose, somewhat like Sammy's; she deleted and inserted, just as he had done on his field-service postcards. <u>Nothing to be written on this side of the galley-proof. If anything else is added to the galley-proof it will be destroyed</u>. No, she did not have to worry; she made her marks with impunity. She spotted colons which were italic instead of roman, brackets which were square instead of round, inconsistent abbreviations, misleading cross-references. Occasionally she made suggestions. She might observe, in looping pencil, that such-and-such a word was in her opinion vulgar rather than colloquial, or that the sense illustrated was figurative rather than transferred. She passed on her galley-proofs to Mr. Rothwell, the joint deputy editor, but never enquired whether her annotations were finally acted upon. Mr. Rothwell, a bearded, taciturn and pacific man, valued her meticulous eyes, her sure grasp of the Dictionary's conventions, and her willingness to take work home if a fascicle was shortly going to press. He remarked to himself and to others that she had a strangely disputatious attitude over words labelled as obsolete. Often she would propose *?Obs.* rather than *Obs.* as the correct marking. Perhaps this had something to do with age, Mr. Rothwell thought; younger folk were perhaps more willing to accept that a word had had its day.

In fact, Mr. Rothwell was only five years younger than she; but Miss Moss—as she had become once more after her disposal of Denis—had aged quickly, almost as a matter of will. The years passed and she grew stout, her hair flew a little more wildly away from her clips, and her spectacle lenses became thicker. Her stockings had a dense, antique look to them, and she never took her raincoat to the dry-cleaner. Younger lexicographers entering her office, where a number of back files were stored, wondered if the faint smell of rabbit-hutch came from the walls, the old Dictionary slips, Miss Moss's raincoat, or Miss Moss herself. None of this mattered to Mr. Rothwell, who saw only the precision of her work. Though entitled by the Press to an annual holiday of fifteen working days, she never took more than a single week.

At first this holiday coincided with the eleventh hour of the eleventh day of the eleventh month; Mr. Rothwell had the delicacy not to ask for details. In later years, however, she would take her week in other months, late spring or early autumn. When her parents died and she inherited a small amount of money, she surprised Mr. Rothwell by arriving for work one day in a small grey Morris with red leather seats. It sported a yellow metal AA badge on the front and a metal GB plate on the back. At the age of fifty-three she had passed her driving-test first time, and manoeuvred her car with a precision bordering on elan.

She always slept in the car. It saved money; but mainly it helped her be alone with herself and Sam. The villages in that thinned triangle south of Arras became accustomed to the sight of an ageing British car the colour of gunmetal drawn up beside the war memorial; inside, an elderly lady wrapped in a travelling-rug would be asleep in the passenger seat. She never locked the car at night, for it seemed impertinent, even disrespectful on her part to feel any fear. She slept while the villages slept, and would wake as a drenched cow on its way to milking softly shouldered a wing of the parked Morris. Every so often she would be invited in by a villager, but she preferred not to accept hospitality. Her behaviour was not regarded as peculiar, and cafés in the region knew to serve her *thé à l'anglaise* without her having to ask.

After she had finished with Thiepval, with Thistle Dump and Caterpillar Valley, she would drive up through Arras and take the D937 towards Béthune. Ahead lay Vimy, Cabaret Rouge, N.D. de Lorette. But there was always one other visit to be paid first: to Maison Blanche. Such peaceful names they mostly had. But here at Maison Blanche were 40,000 German dead, 40,000 Huns laid out beneath their thin black crosses, a sight as orderly as you would expect from the Huns, though not as splendid as the British graves. She lingered there, reading a few names at random, idly wondering, when she found a date just a little later than the 21st January 1917, if this could be the Hun that had killed her Sammy. Was this the man who squeezed the trigger, fed the machine-gun, blocked his ears as the howitzer roared? And see how short a time he had lasted afterwards: two days, a week, a month or so in the mud before being lined up in known and honoured burial, facing out once more towards her Sammy, though separated now not by barbed-wire and <u>50 yds</u> but by a few kilometers of asphalt.

She felt no rancour towards these Huns; time had washed from her any anger at the man, the regiment, the Hun army, the nation that had taken Sam's life. Her resentment was against those who had come later, and whom she refused to dignify with the amicable name of Hun. She hated Hitler's war for diminishing the memory of the Great War, for allotting it a number, the mere first among two. And she hated the way in which the Great War was held responsible for its successor, as if Sam, Denis and all the East Lancashires who fell were partly the cause of that business. Sam had done what he could—he had served and died—and was punished all too quickly with becoming subservient in memory. Time did not behave rationally. Fifty years back to the Somme; a hundred beyond that to Waterloo; four hundred more to Agincourt, or Azincourt as the French preferred. Yet these distances had now been squeezed closer to one another. She blamed it on 1939–1945.

She knew to keep away from those parts of France where the second war happened, or at least where it was remembered. In the early years of the Morris, she had sometimes made the mistake of imagining herself on holiday, of being a tourist. She might thoughtlessly stop in a lay-by, or be taking a stroll down a back lane in some tranquil, heat-burdened part of the country, when a neat tablet inserted in a dry wall would assault her. It would commemorate Monsieur Un Tel, *lâchement assassiné par les Allemands,* or *tué,* or *fusillé,* and then an insulting modern date: 1943, 1944, 1945. They blocked the view, these deaths and these dates; they demanded attention by their recency. She refused, she refused.

When she stumbled like this upon the second war, she would hurry to the nearest village for consolation. She always knew where to look: next to the church, the *mairie,* the railway station; at a fork in the road; on a dusty square with cruelly pollarded limes and a few rusting café tables. There she would find her damp-stained memorial with its heroic *poilu,* grieving widow, triumphant Marianne, rowdy cockerel. Not that the story she read on the plinth needed any sculptural illustration. 67 against 9, 83 against 12, 40 against 5, 27 against 2: here was the eternal corroboration she sought, the historical corrigendum. She would touch the names cut into stone, their gilding washed away on the weather-side. Numbers whose familiar proportion declared the terrible primacy of the Great War. Her eye would check down the bigger list, snagging at a name repeated twice, thrice, four, five six times: one male generation of an entire family taken away to known and honoured burial. In the bossy statistics of death she would find the comfort she needed.

She would spend the last night at Aix-Noulette (101 to 7); at Souchez (48 to 6), where she remembered Plouvier, Maxime, Sergent, killed on 17th December 1916, the last of his village to die before her Sam; at Carency (19 to 1); at Ablain-Saint-Nazaire (66 to 9), eight of whose male Lherbiers had died, four on the *champ d'honneur,* three as *victimes civiles,* one a *civil fusillé par l'ennemi.* Then, the next morning, cocked with grief, she would set off for Cabaret Rouge while dew was still on the grass. There was consolation in solitude and damp knees. She no longer talked to Sam; everything had been said decades ago. The heart had been expressed, the apologies made, the secrets given. She no longer wept, either; that too had stopped. But the hours she spent with him at Cabaret Rouge were the most vital of her life. They always had been.

The D937 did its reminding elbow at Cabaret Rouge, making sure you slowed out of respect, drawing your attention to Brigadier Sir Frank

Higginson's handsome domed portico, which served as both entrance gate and memorial arch. From the portico, the burial ground dropped away at first, then sloped up again towards the standing cross on which hung not Christ but a metal sword. Symmetrical, amphitheatrical, Cabaret Rouge held 6,676 British soldiers, sailors, Marines and airmen; 732 Canadians; 121 Australians; 42 South Africans; 7 New Zealanders; 2 members of the Royal Guernsey Light Infantry; 1 Indian; 1 member of an unknown unit; and 4 Germans.

It also contained, or more exactly had once had scattered over it, the ashes of Brigadier Sir Frank Higginson, Secretary to the Imperial War Graves Commission, who had died in 1958 at the age of sixty-eight. That showed true loyalty and remembrance. His widow, Lady Violet Lindsley Higginson, had died four years later, and her ashes had been scattered here too. Fortunate Lady Higginson. Why should the wife of a brigadier who, whatever he had done in the Great War, had not died, be allowed such enviable and meritorious burial, and yet the sister of one of those soldiers whom the fortune of war had led to known and honoured burial be denied such comfort? The Commission had twice denied her request, saying that a military cemetery did not receive civilian ashes. The third time she had written they had been less polite, referring her brusquely to their earlier correspondence.

There had been incidents down the years. They had stopped her coming for the eleventh hour of the eleventh day of the eleventh month by refusing her permission to sleep the night beside his grave. They said they did not have camping facilities; they affected to sympathise, but what if everybody else wanted to do the same? She replied that it was quite plain that no one else wanted to do the same but that if they did then such a desire should be respected. However, after some years she ceased to miss the official ceremony: it seemed to her full of people who remembered improperly, impurely.

There had been problems with the planting. The grass at the cemetery was French grass, and it seemed to her of the coarser type, inappropriate for British soldiers to lie beneath. Her campaign over this with the Commission led nowhere. So one spring she took out a small spade and a square yard of English turf kept damp in a plastic bag. After dark she dug out the offending French grass and relaid the softer English turf, patting it into place, then stamping it in. She was pleased with her work, and the next year, as she approached the grave, saw no indication of her mending. But when she knelt, she realised that her work had been undone: the French grass was back again. The same had happened when she had surreptitiously planted her bulbs. Sam liked tulips, yellow ones especially, and one autumn she had pushed half a dozen bulbs into the earth. But the following spring, when she returned, there were only dusty geraniums in front of his stone.

There had also been the desecration. Not so very long ago. Arriving shortly after dawn, she found something on the grass which at first she put down to a dog. But when she saw the same in front of 1685 Private W. A. Andrade 4th Bn. London Regt. R. Fus. 15th March 1915, and in front of 675 Private Leon Emanuel Levy The Cameronians (Sco. Rif.) 16th August 1916 aged 21 And the Soul Returneth to God Who Gave It—Mother, she judged it most unlikely that a dog, or three dogs, had managed to find the only three Jewish graves in the cemetery. She gave the caretaker the rough edge of her tongue. He admitted that such desecration had occurred before, also that paint had been sprayed but he always tried to arrive before anyone else and remove the signs. She told him that he might be honest but he was clearly idle. She blamed the second war. She tried not to think about it again.

For her, now, the view back to 1917 was uncluttered: the decades were mown grass, and at their end was a row of white headstones, domino-thin. 1358 Private Samuel M. Moss East Lancashire Regt. 21st January 1917, and in the middle the Star of David. Some graves in Cabaret Rouge were anonymous, with no identifying words or symbols; some had inscriptions, regimental badges, Irish harps, springboks, maple leaves, New Zealand ferns. Most had Christian crosses; only three displayed the Star of David. Private Andrade, Private Levy and Private Moss. A British soldier buried beneath the Star of David: she kept her eyes on that. Sam had written from training camp that the fellows chaffed him, but he had always been Jewy Moss at school, and they were good fellows, most of them, as good inside the barracks as outside, anyway. They made the same remarks he'd heard before, but Jewy Moss was a British soldier, good enough to fight and die with his comrades, which is what he had done, and what he was remembered for. She pushed away the second war, which muddled things. He was a British soldier, East Lancashire Regiment, buried at Cabaret Rouge beneath the Star of David.

She wondered when they would plough them up, Herbécourt, Devonshire, Quarry, Blighty Valley, Ulster Tower, Thistle Dump and Caterpillar Valley; Maison Blanche and Cabaret Rouge. They said they never would. This land, she read everywhere, was "the free gift of the French people for the perpetual resting place of those of the allied armies who fell . . ." and so on. EVERMORE, they said, and she wanted to hear: for all future time. The War Graves Commission, her successive members of parliament, the Foreign Office, the commanding officer of Sammy's regiment, all told her the same. She didn't believe them. Soon—in fifty years or so—everyone who had served in the War would be dead; and at some point after that, everyone who had known anyone who had served would also be dead. What if memory-grafting did not work, or the memories themselves were deemed shameful? First, she guessed, those little stone tablets in the back lanes would be chiselled out, since the French and the Germans had officially stopped hating one another years ago, and it would not do for German tourists to be accused of the cowardly assassinations perpetrated by their ancestors. Then the war memorials would come down, with their important statistics. A few might be held to have architectural interest; but some new, cheerful generation would find them morbid, and dream up better things to enliven the villages. And after that it would be time to plough up the cemeteries, to put them back to good agricultural use: they had lain fallow for too long. Priests and politicians would make it all right, and the farmers would get their land back, fertilised with blood and bone. Thiepval might become a listed building, but would they keep Brigadier Sir Frank Higginson's domed portico? That elbow in the D937 would be declared a traffic hazard; all it needed was a drunken casualty for the road to be made straight again after all these years. Then the great forgetting could begin, the fading into the landscape. The war would be levelled to a couple of museums, a set of demonstration trenches, and a few names, shorthand for pointless sacrifice.

Might there be one last fiery glow of remembering? In her own case, it would not be long before her annual renewals ceased, before the clerical error of her life was corrected; yet even as she pronounced herself an antique, her memories seemed to sharpen. If this happened to the individual, could it not also happen on a national scale? Might there not be, at some point in the first decades of the twenty-first century, one final moment, lit by evening sun, before the whole thing was handed over to the archivists? Might there not be a great looking-back down the mown grass of the decades, might not a gap in the trees discover the curving ranks of slender headstones, white tablets holding up to the eye their bright names and terrifying dates, their harps and springboks, maple leaves and ferns, their Christian crosses and their Stars of David? Then, in the space of a wet blink, the gap in the trees would close and the mown grass disappear, a violent indigo cloud would cover the sun, and history, gross history, daily history, would forget. Is this how it would be?

Richard Bausch

Aren't You Happy for Me?

(UNITED STATES)

"William Coombs, with two *o*'s," Melanie Ballinger told her father over long distance. "Pronounced just like the thing you comb your hair with. Say it."

Ballinger repeated the name.

"Say the whole name."

"I've got it, sweetheart. Why am I saying it?"

"Dad, I'm bringing him home with me. We're getting *married.*"

For a moment, he couldn't speak.

"Dad? Did you hear me?"

"I'm here," he said.

"Well?"

Again, he couldn't say anything.

"Dad?"

"Yes," he said. "That's—that's some news."

"That's all you can say?"

"Well, I mean—Melanie—this is sort of quick, isn't it?" he said.

"Not that quick. How long did you and Mom wait?"

"I don't remember. Are you measuring yourself by that?"

"You waited six months, and you do too remember. And this is five months. And we're not measuring anything. William and I have known each other longer than five months, but we've been together—you know, as a couple—five months. And I'm almost twenty-three, which is two years older than Mom was. And don't tell me it was different when *you* guys did it."

"No," he heard himself say. "It's pretty much the same, I imagine."

"Well?" she said.

"Well," Ballinger said. "I'm—I'm very happy for you."

"You don't sound happy."

"I'm happy. I can't wait to meet him."

"Really? Promise? You're not just saying that?"

"It's good news, darling. I mean I'm surprised, of course. It'll take a little getting used to. The—the suddenness of it and everything. I mean, your mother and I didn't even know you were seeing anyone. But no, I'm—I'm glad. I can't wait to meet the young man."

"Well, and now there's something *else* you have to know."

"I'm ready," John Ballinger said. He was standing in the kitchen of the house she hadn't seen yet, and outside the window his wife, Mary, was weeding in the garden, wearing a red scarf and a white muslin blouse and jeans, looking young—looking, even, happy, though for a long while there had been between them, in fact, very little happiness.

"Well, this one's kind of hard," his daughter said over the thousand miles of wire. "Maybe we should talk about it later."

"No, I'm sure I can take whatever it is," he said.

The truth was that he had news of his own to tell. Almost a week ago, he and Mary had agreed on a separation. Some time for them both to sort things out. They had decided not to say anything about it to Melanie until she arrived. But now Melanie had said that she was bringing someone with her.

She was hemming and hawing on the other end of the line: "I don't know, see, Daddy, I—God. I can't find the way to say it, really."

He waited. She was in Chicago, where they had sent her to school more than four years ago, and where after her graduation she had stayed, having landed a job with an independent newspaper in the city. In March, Ballinger and Mary had moved to this small house in the middle of Charlottesville, hoping that a change of scene might help things. It hadn't; they were falling apart after all these years.

"Dad," Melanie said, sounding helpless.

"Honey, I'm listening."

"Okay, look," she said. "Will you promise you won't react?"

"How can I promise a thing like that, Melanie?"

"You're going to react, then. I wish you could just promise me you wouldn't."

"Darling," he said, "I've got something to tell you, too. Promise me *you* won't react."

She said "Promise" in that way the young have of being absolutely certain what their feelings will be in some future circumstance.

"So," he said. "Now, tell me whatever it is." And a thought struck through him like a shock. "Melanie, you're not—you're not pregnant, are you?"

She said, "How did you *know*?"

He felt something sharp move under his heart. "Oh, Lord. Seriously."

"Jeez," she said. "Wow. that's really amazing."

"You're—*pregnant*."

"Right. My God. You're positively clairvoyant, Dad."

"I really don't think it's a matter of any clairvoyance, Melanie, from the way you were talking. Are you—is it sure?"

"Of course it's sure. But—well, that isn't the really hard thing. Maybe I should just wait."

"Wait," he said. "Wait for what?"

"Until you get used to everything else."

He said nothing. She was fretting on the other end, sighing and starting to speak and then stopping herself.

"I don't know," she said finally, and abruptly he thought she was talking to someone in the room with her.

"Honey, do you want me to put your mother on?"

"No, Daddy. I wanted to talk to you about this first. I think we should get this over with."

"Get this over with? Melanie, what're we talking about here? Maybe I should put your mother on." He thought he might try a joke. "After all," he added, "I've never been pregnant."

"It's not about being pregnant. You *guessed* that."

He held the phone tight against his ear. Through the window, he saw his wife stand and stretch, massaging the small of her back with one gloved hand. *Oh, Mary.*

"Are you ready?" his daughter said.

"Wait," he said. "Wait a minute. Should I be sitting down? I'm sitting down." He pulled a chair from the table and settled into it. He could hear her breathing on the other end of the line, or perhaps it was the static wind he so often heard when talking on these new phones. "Okay," he said, feeling his throat begin to close. "Tell me."

"William's somewhat older than I am," she said. "There." She sounded as though she might hyperventilate.

He left a pause. "That's it?"

"Well, it's how much."

"Okay."

She seemed to be trying to collect herself. She breathed, paused. "This is even tougher than I thought it was going to be."

"You mean you're going to tell me something harder than the fact that you're pregnant?"

She was silent.

"Melanie?"

"I didn't expect you to be this way about it," she said.

"Honey, please just tell me the rest of it."

"Well, what did you mean by that, anyway?"

"Melanie, *you said* this would be hard."

Silence.

"Tell me, sweetie. Please?"

"I'm going to." She took a breath. "Dad, William's sixty—he's—he's sixty—sixty-three years old."

Ballinger stood. Out in the garden his wife had got to her knees again, pulling crabgrass out of the bed of tulips. It was a sunny near-twilight, and all along the shady street people were working in their little orderly spaces of grass and flowers.

"Did you hear me, Daddy? It's perfectly all right, too, because he's really a *young* sixty-three, and *very* strong and healthy, and look at George Burns."

"George Burns," Ballinger said. "George—George Burns? Melanie, I don't understand."

"Come on, Daddy, stop it."

"No, what're you telling me?" His mind was blank.

"I said William is sixty-three."

"William who?"

"Dad. My fiancé."

"Wait, Melanie. You're saying your fiancé, the man you're going to marry, *he's* sixty-three?"

"A young sixty-three,"she said.

"Melanie. Sixty-three?"

"Dad."

"You didn't say six feet three?"

She was silent.

"Melanie?"

"Yes."

"Honey, this is a joke, right? You're playing a joke on me."

"It is not a—it's not that. God," she said. "I don't believe this."

"You don't believe—" he began. "You don't believe—"

"Dad," she said. "I told you—" Again, she seemed to be talking to someone else in the room with her. Her voice trailed off.

"Melanie," he said. "Talk into the phone."

"I know it's hard," she told him. "I know it's asking you to take a lot in."

"Well, no," Ballinger said, feeling something shift inside, a quickening in his blood. "It's—it's a little more than that, Melanie, isn't it? I mean it's not a weather report, for God's sake."

"I should've known," she said.

"Forgive me for it," he said, "but I have to ask you something."

"It's all right, Daddy," she said as though reciting it for him. "I know what I'm doing. I'm not really rushing into anything—"

He interrupted her. "Well, good God, somebody rushed into something, right?"

"Daddy."

"Is that what you call *him*? No, *I'm* Daddy. You have to call him *Grand*daddy."

"That is *not* funny," she said.

"I wasn't being funny, Melanie. And anyway, that wasn't my question." He took a breath. "Please forgive this, but I have to know."

"There's nothing you really *have* to know, Daddy. I'm an adult. I'm telling you out of family courtesy."

"I understand that. Family courtesy exactly. Exactly, Melanie, that's a good phrase. Would you please tell me, out of family courtesy, if the baby is his."

"Yes." Her voice was small now, coming from a long way off.

"I am sorry for the question, but I have to put all this together. I mean you're asking me to take in a whole lot here, you know?"

"I said I understood how you feel."

"I don't think so. I don't think you quite understand how I feel."

"All right," she said. "I don't understand how you feel. But I think I knew how you'd react."

For a few seconds, there was just the low, sea sound of long distance.

"Melanie, have you done any of the math on this?"

"I should've bet money," she said in the tone of a person who has been proven right about something.

"Well, but Jesus," Ballinger said. "I mean he's older than *I* am, kid. He's— he's a *lot* older than I am." The number of years seemed to dawn on him as he spoke; it filed him with a strange, heart-shaking heat. "Honey, nineteen years. When he was my age, I was only two years older than you are now."

"I don't see what that has to do with anything," she said.

"Melanie, I'll be forty-five *all the way* in December. I'm a *young* forty-four."

"I know when your birthday is, Dad."

"Well, good God, this guy's nineteen years older than your own father."

She said, "I've grasped the numbers. Maybe you should go ahead and put Mom on."

"Melanie, you couldn't pick somebody a little closer to my age? Some snot-nosed forty-year-old?"

"Stop it," she said. "Please, Daddy. I know what I'm doing."

"Do you know how old he's going to be when your baby is ten? Do you? Have you given that any thought at all?"

She was silent.

He said, "How many children are you hoping to have?"

"I'm not thinking about that. Any of that. This is now, and I don't care about anything else."

He sat down in his kitchen and tried to think of something else to say. Outside the window, his wife, with no notion of what she was about to be hit with, looked through the patterns of shade in the blinds and, seeing him, waved. It was friendly, and even so, all their difficulty was in it. Ballinger waved back. "Melanie," he said, "do you mind telling me just where you happened to meet William? I mean how do you meet a person forty years older than you are. Was there a senior citizen–student mixer at the college?"

"Stop it, Daddy."

"No, I really want to know. If I'd just picked this up and read it in the newspaper, I think I'd want to know. I'd probably call the newspaper and see what I could find out."

"Put Mom on," she said.

"Just tell me how you met. You can do that, can't you?"

"Jesus Christ," she said, then paused.

Ballinger waited.

"He's a teacher, like you and Mom, only college. He was my literature teacher. He's a professor of literature. He knows everything that was ever written, and he's the most brilliant man I've ever known. You have no idea how fascinating it is to talk with him."

"Yes, and I guess you understand that over the years that's what you're going to be doing a *lot* of with him, Melanie. A lot of talking."

"I am carrying the proof that disproves *you*," she said.

He couldn't resist saying, "Did *he* teach you to talk like that?"

"I'm gonna hang up."

"You promised you'd listen to something *I* had to tell *you*."

"Okay," she said crisply. "I'm listening."

He could imagine her tapping the toe of one foot on the floor: the impatience of someone awaiting an explanation. He thought a moment. "He's a professor?"

"That's not what you wanted to tell me."

"But you said he's a professor."

"Yes, I said that."

"Don't be mad at me, Melanie. Give me a few minutes to get used to the idea. Jesus. Is he a professor emeritus?"

"If that means distinguished, yes. But I know what you're—"

"No, Melanie. It means *retired*. You went to college."

She said nothing.

"I'm sorry. But for God's sake, it's a legitimate question."

"It's a stupid, mean-spirited thing to ask." He could tell from her voice that she was fighting back tears.

"Is he there with you now?"

"Yes," she said, sniffling.

"Oh, Jesus Christ."

"Daddy, why are you being this way?"

"Do you think maybe we could've had this talk alone? What's he, listening on the other line?"

"No."

"Well, thank God for that."

"I'm going to hang up now."

"No, please don't hang up. Please let's just be calm and talk about this. We have some things to talk about here."

She sniffled, blew her nose. Someone held the phone for her. There was a muffled something in the line, and then she was there again. "Go ahead," she said.

"Is he still in the room with you?"

"Yes." Her voice was defiant.

"Where?"

"Oh, for God's sake," she said.

"I'm sorry, I feel the need to know. Is he sitting down?"

"I *want* him here, Daddy. We both want to be here," she said.

"And he's going to marry you."

"Yes," she said impatiently.

"Do you think I could talk to him?"

She said something he couldn't hear, and then there were several seconds of some sort of discussion, in whispers. Finally she said, "Do you promise not to yell at him?"

"Melanie, he wants me to promise not to *yell* at him?"

"Will you promise?"

"Good God."

"Promise," she said. "Or I'll hang up."

"All right. I promise. I promise not to yell at him."

There was another small scuffing sound, and a man's voice came through the line. "Hello, sir." It was, as far as Ballinger could tell, an ordinary voice, slightly lower than baritone. He thought of cigarettes. "I realize this is a difficult—"

"Do you smoke?" Ballinger interrupted him.

"No, sir."

"All right. Go on."

"Well, I want you to know I understand how you feel."

"Melanie says she does, too," Ballinger said. "I mean I'm certain you both *think* you do."

"It was my idea that Melanie call you about this."

"Oh, really. That speaks well of you. You probably knew I'd find this a little difficult to absorb and that's why you waited until Melanie was pregnant, for Christ's sake."

The other man gave forth a small sigh of exasperation.

"So you're a professor of literature."

"Yes, sir."

"Oh, you needn't 'sir' me. After all, I mean I *am* the goddam kid here."

"There's no need for sarcasm, sir."

"Oh, I wasn't being sarcastic. That was a literal statement of this situation that obtains right here as we're speaking. And, really, Mr. . . . It's Coombs, right?"

"Yes, sir."

"Coombs, like the thing you comb your hair with."

The other man was quiet.

"Just how long do you think it'll take me to get used to this? You think you might get into your seventies before I get used to this? And how long do you think it'll take my wife who's twenty-one years younger than you are to get used to this?"

Silence.

"You're too old for my *wife,* for Christ's sake."

Nothing.

"What's your first name again?"

The other man spoke through another sigh. "Perhaps we should just ring off."

"Ring off. Jesus. Ring off? Did you actually say 'ring off'? What're you, a goddam limey or something?"

"I am an American. I fought in Korea."

"Not World War One?"

The other man did not answer.

"How many other marriages have you had?" Ballinger asked him.

"That's a valid question. I'm glad you—"

"Thank you for the scholarly observation, *sir.* But I'm not sitting in a class. How many did you say?"

"If you'd give me a chance, I'd tell you."

Ballinger said nothing.

"Two, sir. I've had two marriages."

"Divorces?"

"I have been widowed twice."

"And—oh, I get it. You're trying to make sure that that never happens to you again."

"This is not going well at all, and I'm afraid I—I—" The other man stammered, then stopped.

"How did you expect it to go?" Ballinger demanded.

"Cruelty is not what I'd expected. I'll tell you that."

"You thought I'd be glad my daughter is going to be getting social security before I do."

The other was silent.

"Do you have any other children?" Ballinger asked.

"Yes, I happen to have three." There was a stiffness, an overweening tone, in the voice now.

"And how old are they, if I might ask."

"Yes, you may."

Ballinger waited. His wife walked in from outside, carrying some cuttings. She poured water in a glass vase and stood at the counter arranging the flowers, her back to him. The other man had stopped talking. "I'm sorry," Ballinger said. "My wife just walked in here and I didn't catch what you said. Could you just tell me if any of them are anywhere near my daughter's age?"

"I told you, my youngest boy is thirty-eight."

"And you realize that if *he* wanted to marry my daughter I'd be upset, the age difference there being what it is." Ballinger's wife moved to his side, drying her hands on a paper towel, her face full of puzzlement and worry.

"I told you, Mr. Ballinger, that I understood how you feel. The point is, we have a pregnant woman here and we both love her."

"No," Ballinger said. "That's not the point. The point is that you, sir, are not much more than a goddam statutory rapist. That's the point." His wife took his shoulder. He looked at her and shook his head.

"What?" she whispered. "Is Melanie all right?"

"Well, this isn't accomplishing anything," the voice on the other end of the line was saying.

"Just a minute," Ballinger said. "Let me ask you something else. Really now. What's the policy at that goddam university concerning teachers screwing their students?"

"Oh, my God," his wife said as the voice on the line huffed and seemed to gargle.

"I'm serious," Ballinger said.

"Melanie was not my student when we became involved."

"Is that what you call it? Involved?"

"Let me talk to Melanie," Ballinger's wife said.

"Listen," he told her. "Be quiet."

Melanie was back on the line. "Daddy? Daddy?"

"I'm here," Ballinger said, holding the phone from his wife's attempt to take it from him.

"Daddy, we're getting married and there's nothing you can do about it. Do you understand?"

"Melanie," he said, and it seemed that from somewhere far inside himself he heard that he had begun shouting at her. "Jee-zus good Christ. Your fiancé was almost *my* age *now* the day you were *born*. What the hell, kid. Are you crazy? Are you out of your mind?"

His wife was actually pushing against him to take the phone, and so he gave it to her. And stood there while she tried to talk.

"Melanie," she said. "Honey, listen—"

"Hang up," Ballinger said. "Christ. Hang it up."

"Please. Will you go in the other room and let me talk to her?"

"Tell her I've got friends. All these nice men in their forties. She can marry any one of my friends—they're babies. Forties—cradle fodder. Jesus, any one of them. Tell her."

"Jack, stop it." Then she put the phone against her chest. "Did you tell her anything about us?"

He paused. "That—no."

She turned from him. "Melanie, honey. What is this? Tell me, please."

He left her there, walked through the living room to the hall and back around to the kitchen. He was all nervous energy, crazy with it, pacing. Mary stood very still, listening, nodding slightly, holding the phone tight with both hands, her shoulders hunched as if she were out in cold weather.

"Mary," he said.

Nothing.

He went into their bedroom and closed the door. The light coming through the windows was soft gold, and the room was deepening with shadows. He moved to the bed and sat down, and in a moment he noticed that he had begun a low sort of murmuring. He took a breath and tried to be still. From the other room, his wife's voice came to him. "Yes, I quite agree with you. But I'm just unable to put this . . ."

The voice trailed off. He waited. A few minutes later, she came to the door and knocked on it lightly, then opened it and looked in.

"What," he said.

"They're serious." She stood in the doorway.

"Come here," he said.

She stepped to his side and eased herself down, and he moved to accommodate her. He put his arm around her, and then, because it was awkward, clearly an embarrassment to her, took it away. Neither of them could speak for a time. Everything they had been through during the course of deciding about each other seemed concentrated now. Ballinger breathed his wife's presence, the odor of earth and flowers, the outdoors.

"God," she said. "I'm positively numb. I don't know what to think."

"Let's have another baby," he said suddenly. "Melanie's baby will need a younger aunt or uncle."

Mary sighed a little forlorn laugh, then was silent.

"Did you tell her about us?" he asked.

"No," she said. "I didn't get the chance. And I don't know that I could have."

"I don't suppose it's going to matter much to her."

"Oh, don't say that. You can't mean that."

The telephone on the bedstand rang, and startled them both. He reached for it, held the handset toward her.

"Hello," she said. Then: "Oh. Hi. Yes, well, here." She gave it back to him.

"Hello," he said.

Melanie's voice, tearful and angry: "You had something you said you had to tell *me*." She sobbed, then coughed. "Well?"

"It was nothing, honey. I don't even remember—"

"Well, I want you to know I would've been better than you were, Daddy, no matter how hard it was. I would've kept myself from reacting."

"Yes," he said. "I'm sure you would have."

"I'm going to hang up. And I guess I'll let you know later if we're coming at all. If it wasn't for Mom, we wouldn't be."

"We'll talk," he told her. "We'll work on it. Honey, you both have to give us a little time."

"There's nothing to work on as far as William and I are concerned."

"Of course there are things to work on. Every marriage—" His voice had caught. He took a breath. "In every marriage there are things to work on."

"I know what I know," she said.

"Well," said Ballinger. "That's—that's as it should be at your age, darling."

"Goodbye," she said. "I can't say any more."

"I understand," Ballinger said. When the line clicked, he held the handset in his lap for a moment. Mary was sitting there at his side, perfectly still.

"Well," he said. "I couldn't tell her." He put the handset back in its cradle. "God. A sixty-three-year-old son-in-law."

"It's happened before." She put her hand on his shoulder, then took it away. "I'm so frightened for her. But she says it's what she wants."

"Hell, Mary. You know what this is. The son of a bitch was her goddam teacher."

"Listen to you—what are you saying about her? Listen to what you're saying about her. That's our daughter you're talking about. You might at least try to give her the credit of assuming that she's aware of what she's doing."

They said nothing for a few moments.

"Who knows," Ballinger's wife said. "Maybe they'll be happy for a time."

He'd heard the note of sorrow in her voice, and thought he knew what she was thinking; then he was certain that he knew. He sat there remembering, like Mary, their early happiness, that ease and simplicity, and briefly he was in another house, other rooms, and he saw the toddler that Melanie had been, trailing through slanting light in a brown hallway, draped in gowns she had fashioned from her mother's clothes. He did not know why that particular image should have come to him out of the flow of years, but for a fierce minute it was uncannily near him in the breathing silence; it went over him like a palpable something on his skin, then was gone. The ache which remained stopped him for a moment. He looked at his wife, but she had averted her eyes, her hands running absently over the faded denim cloth of her lap. Finally she stood. "Well," she sighed, going away. "Work to do."

"Mary?" he said, low; but she hadn't heard him. She was already out the doorway and into the hall, moving toward the kitchen. He reached over and turned the lamp on by the bed, and then lay down. It was so quiet here. Dark was coming to the windows. On the wall there were pictures; shadows, shapes, silently clamoring for his gaze. He shut his eyes, listened to the small sounds she made in the kitchen, arranging her flowers, running the tap. *Mary,* he had said. But he could not imagine what he might have found to say if his voice had reached her.

Ann Beattie

In Amalfi

(UNITED STATES)

On the rocky beach next to the Cobalto, the boys were painting the boats. In June the tourist season would begin, and the rowboats would be launched, most of them rented by the hour to Americans and Swedes and Germans. The Americans would keep them on the water for five or ten minutes longer than the time for which they had been rented. The Swedes, usually thin and always pale, would know they had begun to burn after half an hour and return the boats early. It was difficult to generalize about the Germans. They were often blamed for the beer bottles that washed ashore, although others pointed out that this wasn't likely, because the Germans were such clean, meticulous people. The young German girls had short, spiky hair and wore earrings that looked like shapes it would be difficult to find the right theorem for in a geometry book. The men were more conventional, wearing socks with their sandals, although when they were on the beach they often wore the sandals barefooted and stuffed socks in their pockets.

What Christine knew about the tourists came from her very inadequate understanding of Italian. This was the second time she had spent a month in Amalfi, and while few of the people were friendly, it was clear that some of them recognized her. The beachboys talked to her about the tourists, as though she did not belong to that category. Two of them (there were usually six to ten boys at the beach, working on the boats, renting chairs, or throwing a Frisbee) had asked some questions about Andrew. They wanted to know if it was her father who sat upstairs in the bar, at the same table every day, feet resting on the scrollwork of the blue metal railing, writing. Christine said that he was not her father. Then another boy punched his friend and said, "I told you he was her *marito*." She shook her head no. A third boy—probably not much interested in what his friends might find out, anyway—said that his brother-in-law was expanding his business. The brother-in-law was going to rent hang gliders, as well as motorcycles, in June. The first boy who had talked to Christine said to her that hang gliders were like lawn chairs that flew through the air, powered by lawn mowers. Everyone laughed at this. Christine looked up at the sky, which was, as it had been for days, blue and nearly cloudless.

She walked up the steep stairs to the second tier of the beach bar. Three women were having toast and juice. The juice was in tall, thin glasses, and paper dangled from the straw of the woman who had not yet begun to sip her drink. The white paper, angled away, looked like a sail. Her two friends were watching some men who were wading out into the water. They moved forward awkwardly, trying to avoid hurting themselves on the stones. The other woman looked in the opposite direction where, on one of the craggiest cliffs, concrete steps curved like the lip of a calla lily around the round facade of the building that served as the bar and restaurant of the Hotel Luna.

Christine looked at the women's hands. None of them had a wedding ring. She thought then—with increasing embarrassment that she had been embarrassed—that she should have just told the boys on the beach that she and Andrew were divorced. What had happened was that—worse than meaning to be mysterious—she had suddenly feared further questioning if she told the truth; she had not wanted to say that she was a stereotype: the pretty, bright girl who marries her professor. But then, Europeans wouldn't judge that the same way Americans would. And why would she have had to explain what role he occupied in her life at all? All the boys really wanted to know was whether she slept with him now. They were like all questioners in all countries.

It occurred to her that the Europeans—who seemed capable of making wonderful comedies out of situations that were slightly off kilter—might make an interesting film about her relationship with Andrew: running off to Paris to marry him when she was twenty, and losing her nerve; marrying him two years later, in New York; having an abortion; leaving; reuniting with him a few months later at the same hotel that they had gone to on the first trip to Paris in 1968, and then divorcing the summer after their reunion; keeping in touch for fifteen years; and then beginning to vacation together. He had married during that time, was now divorced, and had twin boys who lived with their mother in Michigan.

She had been sitting at Andrew's table, quietly, waiting for him to reach a point where he could stop in his writing. She was accustomed to doing this. It no longer irritated her that for seconds or minutes or even for half an hour, she could be no more real to him than a ghost. She was just about to pull her chair into the shade when he looked up.

He told her, with great amusement, that earlier that morning an English couple with their teenage son had sat at the table nearby, and that the English-woman, watching him write, had made him a moral example to her son. She thought that he was a man writing a letter home. She had heard him ordering tea, in English, and—he told Christine again, with even more amusement—assumed that he was writing a letter home. "Can you imagine?" Andrew said. "I'd have to have a hell of an original mind to be scribbling away about a bunch of stones and the Mediterranean. Or, to give her credit, maybe she thought I was just overwrought."

She smiled. For anyone to assume that he liked to communicate about anything that might be even vaguely personal was funny itself, in a mordant way, but the funnier thing was that he was so often thrown by people's quite justifiable misperceptions, yet rarely cracked a smile if something was ludicrous. She had noticed early on that he would almost jump for joy when Alfred Hitchcock did his usual routine of passing briefly through his own film, but when she insisted that he watch a tape of Martin Short going into a frenzy as Ed Grimley on *Saturday Night Live,* he frowned like an archaeologist finding something he had no context for and having to decide, rather quickly, whether it was, say, an icon or petrified cow dung.

She had come to realize that what fascinated her about him was his absolute inadequacy when it came to making small talk. He also did not think of one thing as analogous to another. In fact, he thought of most analogies, metaphors, and similes as small talk. Nothing that caught Diane Arbus's eye ever interested him, but he would open a book of Avedon's photographs and examine a group shot of corporate executives as if he were examining a cross section of a chambered nautilus. When something truly interested him, he had a way of curling his fingers as if he could receive a concept in the palm of his hand.

The day before, Andrew's publisher had cabled to see when the book of essays could be expected. For once he was ahead of schedule with his writing, and the cable actually put him in a better mood. There had been some talk, back in the States, of the publisher's coming from Rome, where he had other business, to Atrani, to spend a few days with them. But just as they were leaving the States, Libya had been bombed, flights were canceled, people abandoned their travel plans. In the cable, the publisher made no mention of coming to Italy. There were few Americans anywhere around them: Libya and Chernobyl had obviously kept away those Americans who might have come before the season began.

Christine looked at the sky, wondering how many hang gliders would be up there during the summer. Icarus came to mind, and Auden's poem about the fall of Icarus that she had studied, years ago, in Andrew's poetry class. It was difficult to remember being that person who sat and listened, although she sometimes remembered how happy she had been to feel, for the first time, that she was part of something. Until she went to college and found out that other people were interested in ideas, she had settled for reading hundreds of books and letting her thoughts about what she read pile up silently. In all the years she spent at college in Middletown, she never cease to be surprised that real voices argued and agreed and debated almost throughout the night. Sometimes, involved as she was, the talk would nonetheless become mere sound—an abstraction, equivalent to her surprise, when she left the city and lived in the suburbs of Connecticut, that the sounds of cicadas would overlap with the cries of cats in the night, and that the wind would meld animal and insect sounds into some weird, theremin-like music. Andrew was probably attracted to her because, while others were very intelligent and very pretty, they showed their excitement, but she had been so stunned by the larger world and the sudden comradeship that she had soaked it in silently. He mistook her stunned silences for composure and the composure of sophistication. And now, in spite of everything they had been through, apparently she was still something of a mystery to him. Or perhaps the mystery was why he had stayed so attached to her.

They had lunch, and she sipped juice through one of the thin red plastic straws, playing a child's game of sipping until the juice was pulled to the top of the straw, then putting her tongue over the top, gradually releasing the pressure until the sucked-up juice ran back into the glass. She looked over the railing and saw that only a few beachboys were still there, sanding the boats. Another sat at a table on a concrete slab above the beach, eating an ice cream. Although she could not hear it from where she sat, he was probably listening to the jukebox just inside the other café—the only jukebox she knew of that had American music on it.

"You've been flirting with them," Andrew said, biting his roll.

"Don't be ridiculous," she said. "They see me every day. We exchange pleasantries."

"They see me every day and look right through me," he said.

"I'm friendlier than you are. That doesn't mean I'm flirting."

"*They're* flirting," he said.

"Well, then, it's harmless."

"For you, maybe. One of them tried to run me down with his motorcycle."

She had been drinking her juice. She looked up at him.

"I'm not kidding. I dropped the *Herald*," he said.

The archness with which he spoke made her smile. "You're sure he did it on purpose?" she said.

"You love to blame me for not understanding simple things," he said, "and here is a perfect example of understanding a simple thing. I have put two and two together: they flirt with my wife and then, when they see me crossing the street, they gun their motorcycles to double the insult, and then I look not only like an old fool but a coward."

He had spoken in such a rush that he seemed not to realize that he had called her "my wife." She waited to see if it would register, but it did not.

"They are very silly boys," he said, and his obvious petulance made her laugh. How childish—how sweet he was, and how silly, too, to let on that he had been so rattled. He was sitting with his arms crossed, like an Indian chief.

"They all drive like fools," he said.

"All of them?" she said. (Years ago he had said to her, "You find this true of *all* Romantic poets?")

"All of them," he said. "You'd see what they did if you came into town early in the morning. They hide in alleyways on their motorcycles and they roar out when I cross, and this morning, when I was on the traffic island with the *Herald,* one of them bent over the handlebars and hunched up his back like a cat and swerved as if he were going to jump the curb."

She made an effort not to laugh. "As you say, they're silly boys, then," she said.

Much to her surprise, he stood, gathered up his books and tablet, and stalked off, saying over his shoulder, "A lot you care."

She frowned as he walked away, sorry, suddenly, that she had not been more compassionate. If one of the boys had really tried to run him down, of course she cared.

Andrew had walked off so fast that he had forgotten his cane.

She watched the sun sparkling on the water. It was so beautiful that it calmed her, and then she slowly surveyed the Mediterranean. There were a few windsurfers—all very far out—and she counted two canoes and at least six paddleboats. She stared, wondering which would crisscross first across a stretch of water, and then she turned, having realized that someone was staring at her. It was a young woman, who smiled hesitantly. At another table, her friends were watching her expectantly. With a heavy French accent, but in perfect English, the young woman said, "Excuse me, but if you will be here for just a little while, I wonder if you would do me a favor?"

The woman was squinting in the sun. She was in her late twenties, and she had long, tanned legs. She was wearing white sorts and a green shirt and high heels. The shoes were patterned with grapes and grape leaves. In two seconds, Christine had taken it all in: the elegance, the woman's nice manner—her hopefulness about something.

"Certainly," Christine said. And it was not until the woman slipped the ring off her finger and handed it to her that she realized she had agreed to something before she even knew what it was.

The woman wanted her to wear her ring while she and her companions went boating. They would be gone only half an hour, she said. "My fingers have swollen, and in the cold air on the water they will be small again, and I would spend my whole time being nervous that I would lose my favorite thing." The woman smiled.

It all happened so quickly—and the woman's friends swept her off so fast—that Christine did not really examine the ring until after the giggling and jostling between the woman and her friends stopped, and they had run off, down the steep steps of the Cobalto to the beach below.

The ring was quite amazing. It sparkled so brightly in the sun that Christine was mesmerized. It was like the beginning of a fairy tale, she thought—and imagine: a woman giving a total stranger her ring. It was silver—silver or platinum—with a large opal embedded in a dome. The opal was surrounded by tiny rubies and slightly larger diamonds. It was an antique—no doubt about that. The woman had sensed that she could trust Christine. What a crazy chance to take, with such an obviously expensive ring. Even though she was right, the woman had taken a huge risk. When Christine looked down at the beach, she saw the two men and the beachboy holding the boat steady, and the woman climbing in. Then the men jumped in, shouting something to each other that made all of them laugh, and in only a minute they were quite far from shore. The woman, sitting in back, had her back to the beach.

As he passed, the waiter caught her eye and asked if she wanted anything else.

"*Vino bianco,*" she said. She hardly ever drank, but somehow the ring made

her nervous—a little nervous and a little happy—and the whole odd encounter seemed to require something new. A drink seemed just the thing.

She watched the boat grow smaller. The voices had already faded away. It
was impossible to believe, she thought, as she watched the boat become
smaller and smaller on the sparkling water, that in a world as beautiful as this,
one country would drop bombs on another to retaliate against terrorism. That
fires would begin in nuclear reactors.

Paddleboats zigzagged over water that was now a little choppier than it had
been earlier in the afternoon. A baby was throwing rocks into the water. The
baby jumped up and down, squealing approval of his every effort. Christine
watched two men in straw hats stop to look at the baby and the baby's mother,
close by on the rocks. Around the cliff, going toward the swimming pool chis-
eled out of a cliff behind the Luna bar and restaurant, the boat that Christine
thought held the French people disappeared.

The waiter brought the wine, and she sipped it. Wine and juice were usually cold. Sodas, in cans, were almost always room temperature. The cold wine
tasted good. The waiter had brought, as well, half a dozen small crackers on a
small silver plate.

She remembered, vaguely, reading a story in college about an American
woman in Italy, at the end of the war. The woman was sad and refused to be
made happy—or at least that was probably what happened. She could remember a great sense of frustration in the story—a frustration on the character's
part that carried over into frustrating the reader. The title of the story wouldn't
come to her, but Christine remembered two of the things the woman had demanded: silver candlesticks and a cat.

A speedboat passed, bouncing through white foam. Compared with that
boat, the paddleboats—more of them, suddenly, now that the heat of the day
was subsiding—seemed to float with no more energy than corks.

The wine Christine had just finished was Episcopio, bottled locally. Very little was exported, so it was almost impossible to find Episcopio in the States.
That was what people did: went home and looked at photographs, tried to buy
the wine they had enjoyed at the restaurant. But usually it could not be found,
and eventually they lost the piece of paper on which the name of the wine had
been written.

Christine ordered another glass of wine.

The man she had lived with for several years had given up his job on Wall
Street to become a photographer. He had wanted to succeed at photography
so much that he had convinced her he would. For years she searched magazines for his name—the tiny photo credit she might see just at the fold. There
were always one or two credits a year. There were until recently; in the last
couple of years there had been none that she knew of. That same man, she
remembered, had always surprised her by knowing when Groundhog Day
was and by being sincerely interested in whether the groundhog saw its
shadow when it came out. She and the man had vacationed in Greece, and although she did not really believe that he liked retsina any better than she did,

it was a part of the Greek meals he prepared for their friends several times a year.

She was worrying that she might be thought of as a predictable type: an American woman, no longer young, looking out to sea, a glass of wine half finished sitting on the table in front of her. Ultimately, she thought, she was nothing like the American woman in the story—but then, the argument could be made that all women had something invested in thinking themselves unique.

The man who wanted to be a photographer had turned conversations by asking for her opinion, and then—when she gave her opinion and he acted surprised and she qualified it by saying that she did not think her opinion was universal—he would suggest that her insistence on being thought unrepresentative was really a way of asserting her superiority over others.

God, she thought, finished the wine. No wonder I love Andrew.

It was five o'clock now, and shade had spread over the table. The few umbrellas that had been opened at the beach were collapsed and removed from the poles and wrapped tightly closed with blue twine. Two of the beachboys, on the way to the storage area, started a mock fencing match, jumping nimbly on the rocks, lunging so that one umbrella point touched another. Then one of the boys whipped a Z through the air and continued on his way. The other turned to look at a tall blond woman in a flesh-colored bikini, who wore a thin gold chain around her waist and another chain around her ankle.

Christine looked at her watch, then back at the cliffs beyond which the rowboat had disappeared. On the road above, a tour bus passed by, honking to force the cars coming toward it to stop and back up. There was a tinge of pink to the clouds that had formed near the horizon line. A paddleboat headed for the beach, and one of the boys started down the rocks to pull it in. She watched as he waded into the surf and pulled the boat forward, then held it steady.

In the shade, the ring was lavender-blue. In the sun, it had been flecked with pink, green, and white. She moved her hand slightly and could see more colors. It was like looking into the sea, to where the sun struck stones.

She looked back at the water, half expecting, now, to see the French people in the rowboat. She saw that the clouds were darker pink.

"I paid the lemon man," Andrew said, coming up behind her. "As usual, he claimed there were whole sacks of lemons he had left against the gate, and I played the fool, the way I always do. I told him that we asked for, and received, only one sack of lemons, and that whatever happened to the others was his problem."

Andrew sat down. He looked at her empty wineglass. Or he might have been looking beyond that, out to the water.

"Every week," he sighed, "the same thing. He rings, and I take in a sack of lemons, and he refuses to take the money. Then he comes at the end of the week asking for money for two or three sacks of lemons—only one of which was ever put in my hands. The others never existed." Andrew sighed again. "What do you think he would do if I said, 'But what do you mean, Signor Zito, three sacks of lemons? I must pay you for the *ten* sacks of lemons we received. We have had the most wonderful lemonade. The most remarkable lemon custard. We have baked lemon-meringue pies and mixed our morning orange juice with the juice of fresh-squeezed lemons. Let me give you more money. Let me give you everything I have. Let me pay you anything you want for your wonderful lemons."

His tone of voice was cold. Frightening. He was too often upset, and sometimes it frightened her. She clamped her hand over his, and he took a deep breath and stopped talking. She looked at him, and it suddenly seemed clear that what had been charming petulance when he was younger was now a kind of craziness—a craziness he did not even think about containing. Or what if he was right, and things were not as simple as she pretended? What if the boys she spoke to every day really did desire her and wish him harm? What if the person who wrote that story had been right, and Americans really were materialistic—so materialistic that they became paranoid and thought everyone was out to cheat them?

"What's that?" Andrew said. She had been so lost in her confusion that she started when he spoke.

"What?" she said.

"That," he said, and pulled his hand out from under hers.

They were both looking at the opal ring.

"From one of the beachboys," she said.

He frowned. "Are you telling me that ring isn't real?"

She put her hand in her lap. "No," she said. "Obviously it's real. You don't think one of the boys would be crazy enough about me to give me a real ring?"

"I assume I was wrong, and it's a cheap imitation," he said. "No. I am not so stupid that I think one of those boys gave you an expensive ring. Although I do admit the possibility that you bought yourself a ring."

He raised a finger and summoned the waiter. He ordered tea with milk. He looked straight ahead, to the beach. It was now deserted, except for the mother and baby. The baby had stopped throwing stones and was being rocked in its mother's arms. Christine excused herself and walked across the wooden planks to the bar at the back of the Cobalto, where the waiter was ordering tea from the bartender.

"Excuse me," she said quietly. "Do you have a pen and a piece of paper?"

The man behind the bar produced a pencil and handed her a business card. He turned and began to pour boiling water into a teapot.

She wondered whether the man thought that a pen and a pencil were interchangeable, and whether a business card was the same as a piece of paper. Was he being perverse, or did he not understand her request very well? All right, she thought: I'll keep it brief.

As she wrote, she reminded herself that it was a calm sea, and that the woman could not possibly be dead. "I had to leave," she wrote. "There is no phone at the villa we are renting. I will be here tomorrow at ten, with your ring." She signed her name, then handed the card to the bartender. "It's very important," she said. "A woman is going to come in, expecting to find me. A

Frenchwoman. If you see someone who's very upset—" She stopped, looking at the puzzled expression on the bartender's face. "Very important," she said again. "The woman had two friends. She's very pretty. She's been out boating." She looked at the card she had given the bartender. He held it, without looking at what she had written. "*Grazie*," she said.

"*Prego*," he said. He put the card down by the cash register and then—perhaps because she was looking—did something that struck her as appropriately ironic: he put a lemon on top of the card, to weigh it down.

"*Grazie*," she said again.

"*Prego*," he said.

She went back to the table and sat, looking not toward the cliff beyond which the French people's boat had disappeared, but in the other direction, toward Positano. They said little, but during the silence she decided—in the way that tourists are supposed to have epiphanies on vacations, at sunset— that there was such a thing as fate, and that she was fated to be with Andrew.

When he finished his tea, they rose together and went to the bar and paid. She did not think she was imagining that the owner nodded his head twice, and that the second nod was a little conspiratorial signal.

From the doors that opened onto the balcony outside their bedroom she could see more of the Mediterranean than from the Cobalto; at this vantage pint, high above the Via Torricella, it was almost possible to have a bird's-eye view. From here, the Luna pool was only a dark-blue speck. There was not one boat on the Mediterranean. She heard the warning honking of the bus drivers below and the buzzing sound the motorcycles made. The intermittent noise only made her think how quiet it was most of the time. Often, she could hear the breeze rustling the leaves of the lemon trees.

Andrew was asleep in the room, his breathing as steady as the surf rolling in to shore. He went to bed rather early now, and she often stood on the balcony for a while, before going in to read.

Years ago, when they were first together, she had worn a diamond engagement ring in a Tiffany setting, the diamond held in place by little prongs that rose up and curved against it, from a thin gold band. Now she had no idea what had become of the ring, which she had returned to him, tearfully, in Paris. When they later married, he gave her only a plain gold band. It made her feel suddenly old, to remember things she had not thought about in years—to miss them, and to want them back. She had to stop herself, because her impulse was to go into the bedroom and wake him up and ask him what had become of the ring.

She did go in, but she did not disturb him. Instead, she walked quietly to the bed and sat on the side of it, then reached over and turned off the little bedside lamp. Then she carefully stretched out and pulled the covers over her. She began to breathe in time with his breathing, as she often did, trying to see if, by imitation, she could sink into easy sleep.

With her eyes closed, she remembered movement: the birds sailing between high cliffs, boats on the water. It was possible, standing high up, as she often did in Italy, to actually look down on the birds in their flight: small specks below, slowly swooping from place to place. The tiny boats on the sea seemed no more consequential than sunbeams, glinting on the surface of the water.

Unaccustomed to wearing jewelry, she rubbed the band of the ring on her finger as she began to fall asleep. Although it was not a conscious thought, something was wrong—something about the ring bothered her, like a grain of sand in an oyster.

In time, his breathing changed, and hers did. Calm sleep was now a missed breath—a small sound. They might have been two of the birds she so often thought of, flying separately between cliffs—birds whose movement, which might seem erratic, was always private, and so took them where they wanted to go.

T. Coraghessan Boyle

Rara Avis

(UNITED STATES)

It looked like a woman or a girl perched there on the roof of the furniture store, wings folded like a shawl, long legs naked and exposed beneath a skirt of jagged feathers the color of sepia. The sun was pale, poised at equinox. There was the slightest breeze. We stood there, thirty or forty of us, gaping up at the big motionless bird as if we expected it to talk, as if it weren't a bird at all but a plastic replica with a speaker concealed in its mouth. Sidor's Furniture, it would squawk, loveseats and three-piece sectionals.

I was twelve. I'd been banging a handball against the side of the store when a man in a Studebaker suddenly swerved into the parking lot, slammed on his brakes, and slid out of the driver's seat as if mesmerized. His head was tilted back, and he was shading his eyes, squinting to focus on something at the level of the roof. This was odd. Sidor's roof—a flat glaring expanse of crushed stone and tar relieved only by the neon characters that irradiated the proprietor's name—was no architectural wonder. What could be so captivating? I pocketed the handball and ambled round to the front of the store. Then I looked up.

There it was: stark and anomalous, a relic of a time before shopping centers, tract houses, gas stations, and landfill, a thing of swamps and tidal flats, of ooze, fetid water, and rich black festering muck. In the context of the minutely ordered universe of suburbia, it was startling, as unexpected as a downed meteor or the carcass of a woolly mammoth. I shouted out, whooped with surprise and sudden joy.

Already people were gathering. Mrs. Novak, all three hundred pounds of her, was lumbering across the lot from her house on the corner, a look of bewilderment creasing her heavy jowls. Robbie Matechik wheeled up on his bike, a pair of girls emerged from the rear of the store with jump ropes, an old man in baggy trousers struggled with a bag of groceries. Two more cars pulled in, and a third stopped out on the highway. Hopper, Moe, Jennings, Davidson, Sebesta: the news echoed through the neighborhood as if relayed by tribal drums, and people dropped rakes, edgers, pruning shears, and came running. Michael Donadio, sixteen years old and a heartthrob at the local high school, was pumping gas at the station up the block. He left the nozzle in the customer's tank, jumped the fence,and started across the blacktop, weaving under his pompadour. The customer followed him.

At its height, there must have been fifty people gathered there in front of Sidor's, shading their eyes and gazing up expectantly, as if the bird were the opening act of a musical comedy or an ingenious new type of vending machine. The mood was jocular, festive even. Sidor appeared at the door of his shop with two stockboys, gazed up at the bird for a minute, and then clapped his hands twice, as if he were shooing pigeons. The bird remained motionless, cast in wax. Sidor, a fleshless old man with a monk's tonsure and liver-spotted hands, shrugged his shoulders and mugged for the crowd. We all laughed. Then he ducked into the store and emerged with an end table, a lamp, a footstool, motioned to the stockboys, and had them haul out a sofa and an armchair. Finally he scrawled BIRD WATCHER'S SPECIAL on a strip of cardboard and taped it to the window. People laughed and shook their heads. "Hey, Sidor," Albert Moe's father shouted, "where'd you get that thing—the Bronx Zoo?"

I couldn't keep still. I danced round the fringe of the crowd, tugging at sleeves and skirts, shouting out that I'd seen the bird first—which wasn't strictly true, but I felt proprietary about this strange and wonderful creature, the cynosure of an otherwise pedestrian Saturday afternoon. Had I seen it in the air? people asked. Had it moved? I was tempted to lie, to tell them I'd spotted it over the school, the firehouse, the used-car lot, a hovering shadow, wings spread wider than the hood of a Cadillac, but I couldn't. "No," I said, quiet suddenly. I glanced up and saw my father in the back of the crowd, standing close to Mrs. Schlecta and whispering something in her ear. Her lips were wet. I didn't know where my mother was. At the far end of the lot a girl in a college sweater was leaning against the fender of a convertible while her boyfriend pressed himself against her as if he wanted to dance.

Six weeks earlier, at night, the community had come together as it came together now, but there had been no sense of magic or festivity about the occasion. The Novaks, Donadios, Schlectas, and the rest—they gathered to watch an abandoned house go up in flames. I didn't dance round the crowd that night. I stood beside my father, leaned against him, the acrid, unforgiving stink of the smoke almost drowned in the elemental odor of his sweat, the odor of armpit and crotch and secret hair, the sematic animal scent of him that had always repelled me—until that moment. Janine McCarty's mother was shrieking. Ragged and torn, her voice clawed at the starless night, the leaping flames. On the front lawn, just as they backed the ambulance in and the crowd parted, I caught a glimpse of Janine, lying there in the grass. Every face was shouting. The glare of the fire tore disordered lines across people's eyes and dug furrows in their cheeks.

There was a noise to that fire, a killing noise, steady and implacable. The flames were like the waves at Coney Island—ghost waves, insubstantial, yellow and red rather than green, but waves all the same. They rolled across the foundation, spat from the windows, beat at the roof. Wayne Sanders was white-faced. He was a tough guy, two years older than I but held back in school because of mental sloth and recalcitrance. Police and firemen and wild-eyed neighborhood men nosed round him, excited, like hounds. Even then, in the grip of confusion and clashing voices, safe at my father's side, I knew what they wanted to know. It was the same thing my father demanded of me whenever he caught me—in fact or by report—emerging from the deserted, vandalized, and crumbling house: What were you doing in there?

He couldn't know.

Spires, parapets, derelict staircases, closets that opened on closets, the place was magnetic, vestige of an age before the neat rows of ranches and Cape Cods that lined both sides of the block. Plaster pulled back from the ceilings to reveal slats like ribs, glass pebbled the floors, the walls were paisleyed with aerosol obscenities. There were bats in the basement, rats and mice in the hallways. The house breathed death and freedom. I went there whenever I could. I heaved my interdicted knife end-over-end at the lintels and peeling cupboards. I lit cigarettes and hung them from my lower lip, I studied scraps of pornographic magazines with a fever beating through my body. Two days before the fire I was there with Wayne Sanders and Janine. They were holding hands. He had a switchblade, stiff and cold as an icicle. He gave me Ex-Lax and told me it was chocolate. Janine giggled. He shuffled a deck of battered playing cards and showed me one at a time the murky photos imprinted on them. My throat went dry with guilt.

After the fire I went to church. In the confessional the priest asked me if I practiced self-pollution. The words were formal, unfamiliar, but I knew what he meant. So, I thought, kneeling there in the dark, crushed with shame, there's a name for it. I looked at the shadowy grill, looked toward the source of the soothing voice of absolution, the voice of forgiveness and hope, and I lied. "No," I whispered.

And then there was the bird.

It never moved, not once, through all the commotion at its feet, through all the noise and confusion, all the speculation regarding its needs, condition, origin, species: it never moved. It was a statue, eyes unblinking, only the wind-rustled feathers giving it away for flesh and blood, for living bird. "It's a crane," somebody said. "No, no, it's a herring—a blue herring." Someone else thought it was an eagle. My father later confided that he believed it was a stork.

"Is it sick, do you think?" Mrs. Novak said.

"Maybe it's broke its wing."

"It's a female," someone insisted. "She's getting ready to lay her eggs."

I looked around and was surprised to see that the crowd had thinned considerably. The girl in the college sweater was gone, Michael Donadio was back across the street pumping gas, the man in the Studebaker had driven off. I scanned the crowd for my father: he'd gone home, I guessed. Mrs. Schlecta had disappeared too, and I could see the great bulk of Mrs. Novak receding into her house on the corner like a sea lion vanishing into a swell. After a while Sidor took his lamp and end table back into the store.

One of the older guys had a rake. He heaved it straight up like a javelin, as high as the roof of the store, and then watched it slam down on the pavement.

The bird never flinched. People lit cigarettes, shuffled their feet. They began to drift off, one by one. When I looked around again there were only eight of us left, six kids and two men I didn't recognize. The women and girls, more easily bored or perhaps less interested to begin with, had gone home to gas ranges and hopscotch squares: I could see a few of the girls in the distance, on the swings in front of the school, tiny, their skirts rippling like flags.

I waited. I wanted the bird to flap its wings, blink an eye, shift a foot; I wanted it desperately, wanted it more than anything I had ever wanted. Perched there at the lip of the roof, its feet clutching the drainpipe as if welded to it, the bird was a coil of possibility, a muscle relaxed against the moment of tension. Yes, it was magnificent, even in repose. And, yes, I could stare at it, examine its every line, from its knobbed knees to the cropped feathers at the back of its head, I could absorb it, become it, look out from its unblinking yellow eyes on the street grown quiet and the sun sinking behind the gas station. Yes, but that wasn't enough. I had to see it in flight, had to see the great impossible wings beating in the air, had to see it transposed into its native element.

Suddenly the wind came up—a gust that raked at our hair and scattered refuse across the parking lot—and the bird's feathers lifted like a petticoat. It was then that I understood. Secret, raw, red, and wet, the wound flashed just above the juncture of the legs before the wind died and the feathers fell back in place.

I turned and looked past the neighborhood kids—my playmates—at the two men, the strangers. They were lean and seedy, unshaven, slouching behind the brims of their hats. One of them was chewing a toothpick. I caught their eyes: they'd seen it too.

I threw the first stone.

Robert Olen Butler

Mr. Green

(UNITED STATES)

I am a Catholic, the daughter of a Catholic mother and father, and I do not believe in the worship of my ancestors, especially in the form of a parrot. My father's parents died when he was very young and he became a Catholic in an orphanage run by nuns in Hanoi. My mother's mother was a Catholic but her father was not and, like many Vietnamese, he was a believer in what Confucius taught about ancestors. I remember him taking me by the hand while my parents and my grandmother were sitting under a banana tree in the yard and he said, "Let's go talk with Mr. Green." He led me into the house and he touched his lips with his forefinger to tell me that this was a secret. Mr. Green was my grandfather's parrot and I loved talking to him, but we passed Mr. Green's roost in the front room. Mr. Green said, "Hello, kind sir," but we didn't even answer him.

My grandfather took me to the back of his house, to a room that my mother had said was private, that she had yanked me away from when I once had tried to look. It had a bead curtain at the door and we passed through it and the beads rustled like tall grass. The room was dim, lit by candles, and it smelled of incense, and my grandfather stood me before a little shrine with flowers and a smoking incense bowl and two brass candlesticks and between them a photo of a man in a Chinese mandarin hat. "That's my father," he said, nodding toward the photo. "He lives here." Then he let go of my hand and touched my shoulder. "Say a prayer for my father." The face in the photo was tilted a little to the side and was smiling faintly, like he'd asked me a question and he was waiting for an answer that he expected to like. I knelt before the shrine as I did at Mass and I said the only prayer I knew by heart, The Lord's Prayer.

But as I prayed, I was conscious of my grandfather. I even peeked at him as he stepped to the door and parted the beads and looked toward the front of the house. Then he returned and stood beside me and I finished my prayer as I listened to the beads rustling into silence behind us. When I said "Amen" aloud, my grandfather knelt beside me and leaned near and whispered, "Your father is doing a terrible thing. If he must be a Catholic, that's one thing. But he has left the spirits of his ancestors to wander for eternity in loneliness." It was hard for me to believe that my father was doing something as terrible as this, but it was harder for me to believe that my grandfather, who was even older than my father, could be wrong.

My grandfather explained about the spirit world, how the souls of our ancestors continue to need love and attention and devotion. Given these things, they will share in our lives and they will bless us and even warn us about disasters in our dreams. But if we neglect the souls of our ancestors, they will become lost and lonely and will wander around in the kingdom of the dead no better off than a warrior killed by his enemy and left unburied in a rice paddy to be eaten by black birds of prey.

When my grandfather told me about the birds plucking out the eyes of the dead and about the possibility of our own ancestors, our own family, suffering just like that if we ignore them, I said, "Don't worry, Grandfather, I will always say prayers for you and make offerings for you, even if I'm a Catholic."

I thought this would please my grandfather, but he just shook his head sharply, like he was mad at me, and he said, "Not possible."

"I can," I said.

Then he looked at me and I guess he realized that he'd spoken harshly. He tilted his head slightly and smiled a little smile—just like his father in the picture—but what he said wasn't something to smile about. "You are a girl," he said. "So it's not possible for you to do it alone. Only a son can oversee the worship of his ancestors."

I felt a strange thing inside me, a recoiling, like I'd stepped barefoot on a slug, but how can you recoil from your own body? And so I began to cry. My grandfather patted me and kissed me and said it was all right, but it wasn't all right for me. I wanted to protect my grandfather's soul, but it wasn't in my power. I was a girl. We waited together before the shrine and when I'd stopped crying, we went back to the front room and my grandfather bowed to his parrot and said, "Hello, kind sir," and Mr. Green said, "Hello, kind sir," and even though I loved the parrot, I would not speak to him that day because he was a boy and I wasn't.

This was in our town, which was on the bank of the Red River just south of Hanoi. We left that town not long after. I was seven years old and I remember hearing my grandfather arguing with my parents. I was sleeping on a mat at the back of our house and I woke up and I heard voices and my grandfather said, "Not possible." The words chilled me, but then I listened more closely and I knew they were discussing the trip we were about to go on. Everyone was very frightened and excited. There were many families in our little town who were planning to leave. They had even taken the bell out of the church tower to carry with them. We were all Catholics. But Grandfather did not have the concerns of the Catholics. He was concerned about the spirits of his ancestors. This was the place where they were born and died and were buried. He was afraid that they would not make the trip. "What then?" he cried. And later he spoke of the people of the South and how they would hate us, being from the North. "What then?" he said.

Mr. Green says that, too. "What then?" he has cried to me a thousand times, ten thousand times, in the past sixteen years. Parrots can live for a hundred years. And though I could not protect my dead grandfather's soul, I could take care of his parrot. When my grandfather died in Saigon in 1972, he made sure that Mr. Green came to me. I was twenty-four then and newly married and I still loved Mr. Green. He would sit on my shoulder and take the top of my ear in his beak, a beak that could crush the hardest shell, and he would hold my ear with the greatest gentleness and touch me with his tongue.

I have brought Mr. Green with me to the United Sates of America, and in the long summers here in New Orleans and in the warm springs and falls and even in many days of our mild winters, he sits on my screened-in back porch, near the door, and he speaks in the voice of my grandfather. When he wants to get onto my shoulder and go with me into the community garden, he says, "What then?" And when I first come to him in the morning, he says, "Hello, kind sir."

He loves me. That is, I am the only person who can go near him without his attempting to draw blood. But he loved my grandfather before me, and there are times when he seems to hold the spirit of my grandfather and all his knowledge. Mr. Green sits on my shoulder and presses close to my head and he repeats the words that he has heard from my husband and my children. My children even teach him English words. He says all these things, but without any feeling. The Vietnamese words of my grandfather, however, come out powerfully, like someone very strong is inside him. And whenever he speaks with my grandfather's voice, Mr. Green's eyes dilate and contract over and over, which is a parrot's display of happiness. Yesterday I tried to give him some drops that the veterinarian prescribed for him and Mr. Green said, "Not possible," and even though he is sick, his eyes showed how pleased he was to defy me.

When we all lived in Saigon at last, my grandfather discovered the bird market on Hàm Nghi Street and he would take me there. Actually, in the street market of Hàm Nghi there were animals of all kinds—dogs and monkeys and rabbits and turtles and even wildcats. But when my grandfather took my hand and said to me, "Come, little one," and we walked down Trân Hu'ng Dao, where our house was, and we came to Hàm Nghi, he always took me to the place with the birds.

The canaries were the most loved by everyone who came to the market, and my grandfather sang with them. They all hopped to the side of their cages that was closest to my grandfather and he whistled and hummed and even sang words, songs from the North that he sang quite low, so that only the birds could hear. He did not want the people of Saigon to realize he was from the North. And the canaries all opened their mouths and the air filled with their sounds, their throats ruffling and puffing, and I looked at my grandfather's throat to see if it moved the way the throats of these birds moved. It did not move at all. His skin was slack there, and in all the times I saw him charm the birds, I never saw his throat move, like he didn't really mean the sounds he made. The people all laughed when they saw what he could do and they said that my grandfather was a wizard, but he would just ignore them.

The canaries seemed to be his favorite birds on Hàm Nghi, though he spent time with them all. The dark-plumed ones—the magpies and the blackbirds—were always singing on their own, especially the blackbirds with their orange beaks. My grandfather came near the blackbirds and they were gabbling among themselves and he frowned at them, like they were fools to be content only with their own company. They did not need him to prompt their songs. He growled at them, "You're just a bunch of old women," and we moved on to the doves that were big-eyed and quiet and he cooed at them and he told them how pretty they were and we looked at the moorhens, pecking at the bottoms of their cages like chickens, and the cranes with their wonderful necks curling and stretching.

We visited all the birds and my grandfather loved them, and the first time we went to Hàm Nghi, we ended up at the cages crowded with sparrows. He bent near their chattering and I liked these birds very much. They were small and their eyes were bright, and even though the birds were crowded, they were always in motion, hopping and fluffing up and shaking themselves like my vain friends. I was a quiet little girl, but I, too, would sometimes look at myself in a mirror and primp and puff myself up, even as in public I tried to hold myself apart a little bit from the other girls.

I was surprised and delighted that first day when my grandfather motioned to the birdseller and began to point at sparrows and the merchant reached into the cage and caught one bird after another and he put them all into a cardboard box. My grandfather bought twelve birds and they did not fly as they sat in the box. "Why aren't they flying?" I asked.

"Their wings are clipped," my grandfather said.

This was all right with me. They clearly weren't in any pain and they could still hop and they would never fly away from me. I wouldn't even need a cage for my vain little friends.

I'm sure that my grandfather knew what I was thinking. But he said nothing. When we got home, he gave me the box and told me to take the birds to show my mother. I found her on the back stoop slicing vegetables. I showed her the box and she said that Grandfather was wonderful. She set the box down and told me to stay with her, I could help her. I crouched beside her and waited and I could hear the chattering of the sparrows from the box.

We had always kept chickens and ducks and geese. Some of them were pecking around near us even as I crouched there with my mother. I knew that we ate those animals, but for some reason Hàm Nghi seemed like a different place altogether and the sparrows could only be for song and friendship. But finally my mother finished cutting the vegetables and she reached into the box and drew out a sparrow, its feet dangling from the bottom of her fist and its head poking out of the top. I looked at its face and I knew it was a girl and my mother said, "This is the way it's done," and she fisted her other hand around the sparrow's head and she twisted.

I don't remember how long it took me to get used to this. But I would always drift away when my grandfather went to the sparrow cages on Hàm Nghi. I did not like his face when he bought them. It seemed the same as when he cooed at the doves or sang with the canaries. But I mush have decided that it was all part of growing up, of becoming a woman like my mother, for it was she who killed them, after all. And she taught me to do this thing and I wanted to be just like her and I twisted the necks of the sparrows and I plucked their feathers and we roasted them and ate them and my grandfather would take a deep breath after the meal and his eyes would close in pleasure.

There were parrots, too, on Hàm Nghi. They all looked very much like Mr. Green. They were the color of breadfruit leaves with a little yellow on the throat. My grandfather chose one bird each time and cocked his head at it, copying the angle of the bird's head and my grandfather said, "Hello," or "What's your name?"—things he never said to Mr. Green. The parrots on Hàm Nghi did not talk to my grandfather, though once one of them made a sound like the horns of the little cream and blue taxis that rushed past in the streets. But they never spoke any words, and my grandfather took care to explain to me that these parrots were too recently captured to have learned anything. He said that they were probably not as smart as Mr. Green either, but one day they would speak. Once after explaining this, he leaned near me and motioned to a parrot that was digging for mites under his wing and said, "That bird will still be alive and speaking to someone when you have grown to be an old woman and have died and are buried in the ground."

I am forty-one years old now. I go each day to the garden on the bank of the bayou that runs through this place they call Versailles. It is part of New Orleans, but it is far from the center of the town and it is full of Vietnamese who once came from the North. My grandfather never saw the United States. I don't know what he would think. But I come to this garden each day and I crouch in the rich earth and I wear my straw hat and my black pantaloons and I grow lettuce and collards and turnip greens and mint, and my feet, which were once quite beautiful, grow coarse. My family likes the things I bring to the table.

Sometimes Mr. Green comes with me to this garden. He rides on my shoulder and he stays there for a long time, often imitating the cardinals, the sharp ricochet sound they make. Then finally Mr. Green climbs down my arm and drops to the ground and he waddles about in the garden, and when he starts to bite off the stalk of a plant, I cry, "Not possible" to him and he looks at me like he is angry, like I've dared to use his own words, his and his first master's, against him. I always bring twigs with me and I throw him one to chew on so that neither of us has to back down. I have always tried to preserve his dignity. He is at least fifty years older than me. My grandfather was eighteen when he himself caught Mr. Green on a trip to the highlands with his father.

So Mr. Green is quite old and old people sometimes lose their understanding of the things around them. It is not strange, then, that a few weeks ago Mr. Green began to pluck his feathers out. I went to the veterinarian when it became clear what was happening. A great bare spot had appeared on Mr. Green's chest and I had been finding his feathers at the foot of his perch, so I watched him one afternoon through the kitchen window. He sat there on his perch beside the door of the back porch and he pulled twelve feathers from his chest, one at a time, and felt each with his tongue and then dropped it to the floor. I came out onto the porch and he squawked at me, as if he was doing something private and I should have known better than to intrude. I sat down on the porch and he stopped.

I took Mr. Green to the veterinarian and he said that when parrots do this, it may be because they lack a certain vitamin or mineral. But more often the reason is that the bird is bored. I tried to convince myself that this is what it meant when Mr. Green stopped plucking his feathers as soon as I appeared on the porch. Keep him busy, the doctor said. So I got Mr. Green a new climbing tree with lots of fresh bark to peel and I spent more time with him. I took him to the garden even when he didn't ask to go and I brought my sewing and even some of my cooking—the preparation of the foods—out onto the porch, and while I did these household things, I talked to him. It was just idle chatter but there were plenty of words, and often Mr. Green looked at me sharply as I spoke and I could hear how I sounded, chattering away like a blackbird.

But I felt driven to do something for him. He was old and he was sick and I felt I had to do something. My grandfather took six months to die and he lay in a bed on the top floor of our house and Mr. Green was always on a perch beside him. I remember a wind chime at the window. It was made of brass and I've never had a wind chime in my home because when I hear one, another sound always comes with it, the deep rattling cough of my grandfather. I would visit him in his room with my mother and once he called me back as we were about to leave. I came to him and my mother had gone out the door and I could hear her talking rapidly with my grandmother. My grandfather motioned me to come very near and he twisted his body in the bed. His face crumpled in pain as he did it, but he forced himself because he wanted to tell me a secret. I leaned close to him. "Do you hear them talking?" he said. He nodded toward the door and he obviously meant my mother and grandmother.

"Yes," I said.

He frowned. "How foolish they sound. Chattering and yammering. All the women sound like that. You don't want to grow up sounding like all these foolish women, do you?"

I did not know how to answer his question. I wanted very much to be like my mother, and when my grandfather said this, I felt the recoiling begin inside me and the tears begin to rise. But my mother called my name at that moment and I did not have to find an answer to my grandfather's question. I turned my back on him and ran across the room without saying a word. As I got to the door, however, Mr. Green cried, "What then?" and it sounded as if he had actually finished my grandfather's thought. You will grow up to be a woman—what then?

And maybe he did finish the thought. Parrots are very smart. Mr. Green in particular. And he knows more than just my grandfather's words. The Buddhists believe in the transmigration of souls, though I suppose it's impossible to transmigrate into some creature that's already alive. But after a few days of angry looks from Mr. Green when I filled the porch with talk that was intended to save his life, he began to cry, "Not possible" over and over until I stopped speaking. Perhaps a male voice would have been acceptable to him, but mine was not, and then Mr. Green began to pluck himself once more, even with me sitting there in the room. I went to him when he began to do this and I said, "Not possible," but he ignored me. He did not even raise his head to look at me but tore away at his feathers, each one making a faint popping sound as it came out. Then the next day he began to cough.

I knew the cough well. But I took Mr. Green to the veterinarian and he told me what I expected, that the cough was not the bird's. This was a sound he was imitating. "Did someone in your household recently have a cold or the flu?" the doctor said.

"It is my grandfather," I said.

On the last visit to my grandfather's room he began to cough. My mother went to him and he waved her away. She backed off and I came forward, wanting to help him. He was sitting up now and hunched over and the cough rattled deep inside his chest and then there was a sudden silence and I drew nearer, thinking that my step forward had actually helped, but my grandfather lifted his face and his eyes were very sad, and I knew he was disappointed. My brothers were not yet born and I held my breath so that this silence would go on, but the sound raked up from his chest and filled the room again.

This morning I went to the back porch and Mr. Green was pulling out a feather and he did not acknowledge me, even to taunt me by calling me "sir." He dropped the feather and began to pluck another from beneath his left wing. His chest was naked now and the skin looked as slack as my grandfather's throat. I stood before him and I offered my arm for him to come and sit on my shoulder. Yesterday he had said, "Not possible," but today he said nothing. He dropped a feather and leaned over and bit me hard on my arm. I bled. But I did not move my arm and he looked at me. His eyes were steady in their sadness, fully dilated, as if he was considering all of this. I pushed my arm to him again and he knew that he had no choice, so he climbed on, but he did not go to my shoulder.

I held my arm aloft and carried Mr. Green outside. The sun had still not burned the fog off the bayou and I went straight into the garden. My feet were bare, like a child's, and the earth was soft and wet and I crouched there and I quickly reached to Mr. Green and grasped him at his chest, lifted him and caught him with my other hand before he could struggle. His wings were pinned and he was bigger in my hands than I had ever imagined. But a Vietnamese woman is experienced in these things and Mr. Green did not have a chance even to make a sound as I laid him on his side, pinned him with my knee, slid my hands up and wrung his neck.

I pray for the soul of my grandfather. I do not bear him any anger. Sometimes I go to Mass during the week. Versailles has a Catholic church just for the Vietnamese and the Mass is celebrated in our language. I sit near the back and I look at the section where all the old women go. They take the Eucharist every day of their lives and they sit together wearing their traditional dresses and with their hair in scarves rolled up on their heads and I wonder if that is where I will finally end up, in the old women's section at Mass each day. No one in my church will likely live as long as a parrot. But our savior lived only thirty-three years, so maybe it's not important. There were women around Jesus when He died, the two Marys. They couldn't do anything for Him. But neither could the men, who had all run away.

Peter Carey

The Fat Man in History

(AUSTRALIA)

1.

His feet are sore. The emporium seems endless as he shuffles an odd-legged shuffle with the double-bed sheets under his arm. It is like a nightmare—the exit door in sight but not coming any closer, the oppressive heat, the constant swarm of bodies flowing towards him like insects drawn towards, then repelled by, a speeding vehicle.

He is sweating badly, attempting to look calm. The sheets are badly wrapped. He wrapped them himself, surprising himself with his own nerve. He took the sheets (double, because there were no singles in blue) and walked to the wrapping counter where he pulled out a length of brown paper and set to work. To an assistant looking at him queryingly he said, smiling meekly, "You don't object?" The assistant looked away.

His trousers are large, floppy, and old-fashioned. Fortunately they have very large pockets and the pockets now contain several tins of smoked oysters. The smoked oysters are easy, always in big tubs outside the entrance to the self-service section. He has often wondered why they do this, why put them outside? Is it to make them easier to steal, because they are difficult to sell? Is it their way of providing for him and his friends? Is there possibly a fat man who has retained his position in the emporium? He enjoys himself with these theories, he has a love of such constructions, building ideas like card houses, extending them until he gets dizzy and trembles at their heights.

Approaching the revolving door he hesitates, trying to judge the best way to enter the thing. The door is turning fast, spewing people into the store, last-minute shoppers. He chooses his space and moves forward, bustling to get there in time. Deirdre, as tiny and bird-like as she always was, is thrown out of the revolving door, collides with him, hisses "slob" at him, and scurries into the store, leaving him with a sense of dull amazement, surprise that such a pretty face could express such fear and hatred so quickly.

Of course it wasn't Deirdre. But Alexander Finch reflects that it could have been. As he sadly circles inside the revolving door and walks slowly along the street he thinks how strange it is that the revolution should have produced this one idea that would affect his life so drastically: to be fat is to be an oppressor, to be greedy, to be pre-revolutionary. It is impossible to say if it arose from the people or was fed to them by the propaganda of the revolution. Certainly in the years before the revolution most fat men were either Americans, stooges for the Americans, or wealthy supporters of the Americans. But in those years the people were of a more reasonable mind and could accept the idea of fat men like Alexander Finch being against the Americans and against the old Danko regime.

Alexander Finch had always thought of himself as possessing a lovable face and figure. He had not thought this from any conceit. At school they had called him "Cuddles," and on the paper everyone called him "Teddy" or "Teddy Bear." He had signed his cartoons "Teddy" and when he included himself in a cartoon he was always a bewildered, rotund man with a large bum, looking on the antics of the world with smiling, fatherly eyes.

But somehow, slowly, the way in which the world looked at Alexander Finch and, in consequence, the way Alexander Finch looked at himself altered. He was forced to become a different cartoon, one of his own "Fat Americans": grotesque, greedy, an enemy of the people.

But in the early days after the revolution the change had not taken place. Or, if it had, Finch was too busy to notice it. As secretary of the Thirty-second District he took notes, recorded minutes, wrote weekly bulletins, drafted the ten-day reports to the Central Committee of Seventy-five, and still, somehow, found time to do a cartoon for his paper every day and to remember that General Kooper was spelt with a "K" and not a "C" (Miles Cooper being one of the infamous traitors of the revolution). In addition he was responsible for inspecting and reporting on the state of properties in the Thirty-second District and investigating cases of hardship and poverty wherever he found them. And if, during these early days, he occasionally became involved in unpleasant misunderstandings he regarded them as simply that, nothing more. People were accustomed to regarding all fat officials as either American or Danko men, because only the Americans and their friends had had enough food to become fat on. Occasionally Finch attempted to explain the nature of glandular fat and to point out that he wasn't a real official but rather the cartoonist "Teddy," who had always been anti-Danko.

Finch was occasionally embarrassed by his fatness in the early days when the people were hungry. But, paradoxically, it wasn't until the situation improved, when production had reached and passed the pre-revolutionary figure and when the distribution problems had finally been more or less ironed out, that the fat question came to the fore. And then, of course, food was no problem at all. If anything there was a surfeit and there was talk of dumping grain on the world market. Instead it was dumped in the sea.

Even then the district committees and the Committee of Seventy-five never passed any motions directly relating to fat men. Rather the word "fat" entered slyly into the language as a new adjective, as a synonym for greedy, ugly, sleazy, lazy, obscene, evil, dirty, dishonest, untrustworthy. It was unfair. It was not a good time to be a fat man.

Alexander Finch, now secretary of the clandestine "Fat Men Against The

Revolution," carries his stolen double-bed sheets and his cans of smoke oysters northwards through the hot city streets. His narrow slanting eyes are almost shut and he looks out at the world through a comforting curtain of eyelashes. He moves slowly, a fat man with a white cotton shirt, baggy grey trousers, and a slight limp that could be interpreted as a waddle. His shirt shows large areas of sweat, like daubs, markings deliberately applied. No one bumps him. At the traffic lights he stands to one side, away from the crowds. It seems to be a mutual arrangement.

The sheets under his arm feel heavy and soggy. He is not sure that he has gotten away with it. They may be following him still (he dares not look around), following him to the house, to discover what else he may have stolen. He smiles at the thought of all those empty cans of smoked oysters in the incinerator in the backyard, all those hundreds of cans they will find. And the beer keg Fantoni stole. And the little buddha he stole for Fantoni's birthday but somehow kept for himself, he felt so sorry for (or was it fond of?) the little fat statue. He accuses himself of self-love but reflects that a little self-love is tonic for a fat man in these times.

Two youths run past him, bumping him from either side. He assumes it was intentional but is uncertain. His whole situation is like that, a tyranny of subtlety. To be fired from his job with the only newspaper that had been continually sympathetic to Kooper and his ideas for "slovenliness" and "bad spelling." He had laughed ut loud. "Bad spelling." It was almost a tradition that cartoonists were bad spellers. It was expected of them and his work was always checked carefully for literals. But now they said his spelling was a nuisance and wasteful of time, and anyway he was "generally slovenly in dress and attitude." Did "slovenly" really mean "fat"? He didn't ask them. He didn't wish to embarrass them.

2.

Milligan's taxi is parked in front of the house. The taxi is like Milligan: it is very bright and shiny and painted in stripes of iridescent blue and yellow. Milligan spray-painted it himself. It looks like a dodgem car from Luna Park, right down to the random collection of pink stars stencilled on the driver's door.

Milligan is probably asleep.

Behind Milligan's taxi the house is very still and very drab, painted in the colours of railway stations and schools: hard green and dirty cream. Rust shows through the cream paint on the cast-iron balcony and two pairs of large baggy underpants hang limply from a line on the upstairs verandah.

It is one of six such houses, all identical, surrounded by high blocks of concrete flats and areas of flat waste land where dry thistles grow. The road itself is a major one and still retains some of its pre-revolutionary grandeur: rows of large elms form an avenue leading into the city.

The small front garden is full of weeds and Glino's radishes. Finch opens the front door cautiously, hoping it will be cooler inside but knowing that it won't be. In the half-dark he gropes around on the floor, feeling for letters. There are none—Fantoni must have taken them. He can still make out the dark blotches on the door where May sat and banged his head for three hours. No one has bothered to remove the blood.

Finch stands in the dark passage and listens. The house has the feeling of a place where no one works, a sort of listlessness. May is upstairs playing his Sibelius record. It is very scratched and it makes May morose, but it is the only record he has and he plays it incessantly. The music filters through the heavy heat of the passage and Finch hopes that Fantoni is not in the kitchen reading his "correspondence"—he doesn't wish Fantoni to see the sheets. He shuffles slowly down the passage, past the foot of the high, steep stairs, through the strange little cupboard where Glino cooks his vegetarian meals in two battered aluminium saucepans, and enters the kitchen where Fantoni, wearing a florid Hawaiian shirt and smoking a cigar, is reading his "correspondence" and tugging at the large moustache which partially obscures his small mouth. Finch has often thought it strange that such a large man should have such a small mouth. Fantoni's hands are also small but his forearms are large and muscular. His head is almost clean-shaven, having the shortest of bristles covering it, and the back of his head is divided by a number of strange creases. Fantoni is the youngest of the six fat men who live in the house. An ex-parking officer, aged about twenty-eight, he is the most accomplished thief of them all. Without Fantoni they would all come close to starving, eking out a living on their pensions. Only Milligan has any other income.

Fantoni has connections everywhere. He can arrange food. He can arrange anything but the dynamite he needs to blow up the 16 October Statue. He has spent two months looking for the dynamite. Fantoni is the leader and driving force of the "Fat Men Against The Revolution." The others are like a hired army, fighting for Fantoni's cause which is to "teach the little monkeys a lesson."

Fantoni does not look up as Finch enters. He does not look up when Finch greets him. He does nothing to acknowledge Finch's presence. Because he is occupied with "my correspondence," the nature of which he has never revealed to anyone. Finch, for once, is happy that Fantoni doesn't look up, and continues out onto the porch with the green fibreglass sunroof, past Fantoni's brand-new bicycle and Glino's herbs, along the concrete path, past the kitchen window, and comes to what is known as "the new extensions."

"The new extensions" are two bedrooms that have been added onto the back of the house. Their outside walls are made from corrugated iron, painted a dark, rusty red. Inside they are a little more pleasant. One is empty. Finch has the other. Finch's room is full of little pieces of bric-à-brac—books, papers, his buddha, a Rubens print, postcards from Italy with reproductions of Renaissance paintings. He has an early map of Iceland on the wall above the plywood bedhead, a grey goatskin rug covering the biggest holes in the maroon felt carpet, a Chinese paper lantern over the naked light globe.

He opens the door, steps back a pace, and pulls a huge comic fatman's face to register his disgust to some invisible observer.

The room has no insulation. And with each day of heat it has become hotter and hotter. At 4 A.M. It becomes a little cooler and at 7 A.M. it begins to heat up again. The heat brings out the strange smells of previous inhabitants, strange sweats and hopes come oozing out in the heat, ghosts of dreams and spilt Pine-o-Kleen.

The window does not open. There is no fly-wire screen on the door. He can choose between suffocation and mosquitoes.

Only a year ago he did a series of cartoons about housing conditions. He had shown corrugated-iron shacks, huge flies, fierce rats, and Danko himself pocketing the rent. Danko's men had called on him after the fourth one had appeared. They threatened to jail him for treason, to beat him up, to torture him. He was very frightened, but they did nothing.

And now he is living in a corrugated-iron room with huge blow-flies and the occasional rat. In a strange way it pleases him that he is no longer an observer, but it is a very small pleasure, too small to overcome the sense of despair that the smells and the suffocating heat induce in him.

He opens the roughly wrapped parcel of sheets and arranges them on the bed. The blue is cool. That is why he wanted the blue so badly, because it is cooler than white, and because it doesn't show the dirt so badly. The old sheets have turned a disgusting brown. If they were not listed in the inventory he would take them out and burn them. Instead he rolls them up and stuffs them under the bed.

If Fantoni had seen the sheets there would have been a row. He would have been accused, again, of self-indulgence, of stealing luxuries instead of food. But Fantoni can always arrange sufficient food.

He peels off the clinging, seat-soaked clothes and throws them onto the goatskin rug. Bending over to remove his socks he catches sight of his body. He stands slowly, in amazement. He is Alexander Finch whose father was called Senti but who called himself Finch because he sold American cigarettes on the black market and thought the name Finch very American. He is Alexander Finch, thirty-five years old, very fat, very tired, and suddenly, hopelessly sad. He has four large rolls of fat descending like a flesh curtain suspended from his navel. His spare tyres. He holds the fat in his hand, clenching it, wishing to tear it away. He clenches it until it hurts, and then clenches harder. For all the Rubens prints, for all the little buddhas he is no longer proud or even happy to be fat. He is no longer Teddy. But he is not yet Fantoni or Glino—he doesn't hate the little monkeys. And, as much as he might pretend to, he is never completely convincing. They suspect him of mildness.

He is Finch whose father was called Senti, whose father was not fat, whose mother was not fat, whose grandfather may well have been called Chong or Ching—how else to explain the narrow eyes and the springy black hair?

3.

There are six fat men in the house: Finch, Fantoni, May, Milligan, Glino, and one man who has never divulged his name. The-man-who-won't-give-his-name has been here from the beginning. He is taller, heavier, and stronger than any of the others, Fantoni included. Finch has estimated his weight at twenty-two stone. The-man-who-won't-give-his-name has a big tough face with a broken nose. Hair grows from him everywhere, it issues from his nose, his ears, flourishes in big bushy white eyebrows, on his hands, his fingers and, Finch has noticed, on his large rounded back. He is the only original tenant. It was because of him that Florence Nightingale suggested the place to Fantoni, thinking he would find a friend in another fat man. Fantoni offered accommodation to Milligan. A month or so later Finch and May were strolling along 16 October Avenue (once known as Royal Parade) when they saw three men talking on the upstairs balcony outside Fantoni's room. Fantoni waved. May waved back, Milligan called to them to come up, and they did. Glino moved in a week later, having been sent with a letter of introduction from Florence Nightingale.

It was Fantoni who devise the now legendary scheme for removing the other tenants. And although the-man-who-won't-give-his-name never participated in the scheme, he never interfered or reported the matter to the authorities.

The-man-who-won't-give-his-name says little and keeps to himself. But he always says good-morning and good-night and once discussed Iceland with Finch on the day Finch brought home the map. Finch believes he was a sailor, but Fantoni claims that he is Calsen, an academic, who was kicked out of the university for seducing one of "the little scrawnies."

Finch stands in front of the mirror, his hands digging into his stomach. He wonders what Fantoni would say if he knew that Finch had been engaged to two diminutive girls, Deirdre and Anne, fragile girls with the slender arms of children who had both loved him with a total and unreasonable love, and he them, before the revolution.

4.

May turns his Sibelius record to side two and begins one more letter to his wife. He begins, Dear Iris, just a short note to say everything is all right.

5.

Finch is sitting in the kitchen leafing through the Botticelli book he has just bought. It took half the pension money. Everyone is out. He turns each page gently, loving the expensive paper as much as the reproductions.

Behind him he hears the key in the front door. He puts the book in the cupboard under the sink, among the saucepans, and begins to wash up the milk bottles; there are dozens of them, all dirty, all stinking.

There is cursing and panting in the passage. He can hear Fantoni saying, the little weed, the little fucker. Glino says something. There is an unusual sense of urgency in their voices. They both come into the kitchen at once. Their clothes are covered with dirty but Fantoni is wearing overalls.

Glino says, we went out to Deer Park.

There is an explosives factory at Deer Park. Fantoni has discussed it for months. No one could tell hm what sort of explosive they made out there, but he was convinced it was dynamite.

Fantoni pushes Finch away from the sink and begins to wash the dirt off his hands and face. He says, the little weeds had guns.

Finch looks at Glino, who is leaning against the door with his eyes closed, his hands opening and closing. He is trembling. There is a small scratch on one of his round, smooth cheeks and blood is seeping through his transparent skin. He says, I thought I was going in again, I thought we'd gone for sure.

Fantoni says, shut up, Glino.

Glino says, Christ, if you've ever been inside one of those places you'll never want to see one again.

He is talking about prison. The fright seems to have overcome some of his shyness. He says, Christ I couldn't stand it.

Finch, handing Fantoni a tea towel to dry himself with, says, did you get the dynamite?

Fantoni says, well, what do *you* think! It's past your bedtime.

Finch leaves, worrying about the Botticelli book.

6.

Florence Nightingale will soon be here to collect the rents. Officially she arrives at 8 P.M., but at 7:30 she will arrive secretly, entering through the backyard, and visit Finch in "the new extensions."

Finch has showered early and shaved carefully. And he waits in his room, the door closed for privacy, checking with serious eyes to see that everything is tidy.

These visits are never mentioned to the others, there is an unspoken understanding that they never will be.

There is a small tap on the door and Florence Nightingale enters, smiling shyly. She says, wow, the heat. She is wearing a simple yellow dress and leather sandals that lace up her calves Roman-style. She closes the door with an exaggerated sort of care and tiptoes across to Finch, who is standing, his face wreathed in a large smile.

She says, hello, Cuddles, and kisses him on the cheek. Finch embraces her and pats her gently on the back. He says, the heat . . .

As usual Finch sits on the bed and Florence Nightingale squats yoga-style on the goatskin rug at his feet. Finch once said, you look as if Modigliani painted you. And was pleased that she knew of Modigliani and was flattered by the comparison. She has a long straight face with a nose that is long vertically but not horizontally. Her teeth are straight and perfect, but a little on the long side. But now they are not visible and her lips are closed in a strange calm smile that suggests melancholy. They enjoy their melancholy together, Finch and Florence Nightingale. Her eyes, which are grey, are very big and very wide and she looks around the room as she does each time, looking for new additions.

She says, it got to 103 degrees . . . the steering wheel was too hot to touch.

Finch says, I was shopping. I got a book on Botticelli.

Her eyes begin to circle the room more quickly. She says, where, show me?

Finch giggles. He says, it's in the kitchen cupboard. Fantoni came back while I was reading it.

She says, you shouldn't be frightened of Fantoni, he won't eat you. You've got blue sheets, *double* blue sheets. She raises her eyebrows.

He says, no significance, it was just the colour.

She says, I don't believe you. *Double* blue sheets. Florence Nightingale likes to invent a secret love life for him but he doesn't know why. But they enjoy this, this sexual/asexual flirtation. Finch is never sure what it is meant to be but he has never had any real hopes regarding Florence Nightingale, although in sleep and half-sleep he has made love to her many times. She is not quite frail enough. There is a strength that she attempts to hide with little girl's shyness. And sometimes there is a strange awkwardness in her movements as if some logical force in her mind is trying to deny the grace of her body. She sits on the floor, her head cocked characteristically on one side so her long hair falls over one eye. She says, how's the Freedom Fighter?

The Freedom Fighter was Finch's name for Fantoni. Finch says, oh nothing, we haven't done anything yet, just plans.

She says, I drove past the 16 October Statue—it's still there.

Finch says, we can't get the explosive. Maybe we'll just paint it yellow.

Florence Nightingale says, maybe you should eat it.

Finch loves that. He says, that's good, Nancy, that's really good.

Florence Nightingale says, it's your role, isn't it? The eaters? You should behave in character, the way they expect you to. You should eat everything. Eat the Committee of Seventy-five. She is rocking back and forth on the floor, holding her knees, balancing on her arse.

Finch tries not to look up her skirt. He says, a feast.

She cups her hands to make a megaphone and says, The Fat Men Against The Revolution have eaten General Kooper.

He says, and General Alvarez.

She says, the Central Emporium was devoured last night, huge droppings have been discovered in 16 October Avenue.

He says, you make me feel like the old days, good fat, not bad fat.

She says, I've got to go. I was late tonight. I brought you some cigars, some extra ones for you.

She has jumped up, kissed him, and departed before he has time to thank her. He remains on the bed, nursing some vague disappointment, staring at the goatskin rug.

Slowly he smiles to himself, thinking about eating the 16 October Statue.

7.

Florence Nightingale will soon be here to collect the rents. With the exception of Fantoni, who is in the shower, and Glino, who is cooking his vegetarian meal in his little cupboard, everyone is in the kitchen.

Finch sits on a kerosene drum by the back annexe, hoping to catch whatever breeze may come through.

Milligan, in very tight blue shorts, yellow T-shirt, and blue-tinted glasses, squats beside him, smiling to himself and rubbing his hands together. He has just finished telling a very long and involved story about a prostitute he picked up in his cab and who paid him double to let her conduct her business in the backseat. She made him turn his mirror back to front. No one cares if the story is true or not.

Milligan says, yep.

Milligan wears his clothes like corsets, always too tight. He says it is good for his blood, the tightness. But his flesh erupts in strange bulges from his thighs and stomach and arms. He looks trussed up, a grinning turkey ready for the oven.

Milligan always has a story. His life is a continual charade, a collection of prostitutes and criminals, "characters," beautiful women, eccentric old ladies, homosexuals, and two-headed freaks. Also he knows many jokes. Finch and May sit on the velvet cushions in Milligan's room and listen to the stories, but it is bad for May, who becomes depressed. The evenings invariably end with May in a fury saying, Jesus, I want a fuck, I want a fuck so badly it hurts. But Milligan just keeps laughing, somehow never realizing how badly it affects May.

May, Finch, Milligan, and the-man-who-won't-give-his-name lounge around the kitchen, drinking Glino's homemade beer. Finch has suggested that they wash the dirty milk bottles before Florence Nightingale arrives and everyone has agreed that it is a good idea. However, they have all remained seated, drinking Glino's homemade beer. No one likes the beer, but out of all the things that are hard to steal alcohol is the hardest. Even Fantoni cannot arrange it. Once he managed to get hold of a nine-gallon keg of beer but it sat in the back yard for a year before Glino got hold of a gas cylinder and the gear for pumping it out. They were drunk for one and a half days on that lot, and were nearly arrested en masse when they went out to piss on the commemorative plaque outside the offices of the Fifty-fourth District.

No one says much. They sip Glino's beer from jam jars and look around the room as if considering ways to tidy it, removing the milk bottles; doing something about the rubbish bin—a cardboard box which was full a week ago and from which eggshells, tins, and breadcrusts cascade onto the floor. Every now and then May reads something from an old newspaper, laughing very loudly. When May laughs, Finch smiles. He is happy to see May laughing because when he is not laughing he is very sad and liable to break things and do himself an injury. May's forehead is still scarred from the occasion when he battered it against the front door for three hours. There is still blood on the paintwork.

May wears an overcoat all the time, even tonight in this heat. His form is amorphous. He has a double chin and a drooping face that hangs downwards from his nose. He is balding and worries about losing hair. He sleeps for most of the day to escape his depressions and spends the nights walking around the house, drinking endless glasses of water, playing his record, and groaning quietly to himself as he tries to sleep.

May is the only one who was married before the revolution. He came to this town when he was fired from his job as a refrigerator salesman, and his wife was to join him later. Now he can't find her. She has sold their house and he is continually writing letters to her, care of anyone he can think of who might know her whereabouts.

May is also in love with Florence Nightingale, and in this respect he is no different from the other five, even Fantoni, who claims to find her skinny and undernourished.

Florence Nightingale is their friend, their confidante, their rent collector, their mascot. She works for the revolution but is against it. She will be here soon. Everybody is waiting for her. They talk about what she will wear.

Milligan, staring intently at his large Omega watch, says, peep, peep, peep, on the third stroke . . .

The front door bell rings. It is Florence Nightingale.

The-man-who-won't-give-his-name springs up. He says, I'll get it, I'll get it. He looks very serious but his broken, battered face appears to be very gentle. He says, I'll get it. And sounds out of breath. He moves with fast heavy strides along the passage, his back hunched urgently like a jungle animal, a rhino, ploughing through undergrowth. It is rumoured that he is having an affair with Florence Nightingale but it doesn't seem possible.

They crowd together in the small kitchen, their large soft bodies crammed together around the door. When Florence Nightingale nears the door there is much pushing and shoving and Milligan dances around the outside of the crowd, unable to get through, crying "make way there, make way for the lady with big blue eyes" in his high nasal voice, and everyone pushes every way at once. Finally it is Fantoni who arrives from his shower and says, "For Christ's sake, give a man some *room.*"

Everybody is very silent. They don't like to hear him swear in front of Florence Nightingale. Only Fantoni would do it, no one else. Now he nods to her and indicates that she should sit down on one of the two chairs. Fantoni takes the other. For the rest there are packing cases, kerosene tins, and an empty beer keg which is said to cause piles.

Fantoni is wearing a new safari suit, but no one mentions it. He has sewn insignia on the sleeves and the epaulettes. No one has ever seen this insignia before. No one mentions it. They pretend Fantoni is wearing his white wool suit as usual.

Florence Nightingale sits simply with her hands folded in her lap. She greets them all by name and in turn; to the-man-who-won't-give-his-name she merely says "hello." But it is not difficult to see that there is something between them. The-man-who-won't-give-his-name shuffles his large feet and suddenly smiles very broadly. He says, "Hello."

Fantoni then collects the rent which they pay from their pensions. The rent is not large, but the pensions are not large either. Only Milligan has an income, which gives him a certain independence.

Finch doesn't have enough for the rent. He had meant to borrow the difference from Milligan but forgot. Now he is too embarrassed to ask in front of Fantoni.

He says, I'm a bit short.

Florence Nightingale says, forget it, try and get it for next week. She counts the money and gives everyone a receipt. Finch tries to catch Milligan's eye.

Later, when everyone is smoking the cigars she has brought and drinking Glino's homebrew, she say, I hate this job, it's horrible to take this money from you.

Glino is sitting on the beer keg. He says, what job would you like? But he doesn't look at Florence Nightingale. Glino never looks at anyone.

Florence Nightingale says, I would come and look after you. We could all live together and I'd cook you crêpe Suzettes.

And Fantoni says, but who would bring us cigars then? And everybody laughs.

8.

Everyone is a little bit drunk.

Florence Nightingale says, Glino, play us a tune.

Glino says nothing, but seems to double up even more so that his broad shoulders become one with his large bay window. His fine white hair falls over his face.

Everybody says, come on, Glino, give us a tune. Until, finally, Glino takes his mouth organ from his back pocket and, without once looking up, begins to play. He plays something very slow. It reminds Finch of an albatross, an albatross flying over a vast, empty ocean. The albatross is going nowhere. Glino's head is so bowed that no one can see the mouth organ, it is sandwiched between his nose and his chest. Only his pink, translucent hands move slowly from side to side.

Then, as if changing its mind, the albatross becomes a gypsy, a peddler, or a drunken troubador. Glino's head shakes, his foot taps, his hands dance.

Milligan jumps to his feet. He dances a sailor's dance, Finch thinks it might be the hornpipe, or perhaps it is his own invention, like the pink stars stencilled on his taxi door. Milligan has a happy, impish face with eyebrows that rise and fall from behind his blue-tinted glasses. If he weighed less his face might even be pretty. Milligan's face is half-serious, half-mocking, intent on the dance, and Florence Nightingale stands slowly. They both dance, Florence Nightingale whirling and turning, her hair flying, her eyes nearly closed. The music becomes faster and faster and the five fat men move back to stand against the wall, as if flung there by centrifugal force. Finch, pulling the table out of the way, feels he will lose his balance. Milligan's face is bright red and steaming with sweat. The flesh on his bare white thighs shifts and shakes and beneath his T-shirt his breasts move up and down. Suddenly he spins to one side, drawn to the edge of the room, and collapses in a heap on the floor.

Everyone claps. Florence Nightingale keeps dancing. The clapping is forced into the rhythm of the music and everyone claps in time. May is dancing with Florence Nightingale. His movements are staccato, he stands with his feet apart, his huge overcoat flapping, stamps his feet, spins, jumps, shouts, nearly falls, takes Florence Nightingale around the waist and spins her around and around, they both stumble, but neither stops. May's face is transformed, it is living. The teeth in his partly open mouth shine white. His overcoat is like some magical cloak, a swirling beautiful thing.

Florence Nightingale constantly sweeps long hair out of her eyes.

May falls. Finch takes his place but becomes puffed very quickly and gives over to the-man-who-won't-give-his-name.

The-man-who-won't-give-his-name takes Florence Nightingale in his arms and disregards the music. He begins a very slow, gliding waltz. Milligan whispers in Glino's ear. Glino looks up shyly for a moment, pauses, then begins to play a Strauss waltz.

Finch says, the "Blue Danube." To no one in particular.

The-man-who-won't-give-his-name dances beautifully and very proudly. He holds Florence Nightingale slightly away from him, his head is high and cocked to one side. Florence Nightingale whispers something in his ear. He looks down at her and raises his eyebrows. They waltz around and around the kitchen until Finch becomes almost giddy with embarrassment. He thinks, it is like a wedding.

Glino once said (of prisons): "If you've ever been inside one of those places you wouldn't ever want to be inside one again."

Tonight Finch can see him lying on his bunk in a cell, playing the "Blue Danube" and the albatross and staring at the ceiling. He wonders if it is so very different from that now: they spend their days lying on their beds, afraid to go out because they don't like the way people look at them.

The dancing finishes and the-man-who-won't-give-his-name escorts Florence Nightingale to her chair. He is so large, he treats her as if she were wrapped in crinkly cellophane, a gentleman holding flowers.

Milligan earns his own money. He asks Fantoni, why don't you dance?

Fantoni is leaning against the wall smoking another cigar. He looks at Milligan for a long time until Finch is convinced that Fantoni will punch Milligan.

Finally Fantoni says, I can't dance.

9.

They all walk up the passage with Florence Nightingale. Approaching the front door she drops an envelope. The envelope spins gently to the floor and everyone walks around it. They stand on the porch and wave goodnight to her as she drives off in her black government car.

Returning to the house Milligan stoops and picks up the envelope. He hands it to Finch and says, for you. Inside the official envelope is a form letter with the letterhead of the Department of Housing. It says, Dear Mr Finch, the department regrets that you are now in arrears with your rent. If this matter is not settled within the statutory seven days you will be required to find other accommodation. It is signed, Nancy Bowlby.

Milligan says, what is it?

Finch says, it's from Florence Nightingale, about the rent.

Milligan says, seven days?

Finch says, oh, she has a job to do, it's not her fault.

10.

May has the back room upstairs. Finch is lying in bed in "the new extensions." He can hear Milligan calling to May.

Milligan says, May?

May says, what is it?

Milligan says, come here.

Their voices, Milligan's distant, May's close, seem to exist only inside Finch's head.

May says, what do you want?

Milligan shouts, I want to tell you something.

May says, no you don't, you just want me to tuck you in.

Milligan says, no. No, I don't.

Fantoni's loud raucous laugh comes from even further away.

The-man-who-won't-give-his-name is knocking on the ceiling of his room with a broom. Finch can hear it going, bump, bump, bump. The Sibelius record jumps. May shouts, quit it.

Milligan says, I want to tell you something.

May shouts, no you don't.

Finch lies naked on top of the blue sheets and tries to hum the albatross song but he has forgotten it.

Milligan says, come *here*. May? May, I want to tell you something.

May says, tuck yourself in, you lazy bugger.

Milligan giggles. The giggle floats out into the night.

Fantoni is in helpless laughter.

Milligan says, May?

May's footsteps echo across the floorboards of his room and cross the corridor to Milligan's room. Finch hears Milligan's laughter and hears May's footsteps returning to May's room.

Fantoni shouts, what did he want?

May says, he wanted to be tucked in.

Fantoni laughs. May turns up the Sibelius record. The-man-who-won't-give-his-name knocks on the ceiling with a broom. The record jumps.

11.

It is 4 A.M. and not yet light. No one can see them. As May and Finch leave the house a black government car draws away from the kerb but, although both of them see it, neither mentions it.

At 4 A.M. it is cool and pleasant to walk through the waste lands surrounding the house. There are one or two lights on in the big blocks of flats, but everyone seems to be asleep.

They walk slowly, picking their way through the thistles.

Finally May says, you were crazy.

Finch says, I know.

They walk for a long time. Finch wonders why the thistles grow in these parts, why they are sad, why they only grow where the ground has been disturbed, and wonders where they grew originally.

He says, do they make you sad?

May says, what?

He says, the thistles.

May doesn't answer. Finally he says, you were crazy to mention it. He'll really do it. He'll *really* do it.

Finch stubs his toe on a large block of concrete. The pain seems deserved. He says, it didn't enter my mind—that he'd think of Nancy.

May says, he'll really do it. He'll bloody well eat her. Christ, you know what he's like.

Finch says, I know, but I didn't mention Nancy, just the statue.

May wraps his overcoat around himself and draws his head down into it. He says, he *looks* evil, he *likes* being fat.

Finch says, that's reasonable.

May says, I can still remember what it was like being thin. Did I tell you, I was only six, but I can remember it like it was yesterday. Jesus it was nice. Although I don't suppose I appreciated it at the time.

Finch says, shut up.

May says, he's still trying to blow up that bloody statue and he'll get caught. Probably blow himself up. Then we'll be the ones that have to pinch everything. And we'll get caught, or we'll starve more like it.

Finch says, help him get some dynamite and then dob him in to the cops. While he's in jail he couldn't eat Florence Nightingale.

May says, and we wouldn't eat anything. I wouldn't mind so much if he just wanted to screw her. I wouldn't mind screwing her myself.

Finch says, maybe he is. Already.

May pulls his overcoat tightly around himself and says, no, it's whatshisname, the big guy, that's who's screwing her. Did you see them dancing? It's him.

Finch says, I like him.

May says nothing. They have come near a main road and they wordlessly turn back, keeping away from the streetlights, returning to the thistles.

Finch says, it was Nancy's idea. She said why don't we eat the statue.

May says, you told me already. You were nuts. She was nuts too but she was only joking. You should have known that he's serious about everything. He really wants to blow up everything, not just the fucking statue.

Finch says, he's fascist.

May says, what's a fascist?

Finch says, like Danko . . . like General Kooper . . . like Fantoni. He's going to dig a hole in the backyard. He calls it the barbecue.

12.

In another two hours Finch will have earned enough money for the rent. Fantoni is paying him by the hour. In another two hours he will be clear and then he'll stop. He hopes there is still two hours' work. They are digging a hole among the dock weeds in the backyard. It is a trench like a grave but only three feet deep. He asked Milligan for the money but Milligan had already lent money to Glino and May.

Fantoni is wearing a pair of May's trousers so he won't get his own dirty. He is stripped to the waist and working with a mattock. Finch clears the earth Fantoni loosens; he has a long-handled shovel. Both the shovel and the mattock are new; they have appeared miraculously, like anything that Fantoni wants.

They have chosen a spot outside Finch's window, where it is completely private, shielded from the neighbouring houses. It is a small private spot which Fantoni normally uses for sunbathing.

The top of Fantoni's bristly head is bathed in sweat and small dams of sweat have caught in the creases on the back of his head; he gives strange grunts between swings and carries out a conversation with Finch, who is too exhausted to answer.

He says, I want the whole thing . . . in writing, OK? . . . write it down . . . all the reasons . . . just like you explained it to me.

Finch is getting less and less earth on the shovel. He keeps aiming at the earth and overshooting it, collecting a few loose clods on the blade. He says, yes.

Fantoni takes the shovel from him. He says, you write that now, write all the reasons like you told me, and I'll count that as time working. How's that?

And he is not sure how it is. He cannot believe any of it. He cannot believe that he, Alexander Finch, is digging a barbecue to cook a beautiful girl called Florence Nightingale in the backyard of a house in what used to be called Royal Parade. He would not have believed it, and still cannot.

He says, thanks Fantoni.

Fantoni says, what I want, Finch, is a thing called a rationale . . . that's the word isn't it . . . they're called rationales.

13.

Rationale by A. Finch

The following is a suggested plan of action for the "Fat Men Against The Revolution."

It is suggested that the Fat Men of this establishment pursue a course of militant love, by bodily consuming a senior member of the revolution, an official of the revolution, or a monument of the revolution (e.g. the 16 October Statue).

Such an act would, in the eyes of the revolution, be in character. The Fat Men of this society have been implicitly accused of (among other things) loving food too much, of loving themselves too much to the exclusion of the revolution. To eat a member or monument of the revolution could be seen as a way of turning this over towards the revolution. The Fat Men would incorporate in their own bodies all that could be good and noble in the revolution and excrete that which is bad. In other words, the bodies of Fat Men will purify the revolution.

Alexander Finch shivers violently although it is very hot. He makes a fair copy of the draft. When he has finished he goes upstairs to the toilet and tries, unsuccessfully, to vomit.

Fantoni is supervising the delivery of a load of wood, coke, and kindling in the backyard. He is dressed beautifully in a white suit made from lightweight wool. He is smoking one of Florence Nightingale's cigars.

As Finch descends the stairs he hears a loud shout and then, two steps later, a loud crash. It came from May's room. And Finch knows without looking that May has thrown his bowl of goldfish against the wall. May loved his goldfish.

14.

At dinner Finch watches Fantoni eat the omelette that Glino has cooked for him. Fantoni cuts off dainty pieces. He buries the dainty pieces in the small fleshy orifice beneath his large moustache.

15.

May wakes him at 2 A.M. He says, I've just realized where she is. She'll be with her brother. That's where she'll be. I wrote her a letter.

Finch says, Florence Nightingale.

May says, my wife.

16.

Glino knows. Milligan knows. May and Finch know. Only the-man-who-won't-give-his-name is unaware of the scheme. He asked Fantoni about the hole in the backyard. Fantoni said, it is a wigwam for a goose's bridle.

17.

The deputation moves slowly on tiptoes from Finch's room. In the kitchen annexe someone trips over Fantoni's bicycle. It crashes. Milligan giggles. Finch punches him sharply in the ribs. In the dark, Milligan's face is caught between laughter and surprise. He pushes his glasses back on the bridge of his nose and peers closely at Finch.

The others have continued and are now moving quietly through the darkened kitchen. Finch pats Milligan on the shoulder. He whispers, I'm sorry. But Milligan passes on to join the others where they huddle nervously outside the-man-who-won't-give-his-name's room.

Glino looks to Finch, who moves through them and slowly opens the door. Finch sums up the situation. He feels a dull soft shock. He stops, but the others push him into the room. Only when they are all assembled inside the room, very close to the door, does everybody realize that the-man-who-won't-give-his-name is in bed with Florence Nightingale.

Florence Nightingale is lying on her side, facing the door, attempting to smile. The-man-who-won't-give-his-name seems very slow and very old. He rummages through the pile of clothes beside the bed, his breathing the only sound in the room. It is hoarse, heavy breathing that only subsides after he has found his underpants. He trips getting into them and Finch notices they are on inside out. Eventually the-man-who-won't-give-his-name says, it is generally considered good manners to knock.

He begins to dress now. No one knows what to do. They watch him hand Florence Nightingale her items of clothing so she can dress beneath the sheet. He sits in front of her then, partially obscuring her struggles. Florence Nightingale is no longer trying to smile. She looks very sad, almost frightened.

Eventually Finch says, this is more important, I'm afraid, more important than knocking on doors.

He has accepted some new knowledge and the acceptance makes him feel strong although he has no real idea of what the knowledge is. He says, Fantoni is planning to eat Florence Nightingale.

Florence Nightingale, struggling with her bra beneath the sheet, says, we know, we were discussing it.

Milligan giggles.

The-man-who-won't-give-his-name has found his dressing gown in the cupboard in the corner. He remains there, like a boxer waiting between rounds.

Florence Nightingale is staring at her yellow dress on the floor. Glino and May bump into each other as they reach for it at the same time. They both retreat and both step forward again. Finally it is Milligan who darts forward, picks up the garment, and hands it to Florence Nightingale, who disappears under the sheets once more. Finch finds it almost impossible not to stare at her. He wishes she would come out and dress quickly and get the whole thing over and done with.

Technically, Florence Nightingale has deceived no one.

Glino says, we got to stop him.

Florence Nightingale's head appears from beneath the sheets. She smiles at them all. She says, you are all wonderful . . . I love you all.

It is the first time Finch has ever heard Florence Nightingale say anything so insincere or so false. He wishes she would unsay that.

Finch says, he must be stopped.

Behind him he can hear a slight shuffling. He looks around to see May, his face flushed red, struggling to keep the door closed. He makes wild signs with his eyes to indicate that someone is trying to get in. Finch leans against the door, which pushes back with the heavy weight of a dream. Florence Nightingale slides sideways out of bed and Glino pushes against Finch, who is sandwiched between two opposing forces. Finally it is the-man-who-won't-give-his-name who says, let him in.

Everybody steps back, but the door remains closed. They stand, grouped in a semicircle around it, waiting. For a moment it seems as if it was all a mistake. But finally, the door knob turns and the door is pushed gently open. Fantoni stands in the doorway wearing white silk pyjamas.

He says, what's this, an orgy?

No one knows what to do or say.

18.

Glino is still vomiting in the drain in the backyard. He has been vomiting since dawn and it is now dark. Finch said he should be let off, because he was a vegetarian, but the-man-who-won't-give-his-name insisted. So they made Glino eat just a little bit.

The stench hangs heavily over the house.

May is playing his record.

Finch has thought many times that he might also vomit.

The blue sheet which was used to strangle Fantoni lies in a long tangled line from the kitchen through the kitchen annexe and out into the backyard, where Glino lies retching and where the barbecue pit, although filled in, still smokes slowly, the smoke rising from the dry earth.

The-man-who-won't-give-his-name had his dressing gown ruined. It was soaked with blood. He sits in the kitchen now, wearing Fantoni's white safari suit. He sits reading Fantoni's mail. He has suggested that it would be best if he were referred to as Fantoni, should the police come, and that anyway it would be best if he were referred to as Fantoni. A bottle of Scotch sits on the table beside him. It is open to anyone, but so far only May has taken any.

Finch is unable to sleep. He has tried to sleep but can see only Fantoni's face. He steps over Glino and enters the kitchen.

He says, may I have a drink please, Fantoni?

It is a relief to be able to call him a name.

19.

The-man-who-won't-give-his-name has taken up residence in Fantoni's room. Everybody has become used to him now. He is known as Fantoni.

A new man has also arrived, being sent by Florence Nightingale with a letter of introduction. So far his name is unknown.

20.

> *"Revolution in a Closed Society—A Study of Leadership among the Fat"* by Nancy Bowlby
>
> Leaders were selected for their ability to provide materially for the welfare of the group as a whole. Obviously the same qualities should reside in the heir-apparent, although these qualities were not always obvious during the waiting period; for this reason I judged it necessary to show favouritism to the heir-apparent and thus to raise his prestige in the eyes of the group. This favouritism would sometimes take the form of small gifts and, in those rare cases where it was needed, shows of physical affection as well.
>
> A situation of "crisis" was occasionally triggered, *deus ex machina,* by suggestion, but usually arose spontaneously and had only to be encouraged. From this point on, as I shall discuss later in this paper, the "revolution" took a similar course and "Fantoni" was always disposed of effectively and the new "Fantoni" took control of the group.

The following results were gathered from a study of twenty-three successive "Fantonis." Apart from the "Fantoni" and the "Fantoni-apparent," the composition of the group remained unaltered. Whilst it can be admitted that studies so far are at an early stage, the results surely justify the continuation of the experiments with larger groups.

Angela Carter
The Courtship of Mr. Lyon

(ENGLAND)

Outside her kitchen window, the hedgerow glistened as if the snow possessed a light of its own; when the sky darkened towards evening, an unearthly, re- flected pallor remained behind upon the winter's landscape, while still the soft flakes floated down. This lovely girl, whose skin possesses that same, inner light so you would have thought she, too, was made all of snow, pauses in her chores in the mean kitchen to look out at the country road. Nothing has passed that way all day; the road is white and unmarked as a spilled bolt of bridal satin.

Father said he would be home before nightfall.

The snow brought down all the telephone wires; he couldn't have called, even with the best of news.

The roads are bad. I hope he'll be safe.

But the old car stuck fast in a rut, wouldn't budge an inch; the engine whirred, coughed and died and he was far from home. Ruined, once; then ruined again, as he had learnt from his lawyers that very morning; at the conclusion of the lengthy, slow attempt to restore his fortunes, he had turned out his pock- ets to find the cash for petrol to take him home. And not even enough money left over to buy his Beauty, his girl-child, his pet, the one white rose she said she wanted; the only gift she wanted, no matter how the case went, how rich he might once again be. She had asked for so little and he had not been able to give it to her. He cursed the useless car, the last straw that broke his spirit; then, nothing for it but to fasten his old sheepskin coat around him, abandon the heap of metal and set off down the snow-filled lane to look for help.

Behind wrought-iron gates, a short, snowy drive performed a reticent flour- ish before a miniature, perfect Palladian house that seemed to hide itself shyly behind snow-laden skirts of an antique cypress. It was almost night; that house, with its sweet, retiring, melancholy grace, would have seemed deserted but for a light that flickered in an upstairs window, so vague it might have been the reflection of a star, if any stars could have penetrated the snow that whirled yet more thickly. Chilled through, he pressed the latch of the gate and saw, with a pang, how, on the withered ghost of a tangle of thorns, there clung, still, the faded rag of a white rose.

The gate clanged loudly shut behind him; too loudly. For an instant, that reverberating clang seemed final, emphatic, ominous as if the gate, now closed, barred all within it from the world outside the walled, wintry garden. And, from a distance, though from what distance he could not tell, he heard the most singular sound in the world: a great roaring, as of a beast of prey.

In too much need to allow himself to be intimidated, he squared up to the mahogany door. This door was equipped with a knocker in the shape of a lion's head, with a ring through the nose; as he raised his hand towards it, it came to him this lion's head was not, as he had thought at first, made of brass, but, instead, of gold. Before, however, he could announce his presence, the door swung silently inward on well-oiled hinges and he saw a white hall where the candles of a great chandelier cast their benign light upon so many, many flowers in great, free-standing jars of crystal that it seemed the whole of spring drew him into its warmth with a profound intake of perfumed breath. Yet there was no living person in the hall.

The door behind him closed as silently as it had opened, yet, this time, he felt no fear although he knew by the pervasive atmosphere of a suspension of reality that he had entered a place of privilege where all the laws of the world he knew need not necessarily apply, for the very rich are often very eccentric and the house was plainly that of an exceedingly wealthy man. As it was, when nobody came to help him with his coat, he took it off himself. At that, the crystals of the chandelier tinkled a little, as if emitting a pleased chuckle, and the door of a cloakroom opened of its own accord. There were, however, no clothes at all in this cloakroom, not even the statutory country-garden mackintosh to greet his own squirearchal sheepskin, but, when he emerged again into the hall, he found a greeting waiting for him at last—there was, of all things, a liver and white King Charles spaniel crouched with head intelligently cocked, on the kelim runner. It gave him further, comforting proof of his unseen host's wealth and eccentricity to see the dog wore, in place of a collar, a diamond necklace.

The dog sprang to its feet in welcome and busily shepherded him (how amusing!) to a snug little leather-panelled study on the first floor, where a low table was drawn up to a roaring log fire. On the table, a silver tray; round the neck of the whisky decanter, a silver tag with the legend: *Drink me*, while the cover of the silver dish was engraved with the exhortation: *Eat me*, in a flowing hand. This dish contained sandwiches of thick-cut roast beef, still bloody. He drank the one with soda and ate the other with some excellent mustard thoughtfully provided in a stoneware pot, and, when the spaniel saw to it he had served himself, she trotted off about her own business.

All that remained to make Beauty's father entirely comfortable was to find, in a curtained recess, not only a telephone but the card of a garage that advertised a twenty-four-hour rescue service; a couple of calls later and he had confirmed, thank God, that there was no serious trouble, only the car's age and the cold weather . . . he could pick it up from the village in an hour? And directions to the village, but half a mile away, were supplied, in a new tone of deference, as soon as he described the house from where he was calling.

And he was disconcerted but, in his impecunious circumstances, relieved to hear the bill would go on his hospitable if absent host's account, no question, assured the mechanic. It was the master's custom.

Time for another whisky as he tried, unsuccessfully, to call Beauty and tell her he would be late; but the lines were still down, although, miraculously, the storm had cleared as the moon rose and now a glance between the velvet curtains revealed a landscape as of ivory with an inlay of silver. Then the spaniel appeared again, with his hat in her careful mouth, prettily wagging her tail, as if to tell him it was time to be gone, that this magical hospitality was over.

As the door swung to behind him, he saw the lion's eyes were made of agate.

Great wreaths of snow now precariously curded the rose trees and, when he brushed against a stem on his way to the gate, a chill armful softly thudded to the ground to reveal, as if miraculously preserved beneath it, one last, single, perfect rose that might have been the last rose left living in all the white winter, and of so intense and delicate a fragrance it seemed to ring like a dulcimer on the frozen air.

How could his host, so mysterious, so kind, deny Beauty her present?

Not now distant but close to hand, close as the mahogany front door, rose a mighty, furious roaring; the garden seemed to hold its breath in apprehension. But still, because he loved his daughter, Beauty's father stole the rose.

At that, every window of the house blazed with furious light and a fugal baying, as if a pride of lions, introduced his host.

There is always a dignity about great bulk, an assertiveness, a quality of being more *there* than most of us are. The being who now confronted Beauty's father seemed to him, in his confusion, vaster than the house he owned, ponderous yet swift, and the moonlight glittered on his great, mazy head of hair, on the eyes green as agate, on the golden hairs of the great paws that grasped his shoulders so that their claws pierced the sheepskin as she shook him like an angry child shakes a doll.

This leonine apparition shook Beauty's father until his teeth rattled and then dropped him sprawling on his knees while the spaniel, darting from the open door, danced round them, yapping distractedly, like a lady at whose dinner party blows have been exchanged.

"My good fellow—" stammered Beauty's father; but the only response was a renewed roar.

"Good fellow? I am no good fellow! I am the Beast, and you must call me Beast, while I call you, Thief!"

"Forgive me for robbing your garden, Beast!"

Head of a lion; mane and mighty paws of a lion; he reared on his hind legs like an angry lion yet wore a smoking jacket of dull red brocade and was the owner of that lovely house and the low hills that cupped it.

"It was for my daughter," said Beauty's father. "All she wanted, in the whole world, was one white, perfect rose."

The Beast rudely snatched the photograph her father drew from his wallet and inspected it, first brusquely, then with a strange kind of wonder, almost the dawning of surmise. The camera had captured a certain look she had, sometimes, of absolute sweetness and absolute gravity, as if her eyes might pierce appearances and see your soul. When he handed the picture back, the Beast took good care not to scratch the surface with his claws.

"Take her her rose, then, but bring her to dinner," he growled; and what else was there to be done?

Although her father had told her of the nature of the one who waited for her, she could not control an instinctual shudder of fear when she saw him, for a lion is a lion and a man is a man and, though lions are more beautiful by far than we are, yet they belong to a different order of beauty and, besides, they have no respect for us; why should they? Yet wild things have a far more rational fear of us than is ours of them, and some kind of sadness in his agate eyes, that looked almost blind, as if sick of sight, moved her heart.

He sat, impassive as a figurehead, at the top of the table; the dining room was Queen Anne, tapestried, a gem. Apart from an aromatic soup kept hot over a spirit lamp, the food, though exquisite, was cold—a cold bird, a cold soufflé, cheese. He asked her father to serve them from a buffet and, himself, ate nothing. He grudgingly admitted what she had already guessed, that he disliked the presence of servants because, she thought, a constant human presence would remind him too bitterly of his otherness, but the spaniel sat at his feet throughout the meal, jumping up from time to time to see that everything was in order.

How strange he was. She found his bewildering difference from herself almost tolerable; its presence choked her. There seemed a heavy, soundless pressure upon her in his house, as if it lay under water, and when she saw the great paws lying on the arm of his chair, she thought: they are the death of any tender herbivore. And such a one she felt herself to be, Miss Lamb, spotless, sacrificial.

Yet she stayed, and smiled, because her father wanted her to do so; and when the Beast told her how he would aid her father's appeal against the judgement, she smiled with both her mouth and her eyes. But when, as they sipped their brandy, the Beast, in the diffuse, rumbling purr with which he conversed, suggested, with a hint of shyness, of fear of refusal, that she should stay here, with him, in comfort, while her father returned to London to take up the legal cudgels again, she forced a smile. For she knew with a pang of dread, as soon as he spoke, that it would be so and her visit to the Beast must be, on some magically reciprocal scale, the price of her father's good fortune.

Do not think she had no will of her own; only, she was possessed by a sense of obligation to an unusual degree and, besides, she would gladly have gone to the ends of the earth for her father, whom she loved dearly.

Her bedroom contained a marvellous glass bed; she had a bathroom, with towels thick as fleece and vials of suave unguents; and a little parlour of her own, the walls of which were covered with an antique paper of birds of paradise and Chinamen, where there were precious books and pictures and the flowers grown by invisible gardeners in the Beast's hothouses. Next morning, her father kissed her and drove away with a renewed hope about him that made her glad, but, all the same, she longed for the shabby home of their poverty. The unaccustomed luxury about her she found poignant, because it gave no pleasure to its possessor and himself she did not see all day as if, curious reversal, she frightened him, although the spaniel came and sat with her, to keep her company. Today, the spaniel wore a neat choker of turquoises.

Who prepared her meals? Loneliness of the Beast; all the time she stayed there, she saw no evidence of another human presence but the trays of food had arrived on a dumb waiter inside the mahogany cupboard in her parlour. Dinner was eggs Benedict and grilled veal; she ate it as she browsed in a book she had found in the rosewood revolving bookcase, a collection of courtly and elegant French fairy tales about white cats who were transformed princesses and fairies who were birds. Then she pulled a sprig of muscat grapes from a fat bunch for her dessert and found herself yawning; she discovered she was bored. At that, the spaniel took hold of her skirt with its velvet mouth and gave a firm but gentle tug. She allowed the dog to trot before her to the study in which her father had been entertained and there, to her well-disguised dismay, she found her host, seated beside the fire with a tray of coffee at his elbow from which she must pour.

The voice that seemed to issue from a cave full of echoes, his dark, soft rumbling growl; after her day of pastel-coloured idleness, how could she converse with the possessor of a voice that seemed an instrument created to inspire the terror that the chords of great organs bring? Fascinated, almost awed, she watched the firelight play on the gold fringes of his mane; he was irradiated, as if with a kind of halo, and she thought of the first great beast of the Apocalypse, the winged lion with his paw upon the Gospel, Saint Mark. Small talk turned to dust in her mouth; small talk had never, at the best of times, been Beauty's forte, and she had little practice at it.

But he, hesitantly, as if he himself were in awe of a young girl who looked as if she had been carved out of a single pearl, asked after her father's law case; and her dead mother; and how they, who had been so rich, had come to be so poor. He forced himself to master his shyness, which was that of a wild creature, and so, she contrived to master her own—to such effect that soon she was chattering away to him as if she had known him all her life. When the little cupid in the gilt clock on the mantelpiece struck its miniature tambourine, she was astonished to discover it did so twelve times.

"So late! You will want to sleep," he said.

At that, they both fell silent, as if these strange companions were suddenly overcome with embarrassment to find themselves together, alone, in that room in the depths of winter's night. As she was about to rise, he flung himself at her feet and buried his head in her lap. She stayed stock-still, transfixed; she felt his hot breath on her fingers, the stiff bristles of his muzzle grazing her skin, the rough lapping of his tongue and then, with a flood of compassion, understood: all he is doing is kissing my hands.

He drew back his head and gazed at her with his green, inscrutable eyes, in which she saw her face repeated twice, as small as if it were in bud. Then, without another word, he sprang from the room and she saw, with an indescribable shock, he went on all fours.

Next day, all day, the hills on which the snow still settled echoed with the Beast's rumbling roar: has master gone a-hunting? Beauty asked the spaniel. But the spaniel growled, almost bad-temperedly, as if to say, that she would not have answered, even if she could have.

Beauty would pass the day in her suite reading or, perhaps, doing a little embroidery; a box of coloured silks and a frame had been provided for her. Or, well wrapped up, she wandered in the walled garden, among the leafless roses, with the spaniel at her heels, and did a little raking and rearranging. An idle, restful time; a holiday. The enchantment of that bright, sad pretty place enveloped her and she found that, against all her expectations, she was happy there. She no longer felt the slightest apprehension at her nightly interviews with the Beast. All the natural laws of the world were held in suspension, here, where an army of invisibles tenderly waited on her, and she would talk with the lion, under the patient chaperonage of the brown-eyed dog, on the nature of the moon and its borrowed light, about the stars and the substances of which they were made, about the variable transformations of the weather. Yet still his strangeness made her shiver; and when he helplessly fell before her to kiss her hand, as he did every night when they parted, she would retreat nervously into her skin, flinching at his touch.

The telephone shrilled; for her. Her father. Such news!

The Beast sunk his great head on to his paws. You will come back to me? It will be lonely here, without you.

She was moved almost to tears that she should care for her so. It was in her heart to drop a kiss upon his shaggy mane but, though she stretched out her hand towards him, she could not bring herself to touch him of her own free will, he was so different from herself. But, yes, she said; I will come back. Soon, before the winter is over. Then the taxi came and took her away.

You are never at the mercy of the elements in London, where the huddled warmth of humanity melts the snow before it has time to settle; and her father was as good as rich again, since his hirsute friend's lawyers had the business so well in hand that his credit brought them nothing but the best. A resplendent hotel; the opera, theatres; a whole new wardrobe for his darling, so she could step out on his arm to parties, to receptions, to restaurants, and life was as she had never known it, for her father had ruined himself before her birth killed her mother.

Although the Beast was the source of this new-found prosperity and they talked of him often, now that they were so far away from the timeless spell of his house it seemed to possess the radiant and finite quality of dream and the Beast himself, so monstrous, so benign, some kind of spirit of good fortune who had smiled on them and let them go. She sent him flowers, white roses in return for the ones he had given her; and when she left the florist, she experienced a sudden sense of perfect freedom, as if she had just escaped from an unknown danger, had been grazed by the possibility of some change but, finally, left intact. Yet, with this exhilaration, a desolating emptiness. But her father was waiting for her at the hotel; they had planned a delicious expedition to buy her furs and she was as eager for the treat as any girl might be.

Since the flowers in the shop were the same all the year round, nothing in the window could tell her that winter had almost gone.

Returning late from supper after the theatre, she took off her earrings in front of the mirror; Beauty. She smiled at herself with satisfaction. She was learning, at the end of her adolescence, how to be a spoiled child and that pearly skin of hers was plumping out, a little, with high living and compliments. A certain inwardness was beginning to transform the lines around her mouth, those signatures of the personality, and her sweetness and her gravity could sometimes turn a mite petulant when things went not quite as she wanted them to go. You could not have said that her freshness was fading but she smiled at herself in mirrors a little too often, these days, and the face that smiled back was not quite the one she had seen contained in the Beast's agate eyes. Her face was acquiring, instead of beauty, a lacquer of the invincible prettiness that characterises certain pampered, exquisite, expensive cats.

The soft wind of spring breathed in from the nearby park through the open window; she did not know why it made her want to cry.

There was a sudden urgent, scrabbling sound, as of claws, at her door.

Her trance before the mirror broke; all at once, she remembered everything perfectly. Spring was here and she had broken her promise. Now the Beast himself had come in pursuit of her! First, she was frightened of his anger; then, mysteriously joyful, she ran to open the door. But it was his liver and white spotted spaniel who hurled herself into the girl's arm in a flurry of little barks and gruff murmurings, of whimpering and relief.

Yet where was the well-brushed, jewelled dog who had sat beside her embroidery frame in the parlour with birds of paradise nodding on the walls? This one's fringed ears were matted with mud, her coat was dusty and snarled, she was thin as a dog that has walked a long way and, if she had not been a dog, she would have been in tears.

After that first, rapturous greeting, she did not wait for Beauty to order her food and water; she seized the chiffon hem of her evening dress, whimpered and tugged. Threw back her head, howled, then tugged and whimpered again.

There was a slow, late train that would take her to the station where she had left for London three months ago. Beauty scribbled a note for her father, threw a coat round her shoulders. Quickly, quickly, urged the spaniel soundlessly; and Beauty knew the Beast was dying.

In the thick dark before dawn, the station master roused a sleepy driver for her. Fast as you can.

It seemed December still possessed his garden. The ground was hard as iron, the skirts of the dark cypress moved on the chill wind with a mournful rustle and there were no green shoots on the roses as if, this year, they would not bloom. And not one light in any of the windows, only, in the topmost attic, the faintest smear of radiance on a pane. The thin ghost of a light on the verge of extinction.

The spaniel had slept a little, in her arms, for the poor thing was exhausted. But now her grieving agitation fed Beauty's urgency and, as the girl pushed open the front door, she saw, with a thrust of conscience, how the golden door knocker was thickly muffled in black crêpe.

The door did not open silently, as before, but with a doleful groaning of the hinges and, this time, on to perfect darkness. Beauty clicked her gold cigarette lighter; the tapers in the chandelier had drowned in their own wax and the prisms were wreathed with dreadful arabesques of cobwebs. The flowers in the glass jars were dead, as if nobody had had the heart to replace them after she was gone. Dust, everywhere; and it was cold. There was an air of exhaustion, of despair in the house and, worse, a kind of physical disillusion, as if its glamour had been sustained by a cheap conjuring trick and now the conjurer, having failed to pull the crowds, had departed to try his luck elsewhere.

Beauty found a candle to light her way and followed the faithful spaniel up the staircase, past the study, past her suite, through a house echoing with desertion up a little back staircase dedicated to mice and spiders, stumbling, ripping the hem of her dress in her haste.

What a modest bedroom! An attic, with a sloping roof, they might have given the chambermaid if the Beast had employed staff. A night light on the mantelpiece, no curtains at the windows, no carpet on the floor and a narrow, iron bedstead on which he lay, sadly diminished, his bulk scarcely disturbing the faded patchwork quilt, his mane a greyish rat's nest and his eyes closed. On the stick-backed chair where his clothes had been thrown, the roses she had sent him were thrust into the jug from the washstand but they were all dead.

The spaniel jumped up on the bed and burrowed her way under the scanty covers, softly keening.

"Oh, Beast," said Beauty. "I have come home."

His eyelids flickered. How was it she had never noticed before that his agate eyes were equipped with lids, like those of a man? Was it because she had only looked at her own face, reflected there?

"I'm dying, Beauty," he said in a cracked whisper of his former purr. "Since you left me, I have been sick. I could not go hunting, I found I had not the stomach to kill the gentle beasts, I could not eat. I am sick and I must die; but I shall die happy because you have come to say goodbye to me."

She flung herself upon him, so that the iron bedstead groaned, and covered his poor paws with her kisses.

"Don't die, Beast! If you'll have me, I'll never leave you."

When her lips touched the meat-hook claws, they drew back into their pads and she saw how he had always kept his fists clenched, but now, painfully, tentatively, at last began to stretch his fingers. Her tears fell on his face like snow and, under their soft transformation, the bones showed through the pelt, the flesh through the wide, tawny brow. And then it was no longer a lion in her arms but a man, a man with an unkempt mane of hair and, how strange, a broken nose, such as the noses of retired boxers, that gave him a distant, heroic resemblance to the handsomest of all the beasts.

"Do you know," said Mr. Lyon, "I think I might be able to manage a little breakfast today, Beauty, if you would eat something with me."

Mr. and Mrs. Lyon walk in the garden; the old spaniel drowses on the grass, in a drift of fallen petals.

Raymond Carver

Are These Actual Miles?

(UNITED STATES)

Fact is the car needs to be sold in a hurry, and Leo sends Toni out to do it. Toni is smart and has personality. She used to sell children's encyclopedias door to door. She signed him up, even though he didn't have kids. Afterward, Leo asked her for a date, and the date led to this. This deal has to be cash, and it has to be done tonight. Tomorrow somebody they owe might slap a lien on the car. Monday they'll be in court, home free—but word on them went out yesterday, when their lawyer mailed the letters of intention. The hearing on Monday is nothing to worry about, the lawyer has said. They'll be asked some questions, and they'll sign some papers, and that's it. But sell the convertible, he said—today, *tonight*. They can hold onto the little car, Leo's car, no problem. But they go into court with that big convertible, the court will take it, and that's that.

Toni dresses up. It's four o'clock in the afternoon. Leo worries the lots will close. But Toni takes her time dressing. She puts on a new white blouse, wide lacy cuffs, the new two-piece suit, new heels. She transfers the stuff from her straw purse into the new patent-leather handbag. She studies the lizard makeup pouch and puts that in too. Toni has been two hours on her hair and face. Leo stands in the bedroom doorway and taps his lips with his knuckles, watching.

"You're making me nervous," she says. "I wish you wouldn't just stand," she says. "So tell me how I look."

"You look fine," he says. "You look great. I'd buy a car from you anytime."

"But you don't have money," she says, peering into the mirror. She pats her hair, frowns. "And your credit's lousy. You're nothing," she says. "Teasing," she says and looks at him in the mirror. "Don't be serious," she says. "It has to be done, so I'll do it. You take it out, you'd be lucky to get three, four hundred and we both know it. Honey, you'd be lucky if you didn't have to pay *them*." She gives her hair a final pat, gums her lips, blots the lipstick with a tissue. She turns away from the mirror and picks up her purse. "I'll have to have dinner or something, I told you that already, that's the way they work, I know them. But don't worry, I'll get out of it," she says. "I can handle it."

"Jesus," Leo says, "did you have to say that?"

She looks at him steadily. "Wish me luck," she says.

"Luck," he says. "You have the pink slip?" he says.

She nods. He follows her through the house, a tall woman with a small high bust, broad hips and thighs. He scratches a pimple on his neck. "You're sure?" he says. "Make sure. You have to have the pink slip."

"I have the pink slip," she says.

"Make sure."

She starts to say something, instead looks at herself in the front window and then shakes her head.

"At least call, " he says. "Let me know what's going on."

"I'll call," she says. "Kiss, kiss. Here," she says and points to the corner of her mouth. "Careful," she says.

He holds the door for her. "Where are you going to try first?" he says. She moves past him and onto the porch.

Ernest Williams looks from across the street. In his Bermuda shorts, stomach hanging, he looks at Leo and Toni as he directs a spray onto his begonias. Once, last winter, during the holidays, when Toni and the kids were visiting his mother's, Leo brought a woman home. Nine o'clock the next morning, a cold foggy Saturday, Leo walked the woman to the car, surprised Ernest Williams on the sidewalk with a newspaper in his hand. Fog drifted, Ernest Williams stared, then slapped the paper against his leg, hard.

Leo recalls that slap, hunches his shoulders, says, "You have someplace in mind first?"

"I'll just go down the line," she says. "The first lot, then I'll just go down the line."

"Open at nine hundred," he says. "Then come down. Nine hundred is a low bluebook, even on a cash deal."

"I know where to start," she says.

Ernest Williams turns the hose in their direction. He stares at them through the spray of water. Leo has an urge to cry out a confession.

"Just making sure," he says.

"Okay, okay," she says, "I'm off."

It's her car, they call it her car, and that makes it all the worse. They bought it new that summer three years ago. She wanted something to do after the kids started school, so she went back selling. He was working six days a week in the fiber-glass plant. For a while they didn't know how to spend the money. Then they put a thousand on the convertible and doubled and tripled the payments until in a year they had it paid. Earlier, while she was dressing, he took the jack and spare from the trunk and emptied the glove compartment of pencils, matchbooks, Blue Chip stamps. Then he washed it and vacuumed inside. The red hood and fenders shine.

"Good luck," he says and touches her elbow.

She nods. He sees she is already gone, already negotiating.

"Things are going to be different!" he calls to her as she reaches the driveway. "We start over Monday. I mean it."

Ernest Williams looks at them and turns his head and spits. She gets into the car and lights a cigarette.

"This time next week!" Leo calls again. "Ancient history!"

He waves as she backs into the street. She changes gear and starts ahead. She accelerates and the tires give a little scream.

In the kitchen Leo pours Scotch and carries the drink to the backyard. The kids are at his mother's. There was a letter three days ago, his name penciled on the outside of the dirty envelope, the only letter all summer not demanding payment in full. We are having fun, the letter said. We like Grandma. We have a new dog called Mr. Six. He is nice. We love him. Good-bye.

He goes for another drink. He adds ice and sees that his hand trembles. He holds the hand over the sink. He looks at the hand for a while, sets down the glass, and holds out the other hand. Then he picks up the glass and goes back outside to sit on the steps. He recalls when he was a kid his dad pointing at a fine house, a tall white house surrounded by apple trees and a high white rail fence. "That's Finch," his dad said admiringly. "He's been in bankruptcy at least twice. Look at that house." But bankruptcy is a company collapsing utterly, executives cutting their wrists and throwing themselves from windows, thousands of men on the street.

Leo and Toni still had furniture. Leo and Toni had furniture and Toni and the kids had clothes. Those things are exempt. What else? Bicycles for the kids, but these he had sent to his mother's for safekeeping. The portable air-conditioner and the appliances, new washer and dryer, trucks came for those things weeks ago. What else did they have? This and that, nothing mainly, stuff that wore out or fell to pieces long ago. But there were some big parties back there, some fine travel. To Reno and Tahoe, at eighty with the top down and the radio playing. Food, that was one of the big items. They gorged on food. He figures thousands on luxury items alone. Toni would go to the grocery and put in everything she saw. "I had to do without when I was a kid," she says. "These kids are not going to do without," as if he'd been insisting they should. She joins all the book clubs. "We never had books around when I was a kid," she says as she tears open the heavy packages. They enroll in the record clubs for something to play on the new stereo. They sign up for it all. Even a pedigreed terrier named Ginger. He paid two hundred and found her run over in the street a week later. They buy what they want. If they can't pay, they charge. They sign up.

His undershirt is wet; he can feel the sweat rolling from his underarms. He sits on the step with the empty glass in his hand and watches the shadows fill up the yard. He stretches, wipes his face. He listens to the traffic on the highway and considers whether he should go to the basement, stand on the utility sink, and hang himself with his belt. He understands he is willing to be dead.

Inside he makes a large drink and he turns the TV on and he fixes something to eat. He sits at the table with chili and crackers and watches something about a blind detective. He clears the table. He washes the pan and the bowl, dries these things and puts them away, then allows himself a look at the clock.

It's after nine. She's been gone nearly five hours.

He pours Scotch, adds water, carries the drink to the living room. He sits on the couch but finds his shoulders so stiff they won't let him lean back. He stares at the screen and sips, and soon he goes for another drink. He sits again. A news program begins—it's ten o'clock—and he says, "God, what in God's name has gone wrong?" and goes to the kitchen to return with more Scotch. He sits, he closes his eyes, and opens them when he hears the telephone ringing.

"I wanted to call," she says.

"Where are you?" he says. He hears piano music, and his heart moves.

"I don't know," she says. "Someplace. We're having a drink, then we're going someplace else for dinner. I'm with the sales manager. He's crude, but he's all right. He bought the car. I have to go now. I was on my way to the ladies and saw the phone."

"Did somebody buy the car?" Leo says. He looks out the kitchen window to the place in the drive where she always parks.

"I told you," she says. "I have to go now."

"Wait, wait a minute, for Christ's sake," he says. "Did somebody buy the car or not?"

"He had his checkbook out when I left," she says. "I have to go now. I have to go to the bathroom."

"Wait!" he yells. The line goes dead. He listens to the dial tone. "Jesus Christ," he says as he stands with the receiver in his hand.

He circles the kitchen and goes back to the living room. He sits. He gets up. In the bathroom he brushes his teeth very carefully. Then he uses dental floss. He washes his face and goes back to the kitchen. He looks at the clock and takes a clean glass from a set that has a hand of playing cards painted on each glass. He fills the glass with ice. He stares for a while at the glass he left in the sink.

He sits against one end of the couch and puts his legs up at the other end. He looks at the screen, realizes he can't make out what the people are saying. He turns the empty glass in his hand and considers biting off the rim. He shivers for a time and thinks of going to bed, though he knows he will dream of a large woman with gray hair. In the dream he is always leaning over tying his shoelaces. When he straightens up, she looks at him, and he bends to tie again. He looks at his hand. It makes a fist as he watches. The telephone is ringing.

"Where are you, honey?" he says slowly, gently.

"We're at this restaurant," she says, her voice strong, bright.

"Honey, which restaurant?" he says. He puts the heel of his hand against his eye and pushes.

"Downtown someplace," she says. "I think it's New Jimmy's. Excuse me," she says to someone off the line, "is this place New Jimmy's? This is New Jimmy's, Leo," she says to him. "Everything is all right, we're almost finished, then he's going to bring me home."

"Honey?" he says. He holds the receiver against his ear and rocks back and forth, eyes closed. "Honey?"

"I have to go," she says. "I wanted to call. Anyway, guess how much?"

"Honey," he says.

"Six and a quarter," she says. "I have it in my purse. He said there's no market for convertibles. I guess we're born lucky," she says and laughs. "I told him everything. I think I had to."

"Honey," Leo says.

"What?" she says.

"Please, honey," Leo says.

"He said he sympathizes," she says. "But he would have said anything." She laughs again. "He said personally he'd rather be classified a robber or a rapist than a bankrupt. He's nice enough, though," she says.

"Come home," Leo says. "Take a cab and come home."

"I can't," she says. "I told you, we're halfway through dinner."

"I'll come for you," he says.

"No," she says. "I said we're just finishing. I told you, it's part of the deal. They're out for all they can get. But don't worry, we're about to leave. I'll be home in a little while." She hangs up.

In a few minutes he calls New Jimmy's. A man answers. "New Jimmy's has closed for the evening," the man says.

"I'd like to talk to my wife," Leo says.

"Does she work here?" the man asks. "Who is she?"

"She's a customer," Leo says. "She's with someone. A business person."

"Would I know her?" the man says. "What is her name?"

"I don't think you know her," Leo says.

"That's all right," Leo says. "That's all right. I see her now."

"Thank you for calling New Jimmy's," the man says.

Leo hurries to the window. A car he doesn't recognize slows in front of the house, then picks up speed. He waits. Two, three hours later, the telephone rings again. There is no one at the other end when he picks up the receiver. There is only a dial tone.

"I'm right here!" Leo screams into the receiver.

Near dawn he hears footsteps on the porch. He gets up from the couch. The set hums, the screen glows. He opens the door. She bumps the wall coming in. She grins. Her face is puffy, as if she's been sleeping under sedation. She works her lips, ducks heavily and sways as he cocks his fist.

"Go ahead," she says thickly. She stands there swaying. Then she makes a noise and lunges, catches his shirt, tears it down the front. "Bankrupt!" she screams. She twists loose, grabs and tears his undershirt at the neck. "You son of a bitch," she says, clawing.

He squeezes her wrists, then lets go, steps back, looking for something heavy. She stumbles as she heads for the bedroom. "Bankrupt," she mutters. He hears her fall on the bed and groan.

He waits awhile, then splashes water on his face and goes to the bedroom. He turns the lights on, looks at her, and begins to take her clothes off. He pulls and pushes her from side to side undressing her. She says something in her sleep and moves her hand. He takes off her underpants, looks at them closely under the light, and throws them into a corner. He turns back the covers and rolls her in, naked. Then he opens her purse. He is reading the check when he hears the car come into the drive.

He looks through the front curtain and sees the convertible in the drive, its motor running smoothly, the headlamps burning, and he closes and opens his eyes. He sees a tall man come around in front of the car and up to the front porch. The man lays something on the porch and starts back to the car. He wears a white linen suit.

Leo turns on the porch light and opens the door cautiously. Her makeup pouch lies on the top step. The man looks at Leo across the front of the car, and then gets back inside and releases the handbrake.

"Wait!" Leo calls and starts down the steps. The man brakes the car as Leo walks in front of the lights. The car creaks against the brake. Leo tries to pull the two pieces of his shirt together, tries to bunch it all into his trousers.

"What is it you want?" the man says. "Look," the man says, "I have to go. No offense. I buy and sell cars, right? The lady left her makeup. She's a fine lady, very refined. What is it?"

Leo leans against the door and looks at the man. The man takes his hands off the wheel and puts them back. He drops the gear into reverse and the car moves backward a little.

"I want to tell you," Leo says and wets his lips.

The light in Ernest Williams' bedroom goes on. The shade rolls up.

Leo shakes his head, tucks in his shirt again. He steps back from the car. "Monday," he says.

"Monday," the man says and watches for sudden movement.

Leo nods slowly.

"Well, goodnight," the man says and coughs. "Take it easy, hear? Monday, that's right. Okay, then." He takes his foot off the brake, puts it on again after he has rolled back two or three feet. "Hey, one question. Between friends, are these actual miles?" The man waits, then clears his throat. "Okay, look, it doesn't matter either way," the man says. "I have to go. Take it easy." He backs into the street, pulls away quickly, and turns the corner without stopping.

Leo tucks at his shirt and goes back in the house. He locks the front door and checks it. Then he goes to the bedroom and locks that door and turns back the covers. He looks at her before he flicks the light. He takes off his clothes, folds them carefully on the floor, and gets in beside her. He lies on his back for a time and pulls the hair on his stomach, considering. He looks at the bedroom door, outlined now in the faint outside light. Presently he reaches out his hand and touches her hip. She does not move. He turns on his side and puts his hand on her hip. He runs his fingers over her hip and feels the stretch marks there. They are like roads, and he traces them in her flesh. He runs his fingers back and forth, first one, then another. They run everywhere in her flesh, dozens, perhaps hundreds of them. He remembers waking up the morning after they bought the car, seeing it, there in the drive, in the sun, gleaming.

Patrick Chamoiseau

The Old Man Slave and the Mastiff

(MARTINIQUE)

The fugitive—the African doomed to spend his life on harmful islands—did not even recognize the taste of the night. This unfamiliar night was less dense, more naked; it disoriented him. Far behind him, he heard the dogs, but the acacias had already carried him away from the world of his hunters; and, a man of the open air, he entered thus a new story: where, without him realizing it, time had begun again for him.

—Edouard Glissant

The principle of bones, mineral and living, opaque yet providing clarity.

—Toucher, page 11

The mastiff was a monster. It had also traveled on a boat, endured weeks of a kind of terror. It had also experienced the abyss of a journey on a slave ship. The dark bodies huddled in the hold enveloped that sailing hell in a radiance that the enraged dog could sense and that the sharks pursued across the ocean. Like all those who came to the islands, the mastiff had suffered through the constant undulation of the sea, its unfathomable echoes, the way it swallowed time and irreparably destroyed all private space, and the slow drifting of memory it engendered—the sea that penetrated the body to torment the soul, or break it down and install in its place the petty rhythm of nauseating survivals, of small deaths, of bitter habits, of the martyrdom of living corpses that must adapt to scattering cadences. The mastiff had also experienced brief moments of fresh air (hoisted up onto the bridge by a strangling chain), when, under the sting of the whip, it was forced, like the black captives, to turn in circles to stretch its muscles and to inhale a little iodine from the open sea. The wind itself, dizzying as a rush of shadows, only added to the devastation wreaked by the sea in the dark nights of the ship's hold. The dog moved unsteadily, as weak as a jellyfish. Then it was sent back to the abandoned corner of a back gangway, the hold that was a tomb (its cage).

The dog's look resembled that of the sailors. And worse: the rags that rose from the hold—burdened less by their chains than by their broken spirits, and who sometimes threw themselves overboard into the mouths of the sharks, or who suddenly, arching their bodies, swallowed their own tongues, or even fell with hopeless rage onto the blade of the bayonet that protected a captain's throat—had the same look. Only the ship itself, with its rhythm of waves, the billowing majesty of its tall sails, seemed to live and to keep its prisoners alive. The mastiff was a monster because it had known this despair.

Who knows what European Gehenna it came from. No one even knows the exact color of its fur. It likely changed with the wind. The ship's papers listed the dog as white with a black patch between its eyes. The sailor who slipped its water and salted leather between the bars of the steerage hold described it as black with a white patch on its muzzle. At the Plantation, it seemed black, shimmering, almost a lunar blue, with several white spots that may have grown larger over time. But the slaves the dog caught sometimes saw it (as it tore the tendons out of their legs) as red, or blue-green, or even vested with the orange strength of the heart of a burning fire. Better not even to mention its eyes.

The Master-béké° paid for the dog without bargaining. Most likely he had ordered it directly from Europe. He placed the animal next to him in the carriage. The two young slaves, the little slave girl, and the pottery from Aubagne that he had bought that day were left to pile themselves into the back of a mule cart driven by the old man slave. He was the one who accompanied the Master to the slave auctions when the ships arrived in port in the big city. Those occasions were rare now that the slave trade had been abolished, but there had been a time when the Master went there often, not even always to make a purchase. He would breathe in the atmosphere of the sluggish ships, whose crews (of savages) had experience unknown lands and who sold melancholy objects and old sea maps behind the slaughterhouse. These arrivals filled the taverns with tar-stained tales of ghost ships and women with seaweed hair and senseless revolutions that annulled the blue blood of kings or of nameless tribes of people who threaded their lips with gold straws and drank pure blood in tribute to the sun.

Sometimes the ships entered the port in errant drunkenness. Their shackled cargo was soon discovered, emaciated by hunger and yellowing fever, the ship's steerage and guy ropes abandoned. The orphaned sails had become giant parched leaves, and the ropes untied themselves like hangman's nooses. The crew had been struck down mysteriously. Their barrels of oil, salted meat, or drinking water were all crawling with the same maggots, which seemed to be waiting for (or announcing) the end of time. From each bolt of the bridge small flames rose up, only to flicker out again, leaving behind the deadly smell of the basilisk. No one wanted to buy the abandoned creatures in chains who were pulled from the steerage. Without even feeding them, the Governor chartered a military steamer and shipped them off to some point of no return on the coast of Brazil.

It was, for the old man slave, a moment of confusion: seeing those men who looked so much like him leave the ship, all only half revived from the longest

°*Béké*, a Creole word, indicates the white Creoles of Martinique, members of the old plantation class.

of deaths. The oil that coated their sickly skin blended with their sweat and traces of anguish. Their screams, companion to extreme suffering, had left permanent deposits of garlic-smelling foam in the corners of their mouths. They still carried the odors of the country of Before, its ultimate rhythms, its languages that were already almost lost. The old man slave sensed that they were still in thrall to the gods he remembered vaguely without words. And the ship also moved him. He no longer knew whether he had been born on the Plantation or whether he had known this crossing in the hold, but each tilt of a slave ship in the calm waters of the harbor triggered a primordial reeling inside him. Multiple creaks, muddy shadows, and liquid rays of light inhabited the depths of his spirit, which was drunk on the viscous seaweed and the ship's dances.

After the Master, the old man slave was the first to see the mastiff. The old man slave and the mastiff looked at each other. The mastiff suddenly started to bark. Worse, it jumped forward with a terrible rage, foaming at the mouth, its fur wild like a lion's mane. The Master-béké was delighted with this reaction, convinced that black flesh excited the dog's appetite. He rewarded the dog with a lump of raw meat and some water gathered specially for this purpose during a thunderstorm, and the dog calmed down enough to stop barking at everyone, including the old man slave—who, before the dog's enigmatic fury, had remained as he always was: more opaque and dense than a lump of charcoal burned seven times and then again as many.

They saw each other again every day after that because the Master had placed the animal in an enormous kennel, with wire fences on all four sides, between the main hut and the buildings of the sugar refinery. Everyone had to pass it at some point during the day or week. The monster was always there, at this strategic junction, this inevitable intersection. Stretched out on one side, panting, weary and persecuted, or anxious and high-strung behind the limits of its fence.

The Master-béké had other small Creole dogs. Six or seven. They kept guard over the main hut. They barked at every slave, every unfortunate bird, mongoose, or snake that passed by. They had a savage appetite because they were always kept tied up. When the pack of them escaped, they amused themselves by biting one of the house slaves or tearing apart the leg of an old slave woman who had tripped by the boilers, where they also lapped up the multi-colored crusts of molasses. The Master did not scold them for this. The slaves hated the dogs to an extent that is no longer possible to imagine. Despised them as well. They fed them old poisons that paralyzed them on the spot and prevented their bodies from rotting in their lime-covered graves (the heavy rains were always exhuming their doomed mummies in some corner of the Plantation). But their numbers were never depleted: determined to populate his surroundings with canine terror, the Master constantly bought more of them from an elegant mulatto who had lost all sense of shame.

The day the mastiff arrived at the Plantation, the Creole dogs started howling from a distance. As the carriage approached, they fell into a rage unknown in their breed. Then, once the carriage had entered the main courtyard and the mastiff had jumped to the ground, the dogs were abruptly silent, suddenly overcome by an uneasy calm that would leave them only rarely from then on—when an unexpected slave wandered by the house or when their hysterical senses detected the early signs of an unusually wily hurricane or earthquake.

If the slaves feared those dogs, they were terrified of the mastiff. Its massive body, like a lump of sulfur, its muscles knotted like bubbles of lava, its unbaptized face, its sightless stare. The most terrifying was its silence. It didn't bark. It didn't growl. But there was nothing calm or peaceful about the dog. There was only, above its suspended breath, a searching stare, sharpened narrowed cut sliced, with which it followed the living creatures that passed by its fence. When a Creole dog got loose and prowled around its cage, the mastiff didn't even get up. The prowler would soon lie down with an empty expression, moaning and submissive, bowing to the least blink of the monster's eye.

The Master-béké fed it in a strange and secret way. Quivering meat. Bones sizzling with marrow. Bloody carnalities that he himself had kneaded together in the skull of a Caribbean warrior. It was said that he ground up and added to the mixture wasps, hot peppers, hummingbirds' heads, snake fat, the powdered bones of madmen, the hair of crazy mulatresses, the brains of a *manman-balaou,*° and the bones of mother barracudas. The mastiff devoured it all, less with appetite than with sullen purpose. Within a few months, it had recovered the incredible strength the ship had drained from it. Its body had become even denser. Its muscles were as supple as cables when the Master took it running for hours tied to the end of a rope. The Master on his chestnut horse had to stick to a steady gallop just to keep up with the dog. And the horse, upset at having the dog so close to its hoofs, soon lost even more of its joie de vivre.

People wondered what purpose the monster would serve. The answer wasn't long coming. There was soon, as there was almost every month, a young slave, convinced that he was more resourceful than his predecessors, who was suddenly hit by *the surge.* Let me tell you about *the surge.* The old slaves knew it well: it was an evil kind of impulse vomited up from a forgotten place, a fundamental fever, a curdling of the blood, a malicious seizure, a vibrant voice that threw you off track. You became completely disoriented by an impetuous presence inside you. Your voice took on another sound. You began to reel grotesquely as you walked. A religious tremor shook through your eyelids and cheeks. And your eyes carried the marks of fire seen in the eyes of angered dragons.

The surge could hit you at any moment. It was responsible for the desperate attacks inflicted on the commanders: the slave hands that suddenly clutched at the commanders' throats, the machete that sliced through air, despite the pistol with which the commanders would shoot the knife-wielding madman hopelessly down. The surge threw you into the woods in impossible flight, where the Master pursued you with his Arabian horse and his pack of yapping little dogs. He always caught these runaways, and rare were those

°A female needlefish.

whom the surge could dissolve into the damp shadows of the enormous trees. The Master confirmed this. He never said, "That one got away." He said, "That one evaporated in the woods"—confident that the fugitive had fallen prey to the zombies who, he claimed, infested the forbidden deep woods.

So this slave youth had his surge. And, rather than slitting a commander's throat, he took off, just like that, in the middle of the day, dropping everything with an interminable scream, and fleeing toward the closest trees. A *run-away!* . . . The commanders pursued him for an hour but couldn't pick up his trail. So they alerted the Master by blowing into a conch shell which brought him running. The Master was told of the escape, wrinkled his eyes toward the hills, and listened to the aphonia of the trees. Then he smiled (unexpectedly), but no one had time to wonder why: the mastiff, by the refinery, had begun to growl. Not a bark, but an ammoniacal growl, insolubly evil and acidic, that immediately made it clear to everyone what purpose the dog would serve.

The Master rode toward the fenced-in kennel and led the animal out at the end of a thick rope. The mastiff had stopped growling. It had become attentive, its eyes fixed on the hills as its head seemed to follow an invisible movement. It didn't pull on the rope or try to hurry the pace. In the fugitive's hut, the Master made it sniff some old bedclothes. Then, together, they headed for the silent deep forest that was leafed in permanent mist and lost dreams. The slaves watched as the terrifying procession disappeared. The Master, the horse, the dog: an age-old understanding seemed to tie them together. A melan-combination. They moved as one, with one fatal resolution. Nothing could distract them from their united forward charge.

The Master released the dog as soon as they reached the first bushes. The animal dove in, without barking, without growling. All that could be heard was the unbelievable energy of its paws that hammered down the soil while the Master followed calmly, his gun on his shoulder. What happened then? There wasn't really a then. They shot back out almost immediately. The young black man, a giant sore dragged out at the end of the rope, the dog alert and serious at his side. Everyone could see for themselves, from close up, the damage done by the animal's teeth. And the Master wanted everyone to see it before he tossed his own hot pepper sauce onto the wounds. The dog had torn the young slave apart more savagely than the fiercest of whips or the most hostile of planks with nails could have done. From then on he stuttered and walked like an old man, with a look of ruin on his face.

The mastiff returned to its place in the kennel, relaxed now, attentive and placid again. The old man slave saw it every day but never stopped to look at it, as did the slave children—thoughtlessly, of course. Because each of them, even the craziest, tried to avoid having his smell "taken" by the dog. With your smell in its nostrils, it could sculpt you in its dreams, taste in advance the splendors of your blood, and, worse, it could easily catch you should the surge ever cause you to flee. So people avoided walking near the dog, and the children, having watched slave after slave hunted through the woods, relinquished the idea that the dog was something worth seeing. But no one noticed that the old man slave often walked alongside the kennel. Et cetera times a day, without ever looking directly at the mastiff. Without examining it. Sometimes he even passed by as the Master opened the cage, carried in meat and bloody organs, smiled at the dog, and petted it. And no one noticed that in the presence of this old slave guy, the mastiff became even more attentive, a touch more alert, a stitch more expectant, its iron carcass erect in a state of perfect tension. In Creole, we say: *véyatif o fandan.* *

The mastiff expressed the cruelty of the Master and his plantation. It was poisonously alive. When the old man slave walked along its fence, it followed him with a fiery eye. From time to time, the old guy shot it a look, a furtive and dull look. And their eyes met for seven n^{ths} of a second. This confrontation lasted for several months. The mastiff brought six or seven runaway slaves back from the woods. It tore through the throat of a Congolese woman who had been hit by the surge. As time passed, it became even more harmful. And if the surges still happened (stray attacks, suicides, or volcanic fits of insanity), it became less and less common for someone to run for the woods. The mastiff kept terrifying watch over the spirits of the prisoners. Which is why everyone was stupefied to find out that the old man had defied it.

How could it have been possible, for such an old man, so close to death? I will, without fear of lies or truth, tell you everything I know. But it's not a lot.

The old man has never participated in the slave parties, nor in the evening storytelling sessions during which the speakers explain how to defeat the mastiff. He doesn't dance, doesn't talk, doesn't react to the ringing of the drum. He seems dull, but is able to decipher incomprehensible things. His presence reinforces the drummers' beat. It gives them a mysterious balance and fills them with lightness. Which the old man drinks down as well. The dancers—without realizing it—find, in his presence, a choreography they had never known. The songs surround him as they surround others. But the old singers who tremble with automatic memories (great purveyors of unspeakable words) are, unconsciously, happier when he is there, when he is listening to them. Everyone, without expressing it, suspects that he is a sun of remembrance and tries to live in his light. And he, undaunted, accepts this gift. He plays the drum without playing it. He dances animatedly without moving. He peoples his soul with scattered, crooked, reconstructed things that weave a shimmering memory for him. Often, at night, this memory cripples him with insomnia.

The Papa-Storyteller of the Plantation was a pretty insignificant fellow (a black man from Guinea with small eyes, a body like a plank, and a rounded back). He was transformed when he began to speak (big eyes, sturdy body, and a straight back). He breathed in the life around him in order to sustain his speech. And with this speech he roused life. He spoke and made people laugh. And laughter opened up people's chests, made them expand. His tongue expressed the hates, desires, lost cries, and silences that everyone experienced. When the Master suddenly appeared, with a commander at his side, and sat benevolently at the edge of the circle, with a gallon of rum as a

* Nose to the wind.

special treat, and started to join in with the Krik-Kraks,* the Papa-Storyteller's speech was not disturbed. He continued the same story, through which circulated things that very few people could evaluate. But the old man slave lives on those things. He untangles the obscure words of the stories; he understands hatred, desire, and fear; he knows a thousand stories from Africa, a thousand narrations culled from the forgotten Amerindians, from the Master himself, and from the mastiff, of course.

The Papa-Storyteller's words carry the old man toward strange borders. They give him a body in the bodies of others, memories that belong to everyone and that fill everyone with a wordless throbbing. The Master can't see it, but there are so many overwhelming spirits inside the old man that he must (like the other slaves) exaggerate the passivity of his skin, the helplessness of his gestures, the rhythm of his heart, the outlines of his face. He must *go on* with these forces inside him, disorderly beyond comprehension, which tell him nothing about himself nor about this vast life within such a narrow death.

At night, unable to sleep, trapped inside himself, he faces incomprehensible absences, a suffocating weight, rhythms that are juxtaposed according to the muddled laws that kick out at uncertainty. Worlds are dying deep inside him, but these death throes offer him no respite, nothing but a confusion that only the dance, the drums, and the speech of the Storyteller (with its incomprehensible thrust) can soothe. Which is why he is always so still on those evenings, as he savors the balm that spreads across his wound in search of a meaning. The Storyteller's words do not come to him as words—they carry too many languages, too many cries, too many silences; the story floats like a creation song above his stomach. His throat tightens around impossibilities, and, without participating in the Storyteller's chorus, he *extends his presence to him* like a silent hand. He offers him his spirit, the specters of his memory, the prophetic pains that shimmer through every part of his body—his body, that motionless malignancy in which the Storyteller always finds what he wants.

The surge had shaken the old man many times. No one had known. Some felt it only once in their lives, but he had suffered through it almost every day. Day after day, and more often when it abandoned the others. The first time, it left him curled up on the floor of his hut, in the middle of the night, with an irrepressible desire to scream himself to death, to set off running, to go into spasms, to strangle something. He calmed himself by eating dirt and scraping his forehead against the wall. The friction released a throbbing heat that soothed his spirit. The other times it happened during the day, in the fields, as he was moving sacks, in the port, on the road as he was driving the carriage, or in the grease of the boilers where his life was trickling away. And, each time, his body became a burning rock, an immense cacophony that could not be controlled. He had felt a sudden desire to dance, to pound on the drums, to shout out the incomprehensible sounds that were slicing through his head; but each time he held himself back, knotting together his gestures, his actions,

*In Caribbean storytelling, the speaker often finishes a phrase with the word "krik" to which the audience responds "krak."

and his emotions, like vines around a demented body. In this way he became as serene as an African swamp. Calmer than a water lily. He had to live like a paralyzed man in order to control his constant surges. Not a gesture. Not an unnecessary word. No raised eyebrow, no raised voice. Nothing but an impeccable control over his movements, the slight murmur of his spirit and his gestures, the dance of his blood slowed to a minimum, an eruption that is matched only by the inertia of the most terrible of corpses or the most solid of substances. This is his only way of living and of being—which no one understands—catastrophically alive.

He recognizes in the mastiff the disaster that possesses him. A fury without eyes that attacks from far away. This internal chaos brings with it some things that are not an intimate part of him. He feels himself inhabited by spirits other than his own, while he cannot find himself, his own spirit, anywhere—no backbone of memory, no constructive paradigm, no nerve that remains from a time when he was someone distinct. Nothing but this seething violence, disgust, desire, impossibility: this magma that flourishes on the Plantation and that constitutes the most vital part of him. The mastiff is also like that. But in the animal's impressive ferocity, the disaster has found a convergence: it has transformed itself into a blind faith that is able to overcome the despair born on the ship.

The old slave man does not remember the ship, but he has, so to speak, lived in its hold. His head is filled with that overwhelming misery. He has the taste of the sea on his lips. He hears, even in the middle of the day, the sharks beating their dramatic jaws against the hull. He also has a memory of the sails, the helm, the rigging—as if he had been a member of the crew—and that memory blends with his visions of the country of Before, which are more than visions: women, beings, objects, things of beauty, ugly things that quiver inside him, that are him, and that add to the chaos he has already recognized. The mastiff is like him, but it has at its disposal a wealth of instincts that gives the illusion of meaning to it all. And that meaning mixes with the taste of bloody flesh that the Master has established as the principle of its existence. The dog is the Master's crippled soul. The dog is the slave's suffering double.

Our old man paces around the dog for these obscure reasons. As he copes with his own internal chaos, he is drawn toward the animal. He doesn't even need to look at it—the dog lives in him. The old man's air of absence and death has never fooled the mastiff. The monster sees in him a cartful of possibilities. It feels a bond with this old slave man from whom no wave emanates, nothing but the crude density of an unfathomable material, saturated with moisture and bridled sunlight. The mastiff's cruel vigilance senses them in confusion. With each approach, the old man slave feels the despair roll over him and the chaos drag him under. As he reaches the fence, he struggles with the forces that possess him. They awake, they begin to move, they devastate him even more. *Surge and resurge!*

He had seen the beast throw itself in pursuit of the runaways. Had seen it come back. He had seen the terror that it caused at the slaves' gatherings and how much its presence depleted the energy of their dances. He had heard the Storyteller describe it in terms that went beyond all proportion. This mastiff, he would say, keeps watch over the dead and over hell. He described it as a bird with fur, a horse with feathers, a one-horned buffalo, a voiceless toad man, or a carnivorous flower. Its body, made of mother of water and wounded moon, guarded precious gates. He explained that whoever overcame the dog would open the door to unknown happiness. He depicted the dog on underground journeys, flanked by suns that spat shadows. Sometimes he claimed that the dog was a jailer of a series of lights that were as fluid as the tears of a virgin. He described the dog dressed in palm leaves beside inconceivable tombs where rebirths flowered. He described it eating the undead that were cut into pieces by old men, in accordance with the position of the stars. He announced that the dog was able to sink its eye into the glassy eyes of the dead and awaken nine times three times seven souls. He saw the dog guiding pregnant women along the bridge of fate, leading them to term. He always placed the dog at turning points and fountainheads, at crossings and gulfs, on shortcuts and in passageways. He saw it clothed in leopard's skin, hovering above its master, offering its prophecies to those who would swallow its flesh. He saw it calling forth words that only the prophets were able to name. He saw it riding the solemn shoulders of high priests and fulfilling their liturgies with a cruel wisdom. He saw it swallowed by ghouls, by ogres, by grotesque chimeras until it was transformed into a pure light, the most desirable of all possible lights. The old slave man listened to all of these stories without hearing them, understood without understanding. He could hear only the murmur they set off inside him.

Since the animal arrived, the surges have become terrible. He, who had thought himself in control of this chaos, finds himself submerged in it. He comes to fear the surges. Fears that they will force him into pathetic battle with the commander's trigger or the Master's rifle. Fears that he will no longer be himself and that he will appear before everyone as a runaway slave who did not have the courage to run. It does him no good to turn himself to blind rock before the dog, the dog stirs his tumult to extremes that leave him dazed. In this way, he soon comes to feel that he is dying: his soul chafing, chaos pushing him to scream, his scream his speech, and his speech his statement. So he decides to leave, not to run away, but *to go.*

So he prepares nothing. No salt, no oil, no water, no bit of boiled cabbage. He does not reflect, does not look grimly toward the woods. He becomes even more immobile than before, placid to the extreme. His gestures around the machines become more and more fluid as the chaos hardens inside him. On this day, the sudden, irrepressible force throws him against one of the boilers. His skin touches the hot metal. It sizzles. He believes that he is losing his mind under the force of pain that hits him from all sides. But his lifetime of control gains the upper hand. His skin emerges intact. He cannot see clearly, and he can only just make out the landscape that clouds his eyes. He sees quicksilver cocks celebrating evangelical nights, which molt into snakes before dissolving.

He knows that he is ready.
He doesn't know what for.

This time when he approaches the fence, the mastiff gets up. The old slave man stops. For the first time in so many years, he looks directly at the monster. The latter approaches slowly. Looking straight ahead. Sizing him up. Ears stirring. Foam appearing around its mouth. Immobile in front of the old slave man who stares at it, even more immobile. The old slave man makes a gesture whose meaning he doesn't understand, an imperceptible movement that no one else sees, but that the mastiff follows with his icy pupils.

During the following night, the old slave man experiences not a surge but an explosion. His body falls into helpless convulsions. Heat drowns his limbs. Each object in his hut oozes flaming blood, and the waxed earth of the floor also catches fire. He is surrounded by lights that carve minuscule circles in the air. He battles against these nightmares. He is heard (by whom?) moaning. Then coughing as if in a fever, but no one worries because suffering no longer moves anyone here. Before dawn—as a medicinal light begins to rise from the earth, foretelling the appearance of an innocent sun—the old slave man sits up. He puts on his rough linen tunic. He places his old *bakoua*° jauntily on his head. He picks up his stick and calmly leaves his hut, his steps vibrating with a sacred energy. He walks along the line of huts, the sugarcane rooms where the glowworms watch him pass. When he reaches the first trees, the mastiff stands up, attentive. Although he is already very far, the old slave man feels a shiver run up his spine. He turns around to look at the Plantation where he has worn out his existence. He sees the distant buildings, the chimney of the sugar refinery with its familiar torches. He hears, for the last time, the noise of the now-widowed machines. The shiver disappears when it reaches his neck. Then the old slave man dives into the deep woods. The mastiff's howl tears through the estate, setting off the usual thousand and twelve strange little circuses that disrupt the science of slavery.

Translated from the French by Deborah Treisman

°A handmade straw hat.

Vikram Chandra

Dharma

(I N D I A)

Considering the length of Subramaniam's service, it was remarkable that he still came to the Fisherman's Rest. When I started going there, he had been retired for six years from the Ministry of Defence, after a run of forty-one years that had left him a joint-secretary. I was young, and I had just started working at a software company which had its air-conditioned and very streamlined head offices just off the Fountain, and I must confess the first time I heard him speak it was to chastise me. He had been introduced to me at a table on the balcony, sitting with three other older men, and my friend Ramani, who had taken me there, told me that they had been coming there for as long as they had worked and longer. Subramaniam had white hair, he was thin, and in the falling dusk he looked very small to me, the kind of man who would while away the endless boredom of his life in a bar off Sasoon Dock, and so I shaped him up in my mind, and weighed him and dropped him.

I should have noticed then that the waiters brought his drinks to him without being asked, and that the others talked around his silence but always with their faces turned towards him, but I was holding forth on the miserable state of computers in Bombay. The bar was on the second floor of an old house, looking towards the sea, and you wouldn't have known it was there, there was certainly no sign, and it couldn't be seen from the street. There were old trophy fish, half a century old at least, strung along the walls, and on the door to the bathroom there was a picture of a hill stream cut from a magazine, British by the look of it. When the wind came in from the sea it fluttered old flowered curtains and a 1971 calendar, and I was restless already, but I owed at least a drink to the courtesy of my friend Ramani, who understood my loneliness in Bombay and was maybe trying to mix me in with the right circle. So I watched a navy ship, a frigate maybe, wheel into the sun, sipped my drink (despite everything, I noticed, a perfect gin sling), and listened to them talk.

Ramani had been to Bandra that day, and he was telling them about a bungalow on the seafront. It was one of those old three-storied houses with balconies that ran all the way around, set in the middle of a garden filled with palms and fish ponds. It sat stubbornly in the middle of towering apartment buildings, and it had been empty as far back as anyone could remember, and so of course the story that explained this waste of golden real estate was one of ghosts and screams in the night.

"They say it's unsellable," said Ramani. "They say a Gujarati *seth* bought it and died within the month. Nobody'll buy it. Bad place."

"What nonsense," I said. "These are all family property disputes. The cases drag on for years and years in courts, and the houses lie vacant because no one will let anyone else live in them." I spoke at length then, about superstition and ignorance and the state of our benighted nation, in which educated men and women believed in banshees and ghouls. "Even in the information age we will never be free," I said. I went on, and I was particularly witty and sharp, I thought. I vanquished every argument with efficiency and dispatch.

After a while my glass was empty and I stopped to look for the bearer. In the pause the waves gathered against the rocks below, and then Subramaniam spoke. He had a small whispery voice, a departmental voice, I thought, it was full of intrigues and secrets and nuances. "I knew a man once who met a ghost," he said. I still had my body turned around in the seat, but the rest of them turned to him expectantly. He said, "Some people meet their ghosts, and some don't. But we're all haunted by them." Now I turned, too, and he was looking straight at me, and his white hair stood clearly against the extravagant red of the sunset behind him, but his eyes were shadowed and hidden. "Listen," he said.

On the day that Major General Jago Antia turned fifty, his missing leg began to ache. He had been told by the doctors about phantom pain, but the leg had been gone for twenty years without a twinge, and so when he felt a twisting ache two inches under his plastic knee, he stumbled not out of agony but surprise. It was only a little stumble, but the officers who surrounded him turned away out of sympathy, because he was Jago Antia, and he never stumbled. The younger lieutenants flushed with emotion, because they knew for certain that Jago Antia was invincible, and this little lapse, and the way he recovered himself, how he came back to his ramrod straightness, this reminded them of the metallic density of his discipline, which could see in his grey eyes. He was famous for his stare, for the cold blackness of his anger, for his tactical skill and his ability to read ground, his whole career from the gold medal at Kharakvasla to the combat and medals in Leh and NEFA. He was famous for all this, but the leg was the centre of the legend, and there was something terrible about it, about the story, and so it was never talked about. He drove himself across jungle terrain and shamed men twenty years younger, and it was as if the leg had never been lost. This is why his politeness, his fastidiousness, the delicate way he handled his fork and knife, his slow smile, all these Jago quirks were imitated by even the cadets at the Academy: they wished for his certainty, and believed that his loneliness was the mark of his genius.

So when he left the *bara khana* his men looked after him with reverence, and curiously the lapse made them believe in his strength all the more. They had done the party to mark an obscure regimental battle day from half a century before, because he would never have allowed a celebration for himself. After he left they lolled on sofas, sipping from their drinks, and told stories about him. His name was Jehangir Antia, but for thirty years, in their stories, he had been Jago Antia. Some of them didn't know his real name.

Meanwhile, Jago Antia lay on his bed under a mosquito net, his arms flat by his sides, his one leg out as if at attention, the other standing by the bed, and waited for his dream to take him. Every night he thought of falling endlessly through the night, slipping through the cold air, and then somewhere it became a dream, and he was asleep, still falling. He had been doing it for as long as he could remember, long before para school and long before the drop at Sylhet, towards the hostile guns and the treacherous ground. It had been with him from long ago, this leap, and he knew where it took him, but this night a pain grew in that part of him that he no longer had, and he tried to fight it away, imagining the rush of air against his neck, the flapping of his clothes, the complete darkness, but it was no use. He was still awake. When he raised his left hand and uncovered the luminous dial it was oh-four-hundred, and then he gave up and strapped his leg on. He went into the study and spread out some maps and began to work on operational orders. The contour maps were covered with markers, and his mind moved easily among the mountains, seeing the units, the routes of supply, the staging areas. They were fighting an insurgency, and he knew of course that he was doing good work, that his concentration was keen, but he knew he would be tired the next day, and this annoyed him. When he found himself kneading his plastic shin with one hand, he was so angry that he went out on the porch and puffed out a hundred quick push-ups, and in the morning his puzzled *sahayak* found him striding up and down the garden walk as the sun came up behind a gaunt ridge.

"What are you doing out here?" Thapa said. Jago Antia had never married. They had known each other for three decades, since Jago Antia had been a captain, and they had long ago discarded the formalities of master and batman.

"Couldn't sleep, Thapa. Don't know what it was."

Thapa raised an eyebrow. "Eat well then."

"Right. Ten minutes?"

Thapa turned smartly and strode off. He was a small, round man, not fat but bulging everywhere with the compact muscles of the mountains.

"Thapa?" Jago Antia called.

"Yes."

"Nothing." He had for a moment wanted to say something about the pain, but then the habit of a lifetime asserted itself, and he threw back his shoulders and shook his head. Thapa waited for a moment and then walked into the house. Now Jago Antia looked up at the razor edge of the ridge far above, and he could see, if he turned his head to one side, a line of tiny figures walking down it. They would be woodcutters, and perhaps some of the men he was fighting. They were committed, hardy, and well trained. He watched them. He was better. The sun was high now, and Jago Antia went to his work.

The pain didn't go away, and Jago Antia couldn't sleep. Sometimes he was sure he was in his dream, and he was grateful for the velocity of the fall, and he could feel the cold on his face, the dark, but then he would sense something, a tiny glowing pinpoint that spun and grew and finally became a bright hurling maelstrom that wrenched him back into wakefulness. Against this he had no defence: no matter how tired he made himself, how much he exhausted his body, he could not make his mind insensible to his phantom pain, and so his discipline, honed over the years, was made useless. Finally he conquered his shame, and asked—in the strictest confidence—an Army Medical Corps colonel for medication, and got, along with a very puzzled stare, a bottle full of yellow pills, which he felt in his pocket all day, against his chest. But at night these pills too proved no match for the ferocity of the pain, which by now Jago Antia imagined as a beast of some sort, a low growling animal that camouflaged itself until he was almost at rest and then came rushing out to worry at his flesh, or at the memory of his flesh. It was not that Jago Antia minded the defeat, because he had learnt to accept defeat and casualties and loss, but it was that he had once defeated this flesh, it was he who had swung the *kukri*, but it had come back now and surprised him. He felt outflanked, and this infuriated him, and further, there was nothing he could do about it, there was nothing to do anything about. So his work suffered, and he felt the surprise of those around him. It shamed him more than anything else that they were not disappointed but sympathetic. They brought him tea without being asked, he noticed that his aides spoke amongst themselves in whispers, his headquarters ran—if it was possible—even more efficiently than before, with the gleam of spit and polish about it. But now he was tired, and when he looked at the maps he felt the effort he had to make to grasp the flow of the battle—not the facts, which were important, though finally trivial—but the thrust and the energy of the struggle, the movement of the initiative, the flux and ebb of the chaotic thing. One afternoon he sat in his office, the pain a constant hum just below his attention, and the rain beat down in gusts against the windows, and the gleam of lightning startled him into realizing that his jaw was slack, that he had been staring aimlessly out of the window at the green side of the mountain, that he had become the sort of commander he despised, a man who because of his rank allowed himself to become careless. He knew he would soon make the sort of mistake that would get some of his boys killed, and that was unacceptable: without hesitation he called the AMC colonel and asked to be relieved of his command for medical reasons.

The train ride to Bombay from Calcutta was two days long, and there was a kind of relief in the long rhythms of the wheels, in the lonely clangings of the tracks at night. Jago Antia sat next to a window in a first class compartment and watched the landscape change, taken back somehow to a fifth-grade classroom and lessons on the crops of the Deccan. Thapa had taken a week's leave to go to his family in Darjeeling and was to join up in Bombay later. Jago Antia was used to solitude, but the relief from immediate responsibility brought with it a rush of memory, and he found the unbidden recall of images from the past annoying, because it all seemed so useless. He tried to take up the time usefully by reading NATO journals, but even under the hard edge of his concentration the pain throbbed in time with the wheels, and he found himself remembering an afternoon at school when they had run out of history class to watch two fighter planes fly low over the city. By the time the train pulled into Bombay Central, he felt as if he were covered not only with sweat and grit, but also with an oily film of recollection, and he marched through the crowd towards the taxi stand, eager for a shower.

The house stood in a square plot on prime residential land in Khar, surrounded by new, extravagant constructions coloured the pink and green of new money. But it was mostly dark brown, stained by decades of sea air and monsoon rains, and in the late-afternoon sun it seemed to gather the light about it as it sat surrounded by trees and untidy bushes. There was, in its three stories, in the elegant arches on the balconies, and in the rows of shuttered windows, something rich and dense and heavy, like the smell of gun oil on an old hunting rifle, and the taxi driver sighed, "They don't build them like that anymore."

"No, they're draughty and take a fortune to keep up," said Jago Antia curtly as he handed him the money. It was true. Amir Khan the housekeeper was waving slowly from the porch. He was very old, with a thin neck and a white beard that gave him the appearance of a heron, and by the time he was halfway down the flight of stairs Jago Antia had the bags out of the car and up to the house. Inside, with Amir Khan puffing behind him, he paused to let his eyes take to the darkness, but it felt as if he were pushing his way through something substantial and insidious, more clear than fog but as inescapable. It was still much as he had left it many years ago to go to the Academy. There were the Victorian couches covered with faded flower prints, the gold-rimmed paintings on the wall of his grandparents and uncles. He noticed suddenly how quiet it was, as if the street and the city outside had vanished.

"I'll take these bags upstairs," he said.

"Can't," Amir Khan said. "It's been closed up for years. All just sheets on the furniture. Even your parents slept in the old study. They moved a bed into it."

Jago Antia shrugged. It was more convenient on the ground floor in any case. "It's all right. It's just for a few days. I have some work here. I'll see Tody-walla too."

"What about?"

"Well, I want to sell the house."

"You want to sell the house?"

"Yes."

Amir Khan shuffled away to the kitchen, and Jago Antia heard him knocking about with cups and saucers. He had no intention of using the house again,

and he saw no other alternative. His parents were dead, gone one after another in a year. He had been a distant son, meeting them on leave in Delhi
and Lucknow while they were on vacation. Wherever they had met, far away
from Bombay, he had always seen the old disappointment and weariness
in their eyes. Now it was over, and he wanted not to think about the house
anymore.

"Good, sell this house." It was Amir Khan with a cup of tea. "Sell it."

"I will."

"Sell it."

Jago Antia noticed that Amir Khan's hands were shaking, and he remembered suddenly an afternoon in the garden when he had made him throw ball
after ball to his off side, and his own attempts at elegant square cuts, and the
sun high overhead through the palm trees.

"We'll do something for you," said Jago Antia. "Don't worry."

"Sell it," Amir Khan said. "I'm tired of it."

Jago Antia tried to dream of falling, but his ache stayed with him, and besides
the gusts of water against the windows were loud and unceasing. It had begun
to rain with nightfall, and now the white illumination of lightning threw the
whole room into sharp relief. He was thinking about the Academy, about how
he had been named Jago, two weeks after his arrival. His roommate had found
him at five o'clock on a Saturday morning doing push-ups on the gravel outside their room, and rubbing his eyes he had said, "Antia, you're an enthusi-
ast." He had never known where the nickname Jago came from, but after the
second week nobody except his parents had called him Jehangir again. When
he had won the gold medal for best cadet even the major-general who was
commandant of the Academy had said to him at the reviewing stand, "Good
show, Jago." He had been marked for advancement early, and he had never
betrayed his promise. He was thinking of this, and the wind flapped the curtains above him, and when he first heard the voice far away he thought it was a
trick of the air, but then he heard it again. It was muffled by distance and the
rain but he heard it clearly. He could not make out what it was saying. He was
alert instantly and strapped on his leg. Even though he knew it was probably
Amir Khan talking to himself, flicking away with a duster in the imagined light
of some long-gone day, he moved cautiously, back against the wall. At the bottom of the hallway he paused, and heard it again, small but distinct, above
him. He found the suitcase and went up, his thighs tense, moving in a fluid
half-squat. Now he was truly watchful, because the voice was too young to be
Amir Khan. On the first landing, near an open door, he sensed a rush of
motion on the balcony that ran around the outside of the house; he came to
the corner, feeling his way with his hands. Everything in the darkness appeared as shades, blackness and deeper blackness. He darted a look around
the corner, and the balcony was empty, he was sure of it. He came around the
corner, back against the wall. Then he heard the movement again, not distinct
footsteps but the swish of feet on the ground, one after another. He froze.
Whatever it was, it was coming towards him. His eyes ached in the darkness,

but he could see nothing. Then the white blaze of lightning swept across the lawn, throwing the filigreed ironwork of the railing sharply on the wall, across Jago Antia's belly, and in the long light he saw on the floor the clearly outlined shape of shoes, one after another, the patches of water a sharp black in the light, and as he watched another footprint appeared on the tile, and then another, coming towards him. Before it was dark again he was halfway down the stairs. He stopped, alone with the beating of his heart. He forced himself to stand up straight, to look carefully about and above the staircase for dead ground and lines of fire. He had learnt long ago that professionalism was a much better way to defeat fear than self-castigation and shame, and now he applied himself to the problem. The only possible conclusion was that it had been a trick of the light on the water, and so he was able to move up the staircase, smooth and graceful once again. But on the landing a breath of air curled around his ankle like a flow of cool liquid, and he began to shiver. It was a freezing chill that spread up his thighs and into his groin, and it caught him so suddenly that he let his teeth chatter for a moment. Then he bit down, but despite his straining he could hardly take a step before he stopped again. It was so cold that his fingers ached. His eyes filled with moisture and suddenly the dark was full of soft shadows. Again he heard the voice, far away, melancholy and low. With a groan he collapsed against the banister and slid down the stairs, all the way to the bottom, his leg rattling on the steps. Through the night he tried it again and again, and once he made it to the middle of the landing, but the fear took the strength from his hips, so that he had to crawl on hands and knees to the descent. At dawn he sat shaken and weak on the first step, his arm around the comforting curve of the thick round post.

Finally it was the shock in Thapa's eyes that raised Jago Antia from the stupor he had fallen into. For three days he had been pacing, unshaven and unwashed, at the bottom of the stairs, watching the light make golden shapes in the air. Now Thapa had walked through the front door, and it was his face, slack, and the fact that he forgot to salute that conveyed to Jago Antia how changed he was, how shocking he was.

"It's all right," Jago Antia said. "I'm all right."

Thapa still had his bag in his right hand and an umbrella in the left, and he said nothing. Jago Antia remembered then a story that was a part of his own legend: he had once reduced a lieutenant to tears because of a tea stain on his shirt. It was quite true.

"Put out a change of clothes," he said. "And close your mouth."

The water in the shower drummed against Jago Antia's head and cleared it. He saw the insanity of what had gone on for three days, and he was sure it was exhaustion. There was nothing there, and the important thing was to get to the hospital, and then to sell the house. He ate breakfast eagerly, and felt almost relaxed. Then Amir Khan walked in with a glass of milk on a tray. For three days he had been bringing milk instead of tea, and now when Jago Antia told him to take it back to the kitchen, he said, "Baba, you have to drink it.

Mummy said so. You know you're not allowed to drink tea." And he shuffled away, walking through a suddenly revived age when Jehangir Antia was a boy in knickers, agile and confident on two sunburnt legs. For a moment Jago Antia felt time slipping around him like a dark wave, but then he shook away the feeling and stood up.

"Call a taxi," he said to Thapa.

The doctors at Jaslok were crisp and confident in their poking and prodding, and the hum of machinery comforted him. But Todywalla, sitting in his disorderly office, said bluntly, "Sell that house? Na, impossible. There's something in it."

"Oh don't be ridiculous," said Jago Antia vehemently. "That's absurd."

Todywalla looked keenly at him. Todywalla was a toothless old man with a round black cap squarely on the middle of his head. "Ah," he said. "So you've heard it too."

"I haven't heard a damn thing," Jago Antia said. "Be rational."

"You may be a rationalist," Todywalla said. "But I sell houses in Bombay." He sipped tea noisily from a chipped cup. "There's something in that house."

When the taxi pulled through the gate Thapa was standing in the street outside, talking to a vegetable seller and two other men. As Jago Antia pulled off his shoes in the living room, Thapa came in and went to the kitchen. He came back a few minutes later with a glass of water.

"Tomorrow I will find my cousin at the bank at Nariman Point," he said. "And we will get somebody to come to this house. We shouldn't sleep here."

"What do you mean, somebody?"

"Somebody who can clean it up." Thapa's round face was tight, and there were white crescents around his temples. "Somebody who knows."

"Knows what exactly? What are you talking about?"

Thapa nodded towards the gate. "No one on this street will come near this place after dark. Everyone knows. They were telling me not to stay here."

"Nonsense."

"We can't fight this, *saab*," Thapa said. After a pause: "Not even you."

Jago Antia stood erect. "I will sleep tonight quietly and so will you. No more of this foolishness." He marched into the study and lay on the bed, loosening his body bit by bit, and under the surface of his concentration the leg throbbed evenly. The night came on and passed. He thought finally that nothing would happen, and there was a grey outside the window, but then he heard again the incessant calling. He took a deep breath, and walked into the drawing room. Thapa was standing by the door, his whole body straining away from the stairs. Jago Antia took two steps forward. "Come on," he said. His voice rustled across the room, and both of them jerked. He read the white tightness of terror around Thapa's mouth, and as he had done many times before, he led by example. He felt his legs move far away, towards the stairs, and he did not look behind him to see if Thapa was following. He knew the same pride and shame which was taking him up the stairs would bring Thapa: as long as each saw himself in the other's eyes he would not let the other down. He had tested this in front of machine guns and found it to be true. So now they moved, Thapa a little behind and flanking, up the stairs. This time he came up to the landing and was able to move out, through the door, onto the balcony. He was moving, moving, But then the voice came around a corner and he stood still, feeling a rush in his veins. It was amazing, he found himself thinking, how localized it was. He could tell from moment to moment where it was on the balcony. It was not a trick of the wind, not a hallucination. Thapa was still against the wall, his palms against it, his mouth working back and forth, looking exactly where Jago Antia was. It came closer, and now Jago Antia was able to hear what it was saying: "Where shall I go?" The question was asked with a sob in it, like a tearing hiccup, so close that Jago Antia heard it shake the small frame that asked it. He felt a sound in his own throat, a moan, something like pain, sympathy. Then he felt the thing pause, and though there was nothing but the air he felt it coming at him, first hesitating, then faster, asking again, where shall I go, where, and he backed away from it, fast, tripping over his heels, and he felt the railing of the balcony on his thighs, hard, and then he was falling.

The night was dark below. They plummeted headfirst from the belly of the plane into the cool pit at a thousand feet, and Jago Antia relished the leap into reality. They had been training long enough, and now he did not turn his head to see if the stick was tight because he knew his men and their skill. The chute popped with a flap, and after the jerk he flew the sky with his legs easy in the harness. The only feature he could see was the silver curve of the river far below, and then quite suddenly the dark mass of trees and the swathe of fields. There were no lights in the city of Sylhet, but he knew it was there, to the east, and he knew the men who were in it, defending against him, and he saw the problem clearly and the movements across the terrain below.

Then he was rolling across the ground, and the chute was off. Around him was the controlled confusion of a nighttime drop, and swiftly out of that formed the shape of his battalion. He had the command group around him, and in a few minutes they were racing towards their first objectives. Now he was sweating freely, and the weight of his pistol swung against his hip. He could smell the cardamom seeds his radioman was chewing. In the first grey, to the east, the harsh tearing noise of LMG fire flung the birds out of the trees. *Delta Bravo I have contact over.* As Jago Antia thumbed the mouthpiece, his radioman smiled at him, nineteen and glowing in the dawn. *Delta Bravo, bunkers, platoon strength, I am going in now.* Alpha Company had engaged.

As the day came they moved into the burning city, and the buildings were torn by explosions and the shriek of rockets skimming low over the streets and ringing off the walls. Now the noise echoed and boomed, and it was difficult to tell where it was coming from, but Jago Antia still saw it all forming on his map, which was stained black now with sweat here and there, and dust, and the plaster knocked from the walls by bullets. He was icy now, his mind holding it all, and as an excited captain reported to him he listened silently, and there was the flat crack of a grenade, not far off, and the captain flinched, then blushed as he saw that Jago Antia was calm as if he were walking down a golf course in Wellington, not a street shining with glass, thousands of shards sharp as death, no, he was meditative and easy. So the captain went back to his boys with something of Jago Antia's slow watchfulness in his walk, and he put away his nervousness and smiled at them, and they nodded, crouched behind cracked walls, sure of each other and Jago Antia.

Now in the morning the guns echoed over the city, and a plummy BBC voice sounded over a Bush radio in the remnants of a tailor's shop: "Elements of the Indian Para Brigade are said to be in the outskirts of Sylhet. Pakistani troops are dug in . . ." Jago Antia was looking at the rounded curves of the radio on the tailor's shelf, at the strange white knobs and the dial from decades ago, at the deep brown wood, and a shiver came from low on his back into his heart, a whisper of something so tiny that he could not name it, and yet it broke his concentration and took him away from his body and this room with its drapes of cloth to somewhere else, a flickering vision of a room, curtains blowing in a gusting wind, a feeling of confusion, he shook his head and swallowed. He curled the knob with the back of his hand so that it snapped the voice off and broke with a crack. Outside he could feel the fight approaching a crisis, the keen whiplash of the carbines and the rattle of the submachine guns and the heavier Pakistani fire, cresting and falling like waves but always higher, it was likely the deciding movement. He had learnt the waiting that was the hardest part of commanding, and now the reports came quickly, and he felt the battle forming to a crescendo; he had a reserve, sixty men, and he knew now where he was going to put them. They trotted down the street to the east and paused on a dusty street corner (the relentless braying scream of an LMG near by), and Jung the radioman pointed to a house at the end of the street, a white three-storied house with a decorative vine running down the front in concrete, now chipped and holed. "Tall enough," Jago Antia said: he wanted a vantage point to see the city laid out for him. He started off confidently across the street, and then all the sound in the world vanished, leaving a smooth silence, he had no recollection of being thrown, but now he was falling through the air, down, he felt distinctly the impact of the ground, but again there was nothing, no sound.

After a while he was able to see the men above him as he was lifted, their lips moving serenely even though their faces were twisted with emotion, they appeared curved and bent inwards against a spherical sky. He shut and opened his eyes several times, searching for connections that seemed severed. They carried him into a house. Then he was slowly able to hear again, and with the sound he began to feel the pain. His ears hurt sharply and deep inside his head, in a place in which he had never felt pain before. But he strained and finally he was able to find, inside, some part of himself, and his body jerked, and they held him still. His jaw cracked, and he said: "What?"

It was a mine on the corner, they told him. Now he was fighting it, he was using his mind, he felt his strength coming back, he could find his hands, and he pushed against the bed and sat up. A fiercely moustached nursing-assistant pushed at his shoulders, but he struck the hands away and took a deep breath. Then he saw his leg. Below his right knee the flesh was white and twisted away from the bone. Below the ankle was a shapeless bulk of matter, and the nursing-assistant was looking for the artery, but as Jago Antia watched the black blood seeped out onto the floor. Outside, the firing was ceaseless now, and Jago Antia was looking at his leg, and he realized that he no longer knew where his boys were. The confusion came and howled around his head, and for a moment he was lost. "Cut it off," he said then. "Off."

But, said the nursing-assistant, holding up the useless bandages, but I have nothing, and Jago Antia felt his head swim on an endless swell of pain, it took him up and away and he could no longer see, and it left him breathless and full of loss. "No time. Cut it off now," he said, but the nursing-assistant was dabbing with the bandages. Jago Antia said to Jung: "You do it, now. Quickly." They were all staring at him, and he knew he could not make them cut him. "Give me your *kukri*," he said to Jung. The boy hesitated, but then the blade came out of its scabbard with a hiss that Jago Antia heard despite the ceaseless roar outside. He steadied himself and gripped it with both hands and shut his eyes for a moment, and there was impossibly the sound of the sea inside him, a sob rising in his throat, he opened his eyes and fought it, pulled against it with his shoulders as he raised the *kukri* above his head, against darkness and mad sorrow, and then he brought the blade down below his knee. What surprised him was the crunch it made against the bone. In four strokes he was through. Each was easier. "Now," he said, and the nursing-assistant tied it off. Jago Antia waved off the morphine, and he saw that Jung the radioman was crying. On the radio Jago Antia's voice was steady. He took his reports, and then he sent his reserve in. They heard his voice across Sylhet. "Now then," he said. "Finish it."

The room that Jago Antia woke up in had a cracked white ceiling, and for a long time he did not know where he was, in Sylhet (he could feel an ache under his right knee), in the house of his childhood after a fall from the balcony, or in some other room, unknown: everything seemed to be thrown together in his eyes without shape or distinction, and from moment to moment he forgot the flow of time, and found himself talking to Amir Khan about cricket, and then suddenly it was evening. Finally he was able to sit up in bed, and a doctor fussed about him: there were no injuries, the ground was soft from the rain, his paratrooper's reflexes had turned him in the air and rolled him on the ground, but he was bruised, and a concussion could not be ruled out. He was to stay in bed and rest. When the doctor left Thapa brought in a plate of rice and *dal,* and stood at the foot of the bed with his arms behind him. "I will talk to my cousin tonight."

Jago Antia nodded. There was nothing to say. But when the exorcist came two days later he was not the slavering tribal magician that Jago Antia was expecting, but a sales manager from a large electronics company. Without haste and without stopping he put his briefcase down, stripped off his black pants and white shirt and blue tie, and bathed under the tap in the middle of the garden. Then he put on a white *dhoti* and daubed his forehead with a white powder, and meanwhile Thapa was preparing a *thali* with little mounds of rice and various kinds of coloured paste and a small *diya,* with the wick floating in the oil. Then the man took the *thali* from Thapa and walked slowly into the house, and as he came closer Jago Antia saw that he was in his late forties, that he was heavyset, that he was neither ugly nor handsome. "My name is Thakker," he said to Jago Antia before he sat cross-legged in the middle of the living room, in front of the stairs, and lit the *diya.* It was evening now, and the flame was tiny and flickering in the enormous darkness of the room.

As Thakker began to chant and throw fistfuls of rice from his *thali* into the room Jago Antia felt all the old irritation return, and he was disgusted with himself for letting this insanity gather around him. He walked out into the garden and stood with the grass rustling against his pants. There was a huge bank of clouds on the horizon, mass upon mass of dark heads piled up thousands of feet high, and as he watched a silver dart of lightning flickered noiselessly, and then another. Now his back began to ache slightly, and he shook his head slowly, overwhelmed by the certainty that he no longer knew anything. He turned around and looked up the path, into the house, and through the twilight he could see the tiny gleam of Thakker's *diya,* and as he watched Thakker lifted the *thali* and walked slowly towards the stairs, into the shadow, so that finally it seemed that the flame was rising up the stairs. Then Thapa came out, and they stood in the garden together, and the breeze from the sea was full of the promise of rain. They waited as night fell, and sometimes they heard Thakker's voice, lifted high and chanting, and then, very faint, that other voice, blown away by the gusts of wind. Finally—Jago Antia did not know what time it was—Thakker came down the stairs, carrying the *thali,* but the *diya* was blown out. They walked up to meet him on the patio, under the faint light of a single bulb.

"It is very strong," he said.

"What is it?" said Jago Antia angrily.

Thakker shrugged. "It is most unmovable." His face was drawn and pale. "It is a child. It is looking for something. Most terrible. Very strong."

"Well, get it out."

"I cannot. Nobody can move a child."

Jago Antia felt a rush of panic, like a steady pressure against his chest.

Thapa said, "What can we do?"

Thakker walked past them, down the stairs, and then he turned and looked up at them. "Do you know who it is?" Jago Antia said nothing, his lips held tightly together to stop them from trembling. "It is most powerful because it is a child and because it is helpless and because it is alone. Only one who knows it and who is from its family can help it. Such a person must go up there naked and alone. Remember, alone and naked, and ask it what it seeks." Thakker wiped away the white powder from his forehead slowly, and then he turned and walked away. It was now drizzling, fat drops that fell out of the sky insistently.

Out of the darkness Thakker called. "You must go." Then a pause in which Jago Antia could hear, somewhere, rushing water. "Help him."

At the bottom of the stairs Jago Antia felt his loneliness like a bitterness in his nostrils, like a stench. Thapa watched from the door, remote already, and there seemed to be nothing in the world but the shadows ahead, the creaking of the old house, the wind in the balconies. As Jago Antia walked slowly up the stairs, unbuttoning his shirt, his pulse was rushing in his head, each beat like an explosion, not out of fear anymore but from a kind of anticipation, because now he knew who it was, who waited for him. On the landing he kicked off his shoes and unbuckled his belt, and whispered, "What can you want from me? I was a child too." He walked slowly around the balcony, and the rain dashed against his shoulders and rolled down his back. He came to the end of the balcony, at a door with bevelled glass, and he peered through it, and he could dimly make out the ornate curves of his mother's dressing table, the huge mirror, and beyond that the bed now covered with sheets. He stood with his face against the cool pane. He shut his eyes. Somewhere deep came the poisonous seep of memory, he felt it in his stomach like a living stream, and his mother was looking at him, her eyes unfocussed in a kind of daze. She was a very beautiful woman, and she was sitting in front of her mirror now as she always did, but her hair was untidy, and she was wearing a white sari. He was sitting on the edge of her bed, his feet stuck out, and he was looking at his black shoes and white socks, and he was trying to be very still because he did not know what was going to happen next. He was dressed up, and the house was full of people, but it was very quiet and the only sounds were the pigeons on the balcony. He was afraid to move, and after a while he began to count his breaths, in and out. Then his father came in, he stood next to his mother, put a hand on her shoulder, and they looked at each other for a long time, and he wanted to say that they looked like their picture on the mantelpiece, only older and in white, but he knew he couldn't so he kept himself still and waited. Then his father said to his mother, come, and they rose and he walked behind them a little. She was leaning on his father, and they came down the stairs and everyone watched them. Downstairs he saw his uncles and aunts and other people he didn't know, and in the middle of the room there was a couch and on it lay his brother Sohrab. Sohrab had been laid out and draped in a white sheet. There was a kind of oil lamp with a wick burning near Sohrab's head, and a man was whispering a prayer into his ear. There was a smell of sandalwood in the air. Then his mother said, "Soli, Soli," and his father turned his face away, and a breath passed through the room, and he saw many people crying. That was what they always called Sohrab. He was Soli, and that was how Jehangir always thought of him. His mother was kneeling next to Soli, and his father too, and he was alone, and he didn't know what to do, but he stood straight up, and he kept his hands by his sides. Then two men came forward, and they covered Soli's face, and then other people lifted him up, and they took him through the door, and for a long time he could see them walking through the garden towards the gate. His mother was sitting on the sofa with her sisters, and after a while he turned around and walked up the stairs, and above there was nobody, and he walked through the rooms and around the balcony, and after a while he thought he was waiting for something to happen, but it never did.

Jago Antia's forehead trembled against the glass and now he turned and walked down the corridor that ran around the house, through darkness and sudden light, and he walked by a playroom, and then his father's study, and as he walked he felt that it was walking beside him, in front of him, around him. He heard the voice asking its question, but his own desperate question seemed to twist in his throat and come out only as a sound, a sort of sob of anger. It went into the room that had been his room and Soli's room, and he stopped at the door, his chest shaking, looking at the floor where they had wrestled each other, the bureau between the beds on which they had stacked their books and their toys. The door creaked open under his hand, and inside he sat on this bed, in the middle, where he used to, and they were listening to the Binaca Geet Mala on the radio, Soli loved his radio and the Binaca Geet Mala. He was lying on the bed in his red pyjamas and the song went *Maine shayad tumhe pahale bhi kahin dekha hai,* Soli sang along with it, Jehangir was not allowed to touch the radio, but when Soli was away he sometimes played with the knobs, and once he switched it on and heard a hiss and a voice far away speaking angrily in a language he didn't understand, it scared him and he ran away from it, and Soli found his radio on, and then there was a fight. Jehangir lost the fight, but Soli always won, even with the other boys on the street, he was fearless, and he jumped over walls, and he led them all, and at cricket he was always the captain of one side, and sometimes in the evenings, still in his barrister's clothes, their father watched their games in the garden, and he said that Soli had a lovely style. When he said this the first time Jehangir raised his head and blinked because he understood instantly what his father meant, he had known it all along but now he knew the words for it, and he said it to himself sometimes under his breath, a lovely style, a lovely style. Now Soli raised himself up in bed on an elbow, and Amir Khan brought in two glasses of milk on a tray, and then their mother came in and sat as she did on Soli's bed, and tonight she had *The Illustrated Weekly of India* in her hand, folded open to a tall picture of a man with a moustache and a bat, and she said, "Look at him, he was the Prince." So she told them about Ranjitsinhji, who was really a prince, who went to England where they called him nigger and wog, but he showed them, he was the most beautiful batsman, like a dancer he turned their bouncers to the boundaries with his wrists, he drove with clean elegance, he had good manners, and he said nothing to their insults, and he showed them all he was the best of them all, he was the Prince, he was lovely. After their mother left Soli put *The Illustrated Weekly* in his private drawer, and after that Jehangir would see him take it out and look at it, and sometimes he would let Jehangir look at it, and Jehangir would look at the long face and the pride in the stance and the dark opaque eyes, and he would feel a surge of pride himself, and Soli would have his wiry hand on his shoulder, and they would both say together, Ranjitsinhji, Ranji.

That summer one Sunday afternoon they were dozing in the heat when suddenly Burjor Mama came in and tumbled them both out of bed, roaring what a pair of sleepyhead sissy types, and they laughed with delight because he was their favourite uncle. They knew his arrival meant at least two weeks of unexpected pleasures, excursions to Juhu, sailing trips, films, shows, and sizzling forbidden pavement foods. Their mother came in and hugged him close, and they were embarrassed by her tears, Burjor was her only younger brother and more precious for his profession of soldiering, she was exclaiming now how he was burnt black by the sun, what are they doing to you now, and he was really dark, but Jehangir liked his unceasing whiplike energy and the sharp pointed ends of his handlebar moustache. Barely pausing to thump down his hold-all and his suitcase, he gathered up the whole family, Amir Khan included, and he whisked them off for a drive, and he whistled as he drove. On the way back Jehangir, weighted down with ice cream, fell asleep with his head in his mother's lap, and once for a moment he awoke and saw, close to his face, his mother's hand holding her brother's wrist tenderly and close, her delicate fingers very pale against his skin with the strong corded muscles underneath.

And Jago Antia, walking down the corridor, walking, felt the sticky sleep of childhood and the cosy hum of the car and safety. And then he was at the bottom of a flight of stairs, he knew he had to go up, because it had gone before him, and now he stumbled because the pain came, and it was full of fear, he went up, one two three, and then leaned over, choking. Above him the stairs angled into darkness and the roof he knew so well, and he couldn't move, again he was trembling, and the voice was speaking somewhere ahead, he said, "I don't want to go," but then he heard it again. He knew his hands were shaking, and he said, "All right you bastard, naked, naked," and he tore at the straps, and then the leg rolled down the stairs to the bottom. He went up, hunching, on hands and knees, his lips curled back and breathing in huge gasps.

Burjor Mama bought them a kite. On Monday morning he had to report in Colaba for work, and so Jehangir's mother brought up his pressed uniform and put it on the bed in the guest room. Jehangir lay on the bed next to the uniform and took in its peculiar smell, it was a deep olive green, and the bars on the front were of many colours but mainly red and orange, and above a breast pocket it said, B. MEHTA. Jehangir's mother sat on the bed too and smoothed out the uniform with an open palm, and then Burjor Mama came out of the bathroom in a towel. As he picked up the shirt, Jehangir saw under the *sadra*, under and behind his left arm, a scar shaped like a star, brown and hard against the pale skin. Then Jehangir looked up and he saw his mother's face, tender and proud and a little angry as she looked at Burjor. After breakfast Soli and Jehangir walked with him to the gate, and he said, "See you later, alligators," and in the afternoon they waited on the porch for him, reading comics and sipping at huge glasses of squash. When the taxi stopped at the gate they had run forward, whooping, because even before he was out they had seen the large triangle of the kite, and then they ran up without pause to the roof, Soli holding the kite at the ends, and Jehangir following behind with the roll of string. Jehangir held the roll as Soli spun off the *manjha*, and Soli said, watch your fingers, and Burjor showed them how to tie the kite string, once up, once down, and then they had it up in the air, it was doing spirals and rolls, and Soli said, "*Yaar*, that's a fighting kite!" Nobody was flying to fight with nearby, but when their father came up he laughed and watched them, and when they went down to tea Soli's fingers were cut from the *manjha*, and when Jehangir asked, Burjor Mama said, "It's ground glass on the line."

Now he came up the stairs, his stump bumping on the edges of the stone, and his palm scraped against something metal, but he felt the sting distantly and without interest. The next day Soli lay stretched across the roof, his mouth open. Jago Antia pulled himself up, his arms around a wooden post, and he could see the same two-level roof, Amir Khan's old room to one side, with its sloping roof coming to the green posts holding it up, beyond that the expanse of brick open to the sky, and then a three-foot drop with a metal ladder leading to the lower level of the roof, and beyond that the treetops and the cold stretch of the ocean. He let go of the post and swayed gently in the rain. Soli walked in front of him, his hands looping back the string, sending the kite fluttering strongly through the sky, and Jehangir held the coil and took up the slack. It flew in circles above them. "Let me fly it," Jehangir said. "Let me fly it." But Soli said, "You can't hold this, it'll cut you." "I can hold anything. I can." "You can't, it'll hurt you." "It won't. I won't let it." And Jehangir ran forward, Soli danced away, light and confident, backwards, and then for a moment his face was surprised, and then he was lying below, three feet below on the ground, and the string flew away from him. Jago Antia dropped to his knee, then fell heavily on his side. He pulled himself through the water, to the edge, next to the metal stairs, and he peered down trying to see the bottom but it seemed endless, but he knew it was only three feet below. How can somebody die falling three feet? He heard the voice asking its question, where shall I go, and he roared into the night, "What do you want? What the hell is it you want?" But it wouldn't stop, and Jago Antia knelt on the edge and wept, "What do you want," and finally he said, "Look, look," and he pushed himself up, leaned forward, and let himself go, and he fell: he saw again Soli backing away, Jehangir reaching up trying to take his hand away from the string, Soli holding his hand far up, and Jehangir helpless against his strength. Then Soli smiling, standing, and Jehangir shouting and running forward and jumping, the solid impact of his small body against Soli's legs. Soli's look of surprise, he's falling, reaching wildly. Jehangir's hand under the bottom of Soli's shorts, he holds on and tries, holds and pulls, but then he feels the weight taking him over, and he won't let go, but he hasn't the strength, he's falling with Soli, he feels the impact of the bricks through Soli's body.

When Jago Antia stirred weakly on the roof, when he looked up, it was dawn. He held himself up and said, "Are you still here? Tell me what you want." Then he saw at the parapet, very dim and shifting in the grey light, the shape of a small body, a boy looking down over the edge towards the ocean. As Jago Antia watched, the boy turned slowly, and in the weak light he saw that the boy was wearing a uniform of olive green, and he asked, "Where shall I go?" Jago Antia began to speak, but then his voice caught, because he was remembering his next and seventh birthday, the first party without Soli, and his parents holding him between them, soothing him, saying you must want something, and he looking up at their faces, at the lines in his father's face, the exhaustion in his mother's eyes. Burjor Mama sits on the carpet behind him with head down, and Amir Khan stands behind, and Jehangir shakes his head, nothing. His mother's eyes fill with tears, and she kisses him on the forehead, "Baba, it's all right, let us give you a present," and his heart breaks beneath a surging weight, but he stands up straight, and looking at her and his father, he says, "I want a uniform." So Jago Antia looked at the boy as he came closer, and he saw the small letters above the pocket, J. ANTIA, and the sun came up, and he saw the boy clearly, he saw the enormous dark eyes, and in the eyes he saw his vicious and ravenous strength, his courage and his devotion, his silence and his pain, his whole misshapen and magnificent life, and Jago Antia said, "Jehangir, Jehangir, you're already at home."

Thapa and Amir Khan came up the stairs slowly, and he called out to them. "Come, come. I'm all right." He was sitting cross-legged, watching the sun move in and out of the clouds.

Thapa squatted beside him. "Was it here?"

"He's gone. I saw him, and then he vanished."

"Who?"

Jago Antia shook his head. "Someone I didn't know before."

"What was he doing here then?"

"He was lost." He leaned on both their shoulders, one arm around each, for the descent down the stairs. Somehow, naked and hopping from stair to stair, he was smiling. He knew that nothing had changed. He knew he was still and forever Jago Antia, that for him it was too late for anything but a kind of solitude, that he would give his body to the fire, that in the implacable hills to the north, among the rocks, he and other men and women, each with histories of their own, would find each other for life and for death. And yet he felt free. He sat on the porch, strapping his leg on, and Amir Khan brought out three cups of tea. Thapa wrapped a sheet around Jago Antia, and looking at each other they both laughed. "Thank you," Jago Antia said. Then they drank the tea together.

Sandra Cisneros

Never Marry a Mexican

(U N I T E D   S T A T E S)

Never marry a Mexican, my ma said once and always. She said this because of my father. She said this though she was Mexican too. But she was born here in the U.S., and he was born there, and it's *not* the same, you know.

I'll *never* marry. Not any man. I've known men too intimately. I've witnessed their infidelities, and I've helped them to it. Unzipped and unhooked and agreed to clandestine maneuvers. I've been accomplice, committed premeditated crimes. I'm guilty of having caused deliberate pain to other women. I'm vindictive and cruel, and I'm capable of anything.

I admit, there was a time when all I wanted was to belong to a man. To wear that gold band on my left hand and be worn on his arm like an expensive jewel brilliant in the light of day. Not the sneaking around I did in different bars that all looked the same, red carpets with a black grillwork design, flocked wallpaper, wooden wagon-wheel light fixtures with hurricane lampshades a sick amber color like the drinking glasses you get for free at gas stations.

Dark bars, dark restaurants then. And if not—my apartment, with his toothbrush firmly planted in the toothbrush holder like a flag on the North Pole. The bed so big because he never stayed the whole night. Of course not.

Borrowed. That's how I've had my men. Just the cream skimmed off the top. Just the sweetest part of the fruit, without the bitter skin that daily living with a spouse can rend. They've come to me when they wanted the sweet meat then.

So, no. I've never married and never will. Not because I couldn't, but because I'm too romantic for marriage. Marriage has failed me, you could say. Not a man exists who hasn't disappointed me, whom I could trust to love the way I've loved. It's because I believe too much in marriage that I don't. Better to not marry than live a lie.

Mexican men, forget it. For a long time the men clearing off the tables or chopping meat behind the butcher counter or driving the bus I rode to school every day, those weren't men. Not men I considered as potential lovers. Mexican, Puerto Rican, Cuban, Chilean, Colombian, Panamanian, Salvadorean, Bolivian, Honduran, Argentine, Dominican, Venezuelan, Guatemalan,

Ecuadorean, Nicaraguan, Peruvian, Costa Rican, Paraguayan, Uruguayan, I don't care. I never saw them. My mother did this to me.

I guess she did it to spare me and Ximena the pain she went through. Having married a Mexican man at seventeen. Having had to put up with all the grief a Mexican family can put on a girl because she was from *el otro lado,* the other side, and my father had married down by marrying her. If he had married a white woman from *el otro lado,* that would've been different. That would've been marrying up, even if the white girl was poor. But what could be more ridiculous than a Mexican girl who couldn't even speak Spanish, who didn't know enough to set a separate plate for each course at dinner, nor how to fold cloth napkins, nor how to set the silverware.

In my ma's house the plates were always stacked in the center of the table, the knives and forks and spoons standing in a jar, help yourself. All the dishes chipped or cracked and nothing matched. And no tablecloth, ever. And newspapers set on the table whenever my grandpa sliced watermelons, and how embarrassed she would be when her boyfriend, my father, would come over and there were newspapers all over the kitchen floor and table. And my grandpa, big hardworking Mexican man, saying Come, come and eat, and slicing a big wedge of those dark green watermelons, a big slice, he wasn't stingy with food. Never, even during the Depression. Come, come and eat, to whoever came knocking on the back door. Hobos sitting at the dinner table and the children staring and staring. Because my grandfather always made sure they never went without. Flour and rice, by the barrel and by the sack. Potatoes. Big bags of pinto beans. And watermelons, bought three or four at a time, rolled under his bed and brought out when you least expected. My grandpa had survived three wars, one Mexican, two American, and he knew what living without meant. He knew.

My father, on the other hand, did not. True, when he first came to this country he had worked shelling clams, washing dishes, planting hedges, sat on the back of the bus in Little Rock and had the bus driver shout, You—sit up here, and my father had shrugged sheepishly and said, No speak English.

But he was no economic refugee, no immigrant fleeing a war. My father ran away from home because he was afraid of facing his father after his first-year grades at the university proved he'd spent more time fooling around than studying. He left behind a house in Mexico City that was neither poor nor rich, but thought itself better than both. A boy who would get off a bus when he saw a girl he knew board if he didn't have the money to pay her fare. That was the world my father left behind.

I imagine my father in his *fanfarrón* clothes, because that's what he was, a *fanfarrón.* That's what my mother thought the moment she turned around to the voice that was asking her to dance. A big show-off, she'd say years later. Nothing but a big show-off. But she never said why she married him. My father in his shark-blue suits with the starched handkerchief in the breast pocket, his felt fedora, his tweed topcoat with the big shoulders, and heavy British wing tips with the pin-hole design on the heel and toe. Clothes that cost a lot. Expensive. That's what my father's things said. *Calidad.* Quality.

My father must've found the U.S. Mexicans very strange, so foreign from what he knew at home in Mexico City where the servant served watermelon on a plate with silverware and a cloth napkin, or mangos with their own special prongs. Not like this, eating with your legs wide open in the yard, or in the kitchen hunkered over newspapers. *Come, come and eat.* No, never like this.

How I make my living depends. Sometimes I work as a translator. Sometimes I get paid by the word and sometimes by the hour, depending on the job. I do this in the day, and at night I paint. I'd do anything in the day just so I can keep on painting.

I work as a substitute teacher, too, for the San Antonio Independent School District. And that's worse than translating those travel brochures with their tiny print, believe me. I can't stand kids. Not any age. But it pays the rent.

Any way you look at it, what I do to make a living is a form of prostitution. People say, "A painter? How nice," and want to invite me to their parties, have me decorate the lawn like an exotic orchid for hire. But do they buy art?

I'm amphibious. I'm a person who doesn't belong to any class. The rich like to have me around because they envy my creativity; they know they can't buy *that.* The poor don't mind if I live in their neighborhood because they know I'm poor like they are, even if my education and the way I dress keeps us worlds apart. I don't belong to any class. Not to the poor, whose neighborhood I share. Not to the rich, who come to my exhibitions and buy my work. Not to the middle class from which my sister Ximena and I fled.

When I was young, when I first left home and rented that apartment with my sister and her kids right after her husband left, I thought it would be glamorous to be an artist. I wanted to be like Frida or Tina. I was ready to suffer with my camera and my paint brushes in that awful apartment we rented for $150 each because it had high ceilings and those wonderful glass skylights that convinced us we had to have it. Never mind there was no sink in the bathroom, and a tub that looked like a sarcophagus, and floorboards that didn't meet, and a hallway to scare away the dead. But fourteen-foot ceilings was enough for us to write a check for the deposit right then and there. We thought it all romantic. You know the place, the one on Zarzamora on top of the barber shop with the Casasola prints of the Mexican Revolution. Neon BIRRIA TEPATITLÁN sign round the corner, two goats knocking their heads together, and all those Mexican bakeries, Las Brisas for *huevos rancheros* and *carnitas* and *barbacoa* on Sundays, and fresh fruit milk shakes, and mango *paletas,* and more signs in Spanish than in English. We thought it was great, great. The barrio looked cute in the daytime, like Sesame Street. Kids hopscotching on the sidewalk, blessed little boogers. And hardware stores that still sold ostrich-feather dusters, and whole families marching out of Our Lady of Guadalupe Church on Sundays, girls in their swirly-whirly dresses and patent-leather shoes, boys in their dress Stacys and shiny shirts.

But nights, that was nothing like what we knew up on the north side. Pistols going off like the wild, wild West, and me and Ximena and the kids huddled in one bed with the lights off listening to it all, saying, Go to sleep, babies, it's just firecrackers. But we knew better. Ximena would say, Clemencia, maybe we should go home. And I'd say, Shit! Because she knew as well as I did there was no home to go home to. Not with our mother. Not with that man she married. After Daddy died, it was like we didn't matter. Like Ma was so busy feeling sorry for herself, I don't know. I'm not like Ximena. I still haven't worked it out after all this time, even though our mother's dead now. My half brothers living in that house that should've been ours, me and Ximena's. But that's—how do you say it?—water under the damn? I can't ever get the sayings right even though I was born in this country. We didn't say shit like that in our house.

Once Daddy was gone, it was like my ma didn't exist, like if she died, too. I used to have a little finch, twisted one of its tiny red legs between the bars of the cage once, who knows how. The leg just dried up and fell off. My bird lived a long time without it, just a little red stump of a leg. He was fine, really. My mother's memory is like that, like if something already dead dried up and fell off, and I stopped missing where she used to be. Like if I never had a mother. And I'm not ashamed to say it either. When she married that white man, and he and his boys moved into my father's house, it was as if she stopped being my mother. Like I never even had one.

Ma always sick and too busy worrying about her own life, she would've sold us to the Devil if she could. "Because I married so young, *mi'ja*," she'd say. "Because your father, he was so much older than me, and I never had a chance to be young. Honey, try to understand . . ." Then I'd stop listening.

That man she met at work, Owen Lambert, the foreman at the photo-finishing plant, who she was seeing even while my father was sick. Even then. That's what I can't forgive.

When my father was coughing up blood and phlegm in the hospital, half his face frozen, and his tongue so fat he couldn't talk, he looked so small with all those tubes and plastic sacks dangling around him. But what I remember most is the smell, like death was already sitting on his chest. And I remember the doctor scraping the phlegm out of my father's mouth with a white washcloth, and my daddy gagging and I wanted to yell, Stop, you stop that, he's my daddy. Goddamn you. Make him live. Daddy, don't. Not yet, not yet, not yet. And how I couldn't hold myself up, I couldn't hold myself up. Like if they'd beaten me, or pulled my insides out through my nostrils, like if they'd stuffed me with cinnamon and cloves, and I just stood there dry-eyed next to Ximena and my mother, Ximena between us because I wouldn't let her stand next to me. Everyone repeating over and over the Ave Marias and Padre Nuestros. The priest sprinkling holy water, *mundo sin fin, amén.*

Drew, remember when you used to call me your Malinalli? It was a joke, a private game between us, because you looked like a Cortez with that beard of yours. My skin dark against yours. Beautiful, you said. You said I was beautiful, and when you said it, Drew, I was.

My Malinalli, Malinche, my courtesan, you said, and yanked my head back by the braid. Calling me that name in between little gulps of breath and the raw kisses you gave, laughing from that black beard of yours.

Before daybreak, you'd be gone, same as always, before I even knew it. And it was as if I'd imagined you, only the teeth marks on my belly and nipples proving me wrong.

Your skin pale, but your hair blacker than a pirate's. Malinalli, you called me, remember? *Mi doradita.* I liked when you spoke to me in my language. I could love myself and think myself worth loving.

Your son. Does he know how much I had to do with his birth? I was the one who convinced you to let him be born. Did you tell him, while his mother lay on her back laboring his birth, I lay in his mother's bed making love to you.

You're nothing without me. I created you from spit and red dust. And I can snuff you between my finger and thumb if I want to. Blow you to kingdom come. You're just a smudge of paint I chose to birth on canvas. And when I made you over, you were no longer a part of her, you were all mine. The landscape of your body taut as a drum. The heart beneath that hide thrumming and thrumming. Not an inch did I give back.

I paint and repaint you the way I see fit, even now. After all these years. Did you know that? Little fool. You think I went hobbling along with my life, whimpering and whining like some twangy country-and-western when you went back to her. But I've been waiting. Making the world look at you from my eyes. And if that's not power, what is?

Nights I light all the candles in the house, the ones to La Virgen de Guadalupe, the ones to El Niño Fidencio, Don Pedrito Jaramillo, Santo Niño de Atocha, Nuestra Señora de San Juan de los Lagos, and especially, Santa Lucia, with her beautiful eyes on a plate.

Your eyes are beautiful, you said. You said they were the darkest eyes you'd ever seen and kissed each one as if they were capable of miracles. And after you left, I wanted to scoop them out with a spoon, place them on a plate under these blue blue skies, food for the blackbirds.

The boy, your son. The one with the face of that redheaded woman who is your wife. The boy red-freckled like fish food floating on the skin of water. That boy.

I've been waiting patient as a spider all these years, since I was nineteen and he was just an idea hovering in his mother's head, and I'm the one that gave him permission and made it happen, see.

Because your father wanted to leave your mother and live with me. Your mother whining for a child, at least *that.* And he kept saying, Later, we'll see, later. But all along it was me he wanted to be with, it was me, he said.

I want to tell you this evenings when you come to see me. When you're full of talk about what kind of clothes you're going to buy, and what you used to be like when you started high school and what you're like now that you're almost finished. And how everyone knows you as a rocker, and your band, and your new red guitar that you just got because your mother gave you a choice, a guitar or a car, but you don't need a car, do you, because I drive you everywhere. You could be my son if you weren't so light-skinned.

This happened. A long time ago. Before you were born. When you were a moth inside your mother's heart. I was your father's student, yes, just like you're mine now. And your father painted and painted me, because he said, I was his *doradita,* all golden and sun-baked, and that's the kind of woman he likes best, the ones brown as river sand, yes. And he took me under his wing and in his bed, this man, this teacher, your father. I was honored that he'd done me the favor. I was that young.

All I know is I was sleeping with your father the night you were born. In the same bed where you were conceived. I was sleeping with your father and didn't give a damn about that woman, your mother. If she was a brown woman like me, I might've had a harder time living with myself, but since she's not, I don't care. I was there first, always. I've always been there, in the mirror, under his skin, in the blood, before you were born. And he's been here in my heart before I even knew him. Understand? He's always been here. Always. Dissolving like a hibiscus flower, exploding like a rope into dust. I don't care what's right anymore. I don't care about his wife. She's not *my* sister.

And it's not the last time I've slept with a man the night his wife is birthing a baby. Why do I do that, I wonder? Sleep with a man when his wife is giving life, being suckled by a thing with its eyes still shut. Why do that? It's always given me a bit of crazy joy to be able to kill those women like that, without their knowing it. To know I've had their husbands when they were anchored in blue hospital rooms, their guts yanked inside out, the baby sucking their breasts while their husband sucked mine. All this while their ass stitches were still hurting.

Once, drunk on margaritas, I telephoned your father at four in the morning, woke the bitch up. Hello, she chirped. I want to talk to Drew. Just a moment, she said in her most polite drawing-room English. Just a moment. I laughed about that for weeks. What a stupid ass to pass the phone over to the lug asleep beside her. Excuse me, honey, it's for you. When Drew mumbled hello I was laughing so hard I could hardly talk. Drew? That dumb bitch of a wife of yours, I said, and that's all I could manage. That stupid stupid stupid. No Mexican woman would react like that. Excuse me, honey. It cracked me up.

He's got the same kind of skin, the boy. All the blue veins pale and clear just like his mama. Skin like roses in December. Pretty boy. Little clone. Little cells split into you and you and you. Tell me, baby, which part of you is your mother. I try to imagine her lips, her jaw, her long long legs that wrapped themselves around this father who took me to his bed.

This happened. I'm asleep. Or pretend to be. You're watching me, Drew. I feel your weight when you sit on the corner of the bed, dressed and ready to go, but now you're just watching me sleep. Nothing. Not a word. Not a kiss. Just sitting. You're taking me in, under inspection. What do you think already?

I haven't stopped dreaming you. Did you know that? Do you think it's strange? I never tell, though. I keep it to myself like I do all the thoughts I think of you.

After all these years.

I don't want you looking at me. I don't want you taking me in while I'm asleep. I'll open my eyes and frighten you away.

There. What did I tell you? *Drew? What is it?* Nothing. I'd knew you'd say that.

Let's not talk. We're no good at it. With you I'm useless with words. As if somehow I had to learn to speak all over again, as if the words I needed haven't been invented yet. We're cowards. Come back to bed. At least there I feel I have you for a little. For a moment. For a catch of the breath. You let go. You ache and tug. You rip my skin.

You're almost not a man without your clothes. How do I explain it? You're so much a child in my bed. Nothing but a big boy who needs to be held. I won't let anyone hurt you. My pirate. My slender boy of a man.

After all these years.

I didn't imagine it, did I? A Ganges, an eye of the storm. For a little. When we forgot ourselves, you tugged me, I leapt inside you and split you like an apple. Opened for the other to look and not give back. Something wrenched itself loose. Your body doesn't lie. It's not silent like you.

You're nude as a pearl. You've lost your train of smoke. You're tender as rain. If I put you in my mouth you'd dissolve like snow.

You were ashamed to be so naked. Pulled back. But I saw you for what you are, when you opened yourself for me. When you were careless and let yourself through. I caught that catch of the breath. I'm not crazy.

When you slept, you tugged me toward you. You sought me in the dark. I didn't sleep. Every cell, every follicle, every nerve, alert. Watching you sigh and roll and turn and hug me closer to you. I didn't sleep. I was taking *you* in that time.

Your mother? Only once. Years after your father and I stopped seeing each other. At an art exhibition. A show on the photographs of Eugène Atget. Those images, I could look at them for hours. I'd taken a group of students with me.

It was your father I saw first. And in that instant I felt as if everyone in the room, all the sepia-toned photographs, my students, the men in business suits, the high-heeled women, the security guards, everyone, could see me for what I was. I had to scurry out, lead my kids to another gallery, but some things destiny has cut out for you.

He caught up with us in the coat-check area, arm in arm with a redheaded Barbie doll in a fur coat. One of those scary Dallas types, hair yanked into a ponytail, big shiny face like the women behind the cosmetic counters at Neiman's. That's what I remember. She must've been with him all along, only I swear I never saw her until that second.

You could tell from a slight hesitancy, only slight because he's too suave to hesitate, that he was nervous. Then he's walking toward me, and I didn't know what to do, just stood there dazed like those animals crossing the road at night when the headlights stun them.

And I don't know why, but all of sudden I looked at my shoes and felt ashamed at how old they looked. And he comes up to me, my love, your father, in that way of his with that grin that makes me want to beat him, makes me want to make love to him, and he says in the most sincere voice you ever heard, "Ah, Clemencia! *This* is Megan." No introduction could've been meaner. *This* is Megan. Just like that.

I grinned like an idiot and held out my paw—"Hello, Megan"—and smiled too much the way you do when you can't stand someone. Then I got the hell out of there, chattering like a monkey all the ride back with my kids. When I got home I had to lie down with a cold washcloth on my forehead and the TV on. All I could hear throbbing under the washcloth in that deep part behind my eyes: *This* is Megan.

And that's how I fell asleep, with TV on and every light in the house burning. When I woke up it was something like three in the morning. I shut the lights and TV and went to get some aspirin, and the cats, who'd been asleep with me on the couch, got up too and followed me into the bathroom as if they knew what's what. And then they followed me into bed, where they aren't allowed, but this time I just let them, fleas and all.

This happened, too. I swear I'm not making this up. It's all true. It was the last time I was going to be with your father. We had agreed. All for the best. Surely I could see that, couldn't I? My own good. A good sport. A young girl like me. Hadn't I understood . . . responsibilities. Besides, he could *never* marry *me*. You didn't think . . . ? *Never marry a Mexican. Never marry a Mexican* . . . No, of course not. I see. I see.

We had the house to ourselves for a few days, who knows how. You and your mother had gone somewhere. Was it Christmas? I don't remember.

I remember the leaded-glass lamp with the milk glass above the dining-room table. I made a mental inventory of everything. The Egyptian lotus design on the hinges of the doors. The narrow, dark hall where your father and I had made love once. The four-clawed tub where he had washed my hair and rinsed it with a tin bowl. This window. That counter. The bedroom with its light in the morning, incredibly soft, like the light from a polished dime.

The house was immaculate, as always, not a stray hair anywhere, not a flake of dandruff or a crumpled towel. Even the roses on the dining-room table held their breath. A kind of airless cleanliness that always made me want to sneeze.

Why was I curious about this woman he lived with? Every time I went to the bathroom, I found myself opening the medicine cabinet, looking at all the things that were hers. Her Estée Lauder lipsticks. Corals and pinks, of course. Her nail polishes—mauve was as brave as she could wear. Her cotton balls and blonde hairpins. A pair of bone-colored sheepskin slippers, as clean as the day she'd bought them. On the door hook—a white robe with a MADE IN ITALY label, and a silky nightshirt with pearl buttons. I touched the fabrics. *Calidad.* Quality.

I don't know how to explain what I did next. While your father was busy in the kitchen, I went over to where I'd left my backpack, and took out a bag of gummy bears I'd bought. And while he was banging pots, I went around the house and left a trail of them in places I was sure *she* would find them. One in her lucite makeup organizer. One stuffed inside each bottle of nail polish. I untwisted the expensive lipsticks to their full length and smushed a bear on the top before recapping them. I even put a gummy bear in her diaphragm case in the very center of that luminescent rubber moon.

Why bother? Drew could take the blame. Or he could say it was the cleaning woman's Mexican voodoo. I knew that, too. It didn't matter. I got a strange satisfaction wandering about the house leaving them in places only she would look.

And just as Drew was shouting, "Dinner!" I saw it on the desk. One of those wooden babushka dolls Drew had brought her from his trip to Russia. I know. He'd bought one just like it for me.

I just did what I did, uncapped the doll inside a doll inside a doll, until I got to the very center, the tiniest baby inside all the others, and this I replaced with a gummy bear. And then I put the dolls back, just like I'd found them, one inside the other, inside the other. Except for the baby, which I put inside my pocket. All through dinner I kept reaching in the pocket of my jean jacket. When I touched it, it made me feel good.

On the way home, on the bridge over the *arroyo* on Guadalupe Street, I stopped the car, switched on the emergency blinkers, got out, and dropped the wooden toy into that muddy creek where winos piss and rats swim. The Barbie doll's toy stewing there in that muck. It gave me a feeling like nothing before and since.

Then I drove home and slept like the dead.

These mornings, I fix coffee for me, milk for the boy. I think of that woman, and I can't see a trace of my lover in this boy, as if she conceived him by immaculate conception.

I sleep with this boy, their son. To make the boy love me the way I love his father. To make him want me, hunger, twist in his sleep, as if he'd swallowed glass. I put him in my mouth. Here, little piece of my *corazón*. Boy with hard thighs and just a bit of down and a small hard downy ass like his father's, and that back like a valentine. Come here, *mi cariñito*. Come to *mamita*. Here's a bit of toast.

I can tell from the way he looks at me, I have him in my power. Come, sparrow. I have the patience of eternity. Come to *mamita*. My stupid little bird. I don't move. I don't startle him. I let him nibble. All, all for you. Rub his belly. Stroke him. Before I snap my teeth.

What is it inside me that makes me so crazy at 2 A.M.? I can't blame it on alcohol in my blood when there isn't any. It's something worse. Something that poisons the blood and tips me when the night swells and I feel as if the whole sky were leaning against my brain.

And if I killed someone on a night like this? And if it was *me* I killed instead, I'd be guilty of getting in the line of crossfire, innocent bystander, isn't it a shame. I'd be walking with my head full of images and my back to the guilty. Suicide? I couldn't say. I didn't see it.

Except it's not me who I want to kill. When the gravity of the planets is just right, it all tilts and upsets the visible balance. And that's when it wants out from my eyes. That's when I get on the telephone, dangerous as a terrorist. There's nothing to do but let it come.

So. What do you think? Are you convinced now I'm as crazy as a tulip or a taxi? As vagrant as a cloud?

Sometimes the sky is so big and I feel so little at night. That's the problem with being cloud. The sky is so terribly big. Why is it worse at night, when I have such an urge to communicate and no language with which to form the words? Only colors. Pictures. And you know what I have to say isn't always pleasant.

Oh, love, there. I've gone and done it. What good is it? Good or bad, I've done what I had to do and needed to. And you've answered the phone, and startled me away like a bird. And now you're probably swearing under your breath and going back to sleep, with that wife beside you, warm, radiating her own heat, alive under the flannel and down and smelling a bit like milk and hand cream, and that smell familiar and dear to you, oh.

Human beings pass me on the street, and I want to reach out and strum them as if they were guitars. Sometimes all humanity strikes me as lovely. I just want to reach out and stroke someone, and say There, there, it's all right, honey. There, there, there.

Jim Crace

The Prospect from the Silver Hills

(ENGLAND)

The company agent—friendless, single, far from home—passed most days alone in a cabin at Ibela-hoy, the Hill Without a Hat. His work was simple. Equipped with a rudimentary knowledge of mineralogy, neat, laborious handwriting, and a skill with ledgers, he had been posted to the highlands to identify the precious metals, the stones, the ores, that (everybody said) were buried there.

This was his life: awake at dawn, awake all day, awake all night. Phrenetic insomnia was the term. But there were no friends or doctors to make the diagnosis. The agent simply—like a swift, a shark—dared not sleep. He kept moving. He did not close his eyes. At night, at dawn, in the tall heat of the day, he looked out over the land and, watching the shades and colors of the hill and its valley accelerate and reel, he constructed for himself a family and a life less solitary than the one he was forced to live. He took pills. He drank what little spirits arrived each month with his provisions. He exhausted himself with long, aimless walks among the boulders and dry beds. Sometimes he fell forward at work, his nose flattened among the gravels on the table, his papers dampened by saliva, his tongue slack. But he did not sleep or close his eyes, though he was still troubled by chimeras, daydreams, which broke his concentration and, because he was conscious, seemed more substantial and coherent than sleeping dreams. As the men had already remarked among themselves when they saw the sacs of tiredness spreading across his upper cheeks and listened to his conversation, the company agent either had a fever or the devil had swapped sawdust for his brain.

Several times a week one of the survey gangs arrived in a company mobile drilling rig to deposit drill cores of augered rock and sand, pumice and shale, and provide the company agent with a profile of the world twenty meters below his feet. He sorted clays as milky as nutsap and eggstones as worn and weathered as a saint's beads into sample bags. Each rock, each smudge of soil, was condemned. Nothing. Nothing. Nothing. A trace of tin. Nothing.

Once, when he had been at Ibela-hoy for only a few weeks, one of the survey gangs offered to take him down to the lumber station, where the woodsmen had established a good still and an understanding with some local women. He sat in the cab of the mobile drilling rig and talked nonstop. That's the loneliest place, he told them, as the rig descended from the cabin. There aren't even ghosts. He spoke, too, about the wife and children, the companionable life, which he had concocted in his daydreams. How he wished he had a camera at home, he told the men. Then he could have shown them photographs of his family, of his garden in the city, his car, his wedding day.

The men indulged him. He was still a stranger, they reasoned, and starved of company, missing home. He would quiet down once he had a glass in his hand. But they were wrong. He became louder with every sip. He spoke in a voice which sent the women back into their homes, which sent the men early to bed. The voice said, My sadness is stronger than your drink. Nothing can relieve it. Nothing. A trace of tin. Nothing.

He daydreamed: a lifetime of finding nothing. He dreamed of prospecting the night sky and locating a planet of diamonds or an old, cooled sun of solid gold. But then the company had no need for diamonds or gold. Find us sand, they instructed. Find us brown mud. Send us a palmful of pebbles. He dreamed again, and produced a twist of earth and stone which contained new colors, a seam of creamy nougat in a funnel of tar. His dream delivered the funnel to his company offices. Soon secretaries typed Ibela-hoy for the first time—and a name was coined for the new mineral which he had unearthed. Then his dream transported friends and family to Ibela-hoy. They walked behind him as he set out to map the creamy seam. Together they charted an area the shape of a toadstool. A toadstool of the newest mineral in the world. His daydream provided a telephone and a line of poles. He telephoned the company with the good news. They referred him to the agency and then to the ministry. His calls were bounced and routed between switchboards and operators and his story retold a dozen times—but nobody was found with sufficient authority to accept such momentous information or to order his return to home, to sleep.

Send me a dream, he said aloud, in which my wife and my children are brought to the cabin. When I wake, they are there. When I sleep, they are there. We sit at the same table. The two boys tumble on the bed. The baby stands on my thighs with crescent legs and tugs at my nose and hair. My wife and I sit together slicing vegetables at the table. But when he had finished speaking there was no reply from among the rocks, no promises. He spoke again, in whispers. Have pity, he said.

Sometimes he wrapped his arms around boulders, warmed by the sun, and embraced them. My wife, he said. He kissed boulders.

Now the men kept their distance. They were polite, but no longer generous. There were no more invitations to visit the lumber station, and they became watchful on those occasions when they brought drill cores to the cabin. Does this man know his business? they asked among themselves. Can he be trusted to know marl from marble? They waited awkwardly at his door or stood at his window as their plugs of earth were spread and sorted on his bench, the soils washed and sieved, the stones stunned and cracked, the unusual flakes of rocks matched with the specimens in the mineral trays. His fatigue—the second stage—had hardened his concentration. He was engrossed. He lowered his head and smelled the soil. He sucked the roundest pebbles. He rubbed stones on the thighs of his trousers and held them to the light. No, nothing, he told them. But when they sat in their camps and looked up from the valley late at night, a light still burned in the agent's cabin and they could see him holding their stones to his oil flame and talking to their earth in his skinned and weary voice.

At first the sorted, worthless plugs were dumped each day in a rough pile at the side of the cabin. The clays of the valley consorted with the volcanic earths of Ibela-hoy. Flints jostled sandstones, topsoils ran loose among clods, the rounded pebbles of the riverbed bubbled in the wasteland shales. He was struck how—held and turned in the daylight—each stone was a landscape. Here was a planet, a globe, with the continents gray and peninsular, the seas cold and smooth to the touch. And here was a coastline, one face the beach, four faces cliff, and a rivulet of green where the children and donkeys could make their descent. And here, twisted and smoothed by the survey drill, were the muddied banks of rivers and the barks of trees modeled and reduced in deep, toffee earth. But in the dump, their shapes and colors clashed and were indecent. He remembered how, when he was a child, they had buried his father. The grave was open when the body came. There were clays and flints piled on the yellow grass. The bottom of his father's trench had filled with water. The digger's spade had severed stones. They said that, in ancient times when humankind went naked and twigged for termites and ate raw meat, the dead were left where they fell. What the animals did not eat became topsoil, loam. The company agent had wished for that, had dreamed of his father free of his grave and spread out on the unbroken ground as calm and breathless as frost. But he could not look at that open grave, those wounded flints, without tears. He could not look at road works, either. Or a ploughed field. Or a broken wall. And whenever he had stared at that squinting corner of his room where the ceiling plaster had fallen and the broken roof laths stuck through, his chest (what was the phrase?) shivered like a parched pea and he dared not sleep. The ceiling doesn't leak, his mother said. It's you that leaks, not it.

Now he wept when he passed the waste pile, when he was drawn at night to stand before it with a lamp or summoned to salvage one lonely stone for his pocket or his table. Sometimes it seemed that the pile was an open wound or a slaughterhouse of stones. But the longer he stood, the more it seemed that a piece of the world had been misplaced and abandoned at his cabin side.

Then he took a spade and dug a pit behind the waste pile. First he gathered the chipped yellow stones which lay on the surface and placed them together in a bucket. And then he removed the thin soil crust and piled it neatly onto a tarpaulin. Each individual layer was dug out and piled separately, until the pit was shoulder deep. The continents and planets, the landscapes and coastlines of the waste dump were shoveled into the pit and one by one, in order, the layers of Ibela-hoy were put back in place. Then he scattered the chipped yellow stones onto the bulging ground.

When the gangs delivered drill cores, they noticed that the waste had gone. I buried it, he said. I put it back. He showed them where the swollen ground was setting. Well, they said, that's very neat and tidy. Or, Is that what you're paid to do, fool about with spades? His replies made no sense to them. They continued to talk with him roughly or to humor him with banter. What should we do for him, they asked among themselves, to bring him back to earth? Should we write, they wondered, to his wife and children or to the boss? Should we let him be and let the illness pass? Some of the kinder, older men went to talk with him, to offer help, to exchange a word or two about the samples on his bench. Yet he seemed indifferent to them and those funnels of earth and stone which could earn them all a fortune. Was that the yellow of bauxite or the rose of cinnabar or the fire blue of opal? The company agent did not seem to share their excitement or their interest. But when at last they left him in peace, he turned to the samples on his bench and sorted through them with unbroken attention. A stone of apple green he removed and walked with it into the valley, where in a cave there were lichens of the same color. A fistful of grit he scattered in the grass so that it fell among the leaf joints like sleet. A round stone he placed on the riverbed with other round stones. A gray landscape in an inch of granite he stood in the shadow of the grayest rock. A chip of pitchblende was reunited with black soil.

Once a month, when his provisions were delivered together with letters from home, the company agent presented his report and sent back to the city any minerals or gemstones which were worthy of note. Once he had found a fragment of platinum in a sample from the plateau beyond the hill. He and the gang waited a month for the company's response. Low-quality platinum, they said. No use to us. And once he had identified graphite among the native carbons. But again, the company was unimpressed. Now he wrapped a piece of damp clay and placed it in a sample bag. Its colors were the colors of pomegranite skins. Its odor was potatoes. He sealed the bag and sent it to the company. Urgent, he wrote on the label. Smell this! And, in the second month, he sent them a cube of sandstone and wrote: See the landscape, the beach, the pathway through the rocks. And later they received the palmful of pebbles that they had requested in his dream.

Alarms rang. Secretaries delivered the agent's file to the company bosses. They searched the certificates and testimonials for any criminal past. Was he a radical? Had he been ill? What should they make of clay, sandstone, pebbles? They called his mother to the offices and questioned her. She showed them her son's monthly letters and pointed to those parts where he spoke of insomnia, a slaughterhouse of stones, and a family that never was. He misses home, she said. Why would he send worthless soil and cryptic notes in sample bags? She could not say, except that he had always been a good man, quick to tears. If only he had married, found a girl to love, had children perhaps . . . then who can guess what might have been? But worthless soil? Still she could not say.

The bosses sent their man to Ibela-hoy in their air-conditioned jeep to bring the agent home and to discover what had been going on. The brick and tarmac of the town and villages lasted for a day. The bosses' man passed the night at the Rest House, where the valley greens rose to the implacable evening monochromes of the hills. In the morning, early, he drove onto the bouldered track along the valley side. The Hill Without a Hat swung across his windshield in the distance. On the summit of the ridge the track widened and cairns marked the route down into the valley of Lekadeeb and then up again towards Ibela-hoy. He stood with his binoculars and sought out the company agent's cabin in the hollow of the hill. He saw the company mobile parked at the door and the antics of men who seemed intoxicated with drink or horseplay. A survey team had returned from the far valley bluffs some days ahead of schedule and hurried to the agent's cabin. The men were wild. They had found silver. They had recognized small fragments in their drill cores and had excavated in the area for larger quantities. They placed a half-dozen jagged specimens on the company agent's bench. Tell us it isn't silver, they challenged him. He looked at one piece of silver shaped like a stem of ginger but metallic gray in color with puddles of milky-white quartz. What he saw was a bare summit of rock in sunshine. But the snow in its crevices was too cold to melt. I'll do some tests, he said.

The men sat outside in their drilling mobile and waited for his confirmation that at last their work had produced minerals of great value. There were bonuses to be claimed, fortunes to be made, celebrations, hugging, turbulent reunions with wives and children to anticipate. The company agent turned the snowy summit in his hand and divined its future. And its past. Once the word "silver" was spoken in the company offices, Ibela-hoy could count on chaos: there would be mining engineers, labor camps, a village, roads, bars, drink, soldiers. Bulldozers would push back the soil and roots of silver would be grubbed like truffles from the earth. Dynamite, spoil heaps, scars. And he, the company agent, the man who spilled the beans, would have no time to reconcile the stones, the dreams, the family, the fatigue, the sleeplessness which now had reached its final stage. The turmoil had begun already. He heard the smooth engine of the company jeep as it labored over the final rise before the cabin. He saw the bosses' man climb out with his folder and his suit and pause to talk with the men who waited inside the mobile's cab. Arms were waved and fingers pointed towards the bluffs where silver lay in wait.

I'll put it back, he said.

By the time the bosses' man had walked into the cabin with a string of false and reassuring greetings on his lips, the company agent had pocketed the half-dozen pieces of silver and had slipped away into the rocks behind the cabin. He climbed as high as was possible without breaking cover and crouched in a gully. He toyed with the stones on the ground, turning them in his palms, and waited for night. He watched as the bosses' man ran from the cabin and the survey gang jumped from their mobile and searched the landscape for the agent. He watched as they showed the bosses' man where he had buried the waste heap, the world misplaced. He watched as the gang brought picks and shovels and, insensitive to topsoils and chipped yellow stones, dug into the slaughterhouse. He watched the bosses' man crouch and shake his head as he sorted through the debris for the gold, the agate, the topaz which the men promised had been buried, hidden there. It was, they said, a matter for the madhouse or the militia. They'd watched the agent for a month or two. He had hugged boulders. He had hidden gemstones, their gemstones, company gemstones, throughout the valley. They'd seen him walking, crouching, placing gemstones in the shade of rocks, in the mouth of caves, under leaves.

A bare summit of rock in sunshine was the location of his dream. There were crevices of unbroken snow and pats of spongy moss. He was naked. There were no clothes. He squatted on his haunches and chipped at flints. Someone had caught a hare—but nobody yet knew how to make fire, so its meat was ripped apart and eaten raw. They washed it down with snow. The carcass was left where it fell. The two boys played with twigs. The baby stood on crescent legs and tugged at grass. He and the woman delved in the softer earth for roots to eat and found silver, a plaything for the boys. He conjured in his dream a world where the rocks were hot and moving, where quakes and volcanoes turned shales to schists, granite to gneiss, limestone to marble, sandstone to quartz, where continents sank and rose like kelp on the tide.

When it was light, he unwrapped himself from the embrace of the boulder where he had passed the night and began to traverse the valley towards the high ground and the rocks where snow survived the sun. His aimless walks had made his legs strong, and his mind was soaring with a fever of sleeplessness. He walked and talked, his tongue guiding his feet over the rocks, naming what passed beneath. Molten silicates, he said as his feet cast bouncing shadows over salt-and-pepper rocks. Pumice, he said to the hollows. Grass.

In two hours the company agent had reached the ridge where the winds seemed to dip and dive and hug the earth. He turned to the south and, looking down into the valley, he saw the men and the trucks at his cabin and the twist of smoke as breakfast was prepared. Bring my wife and children, he said. And one man, standing at the hut with a hot drink resting on the hood of the air-conditioned jeep, saw him calling there and waved his arms. Come down, he said. Come back.

But the company agent walked on until he found that the earth had become slippery with ice and the air white like paper. He looked now for gray rocks, metallic gray, and found them at the summit of his walk, his rendezvous. There was no easy path; the boulders were shoulder height and he was forced to squeeze and climb. But his hands were taking hold of crevices fossilized with snow, and soon, at last, he stood upon the landscape that he had sought, glistening, winking gray with puddles of milky-white quartz. He took the six jagged specimens from his pocket. I am standing here, he said, pointing at an ounce of silver. He took the pieces and placed them in a streak of snow where their colors matched the rock and where, two paces distant, they disappeared for good.

In the afternoon he watched the first helicopter as it beat about the hills, its body bulbous ended like a floating bone. And then, close by, he heard the grinding motors of the jeep as it found a route between the rocks and stalled. He heard voices and then someone calling him by his first name. Was it his son? He walked to the edge of his gray platform and looked down on the heads of the bosses' man, a soldier, and two of the survey gang. Climb down, they said. We're going to take you home. A holiday. I have my job to do, he said. Yes, they said, we all have jobs to do. We understand. But it's cold up here and you must be tired and hungry. Climb down and we'll drive you back to the city. No problems. No awkward questions. Your mother's waiting. Just show us what is hidden and you can be with your family.

Bring my family here, he said. Bring my wife and children here. The men looked at each other, and then one of the survey gang spoke. You have no wife and children, he said. You lied. The company agent picked up the largest stone and flung it at the men. It landed on the hood of the jeep and its echo was as metallic, as full of silver, as the gray hill.

Leave him there, they said. Let hunger bring him down.

It was cold that night above Ibela-hoy. But there was warmth in numbers. The company agent and his wife encircled their children, their breath directed inwards, their backs turned against the moon. And in the morning when the sun came up and the colors of the hill and its valley accelerated from gray and brown to red and green to white, the company agent gathered stones for his family and they breakfasted on snow.

Edwidge Danticat

Night Women

(HAITI)

I cringe from the heat of the night on my face. I feel as bare as open flesh. Tonight I am much older than the twenty-five years that I have lived. The night is the time I dread most in my life. Yet if I am to live, I must depend on it.

Shadows shrink and spread over the lace curtain as my son slips into bed. I watch as he stretches from a little boy into the broom-size of a man, his height mounting the innocent fabric that splits our one-room house into two spaces, two mats, two worlds.

For a brief second, I almost mistake him for the ghost of his father, an old lover who disappeared with the night's shadows a long time ago. My son's bed stays nestled against the corner, far from the peeking jalousies. I watch as he digs furrows in the pillow with his head. He shifts his small body carefully so as not to crease his Sunday clothes. He wraps my long blood-red scarf around his neck, the one I wear myself during the day to tempt my suitors. I let him have it at night, so that he always has something of mine when my face is out of sight.

I watch his shadow resting still on the curtain. My eyes are drawn to him, like the stars peeking through the small holes in the roof that none of my suitors will fix for me, because they like to watch a scrap of the sky while lying on their naked backs on my mat.

A firefly buzzes around the room, finding him and not me. Perhaps it is a mosquito that has learned the gift of lighting itself. He always slaps the mosquitoes dead on his face without even waking. In the morning, he will have tiny blood spots on his forehead, as though he had spent the whole night kissing a woman with wide-open flesh wounds on her face.

In his sleep he squirms and groans as though he's already discovered that there is pleasure in touching himself. We have never talked about love. What would he need to know? Love is one of those lessons that you grow to learn, the way one learns that one shoe is made to fit a certain foot, lest it cause discomfort.

There are two kinds of women: day women and night women. I am stuck between the day and night in a golden amber bronze. My eyes are the color of dirt, almost copper if I am standing in the sun. I want to wear my matted tresses in braids as soon as I learn to do my whole head without numbing my arms.

Most nights, I hear a slight whisper. My body freezes as I wonder how long it would take for him to cross the curtain and find me.

He says, "Mommy."

I say, *"Darling."*

Somehow in the night, he always calls me in whispers. I hear the buzz of his transistor radio. It is shaped like a can of cola. One of my suitors gave it to him to plug into his ears so he can stay asleep while Mommy *works*.

There is a place in Ville Rose where ghost women ride the crests of waves while brushing the stars out of their hair. There they woo strollers and leave the stars on the path for them. There are nights that I believe that those ghost women are with me. As much as I know that there are women who sit up through the night and undo patches of cloth that they have spent the whole day weaving. These women, they destroy their toil so that they will always have more to do. And as long as there's work, they will not have to lie next to the lifeless soul of a man whose scent still lingers in another woman's bed.

The way my son reacts to my lips stroking his cheeks decides for me if he's asleep. He is like a butterfly fluttering on a rock that stands out naked in the middle of a stream. Sometimes I see in the folds of his eyes a longing for something that's bigger than myself. We are like faraway lovers, lying to one another, under different moons.

When my smallest finger caresses the narrow cleft beneath his nose, sometimes his tongue slips out of his mouth and he licks my fingernail. He moans and turns away, perhaps thinking that this too is a part of the dream.

I whisper my mountain stories in his ear, stories of the ghost women and the stars in their hair. I tell him of the deadly snakes lying at one end of a rainbow and the hat full of gold lying at the other end. I tell him that if I cross a stream of glass-clear hibiscus, I can make myself a goddess. I blow on his long eyelashes to see if he's truly asleep. My fingers coil themselves into visions of birds on his nose. I want him to forget that we live in a place where nothing lasts.

I know that sometimes he wonders why I take such painstaking care. Why do I draw half-moons on my sweaty forehead and spread crimson powders on the rise of my cheeks. We put on his ruffled Sunday suit and I tell him that we are expecting a sweet angel and where angels tread the hosts must be as beautiful as floating hibiscus.

In his sleep, his fingers tug his shirt ruffles loose. He licks his lips from the last piece of sugar candy stolen from my purse.

No more, no more, or your teeth will turn black. I have forgotten to make him brush the mint leaves against his teeth. He does not know that one day a woman like his mother may judge him by the whiteness of his teeth.

It doesn't take long before he is snoring softly. I listen for the shy laughter of his most pleasant dreams. Dreams of angels skipping over his head and occasionally resting their pink heels on his nose.

I hear him humming a song. One of the madrigals they still teach children on very hot afternoons in public schools. *Kompè Jako, domé vou?* Brother Jacques, are you asleep?

The hibiscus rustle in the night outside. I sing along to help him sink deeper into his sleep. I apply another layer of the Egyptian rouge to my cheeks. There are some sparkles in the powder, which make it easier for my visitor to find me in the dark.

Emmanuel will come tonight. He is a doctor who likes big buttocks on women, but my small ones will do. He comes on Tuesdays and Saturdays. He arrives bearing flowers as though he's come to court me. Tonight he brings me bougainvillea. It is always a surprise.

"How is your wife?" I ask.

"Not as beautiful as you."

On Mondays and Thursdays, it is an accordion player named Alexandre. He likes to make the sound of the accordion with his mouth in my ear. The rest of the night, he spends with his breadfruit head rocking on my belly button.

Should my son wake up, I have prepared my fabrication. One day, he will grow too old to be told that a wandering man is a mirage and that naked flesh is a dream. I will tell him that his father has come, that an angel brought him back from Heaven for a while.

The stars slowly slip away from the hole in the roof as the doctor sinks deeper and deeper beneath my body. He throbs and pants. I cover his mouth to keep him from screaming. I see his wife's face in the beads of sweat marching down his chin. He leaves with his body soaking from the dew of our flesh. He calls me an avalanche, a waterfall, when he is satisfied.

After he leaves at dawn, I sit outside and smoke a dry tobacco leaf. I watch the piece-worker women march one another to the open market half a day's walk from where they live. I thank the stars that at least I have the days to myself.

When I walk back into the house, I hear the rise and fall of my son's breath. Quickly, I lean my face against his lips to feel the calming heat from his mouth.

"Mommy, have I missed the angels again?" he whispers softly while reaching for my neck.

I slip into the bed next to him and rock him back to sleep.

"Darling, the angels have themselves a lifetime to come to us."

Lydia Davis
The House Behind

(UNITED STATES)

We live in the house behind and can't see the street: our back windows face the gray stone of the city wall and our front windows look across the courtyard into the kitchens and bathrooms of the front house. The apartments inside the front house are lofty and comfortable, while ours are cramped and graceless. In the front house, maids live in the neat little rooms on the top floor and look out upon the spires of St-Etienne, but under the eaves of our house, tiny cubicles open in darkness onto a dusty corridor and the students and poor bachelors who sleep in them share one toilet by the back stairwell. Many tenants in the front house are high civil servants, while the house behind is filled with shopkeepers, salesmen, retired post-office employees, and unmarried schoolteachers. Naturally, we can't really blame the people in the front house for their wealth, but we are oppressed by it: we feel the difference. Yet this is not enough to explain the ill will that has always existed between the two houses.

I often sit by my front window at dusk, staring up at the sky and listening to the sounds of the people across from me. As the hour passes, the pigeons settle over the dormers, the traffic choking the narrow street beyond thins out, and the televisions in various apartments fill the air with voices and the sounds of violence. Now and again, I hear the lid of a metal trash can clang below me in the courtyard, and I see a shadowy figure carry away an empty plastic pail into one of the houses.

The trash cans were always a source of embarrassment, but now the atmosphere has sharpened: the tenants from the house in front are afraid to empty their trash. They will not enter the courtyard if another tenant is already there. I see them silhouetted in the doorway of the front hall as they wait. When there is no one in the courtyard, they empty their pails and walk quickly back across the cobblestones, anxious not to be caught there alone. Some of the old women from the house in front go down together, in pairs.

The murder took place nearly a year ago. It was curiously gratuitous. The murderer was a respected married man from our building and the murdered woman was one of the few kind people in the front house; in fact, one of the few who would associate with the people of the house behind. M. Martin had no real reason to kill her. I can only think that he was maddened by frustration: for years he had wanted to live in the house in front, and it was becoming clear to him that he never would.

It was dusk. Shutters were closing. I was sitting by my window. I saw the two of them meet in the courtyard by the trash cans. It was probably something she said to him, something perfectly innocent and friendly yet which made him realize once again just how different he was from her and from everyone else in the front house. She never should have spoken to him—most of them don't speak to us.

He had just emptied his pail when she came out. There was something so graceful about her that although she was carrying a garbage pail, she looked regal. I suppose he noticed how even her pail—of the same ordinary yellow plastic as his—was brighter, and how the garbage inside was more vivid than his. He must have noticed, too, how fresh and clean her dress was, how it wafted gently around her strong and healthy legs, how sweet the smell was that rose from it, and how luminous her skin was in the fading daylight, how her eyes glimmered with the constant slightly frenetic look of happiness that she wore, and how her light hair glinted with silver and swelled under its pins. He had stooped over his pail and was scraping the inside of it with a blunt hunting knife when she came out, gliding over the cobblestones toward him.

It was so dark by then that only the whiteness of her dress would have been clearly visible to him at first. He remained silent—for, scrupulously polite, he was never the first to speak to a person from the front house—and quickly turned his eyes away from her. But not quickly enough, for she answered his look and spoke.

She probably said something casual about how soft the evening was. If she hadn't spoken, his fury might not have been unleashed by the gentle sound of her voice. But in that instant he must have realized that for him the evening could never be as soft as it was for her. Or else something in her tone—something too kind, something just condescending enough to make him see that he was doomed to remain where he was—pushed him out of control. He straightened like a shot, as though something in him had snapped, and in one motion drove his knife into her throat.

I saw it all from above. It happened very quickly and quietly. I did not do anything. For a while I did not even realize what I had seen: life is so uneventful back here that I have almost lost the ability to react. But there was also something arresting in the sight of it: he was a strong and well-made man, an experienced hunter, and she was as slight and graceful as a doe. His gesture was a classically beautiful one; and she slumped down onto the cobblestones as quietly as a mist melting away from the surface of a pond. Even when I was able to think, I did not do anything.

As I watched, several people came to the back door of the house in front and the front door of our own house and stopped short with their garbage pails when they saw her lying there and him standing motionless above her. His pail stood empty at his feet, scraped clean, the handle of her pail was still clenched in her hand, and her garbage had spilled over the stones beside her, which was, strangely, almost as shocking to us as the murder itself. More and more tenants gathered and watched from the doorways. Their lips were moving, but I could not hear them over the noise of the televisions on all sides of me.

I think the reason no one did anything right away was that the murder had taken place in a sort of no-man's-land. It if had happened in our house or in theirs, action would have been taken—slowly in our house, briskly in theirs. But, as it was, people were in doubt: those from the house in front hesitated to lower themselves so far as to get involved in this, and those from our house hesitated to presume so far. In the end it was the concierge who dealt with it. The body was removed by the coroner and M. Martin left with the police. After the crowd had dispersed, the concierge swept up the spilled garbage, washed down the cobblestones, and returned each pail to the apartment where it belonged.

For a day or two, the people of both houses were visibly shaken. Talk was heard in the halls: in our house, voices rose like wind in the trees before a storm; in theirs, rich confident syllables rapped out like machine-gun fire. Encounters between the tenants of the two houses were more violent: people from our house jerked away from the others, if we met them in the street, and something in our faces cut short their conversations when we came within earshot.

But then the halls grew quiet again, and for a while it seemed as though little had changed. Perhaps this incident had been so far beyond our understanding that it could not affect us, I thought. The only difference seemed to be a certain blank look on the faces of the people in my building, as though they had gone into shock. But gradually I began to realize that the incident had left a deeper impression. Mistrust filled the air, and uneasiness. The people of the house in front were afraid of us here behind, now, and there was no communication between us at all. By killing the woman from the house in front, M. Martin had killed something more: we lost the last traces of our self-respect before the people from the house in front, because we all assumed responsibility for the crime. Now there was no point in pretending any longer. Some, it is true, were unaffected and continued to wear the rags of their dignity proudly. But most of the people in the house behind changed.

A night nurse lived across the landing from me. Every morning when she came home from work, I would wake to hear her heavy iron key ring clatter against the wooden door of her apartment, her keys rattle in the keyholes. Late in the afternoon she would come out again and shuffle around the landing on little cloth pads, dusting the banisters. Now she sat behind her door listening to the radio and coughing gently. The older Lamartine sister, who used to keep her door open a crack and listen to conversations going on in the hallway—occasionally becoming so excited that she stuck her sharp nose in the crack and threw out a comment or two—was now no longer seen at all except on Sundays, when she went out to early-morning Mass with a blue veil thrown over her head. My neighbor on the second floor, Mme Bac, left her laundry out for days, in all weathers, until the sour smell of it rose to me where I sat. Many tenants no longer cleaned their doormats. People were ashamed of their clothes, and wore raincoats when they went out. A musty odor filled the hallways: delivery boys and insurance salesmen groped their way up and down the stairs looking uncomfortable. Worst of all, everyone became surly and mean: we stopped speaking to one another, told tales to outsiders, and left mud on each other's landings.

Curiously enough, many pairs of houses in the city suffer from bad relations like ours: there is usually an uneasy truce between the two houses until some incident explodes the situation and it begins deteriorating. The people in the front houses become locked in their cold dignity and the people in the back houses lose confidence, their faces gray with shame.

Recently I caught myself on the point of throwing an apple core down into the courtyard, and I realized how much I had already fallen under the influence of the house behind. My windowpanes are dim and fine curlicues of dust line the edges of the baseboards. If I don't leave now, I will soon be incapable of making the effort. I must lease an apartment in another section of the city and pack up my things.

I know that when I go to say goodbye to my neighbors, with whom I once got along quite well, some will not open their doors and others will look at me as though they do not know me. But there will be a few who manage to summon up enough of their old spirit of defiance and aggressive pride to shake my hand and wish me luck.

The hopeless look in their eyes will make me feel ashamed of leaving. But there is no way I can help them. In any case, I suspect that after some years things will return to normal. Habit will cause the people here behind to resume their shabby tidiness, their caustic morning gossip against the people from the house in front, their thrift in small purchases, their decency where no risk is involved—and as the people in both houses move away and are replaced by strangers, the whole affair will slowly be absorbed and forgotten. The only victims, in the end, will be M. Martin's wife, M. Martin himself, and the gentle woman M. Martin killed.

Daniele del Giudice

All Because of the Mistake

(ITALY)

There is neither a precise moment nor an agreed day, no forewarning conveyed by any external sign, by any alteration in behavior or change in the surrounding landscape, no visible deviation from humdrum routine—the sun striking across the runway, the runway stretching towards the sea—nothing whatsoever to give any indication that, for you, that moment has arrived when, as in the blackest of nightmares, you find yourself in an airplane without passengers, without pilots, without any living being apart from yourself. There is no ban on talking aloud, no one will even notice if you sing or if you break into a sweat, you may turn to your right and stare at the place normally filled by your instructor, you may consider that emptiness the most painful of all representations of the absolute void or as the most poignant of all sensations of abandonment. You are, of course, at liberty to haul back the levers, switch off the propeller, open the doors, undo the safety belts, climb out waving your arms over your head, and leave it to someone else to come and move the plane you are abandoning where it stands, lined up at the beginning of the runway for your first solo takeoff. An immensely wise decision, perhaps even an honorable decision, but do you dare make such a decision? Your instructor is outside the hangar, looking on with no less perplexity, with no less concern than you are showing yourself; you are familiar with the mannerisms of flying instructors, with that way they have of gazing at the sky which makes them one with soothsayers, meteorologists and worried fathers: inside the airfield, all traffic has been suspended for your first solo takeoff; however early it may be and however deserted the surroundings seem, there is always a vast, unsuspected audience for anyone about to cut a pathetic figure.

So there you are, whatever instinct or pain or malformation of the unconscious may have led you to believe yourself capable of facing such a situation, there you are with your feet desperately jammed on the brakes to stop the plane making up its mind for you, and taxiing down the runway by itself, presumably for its own first solo takeoff; at this point, turning back would be more complicated than carrying on, so, having made the most detailed arrangements to box yourself in, you can once more delude yourself that you have no choice, and that now, at the very last minute, tense and silent, your only wish is to see how it will all end, to go through with it, to make for the far point on the runway, for that moment of disequilibrium which, as you lift your shadow from the earth, accompanies the ascent and the climb into the skies.

A matter of moments ago, arms imperturbably folded, a flying instructor had been seated at your side as your shield against all responsibility for error (the God Error) or accident; a matter of moments ago the day was unremarkable and unpredictable, and you ache to return to that moment, or even to the one preceding it, to the moment of heedless tranquility on the apron as you carried out routine checks, moving round the aircraft as though it were freshly delivered from the factory and you were its first inspector, whereas you were no more than an apprentice pilot on a plane meticulously checked by mechanics that day, every day: you would gladly return to the time when you sat in the cockpit fingering the instruments, ticking off items from a checklist you knew by heart, following a daily liturgy, reciting prayers from a manual of "All OK," waiting for that very last moment when, as was his wont, your instructor, one of those people who never had time to dally, would finally clamber aboard and allow the engine to be started up. Bruno was not simply a captain, he was an Indian chief, an old-style Indian chief of few words and fewer explanations. Bruno was a teacher who disdained explanations, and how this was possible in matters of such delicacy will be explained later on. For Bruno, it was an article of faith that the concept of maneuver entailed absolute discipline and rigor, but his concern was with intuition; a correctly executed maneuver was less than nothing, scarcely the bare minimum, as he did not exactly say but certainly made you understand; flying was more than the nicely executed maneuver. He never explained, he behaved as though you were already aware and what you did not know, that is everything, you were left to pick up from the silence of his eyes and expressions, from his way of bringing you up short during maneuvers with swift, wordless gestures of a finger pointed towards instruments or stabbing outwards towards the far horizon or towards some invisible checkpoint in the skies; this for him was learning. Never, ever would this man have hinted that the time for your solo flight had come. Like everyone else, you prayed that it came between the sixth and eighth hour of dual-control training, otherwise, of this you were certain, it would never come at all.

Finally Bruno had climbed on board and you had begun to wait: to wait for him to place those schoolmasterly spectacles over his nose and to transcribe the initial data relating to the flight, to wait for that wave of the hand which meant switch on the engine and let's go, to wait for clearance from the tower to begin taxying, and then, once parked at the end of the runway, clearance for lineup and takeoff. Waiting was as much part of flight as flying itself, waiting, checking and double-checking; there is always some worthwhile means of filling in waiting time, there is always something on board to be attended to in the final moments before you push the lever and bounce slowly forward, and, thinking it over now, you should have seen to it then. When the cosmic order of things, or the concatenation of events or the sheer force of coincidence had finally arranged themselves for liftoff, there you were applying power, releasing the brakes, staring at the rev counter and the anemometer, using the ped-

als to control the aircraft's right-left yawing movements. The run-up to takeoff
is a metamorphosis: here is a pile of metal transforming itself into an airplane
by the power of the air itself, each takeoff is the birth of an aircraft, this time
like all the others you had had the same experience, the same wonder at each
metamorphosis. Towards the end of the metamorphosis and of the runway,
you feel the airplane surging upwards, no longer a creature of earth; too many
leaps, too much yawing this way and that, you can no longer keep it on earth,
better fly than race like this, your part is simply to wait for it to become an airplane, to wish that the transformation had already occurred; at that point, it
sometimes rises up under its own force, calming itself as it rises, at other times
it needs just a gentle, very gentle invitation from the control column. You had
issued the invitation with delicacy, the merest millimeter so as not to wrench
the plane roughly from earth, then you had casually pulled one more time, as
though repeating a word spoken too low and unheard. You pulled gently but
the plane did not respond. You gave a longer pull but the plane declined to
follow you. You pulled firmly but still the plane did not lift off. You had looked
out onto the runway and realized that you were more than halfway down its
length, you saw the strip of sea beyond the mouth of the harbor, look at how
it's rushing towards you, no, look at the dashboard and the dials, concentrate!
and you went over the instruments one by one, as though pleading with each
of them to side with you in some street brawl, and they did, everything was
all right, but still the aircraft refused to leave the ground. Without turning
around, you sought out Bruno's profile, a profile carved in stone, arms crossed,
gaze unflinching, as though waiting: but there was nothing to wait for, the runway was ending, the aircraft was not lifting and you no longer had sufficient
room to brake. Concentrate yet more intensely, stare at the instrument panel,
stare harder, and by the sheer effort of staring you finally spot it: that's what
was wrong, how could you have missed it? The flaps had not been released,
the flap lever was still up, flap maneuver zero, you had forgotten the flaps.
There must be some forty meters of runway remaining, not a centimeter
more, then the sea; you had endeavored to slip your hand from the engine
control to the flaps without Bruno noticing, you had desperately struggled to
lower that lever, the end of the runway perilously close, your left hand still
clutching the column, the right almost furtively giving the lever a sharp blow.
Such was the accumulated speed that the moment the flaps began to descend
from the trailing edge of the wings, the plane was sucked up, seized bodily,
raised from the earth as though liberated, wrenched up above the embankment at the end of the runway, above the harbor mouth, above the bay and out
over the sea.

Bruno's silence had immediately appeared to you a matter of concern; better say something. You had said, *We* forgot the flaps, in an offhand tone, with
an ironic plural which implicated him in the oversight, even though he would
never have forgotten the flaps; you were at the controls and it was entirely
your responsibility, as well you knew. Bruno made no answer and you continued your ascent while waiting for further orders. After takeoff he would announce the flight plan, the items which might feature on today's menu: stalls

and spins? sharp turns? navigation? engine trouble? radar approach to an airport? But Bruno uttered not a word, nothing, not the merest glance; he did no more than make a wide circular gesture with one hand, a downward, spiralling movement which conveyed a swerve over the sea, a rapid return to the island, an immediate landing. The gesture's abruptness suggested that for you the landing would be definitive and permanent. So that was the plan.

The fear of a short time previously, the fear of the runway coming to an end, was as nothing compared to the desolation of the present, when even your soul seemed to be blushing; had it been possible, you would have got out there and then, in midair, leaving him to take charge of the airplane; your next hope was to make at least a dignified farewell with a good landing, or more precisely a perfect landing, the sort of masterpiece of a landing that would have shown him what you were capable of; but on the final approach, over the trees which seem inexplicably to ring every airfield, you ran into a spot of turbulence: slight shudder of the airplane, immediate correction, landing on one wheel, bounce, land again, further bounce, land. You made straight for the hangar, you simply wanted to get there as quickly as possible, but just as you were turning onto the taxiway, you had felt a resistance on the pedals; I can't even turn on land, you said to yourself, when it occurred to you that Bruno had his foot on the pedal on his side and was making the plane pull up at the side of the runway. What was wrong now? You had cut the revs so low that the propeller was barely turning. Bruno had given you a rapid glance, then looking at you more squarely had said, How do you feel about going up on your own?

Don't pretend, you understood perfectly, the whole thing happened only a few moments ago; of course you understood perfectly, but had to run the entire gamut of emotions before regaining your balance, and even then you needed another pause before getting sufficient grip on yourself not to appear too delighted or too smug. You were then able to reply, Yes, if you're sure, why not? Bruno switched on the radio, asked the tower to suspend the traffic over the airfield, explained the reason why. Then he turned to you and said, You do know it's going to be a bit different, it will take off more quickly, climb much faster. I'll be standing here at the edge of the airfield, make all your calls to me as though you were talking to the tower. He gave you a last look as though you were an item on the final checklist, taking in what was showing on your face, the controls, the fastened safety belts, the cockpit. He even stopped as he climbed down to check that the door was properly closed.

On your own, here you are on your own, the solo pilot, as it will be recorded in the aeronautical registers. The word "solo" makes you sound like a violinist, when all you are is a person on your own inside an airplane in the middle of a runway, now speaking into the radio and communicating that you are lined up ready for takeoff, even if you still can't quite believe it yourself; lined up you undoubtedly are, but whether you are ready is another matter. Bruno replies "cleared" and reminds you of wind strengths, wind patterns and directions, but who's going to have time to think about the wind, to figure out where it's coming from and how strong it might be? In a moment or two there may be time, once you have pushed forward the levers and started to lift the soles of your feet from the pedals, then there may be time. The plane moves, quarter way down the runway you ask yourself why on earth Bruno ever decided to let you do it instead of kicking you out for good, halfway down you begin to feel tremors of something called responsibility, even if you are not clear whose, then gradually as the machine transforms itself into an airplane, you too transform yourself into Bruno and assume command of yourself, and in this new dimension you pull yourself together, check yourself and correct yourself as though you were a schoolboy. There are things to do, and these cancel out every other thought, and only after doing the things that needed doing, after closing the things that needed to be closed, opening the things that needed to be opened and regulating the things that needed to be regulated, only now that the plane has levelled out in the sky can you, in the light morning mist, look out over the sea and the horizon and see them for the first time not merely as reference points for checking turns, ascents and descents but as a landscape to which from now on you could belong, just as on earth you belong to the rivers and mountains.

You glide along the coast in a fantasy of immobility and timelessness, on the right the island, on the left the sea, you glide along thinking of the first time you made the ascent with Bruno, the first time, the orientation and test flight, preceding even the medical examination, you flew without putting a hand on the controls, seated on the right, relishing the panorama as Bruno soared calmly into the skies, at one point turning to you and asking if your seat belt was fastened properly, you had replied yes, offhandedly, and he pulled out his glasses, bent over a metal plate in the middle of the instrument panel where a notice in English indicated the aerobatic capability of the plane and, without lifting his hand from the control column, ran his fingers over the embossed lettering: no more than three spins, he read aloud, as though he did not already know that plane through and through, or as though it were essential for you to be made aware that after the third spin it was curtains; then, without a word, he had removed his glasses and sent the airplane careering into a nosedive, spinning as it went, without warning every part of you was pitched forward as you both plunged downwards still seated, the plane rotating on its axis, while down below the shoreline and the beach spun crazily round as they did in films, three spins he had said, but you seemed to have done thirty or three hundred already, I'm going to die with this man I don't know; but how were you to know then that Bruno was Bruno, that he had been an aerobatic pilot and a test pilot and that in the postwar years he had earned his living doing pirouettes at air shows, or that he had notched up thirty thousand flying hours on every type of plane. You prayed to God that this white-haired gentleman knew what he was about and that he had the skills to match, that the airplane would not disintegrate, that the dizzying, spinning plunge would stop at once.

It was no better the second time when, without more ado, he made you sit on the left, in the pilot's seat, no less! Out of the vast array of instruments, dials and electronic odds and ends that make up a control panel, he explained no more than the indispensable minimum before telling you to take off and head straight for the open sea. It was a grey, overcast day, and when that dense greyness had become one all-enveloping, impenetrable, hypnotic mass, Bruno turned to you quite suddenly with the words, Let's go back, where's the airfield? You glanced over your shoulder to look through the windows at the rear, but the view behind was the same as the view ahead, grey and more grey as far as the eye could see, with not a speck of land in sight, nothing which was in any respect distinguishable from that terrifying, flat, blinding calm. You in your turn asked, Yes, exactly, where is the airfield? Bruno shrugged his shoulders. You're in charge, he said, it's up to you to know these things and get us home. To start with, you swung to the left, purely out of intuition, for then you knew next to nothing about compasses or back courses, and all those position-finding instruments were a closed book to you. Guided by nothing more than a memory of the space and an instinctive orientation, you turned left and left again, and when it seemed you had gone far enough you straightened up. You turned to Bruno in the hope of some sign of assent or dissent, but were rewarded with another shrug. You ploughed on in the greyness, leaning forward against the windscreen so as to see better, to guess the lie of a coast, but there was no trace of any coastline; you peered in every direction but nowhere was there any sign of land until, in the all-encompassing greyness, a greyer, finer and more distant line appeared; it was the coast, but what coast, and at which point? Well done, you had sighted land, but the airfield was not there, nor was the city nor even the lagoon. You were too far to the south. When the coast took on the feel of a real landscape, Bruno gave directions with the gestures of a camel driver. In future, he said, when you take off remember to make a note of the position, if you intend going back, that is.

Bruno's voice on the radio now asks you to come in to land; the first solo landing is, of necessity, the reverse of the first solo takeoff, and God help you if it were otherwise! Bruno's voice on the radio always has a touch of uncertainty and concern, as once you had occasion to notice in the control tower, listening in with an operator. Bruno sidles cautiously up to words as though coming from somewhere he prefers not to name, giving the impression that words are the last resort when all alternatives have failed. On this occasion, the tone is deeper and the worry greater, perhaps because the trees at the bottom of the runway block his sight of you, and from the ground he asks your position in strict aeronautical jargon, and immediately afterwards asks in everyday language if everything is OK, and you give the position in aeronautical jargon and reply yes, everything's fine. And finally, while you go through the downwind checks, while you remove the antifreeze and enrich the mixture and cut back on engine speed and set the flaps at ten degrees, finally it occurs to you that the first takeoff is the meeting of two fears—yours and his, the mutual, shared fears of two people obliged to face the one event with only partial knowledge. What does Bruno know about you? Nothing at all. Mere intuition. Has he ever witnessed your hysterical scenes? Your moments of total abstraction? Has he ever seen you experience those moments of rapture, when you lose yourself in a void and leave behind your body like yesterday's newspaper to fill a spot you have vacated? Or those moments of ice-cold, bitter, deaf rage or pure hatred—those forces of evil to which you would so happily give vent? And what would Bruno say if he knew that leaving the airfield in the evening and walking home, you enjoyed keeping time to ditties of your own composition, like:

> *The night has arrived*
> *The planes are asleep*
> *The tower is dark*
> *The fax makes a bleep*

If you were in Bruno's shoes, would you entrust a plane to a man like that? What can have made him believe you were up to it, what does Bruno know about you? Only what he may have deduced from a very limited area, such as piloting a plane, an aptitude and activity which can, admittedly, be subject to scrutiny, but for the rest, for all the other things about a person, the things that matter and would matter more than anything else in those crucial moments of midair emergency, he can only go by intuition and deduction from those acts, those few acts he has seen you carry out; this is the risk he is running, what if there were engine trouble right now? An engine has no way of knowing who is at the controls, chance never takes circumstances or a pilot's experience into consideration. The other person, who just happens to be you, ought to have adequate self-knowledge, or at least that's the hope, but who can say if he really has that grasp of aeronautics, that pilot's know-how which at this moment of his life, on his first solo landing, now seem to him so crucial, and it's here that your greatest risk lies. As the final turn to the left brings the city into view, with the island on the right and the airfield straight ahead, speak into the radio, call on final, flaps out, landing gear down, landing lights. There's Bruno, a tiny figure standing on the grass border of the runway, looking upwards, walkie-talkie clasped to ear, That's just fine, he murmurs, just fine, you repeat to yourself, checking distance and trim. You are sitting on an accumulated inheritance of speed and height waiting to be dissipated and run down, the descent is the richest moment of flight (the body is the prime gauge of this wasting bonanza, of this wealth dispersed in descent and free fall, of the pure joy of refound weight and gravity), drop the nose of the aircraft, let it go, let yourself go, come down in a gentle glide over the trees, if you were not so tense and concentrated you would notice the shadow projected ahead of you by the sun at your back and could watch it expand on the grass and touch down a few moments ahead of you, your shadow has landed, your plane following it down, let yourself go, place the central wheels on the grass and for a moment keep the aircraft suspended in that position, a moment later the nosewheel touches down, leaving you only to brake, gradually, decisively, to brake until the thing carrying you, on which you are seated, slows down and ceases to be an airplane.

All that's left is to make your way to the hangar, *taxi to park*, the last maneuver cleared by Bruno over the radio before handing you over to the control tower, now that the airfield has reopened for traffic; it may be simply a clearance to backtrack off the runway, but in your mind it is a clearance of vast import, the first step in an enterprise just beginning and which could be ended only by some terminal event, an overriding clearance bringing with it many small, accompanying clearances, like the clearance to receive less severe treatment from the mechanic standing there, crossed forearms aloft—the sign for flight terminated, engines off, complete stop—at the end of the yellow line you are meticulously following with the nosewheel.

(If there existed some compartment of the memory reserved for first times, you think as you check that everything is switched off, you would place first takeoff alongside first lovemaking, for the intensity of the two is identical, however curious it may seem that for you the first and most overwhelming fusion with another human being should be put on the same level as the first and most total loneliness of all—the utter solitude of the solo pilot.)

And, when you climb out of the cockpit, there can be numbered among the innovations that distant hint, if not exactly of a smile at least of a less glowering expression from Bruno, accompanied by a new informality of address that betokens friendship, but an informality which in no way reduces the distance between the two of you, quite the reverse, and which does not alter his general demeanor, even if later in his office—if "office" is the right word for a forties desk, a rack of aeronautical maps, a rocking chair and a monitor showing a cloud-covered Italy as seen at this moment from a meteorological satellite—this tentative informality will permit you, while that instructor himself, dressed in his unvarying captain's uniform of dark tie over white shirt, sits down to put his signature to your first solo takeoff, to take advantage of this newfound confidentiality and ask why today precisely, why this morning of all mornings when you had just forgotten the flaps and came near to ending up in the sea; and will permit him, with a rapid, puzzled glance, to reply to you—Why today? plainly incredulous that you have not grasped. The mistake, because of the mistake, you saw the mistake yourself. The tone is offhand, whispered, as though he were repeating something obvious and, more importantly, secret. When else? he concludes, handing you back your logbook.

As soon as you are outside, you stop in the slanting light of the morning and leaf through the pages, searching out the handwriting, the signature which definitively enrolls you in the halls of celestial error, where each error is a scar, but not one which will ward off further relapses.

Translated from the Italian by Joseph Farrell

Junot Díaz

Ysrael

(DOMINICAN REPUBLIC)

1.

We were on our way to the colmado for an errand, a beer for my tío, when Rafa stood still and tilted his head, as if listening to a message I couldn't hear, something beamed in from afar. We were close to the colmado; you could hear the music and the gentle clop of drunken voices. I was nine that summer, but my brother was twelve, and he was the one who wanted to see Ysrael, who looked out towards Barbacoa and said, We should pay that kid a visit.

2.

Mami shipped me and Rafa out to the campo every summer. She worked long hours at the chocolate factory and didn't have the time or the energy to look after us during the months school was out. Rafa and I stayed with our tíos, in a small wooden house just outside Ocoa; rose bushes blazed around the yard like compass points and the mango trees spread out deep blankets of shade where we could rest and play dominos, but the campo was nothing like our barrio in Santo Domingo. In the campo there was nothing to do, no one to see. You didn't get television or electricity and Rafa, who was older and expected more, woke up every morning pissy and dissatisfied. He stood out on the patio in his shorts and looked out over the mountains, at the mists that gathered like water, at the brucal trees that blazed like fires on the mountain. This, he said, is shit.

Worse than shit, I said.

Yeah, he said, and when I get home, I'm going to go crazy—chinga all my girls and then chinga everyone else's. I won't stop dancing either. I'm going to be like those guys in the record books who dance four or five days straight.

Tío Miguel had chores for us (mostly we chopped wood for the smoke-house and brought water up from the river) but we finished these as easy as we threw off our shirts, the rest of the day punching us in the face. We caught jaivas in the streams and spent hours walking across the valley to see girls who were never there; we set traps for jurones we never caught and toughened up our roosters with pails of cold water. We worked hard at keeping busy.

I didn't mind these summers, wouldn't forget them the way Rafa would.

Back home in the Capital, Rafa had his own friends, a bunch of tígueres who liked to knock down our neighbors and who scrawled chocha and toto on walls and curbs. Back in the Capital he rarely said anything to me except Shut up, pendejo. Unless, of course, he was mad and then he had about five hundred routines he liked to lay on me. Most of them had to do with my complexion, my hair, the size of my lips. It's the Haitian, he'd say to his buddies. Hey Señor Haitian, Mami found you on the border and only took you in because she felt sorry for you.

If I was stupid enough to mouth off to him—about the hair that was growing on his back or the time the tip of his pinga had swollen to the size of a lemon—he pounded the hell out of me and then I would run as far as I could. In the Capital Rafa and I fought so much that our neighbors took to smashing broomsticks over us to break it up, but in the campo it wasn't like that. In the campo we were friends.

The summer I was nine, Rafa shot whole afternoons talking about whatever chica he was getting with—not that the campo girls gave up ass like the girls back in the Capital but kissing them, he told me, was pretty much the same. He'd take the campo girls down to the dams to swim and if he was lucky they let him put it in their mouth or in their asses. He'd done La Muda that way for almost a month before her parents heard about it and barred her from leaving the house forever.

He wore the same outfit when he went to see these girls, a shirt and pants that my father had sent him from the States last Christmas. I always followed Rafa, trying to convince him to let me tag along.

Go home, he'd say. I'll be back in a few hours.

I'll walk you.

I don't need you to walk me anywhere. Just wait for me.

If I kept on he'd punch me in the shoulder and walk on until what was left of him was the color of his shirt filling in the spaces between the leaves. Something inside of me would sag like a sail. I would yell his name and he'd hurry on, the ferns and branches and flower pods trembling in his wake.

Later, while we were in bed listening to the rats on the zinc roof he might tell me what he'd done. I'd hear about tetas and chochas and leche and he'd talk without looking over at me. There was a girl he'd gone to see, half-Haitian but he ended up with her sister. Another who believed she wouldn't get pregnant if she drank a Coca-Cola afterwards. And one who was pregnant and didn't give a damn about anything. His hands were behind his head and his feet were crossed at the ankles. He was handsome and spoke out of the corner of his mouth. I was too young to understand most of what he said, but I listened to him anyway, in case these things might be useful in the future.

3.

Ysrael was a different story. Even on this side of Ocoa people had heard of him, how when he was a baby a pig had eaten his face off, skinned it like an orange. He was something to talk about, a name that set the kids to screaming, worse than el Cuco or la Vieja Calusa.

I'd seen Ysrael my first time the year before, right after the dams were finished. I was in town, farting around, when a single-prop plane swept in across the sky. A door opened on the fuselage and a man began to kick out tall bundles that exploded into thousands of leaflets as soon as the wind got to them. They came down as slow as butterfly blossoms and were posters of wrestlers, not politicians, and that's when us kids started shouting at each other. Usually the planes only covered Ocoa, but if extras had been printed the nearby towns would also get leaflets, especially if the match or the election was a big one. The paper would cling to the trees for weeks.

I spotted Ysrael in an alley, stooping over a stack of leaflets that had not come undone from its thin cord. He was wearing his mask.

What are you doing? I said.

What do you think I'm doing?

He picked up the bundle and ran down the alley, away from me. Some other boys saw him and wheeled around, howling but, coño, could he run.

That's Ysrael! I was told. He's ugly and he's got a cousin around here but we don't like him either. And that face of his would make you sick!

I told my brother later when I got home and he sat up in his bed. Could you see under the mask?

Not really.

That's something we got to check out. I hear it's bad.

The night before we went to look for him my brother couldn't sleep. He kicked at the mosquito netting and I could hear the mesh tearing just a little. My tío was yukking it up with his buddies in the yard. One of tío's roosters had won big the day before and he was thinking of taking it to the Capital.

People around here don't bet worth a damn, he was saying. Your average campesino only bets big when he feels lucky and how many of them feel lucky?

You're feeling lucky right now.

You're damn right about that. That's why I have to find myself some big spenders.

I wonder how much of Ysrael's face is gone, Rafa said.

He has his eyes.

That's a lot, he assured me. You'd think eyes would be the first thing a pig would go for. Eyes are soft. And salty.

How do you know that?

I licked one, he said.

Maybe his ears.

And his nose. Anything that sticks out.

Everyone had a different opinion on the damage. Tío said it wasn't bad but the father was very sensitive about anyone taunting his oldest son, which explained the mask. Tía said that if we were to look on his face we would be sad for the rest of our lives. That's why the poor boy's mother spends her day in church. I had never been sad more than a few hours and the thought of that sensation lasting a lifetime scared the hell out of me. My brother kept pinching my face during the night, like I was a mango. The cheeks, he said. And the chin. But the forehead would be a lot harder. The skin's tight.

All right, I said. Ya.

The next morning the roosters were screaming. Rafa dumped the ponchera in the weeds and then collected our shoes from the patio, careful not to step on the pile of cacao beans Tía had set out to dry. Rafa went into the smokehouse and emerged with his knife and two oranges. He peeled them and handed me mine. When we heard Tía coughing in the house, we started on our way. I kept expecting Rafa to send me home and the longer he went without speaking, the more excited I became. Twice I put my hands over my mouth to stop from laughing. We went slow, grabbing saplings and fenceposts to keep from tumbling down the rough brambled slope. Smoke was rising from the fields that had been burned the night before, and the trees that had not exploded or collapsed stood in the black ash like spears. At the bottom of the hill we followed the road that would take us to Ocoa. I was carrying the two Coca-Cola empties Tío had hidden in the chicken coop.

We joined two women, our neighbors, who were waiting by the colmado on their way to mass.

I put the bottles on the counter. Chicho folded up yesterday's *El Nacional*. When he put fresh Cokes next to the empties, I said, We want the refund.

Chicho put his elbows on the counter and looked me over. Are you supposed to be doing that?

Yes, I said.

You better be giving this money back to your tío, he said. I stared at the pastelitos and chicharrón he kept under a fly-specked glass. He slapped the coins onto the counter. I'm going to stay out of this, he said. What you do with this money is your own concern. I'm just a businessman.

How much of this do we need? I asked Rafa.

All of it.

Can't we buy something to eat?

Save it for a drink. You'll be real thirsty later.

Maybe we should eat.

Don't be stupid.

How about if I just bought us some gum?

Give me that money, he said.

OK, I said. I was just asking.

Then stop. Rafa was looking up the road, distracted; I knew that expression better than anyone. He was scheming. Every now and then he glanced over at the two women, who were conversing loudly, their arms crossed over their big chests. When the first autobus trundled to a stop and the women got on, Rafa watched their asses bucking under their dresses. The cobrado leaned out from the passenger door and said, Well? And Rafa said, Beat it, baldie.

What are we waiting for? I said. That one had air conditioning.

I want a younger cobrador, Rafa said, still looking down the road. I went to the counter and tapped my finger on the glass case. Chicho handed me a pastelito and after putting it in my pocket, I slid him a coin. Business is business, Chicho announced but my brother didn't bother to look. He was flagging down the next autobus.

Get to the back, Rafa said. He framed himself in the main door, his toes out in the air, his hands curled up on the top lip of the door. He stood next to the cobrador, who was a year or two younger than he was. This boy tried to get Rafa to sit down but Rafa shook his head with that not-a-chance grin of his and before there could be an argument the driver shifted into gear, blasting the radio. *La chica de la novela* was still on the charts. Can you believe that? the man next to me said. They play that vaina a hundred times a day.

I lowered myself stiffly into my seat but the pastelito had already put a grease stain on my pants. Coño, I said and took out the pastelito and finished it in four bites. Rafa wasn't watching. Each time the autobus stopped he was hopping down and helping people bring on their packages. When a row filled he lowered the swing-down center seat for whoever was next. The cobrador, a thin boy with an Afro, was trying to keep up with him and the driver was too busy with his radio to notice what was happening. Two people paid Rafa—all of which Rafa gave to the cobrador, who was himself busy making change.

You have to watch out for stains like that, the man next to me said. He had big teeth and wore a clean fedora. His arms were ropy with muscles.

These things are too greasy, I said.

Let me help. He spit in his fingers and started to rub at the stain but then he was pinching at the tip of my pinga through the fabric of my shorts. He was smiling. I shoved him against his seat. He looked to see if anybody had noticed.

You pato, I said.

The man kept smiling.

You low-down pinga-sucking pato, I said. The man squeezed my bicep, quietly, hard, the way my friends would sneak me in church. I whimpered.

You should watch your mouth, he said.

I got up and went over to the door. Rafa slapped the roof and as the driver slowed the cobrador said, You two haven't paid.

Sure we did, Rafa said, pushing me down into the dusty street. I gave you the money for those two people there and I gave you our fare too. His voice was tired, as if he got into these discussions all the time.

No you didn't.

Fuck you I did. You got the fares. Why don't you count and see?

Don't even try it. The cobrador put his hands on Rafa but Rafa wasn't having it. He yelled up to the driver, Tell your boy to learn how to count.

We crossed the road and went down into a field of guineo; the cobrado was shouting after us and we stayed in the field until we heard the driver say, Forget them.

Rafa took off his shirt and fanned himself and that's when I started to cry.

He watched for a moment. You, he said, are a pussy.

I'm sorry.

What the hell's the matter with you? We didn't do anything wrong.

I'll be OK in a second. I sawed my forearm across my nose.

He took a look around, drawing in the lay of the land. If you can't stop crying, I'll leave you. He headed towards a shack that was rusting in the sun.

I watched him disappear. From the shack you could hear voices, as bright as chrome. Columns of ants had found a pile of meatless chicken bones at my feet and were industriously carting away the crumbling marrow. I could have gone home, which was what I usually did when Rafa acted up, but we were far—eight, nine miles away.

I caught up with him beyond the shack. We walked about a mile; my head felt cold and hollow.

Are you done?

Yes, I said.

Are you always going to be a pussy?

I wouldn't have raised my head if God himself had appeared in the sky and pissed down on us.

Rafa spit. You have to get tougher. Crying all the time. Do you think our papi's crying? Do you think that's what he's been doing the last six years? He turned from me. His feet were crackling through the weeds, breaking stems.

Rafa stopped a schoolboy in a blue and tan uniform, who pointed us down a road. Rafa spoke to a young mother, whose baby was hacking like a miner. A little further, she said and when he smiled she looked the other way. We went too far and a farmer with a machete showed us the easiest loop back. Rafa stopped when he saw Ysrael standing in the center of a field; he was flying a kite and despite the string he seemed almost unconnected to the distant wedge of black that finned back and forth in the sky. Here we go, Rafa said. I was embarrassed. What the hell were we supposed to do?

Stay close, he said. And get ready to run. He passed me his knife, then trotted down towards the field.

4.

The summer before I pegged Ysrael with a rock and the way it bounced off his back I knew I'd clocked a shoulder blade.

You did it! You fucking did it! the other boys yelled.

He'd been running from us and he arched in pain and one of the other boys nearly caught him but he recovered and took off. He's faster than a mongoose, someone said, but in truth he was even faster than that. We laughed and went back to our baseball games and forgot him until he came to town again and then we dropped what we were doing and chased him. Show us your face, we cried. Let's see it just once.

5.

He was about a foot bigger than either of us and looked like he'd been fattened on that supergrain the farmers around Ocoa were giving their stock, a new product which kept my tío up at night, muttering jealously, Proxyl Feed 9, Proxyl Feed 9. Ysrael's sandals were of stiff leather and his clothes were North American. I looked over at Rafa but my brother seemed unperturbed.

Listen up, Rafa said. My hermanito's not feeling too well. Can you show us where a colmado is? I want to get him a drink.

There's a faucet up the road, Ysrael said. His voice was odd and full of spit. His mask was handsewn from thin blue cotton fabric and you couldn't help but see the scar tissue that circled his left eye, a red waxy crescent, and the saliva that trickled down his neck.

We're not from around here. We can't drink the water.

Ysrael spooled in his string. The kite wheeled but he righted it with a yank.

Not bad, I said.

We can't drink the water around here. It would kill us. And he's already sick.

I smiled and tried to act sick, which wasn't too difficult. I was covered with dust and I saw Ysrael looking us over.

The water here is probably better than up in the mountains, he said.

Help us out, Rafa said in a low voice.

Ysrael pointed down a path. Just go that way, you'll find it.

Are you sure?

I've lived here all my life.

I could hear the plastic kite flapping in the wind; the string was coming in fast. Rafa huffed and started on his way. We made a long circle and by then Ysrael had his kite in hand—the kite was no handmade local job. It had been manufactured abroad.

We couldn't find it, Rafa said.

How stupid are you?

Where did you get that? I asked.

Nueva York, he said. From my father.

No shit! Our father's there too! I shouted.

I looked at Rafa, who, for an instant, frowned. Our father only sent us letters and an occasional shirt or pair of jeans at Christmas.

What the hell are you wearing that mask for anyway? Rafa asked.

I'm sick, Ysrael said.

It must be real hot.

Not for me.

Don't you take it off?

Not until I get better. I'm going to have an operation soon.

You better watch out for that, Rafa said. Those doctors will kill you faster than the guardia.

These are American doctors.

Rafa sniggered. You're lying.

I saw them last spring. They want me to go next year.

They're lying to you. They probably just felt sorry.

Do you want me to show you where the colmado is or not?

Sure.

Follow me, he said, wiping the spit on his neck. At the colmado he stood off while Rafa bought me the Cola. The owner was playing dominos with the beer delivery man and didn't bother to look up, though he put a hand in the air for Ysrael. He had that lean look of every colmado owner I'd ever met. On the way back to the road I left the bottle with Rafa to finish and caught up with Ysrael, who was ahead of us. Are you still into wrestling? I asked.

He turned to me and something rippled under the mask. How did you know that?

I heard, I said. Do they have wrestling in the States?

I hope so.

Are you a wrestler?

I'm a great wrestler. I almost went to fight in the Capital.

My brother laughed, swigging on the bottle.

You want to try it, pendejo?

Not right now.

I didn't think so.

I tapped his arm. The planes haven't dropped anything this year.

It's still too early. The first Sunday of August is when it starts.

How do you know?

I'm from around here, he said. The mask twitched. I realized he was smiling and then my brother brought his arm around and smashed the bottle on top of his head. It exploded, the thick bottom spinning away like a crazed eyeglass and I said, Holy fucking shit. Ysrael stumbled once and slammed into a fencepost that had been sunk into the side of the road. Glass crumbled off his mask. He spun towards me, then fell down on his stomach. Rafa kicked him in the side. Ysrael seemed not to notice. He had his hands flat in the dirt and was concentrating on pushing himself up. Roll him on his back, my brother said and we did, pushing like crazy. Rafa took off his mask and threw it spinning into the grass.

His left ear was a nub and you could see the thick veined slab of his tongue through a hole in his cheek. He had no lips. His head was tipped back and his eyes had gone white and the cords were out on his neck. He'd been an infant when the pig had come into the house. The damage looked old but I still jumped back and said, Rafa, let's go! Rafa crouched and using only two of his fingers, turned Ysrael's head from side to side.

6.

We went back to the colmado where the owner and the delivery man were now arguing, the dominos chattering under their hands. We kept walking and after one hour, maybe two, we saw an autobus. We boarded and went right to the back. Rafa crossed his arms and watched the fields and roadside shacks scroll past, the dust and smoke and people almost frozen by our speed.

Ysrael will be OK, I said.

Don't bet on it.

They're going to fix him.

A muscle fluttered between his jaw bone and his ear. Yunior, he said tiredly. They aren't going to do shit to him.

How do you know?

I know, he said.

I put my feet on the back of the chair in front of me, pushing on an old lady, who looked back at me. She was wearing a baseball cap and one of her eyes was milky. The autobus was heading for Ocoa, not for home.

Rafa signaled for a stop. Get ready to run, he whispered.

I said, OK.

Patricia Duncker

Betrayal

(ENGLAND)

Hélène held a dinner party to which she invited all her ex-lovers. Her most recent ex-lovers. I was the only person there who hadn't been to bed with her. Unfortunately, I was late. Thus, when I arrived, there were three faces shimmering with jealousy, arranged around the table. The post of Hélène's lover, usually occupied by at least two women who were never allowed to meet, theoretically out of respect for both but in fact to avoid broken crockery and nasty scenes, was currently held on short-term renewable contract by a ravishingly beautiful ballet dancer with supple encircling arms and a back like a concrete curtain wall. She was hindering Hélène's cooking by administering torrents of kisses. The three other women watched, furious.

"Hello everyone," I cried, realizing that the only lover I knew was the ballet dancer.

I tried to create an amiable diversion. I was the only person not close to an outburst of hysterical murderousness. I unloaded my box. I was carrying alcohol, oranges and eggs. All the different colours looked charming on the table. Everyone smiled and clapped. The tension ebbed.

"Do you know Louise?" accused one of the jealous faces as the ballet dancer coiled herself around me.

"Oh yes, we've met," I said cautiously.

"Today is my birthday. I can do anything," cried Louise and involved herself sexually with casseroles and cooking pots.

I sat down to look at the row of ex-lovers. One was very fat, one was very thin and one was very small. I decided that I was under an obligation to become an ex-lover as I am very tall, in order to complete the row. They were all creative, interesting women, their faces twisted with jealousy. Louise made love to the herrings, then we got two each, bristling with butter and parsley. Hélène enjoyed every moment of our discomfort.

"And how is Anna?" asked one of the ex-lovers, suddenly turning very nasty as we melted our square sugars in tiny cups. Anna is the most beautiful woman I have ever seen. Anna is Hélène's other lover. Anna has tenure in the post.

"Ah . . . *ça va*," said Hélène uneasily. Louise rumbled like Etna. All the ex-

lovers looked pleased. Hélène and I looked at each other shiftily, like suspected conspirators.

The ex-lovers pushed off at midnight. I discovered that they were all staying together like the three musketeers. Louise was dancing in front of the mirror in the bathroom. Hélène and I smoked at the bottom of the garden. Her
city seems unlighted in the night; the only spotlit monument is the cathedral, a
massive red-brick fortress in which the local Protestants were massacred. It is
full of famous fifteenth-century sculptures attributed to an Italian master of
Giotto's school. All the women look shifty, with ambiguous eyes. The Mag-
dalens cover their pots, the Virgins pull their robes around them, Judith is
no better than she ought to be. Hélène loves the cathedral. This is entirely
suitable.

We watched the red turrets burning in the warm night. It was my serve.

"Hélène, I know that this is going to sound silly as you obviously had a sce-
nario of some kind in mind. But why on earth did you invite them all on the
same evening?"

She stared at me resentfully, like a child being bullied. "Chantal did that to
me. Invited all her ex-lovers. And they were all friends. Friends! Can you
imagine? They got on. And I was the only woman there who was a cauldron of
jealousy. I thought I'd explode."

I looked at her. I was about to say something patronizing and brutal about
petty vendettas and revenges that ruined good dinners. But I thought better
of it and smiled wearily. "Let's have a beer," I said.

I have never been in love with Hélène, but I am very fond of her.

Do heterosexual people permit themselves the luxury of breaking up, then
hating each other for ever—with impunity? Do they just vanish into that great
safe sea of other heterosexuals and never see one another again? Martin tells
me that gay men sometimes never know who it is that they have just sucked
off. I said that it must be odd to kiss only cocks, not faces. He said that he liked
the mystery and that cocks were often more honest than faces. And then
again, I do know gay men, Martin among them, who have devastating love affairs, every bit as horrendous as our own, and storm out of rooms, smashing
glasses against potted plants. I have seen poets pinned against radiators, facing
accusations of infamy which revealed the Tolstoyan dimensions of the ac-
cuser's imagination. Or perhaps the astonishing sexual talents of the accused.
Jealousy magnifies, distorts, like a fairground mirror. It turns the lover and the
beloved into monsters.

With us it is not possible to run away from the past. Your ex-lover is your
present lover's ex-lover but one, which is when she was with you. And if you
try to escape the enchanted castle by advertisements in another area you'll
find that the woman who replies was lovers with your first lover after she was
married and before she came out for real this time and hasn't she changed?
The silk twist that binds us is unbreakable, invisible, eternal. It is like God's
love: theoretical, ever-present and stifling. We meet what is actually just one of

the facts of life in small communities with a barrage of ideologies—lesbian ethics, significant friendship and political continuity. Sometimes this works. As it did with Chantal's ex-lovers who all but formed a collective. More often it is simply a veil for resentment, insecurity, violence and hypocrisy. Real feeling, brutal but honest, is channelled into decent behaviour in a fashion worthy of an English village church flower committee. Mind you, I'm not an enemy of decent behaviour and when I lived in an English village one of those nice tight-curled, blue-rinsed old ladies drove one of the others on the flower rota to a nervous breakdown. I told my mother all about it. "Oh yes," she said, "they're all lesbians."

Well, Hélène and Louise got up and went off to work the next morning. Not particularly early. I heard them making love in a welter of shrieks and cries. It sounded fun. I stroked the cat. She's an interesting cat. Multicoloured, and she dreams. God knows what about. Sometimes in the night she turns circles at the bottom of the bed, spitting and growling. Hélène told me that one rare night when she was sleeping alone she took the harlequin cat to bed with her. In the grip of a nightmare the cat bit her ear and she had to have an anti-tetanus injection. "How did you do that?" asked the doctor. "My cat bit me in her dreams," said Hélène and the doctor went away shaking his head. "You could put an earring through it," I suggested.

I walked round the town. It was quiet, sunny and free of tourists. The British and the Dutch arrive in July. By the time they get this far south they've already caught the sun. The British have become pink shrimps with densely packed freckles. The Dutch are a magnificent toasted brown. The British have thermos flasks and are carrying melted plastic sacs of freezing fluid in their picnic boxes. The Dutch wear anti-nuclear T-shirts and new trainers. I watch them going into their hotels. This time of year the terrace under the cathedral is empty. So I sat down with a coffee, my blue note book and a sense of well-being. I was still writing when Hélène's Mercedes cruised round the corner.

Hélène is not rich. She inherited a bit of money last year, but she spent that on a laser photocopier and a new computer. She's always had the Mercedes. It's one of those 1968 models with fins, leather seats and a walnut dashboard. She loves it so much that I always say it's her other lover. The third lover, who is never in danger of becoming her ex-lover. She's put in seat belts, even at the back, and she has a mechanic who loves it as much as she does. Early in the spring she got all the rust done and gave it a respray. It's the original colour now—luxurious, strokeable cream.

"Get in quick," said Hélène, "we'll pick up Louise."

"Where are we going?"

"The Conquistadora. You wanted to see everyone, didn't you?"

"Hélène. Do you know what you're doing?"

"Of course I do. It's all arranged."

Anna runs the Conquistadora. With her ex-lover. The one before Hélène. Mine not to reason why. I felt like declaring that she could certainly do as she liked, but that I was just an ordinary person who poured acid on her verrucas every morning.

So we drove away across hills, past fields rampant with poppies, banks over-flowing with wild daisies. The corn was rising fast in the May days. I cheered up as the Mercedes cruised over the hills like Aladdin's carpet. Sunk in leather and cushions, my feet on wool mats, it was like driving along in a private club. The sun laid little warm kisses all along my arm. Louise was doing the same thing to Hélène. Nobody had premonitions of disaster.

It's always exciting arriving in cities. Even the obligatory ten kilometres of horror, half-made roads, dank canals and pink-brick high-rise blocks were in-teresting. I looked around, enjoying the mixture of flash investment and de-crepitude. The Conquistadora is a discreet private club in a back street. It's surprisingly light inside. They don't have a licence to sell hard liquor, but they do beer, coffee and cocktails. They serve food. The cook is Spanish and she's called Maria. Her food is worth fighting for and so is she. Anna says that Maria is courted with flowers every evening, by the woman she had chatted to the night before. She's employed to be nice to everyone. So everyone is in love with her. I once asked for her photograph. She gave me one from a stash she keeps under the bar. We were early. So only Maria and Anna's ex-lover were there. Both of them were cleaning glasses and smiling at each other.

I bought everyone a drink. Anna and her ex-lover are on Weight Watchers, so they only drink Vittel. Nobody here believes in learning to love their natural body weight. The dominant ideology, as seen on TV, says that we all have to be as thin as pencils; so we are. And if you aren't, you join Weight Watchers and diet. We were all pleasantly relaxed and the bar began to fill up at dusk. Then Anna walked in.

A woman who is brazen enough to hold an exclusively ex-lovers dinner party should not flinch when her two current lovers, both of whom are quite aware of the situation and who the other one is, actually, finally, eventually meet. Anna knew it wasn't me, so it had to be the other one. The tall one with the back like an engineering construction and the arms like fluid tentacles. Anna kissed me. Hélène slunk into a corner. Louise looked into her drink.

Anna is very, very beautiful. You'd think she's older than she is. She has black hair, cut like an Italian page boy, and wonderful brown eyes. She's the sort of woman who poisons your wine if you don't make love well, but covers you in roses if you do. She's tireless, dynamic, organized. Other women grow in her soil as if she were pure fertilizer. She stays close friends with all her ex-lovers.

"Well," she said, smiling at Hélène, "aren't you going to introduce me?"

Hélène hid guiltily under a table. And so it was I who introduced Anna to Louise. They kissed each other very cautiously, three times, one cheek after the other. Then they stepped back. Anna smiled. I told you, didn't I. Anna is the most beautiful woman I know. Louise thought so too. I could tell that she did. They liked each other. That was dreadful, it really was adding irony to in-jury. And so the evening began.

In some ways it went well. Maria's food was spicy and peculiar. Anna's ex-lover was pleased with the situation, played soft music and was charming to her customers. All our friends came up to join us. We sat at a large table, argued about politics, the war, books, moaned about money and unemployment, gossiped about the past. We ordered more wine. Christelle came in at around ten o'clock. I abandoned my self-appointed post as amiable distraction to talk to her, just us, at another table.

"How's it going?" I asked her.

"Oh, fine. Really fine. I'm just starting my third year at the hospital and I'm off on a *stage* next Monday. Paediatrics. A hospital in the Pyrénées. Just three weeks. I'm looking forward to it. *Ça va me changer mes idées.* I've had a bit of a problem. No, not with Isabelle. She's not a lesbian, you know. She's straight. But she's still my best friend. Well yes, at the beginning she had all the usual prejudices. She actually said that she couldn't stand lesbians. So I said, well, do you like me, *parce que moi, je suis comme ça.* I know it's taking a risk. But it worked. She was really shaken. She realized that she was quite wrong about women like us. And she didn't drop me. She started asking questions. We came here once. She really liked it. She liked the way that the women were all dressed up. And that we chatted about ordinary things. Funny, isn't it, the ideas people have. She did have a boyfriend, but it wasn't going too well with him. He wanted it all his own way; so she packed it in and told him to push off. Then suddenly, when I was round at her house, her parents—it was her mother at first—started in on me. Really nasty. Saying how I wasn't welcome there as I wasn't the kind of person they wanted to have around. But nothing explicit. Well, I went away at once and I wouldn't go into the house again. I just sound the horn at the gate and Isabelle comes out. I asked her what on earth had gone wrong as her parents had always been so sweet to me before. God, they've known me since the *sixième.* I've always been her best friend. And she said that she'd tackled her dad and he'd said that he wasn't born yesterday and he could see that I was *comme ça* and he didn't want his daughter being led astray by women like that. Is it written all over my face? Or my clothes? Do I look like a lesbian? What does a lesbian look like? We all look different, don't we? Was it that I didn't talk about boyfriends? Or bring one round? *Merde,* I had to tell Isabelle straight out. She's my very best friend and she hadn't noticed. So what's so special about her parents? My parents know. They accept it. But I wouldn't want my mother to hear people criticizing me in the street. Or getting phone calls. It's all caused problems for Isabelle. She won't drop me. She's too loyal. I know, I thought that too. And it's because of that honesty and courage that she's still my best friend. Even if she is straight. But she's quarrelled with her parents and she's very upset."

"Did her boyfriend know that you were a lesbian?" I asked.

She look astonished.

"Yes, he did. He must have done. I think Isabelle told him."

"Look no further than the ex-lover," I said.

Sometimes we betray each other unforgivably, giving away kingdoms, selling the pass to the enemy for a lot less than thirty pieces of silver. But sometimes we betray each other in tiny ways. Over very ordinary things.

All was not well within the eternal triangle. Anna had noticed something which she did not like. It was eleven o'clock and the room was full of smoke. The meal was over and tempers were bottoming out. The bar was overladen with women, leaning inwards like chickens over their millet dispenser. Someone chose very loud music. Louise got up to go to the loo and Anna immediately asked Hélène to step outside. A deadly hush, worthy of the moment when the saloon door swings open and the gunslinger walks in, descended over our table. But some little part of us was excited and delighted. We all turned white as daisies. Louise came out of the loo and saw at once that Anna, who had been looking dangerous, had gone. Nor was there any sign of Hélène.

"Let's dance," cried Louise, seizing my arm with her double-jointed tentacle. That was the signal, I suppose. The room suddenly erupted with pure joy. We waltzed, we tangoed, we smooched. We even did a Russian dance, bobbing about on our buttocks, flinging our legs out with maniacal enthusiasm. We menaced the floor-boards, thumping out splintering rhythms. The entire café-restaurant joined us. Someone starting taking photographs. Someone mean bought two rounds of drinks and paid for them with a 500 franc note. Anna's ex-lover sellotaped it to the bar mirror as a trophy. We yelled for more wine. I must have given myself a hernia. Louise danced with every woman in the house, bewitching them all with her strength and grace. We clapped. We cheered. We wanted more. We were all young and in love. We didn't notice when Anna came back into the bar, her face silent and blank.

Exuberance subsided into stupor at about two o'clock. Louise and I waltzed down the street and stumbled into the glistening creamy Mercedes. Hélène was weeping over the steering wheel. Huge heart-rending sobs pouring over the upholstery.

We put the car into the *lavage* at Intermarché late next morning to wash away the trauma of the night. I stood beside Hélène watching the rainbow dervishes glitter and whirl. We were hollow-eyed, hung over and depressed. It was not a moment to bother with tact.

"So you didn't tell her you were still sleeping with Louise?" I said bluntly.

"How could I?"

"Well, you told her that you were still sleeping with that other woman last year, didn't you?"

"Of course. We have no secrets. It's very important to be utterly honest."

"I see."

"I would have told her."

"But she noticed before you had the chance to do so."

Hélène shrugged remorsefully. "I'm in a dreadful state," she said.

We stood watching her 1968 Mercedes becoming gradually whiter with foam.

A week later Hélène rang me up and said "Hello" in a very shaky voice.

"I've finished with Louise."

"Oh God, was it awful?"

"She shouted and cried and made a scene in the street."

"Did she come round to see you at the house?"

"Yes. Once. And Anna was there."

"Oh my God."

"Anna sat at the bottom of the garden while Louise blacked my eye. It's still yellow round the edges."

"Oh no," I groaned weakly, "she actually hit you."

"And then she came round the next morning to apologize and that was much worse. She sat on my lap for three hours and we both cried ourselves into hysterics. Then Chantal came past on her way to her judo lesson and she started crying too."

"Listen," I said, "don't go anywhere. I'm coming down to see you."

But Hélène's eye recovered its usual sensuous lustre and our community re-established its equilibrium. Louise still wasn't speaking to Hélène; and so we all waited patiently for Louise to get over it and come round. Wounded feelings are a luxury most of us are unable to afford. Pride is never a cheerful longterm companion. You get lonely after a while. But Louise didn't come round. Hélène sent her a little note. Louise sent it back. I sent her a card. Louise rang me up and said that she didn't feel like dancing any more. It's very hard being someone's ex-lover. We all are. But that doesn't make it any easier.

The days were getting colder when I pulled in at the petrol pump by the *lavage*. The boy on the pump looked at me hard, then lit up with instant recognition.

"It was you, wasn't it? Who put the car into the *lavage*. And left all the windows open."

"No. Not me."

But someone with a really nice old Mercedes had done it. Paid for a forty franc wash and had the *mousse* foaming all over the leather seats, hand-stitched cushions and into the shopping bags. She had stood there screaming as the water poured in every pore, into the body of the car. Screaming, but powerless to stop the dancing rainbow whirls.

Only one person in town drove an elderly Mercedes. I walked thoughtfully down the cat food section, peering at cans of Gourmet and Sheba. Suddenly a woman's arm snaked around my waist and I abandoned my trolley in a waltz. Louise took the lead, guiding my steps, her eyes glittering like fencing rapiers. I hugged her and she laughed.

"You did it."

"I never did."

"You're dancing."

She smiled.

Duong Thu Huong
Reflections of Spring

(VIETNAM)

It's not because of that evening. But since then, thoughts of her hadn't left his mind. They would linger for a while, then rush at him like a gust of wind, throwing his thoughts into chaos and disrupting his equanimity, leaving behind vague and anguished longings. That evening, he was returning to Hanoi from a midland province. An economic planner, he was used to these long, tedious trips. Dozing in his seat on the bus, he was awoke by loud clanking sounds coming from the engine. The driver lifted the hood and moaned:

"Can't make it to Hanoi this evening. The radiator is broken . . ."

The passengers got off the bus to walk around and to breathe in the pleasant air of the midland area. Yellow fields ran to the horizon. In the distance, one could see the uneven peaks of dark green hills, like a clique of moss-covered snails resting on a carpet of rice paddies. The yellow of ripe rice was pale in the fading sun, but it flared up in spots, as if still soaked in light. At the edge of the road, the harvested field had a soft pink glow, as gentle as adolescent love. The autumn breeze made him feel light-headed: He was free from projects, reports, criticisms, approvals—all hindrances and distractions. It was an unusual feeling, this clarity. He walked briskly along.

By the side of the road was a row of houses. Their uneven roofs and white walls gave a strong warmth to the landscape. Butted up against each other, the houses were fronted by a mishmash of verandahs in different styles. In the small yards were tree stumps and piles of bricks. Nearby, pigeon coops perched on tree branches. At the base of a mound of shiny yellow straw, smelling of harvest, an old hen led her chicks, cluck-clucking, searching for food. A crude red and green sign announced a bicycle repair shop. In front, a dangling flat wire wobbled with each gust of wind. Bunches of bananas, suspended from hooks, hovered over the heads of diners in the cheap restaurants.

The serenity and melancholic air of the small town enchanted him. He didn't know what he was thinking, but he walked up and down the streets admiring the familiar views, especially the shrubs and poinciana plants behind the houses. The yellow flowers bloomed in the quiet evening.

"Uncle, come in for a drink. We have country rice pies and sticky-rice cakes."

An old woman behind a small glass display case leaned forward to greet her customer. He was a little surprised; it had been a long time since he heard such a natural, friendly greeting from a shopkeeper. He walked in and sat down on a long bench. He didn't know why he had walked in; he wasn't hungry, thirsty or in need of a smoke from the water pipe. But he had a strong intuition he was waiting for something. It was vague yet urgent. His heart beat anxiously. The shopkeeper leisurely poured out a bowl of green tea for her customer. Then she sat back, chewed her betel nut and said nothing. He raised the bowl of tea, took a sip and looked around. A gust of wind whirled some yellow leaves. From a distance, they looked like tiny gold grains that nature had generously scattered.

He had known all of this at one time. They were images from his past, although he wasn't aware of it. He felt increasingly uneasy.

"Grandma, should I make more rice wafers?"

A girl's voice echoed from inside the house. The sound of her voice startled him. He almost got up to rudely peer into the other room. But he restrained himself. The shop owner's granddaughter came out from the back:

"I baked ten more rice wafers, Grandma. There's none left in the basket!"

Seeing him, the girl stepped back cautiously. The old woman opened the bag and took out a bunch of small rice pancakes. "Bake twenty small ones for Grandma. They're easier to sell." The girl answered "yes" in a low voice and leaned over the earthenware basin to blow into the fire. The white ashes flew up, danced in the air and gently landed on her shiny black hair. Her teenage face was smooth and ruddy as a ripe fruit. Her nose was straight and graceful. She had a simple haircut, parted down the middle. He couldn't take his eyes off her; his heart beat excitedly.

"This is it!"

This unspoken sentiment had echoed within him as the girl came out . . . Twenty-three years ago, when he was in the tenth grade and a boarder in a small town, there was a similarly pretty and well-behaved girl. The same earthenware basin and red coals throwing off cinders, the same ruddy cheeks and round wrists . . . but the girl from his memory had a long hollow trace on her forehead. There were the same poinciana flowers and tiny yellow leaves, scattered by gusts of wind, dotting the ground in autumn, when sounds from the radio mixed with rustling from the unharvested rice paddies and the incessant noises of insects—the lazy, forlorn music of a small town.

It was odd how deeply buried these memories were. He was very poor then. Each month, his mother would send him only three *dong* for pocket money and 10 kilograms of rice. But he studied harder than all the other boys in his class, who called him a bookworm. The pretty girl lived next door to the house where he rented his room. She used to lean her arms against the fence and listen to him memorize poems out loud. Her mother was a food vendor; she would squat in front of the earthenware basin to bake rice wafers for her mother. At night, when he studied, she also lit an oil lamp and sat under the carambola tree to do her homework. At 10 o'clock, as his face was still buried in a book, she would hoist a carrying pole onto her shoulder to go get water for her family. She was a good student and never needed his help. Still, she would look at him admiringly as he diagrammed a geometric problem, or as he closed his eyes and recited, smooth as soup, a long poem. By the time she came back with the water, he would be ready for bed. He was so hungry he had to literally tighten his belt. It was then she would bring him a piping hot rice wafer. The two of them didn't say much. Usually, he just smiled:

"What luck, my stomach was growling."

He never bothered to thank her. But they both felt that they needed to see each other, look at each other's faces and talk about nothing. Neither of them dared to ask too deeply about the other. Truth is, there was nothing more to ask . . . Her piping hot wafers; the hollow trace on her forehead; the bright face; the understanding looks when he was homesick, sitting all bunched up during cold, rainy evenings.

He suddenly remembered all these things. All of them. He now understood what he had been waiting for that evening. It had arrived. That beautiful, sweet, distant memory. A memory, buried for more than twenty years, awakened suddenly by a gust of wind.

The young girl, who was fanning the fire, looked up: "Grandma, I've finished ten . . . Give me a hand . . ."

She gave the stack of yellow cakes to the old woman and glanced curiously at the strange customer. He rotated the tea bowl in his hands while staring at her. She became flustered and clumsily swatted a lump of coal to the ground with her fan. She picked it up immediately, threw it back into the basin, then blew on her two fingers to cool them off, her brows knit in a frown.

"Now she looks like a twelve-year-old. The other girl was older, and more pretty," he thought.

Once, he didn't have enough money to buy textbooks. It wasn't clear how she found out. That night, along with the wafers, she also gave him a small envelope. He opened it: inside was a small stack of bills. The notes were so new you could smell the aroma of paper and ink. It was her New Year's money. He sat motionless. It looked like she had been hoarding it for ten months and hadn't touched it. "But what did I do that day?" After graduating, he was preoccupied with taking the university admissions exam. After his acceptance, knowing he was going away, he excitedly took care of the paperwork, merrily said goodbye to everyone, then took a train straight for Hanoi.

"Why didn't I say goodbye to the girl? No, I was about to, but it was getting too close to my departure date. I was rushed by my relatives. And intimidated by such an opportunity . . ."

And after that? A fresh environment; a strange city; life's frantic rhythm made him dizzy; bright lights; streetcars; the first parties where he felt awkward, provincial, out of place; teahouses; the blackboard in the classroom; new girlfriends . . .

"Eat the hot rice wafers, Uncle. It's aromatic in your mouth. In Hanoi, you don't get country treats like this." The old shopkeeper gave him a small rice wafer. Its fluffy surface was speckled with golden sesame seeds—very appetizing. He broke off a small piece and put it in his mouth. It was a taste he had long forgotten about.

"I used to think rice wafers were the most delicious food on earth," he thought. He remembered studying at night, particularly nights when he had to memorize history and biology lessons—two damnable subjects when he was so hungry waiting for her footsteps near the fence that his mouth could taste the deliciously baked rice flour and the fatty sesame seeds . . . that taste and smell . . . and her wet eyes looking at him, as she rested her arms on the windowsill and smiled:

"I knew you were hungry, Brother. I get pretty hungry at night also. Mother told me to go into town tomorrow to buy cassava so we can have something extra to eat at night." The next day she brought him pieces of boiled cassava. At eighteen, eating them, he also thought her boiled cassava was the most delicious food on earth. Once, she gave him cassava wrapped in banana leaves. It was steaming hot. As he yanked his arms back, she grabbed both his hands and the hot cassava. She let go immediately, her eyes wide in astonishment. As for him, he was as dizzy as he had been that one holiday morning, when he had drunk too much sweet wine . . .

"I really did love her back then . . . I really did love . . ." Then why hadn't he gone back to that town to find her? Finished with his studies, he was assigned a job by the government. Then he had to apply for housing. Then he was involved with a female colleague. Life worries. There was a secret agreement, then the marriage license. That was his wife, unattractive yet dogged in her pursuit of his love, who used every trick imaginable to make him yield to the harsh demands of necessity . . . And then what? Children. Problems at work. A promotion. Steps forward and backward. Years spent overseas to get a doctorate degree . . . Everything has to be tabulated.

"Is the wafer good, Uncle?" the old woman asked.

"Very good, Grandmother," he answered. Crumbs fell onto his knees and he brushed them off. The old hen came over, cluck clucking for her chicks to come pick the crumbs.

"Why didn't I look for her? Why did I . . . Well, I had to achieve, at all costs, the planning targets for operative 038 . . . And, to raise my kids, I had to teach to supplement my income. My daughters don't resemble me; they are like their mother, ugly, stuck-up . . . But do I love my wife? Probably not . . . Most likely not. I've never tingled because of that woman like I did years ago waiting for the sounds of the little girl's footsteps. Especially in the afternoon, with everyone gone, when she washed her hair—with her cheeks dripping wet and strands of hair nappy on her temples. As she dried her hair, one hand on the fence, she would smile because she knew I was secretly admiring her . . . As for my wife, there's never any suspense; I never look forward to seeing her, nor feel empty when we're apart. Back then, going home to get rice, how I anticipated seeing the little girl again, even after only a day . . . My wife needed a husband and she found me. As for me . . ."

This thought nearly drove him mad. He stood up abruptly. The girl fanning the fire stared at him, her eyes black as coal, a deep dimple on one cheek.

He paid the old woman and started walking toward the bus. He wanted to return to Hanoi immediately. He wanted to forget these thoughts . . .

But the bus wasn't fixed until 2 in the morning. They returned to Hanoi by dawn. He returned to his daily life, to his daily business and worries . . . The thoughts of the little girl never left him. They would circle back like the hands on a watch.

"Why didn't I go find her back then? I surely would have had a different wife. And who knows . . ." The little girl is thirty-eight now, but to him she's still fifteen. She is his true love, but why do people only find out these things twenty years later? He flicked the cigarette ashes into the fancy pink ashtray and watched the tiny embers slowly die. On the bed, his wife sleepily raised her head:

"Why are you up so late, dear? Are you admiring me?"

"Yes, yes, I'm admiring you," he answered, squashing the cigarette butt in the ashtray. His wife had just bought an embroidered dress from Thailand and had asked what he thought of it three times already.

"Go to bed, dear."

"I still have work to do."

"I wonder where the little girl is living now? What is she doing? Maybe I can take a bus there tomorrow. No, no, that's not possible." He saw clearly that to walk away silently twenty-three years ago was wrong. How could he possibly go back, when he had dismissed love so easily?

He retrieved the cigarette butt and lit it again. The ember returned to his lips.

A garden full of shades. Carambolas on the ground like fallen stars. And the smell of ripe carambolas. And her wet eyes. Her head tilted as she stood near the fence . . .

"But I was very shy then. I didn't dare to make any vow . . . Stop denying it—it is useless when it comes to love." He knew he had loved her and she had loved him, but he was impatient to get out of there because he was dazzled by his own prospects. During the last hectic days, he did brood over a petty calculation. He did plan to . . . but never realized it.

"It wasn't like that, because . . .

"Sure it was.

"It wasn't like that . . .

"Yes, and you can't be forgiven . . ."

He threw the cigarette butt into the ashtray and flopped into an armchair. The polyester-covered cushions weren't as comfortable as usual. He stood up again, went to the window and pushed the glass panes open.

"It's cold, honey," his wife shrieked.

He didn't turn around, but answered gruffly:

"Then use the blanket."

Many stars lit up the night sky. He suddenly smelled the scent of fresh straw, of harvest. This familiar smell shrouded the neighborhood, a fragrance to stir one's soul. The poinciana flowers bloomed in the evening . . . Everything revived—vague, spurious, yet stark enough to make him bitter. His head was spinning.

He lit a second cigarette and slapped himself on the forehead.

"What is going on?"

There was no answer. Only a rising tremolo of rice stalks and leaves rustling. Again, the swirling sky over the crown of the carambola tree; her smooth, firm arms on the windowsill as she smiled at him. White teeth like two rows of corn. His love had returned, right now, within him. He walked unconsciously to the mirror. His hair had begun to gray. Lines were etched all over his cheeks. Behind the glasses, his eyes had started to become lifeless. He drew deeply on the cigarette then exhaled. The pale blue smoke billowed shapelessly, like the confusions in his life.

His report contained many interesting proposals and was very well received, a complete success. Both his bosses and rivals were equally impressed. He himself didn't know how he had managed to do it. All the endless nights, walking back and forth, watching smoke rise then evaporate, when he had thought of her. She, the object of his true love—a love not shared, not articulated, what does it all add up to? But these soothing, melancholic memories had kept him awake at night, and he had written his report during these late hours, as he tried to recover what had disappeared from his life.

At the conference, people were admiring the exhibits illustrating his proposals. He had succeeded almost completely. Even his enemies were congratulating him. He smiled, shook hands and thanked everybody before slipping out into the hallway. Alone.

His closest colleague ran out to find him. The man looked him in the eye and said:

"The newspaper photographers are waiting for you. What's wrong, Brother? Are you in love?"

"Me, in love?" he chuckled, then snapped, "Me, love?! Are you mad? Me still in love . . . a steel-and-cement man, a . . . and with my hair turning . . ."

He didn't finish his sentence, but rushed out the gate. He walked down a little lane. For some reasons, his eyes were stinging, as if smoke had blown into them. Where's that hamlet, that town? With pigeon coops and piles of straw in the yards. And poinciana flowers blooming in the evening sun. And the windswept rice paddies, with their ripe stalks rustling. And the harvested fields glowing, a soft pink, distant . . .

Translated from the Vietnamese by Nguyen Nguyet Cam and Linh Dinh

Deborah Eisenberg

The Girl Who Left Her Sock on the Floor

(UNITED STATES)

Jessica dangled a sock between her thumb and forefinger, studied it, and let it drop. "There are times," she said, "one wearies of rooming with a pig."

Pig. Francie checked to see what page she was on and slammed *World History* shut. "Why not go over to the nice, clean library?" she said. "You could go to the nice, clean library, and you could think nice, clean thoughts. I'll just root round here in the homework." She pulled her blanket up and turned to the window, her eyes stinging.

Faint, constant crumblings and tricklings . . . Outside, spring was sneaking up under the cradle of snow in the valley, behind the lacy gray air that veiled everything except the girl, identifiable as hardly more than the red dot of her jacket, who was winding up the hill toward the dorm.

Jessica sighed noisily and dumped a stack of clothing into a drawer. "I will get to that stuff, please, Jessica," Francie said, "if you'll just kindly leave it."

Jessica gazed sorrowfully at Francie's ear, then bent down to retrieve a dust-festooned sweatshirt from beneath Francie's bed.

"You know," Francie said, "there are people in the world—not many, but a few—to whom the most important thing is not whether there happens to be a sock on the floor. There are people in the world who are not afraid to face reality, to face the fact that the floor is the natural place for a sock, that the floor is where a sock just naturally goes when it's off. But do we fearless few have a voice? No. No, these are words which must never be spoken—true, Jessica? This is a thought which must never be thought."

It was Cynthia in the red jacket, the secretary, Francie saw now—not one of the students. Cynthia wasn't much older than the seniors, but she lived in town and never came to meals. "Right, Jessica?" Francie said.

There was some little oddness about seeing Cynthia outside the office—as if something were leaking somewhere.

"Jessica?" Francie said. "Oh, well. '*But the poor, saintly girl had gone deaf as a post. The end.*'"

Jessica's voice sliced between Francie and the window. "Look, Francie, I don't want to trivialize your pain or anything, but I'm getting kind of bored over here. Besides which, I am not your personal maid."

"Oink oink," Francie said. "Grunt, grunt. *'Actually, not the end, really, at all, because God performed a miracle, and the beautiful deaf girl could hear again, though everything from that moment on sounded to her as the gruntings of pigs.'*"

"*As* the gruntings of pigs?" Jessica demanded. "Sounded *as* gruntings?"

"Oink oink," Francie said. She opened *World History* to page 359 again. "An Artist's Conception of the Storming of the Bastille." Well, and who were "Editors Clarke & Melton," for that matter, to be in charge of what was going on? To decide which, out of all the things that went on, were *things that had happened?* Yeah. "World History: The Journey of Two Editors and Their Jobs," Why not a picture of people trapped in their snooty boarding school with their snooty roommates? "Anyhow, guess what, next year we both get to pick new roommates."

"If we're both still here," Jessica said. "Besides, that's then—"

"What does *that* mean?" Francie said.

"You don't have to shout at me all the time," Jessica said. "Besides, as I was saying, that's then and this is now. And if I were you, I'd stop calling Mr. Klemper 'Sex Machine.' Sooner or later someone's going to—"

But just then the door opened, and the girl, Cynthia, was standing there in her red jacket. "Frances McIntyre?" Cynthia said. She stared at Francie and Jessica as though she had forgotten which one Francie was. And Francie and Jessica stared back as though they had forgotten, too. "Frances McIntyre, Mrs. Peck wants to see you in the Administration Building."

Jessica watched, flushed and round-eyed, as Francie put on her motorcycle jacket and work boots. "You're going to freeze like that, Francie," Jessica said, and then Cynthia held the door open.

"Francie—" Jessica said. "Francie, do you want me to go with you?"

Francie had paused on the threshold. She didn't turn around, and she couldn't speak. She shook her head.

What had she done? What had been seen or heard or said? Had someone already told Mr. Klemper? Was it cutting lacrosse? Had she been reported smoking again in back of the Science Building? Because if she had she was out. Out. Out. End. The end of her fancy scholarship, the end of her education, the end of her freedom, the end of her future. No, the beginning of a new future, her real future, the one that had been lying in wait for her all along, whose snuffly breathing she could hear in the dark. She'd live out her days as a checkout girl, choking on the toxic vapors of household cleaners and rotting baked goods, trudging home in the cold to rot, herself, in the scornful silence of her bulky, furious mother. Her mother, who had slaved to give ungrateful Francie this squandered opportunity. Her mother, who wouldn't tolerate a sock on the floor for as long as one instant.

Mrs. Peck's bleached blue eyes stared at Francie as Francie stood in front of her, shivering, each second becoming more vividly aware that her jacket, her little, filmy dress, her boots, her new nose ring all trod on the boundaries of the dress code. "Do sit down, please, Frances," Mrs. Peck said.

Mrs. Peck was wearing, of course, a well-made and proudly unflattering suit. On the walls around her were decorative, framed what-were-they-called, Francie thought—Wise Sayings. "I have something very, very sad, I'm afraid, to tell you, Frances," Mrs. Peck began.

Out, she was *out*. Francie's blood howled like a storm at sea; her heart pitched and tossed.

But Mrs. Peck's voice—what Mrs. Peck's voice seemed to be saying, was that Francie's mother was dead.

"What?" Francie said. The howling stopped abruptly, as though a door had been shut. "My mother's in the hospital. My mother broke her hip."

Mrs. Peck bowed her head slightly, over her folded hands. "EVERYTHING MUST BE TAKEN SERIOUSLY, NOTHING TRAGICALLY," the wall announced over her shoulder. "FORTUNE AND HUMOR GOVERN THE WORLD."

"My mother has a broken hip," Francie insisted. "Nobody dies from a broken fucking *hip*."

Mrs. Peck's eyes closed for a moment. "There was an embolism," she said. "Apparently, this is not unheard of. Patients who greatly exceed an ideal weight . . . That is, a Miss Healy called from the hospital. Do you remember Miss Healy? A student nurse, I believe. I understand you met each other when you went to visit your mother several weeks ago. Your mother must have tried to get up sometime during the night. And most probably—" Mrs. Peck frowned at a piece of paper and put on her glasses. "Yes. Most probably, according to Miss Healy, your mother wished to go to the toilet. Evidently, she would have fallen back against her pillow. The staff wouldn't have discovered her death until morning."

Bits of things were falling around Francie. " 'Wouldn't have'?" she plucked from the air.

"This is, of course, a reconstruction," Mrs. Peck said. "Miss Healy came on duty this afternoon. Your mother wasn't there, and Miss Healy became concerned that perhaps no one had thought to notify you. A thoughtful young woman. I had the impression she was acting outside official channels, but . . ."

"But *all's well that ends well*," Francie said.

Mrs. Peck's eyes rested distantly on Francie. "I wonder," she said. "It might be possible, under the terms of your scholarship, to arrange for some therapy when you return." Her gaze wandered up the chattering wall. "A hospital must be a terribly difficult thing to administer," she remarked to it graciously. "I have absolutely no one to bring you to Albany, Frances, I'm afraid. I'll have to call someone in your family to come for you."

Francie gasped. "You can't!" she said.

Mrs. Peck frowned. She appeared to be embarrassed. "Ah," she said, no doubt picturing, Francie thought, some abyss of mortifying circumstances. "In that case . . ." she said. "Yes. I'll have Mr. Klemper cancel French tomorrow, and he—"

"Why can't I take the morning bus?" Francie said. "I've taken that bus a thousand times." She was going red, she knew; one more second and she'd cry. "Don't cancel French," she said. "I always take that bus. *Please.*"

Mrs. Peck's glance strayed up the wall again, and hesitated. "HONI SOIT QUI MAL Y PENSE," Francie read.

Mrs. Peck took off her glasses and rubbed the bridge of her nose. "Miss Healy," she mused. "Such an unsuitable name for a nurse, isn't it. People must often make foolish remarks."

How could it be true? How could Francie be on the bus now, when she should be at school? The sky hadn't changed since yesterday, the trees and fields out the windows hadn't changed; Francie could imagine her mother just as clearly as she'd ever been able to, so how could it be true?

And yet her mother would have been dead while she herself had been asleep, dreaming. Of what? Of what? Of Mr. Davis, probably. Not of her mother, not dreaming of a little wad of blood coalescing like a pearl in her mother's body, preparing to wedge itself into her mother's heart.

If you were to break, for example, your hip, there would be the pain, the proof, telling you all the time it was true: *that's then and this is now.* But this thing—each second it had to be true all over again; she was getting hurled against each second. *Now.* And *now again—thwack!* Maybe one of these seconds she'd smash right through and find herself in the clear place where her mother was alive, scowling, criticizing . . .

Out the window, snow was draining away from the patched fields of the small farms, the small, failing farms. Rusted machinery glowed against the sky in fragile tangles. Her mother would have been dead while Francie got up and took her shower and worried about being late to breakfast and went to biology and then to German and then dozed through English and then ate lunch and then hid in the dorm instead of playing lacrosse and then quarreled with Jessica about a sock. At some moment in the night her mother had gone from being completely alive to being completely dead.

The passengers were scraggy and exhausted-looking, like a committee assigned to the bus aeons earlier to puzzle out just this sort of thing—part of a rotating team whose members were picked up and dropped off at stations looping the planet. How different they were from the team of sleek girls at school, who already knew everything they needed to know. Which team was Francie on? Ha-ha. She glanced at the man across the aisle, who nodded commiseratingly between bites of the vile-smelling food he lifted from a plastic-foam container on his lap.

All those hours during which her life (along with her mother) had gone from being one thing to being another, it had held its shape, like a car window Francie once saw hit by a rock. The rock hit, a web of tiny, glittering lines fanned out, and only a minute or so later had the window tinkled to the street in splinters.

The dazzling, razor-edged splinters had tinkled around Francie yesterday afternoon in Mrs. Peck's voice. "Your family." "Have someone in your family come for you." Well, fine, but where on earth had Mrs. Peck got the idea there *was* anyone in Francie's family?

From Francie's mother, doubtless, the world's leading expert in giving people ideas without having to say a single word. "A proud woman" was an observation people tended to make, vague and flustered after encountering her. But what did that mean, "proud"? Proud of her poverty. Proud of her poor education. Proud of her unfashionable size. Proud of bringing up her Difficult Daughter. Without an Iota of Help. So what was the difference, when you got right down to it, between pride and shame?

Francie had a memory, one of her few from early childhood, that never altered or dimmed, however often it sprang out: herself in the building stairwell with Mrs. Dougherty, making Mrs. Dougherty laugh. She could still feel her feet fly up as her mother grabbed her and pulled her inside, still hear the door slam. She could still see (and yet this was something she could never have seen, really) skinny Mrs. Dougherty cackling alone in the hall. *"How could you embarrass me like that?"* her mother said. The wave of shock and outrage and humiliation engulfed Francie again with each remembering; she felt her mother's fierce grip on her arm. Francie was an embarrassment. What on earth could she have been doing in the hall? An *embarrassment*. Well, *so be it*.

On the day she had brought Francie all the way from Albany to be interviewed at school, Francie's mother—wearing gloves!—had a private conversation with Mrs. Peck. Francie sat in the outer office and waited. Cynthia had been typing demurely, and occasionally other girls would come through— perfect girls, beautiful and beautifully behaved and sly. Francie could just picture their mothers. When she eventually did see some—Jessica's tall, chestnut-haired mother among them—it turned out that her imagination had not exaggerated.

Waiting in the outer office, Francie feared (Francie hoped) she was to be turned ignominiously away. Instead, she was confronted by Mrs. Peck's withering smile of welcome; Mrs. Peck was gluttonous for Francie's test scores. That Francie and her mother looked, each in her own way, so entirely *unsuitable* appeared to increase, rather than diminish, their desirability.

When her mother and Mrs. Peck emerged from the office together that afternoon, a blaze of triumph and contempt crackled behind the veneer of patently suspect humility on her mother's face. Mrs. Peck, on the other hand, looked as if she'd been bonked on the head with a plank.

Surely it was during that conference that Francie's family had been born. Her mother's gift (the automatic nuancing of the unspoken) and Mrs. Peck's mandate (to heap distinction upon herself) had intertwined to generate little tendrils of plausible realities. Which were now generating tendrils of their own: an imaginary church with imaginary relatives—*suitable* relatives— wavering behind viscous organ music and bearing with simple dignity their imaginary grief. Oh, her poor mother! Her poor mother! What possible business was it of Mrs. Peck's *when* her mother had wanted to go to the toilet for the last time?

Several companionable tears made their way down Francie's face, turning from hot to cold. The sensation consoled her as long as it lasted. When she opened her eyes, she saw the frayed outskirts of town.

Francie climbed the stairs cautiously, lest creakings draw the still gregarious Mrs. Dougherty to her peephole. She paused with her key in the lock before contaminating irreversibly the silence, her mother's special silence, which, she thought, a person had to shout to be heard over. Francie leaned her head against the door's cool plane, listening, then turned the key. The lock's tumbling sounded like a gunshot.

A little colorless sunlight had forced its way around the neighboring buildings and lay, exhausted, across the floor. A fine coating of city grime sealed the sills in front of the closed windows like insulation. Her mother's bed was tightly made; the bedspread was as mute as the surface of a lake into which a clue had been dropped long before.

The only disorder in the kitchen was a cup Francie had left in the sink when she'd come to see her mother in the hospital three weeks earlier, still full of dark liquid in which velvety spots had begun to blossom. Francie sat down at the table. The night she'd finally dared to ask her mother what had happened to her father they'd been in here, just finishing the dishes. Francie remembered: her mother was holding a white dish towel; she started to speak.

Too late, then, for Francie to retract the question—a question that had been clogging her mouth ever since the day, years before, when Corkie Patterson had pummeled into her the concept that every single person on earth had a father. As Francie clutched the wet counter her mother spoke of the sound—the terrible fused sound of brakes and the impact—the crowds out the window, which at first hid everything, the siren circling down on their block like a hawk. She did not use the word "blood," but when she finished her story and left the room without so much as a glance for Francie, Francie lifted her dripping fingers and stared at them.

After that, Francie's mother was even more unyielding, as though she were ashamed of her husband's death, or ashamed to have spoken of it. And Francie's father evaporated without a trace. Francie had only cryptic fragments from before that night in the kitchen with which to assemble the story: her parents married at eighteen, she'd figured out. Had they loved each other? The undiminishing vigor of her mother's resentment toward absolutely everything was warming, in its way—there must have been love to produce all that hatred.

The bathroom, too, was clean—spotless, actually, except for a tiny smudge on the mirror. A fingerprint. Hers? Her mother's? She peered past it, into her own face. Had he ever known there was to be a baby? Just think—things that you did went on and on, turning into situations, for example. Into people . . .

As little as Francie knew about him, it would be infinitely more than he could have known about her. There were no pictures, but if she were to subtract her mother's eyes . . . In just a few years, she would see changes in her face that her father had not lived to see in his.

"In a few years!" Bad enough she had to deal with "in a few minutes." *When you return*, Mrs. Peck had said. Well, sure, a person couldn't just stay at school, probably, when her mother died. But what on earth was she supposed to do here?

Her mother would have told her. Francie snatched open a drawer and out flew the fact of her mother's slippery, pinkish heap of underwear. Her mother's toothbrush sat next to the mirror in a glass. In the mirror, past the fingerprint, her mother's eyes lay across her own reflection like a mask.

The hospital floated in the middle of a vast ocean of construction, or maybe it was demolition; a nation in itself, of which all humans were, at every moment, potential citizens. The inevitable false move, and it was wham, onto the gurney, with workers grabbing smocks and gloves to plunge into the cavity of you, and the lights that burned all night. Outside this building you lived as though nothing were happening to you that you didn't know about. But here, there was simply no pretending.

Cynthia had come up the hill, Mrs. Peck had sent Francie home, and now here she was—completely lost; she'd come in the wrong entrance. People passed, in small groups, not touching or speaking. The proliferating corridors and rotundas bloomed with soft noises—chiming, and disembodied announcements, and the muted tapping of canes and rubber shoes and walkers. The ceilings and floors were the same color and had the same brightness; metal winked, signaling between wheelchairs and bedrails. Francie tried to suppress the notion, which had popped up from somewhere like a groundhog, that her mother was still alive, lost here somewhere herself.

Two unfamiliar nurses sat at a desk at the mouth of the wing where Section E, Room 418, was. In their crisp little white hats they appeared to be exempt from error. They looked up as Francie approached, and their faces were blank and tired, as if they knew Francie through and through—as if they knew everything there was to know about this girl in the short, filmy dress and motorcycle jacket and electric-green socks, who was coming toward them with so much difficulty, as if the air were filled with invisible restraints.

But, as it turned out, when Francie tried to explain herself, using (presumably) key, she thought, words, like "Kathryn McIntyre," and "Room 418," and "dead," even then neither of the nurses seemed to understand. "Did you want to speak to a doctor?" one of them said.

A tiny, hot beading of sweat sprang out all over Francie. From the moment she was born people had been happy to tell her what to do, down to the most minute detail; Eds. Clarke & Melton knew just what was happening; there were admonitions and exhortations plastered all over the walls—this is how to behave, this is what to think, this is how to think it, that's then, this is now, this is where to put your sock—but no one had ever said one little thing that would get her through any five given minutes of her life!

She stared at the nurse who had spoken: *Say it*, Francie willed her, but the nurse instead turned her attention to a form attached to a clipboard. "Is Miss Healy around?" Francie asked after a minute.

The fact was, Francie would not have recognized Miss Healy; she'd hardly noticed the broad-faced, slightly clumsy-looking girl who'd been changing the water in a vase of flowers as Francie had listened to her mother describe, with somber gloating, the damage to her body, the shock of finding herself on the ice with her pork chop and canned peaches and so forth strewn around her, the pitiable little trickle of milk she had watched flow from the ruined carton into the filthy slush before she understood that she couldn't move.

"She never complained," Miss Healy was saying, in a melancholy, slightly adenoidal voice. "She was such a pleasant person. You could tell the pain she was in, but she never said a word." Miss Healy directed her mournful recital toward Francie's elbow, as if she were in danger of being derailed by Francie's face. "And when the people from her office brought candy and flowers? She was just so *polite*. Even though you could see those things were not what she wanted."

Oh, great. Who but her mother could get someone to say that her pain was obvious but that she never complained? Who but her mother could get someone to say she was polite even though everyone could tell she didn't want their gifts? No doubt about it, the body they'd carted off almost a day and a half ago from Room 418 had been her mother's—Miss Healy had just laid waste, in her squelchy voice, to *that* last wisp of hope.

"The thing is," Francie said, "what am I supposed to do?"

"To do?" Miss Healy said. Her look of suffering was momentarily whisked away. "I mean, unfortunately, your mother's dead."

"No, I know," Francie said. "I get that part. I just don't know what to *do*."

Miss Healy looked at her. Clearly Francie was turning out to be, unlike her mother, *not a pleasant person*. "Well, you'll want to grieve, of course," Miss Healy said, as if she were remembering a point from a legal document. "Everyone needs closure." She frowned, then unexpectedly addressed, after all, Francie's problem. "I'll call downstairs so you can see her."

Fading smells of bodies clung to the air like plaintive ghosts, their last friendly overtures vanquished by the stronger smells of disinfectants. An indecipherable muttering came from other ghosts, sequestered in a TV suspended from the ceiling. Outside the window huge, predatory machines prowled among mounds of trash.

Miss Healy returned. "Mrs. McIntyre isn't downstairs. I'm really sorry—I guess they've sent her on."

They? On? If only there were someone around to take over. Anyone. Jessica, even. At least Jessica would be able to ask some sensible question. "On . . ." Francie began uncertainly, and Jessica gave her a little shove. "On where?"

"Oh," Miss Healy said. "Well, I mean, does your family use any in particular?"

Francie stared: Where would Jessica even begin with that one?

"Does your family have a particular one they like," Miss Healy explained. "Mortuary."

"It's just me and mother," Francie said.

Miss Healy nodded, as if this confirmed her point. "Uh-huh. So they'd have sent her on to whatever place was specified by the next of kin."

Francie felt Jessica start to giggle. "It's just me and mother," Francie said again.

"Just whoever your mother put down on the AN37-53," Miss Healy said. "Not literally the next of kin necessarily—she couldn't have used you, for instance, because you're a minor. But just, if there's no spouse, people might put down someone at their office, say. Or she might have used that nice friend of hers who came to visit once, Mrs. Dougherty."

Yargh. It wasn't enough that her mother had died—no, they had to toss her out, into that huge, melted mob, *the dead,* who couldn't speak for themselves, who were too indistinguishable to be remembered, who would be used to prove anything, who could be represented any way at all! "My mother *hates* everyone at her office," Francie said. "My mother *hates* Mrs. Dougherty. Mother calls Mrs. Dougherty that buggy Irish slut."

Miss Healy drew back. "Well, I guess your mom wasn't expecting to *die,* exactly, when she filled out that form," she said, and then recovered herself. "There, now. I'll call down again. Even *this* crazy morgue has files, I guess."

Out the window a wrecking ball swung toward a solitary wall. Miss Healy hesitated. She seemed to be waiting for something. "I called that lady at the school," she said. She stood looking at Francie, and Francie realized that she and Miss Healy must be almost the same age. "I just didn't figure there'd be some other way you'd know."

"How did mother get all the way out here?" Francie asked the man who greeted her.

The man's little smile intensified the ruefulness of his expression. "We get a lot of folks out this way," he said. "You might be surprised."

"That's what I meant." Francie said. "I meant I was surprised."

The man jumped slightly, as if Francie had gummed him on the ankle, and then smiled ruefully again. "Serving all faiths," he explained, gesturing at a sign on the wall. *"Serving all faiths,"* Francie read. *"Owned and operated by Luther and Theodore T. Ade. When you're in need, call for Ade."* "Also," the man added, "competitive pricing. But mainly, first in the phone book."

He disappeared behind a door, and Francie jogged from foot to foot to warm herself—it had been a long walk from the last stop on the bus line. She looked around. Not much to see: a counter holding some file folders, a calendar and a mirror on the wall, several chairs, and a round table on which lay a dog-eared copy of *Consumer Reports.* So this was where her mother had got to—nowhere at all.

"Won't be another minute." The man was back in the room. "Teddy T.'s just doing the finishing touches."

Finishing touches? Francie blanched—she'd almost forgotten what this place was. "You're not using lipstick, are you?" she managed to say. "Mother hated it."

The man glanced rapidly at the mirror and then back at Francie.

"Lipstick," Francie said. "On her."

" 'On her . . .' " the man said. As he stared at Francie, the room lost its color and flattened; swarming black dots began to absorb the table and the counter and the mirror. "I'm very sorry if that's what you had in mind, Miss, ah . . ." dots streamed out of the dot man to say. The riffling of file folders amplified into a deafening splash of dots, and then Francie heard, "I'm very, very sorry, because those were definitely not the instructions. I've got the fax right here—from your dad, right? Yup, Mr. McIntyre."

Francie's vision and hearing cleared before her muscles got a grip on themselves. She was on the floor, splayed out, confusingly, as her mother must have been on the ice, and the man was kneeling next to her, holding a glass of water, although, also confusingly, her hair and clothing were drenched—sweat, she noted, amazed.

"O.K. now?" the man asked. Next to him was a cardboard box, about two feet square, tied up with twine.

Francie nodded.

"Happens," the man said, sympathetically.

Francie finished the water slowly and carefully while the man fetched a little wooden handle and affixed it to the twine around the box. Things had gone far beyond misrepresentation now.

"And here's the irony," the man said. "We deliver."

All night long, Francie fell, plummeting through the air. When she finally managed to pry herself awake with the help of the pale wands of light along the blinds, she found herself sprawled forcefully back on her mattress, aching, as if she'd been hurled from a great height. On the kitchen floor was the cardboard box. Francie hefted it experimentally—yesterday it had been intolerably heavy; this morning it was intolerably light.

O.K., first in the phone book, true enough. ("See display ad, page 182.") "Hi," Francie said when the man answered. "This is Francie McIntyre. The girl who fainted yesterday? Could you—" For an instant, Miss Healy stood in front of her again, looking helpless. "First of all," Francie said. "I mean, thanks for the water. But second of all, could you give me my father's address, please? And, I guess, his name."

Kevin McIntyre—not all that amazing, once you got your head around the notion that he happened to be alive. And he lived on a street called West Tenth, in New York City. Francie looked out the window to the place where there had been for some years now a silently shrieking crowd and a puddle of blood, into which long, splotty raindrops were now falling. Strange—it was raining into the puddle, but at the level of the window it was snowing.

In the closet she found an old plastic slicker. She took it from the hanger and wrapped it around the cardboard box, securing it roughly with tape. Yes, everything had to be *just right*. But the only thing she'd actually *said* to Francie in all these sixteen years was a lie.

Francie looked around at the bluish stillness. "Hello hello," she called. Was that her voice? Was that her mother's silence fading? What had become of everything that had gone on here? "Hello hello," she said. "Hello hello hello hello . . ."

The bus ticket cost Francie eighteen dollars. Which left not all that much of the seventy-three and a bit that she'd saved up, fortunately, to get her back to school and, in fact, Francie thought, to last for the rest of her life. "But, hey," Jessica returned just long enough to point out, "you'll be getting free therapy."

Francie put her box on the overhead rack and scrambled to a window seat. *West Tenth Street.* West of what? The tenth of how many? How on earth was she going to find her way around? If only her mother had let her go last year when Jessica invited her to spend Thanksgiving in New York with her family. But Francie's mother had been able to picture Jessica's mother just as easily as Francie had been able to. "Out of the question," she'd said.

". . . if *there's no spouse* . . ." So, her mother must have used his name on that form! They must never have got a divorce. Could he be a bigamist? Some people were. And he might think Francie was coming to blackmail him. He might decide to kill her right then and there—just reach over and grab a . . . a . . .

Well, one thing—he wasn't living on the street; she had his address. And he wasn't totally feebleminded; he'd sent a fax. Whatever he was, at least what he wasn't was everything except that. And the main thing he wasn't, for absolute certain, was a guy who'd been mashed by a bus.

"Would you like a hankie?" the lady in the seat next to Francie's asked, and Francie realized that she had wiped her eyes and nose on her sleeve. "I have one right here."

"Oh, wow," Francie said gratefully, and blew her nose on the handkerchief the lady produced from a large, shabby cloth sack on her lap.

Despite the shabbiness of the sack, Francie noticed, the lady was tidy. And pretty. Not pretty, really, but exact—with exact little hands and an exact little face. "Do you live in New York?" she asked Francie.

"I've never even been there," Francie said. "My roommate from school invited me to visit once, but my mother wouldn't let me go." Jessica's family had a whole apartment building to themselves, Jessica had told her; she'd called it a "brownstone." It was when Francie had foolishly reported this interesting fact that her mother put her foot down. "Actually," Francie added, "I think my mother was afraid. We had a giant fight about it."

"A mother worries, of course," the lady said. "But it's a lovely city. People tend to have exaggerated fears about New York."

"Yeah," Francie said. "Well, I guess maybe my mother had exaggerated fears about a lot of things. She—" The box! Where was the box? Oh, there— on the rack. Francie's heart was beating rapidly; clashing in her brain were the desire to reveal and the desire to conceal what had become, in the short course of the conversation, a secret. "Do you live in New York?" she asked.

"Technically, no," the lady said. "But I've spent a great deal of happy time there. I know the city very well."

Francie's jumping heart flipped over. "Have you ever been to West Tenth Street?" she asked.

"I have," the lady said.

Francie didn't dare look at the lady. "Is it a nice street?" she asked carefully.

"Very nice," the lady said. "All the streets are very nice. But it seems a strange day to be going there."

"It's strange for me," Francie said loudly. "My mother died."

"I'm terribly sorry," the lady said. "My mother died as well. But evidently no one was hurt in the accident."

"Huh?" Francie said.

"Amazing as it seems," the lady said, "I believe no one was hurt. Although, you'd think, wouldn't you, that an accident of that sort—a blimp, simply sailing into a building . . ."

Francie felt slightly sickened—she wasn't going to have another opportunity to tell someone for the first time that her mother had died, to learn what that meant by hearing the words as she said them for the first time. "How could a blimp just go crashing into a building?" she said crossly.

"These are things we can't understand," the lady said with dignity.

Oops, Francie thought—she was really going to have to watch it; she kept being mean to people, and just completely by mistake.

" 'How could such-and-such a thing happen?' we say," the lady said. "As if this moment or that moment were fitted together, from . . . bits, and one bit or another bit might be some type of mistake. 'There's the building,' people say. 'It's a building. There's the blimp. It's a blimp.' That's the way people think."

Francie peered at the lady. "Wow . . ." she said, considering.

"You see, people tend to settle for the first explanation. People tend to take things at face value."

"Oh, definitely," Francie said. "I mean, absolutely."

"But a blimp or a building cannot be a mistake," the lady said. "Obviously. A blimp or a building are evidence. Oh, goodness—" she said as the bus slowed down. She stood up and gave her sack a little shake. "Here I am."

"Evidence . . ." Francie frowned; Cynthia's red jacket flashed against the snow. "Evidence, of, like . . . the future?"

"Well, more or less," the lady said, a bit impatiently, as the bus stopped in front of a small building. "Evidence of the present, really, I suppose. You know what I mean." She reached into her sack and drew out some papers. "You seem like a very sensitive person—I wonder if you'd be interested in learning about my situation. This is my stop, but you're welcome to the document. It's extra."

"Thank you," Francie said, although the situation she'd really like to learn about, she thought, was her own. "Wait—" The lady was halfway down the aisle. "I've still got your handkerchief—"

"Just hold on to it, dear," the lady called back. "I think it's got your name on it."

The manuscript had a title. *The Triumph of Untruth: A Society That Denies the Workings of the World Puts Us at Even Greater Risk.* "I'd like to introduce myself," it began. "My name is Iris Ackerman."

Hmm, Francie thought: Two people with situations, sitting right next to each other. Coincidence? She glanced up. The sickening thing was, there were a lot of people on this bus.

"My name is Iris Ackerman," Francie read again. "And my belief is that one must try to keep an open mind in the face of puzzling experiences, no matter how laughable this approach may subsequently appear. For many years I maintained the attitude that I was merely a victim of circumstance, or chance, or perhaps now my reluctance to accept the ugliness of certain realities will be considered (with hindsight!) willful obtuseness."

Francie's attention sharpened—she read on. "Certainly my persecution (by literally thousands of men, on the street, in public buildings, and even, before I was forced to flee it, in my own apartment) is a known fact. (One, or several, of these ruffians went so far as to hide himself in my closet, and even under my bed, when least expected.)

"Why, you ask, should so large and powerful an organization concentrate its efforts on tormenting a single individual? This I do not know. It is not (please believe me) false humility that causes me to say I do not consider myself to be in any way 'special.' "

Francie sighed. She rested her eyes for a moment on the weedy lot moving by out the window. Not much point, probably, trying to figure out what Iris had been talking about. Yup, she should have known the minute Iris said the word "blimp."

"I know only," the manuscript continued, "that there was a moment when I fell into the channel, so to speak, of what was ultimately to be revealed as 'my life': In the fall of 1965, when I was twenty years old, I encountered a mathematics professor, an older man, whom I respected deeply. I became increasingly fascinated by certain theories he held regarding the nature of numbers, but he, alas, misunderstood my youthful enthusiasm, and although he had a wife and several children, I was soon forced to rebuff him.

"I continued to feel nothing but the purest and most intense admiration for him, and would gladly have continued our acquaintance. Nevertheless, this professor (Doctor N.) terminated all contact with me (or affected to do so), going so far as to change his telephone number to an unlisted one. Yet, at the same time, he began to pursue me in secret.

"For a period of many months I could detect only the suggestion of his presence—a sort of emanation. Do you know the sensation of a whisper? Or there would sometimes be a telltale hardening, a *crunchiness*, near me. Often, however, I could detect nothing other than a slight discoloration of the atmosphere . . . And then, one day, as I was walking to the library, he was there.

"It was a day of violent heat. People were milling on the sidewalks, waiting. One felt one was penetrating again and again a poisonous, yellow-gray screen that clung to the mouth and the nostrils. I had almost reached the library when I understood that he was behind me. So close, in fact, that he could fit his body to mine. I had never imagined how hard a man's arms could feel! His legs, too, which were pressed up against mine, were like iron, or lead, and he dug his chin into my temple as he clamped himself around me like a butcher about to slash the throat of a calf. I cried out; the bloated sky split, and out poured a filthy rain. The faces of all the people around me began to wash away in inky streaks. A terrible thing had happened to me—A terrible thing had happened—*it was like water gushing out of my body.*

"Since then, my life has not belonged to me. Why do I not go to the authorities? Of course, I have done so. And they have added their mockery to the mockery of my tormentors: *Psychological help!* Tell me: Will 'psychological help' alter my history? Will 'psychological help' locate Dr. N.? Any information regarding my case will be fervently appreciated. Please contact: Iris Ackerman, P.O. Box 139775, Rochester, N.Y. Yours sincerely, Iris Ackerman."

Enclaves of people wrapped in ragged blankets huddled against the walls of the glaring station. Policeman sauntered past in pairs, fingering their truncheons. Danger at every turn, Francie thought. Poor Iris—it was horrible to contemplate. And obviously love didn't exactly clarify the mind, either.

You had to give her credit, though—she was brave. At least she tried to figure things out, instead of just consulting, for example, the wall. To *really* figure things out. Francie blew her nose again. For all the good that did.

Any information regarding my case will be fervently appreciated. But this was not the moment, Francie thought, to lose her nerve. The huge city was just outside the door, and there was no one else to go to West Tenth Street. There was no one else to hear what she had to hear. There was no one else to remember her mother with accuracy. There was no one else to not get the story wrong. There was no one else to reserve judgment. Francie closed one hand tightly around her new handkerchief, and with the other she gripped the handle on her box. The city rose up around her through a peach-colored sunset; now there was no more time.

The man who stood at the door of the apartment (K. McIntyre, #4B) was nice-looking. Nice-looking, and weirdly unfamiliar, as if the whole thing, maybe, were a complete mistake. Francie thought over and over in the striated extrusion of eternity (that was then and this is then; that was now and this is now) it had taken the door to open.

She was filthy, she thought. She smelled. She'd been wearing the same dress, the same socks, for days.

"Can I help you?" he said.

He had no idea why she was there! "Kevin McIntyre?" she said.

"Not back yet," he said. His gaze was pleasant—serene and searching. "Any minute."

He brought her into a big room and sat her down near a fireplace, in a squashy chair. He reached for the chain of a lamp, but Francie shook her head.

"No?" He looked at her. "I'm having coffee," he said. "Want a cup? Or something else—water? Wine? Soda?"

Francie shook her head again.

"Anyhow," he said. "I'm Alex. I'll be in back if you want me."

Francie nodded.

"Can I put your package somewhere for you, at least?" he asked, but Francie folded her arms around the box and rested her cheek against its plastic wrapping.

"Suit yourself," the man said. He paused at the entrance to the room. "You're not a very demanding guest, you know."

Francie felt his attention hesitate and then withdraw. After a moment, she raised her head—yes, he was gone. But then there he was again in the entranceway. "Strange day, huh?" he paused there to say. "Starting with the blimp."

The night before Francie left school, when she'd known so much more about her mother and father than she knew now, she and Jessica had lain in their beds, talking feverishly. "Anything can happen at any moment," Jessica kept exclaiming. "Anything can just *happen.*"

"It's worse than that," Francie had said (and she could still close her eyes and see Cynthia coming up that hill). "It's much, much worse." And Jessica had burst into noisy sobs, as if she knew exactly what Francie meant, as if it were she who had brushed against the burning cable of her life.

Her body, Francie noticed, felt as if it had been crumpled up in a ball—she should stretch. *Strange day.* Well, true enough. That was something they could all be sure of. This room was really nice, though. Pretty and pleasantly messy, with interesting stuff all over the place. Interesting, nice stuff . . .

Twilight was thickening like a dark garden, and paintings and drawings glimmered behind it on the walls. As scary as it was to be waiting for him, it was nice to be having this quiet time. This quiet time together, in a way.

Peach, rose, pale green—yes, poor guy: it might be a moment he'd look back on—last panels of tinted light were falling through the window. He might be walking up the street this very second. Stopping to buy a newspaper.

She closed her eyes. He fished in his pocket for change, and then glanced up sharply. Holding her breath, Francie drew herself back into the darkness. *It's your imagination,* she promised; he was going to have to deal with her soon enough—no sense making him see her until he actually had to.

Nathan Englander

The Twenty-seventh Man

(UNITED STATES)

The orders were given from Stalin's country house at Kuntsovo. He relayed them to the agent in charge with no greater emotion than for the killing of kulaks or clergy or the outspoken wives of very dear friends. The accused were to be apprehended the same day, to arrive at the prison gates at the same moment, and—with a gasp and simultaneous final breath—be sent off to their damnation in a single rattling burst of gunfire.

It was not an issue of hatred, only one of allegiance. For Stalin knew there could be loyalty to only one nation. What he did not know so well were the authors' names on his list. When it was presented to him the next morning, he signed the warrant anyway, though there were now twenty-seven and yesterday there had been twenty-six.

No matter, except maybe to the twenty-seventh.

The orders left little room for variation, and none for tardiness. They were to be carried out in secrecy and—the only point that was reiterated—simultaneously. But how were the agents to get the men from Moscow and Gorky, Smolensk and Penza, Shuya and Podolsk, to the prison near the village of X at the very same time?

The agent in charge felt his strength was in leadership and gave up the role of strategist to the inside of his hat. He cut the list into strips and sprinkled them into the freshly blocked crown, mixing carefully so as not to disturb its shape. Most of these writers were in Moscow. The handful who were in their native villages, taking the waters somewhere, or locked in a cabin trying to finish their seminal work, would surely receive a stiff cuffing when a pair of agents, aggravated by the trek, stepped through the door.

After the lottery, those agents who had drawn a name warranting a long journey accepted the good-natured insults and mockery of friends. Most would have it easy, nothing more to worry about than hurrying some old rebel to a car, or getting their shirts wrinkled in a heel-dragging, hair-pulling rural scene that could be as messy as necessary in front of a pack of superstitious peasants.

Then there were those who had it hard. Such as the two agents assigned to

Vasily Korinsky, who, seeing no way out, was prepared to exit his bedroom quietly but whose wife Paulina struck the shorter of the two officers with an oriental-style brass vase. There was a scuffle, Paulina was subdued, the short officer taken out unconscious, and a precious hour lost on their estimated time.

There was the pair assigned to Moishe Bretzky, a true lover of vodka and its country of origin. One would not have pegged him as one of history's most sensitive Yiddish poets. He was huge, slovenly, and smelly as a horse. Once a year, during the Ten Days of Penitence, he would take notice of his sinful ways and sober up for Yom Kippur. Immediately after breaking the fast, he would grab pen and pad to write furiously for weeks at a time in his sister's ventless kitchen—the shroud of atonement still draped over his splitting head. He would toast the finished work with a brimming shot of vodka, the thimble tiny against his thumb. As the last drop rolled back in his throat, the thirst would begin to rage, and off he would go for another year. His sister's husband would have put an end to this annual practice if it weren't for the rubles he received for the sweat-curled pages Bretzky abandoned.

It took the whole of the night for the two agents to locate Bretzky. They tracked him down in one of the whorehouses that did not exist, and if they did, government agents surely did not frequent them. Nonetheless, having escaped notice, they slipped into the room. Bretzky was passed out on his stomach with a smiling trollop pinned under each arm. The time-consuming process of freeing the whores, getting Bretzky upright, and moving him into the hallway reduced the younger man to tears.

The senior agent left his partner in charge of the body while he went to chat with the senior woman of the house. Introducing himself numerous times as if they had never met, he explained his predicament and enlisted the help of a dozen women.

Twelve of the house's strongest companions—in an array of pink and red robes, froufrou slippers, and painted toenails—carried the giant bear to the waiting car amid a roar of giggles. It was a sight Bretzky would have enjoyed tremendously had he been conscious.

The least troubling of the troublesome abductions was that of Y. Zunser, oldest of the group and a target of the first serious verbal attacks on the cosmopolitans back in '49. In the February 19 edition of *Literaturnaya Gazeta* he had been criticized as an obsolete author, accused of being anti-Soviet, and chided for using a pen name to hide his Jewish roots. In that same edition they printed his real name, Melman, stripping him of the privacy he had so enjoyed.

Three years later they came for him. The two agents were not enthusiastic about the task. They had shared a Jewish literature instructor in high school, whom they admired despite his ethnicity and who even coerced them into writing a poem or two. Both were rather decent fellows, and capturing an eighty-one-year-old man did not exactly jibe with their vision of bravely serving the Party. They were simply following instructions. But somewhere amidst their justifications lay a deep fear of punishment.

It was not yet dawn, and Zunser was already dressed, sitting with a cup of tea. The agents begged him to stand up on his own, one of them trying the name Zunser and the other pleading with Melman. He refused.

"I will neither resist nor help. The responsibility must rest fully upon your conscience."

"We have orders," they said.

"I did not say you were without orders. I said that you have to bear responsibility."

They first tried lifting him by his arms, but Zunser was too delicate for the maneuver. Then one grabbed his ankles while the other clasped his chest. Zunser's head lolled back. The agents were afraid of killing him, an option they had been sternly warned against. They put him on the floor, and the larger one scooped him up, cradling the old man like a child. On their way out, they came upon a portrait of Zunser's deceased wife.

Zunser fancied the picture had a new moroseness to it, as if the sepia-toned eyes of his wife might well up and shed a tear. He spoke aloud. "No matter, Katya. Life ended for me the day of your death; everything since has been but nostalgia." The agent shifted the weight of the romantic in his arms and headed out the door.

The solitary complicated abduction that took place out of Moscow was the one that should have been the easiest of the twenty-seven. It was the simple task of removing Pinchas Pelovits from the inn on the road that ran to X and the prison beyond.

Pinchas Pelovits had constructed his own world with a compassionate god and a diverse group of worshipers. In it, he tested these people with moral dilemmas and tragedies—testing them sometimes more with joy and good fortune. He recorded the trials and events of this world in his notebooks in the form of stories and novels, essays, poems, songs, anthems, tales, jokes, and extensive histories that led up to the era in which he dwelled.

His parents never knew what label to give their son, who wrote all day but did not publish, who laughed and cried over his novels but was gratingly logical in his contact with the everyday world. What they did know was that Pinchas wasn't going to take over the inn.

When they became too old to run the business, the only viable option was to sell out at a ridiculously low price—provided the new owners would leave the boy his room and feed him when he was hungry. Even when the business became the property of the state, Pinchas, in the dreamer's room, was left in peace; *why bother, he's harmless, sort of a good luck charm for the inn, no one even knows he's here, maybe he's writing a history of the place and we'll all be made famous.* He wasn't. But who knows, maybe he would have, had his name—mumbled on the lips of travelers—not found its way onto Stalin's list.

The two agents assigned Pinchas arrived at the inn driving a beat-up droshky and posing as the sons of now-poor landowners, a touch they thought might tickle their superiors. One carried a Luger (a trinket he brought home from the war), and the other kept a billy club stashed in his boot. They found the narrow hallway with Pinchas's room and knocked lightly on his door. "Not hungry," was the response. The agent with the Luger gave the door a hip check; it didn't budge. "Try the handle," said the voice. The agent did, swinging it open.

"You're coming with us," said the one with the club in his boot.

"Absolutely not," Pinchas stated matter-of-factly. The agent wondered if his "you're coming with us" had sounded as bold.

"Put the book down on the pile, put your shoes on, and let's go." The agent with the Luger spoke slowly. "You're under arrest for anti-Soviet activity."

Pinchas was baffled by the charge. He meditated for a moment and came to the conclusion that there was only one moral outrage he'd been involved in, though it seemed to him a bit excessive to be incarcerated for it.

"Well, you can have them, but they're not really mine. They were in a copy of a Zunser book that a guest forgot, and I didn't know where to return them. Regardless, I studied them thoroughly. You may take me away." He proceeded to hand the agents five postcards. Three were intricate pen-and-ink drawings of a geisha in various positions with her legs spread wide. The other two were identical photographs of a sturdy Russian maiden in front of a painted tropical background wearing a hula skirt and making a vain attempt to cover her breasts. Pinchas began stacking his notebooks while the agents divvied the cards. He was sad that he had not resisted temptation. He would miss taking his walks and also the desk upon whose mottled surface he had written.

"May I bring my desk?"

The agent with the Luger was getting fidgety. "You won't be needing anything, just put on your shoes."

"I'd much prefer my books to shoes," Pinchas said. "In the summer I sometimes take walks without shoes but never without a novel. If you would have a seat while I organize my notes—" and Pinchas fell to the floor, struck in the head with the pistol grip. He was carried from the inn rolled in a blanket, his feet poking forth, bare.

Pinchas awoke, his head throbbing from the blow and the exceedingly tight blindfold. This was aggravated by the sound of ice cracking under the droshky wheels as happens along the river route west of X. "The bridge is out on this road," he told them. "You'd best cut through the old Bunakov place. Everybody does it in winter."

The billy club was drawn from the agent's boot, and Pinchas was struck on the head once again. The idea of arriving only to have their prisoner blurt out the name of the secret prison was mortifying. In an attempt to confound him, they turned off on a clearly unused road. There are reasons that unused roads are not used. It wasn't half a kilometer before they had broken a wheel and it was off to a nearby pig farm on foot. The agent with the gun commandeered a donkey-drawn cart, leaving a furious pig farmer cursing and kicking the side of his barn.

The trio were all a bit relieved upon arrival: Pinchas because he started to get the idea that this business had to do with something more than his minor infraction, and the agents because three other cars had shown up only minutes before they had—all inexcusably late.

By the time the latecomers had been delivered, the initial terror of the other twenty-three had subsided. The situation was tense and grave, but also unique. An eminent selection of Europe's surviving Yiddish literary community was being held within the confines of an oversize closet. Had they known they were going to die, it might have been different. Since they didn't, I. J. Manger wasn't about to let Mani Zaretsky see him cry for *rachmones*. He didn't have time to anyway. Pyotr Kolyazin, the famed atheist, had already dragged him into a heated discussion about the ramifications of using God's will to drastically alter the outcome of previously "logical" plots. Manger took this to be an attack on his work and asked Kolyazin if he labeled everything he didn't understand as illogical. There was also the present situation to discuss, as well as old rivalries, new poems, disputed reviews, journals that just aren't the same, up-and-coming editors, and of course the gossip, for hadn't they heard that Lev had used his latest manuscript for kindling?

When the noise got too great, a guard opened the peephole in the door to find that a symposium had broken loose. As a result, by the time numbers twenty-four through twenty-seven arrived, the others had already been separated into smaller cells.

Each cell was meant to house four prisoners, and contained three rotting mats to sleep on. In a corner was a bucket. There were crude holes in the wood plank walls, and it was hard to tell if the captors had punched them as a form of ventilation or if the previous prisoners had painstakingly scratched them through to confirm the existence of a world outside.

The four latecomers had lain down immediately, Pinchas on the floor. He was dazed and shivering, stifling his moans so the others might rest. His companions did not even think of sleep: Vasily Korinsky because of worry about what might be the outcome for his wife; Y. Zunser because he was trying to adapt to the change (the only alteration he had planned for in his daily routine was death, and that in his sleep); Bretzky because he hadn't really awakened.

Excepting Pinchas, none had an inkling of how long they'd traveled, whether from morning until night or into the next day. Pinchas tried to use his journey as an anchor, but in the dark he soon lost his notion of time gone by. He listened for the others' breathing, making sure they were alive.

The lightbulb hanging from a frayed wire in the ceiling went on. This was a relief; not only an end to the darkness but a separation, a seam in the seeming endlessness.

They stared unblinking into the dim glow of the bulb and worried about its abandoning them. All except Bretzky, whose huge form already ached for a vodka and who dared not crack an eye.

Zunser was the first to speak. "With morning there is hope."

"For what?" asked Korinsky out of the side of his mouth. His eyes were pressed up against a hole in the back wall.

"A way out," Zunser said. He watched the bulb, wondering how much electricity there was in the wire, how he would reach it, and how many of them it would serve.

Korinsky misunderstood the statement to be an optimistic one. "Feh on your way out, and feh on your morning. It's pitch-dark outside. Either it's night, or we're in a place with no sun. I'm freezing to death."

The others were a bit shocked when Bretzky spoke: "Past the fact that you are not one of the whores I paid for and this is not the bed we fell into, I'm uncertain. Whatever the situation, I shall endure it, but without your whining about being cold in front of an old man in shirtsleeves and this skinny one with no shoes." His powers of observation were already returning, and Yom Kippur still months away.

"I'm fine," said Pinchas. "I'd much rather have a book than shoes."

They all knitted their brows and studied the man; even Bretzky propped himself up on an elbow.

Zunser laughed, and then the other three started in. Yes, it would be much better to have a book. Whose book? Surely not the pamphlet by that fool Horiansky—this being a well publicized and recent failure. They laughed some more. Korinsky stopped, worrying that one of the other men in the room might be Horiansky. Horiansky, thankfully, was on the other end of the hall and was spared that final degradation before his death.

No one said another word until the lightbulb went off again, and then they remained silent because it was supposed to be night. However, it was not. Korinsky could see light seeping through the holes and chinks in the boards. He would tell them so when the bulb came back on, if it did.

Pinchas could have laughed indefinitely, or at least until the time of his execution. His mind was not trained, never taught any restraint nor punished for its reckless abandon. He had written because it was all that interested him, aside from his walks, and the pictures at which he had peeked. Not since childhood had he skipped a day of writing.

Composing without pen and paper, he decided on something short, something he could hone, add a little bit to every day until his release.

Zunser felt the coldness of the floor seeping into his bones, turning them brittle. It was time anyway. He had lived a long life, enjoyed recognition for something he loved doing. All the others who had reached his level of fame had gone to the ovens, or were in America. How much more meaningless was success with the competition gone? Why write at all when your readers have been turned to ash? Never outlive your language. Zunser rolled onto his side.

Bretzky sweated the alcohol out of his blood. He tried to convince himself that it was a vision of drink, a clearer vision because he was getting older, but a hallucination nonetheless. How many times had he turned, after hearing his name called, to find no one? He fumbled for a breast, a soft pink cheek, a swatch of satin, and fell asleep.

Before closing his eyes only to find more darkness, Pinchas recited the first paragraph a final time:

> The morning that Mendel Muskatev awoke to find his desk was gone, his room was gone, and the sun was gone, he assumed he had died. This worried him, so he said the prayer for the dead, keeping himself in mind. Then he wondered if one was allowed to do such a thing, and worried instead that the first thing he had done upon being dead was sin.

When the light came on, Korinsky stirred noticeably, as if to break the ice, as if they were bound by the dictates of civilized society. "You know it isn't morning, it's about nine o'clock or ten, midnight at the latest."

Pinchas was reciting his paragraph quietly, playing with the words, making changes, wishing he had a piece of slate.

Korinsky waited for an answer, staring at the other three. It was hard to believe they were writers. He figured he too must be disheveled, but at least there was some style left in him. These others, a drunk, an incontinent old curmudgeon and an idiot, could not be of his caliber. Even the deficient Horiansky would be appreciated now. "I said, it's not morning. They're trying to fool us, mess up our internal clocks."

"Then go back to sleep and leave us to be fooled." Bretzky had already warned this sot yesterday. He didn't need murder added to his list of trumped-up charges.

"You shouldn't be so snide with me. I'm only trying to see if we can maintain a little dignity while they are holding us here."

Zunser had set himself up against a wall. He had folded his mat and used it like a chair, cushioning himself from the splinters. "You say 'holding' as if this is temporary and in the next stage we will find ourselves someplace more to our liking."

Korinsky looked at Zunser, surveying him boldly. He did not like being goaded, especially by some old coot who had no idea to whom he was talking.

"Comrade." He addressed Zunser in a most acerbic tone. "I am quite sure my incarceration is due to bureaucratic confusion of some sort. I've no idea what you wrote that landed you here, but I have an impeccable record. I was a principal member of the Anti-Fascist Committee, and my ode, *Stalin of Silver, Stalin of Gold,* happens to be a national favorite."

" 'We spilled our blood in revolution, only to choke on Stalin's pollution.' " Bretzky quoted a bastardization of Korinsky's ballad that had been popularized by naughty children and drunk republicans.

"How dare you mock me!"

"I've not had the pleasure of hearing the original," Zunser said, "but I must say the mockery is quite entertaining."

" 'Our hearts cheered as one for revolution, now we bask in the glory of great Stalin's solution.' " All three heads turned to Pinchas, Korinsky's the quickest.

"Perfect." Korinsky sneered at the other two men. "I must say it is nice to be in the presence of at least one fan."

Among the many social interactions Pinchas had never before been involved in, this was one. He did not know when adulation was being requested.

"Oh, I'm no fan, sir. You're a master of the Yiddish language, but the core of all your work is flawed by a heavy-handed party message that has nothing to do with the people about whom you write." This with an eloquence which to Korinsky sounded like the fool was condescending.

"The characters are only vehicles, fictions!" He was shouting at Pinchas. Then he caught himself shouting at an idiot, while the other two men convulsed with laughter.

"They are very real," said Pinchas before returning to his rocking and mumbling.

"What are you two fops making fun of? At least I have a body of work that is read."

Bretzky was angry again. "Speak to me as you like. If it begins to bother me too much, I'll pinch your head off from your neck." He made a pinching motion with his massive fingers. "But I must warn you against speaking to your elders with disrespect. Furthermore, I have a most cloudy feeling that the face on the old man also belongs to the legendary Zunser, whose accomplishments far exceed any of the writers, Yiddish or otherwise, alive in Russia today."

"Zunser?" said Korinsky.

"Y. Zunser!" screamed Pinchas. He could not imagine being confined with such a singular mind. Pinchas had never even considered that Zunser was an actual person. My god, he had seen the great seer pee into a bucket. "Zunser," he said to the man. He stood and banged his fist against the door, screaming "Zunser" over and over again, like it was a password his keepers would understand and know the game was finished.

A guard came down the hall and beat Pinchas to the floor. He left them a bowl of water and a few crusts of black bread. The three ate quickly. Bretzky held up the casualty while Zunser poured some water into his mouth, made him swallow.

"The man is crazy, he is going to get us all killed." Korinsky sat with his eye against a knothole, peering into the darkness of their day.

"Maybe us, but who would dare to kill the poet laureate of the Communist empire?" Bretzky's tone was biting, though his outward appearance did not reflect it. He cradled Pinchas's limp form while Zunser mopped the boy's brow with his sleeve.

"This is no time for joking. I was going to arrange for a meeting with the warden, but that lunatic's screaming fouled it up. Swooning like a young girl. Has he never before met a man he admired?" Korinsky hooked a finger through one of the larger holes, as if he were trying to feel the texture of the darkness outside. "Who knows when that guard will return?"

"I would not rush to get out," said Zunser. "I can assure you there is only one way to exit."

"Your talk gets us nowhere." Korinsky stood and leaned a shoulder against a cold board.

"And what has gotten you somewhere?" said Zunser. "Your love ballads to the regime? There are no hoofbeats to be heard in the distance. Stalin doesn't spur his horse, racing to your rescue."

"He doesn't know. He wouldn't let them do this to me."

"Maybe not to you, but to the Jew that has your name and lives in your house and lies next to your wife, yes." Zunser massaged a stiffening knee.

"It's not my life. It's my culture, my language. No more."

"Only your language?" Zunser waved him away. "Who are we without Yiddish?"

"The four sons of the Passover seder, at best." Korinsky sounded bitter.

"This is more than tradition, Korinsky. It's blood." Bretzky spat into the pail. "I used to drink with Kapler, shot for shot."

"And?" Korinsky kept his eye to a hole but listened closely.

"And have you seen a movie directed by Kapler lately? He made a friend-ship with the exalted comrade's daughter. Now he is in a labor camp—if he's alive. Stalin did not take too well to Jewish hands on his daughter's pure white skin."

"You two wizards can turn a Stalin to a Hitler."

Bretzky reached over and gave Korinsky a pat on the leg. "We don't need the Nazis, my friend."

"Feh, you're a paranoid, like all drunks."

Zunser shook his head. He was tiring of the Communist and worried about the boy. "He's got a fever. And he's lucky if there isn't a crack in that head." The old man took off his shoes and put his socks on Pinchas.

"Let me," said Bretzky.

"No," Zunser said. "You give him the shoes, mine won't fit him." Pinchas's feet slipped easily into Bretzky's scuffed and cracking shoes.

"Here, take it." Korinsky gave them his mat. "Believe me, it's not for the mitzvah. I just couldn't stand to spend another second trapped with your righ-teous stares."

"The eyes you feel are not ours," said Zunser.

Korinsky glowered at his wall.

Pinchas Pelovits was not unconscious. He had only lost his way. He heard the conversations, but paid them little heed. The weight of his body lay on him like a corpse. He worked on his story, saying it aloud to himself, hoping the others would hear and follow it and bring him back.

Mendel figured he'd best consult the local rabbi, who might be able to direct him in such matters. It was Mendel's first time visiting the rabbi in his study—not having previously concerned himself with the nuances of worship. Mendel was much surprised to find the rabbi's study was of the exact dimensions of his missing room. In fact, it appeared that the volume of Tractate the man was poring over rested on the missing desk.

The bulb glowed. And with light came relief. What if they had been left in the darkness? They hated the bulb for its control, such a flimsy thing.

They had left a little water for the morning. Again, Bretzky held Pinchas while Zunser tipped the bowl against the boy's lips. Korinsky watched, wanting to tell them to be careful not to spill, to make sure they saved some for him.

Pinchas sputtered, then said, "Fine, that's fine." He spoke loudly for someone in such apparent ill health. Zunser passed the bowl to Korinsky before taking his own sip.

"Very good to have you with us," said Zunser, trying to catch the boy's eyes with his own. "I wanted to ask you, why is my presence so unsettling? We are all writers here, if I understand the situation correctly."

Zunser used Bretzky to belabor the point. "Come on, tell the boy who you are."

"Moishe Bretzky. They call me The Glutton in the gossip columns."

Zunser smiled at the boy. "You see. A big name. A legend for his poetry, as much for his antics. Now, tell us. Who are you?"

"Pinchas Pelovits."

None had heard the name. Zunser's curiosity was piqued. Bretzky didn't care either way. Korinsky was only further pained at having to put up with a madman who wasn't even famous.

"I am the one who doesn't belong here," Pinchas said. "Though if I could, I'd take the place of any of you."

"But you are not here in place of us, you are here as one of us. Do you write?"

"Oh, yes, that's all I do. That's all I've ever done, except for reading and my walks."

"If it makes any difference, we welcome you as an equal." Zunser surveyed the cubicle. "I'd much rather be saying this to you in my home."

"Are you sure I'm here for being a writer?" He looked at the three men.

"Not just for being a writer, my friend." Bretzky clapped him lightly on the back. "You are here as a subversive writer. An enemy of the state! Quite a feat for an unknown."

The door opened, and all four were dragged from the cell and taken by a guard to private interrogation chambers—Bretzky escorted by three guards of his own. There they were beaten, degraded, made to confess to numerous crimes, and to sign confessions that they had knowingly distributed Zionist propaganda aimed at toppling the Soviet government.

Zunser and Pinchas had been in adjoining chambers and heard each other's screams. Bretzky and Korinsky also shared a common wall, though there was silence after each blow. Korinsky's sense of repute was so strong that he stifled his screaming. Bretzky did not call out. Instead he cried and cried. His abusers mocked him for it, jeering at the overgrown baby. His tears did not fall from the pain, however. They came out of the sober realization of man's cruelty and the picture of the suffering being dealt to his peers, especially Zunser.

Afterward, they were given a fair amount of water, a hunk of bread, and some cold potato-and-radish soup. They were returned to the same cell in the darkness. Zunser and Pinchas needed to be carried.

Pinchas had focused on his story, his screams sounding as if they were coming from afar. With every stripe he received, he added a phrase, the impact reaching his mind like the dull rap of a windowpane settling in its sash:

> "Rabbi, have you noticed we are without a sun today?" Mendel asked by way of an introduction.
>
> "My shutters are closed against the noise."
>
> "Did no one else mention it at morning prayers?"
>
> "No one else arrived," said the rabbi, continuing to study.
>
> "Well, don't you think that strange?"
>
> "I had. I had until you told me about this sun. Now I understand—no sensible man would get up to greet a dawn that never came."

They were all awake when the bulb went on. Zunser was making peace with himself, preparing for certain death. The fingers of his left hand were twisted and split. Only his thumb had a nail.

Pinchas had a question for Zunser. "All your work treats fate as if it were a mosquito to be shooed away. All your characters struggle for survival, and you choose to play the victim. You had to have known they would come."

"You have a point," Zunser said, "a fair question. And I answer it with another: Why should I always be the one to survive? I watched Europe's Jews go up the chimneys. I buried a wife and a child. I do believe one can elude the fates. But why assume the goal is to live?" Zunser slid the mangled hand onto his stomach. "How many more tragedies do I want to survive? Let someone take witness of mine."

Bretzky disagreed. "We've lost our universe, this is true. Still, a man can't condemn himself to death for the sin of living. We can't cower in the shadows of the camps forever."

"I would give anything to escape," said Korinsky.

Zunser turned his gaze toward the bulb. "That is the single rule I have maintained in every story I ever wrote. The desperate are never given the choice. It bores the gods."

"Then," asked Pinchas, and to him there was no one else but his mentor in the room, "you don't believe there is any reason I was brought here to be with you. It isn't part of anything larger, some cosmic balance, a great joke of the heavens."

"I think that somewhere a clerk made a mistake."

"That," Pinchas said, "I cannot bear."

All the talking had strained Zunser, and he coughed up a bit of blood. Pinchas attempted to help Zunser but couldn't stand up. Bretzky and Korinsky started to their feet. "Sit, sit," Zunser said. They did, but watched him closely as he tried to clear his lungs.

Pinchas Pelovits spent the rest of the day on the last lines of his story. When the light went out, he had already finished.

They hadn't been in darkness long when they were awakened by the noise and the gleam from the bulb. Korinsky immediately put his eye to the wall.

"They are lining up everyone outside. There are machine guns. It is morning, and everyone is blinking as if they were newly born."

Pinchas interrupted. "I have something I would like to recite. It's a story I wrote while we've been staying here."

"Go ahead," said Zunser.

"Let's hear it," said Bretzky.

Korinsky pulled the hair from his head. "What difference can it make now?"

"For whom?" asked Pinchas and then proceeded to recite his little tale:

The morning that Mendel Muskatev awoke to find his desk was gone, his room was gone, and the sun was gone, he assumed he had died. This worried him, so he said the prayer for the dead, keeping himself in mind. Then he wondered if one was allowed to do such a thing, and worried instead that the first thing one had done upon being dead was sin.

Mendel figured he'd best consult the local rabbi, who might be able to direct him in such matters. It was Mendel's first time visiting the rabbi in his study—not having previously concerned himself with the nuances of worship. Mendel was much surprised to find that the rabbi's study was of the exact dimensions of his missing room. In fact, it appeared that the volume of Tractate the man was poring over rested on the missing desk.

"Rabbi, have you noticed we are without a sun today?" Mendel asked by way of an introduction.

"My shutters are closed against the noise."

"Did no one else mention it at morning prayers?"

"No one else arrived," said the rabbi, continuing to study.

"Well, don't you think that strange?"

"I had. I had until you told me about this sun. Now I understand—no sensible man would get up to greet a dawn that never came."

"This is all very startling, Rabbi. But I think we—at some point in the night—have died."

The rabbi stood up, grinning. "And here I am with an eternity's worth of Talmud to study."

Mendel took in the volumes lining the walls.

"I've a desk and a chair and a *shtender* in the corner should I want to stand," said the rabbi. "Yes, it would seem I'm in heaven." He patted Mendel on the shoulder. "I must thank you for rushing over to tell me." The rabbi shook Mendel's hand and nodded good-naturedly, already searching for his place in the text. "Did you come for some other reason?"

"I did," said Mendel, trying to find a space between the books where once there was a door. "I wanted to know"—and here his voice began to quiver—"which one of us is to say the prayer?"

Bretzky stood. "Bravo," he said, clapping his hands together. "It's like a shooting star. A tale to be extinguished along with the teller." He stepped forward to meet the agent in charge at the door. "No, the meaning, it was not lost on me."

Korinsky pulled his knees into his chest, hugged them. "No," he admitted, "it was not lost."

Pinchas did not blush or bow his head. He stared at Zunser, wondered what the noble Zunser was thinking, as they were driven from the cell.

Outside all the others were being assembled. There were Horiansky and Lubovitch, Lev and Soltzky. All those great voices with the greatest stories of their lives to tell, and forced to bring them to the grave. Pinchas, having increased his readership threefold, had a smile on his face.

Pinchas Pelovits was the twenty-seventh, or the fourteenth from either end, if you wanted to count his place in line. Bretzky supported Pinchas by holding up his right side, for his equilibrium had not returned. Zunser supported him on the left, but was in bad shape himself.

"Did you like it?" Pinchas asked.

"Very much," Zunser said. "You're a talented boy."

Pinchas smiled again, then fell, his head landing on the stockingless calves of Zunser. One of his borrowed shoes flew forward, though his feet slid backward in the dirt. Bretzky fell atop the other two. He was shot five or six times, but being such a big man and such a strong man, he lived long enough to recognize the crack of the guns and know that he was dead.

Victor Erofeyev

The Parakeet

(RUSSIA)

In response to your inquiry, most esteemed Spiridon Yermolaevich, to wit: what fate has been determined for your son, Yermolai Spiridonovich Spirkin, who compelled a dead bird to undertake unnatural flight, I shall not respond immediately. And why not? Because, my dear sir, I must admit I would be ashamed to do so. My bosom was rent with emotion as I read your petition, written in the blood of paternal feeling. You have disquieted me, Spiridon Yermolaevich, shattered me! Words cannot render the anguish you have unleashed upon me, only the howl of the beast. However, I harbor no complaint against you. I sensed in my heart your paternal urge to defend your son, Yermolai Spiridonovich, before legal authority, implying in obscure words that your son, Yermolai Spiridonovich, was since his earliest youth possessed, as it were, of a mighty love for those of God's creatures capable of flight. I allow as to the correctness of your implication. I shall say even more. Every child is subject to a weakness for birds, capturing them in groves and forests, as well as in open fields and in gardens with snares, or buying them with their coppers at the bird market, in order to lock the bird in a cage, especially if it be a songbird. In such actions the law discerns nothing blameworthy and thus indulges them in their innocent amusements. And so, of course, it must be—there is a time and place for amusements, but world culture, most esteemed Spiridon Yermolaevich, is, in my most humble opinion, wont rather to think in *symbols*, the interpretation of which is a matter for learned men. Since ancient times, for example, there has been a fashion for divination by the entrails of birds that fly by. If, on the other hand, some living bird were to fly into a room of your house, be it no more than a goldfinch, would you be pleased at such a circumstance, Spiridon Yermolaevich? No, you would not be pleased at such a circumstance. And why not? You would not, I reply, because you would see that as a terrible *symbol*. I am prepared to recount any number of such scenes of human benightedness, but I strive, however, toward a conclusion that has direct bearing on your son, Yermolai Spiridonovich: the bird is a creature which disturbs the soul, the bird is a mysterious creature, not subject to our whims, and so any pranks with it are a bad business. And indeed, what sort of shenanigans is your little boy up to? He plays pranks! Yermolai Spiridonovich pleases to play pranks with a dead parakeet—an especially suspicious bird. The parakeet is a *symbol* in and of itself, and the devil himself couldn't figure out how to interpret it, inasmuch as all of world culture since its inception hasn't managed to do anything more than gossip about it as about some beloved idol. Moreover, it is an overseas bird. And you, Spiridon Yermolaevich, with such frivolousness as had better been applied elsewhere, scribble in your inquiry that your boy's amusement, so you say, was of an utterly innocent nature. Of small matter, you think! My son, you say, Yermolai Spiridonovich, took the eternally departed parakeet, nicknamed Semyon, climbed nimbly to the roof of your own home, which is located on Swan Street, and began tossing it upward, like Ivanushka the Fool, reckoning that the dead creature would, in its airy native venue, find a second breath, take wing and give a chirp, that is, in a certain sense, even be resurrected. Judging from your hasty words, there was in this deed of Yermolai Spiridonovich's more a want of consideration than any base design, more a surfeit of morbid fantasy, a weakening of nerves and trembling throughout the body, than any tidy plan and intrigue. Whereupon you, understandably indignant over his actions, volunteer to flog your boy, Yermolai Spiridonovich, with a lash and without any leniency. It's a clear case of paternal feelings! I repeat once again: we have no complaint against you, Spiridon Yermolaevich, on this account. You are an honorable man and for the time being you remain as such. But deign to understand us as well, we who have likewise served the fatherland all these many years, place yourself in my position, for example. Why, if such experiments were to become more frequent, what then? And what if the overseas trash were to ascend? According to the assurance of your mad son, Yermolai Spiridonovich, the bird did indeed flap its unclean wings a couple of times—that is, displayed a certain attempt at resurrection! Well, what if all of a sudden, contrary to our expectations, it up and actually was resurrected? In what terms would we explain this particular circumstance to our countrymen, so trusting in our best intentions? I become lost in fatal conjecture . . .

WOULDN'T WE BE FINE FOOLS!

Eh! What's there to say! Your boy, Yermolai Spiridonovich, turned out to be of a delicate, one might even say frail, build. We were amazed. What had he become? Well, young man, I inquired of Yermolai Spiridonovich, having given him a good looking over, answer the question: with what intent did you dig the bird up from its place of interment, or, in other words, from the cesspool? Whatever in hell possessed you, we must ask, to exhume it? He answered meekly, but hurriedly and with undeniable courtesy, aiding himself in his answer with his little white hand, with his little hand, don't you know, he aided himself so that it would come out more accessibly. I went on the alert observing manners like these. I saw that not only his build, but his manners, too, are alien, mere civility and nothing more. You don't have a Yiddle in the woodpile with that one, do you Spiridon Yermolaevich? He kept trying to get me to understand, he aided himself, you see, with his little hand—a pretty sight, you might say. But the trick didn't work—this is not a circus! And I sit and note to myself: this pickle's not from our brine! And what did his words add up to?

What sort of picture was taking shape? Tell the story, I say, from the very beginning, and don't wave your little white hand in front of my nose, I won't stand for it! He broke down into a profusion of excuses, as if I needed excuses from him, as if in offering these excuses of his he somehow came forward as my benefactor! But I keep silent. However, in the meantime, I ask him: so you, Yermolai Spiridonovich, wished to resurrect the bird, but this bird, according to competent witnesses, was already sorely afflicted by worms of the earth, didn't you notice? Worms as white as your little fingers? They clung all over it, just as the ants did, they partook of that feast . . . And could such a bird be resurrected? And how did you not recoil at taking it into your pampered hands? He answers, hanging his head: what about the Phoenix bird? I see, my dear sir, Spiridon Yermolaevich, that your boy, Yermolai Spiridonovich, is clever beyond his years. The Phoenix bird, indeed! From where, we ask, do you have knowledge about such a Phoenix bird; what is it, I ask? It, says he, was a certain red-feathered eagle that flew from Arabia to ancient Egypt; there it burned itself up alive after it had lived to the venerable age of five hundred years, and then it was reborn from its ashes, young and hale, hence worms are no obstacle here . . . He's managed that cleverly, I see. What, I ask, is the point of this fable about the red-feathered eagle? How, I continue the question, have you fallen into a life in which you believe in heathen lore? He answers once again evasively: a fable, he says, is meant to be wondrous. Don't you try to wriggle out of it, I tell him, don't you keep denying it or, I'm telling you, I'll give you a fable you'll never forget! Now, out with the whole truth, you hooligan! But, he screamed with emotion, I'm telling you the pure and honest truth! And again he fluttered his little hand. Well, God bless you, then you talk, and we shall sit and listen. Only don't get excited, don't scream. At whom, I say, are you screaming? At whom, so to speak, are you raising your voice?! I, Yermolai, could be your father, and you have taken it into your head to scream at me! He is silent. He flushed. Could I, I ask, be your father, or couldn't I? Why, he answers, couldn't you be? I am appealing to you just as if you were my own father . . . See that, I think to myself, he is already calling me his own father, squirming like a horny wench . . . There is more here than meets the eye. I am curious: and this parakeet of yours, turquoise in hue, nicknamed Semyon—is he, as I suspect, also some kind of *symbol,* or what? Everything in world culture, Spiridon Yermolaevich, is *symbols,* nothing but *symbols,* wherever you cast your glance, especially parakeets. And he, your son, Yermolai Spiridonovich, in answer takes recourse to a childish lament, relates the story, well known to us, of the death of the parakeet called Semyon in the family of the physician to the boyars, Agafon Yelistratovich, your neighbor on Swan Street, who purchased the overseas bird for the amusement of his two small children: five-year-old Tatyana Agafonovna and the three-year-old sniveler Ezdra Agafonovich; he purchased it, as was customary, at the bird market, from the Dutch merchant Van Zaam, or, as we call him, Timofei Ignatievich. That merchant, Timofei Ignatievich, is in no way remarkable, mild as he is of manner, except for a scar on his Dutch nose which he received in our climes as a result of a minor scuffle with his wife. I initiate you into these particulars so that you, Spiridon Yermolaevich, might know that I work for the bread I eat: without the particulars you won't get the picture, the more so if there is foul play. And so your neighbor, Agafon Yelistratovich, purchased an overseas parakeet of diminutive stature, perhaps for the sake of thrift, and it was christened Semyon. The bird was locked, as was customary, in a cage. It was fed, from what Tatyana Agafonovna says, with wheat. But that parakeet, known mournfully for its, thank God, unsuccessful resurrection, resolutely refused to eat the wheat or other sundry feed, flouted its overseas airs, and, despite the children's ministrations, started to die, by reason of a voluntary hunger strike. On the third day Semyon died to the general lament of Tatyana Agafonovna and Ezdra Agafonovich, the three-year-old sniveler: which villain still does not talk, or pretends not to. The agony lasted three and a half hours, during the afternoon, and ended with the natural death of the bird.

In such terms does your son, Yermolai Spiridonovich, relate this story, whereupon he turns into its principal personage. But not all at once. As was customary, after the bird's death, its burial service was conducted in the cesspool, in order that infection not be spread. At the burial there gathered a small crowd of twenty-six snouts, drawn by the yelps of the physician's juvenile spawn. As was related to Yermolai Spiridonovich, who himself took part in the funeral procession in the capacity of an observer, he passed the night before the procession in auditory hallucinations, in spite of the boyar physician Agafon Yelistratovich's having pledged to his children to buy them as replacement for the defunct parakeet something even more amusing, such as a goat. In the morning Yermolai Spiridonovich left home with the firmly set intention of rescuing the bird from its cold grave when it was drizzling, increasing the amount of mud on the streets, and Mam'selle Shchelgunov from the window of her parental home, during a break between her harp-playing lessons, distinctly saw your son, Yermolai Spiridonovich, scrabbling with his fingernails to take the parakeet from the cesspool, his appearance recalling nothing so much as a mangy cat, she said, with a hankering to treat itself to some dainty morsels of carrion. The following disgrace is somewhat familiar to you, my dear Spiridon Yermolaevich, judging by your thoughtless question, one surprising coming from a man in the service. How ever did you contrive to raise a madman, and one who subsequently came to be a real troublemaker into the bargain! How? About this you keep silent, supplicating for your son, but I would like to know, as a lesson for others. For I immediately grasped, as soon as he came before me, that he was not at all our sort, however much he might pretend, and I said to him, when he finished: and now, boy, let's have the whole truth. And he lips back at me that that's it, he says, that *is* the whole truth! Shall we then make a wager, I say, that that is not all? My young stalwarts are standing in the doorway, in their red caps, grinning. Hey, I say, don't be so quick, you jokers, to bare your teeth, maybe the young man will change his mind, will even win a hundred rubles from me with an honorable discharge thrown in. Uh-uh, my stalwarts shake their heads, he won't win, he's an out-and-out prevaricator, wherever he came from. Shut up, I say, don't give me your premature judgments!—and I turn to your son, the dear youth, moving up close: Have the guts for this, Yermolayushka? Yermolai says to me, recoiling: I have nothing more to say. I told you everything. But, believe me, I did nothing wrong . . . It turns out, then, that it was some sort of childish tantrum that made you decide to dig up the bird, is that so, Yermolayushka? You dug up the bird and nimbly hopped up onto the roof. And whispered tenderly: Fly, my Seymon! Fly, my little pigeon! And Semyon the worm-eaten turquoise parakeet flapped his turquoise wings, flapped a couple of times in blind hope of returning to his former life . . . "And here," I said then, angry now, "here you are, Yermolayushka, here you have a SYMBOL!" "There's no *symbol* here!" wailed your son, that silly goose, Yermolai Spiridonovich, "there's none!" "Now you just go and tell that story to somebody else . . ." "Why is it," Yermolai Spiridonovich replies to me, "that you imagine *symbols* appearing everywhere?" I fell silent and stared piercingly at that youngster of yours, Spiridon Yermolaevich, and after wiping my bald spot with a napkin, I answered, "They appear to me, my fine Yermolai Spiridonovich, because world culture, may the Lord forgive me, since its very birth, as the wisest of men assure us, has been stuffed with *symbols,* and there's no way for us, no matter how hard we try, to spring ourselves from that cage!" And I struck him, your brown-eyed boy, right in the teeth with all my soul, because I'd grown weary, I took preventive measures, but my fist . . . well, you, Yermolaich, know. And so his teeth spattered in various directions, just like pearls from a broken string—they spattered and tumbled. We were silent for a while . . . When our beloved Yermolai Spiridonovich came to, he looked at me with his gap-toothed mouth in surprise. Why, says he, such unkindness? It's all right, I assure him, don't cry, new ones will grow in! My stalwarts stand in the doorway, in red caps, ready to bust a gut. But Yermolai Spiridonovich himself is cheerless, counting his losses, and he doesn't even smile at the joke. It is proper to smile, I admonish him, when your elders joke with you and could be your father. You were the one, I exclaim, who taught us to laugh at jokes when you did the trick with the parakeet!

We tormented and tortured your son, Yermolai Spiridonovich, we couldn't have done otherwise, we've not been taught any other way. We marveled at his frailness of build. A gallant little thing! We tormented him for the most part in ways that would gladden the soul. We plunged him, for example, into manure muck over his head: we told him to wallow; we impaled him, blindfolded, on purpose, you understand, using in place of a spike the manly tool of our sturdy Fedka, known as The Veteran. Do you remember him, Spiridon Yermolaevich? He remembers you well, he says that as lads you once went at it in a game of lapta, together with Sashka Shcherbakov, who drowned last winter in a hole in the ice. We also let ants loose into his prong; we blew him up through his shitter like a frog with the aid of an English pump; we tore his nostrils and fingernails with pliers; we called some women of shame and bade him, Yermolai Spiridonovich, lick their shameful ulcers that they might be healed. He licked. Well, what else is there to tell you? Finally we tore off his knackers—as useless. We threw them to the dogs. At least they got some use out of them. What good would they do him? Do we, my dear Spiridon Yermolaevich, need an heir of his? I don't think we do. And the way in which he suffered this loss

was again painfully intemperate, he was angered and became abusive upon returning to consciousness. He called us beasts and barbarians, which is even
unfair. Screaming while on the rack is, of course, not forbidden, they all
scream on it, but why the insults? We are not independent people, our duties
demand that we execute serious orders, and he tells us that for this we are, as
he says, barbarians. No, my dear friend, by and large it's you who turns out to
be an utter barbarian, it's you who went against the natural order of things, not
we, and when he's on the rack, what's on a man's mind is on his tongue as well,
as is observed of drunken people, and consequently my supposition regarding
his not being our sort, my good sir, has been confirmed with every passing
hour. I, thank God, know my business, I earn my bread, and therefore I have
an idea of how our kind of people scream on the rack and how those who
aren't our kind do. One of ours would never call me a barbarian, because he
doesn't think that way, but your scoundrel admitted that he did. He behaved, I
regret to inform you, rather cowardly. After the manure muck, when he'd had
a good puke, he begged for mercy and, like a little child, promised that he
wouldn't do it any more, and said that in the future he wouldn't put on airs,
that he'd behave quietly and would eagerly serve the state. That's all fine—but
who needs his contrition? Still, we asked him anyway: dispel our doubts, we
said, concerning the resurrection of the parakeet nicknamed Semyon. Perhaps
there was some discord between you and your neighbor Agafon Yelistratovich? In his denunciation of Agafon Yelistratovich he said that there didn't
seem to be any discord, but this physician, he said, was a drunken sot, which is
why he doctored people with a shaky hand. We, to be sure, know Agafon Yelistratovich as a man of excellent record, and we responded to the denunciation
regarding sottish drunkenness with total indignation. However, how could you
explain that not even three days had passed since the moment of purchase of
the parakeet when the parakeet keeled over in horrible convulsions, as if
someone had poisoned it, and even earlier had seemed sick, did not chirp, and
went off its feed? Wait, wait, I thought, let me figure this out. I wiped my raspberry bald patch with a napkin and, subsequently, I asked Yermolai Spiridonovich, your son, having previously squeezed his scrotum (which at that
time continued as yet to depend from his person), as a preventive measure:
in case of deception. Wait, wait, weren't you, I asked, the scum who himself poisoned the overseas bird with the desire to vex your neighbor, the boyars' physician Agafon Yelistratovich, and his despondent children as well,
Tatyana Agafonovna and Ezdra Agafonovich? No, answered your son, Yermolai Spiridonovich, bug-eyed from pain, no, no-o-o!!!—and his pretty little
eyes turned white, and we bit our little lip, didn't we, because it hurt us, didn't
it. "No-o-o! . . . I mean Ye-e-e-e-s!!!" We squeezed harder, we were trying to
understand: did he say yes or no? "Yes! yes! It was me!" Yermolai Spiridonovich screams at me, as if he took me for somebody deaf. "Me! I did it," he
said, "to vex them!!!" "Well fine, then. To vex them—but why?" Ow, he
screams, it hurts! let me go! and he is twitching all over, the poor thing. Let
me go! I can't think like this! Then don't think, we say, just answer—but
we loosened up a bit, for we were afraid he'd bite his tongue, and how would

he be able to have a conversation then? "I wanted to vex him," he explains, "because I didn't like him . . ." "Why didn't you?" we squeezed again a little more . . . "Because," he screamed, "he served the fatherland honorably!" "So that's it!" I say. "You should have said that in the beginning! Well, rest, dear boy . . ." And when he had rested, I say: but didn't you want to poison Agafon Yelistratovich as well as the bird? He keeps mum, he's thinking. I was just getting ready to squeeze when he answers: yes! Well, you can see for yourself what kind of story we have here, my esteemed Spiridon Yermolaevich, but we decided, all the same, not to rush: we are mistrustful people, pardon the expression. Next day we took him for a little jaunt on the rack, he could use that, he's a bit stooped, don't you think, Spiridon Yermolaevich, it wouldn't hurt to straighten him up while we're at it. It's an excruciatingly funny line of work, I warrant, especially if it's a wench, but let me tell you, your son is a delicate fruit, just like a wench, if not better . . . But I don't dare weary you any more with details, allow me to make just one digression of a purely physiological sort. You and I, Spiridon, would be as useless as philosophers and con artists had we not noted mankind's great passion for torture. How come the state protects its loyal citizens by law from arbitrary rule and petty tyranny? It protects them because otherwise the people in the state would die out after destroying and torturing each other . . . For example, the wenches don't do anything for my prong, it lies motionless, doesn't sense any distinction between their minimal particularities, having sampled quite a few of them, but when I get ready to really put the screws hard to a man, with all the authority vested in me by the state, I can't help it, it looks up to the sky, and sometimes I get so worked up that I spatter my britches all over, and my old lady thinks that I've been getting a little something on the side, but she's wrong, I'm just returning home from work . . . This passion is a profound mystery, and philosophers are in the main silent about it, burying their heads in their shoulders like ostriches; it's a mystery more significant than rolling your finger around in your sixth hole, Spiridon, you turn your insides out and still don't know something from nothing. But, at the same time, I like the humble sufferers, the ones who only fart and quack when they're on the rack, I respect them, and I wouldn't ever swap a sufferer like that for a hundred Englishmen, because torture and suffering are a thing pleasing unto God, and what's an Englishman?—shit and nothing more! Or let's say we take the prophet Elisha, who some children mocked one day for being bald. Look, baldy! . . . A minor insult: it's proper for any man of worth to have a bald spot. And Elisha didn't say a mean word to the children, he set two she-bears on them, and they tore forty-two children to pieces . . . And there, brother Spiridon, you and I have food for thought: an edifying picture!—and here you go writing inquiries, besmirching paper all for naught. I have no doubt that a man will sell out anyone and anything, you just have to approach him slowly, don't scare him—just give us time! But we're not given time, we're hurried, pressed, rushed. That's why things get bungled up in our business, and because of that, Spiridon, the screwups multiply . . .

And now you be the judge, Spiridon Yermolaevich, what would have

happened if that worm-ravaged parakeet had ascended? WOULDN'T WE BE
FINE FOOLS! And, according to your troublemaker's words, it did flap its wings
a couple of times, although later on the rack he recanted his careless words.
But, you know, that louse got all tangled up in his words towards the end! You
see, either he himself poisoned the bird, or, he says, it was together with Agafon Yelistratovich, in order to test the poison, or—it even came to this, I'll tell
you in confidence—he made a denunciation to the effect that you, his own father, Spiridon Yermolaevich, goaded him into exhuming the dead creature. At
this point (or was it, perhaps, earlier?) we tore off his knackers to teach him
not to shoot his mouth off like that about his father for no good reason, tore
them off and tossed them right to the dogs: let them have a little treat . . . And
now he's agreeable to everything, ready to sign everything, to confirm anything we say, he responds affirmatively to every question. What good does that
do, you be the judge? We see that he wants to undermine the investigation,
set it onto a false trail, conceal the shameful truth. But we came, via a round-
about way, to the truth, arrived, in the bitter end, at the shared opinion that
your boy, Yermolai Spiridonovich, wanted to resurrect the parakeet in order to
prove the superiority of the overseas bird over our own sparrows and thereby
to diminish our pride, to hold us up to the world in a ridiculous and incorrect
light. When Yermolai Spiridonovich and I came to share that common opinion, we embraced in our joy: a job well done, I say, is its own reward, bring us,
my stalwarts, wine and viands, we shall make merry! And my stalwarts bring
us white salmon, suckling pigs and lambs, sundry soufflés and a wine that has
the playful name, Madonna's Milk. We ate and then shot the breeze . . .

However, I dimly suspect that you, Spiridon, inflamed by paternal feeling,
which we cannot hold against you, are further interested in the matter of what
became of your son, the unforgettable, fondly remembered, Yermolayushka.
And what could become of him? Nothing became of him. Everything, thank
God, turned out for the best. Early the next morning, at about five, when the
sun's brilliant orb gilded the poppy-head domes of our holy churches, he and
I went slowly up, arm in arm, to the bell tower. We feasted our eyes. All
around lay our capital city in mellow morning sleep and fog, the cocks were
crowing and the orchards resounding. The granaries, the thoroughfares, the
locomotive whistles, the university—all was in its place. The river ran like a
silvery serpent through the city, and on the far bank, high up, there stood a
pinewood—a sight to behold! And what an aroma, Spiridon, wafted up from
the grasses. The scent of clover, Spiridon, and a heavy scent it was! "Glorious!"
I uttered, looking about. "Glorious!" uttered Yermolai Spiridonovich. I looked
at him from the side. I'll say just one word about him: gorgeous! Even his
hungover pallor, shading into a delicate blueness, enhanced his appearance.
Unwittingly beguiled by lascivious demons, he had arrived at the hour of his
deliverance, and, foretasting his new life, he was beatified in advance. "Well,
Godspeed!" I said, and I led him by the arm to the ledge of the belfry. "Fly,
Yermolayushka! Fly, my pigeon!" Spreading his arms out to form a cross, he
stepped into the emptiness. For just a minute I was almost seized by the torment of doubt: what if he were to ascend like a turquoise parakeet, to the

demons' delight? With a certain disquiet I leaned over the railing and glanced below. Thank God! Smashed! Flopped down nicely, I could see, with his brains splattered like a ripe melon all over the pavement. My stalwarts in red hats ran to cover Yermolai Spiridonovich with a piece of state-issue cloth. I crossed myself.

Don't grieve, Spiridon Yermolaevich! Forget it, don't grieve! As if he were worth grieving over! Don't pine for the scoundrel! He testified against you, too, but I hid that document, didn't let it go any further. When your paternal feelings have cooled down, pay me a call: we'll go to the bathhouse, steam ourselves, drink some beer. My old lady brews a good strong beer, it really hits the spot! Drop by whenever you feel like it, forget the formalities. You'll still father a few more kids, you seem to be a real man, still in good working shape, even if you are getting a bit on up there. And if you don't father any more—it's no big deal, you'll do just fine. There are plenty as it is! And your boy, Yermolai Spiridonovich, he's gone straight up to heaven for sure: a martyr will always get to heaven, even if his cause is wrong. And he looks down on us tenderly from there, plays with his turquoise parakeet, strokes its little feathers—and gives thanks. When you think about it, when you picture that, you even get jealous, Spiridon, honest to God you do . . . Well, fine, then, to hell with him, let him rejoice!

Translated from the Russian by Leonard J. Stanton

Péter Esterházy

Roberto Narrates

(HUNGARY)

"Ignorance does not protect innocence," crowed Roberto, deciding not to make allowances for me after all and launching into the story of the witch who dwells up by the Danube-Breg source, where, in her fury and her boredom, she keeps switching on her cassette recorder to recite the great and true story of the Danube, the smallest and briefest of smiles only flickering across her otherwise dark face when she hears the word Tulcea played back in her own voice. This woman, so the story went, would give birth to horrible monstrosities and sell them at a very good price. It had all begun during the boiling hot days of haymaking when she was still a girl. They'd gone and got her pregnant, and to keep it hidden she covered herself up tight, her stomach, so tight that the kid got squashed, and the circus offered her good money for it. And that's what gave her the idea. Later she could plop out the required shape almost to order. Our host, the Baron, shook his head in disapproval. He was busy waltzing to "The Blue Danube" with the gardener.

Uncle Adalbert was a peculiar little man, short and fidgety, like a ladies' hairdresser. He counted as one of the richest men in Germany, or rather, he owned one of the largest estates, woodlands in particular. We were somehow related, at least in so far as we addressed each other in the *"du"* form in German. When I asked at home exactly how we were related, my father, who took only a marginal interest in genealogy (and understandably, too, for people are usually related *to* him, although it should be added that he exhibits in all this a genuine modesty, which this sentence is unable to suggest), answered, with the indifference such questions always elicited from him, that "one" was usually related to us through the Lichtensteins, and he watched me slyly to see whether I took him seriously or not.

The Baron was only eighteen years old when he took up his duties, so to speak, his parents having died in a car accident on their annual trip to see the Bayreuth *Ring*. (In those days I didn't know what the *Ring* was, and I confused Bayreuth with Beirut. Accordingly, I posed a few politely interested, gentlemanly questions, which must have created a rather bizarre impression.) Uncle Adalbert started out as a highly talented atomic physicist, Dirac's prize pupil ("the brightest of the bunch"), and it was not his great estates which put an end to his scientific career, but a tick bite from which he got meningitis, just like Sarolta Monspart—if the name means anything to anyone. For weeks he hovered between life and death with tiny muscular spasms running all the way down his body, just like a peaceful Danube bay ruffled by an evening breeze. His heartbeat slowed almost to a standstill. (Incidentally, there are two types of tick [*Ixodes ricinus*], Eastern and Western, with the Alps constituting a kind of border in between. The consequences of Eastern bloodsucking can be more severe, although the reasons for this have not as yet been scientifically explained. In Hungary, in spite of the fact that it is on the eastern side of the Alps, one finds both this kind, and the other.) When he recovered, his brain no longer functioned in its former, reliable fashion. It was rather like a beautiful Brussels lace shawl in which moth-eaten, burnt and mouldy patches alternate with the perfect, unblemished squares. And one could never tell just how much he knew about all this, which made him very difficult to get on with. But not, of course, for a child, who could see at once that he was dealing with an idiot who was much cleverer than everyone else. Since his illness, his days had been filled with two activities: hunting and dancing.

"Slow waltz!" he called out to someone in the room, who was meant to jump up and dance with him at once as the music miraculously began to play. "Cha-cha-cha!" our host cried out anew in the middle of the dance, and the music immediately changed. (How, I never knew.) Uncle Adalbert danced with ease and devotion, his face radiating a sublime, contented glow. Whenever he stumbled they thrust an armchair beneath him, into which he would collapse. In the silence Tante Maria immediately opened a bottle of champagne. There was something decidedly grand about the whole madness. Perhaps because here it seemed authentic and valid.

That it was champagne we drank on these long, late afternoons—there was no breakfast, we each took lunch in our own rooms, and only met in the afternoon, in the downstairs drawing room, neighbours, guests, always some ten to twelve people dressed in suits, while in the evening we met in the drawing room, or rather, inner garden, upstairs, in dinner jackets—that it was champagne we drank I had no idea at the time. To myself I called it "fizzy wine," which wasn't good as wine at all, it tickled and scratched, but this tickling was quite nice. Sekt, they called it, and I'd have only understood a word like champagne.

"Don't even think of praying," Roberto threatened at bedtime. Our bedrooms opened into each other. We swaggered about in our new night garb, pirouetting like a couple of angels. I laughed at Roberto—in those days I found it impossible not to pray. I think he had the whole thing planned, because he stroked my head, we got into bed, and he turned out the light. We said nothing. I waited. Silence. I gave up.

"No story today?" He did not reply. I ran over to his bed and climbed in beside him. It was nice and warm. (My father's bed was always cold, my mother's always warm. No value judgement intended.) He still said nothing. He lay on his back staring up at the ceiling, his hands folded on his chest like a corpse. I turned on my side and, resting my head on his shoulder, nestled against him.

Everything had grown too serious, and this frightened me, because I didn't understand.

"Why don't you say something?" he asked suddenly. "You can see that I can't speak. Why don't you help me?" This frightened me all the more. You just don't say such things to a child. "What kind of man do you think I am?" His gaze on the ceiling. Helpfully, terror-stricken, I said:

"Roberto, you're an idiot."

We woke up too early for lunch, and without the appropriate slovenliness. We squinted at each other to check who was awake and who unable to meet the minimal requirements of leisurely life—that is to say, to wait for the sun to shine on one's belly before even contemplating climbing out of bed. My head was still on his shoulder. He always told me a story, every day, whether at bedtime or in the morning or in the middle of the afternoon, during one of our excursions, or even in the company of others he'd whisper a sentence in my ear, if only a line of poetry, or a weighty, merry secret, but there was always a story. This isn't a story—I bristled at once—after all it's about us, because it's about a traveller who's sailing up the Danube, who "throws yet another sleepy glance towards Donaueschingen." What did I mean about us? he said with a dismissive wave of the hand, more disappointed than angry, anybody! anybody! about us? what's that supposed to mean? And if I look back at all those stories now it isn't myself I see, nor even my wonderful scoundrel of an uncle, but someone I know, not a relative, not even a Hungarian, nor a Serb, nor a Czech, not anyone, but that isn't true either, rather, sometimes this, sometimes that, neither likable nor unpleasant, but someone who simply *is*— although I agree with Várhegyi's observation that it is an unforgivable arrogance on the part of a human being if he *sees* that everything is okay—and above all that someone who created this *is,* someone (more exaltedly: the someone) who created this rotten twentieth century *is* in his own image, yes indeed, that much-questioned and highly-questionable someone. They were like my mother's old stories, there too one could always see (*the mother allowed her son to see*) that the story was born of the events of that day, and there too I had always wanted to ask who was who, and which one was I, Porky the pig or Suzy the Sow, or was I the cocodile, or the air, or the river? And mother, just like Roberto, would simply nod huffily, it would seem that *they* didn't like this who's who.

THE TRAVELLER INTRODUCES HIMSELF

The traveller began travelling. He cast a sleepy glance at Donaueschingen. He was a professional traveller; travelling was his occupation. In his younger days he had concocted great literary plans, and had with his literary efforts in his homeland, which is called Hungary, and where Hungarians live, who speak Hungarian, or, more accurately, throw Hungarian words in one another's faces, eat Hungarian, chomping Hungarian meat between their Hungarian teeth, make Hungarian love, with their Hungarian heads resting on Hungarian thighs, are born Hungarian, and die Hungarian, with Hungarian light

falling on their cradles and Hungarian soil falling on their coffins, on their velvety or, as the case may be, wasted Hungarian bodies, and they live Hungarian, in his homeland, that treasure chest which lay like a treasure chest in
the lap of the Carpathians, he, with his literary efforts had even made a name
for himself, but then, when it became clear that even God had created him to
be a traveller, he became a traveller.

He travelled on commission. He would be hired by this or that illustrious
gentleman or shabby country, and then he would set off on his travels.

Just between ourselves, he hated travelling, and loved nothing more than to sit
around in his study. No, that's not true. His soul was the soul of a traveller, in
so far as he had several souls, and in his more ambitious moments he felt he
had as many as he liked. It is always possible that "one" is more than "several,"
but he didn't give this much thought. To put it bluntly, he didn't give death
much thought. Although, as far as death was concerned, he was no virgin. He
had stood beside the grave before, sobbing, silent, numb, he knew what it
meant to lose a parent, to cry, to feel pain, he knew what black stood for, but
his life did not stand in the shadow of death, even though life does stand in the
shadow of death. All this may well be called paradoxical, or, better still, comi-
cal, because it was for precisely this reason that Contractors (Hirers) engaged
him, for in essence they sent him out into death. The traveller was immortal,
in so far as he thought of himself as such.

APPENDIX TO THE TRAVELLER
INTRODUCES HIMSELF

"It is Christmas-time as I write these lines, and the Christmas of '89 in Central
Europe is not a festival of peace and love. To put it nicely, I'd say it was a festival of freedom. But for days now I've sat glued to the television, watching the
formation of my own destiny, just as the Americans once followed the Second
World War; *Schwarzwaldklinik.* ° Weeping faces and the crackle of gunfire
in the background. Broadcast live. A man of about my age from Temesvár
says that he was just walking by the banks of the Bega, his child on his shoulders, when he heard shooting. I simply couldn't believe it had anything to do
with us, he says in tears. His son shook slightly, then fell. By this time the
Securitate-murderers were already beside them. They threw the child into the
river like a cat, and handcuffed the man. But they forgot to shoot him.—It is
Christmas, but again and again I have to wrestle with my hatred. At least to
reach the point where I feel ashamed. But I am motionless.

"I simply couldn't believe that all that was happening had anything to do
with me."

° *Schwarzwaldklinik.* A popular German soap opera

TRAVELLER'S FATHER HELPS OUT

When he received his first commission—to prepare "a travelogue about the Danube, in his own very individual style, spiced with ironical reflections, from, shall we say, the Black Forest to the Black Sea"—and it suddenly occurred to him that, once upon a time, it had been with precisely such a Danube tour that his father had rewarded him for passing his matriculation, he decided to pay the old man a visit. He waited for it to get dark, to avoid arousing the suspicion of the neighbours, then with base but agile movements, tied the ageing man to one of the three trees his mother had planted some thirty years before—the three birches, which had grown aslant in the constant north wind, like three hardy travellers pressing on against a headwind (south wind!). When the old man was so tightly bound that he could not move an inch, the traveller began, coolly, full of love and gratitude, and with blows that were not so much hard as agile, yet brutal all the same, to beat every last Danube story out of his father.

His father did not give in easily, for he had little faith in his son, who for his part carried on with his beating regardless. Then he wiped his father down with a flannel, washed and dried him, and they both sat down at the garden table and drank whatever kind of alcohol they could find in the house, wine, beer, schnapps, Unicum, eggnog, aftershave.

DESCRIPTION OF TRAVELLER'S DUTIES

The traveller could be hired for longer or shorter voyages, groups or individuals, in principle or in practice. There were special offers too, for voyages in time, for example ("Check out the Peace of Karlowitz!")—the latter being the so-called Orlando-Step-Package. All this he posted on a small, modest plaque outside his house. He even prepared fliers.

Do you wish to travel? Do you suffer from the illusion that you can simply head off? You think you just have to find a travel agent and basta? You are mistaken. This century does not favour the traveller. This is the century of the tourist. The Tourist does not travel: he simply changes places. He goes somewhere. (Where? Where? Oh where shall we go?) He is the century's degenerate traveller, who timidly flees into the future. When he has unpacked his bags in one of those hotels which are the same the world over, and lies down on the beach that comes with such hotels, he pronounces haughtily: "We'll come back next year too," and "Let's make a note of this, this bodega!"
Is this enough for you?
For me it would be the end of the world.
The hired traveller brings the whole world to your doorstep. In all its splendour. The traveller will uplift and ennoble. Identity problems? Hire a traveller. A hired traveller is not a solution, but a possibility. Your tragic existence will know no bounds. At the centre of it all you will—in Van Cha's words—still not find the One who dissolves all contradictions, but will confront chaos, lack, the abyss, the unfulfilled, the tension between coming into being and

passing away. Everything depends on what you do with the "I." You will re-
main unable to view as a superfluous burden that which is better forgotten;
on the contrary, you will drag your "I" behind you wherever you go, be it to
heaven or to hell. The Westerner will be astonished to discover that the two
are not so very different after all. The hired traveller will put an end to this
astonishment. You will be like a pilgrim who carries a pianino on his back and
finds the world a little uncomfortable . . . The traveller is always himself, and
as such is infinite. Hire a traveller and you hire infinity! A promenade in the
soft lap of Nature, among other things! Fare-stage concession! Timeplay—
spaceplay! Gather personal experiences! Be traditional and up-to-date.

In fact he was only and exclusively a Danube-traveller. He simply couldn't count the times he'd stood at Donaueschingen. He was well known there. Look, there's that Hungarian, they would whisper. They awaited his arrival, as if waiting for spring after a long winter.

Being a Danube-traveller was in no way a limitation. The contract would always contain a sub-clause (generally 8/y) in which the traveller stated: *What constitutes the Danube is for me to decide.* He had little patience for those contractors who dragged their feet (or simply pulled faces) when they received a bill from Los Angeles. "I'm here on the hills of Pacific Palisades. Looking for the agreed river. Good news: I can't find it. STOP." Surely that was more reassuring than if he were to scurry up and down the hills and finally find a way into the Pacific Ocean. It is the traveller's duty to be vigilant, attentive, and tactful—vis-à-vis the river. Anyone might be the Danube! (Beuys).

It is also true, as it soon became clear, that if anything (etc.) might be the Danube, then the best thing of all would be if the Danube were the Danube. The acceptance of a refined, subjective (indeed subjectivistic), provisional and sophisticated consensus would afford particular pleasure to . . . Well? To whom? As if, instead of taking one right turn, we'd taken three to the left. To the subject. Every journey is an inner journey. That is to say, the traveller goes off in search of himself. Not as if there were actually someone to search for. The traveller is under obligation *not* to be an individual; that is, he must stagger between being somebody and nobody. He is to be the infinite, or, with more false-modesty, to be being itself, to be pure form, a carrel, a creel, a cell, full of books, full of fish, full of chains.

Translated from the Hungarian by Richard Aczel

Nuruddin Farah

My Father, the Englishman, and I

(SOMALIA)

To Mina, all my love

I would have been as high, standing, as the knees of a full-grown pygmy sitting when I first met a European, to wit an Englishman, the Administrator of the Ogaden, with whom my father worked as an interpreter. I wasn't quite three when, responding to an urgent summons, my father took me with him, well aware that I didn't want to meet up with the colonial officer. My mother's undisguised aversion to the white man was no secret, but this in and of itself could not explain why I declined the Englishman's offers of boiled sweets and other presents.

Being my mother's favorite child, I suspect I harbored resentments not only toward the Englishman but toward my father, too—what with my dad's unpredictable furies, his hopeless rages which I would encounter later in life, and his sudden loss of temper when he was not having his way with you. My father was kindness itself to non-family, temperamental with his dependents. But he cut the figure of a most obliging vassal to the Englishman. You might have thought he was the white man's general factotum, doing his bidding and never speaking an unkind word about him.

It was a feat of great magnitude to convince myself not to stuff the boiled sweet the Englishman had sent along with my father, because in those days mine was a mouth-centered universe. Not admitting to being tempted, I now had my right thumb shoved into my mouth and my left tight around the un-eaten sweet, while I remained in contact with my father, who held on to my wrist, pulling me as though I were a sandbag. I had a great urge to eat the sweet but didn't, in deference to my mother's unspoken wish. Later I would realize that a history of loyalties was being made then.

I remember my parents raising their voices over the matter earlier, my mother disapproving of my father's wretched acceptance of his lowly status in the hierarchy of colonial dispensation. When, years later, in a heated argument, my mother accused my father of "political pimping," my memory revisited this incident.

Anyway, I would have stayed with my mother if I could have, my mother who had lately been incontinent of sorrow, something I was too young to understand. I left the house wrapped in sadness. Often I had little difficulty getting my words out when in the company of my mother, whereas with others I had the habit of choking on my speech. Today it felt as though I had swallowed my tongue. I loved my mother, whom I thought of as my sanctuary, her silences generous as openings embracing my stammers.

I regret I do not have my mother to corroborate my versions of these happenings. As fate would have it, I was not able to exchange my memories with her before she died.

Above all, I remember hands: hands pulling me, hands pushing me. I see the Englishman reaching, striving to take hold of me. My father's open palm pushes me from behind, urging me forward toward the white man's looming face. Or are we dealing with memory as a rogue, memory willfully vandalizing the integrity of a remembrance and reshaping the past so as to confirm the present? Perhaps not. Because I am not the only one who associates my father with hands—hands not giving but reaching out to hit. One of my older brothers whom my father often struck for being mischievous reiterates that one did not know if our father's hands were about to make a monkey of one or, in a bid to encourage one, pat one on the head.

If I went with my father to be with the Englishman, it was because I was given little choice. I had to make do with the makeshift of emotions which I had built around myself, emotions meant to protect me from psychological harm. For I had wised up to this before my third year and knew, as though by instinct, that my father might punish me for my lack of deference toward the Englishman. Too clever by half, I took a step forward if only to humor him and made sure not a truant tear would betray my genuine feelings. By Jove, it was difficult not to submit to the desire to weep or to cringe with embarrassment as the Englishman embraced me.

It was such a relief to see that my father appeared pleased!

There was a pattern to the relationship between my father and the Englishman, my father speaking only when spoken to or after he had been given the go-ahead. It struck me as if my old man stood in relation of a student repeating what a teacher had said. What I could not have known was that in his capacity as a vassal to the British Empire, my father translated into Somali whatever the Englishman had uttered in Swahili.

No sooner had the Englishman sat me on his lap than I sensed a change in my surroundings. For we were joined by the stifled murmurs of a dozen or so men, preceded by the noise of *jaamuus*-sandaled feet being dragged heavily across the floor. And I was suddenly heir to the sad expressions on the newly arrived men's faces, the sorrow of the eunuched. I might have thought that my sense of powerlessness was no different from theirs had I known then, as I know now, that the clan elders were gathered in the Englishman's spacious office to sport with the tangles of history, putting their thumbs to a treaty Ethiopia and Britain had prepared with the connivance of the Americans. I'm not certain of the future date in the same calendar year 1948 when the fate of the Ogaden was decided and put in the hands of expansionist Ethiopia.

What was my role in this ignoble affair? I lay in the embrace of the Englishman; I felt the tremors of words dressed in the garb of authority coming into contact with my heartbeat before they were translated into Somali by my father; and I did nothing. If I had resisted being the Englishman's booty, which he received without firing a bullet, would matters have been different? If I had fussed so as to prevent my father from translating the ignominious words of the Englishman into Somali, would the Ogaden have been dealt a fairer hand?

I remember the elders of the clan entering into a cantankerous argument with my father, who in all likelihood was discouraging them from standing up to the Englishman. Left out of the debate altogether, the Englishman rose up to ride the high horse of rage the powerful so often mount: and there was silence. It was then that I entered the fray, letting out a shriek of outrage wrung out of the primeval beginnings of all my years. Apologizing to me, the Englishman adjourned the meeting till another day.

At a subsequent meeting, the clan elders placed their thumbs over the allotted space in the treaty they signed. Had I been present, or had my mother been consulted, maybe this would not have occurred.

Richard Ford

Optimists

(UNITED STATES)

All of this that I am about to tell happened when I was only fifteen years old, in 1959, the year my parents were divorced, the year when my father killed a man and went to prison for it, the year I left home and school, told a lie about my age to fool the Army, and then did not come back. The year, in other words, when life changed for all of us and forever—ended, really, in a way none of us could ever have imagined in our most brilliant dreams of life.

My father was named Roy Brinson, and he worked on the Great Northern Railway, in Great Falls, Montana. He was a switch-engine fireman, and when he could not hold that job on the seniority list, he worked the extra-board as a hostler, or as a hostler's helper, shunting engines through the yard, onto and off the freight trains that went south and east. He was thirty-seven or thirty-eight years old in 1959, a small, young-appearing man, with dark blue eyes. The railroad was a job he liked, because it paid high wages and the work was not hard, and because you could take off days when you wanted to, or even months, and have no one to ask you questions. It was a union shop, and there were people who looked out for you when your back was turned. "It's a workingman's paradise," my father would say, and then laugh.

My mother did not work then, though she *had* worked—at waitressing and in the bars in town—and she had liked working. My father thought, though, that Great Falls was coming to be a rougher town than it had been when he grew up there, a town going downhill, like its name, and that my mother should be at home more, because I was at an age when trouble came easily. We lived in a rented two-story house on Edith Street, close to the freight yards and the Missouri River, a house where from my window at night I could hear the engines as they sat throbbing, could see their lights move along the dark rails. My mother was at home most of her time, reading or watching television or cooking meals, though sometimes she would go out to movies in the afternoon, or would go to the YWCA and swim in the indoor pool. Where she was from—in Havre, Montana, much farther north—there was never such a thing as a pool indoors, and she thought that to swim in the winter, with snow on the ground and the wind howling, was the greatest luxury. And she would come home late in the afternoon, with her brown hair wet and her face flushed, and in high spirits, saying she felt freer.

The night that I want to tell about happened in November. It was not then a good time for railroads—not in Montana especially—and for firemen not at all, anywhere. It was the featherbed time, and everyone knew, including my father, that they would—all of them—eventually lose their jobs, though no one knew exactly when, or who would go first, or, clearly, what the future would be. My father had been hired out ten years, and had worked on coal-burners and oil-burners out of Forsythe, Montana, on the Sheridan spur. But he was still young in the job and low on the list, and he felt that when the cut came young heads would go first. "They'll do something for us, but it might not be enough," he said, and I had heard him say that other times—in the kitchen, with my mother, or out in front, working on his motorcycle, or with me, fishing the whitefish flats up the Missouri. But I do not know if he truly thought that or in fact had any reason to think it. He was an optimist. Both of them were optimists, I think.

I know that by the end of summer in that year he had stopped taking days off to fish, had stopped going out along the coulee rims to spot deer. He worked more then and was gone more, and he talked more about work when he was home: about what the union said on this subject and that, about court cases in Washington, D.C., a place I knew nothing of, and about injuries and illnesses to men he knew, that threatened their livelihoods, and by association with them, threatened his own—threatened, he must've felt, our whole life.

Because my mother swam at the YWCA she had met people there and made friends. One was a large woman named Esther, who came home with her once and drank coffee in the kitchen and talked about her boyfriend and laughed out loud for a long time, but who I never saw again. And another was a woman named Penny Mitchell whose husband, Boyd, worked for the Red Cross in Great Falls and had an office upstairs in the building with the YWCA, and who my mother would sometime play canasta with on the nights my father worked late. They would set up a card table in the living room, the three of them, and drink and eat sandwiches until midnight. And I would lie in bed with my radio tuned low to the Calgary station, listening to a hockey match beamed out over the great empty prairie, and could hear the cards snap and laughter downstairs, and later I would hear footsteps leaving, hear the door shut, the dishes rattle in the sink, cabinets close. And in a while the door to my room would open and the light would fall inside, and my mother would set a chair back in. I could see her silhouette. She would always say, "Go back to sleep, Frank." And then the door would shut again, and I would almost always go to sleep in a minute.

It was on a night that Penny and Boyd Mitchell were in our house that trouble came about. My father had been working his regular bid-in job on the switch engine, plus a helper's job off the extra-board—a practice that was illegal by the railroad's rules, but ignored by the union, who could see bad times coming and knew there would be nothing to help it when they came, and so would let men work if they wanted to. I was in the kitchen, eating a sandwich alone at the table, and my mother was in the living room playing cards with Penny and Boyd Mitchell. They were drinking vodka and eating the other sandwiches my mother had made, when I heard my father's motorcycle outside in the dark. It was eight o'clock at night, and I knew he was not expected home until midnight.

"Roy's home," I heard my mother say. "I hear Roy. That's wonderful." I heard chairs scrape and glasses tap.

"Maybe he'll want to play," Penny Mitchell said. "We can play four-hands."

I went to the kitchen door and stood looking through the dining room at the front. I don't think I knew something was wrong, but I think I knew something was unusual, something I would want to know about firsthand.

My mother was standing beside the card table when my father came inside. She was smiling. But I have never seen a look on a man's face that was like the look on my father's face at that moment. He looked wild. His eyes were wild. His whole face was. It was cold outside, and the wind was coming up, and he had ridden home from the train yard in only his flannel shirt. His face was red, and his hair was strewn around his bare head, and I remember his fists were clenched white, as if there was no blood in them at all.

"My God," my mother said. "What is it, Roy? You look crazy." She turned and looked for me, and I knew she was thinking that this was something I might not need to see. But she didn't say anything. She just looked back at my father, stepped toward him and touched his hand, where he must've been coldest. Penny and Boyd Mitchell sat at the card table, looking up. Boyd Mitchell was smiling for some reason.

"Something awful happened," my father said. He reached and took a corduroy jacket off the coat nail and put it on, right in the living room, then sat down on the couch and hugged his arms. His face seemed to get redder then. He was wearing black steel-toe boots, the boots he wore every day, and I stared at them and felt how cold he must be, even in his own house. I did not come any closer.

"Roy, what is it?" my mother said, and she sat down beside him on the couch and held his hand in both of hers.

My father looked at Boyd Mitchell and at his wife, as if he hadn't known they were in the room until then. He did not know them very well, and I thought he might tell them to get out, but he didn't.

"I saw a man be killed tonight," he said to my mother, then shook his head and looked down. He said, "We were pushing into that old hump yard on Ninth Avenue. A cut of coal cars. It wasn't even an hour ago. I was looking out my side, the way you do when you push out a curve. And I could see this one open boxcar in the cut, which isn't unusual. Only this guy was in it and was trying to get off, sitting in the door, scooting. I guess he was a hobo. Those cars had come in from Glasgow tonight. And just the second he started to go off, the whole cut buckled up. It's a thing that'll happen. But he lost his balance just when he hit the gravel, and he fell backwards underneath. I looked right at him. And one set of trucks rolled right over his foot." My father looked at my mother then. "It hit his foot," he said.

"My God," my mother said and looked down at her lap.

My father squinted. "But then he moved, he sort of bucked himself like he was trying to get away. He didn't yell, and I could see his face. I'll never forget that. He didn't look scared, he just looked like a man doing something that was hard for him to do. He looked like he was concentrating on something. But when he bucked he pushed back, and the other trucks caught his hand." My father looked at his own hands then, and made fists out of them and squeezed them.

"What did you do?" my mother said. She looked terrified.

"I yelled out. And Sherman stopped pushing. But it wasn't that fast."

"Did you do anything then," Boyd Mitchell said.

"I got down," my father said, "and I went up there. But here's a man cut in three pieces in front of me. What can you do? You can't do very much. I squatted down and touched his good hand. And it was like ice. His eyes were open and roaming all up in the sky."

"Did he say anything?" my mother said.

"He said, 'Where am I today?' and I said to him, 'It's all right, bud, you're in Montana. You'll be all right.' Though, my God, he wasn't. I took my jacket off and put it over him. I didn't want him to see what had happened."

"You should've put tourniquets on," Boyd Mitchell said gruffly. "That could've helped. That could've saved his life."

My father looked at Boyd Mitchell then as if he had forgotten he was there and was surprised that he spoke. "I don't know about that," my father said. "I don't know anything about those things. He was already dead. A boxcar had run over him. He was breathing, but was already dead to me."

"That's only for a licensed doctor to decide," Boyd Mitchell said. "You're morally obligated to do all you can." And I could tell from his tone of voice that he did not like my father. He hardly knew him, but he did not like him. I had no idea why. Boyd Mitchell was a big, husky, red-faced man with curly hair—handsome in a way, but with a big belly—and I knew only that he worked for the Red Cross, and that my mother was a friend of his wife's, and maybe of his, and that they played cards when my father was gone.

My father looked at my mother in a way I knew was angry. "Why have you got these people over here now, Dorothy? They don't have any business here."

"Maybe that's right," Penny Mitchell said, and she put down her hand of cards and stood up at the table. My mother looked around the room as though an odd noise had occurred inside of it and she couldn't find the source.

"Somebody definitely should've done something," Boyd Mitchell said, and he leaned forward on the table toward my father. "That's all there is to say." He was shaking his head no. "That man didn't have to die." Boyd Mitchell clasped his big hands on top of his playing cards and stared at my father. "The unions'll cover this up, too, I guess, won't they? That's what happens in these things."

My father stood up then, and his face looked wide, though it looked young, still. He looked like a young man who had been scolded and wasn't sure how he should act. "You get out of here," he said in a loud voice. "My God. What a thing to say. I don't even know you."

"I know you, though," Boyd Mitchell said angrily. "You're another featherbedder. You aren't good to do anything. You can't even help a dying man. You're bad for this country, and you won't last."

"Boyd, my goodness," Penny Mitchell said. "Don't say that. Don't say that to him."

Boyd Mitchell glared up at his wife. "I'll say anything I want to," he said. "And he'll listen, because he's helpless. He can't do anything."

"Stand up," my father said. "Just stand up on your feet." His fists were clenched again.

"All right, I will," Boyd Mitchell said. He glanced up at his wife. And I realized that Boyd Mitchell was drunk, and it was possible that he did not even know what he was saying, or what had happened, and that words just got loose from him this way, and anybody who knew him knew it. Only my father didn't. He only knew what had been said.

Boyd Mitchell stood up and put his hands in his pockets. He was much taller than my father. He had on a white Western shirt and whipcords and cowboy boots and was wearing a big silver wristwatch. "All right," he said. "Now I'm standing up. What's supposed to happen?" He weaved a little. I saw that.

And my father hit Boyd Mitchell then, hit him from across the card table—hit him with his right hand, square into the chest, not a lunging blow, just a hard, hitting blow that threw my father off balance and made him make a *chuffing* sound with his mouth. Boyd Mitchell groaned, "Oh," and fell down immediately, his big, thick, heavy body hitting the floor already doubled over. And the sound of him hitting the floor in our house was like no sound I had ever heard before. It was the sound of a man's body hitting a floor, and it was only that. In my life I have heard it other places, in hotel rooms and in bars, and it is one you do not want to hear.

You can hit a man in a lot of ways, I know that, and I knew that then, because my father had told me. You can hit a man to insult him, or you can hit a man to bloody him, or to knock him down, or lay him out. Or you can hit a man to kill him. Hit him that hard. And that is how my father hit Boyd Mitchell—as hard as he could, in the chest and not in the face, the way someone might think who didn't know about it.

"Oh my God," Penny Mitchell said. Boyd Mitchell was lying on his side in front of the TV, and she had gotten down on her knees beside him. "Boyd," she said. "Are you hurt? Oh, look at this. Stay where you are, Boyd. Stay on the floor."

"Now then. All right," my father said. "Now. All right." He was standing against the wall, over to the side of where he had been when he hit Boyd Mitchell from across the card table. Light was bright in the room, and my father's eyes were wide and touring around. He seemed out of breath and both his fists were clenched, and I could feel his heart beating in my own chest. "All right, now, you son of a bitch," my father said, and loudly. I don't think he was even talking to Boyd Mitchell. He was just saying words that came out of him.

"Roy," my mother said calmly. "Boyd's hurt now. He's hurt." She was just looking down at Boyd Mitchell. I don't think she knew what to do.

"Oh, no," Penny Mitchell said in an excited voice. "Look up, Boyd. Look up at Penny. You've been hurt." She had her hands flat on Boyd Mitchell's chest, and her skinny shoulders close to him. She wasn't crying, but I think she was hysterical and couldn't cry.

All this had taken only five minutes, maybe even less time. I had never even left the kitchen door. And for that reason I walked out into the room where my father and mother were, and where Boyd and Penny Mitchell were both of them on the floor. I looked down at Boyd Mitchell, at his face. I wanted to see what had happened to him. His eyes had cast back up into their sockets. His mouth was open, and I could see his big pink tongue inside. He was breathing heavy breaths, and his fingers—the fingers on both his hands—were moving, moving in the way a man would move them if he was nervous or anxious about something. I think he was dead then, and I think even Penny Mitchell knew he was dead, because she was saying, "Oh please, please, please, Boyd."

That is when my mother called the police, and I think it is when my father opened the front door and stepped out into the night.

All that happened next is what you would expect to happen. Boyd Mitchell's chest quit breathing in a minute, and he turned pale and cold and began to look dead right on our living-room floor. He made a noise in his throat once, and Penny Mitchell cried out, and my mother got down on her knees and held Penny's shoulders while she cried. Then my mother made Penny get up and go into the bedroom—hers and my father's—and lie on the bed. Then she and I sat in the brightly lit living room, with Boyd Mitchell dead on the floor, and simply looked at each other—maybe for ten minutes, maybe for twenty. I don't know what my mother could've been thinking during that time, because she did not say. She did not ask about my father. She did not tell me to leave the room. Maybe she thought about the rest of her life then and what that might be like after tonight. Or maybe she thought this: that people can do the worst things they are capable of doing and in the end the world comes back to normal. Possibly, she was just waiting for something normal to begin to happen again. That would make sense, given her particular character.

Though what I thought myself, sitting in that room with Boyd Mitchell dead, I remember very well, because I have thought it other times, and to a degree I began to date my real life from that moment and that thought. It is this: that situations have possibilities in them, and we have only to be present to be involved. Tonight was a very bad one. But how were we to know it would turn out this way until it was too late and we had all been changed forever? I realized though, that trouble, real trouble, was something to be avoided, inasmuch as once it has passed by, you have only yourself to answer to, even if, as I was, you are the cause of nothing.

In a little while the police arrived to our house. First one and then two more cars with their red lights turning in the street. Lights were on in the neighbors' houses—people came out and stood in the cold in their front yards watching, people I didn't know and who didn't know us. "It's a circus now," my mother said to me when we looked through the window. "We'll have to move somewhere else. They won't let us alone."

An ambulance came, and Boyd Mitchell was taken away on a stretcher, under a sheet. Penny Mitchell came out of the bedroom and went with them, though she did not say anything to my mother, or to anybody, just got in a police car and left into the dark.

Two policemen came inside, and one asked my mother some questions in the living room, while the other one asked me questions in the kitchen. He wanted to know what I had seen, and I told him. I said Boyd Mitchell had cursed at my father for some reason I didn't know, then had stood up and tried to hit him, and that my father had pushed Boyd, and that was all. He asked me if my father was a violent man, and I said no. He asked if my father had a girlfriend, and I said no. He asked if my mother and father had ever fought, and I said no. He asked me if I loved my mother and father, and I said I did. And then that was all.

I went out into the living room then, and my mother was there, and when the police left we stood at the front door, and there was my father outside, standing by the open door of a police car. He had on handcuffs. And for some reason he wasn't wearing a shirt or his corduroy jacket but was bare-chested in the cold night, holding his shirt behind him. His hair looked wet to me. I heard a policeman say, "Roy, you're going to catch cold," and then my father say, "I wish I was a long way from here right now. China maybe." He smiled at the policeman. I don't think he ever saw us watching, or if he did he didn't want to admit it. And neither of us did anything, because the police had him, and when that is the case, there is nothing you can do to help.

All this happened by ten o'clock. At midnight my mother and I drove down to the city jail and got my father out. I stayed in the car while my mother went in—sat and watched the high windows of the jail, which were behind wire mesh and bars. Yellow lights were on there, and I could hear voices and see figures move past the lights, and twice someone called out, "Hello, hello. Marie, are you with me?" And then it was quiet, except for the cars that drove slowly past ours.

On the ride home, my mother drove and my father sat and stared out at the big electrical stacks by the river, and the lights of houses on the other side, in Black Eagle. He had on a checked shirt someone inside had given him, and his hair was neatly combed. No one said anything, but I did not understand why the police would put anyone in jail because he had killed a man and in two hours let him out again. It was a mystery to me, even though I wanted him to be out and for our life to resume, and even though I did not see any way it could and, in fact, knew it never would.

Inside our house, all the lights were burning when we got back. It was one o'clock and there were still lights in some neighbors' houses. I could see a man at the window across the street, both his hands to the glass, watching out, watching us.

My mother went into the kitchen, and I could hear her running water for coffee and taking down cups. My father stood in the middle of the living room and looked around, looking at the chairs, at the card table with cards still on it, at the open doorways to the other rooms. It was as if he had forgotten his own house and now saw it again and didn't like it.

"I don't feel I know what he had against me," my father said. He said this to me, but he said it to anyone, too. "You'd think you'd know what a man had against you, wouldn't you, Frank?"

"Yes," I said. "I would." We were both just standing together, my father and I, in the lighted room there. We were not about to do anything.

"I want us to be happy here now," my father said. "I want us to enjoy life. I don't hold anything against anybody. Do you believe that?"

"I believe that," I said. My father looked at me with his dark blue eyes and frowned. And for the first time I wished my father had not done what he did but had gone about things differently. I saw him as a man who made mistakes, as a man who could hurt people, ruin lives, risk their happiness. A man who did not understand enough. He was like a gambler, though I did not even know what it meant to be a gambler then.

"It's such a quickly changing time now," my father said. My mother, who had come into the kitchen doorway, stood looking at us. She had on a flowered pink apron, and was standing where I had stood earlier that night. She was looking at my father and at me as if we were one person. "Don't you think it is, Dorothy?" he said. "All this turmoil. Everything just flying by. Look what's happened here."

My mother seemed very certain about things then, very precise. "You should've controlled yourself more," she said. "That's all."

"I know that," my father said. "I'm sorry. I lost control over my mind. I didn't expect to ruin things, but now I think I have. It was all wrong." My father picked up the vodka bottle, unscrewed the cap and took a big swallow, then put the bottle back down. He had seen two men killed tonight. Who could've blamed him?

"When I was in jail tonight," he said, staring at a picture on the wall, a picture by the door to the hallway. He was just talking again. "There was a man in the cell with me. And I've never been in jail before, not even when I was a kid. But this man said to me tonight, 'I can tell you've never been in jail before just by the way you stand up straight. Other people don't stand that way. They stoop. You don't belong in jail. You stand up too straight.'" My father looked back at the vodka bottle as if he wanted to drink more out of it, but he only looked at it. "Bad things happen," he said, and he let his open hands tap against his legs like clappers against a bell. "Maybe he was in love with you, Dorothy," he said. "Maybe that's what the trouble was."

And what I did then was stare at the picture on the wall, the picture my father had been staring at, a picture I had seen every day. Probably I had seen it a thousand times. It was two people with a baby on a beach. A man and a woman sitting in the sand with an ocean behind. They were smiling at the camera, wearing bathing suits. In all the times I had seen it I'd thought that it was a picture in which I was the baby, and the two people were my parents. But I realized as I stood there, that it was not me at all; it was my father who was the child in the picture, and the parents there were his parents—two people I'd never known, and who were dead—and the picture was so much older than I had thought it was. I wondered why I hadn't known that before, hadn't understood it for myself, hadn't always known it. Not even that it mattered. What mattered was, I felt, that my father had fallen down now, as much as the man he had watched fall beneath the train just hours before. And I was as helpless to do anything as he had been. I wanted to tell him that I loved him, but for some reason I did not.

Later in the night I lay in my bed with the radio playing, listening to news that was far away, in Calgary and in Saskatoon, and even farther, in Regina and Winnipeg—cold, dark cities I knew I would never see in my life. My window was raised above the sill, and for a long time I had sat and looked out, hearing my parents talk softly down below, hearing their footsteps, hearing my father's steel-toed boots strike the floor, and then their bedsprings squeeze and then be quiet. From out across the sliding river I could hear trucks—stock trucks and grain trucks heading toward Idaho, or down toward Helena, or into the train yards where my father hostled engines. The neighborhood houses were dark again. My father's motorcycle sat in the yard, and out in the night air I felt I could hear even the falls themselves, could hear every sound of them, sounds that found me and whirled and filled my room—could even feel them, cold and wintry, so that warmth seemed like a possibility I would never know again.

After a time my mother came in my room. The light fell on my bed, and she set a chair inside. I could see that she was looking at me. She closed the door, came and turned off my radio, then took her chair to the window, closed it, and sat so that I could see her face silhouetted against the streetlight. She lit a cigarette and did not look at me, still cold under the covers of my bed.

"How do you feel, Frank," she said, smoking her cigarette.

"I feel all right," I said.

"Do you think your house is a terrible house now?"

"No," I said.

"I hope not," my mother said. "Don't feel it is. Don't hold anything against anyone. Poor Boyd. He's gone."

"Why do you think that happened?" I said, though I didn't think she would answer, and wondered if I even wanted to know.

My mother blew smoke against the window glass, then sat and breathed. "He must've seen something in your father he just hated. I don't know what it was. Who knows? Maybe your father felt the same way." She shook her head and looked out into the streetlamp light. "I remember once," she said. "I was still in Havre, in the thirties. We were living in a motel my father part-owned out Highway Two, and my mother was around then, but wasn't having any of us. My father had this big woman named Judy Belknap as his girlfriend. She was an Assiniboin. Just some squaw. But we used to go on nature tours when he couldn't put up with me anymore. She'd take me. Way up above the Milk River. All this stuff she knew about, animals and plants and ferns—she'd tell me all that. And once we were sitting watching some gadwall ducks on the ice where a creek had made a little turn-out. It was getting colder, just like now. And Judy just all at once stood up and clapped. Just clapped her hands. And all these ducks got up, all except for one that stayed on the ice, where its feet were frozen, I guess. It didn't even try to fly. It just sat. And Judy said to me, 'It's just a coincidence, Dottie. It's wildlife. Some always get left back.' And that seemed to leave her satisfied for some reason. We walked back to the car after that. So," my mother said. "Maybe that's what this is. Just a coincidence."

She raised the window again, dropped her cigarette out, blew the last smoke from her throat, and said, "Go to sleep, Frank. You'll be all right. We'll all survive this. Be an optimist."

When I was asleep that night, I dreamed. And what I dreamed was of a plane crashing, a bomber, dropping out of the frozen sky, bouncing as it hit the icy river, sliding and turning on the ice, its wings like knives, and coming into our house where we were sleeping, leveling everything. And when I sat up in bed I could hear a dog in the yard, its collar jingling, and I could hear my father crying, "Boo-hoo-hoo, boo-hoo-hoo"—like that, quietly—though afterward I could never be sure if I had heard him crying in just that way, or if all of it was a dream, a dream I wished I had never had.

The most important things of your life can change so suddenly, so unrecoverably, that you can forget even the most important of them and their connections, you are so taken up by the chanciness of all that's happened and by all that could and will happen next. I now no longer remember the exact year of my father's birth, or how old he was when I last saw him, or even when that last time took place. When you're young, these things seem unforgettable and at the heart of everything. But they slide away and are gone when you are not so young.

My father went to Deer Lodge Prison and stayed five months for killing Boyd Mitchell by accident, for using too much force to hit him. In Montana you cannot simply kill a man in your living room and walk off free from it, and what I remember is that my father pleaded no contest, the same as guilty.

My mother and I lived in our house for the months he was gone. But when he came out and went back on the railroad as a switchman the two of them argued about things, about her wanting us to go someplace else to live—California or Seattle were mentioned. And then they separated, and she moved out. And after that I moved out by joining the Army and adding years to my age, which was sixteen.

I know about my father only that after a time he began to live a life he himself would never have believed. He fell off the railroad, divorced my mother, who would now and then resurface in his life. Drinking was involved in that, and gambling, embezzling money, even carrying a pistol, is what I heard. I was apart from all of it. And when you are the age I was then, and loose on the world and alone, you can get along better than at almost any other time, because it's a novelty, and you can act for what you want, and you can think that being alone will not last forever. All I know of my father, finally, is that he was once in Laramie, Wyoming, and not in good shape, and then he simply disappeared from view.

A month ago I saw my mother. I was buying groceries at a drive-in store by the interstate in Anaconda, Montana, not far from Deer Lodge itself, where my father had been. It had been fifteen years, I think, since I had seen her, though I am forty-three years old now, and possibly it was longer. But when I saw her I walked across the store to where she was and I said, "Hello, Dorothy. It's Frank."

She looked at me and smiled and said, "Oh, Frank. How are you? I haven't seen you in a long time. I'm glad to see you now, though." She was dressed in blue jeans and boots and a Western shirt, and she looked like a woman who could be sixty years old. Her hair was tied back and she looked pretty, though I think she had been drinking. It was ten o'clock in the morning.

There was a man standing near her, holding a basket of groceries, and she turned to him and said, "Dick, come here and meet my son, Frank. We haven't seen each other in a long time. This is Dick Spivey, Frank."

I shook hands with Dick Spivey, who was a man younger than my mother but older than me—a tall, thin-faced man with coarse blue-black hair—and who was wearing Western boots like hers. "Let me say a word to Frank, Dick," my mother said, and she put her hand on Dick's wrist and squeezed it and smiled at him. And he walked up toward the checkout to pay for his groceries.

"So. What are you doing now, Frank," my mother asked, and put her hand on my wrist the way she had on Dick Spivey's, but held it there. "These years," she said.

"I've been down in Rock Springs, on the coal boom," I said. "I'll probably go back down there."

"And I guess you're married, too."

"I was," I said. "But not right now."

"That's fine," she said. "You look fine." She smiled at me. "You'll never get anything fixed just right. That's your mother's word. Your father and I had a marriage made in Havre—that was our joke about us. We used to laugh about it. You didn't know that, of course. You were too young. A lot of it was just wrong."

"It's a long time ago," I said. "I don't know about that."

"I remember those times very well," my mother said. "They were happy enough times. I guess something *was* in the air, wasn't there? Your father was so jumpy. And Boyd got so mad, just all of a sudden. There was some hopelessness to it, I suppose. All that union business. We were the last to understand any of it, of course. We were trying to be decent people."

"That's right," I said. And I believed that was true of them.

"I still like to swim," my mother said. She ran her fingers back through her hair as if it were wet. She smiled at me again. "It still makes me feel freer."

"Good," I said. "I'm happy to hear that."

"Do you ever see your dad?"

"No," I said. "I never do."

"I don't either," my mother said. "You just reminded me of him." She looked at Dick Spivey, who was standing at the front window, holding a sack of groceries, looking out at the parking lot. It was March, and some small bits of snow were falling onto the cars in the lot. He didn't seem in any hurry. "Maybe I didn't appreciate your father enough," she said. "Who knows? Maybe we weren't even made for each other. Losing your love is the worst thing, and that's what we did." I didn't answer her, but I knew what she meant, and that it was true. "I wish we knew each other better, Frank," my mother said to me. She looked down, and I think she may have blushed. "We have our deep feelings, though, don't we? Both of us."

"Yes," I said. "We do."

"So. I'm going out now," my mother said. "Frank." She squeezed my wrist, and walked away through the checkout and into the parking lot, with Dick Spivey carrying their groceries beside her.

But when I had bought my own groceries and paid, and gone out to my car and started up, I saw Dick Spivey's green Chevrolet drive back into the lot and stop, and watched my mother get out and hurry across the snow to where I was, so that for a moment we faced each other through the open window.

"Did you ever think," my mother said, snow freezing in her hair. "Did you ever think back then that I was in love with Boyd Mitchell? Anything like that? Did you ever?"

"No," I said. "I didn't."

"No, well, I wasn't," she said. "Boyd was in love with Penny. I was in love with Roy. That's how things were. I want you to know it. You have to belive that. Do you?"

"Yes," I said. "I believe you."

And she bent down and kissed my cheek through the open window and touched my face with both her hands, held me for a moment that seemed like a long time before she turned away, finally, and left me there alone.

Eduardo Galeano

The Story of the Lizard Who Had the Habit of Dining on His Wives

(U R U G U A Y)

At the edge of the river, hidden by the tall grass, a woman is reading.

Once upon a time, the book tells, there lived a man of very great substance. Everything belonged to him: the town of Lucanamarca, everything around it, the dry and the wet, the tamed and the wild, all that had memory, all that had oblivion.

But that lord of all things had no heir. Every day his wife offered a thousand prayers, begging for the blessing of a son, and every night she lit a thousand candles.

God was fed up with the demands of that persistent woman, who asked for what He had not wished to grant. Finally, either to avoid having to hear her voice any longer or from divine mercy, He performed the miracle. And joy descended on that household.

The child had a human face and the body of a lizard.

With time, he spoke, but he slithered along on his belly. The finest teachers from Ayacucho taught him to read, but his claws prevented him from writing.

At the age of eighteen, he asked for a wife.

His well-heeled father found him one, and the wedding was celebrated with great pomp in the priest's house.

The first night, the lizard threw himself on his wife and devoured her. When the sun rose, in the marriage bed there was only the widower asleep, surrounded by small bones.

The lizard then demanded another wife, and there was another wedding and another devouring, and the glutton asked for yet another, and so on.

Fiancées were never lacking. In the households of the poor, there was always some spare girl.

His scaly belly lapped by river water, Dulcidio is taking his siesta.

Opening one eye, he sees her. She is reading. Never before in his life has he seen a woman wearing glasses.

Dulcidio pokes forward his long snout:

—*What are you reading?*

She lowers her book, looks at him calmly, and replies:

—*Legends.*

—*Legends?*

—*Ancient voices.*

—*What for?*

She shrugs her shoulders:

—*Company.*

This woman does not seem to be from the mountains, nor the jungle, nor the coast.

—*I know how to read too,* says Dulcidio.

She closes her book and turns her face away.

Before the woman disappears, Dulcidio manages to ask:

—*Where are you from?*

The following Sunday, when Dulcidio wakes from his siesta, she is there. Bookless, but wearing glasses.

Sitting on the sand, her feet hidden under many bright-colored skirts, she is very much there, rooted there. She casts her eye on the intruder.

Dulcidio plays all his cards. He raises a horny claw and waves it toward the blue mountains on the horizon.

—*Everything you see and don't see, it's all mine.*

She does not even glance at the vast expanse, and remains silent. A very silent silence.

The heir presses on. Many lambs, many Indians, all his to command. He is lord of all that expanse of earth and water and air, and also of the small strip of sand she sits on.

—*But you have my permission,* he assures her.

Tossing her long black tresses, she bows:

—*Thank you.*

Then the lizard adds that he is rich but humble, studious, a worker and above all a gentleman who wishes to make a home but has been doomed to widowerhood by the cruelties of fate.

She looks away. Lowering her head, she reflects on the situation.

Dulcidio hovers.

He whispers:

—*May I ask a favor of you?*

And he turns his side to her, offering his back.

—*Would you scratch my shoulder? I can't reach.*

She puts out her hand to touch the metallic scales, and exclaims:

—*It's like silk.*

Dulcidio stretches, closes his eyes, opens his mouth, stiffens his tail, and feels as he has never felt.

But when he turns his head, she is no longer there.

He looks for her, rushing full tilt across the field of tall grass, back and forth, on all sides. No trace of her. The woman has evaporated, as before.

The following Sunday, she does not come to the riverbank. Nor the next Sunday. Nor the following one.

Since he first saw her, he sees only her and nothing but her.

The famous sleeper no longer sleeps, the glutton no longer eats.

Dulcidio's bedroom is no longer the pleasant sanctuary he took his rest in, watched over by his dead wives. Their photographs are all there, covering the walls from top to bottom, in heart-shaped frames garlanded with orange blossom; but Dulcidio, now condemned to solitude, lies slumped into his cushions and into despair. Doctors and medicine men come from all over, but can do nothing for the course of his fever and the collapse of everything else.

With his small battery radio, bought from a passing Turk, Dulcidio spends his nights and days sighing and listening to melodies long out of fashion. His parents, despairing, watch him pine away. He no longer asks for a wife, declaring *I'm hungry.* Now he pleads, *I am made a poor beggar for love,* and in a broken voice, and showing an alarming tendency to rhyme, he

> *pays painful homage to that certain She*
> *who stole his soul and his serenity.*

The whole populace sets out to find her. Searchers scour heaven and earth, but they do not even know the name of the vanished one, and no one has seen a woman wearing glasses in the neighborhood or beyond.

One Sunday afternoon, Dulcidio has a premonition. He gets up, in pain, and sets out painfully for the riverbank.

She is there.

In floods of tears, Dulcidio announces his love for the elusive and indifferent dream-girl. He confesses that he *has died of thirst for the honeys of your mouth,* allows that *I don't deserve your disregard, my beautiful dove,* and showers her with compliments and caresses.

The wedding day arrives. Everyone is delighted, for the people have gone a long time without a fiesta, and Dulcidio is the only one there of the marrying kind. The priest gives him a good price, as a special client.

Guitar music engulfs the sweethearts, the harp and the violins sound in all their glory. A toast of everlasting love is raised to the happy pair, and rivers of punch flow under the great bouquets of flowers.

Dulcidio is sporting a new skin, pink on his shoulders and greenish blue on his prodigious tail.

When at last the two are alone and the hour of truth arrives, he declares to her:

—*I give you my heart, for you to tread on.*

She blows out the candle in a single breath, lets fall her wedding dress, spongy with lace, slowly removes her glasses, and tells him, *Don't be an asshole, knock off the bullshit*. With one tug, she unsheathes him like a sword, flings his skin on the floor, embraces his naked body, and sets him on fire.

Afterward Dulcidio sleeps deeply, curled up against this woman, and dreams for the first time in his life.

She eats him while he is still sleeping. She goes on consuming him in small bites, from head to tail, making little sound and chewing as gently as possible, taking care not to wake him, so that he will not carry away a bad impression.

Translated from the Spanish by Mark Fried

Hervé Guibert

The Hammam

(FRANCE)

The woman, behind her glass window with her violet water and eau de Cyprus, her hair creams, the faded prices on her wash mitts and cupping glasses, her discolored plastic roses, stares at the visitor a long time, and asks him in a businesslike tone if this is his first visit. She is reading a photo-novel. The Hammam V is a very undistinguished sort of establishment, located inside a courtyard, its entrance marked by a sign on the street, its mosaic facade symmetrically aligned with two lanterns, the glass of one of which is broken and wrapped in a plastic bag. A notice at the entrance indicates the business hours, the days reserved exclusively for men or for women, as the hammam is ritually a place where men go to relieve their bodies of fat, and their souls of vice. The establishment—for baths, massage, and relaxation, as the sign indicates—is composed of cubicles innocuously spaced on either side of a corridor. These cubicles remain empty. Directly opposite the cashier is a frosted glass door with the words *Steam Bath* written on it, beyond which a long steep staircase descends. A triangular-shaped mirror, dotted with specks of silver and lightly veiled in steam, suddenly reflects one's hunched image, for the vault is low. The combined odor, slightly sour and salty, of the steam, perspiration, soap, and the long-awaited softening of plantar arches irritates the nostrils at first. At the bottom of the stairs, the visitor drifts between several possibilities: doors of frosted glass with hot water seeping beneath them, the sound of showers, a screen that reveals white shapes sleeping on mats in a dark room, a Moorish-style bar in red and yellow, and, just to the right, a dressing room decorated in the same colors. The man at the bar takes the little ticket with the word *Hammam* stamped on it in blue ink and repeats the cashier's question, like a password, to the unfamiliar face: "Is this your first visit?" He hands him a white robe and a warm towel, and demands a tip. His skin is brown; one of his eyes dead. The visitor undresses before a locker of his own choosing, among the lacquered red and yellow wall panels studded with mirrors. Men lurking in the shadows are eyeing him already. An almost black hand with a shiny gold ring clutches the door to the toilets, the rest of the body hidden but for its spread bare feet.

The arch of the foot passes indifferently from slightly sticky black linoleum to cracked white tiles, laid on a slope to allow the water to drain; the contact is rather unpleasant, and can even prompt a shudder if one considers how readily fungi and greenish mosses cling to such surfaces. The showers, level with the floor, are spread out in a row, parallel, along the full length of the main room, which is bounded by a pool of green water, embellished with rock work onto which falls the soft light of a glass roof. A tall, spiral metal staircase rises above the surface of the water, which is empty but surrounded by seated men who wink at the visitor while openly squeezing their genitals and smile to show him their gold teeth. The men shower naked in a line, using one hand to pull an iron chain that releases the water, lathering their heads, soaping their long brown genitals at great length. In the far right corner of this main room, whose walls pierced with sheets of clear glass enable the visitor to see inside the relaxation rooms and the neighboring rooms for scalding oneself, is another door of frosted glass opening onto a dark space entirely filled with thick white steam, which is pierced only by the vacillating yellow glare of a lamp. At the center of this room is a pyramid of stairs, whose graduated sides are lined with an iron ramp. At the very top of this pyramid, one can make out the silhouettes of two men standing face to face, one of whom is shaving with a little hand razor. The walls are entirely scaled and thoroughly brushed with the excrement one wished to make disappear. But the cylindrical mouth that dispenses the steam and burns the tips of one's fingers as they near it is decorated with a delicate painting of a heron catching a fish with the tip of its beak.

The effeminate white man standing behind the bar, amid old aperitif bottles and a tap handle, whispers stories of lechery in Hammamet, while smoothing the lacquered waves of his hair with the hollow of his palm. A small numbered board, whose slots house the drink checks, is surrounded by plastic roses. The tiles are black and white, diamond-shaped, and the archways are decorated with Christmas garlands; someone has painted a moon and the yellow hills of a desert on the walls and, more delicately, palm trees on the mirrors to hide the cracks. High up, above an angel in white plaster, the twin to the one at the entrance which no longer spouts a stream of water, is a television set broadcasting the marriage of Queen Elizabeth, followed by fleets of military jets. Men girded in white loincloths read magazines, limply stretched out on the red, imitation-leather benches, drinking orangeade. Between the bar and the shower room, a shelf edged with mirrors, embedded in the wall, holds large hair dryers in the shape of snails and small red plastic brushes. One of the men, sometimes already dressed, smoothes and waves his thick black hair.

The various rooms, pierced as we said with sheets of glass, hide nothing; they merely muffle the sounds. From the dry steam room, where the light of a glass roof falls on the slats of wood worn almost gray, and on a fat body lying curled up on a curved mat hollowed out like a hammock, one can make out through the glass, just above a verminous sink, the man from the bar leaning on his counter, but one cannot hear that he is talking about the crudeness of Arab customs; and on the other side, in the half-light of the relaxation room, dozing white shapes are again visible. The white linen spread across the wood seems to wrinkle instantly, crumpled by the sour and salty steam.

The metal staircase above the pool's pale-green trickling climbs until it reaches a long corridor, also red and yellow, lit by daylight, and bordered on each side by half-open doors, behind which men, reclining or seated alone in their own little rooms, wink at the passing visitor, their grins invariably revealing one of their gold teeth, and squeeze their genitals. Other men, who have kept their long robes on, lean against the partitions, and wait indefinitely in the silence. Some wear their towels around their necks like scarves, or like turbans on their heads. They don't talk to each other. Each tiny room has a wooden plank covered with a red, imitation-leather mattress, and a little marble ledge with an ashtray attached to the wall. Each room is closed and sealed by a frosted-glass window. Through the doors one catches sight of an eagle tattooed on an arm, or a gold chain bracelet circling a fat hand (gold flashes too, repeatedly, amid smiles and silent invitations). Certain doors are shut. A white man with thick flesh opens one of them and collapses against the door frame, sweating, disheveled, holding his robe closed like a woman hiding her breasts, limp wrists encircled in brightly colored bracelets. The circumcised members of dark-skinned men are often notched with little goosebumps of whiter flesh.

The visitor returns to the bar to pay his tab and asks the barman with the dead eye to open the door to his dressing room. On the way out, he examines the row of little bottles of eau de cologne, Cyprus and Pompeii water behind the cashier's glass cage; they cost only four francs and must not be high in quality. He decides to buy the most discreet one, from Pompeii, which the cashier hands him, and once home he injures himself, as if deliberately, while opening the little steel cap that seals the bottle, gashing the skin of his hand in several places, the steel sliding under his nail.

Translated from the French by Carol Volk

Abdulrazak Gurnah

Escort

(TANZANIA)

I think he saw me approaching, but for his own reasons made no sign. I stood by the open rear door of the car and waited for him to look up. He folded his newspaper and slid out of the door, glancing at me for a second with intense dislike. I stood still, my body emptying in tremors of surprise. Perhaps it was not dislike, merely irritation at the unavoidable, frustration with the inescapable tedium of existence, a disaffection. But it felt like dislike. He tilted his chin forward slightly, inviting me to state my business. When I told him the name of the hotel, he nodded, as if this was the lesser imposition, as if he had expected me to name an impossible destination. I sat beside him in the front, daring the beast, but also conceding to the angry possibilities my appearance seemed to suggest to him—sitting beside him so he could see I was not as deserving of dislike as he had first thought. I did not see how I could avoid finding out about his anger.

The car seat was lumpy and hard (and green), its vinyl upholstery cracked with age. Sharp-edged corners of it curled up like raw hide and pricked me through my shirt as the car swerved out of the taxi-stand. On the dashboard, there were empty recesses and tangled wires where the lighter, or the radio or the glove-compartment, might have been. Or rather they were not quite empty, as rolled-up pieces of paper were stuffed into their corners, and a rag which was grey with use hung to dry through one of the holes.

As we slowed in the lunch-time traffic, he glanced at the briefcase I held in my lap. Then he raised his eyes to look at my face while I pretended to be unaware of his gaze. "Where have you come from?" he asked, modulating his voice to make the question less abrupt, but still managing to sound as if he was snarling with resentment. None the less, he asked his question as if he expected that I would defer to his right to ask it. *Unatoka wapi?* He lurched us into motion again, then leaned back and rested his cocked elbow on the car window. He was lean and tense, his face hollowed with an expectation of disregard. Or so I thought as I turned to give his question my attention. Something grim and tormented in his mobile face made me think of him as someone who had lived a life of danger, and made him seem capable of deliberate cruelty to ease his own pain. I felt fear and distaste for my curiosity and wanted the journey to end as soon as possible. I should have walked away at once after that first bitter look. He glanced again at the case and a shadow of a smile passed over his face, mocking what he took to be my self-importance. It was only a cheap plastic thing with hard sharp handles and a clumsy zip, which I expected to last no more than a few months and which did not deserve such caustic scrutiny.

"Where?" he asked, this time nodding towards the case to include it in his regard.

"Uingereza," I said. *England.* I spoke gently, distractedly, to show how uninterested I was in the conversation.

He snorted softly. "Student?"

He meant was I one of those who had gone out to make good in the world and returned with only stories and a cheap briefcase. Was I one of those failures who worked as something shamefully menial and sent back tales of endless studies and clever arrangements that were bound to yield a little fortune in good time? His face was cheerful with malice as he waited to see how I would squirm out a reply. When he got going I expected he would tell me that he had to stay behind and look after an ailing family while everybody ran off, and this despite the expectations his teachers and mentors had of him when he was young. I told him I was a teacher and he snorted again, this time unambiguously. Is that all?

The lunch-time crowds were in their eternal haste, streaming across the road at the slenderest hesitation by a motorist. The taxi-driver was affronted by these liberties and leaned on his horn whenever a car ahead of him allowed pedestrians to get the better of the driver. A group of Indian schoolboys in their early teens, strolling between the cars and chatting spiritedly, drew a long blast of the horn and mean words from him. *Filthy shit-scrapers. What are they playing at?* The traffic was heaviest by the Post Office. Crowds of people walked the pavements, some men in shirts and ties hurrying, busy-busy-busy, while others were more deliberate, stopping now and then to look at the shoddy wares of the pavement-traders.

"Uingereza," he said, singing the name as he turned left towards the docks, where my hotel was. "Uingereza," he repeated."A land of luxury."

"Have you visited there?" I asked, and could hear the tone of surprised disbelief in my voice. You? After all the struggle to make headway against that brazen and self-besotted culture, to find such casual reference made to the wretched place. A land of luxury.

The taxi-driver leaned savagely on the horn to clear a water-cart off the road ahead of him. For a minute or so he seemed lost in bitter affront at the water-seller's existence, shouting and waving his right arm out of the window as if any second he would leap out of the car and overturn the whole cartful of cans. The dock-workers who were buying their lunch at the road-side kiosks, and who were the water-seller's customers, waved cheerfully at the taxi-driver. He swung his car out around the cart and gave a long blast on his horn.

"Do you have relatives in England?" I asked. I could not imagine that someone who made a living, with such ill-humour, driving the dilapidated taxi we were travelling in, could make the money to afford staying even one night in a stinking bed and breakfast in that land of luxury.

"I used to live there," he said, then turned to look at me quickly and grinned. We had now come off the main road and were weaving behind the docks, past warehouses and the loco-yard, on the last stretch before the hotel. He had to concentrate on the heaving road, with its gorge-like pot-holes and steep embankments for the railway lines. He started to speak but the crises on the roads came too fast one after another, and he shook his head, not wanting to spoil his story. It seemed the work of madness to put the hotel where it was, the other side of yards littered with derelict machinery and workers' garbage, but the hotel was there before the docks and the railways had turned into a sprawling shambles, and before the road had died.

"I had a malaya, one of these European whores. She took me there, and France, and even Australia. We went everywhere. She paid for everything. You hear these stories from people and you think they're telling lies, dreaming about European whores with money and no sense. I thought so, until I picked up my malaya." He had stopped outside the hotel by this time, his car shuddering idly in neutral. "Slim. She used to call me Slim," he said as he took his fare, his face covered in smiles at the memory. "The name is Salim. I'm always there by the Post Office taxi-rank. Come by any time."

I had found the hotel by chance. The Immigration Officer had explained that he could not give me an entry permit unless I gave an address in the country on my form. He said this apologetically, because after seeing the place of birth on my passport he had spoken enthusiastically about Zanzibar, where he too had relatives. He showed me a list of hotels—*Whichever you like,* he said. *You don't have to stay there. Just for the form.* So I picked one, and when I found a cab outside the airport it was the only name I could remember. Its inaccessibility, and the intimidating silence of the loco-yard and warehouses outside working hours, suited me as it meant that no one came to visit me, as they might have done if I had been staying in one of the glittery palaces on the other side of town with their casinos and pool-side combos.

So it was a surprise to have the receptionist ring the following evening to announce a visitor. It was Salim, of course. It never occurred to me that he would come, but now that he was here, it seemed as if I had known all along that he would turn up. He was dressed in a silky green shirt with a pattern of white flowers and blue outrigger canoes—short-sleeved with one handle of his sunglasses visible in his chest-pocket. His corduroy jeans were loose round the waist, and were gathered into folds by the wide, buckled belt he wore. He insisted on buying me a drink, and bought the barman one as well. The bar was almost empty; the Belgian couple who owned the hotel and who were entertaining a friend were the only other people there. *Ces gens sont impossibles,* their guest said in exasperation, raising her voice with untroubled assurance. These people are impossible. She was a slim, well-groomed woman in her forties, sleek with self-regard. Salim glanced at the three Europeans for a moment, as if he had understood what they had said, but they seemed unaware of him.

"She bought me this, my malaya," Salim said, picking delicately at his shiny shirt and then taking a fuller pinch of the blue corduroy jeans. He was smiling, not mocking this time, and didn't mind including the barman in his circle. "Do you want to know how she found me?" He waited until both the barman and I nodded. "OK, I'll tell you. She was a fare outside the Tumbili Hotel, out on the northern coast. Do you know that one? I saw her standing under a tree near the entrance, as if she was waiting for someone. Usually they don't come out until the hotel servants come to fetch us into the drive. Have you seen what they make those baboons wear? They bring them down from the hills back there and dress them in yellow bibs and black bow-ties, and then make them pay for their costumes. I know this." The barman was dressed in a white shirt, a black bow-tie and a yellow apron around his middle—and he probably had to pay for his costume as well, but he managed not to look uncomfortable.

"Anyway," Salim continued, "I guessed she was waiting there for someone to collect her but I thought I'd try anyway. She wasn't young, but she wasn't that old either. She listened to me for a moment, you know, as I gave her the usual chatter about a tour at government-fixed tariffs, and then she got in the car. I drove her around all day, as far as Malindi, Wiatamu, Takaungu. I told her all about those places, making things up when I felt like it or when she asked difficult things. In the evening, as I was driving her back to her hotel, she made me pull up by a beach, and we did it there. On the sand, in the open, like a couple of dogs. It was like that every day. I picked her up in the morning, drove her places, told her stories, then took her to the beach after it got dark. After a few days of this, she told me to go to Ulaya with her. She fixed everything. The tickets, the passport. She paid for it all."

"You must have been very good on that beach," I said, unwillingly, for something to say, because I did not believe that any woman so casually approached would look at Salim and not see danger, and anyway I did not want to listen to another story of frenzied European lust for the African cock. The barman laughed soundlessly, and Salim glanced at the two of us one by one, looking a little wounded.

"Call me Slim," he said, then emptied his glass and pushed it slightly towards me. "It isn't such a lot of money if you're changing from foreign. You know that. And anyway, she had plenty."

I paid for his drink and sat listening to some more of the story of his malaya. Her marriage had ended, and she had taken her share of the money and decided to travel. She took him to Liverpool, where she was born and from where her parents had emigrated to Australia when she was a baby. Was it difficult for him? With her? He shrugged. She took care of everything, showing him things, and the bitch wanted sex every day, sometimes two or three times in a day. It wasn't difficult. They stayed for several weeks. He made a couple of friends who lived nearby, both Muslims, one Somali and the other from Mauritius, and they taught him how to get dole. Then he and his malaya lived a life of luxury. The English government is very stupid. Liverpool is full of blacks, rough bastards who do what they like, and the government just gives them money. English women were always touching him, stroking his hair, squeezing up to him and buying him drinks. After a few minutes of this I said goodbye and left. I had some letters to write, I said.

He was back the next evening, with another flowery shirt. I had asked the receptionist to say I was not in but perhaps he was bound to other loyalties I did not understand. I thought I might throw a word over my shoulder as I walked past the desk, but I saw that a different young man was on duty. "I bought this in Australia," Salim said, picking at his shirt. "We went there after a few days in France. Betty. Her name was Betty. Bethany, some kind of religious name, but she called herself Betty. Do you want to go to a club tomorrow night? You still have another night here, don't you? There is a nice place on the other side of Majengo. None of this tourist trash. We'll go there tomorrow. Australian women want it all the time, but their men have no nyege. So the women are always on fire. Blazing with heat. And my malaya didn't mind if I went with them." There was a great deal more of this, with some details of the arrangements the women made to see him and their shameless abandon afterwards.

"What brought you back to this place?" I asked in the end, trying to force the tale to its conclusion.

"You have to stop playing some time," he said disdainfully, "and return to be with your people. Anywhere else, you only end up being a clown."

That seemed a good moment to say goodbye, but Salim was quite business-like in refusing to let me go. He took hold of my wrist and held on while he ordered another round of drinks on my bill. The barman served us, made me sign the chit and retreated, carefully keeping his eyes away from Salim's hand on my wrist. We were the only people in the bar. Once the drinks were in front of us, he let go of me with a grin, leaving a cold circle of flesh where his hand had gripped me. I stood up to leave, and I saw him consider saying something and then change his mind. "What about your drink? Never mind, I'll have it. See you tomorrow, then," he said. "You haven't forgotten about the club, have you?"

All day I tried not to think of what I would do when he turned up. I had put the day aside to write up the notes of some of the visits and interviews that I had accumulated over the previous week, and it was the worst kind of thing to be doing while Salim's visit loomed. There was neither virtue nor pain in writing up notes, nothing to distract or excite, just a wearing attention to events whose impact had already passed. By evening, I had persuaded myself that it was silly of me to be so squeamish. I had come to find out what I could about a little-known poet called Pandu Kasim, who had lived here at the turn of the century, to see if I could work up anything about him, and a night-club on the other side of Majengo was nothing to do with that. But it couldn't do any harm, and might even help. My enquiries had not revealed anything interesting about Pandu Kasim, and perhaps a night-club which had Salim as a patron might. I would never choose to see such sights, and would be content to say that I knew the town well without any acquaintance with its greasy under-belly, but what harm could it do apart from making me queasy. I was not looking forward to being brought into Salim's circle of friends, whom I expected to be of the same hair-raising ilk as Salim himself, but I only had just under two more days left before returning to England. I could not imagine that much harm would befall me in that time. The notes would have to wait, and I might have to spend a tedious evening listening to stories of sexual triumph over laughably gullible women, but was that not better than trying to chase Salim away and finding myself the subject of his malice and rage?

So by the time Salim arrived I was ready for him. I was even beginning to think that he would not turn up just to punish me for my scepticism about his stories. He was sitting gloomily in his car when I came down, and started up after a mumbled greeting. That charming welcome made me tremble with foreboding. Why had I not simply told him to go away? I stared ahead of me, not attending to where we were going though I had a good idea of where we were. But my attention must have wandered because I suddenly realised that Salim had turned off the road and was driving on a bumpy and unlit track. The bushes pressed in all around us. The horizontal rays of the car-lights made the sensation more oppressive, as if we were underground. It had been a pleasant, breezy evening, but in this tunnel the air was steamy and smelled of wet earth. Salim turned to glance at me, and I saw him grinning. "Not much longer now," he said and began to hum. A dog yelped in the night and a moment later the dark bushes were agitated by the sounds of passage. In another moment, Salim forced the car over a little mound and entered a clearing surrounded by huge dark trees. There was another car parked outside one of the houses. There must have been three or four other houses, but it was impossible to tell in that light. He parked his car alongside the other and we got out.

The club turned out to be the front room of a mud and wattle house, ill-lit by one kerosene lamp. Two other men were already there, and they rose to greet us as if they were expecting us. "This is our guest from Uingereza," Salim said, grinning.

One of the men looked about Salim's age, and had a similar aggravated appearance. The other was younger and bigger, and when he glanced at me I saw an involuntary smirk cross his mouth. His name was Majid. I did not catch the name of the older man at first. (It turned out to be Buda.) Even before we sat down around the rough old table, Majid was shouting for beer. From the back room appeared a woman of uncertain middle age, in a tight dress worn with use and stained black under the arm-pits. Her head was covered with a scarf of the same material, and around her middle she wore a faded kanga. After a few moments of frenzied banter and some forced hilarity, she went away again to prepare the food my jolly companions had asked for.

There were empty beer bottles on the table, and these would remain there as trophies of the drinkers' exploits. Majid and the other man had half-full ones each, from which they drank now and then, tipping the bottles swaggeringly to their lips when the beer frothed. They were big bottles. And not a glass in sight. I had imagined something different when Salim said we should go to the club, not a dark house in a wood where men gathered for a secretive drink.

"They'll be bringing some more," Buda said reassuringly. His expression was that cross between barely suppressed temper and a moping, sulking malice that I had seen in Salim. Maybe it was the drink. You had to be serious, even obsessive, about the stuff to be a drinker in a Muslim town like this, where discretion was impossible and discovery inevitable. Perhaps the guilt of transgression generated an angry self-contempt, or the necessity to consume whatever destructive poison was available in a culture of scarcity produced those looks of pain. Or maybe it was an unassuaged resentment that drove men such as these to drink despite everything. How could I know?

"I can see you people did not bother going to the maghreb prayer today," Salim said with rasping ill-humour, nodding at the empties on the table. The two men laughed at his sarcasm and Salim reluctantly smiled, his clenched face creasing briefly. He looked as if he was burning.

Buda was short and plump, even fat, but his body looked hard and tight, as if his plumpness was not to do with indulgence but with something more calculating then mere pleasure. He scowled at me before he spoke, playfully, playing at being monsters. "Tell us the news from Uingereza. Is it true they have trains that travel under water there?"

"Listen to this savage," Salim cried. "Have you never heard of the Underground?"

"You're going to make this Englishman think we're all as ignorant as you," Majid said, without a hint of pleasantry in his voice.

A girl in a torn and soiled shift came from the inner room, carrying two bottles of beer. Her eyes were intensely blank, looking through what they encountered with some concentration. She put one of the beer bottles in front of me. As she leaned forward I saw through a tear in the shift under her armpit that her body was young and full. She put the other bottle in front of Salim, who stroked her buttocks and made her wince.

"Aziza, our friend from Ulaya wants you," Majid said abruptly, laughing with two loud barks.

She turned her eyes towards me with a look of mild interest. Then she stood waiting, as if to see what would happen next.

"Go with her," Salim said, grinning at me like a cadaver. I saw her wince again.

I looked at the girl, at her small pointed face and her slim young body, and I saw no resistance there. I shook my head and her eyes fell. Majid laughed and stood up. The girl turned back towards the inner room, her hands already pulling up folds of her shift as Majid swaggered at her heels. Buda smiled gently and began to ask me questions about England. Salim answered most of them, calling me in now and then to say a confirming word or two. I thought I heard a sharp voice at one point which made the flame of the kerosene lamp flicker. Majid was in there for what seemed a long time, and when he came out he was beaming, his glossy face sleek with health.

"Thirsty work," he said, reaching for what remained in his bottle. He drained it off and put the bottle down with a conquering smile. "It's the Englishman's round, I think."

They called for Aziza and she came in a moment later, her eyes as vacant as before, the corners of her mouth turned down. I ordered beers for them and said to Salim that I would like to go when he had finished his drink. What about the food we had ordered, Buda asked. I had work to do, I said. Buda rose and followed softly behind the girl after she had brought the beer.

"What work?" Majid asked, unsmiling. "Don't you like women? Go and work in there. Or don't you like women? She won't have anything to do with him," he said, pointing a chin at Salim. "What did you do to her?"

Salim took a long pull at his bottle. "We have to go to a wedding," he said when he had finished. "So we'll leave you to your filthy games."

"What did you do to her, you pervert?" Majid asked, grinning for the sheer joy of his life.

We arrived at the wedding just in time to see the procession of family and friends escorting the groom to the door of the bride's house. Two drummers, skinny young men who looked alike, played with tense impassive faces, their eyes turned inwards in all that noise. Palm-frond arches decorated the house, and a garland of coloured lights ran across the front wall. From the house's interior came voices of women singing, which were suddenly transformed into a gleeful burst of ululations as the groom reached the door. The crowd milled around, shouting ribald comments at the groom, then breaking into a loud shout as he was admitted inside. Youngsters' eyes began wandering anxiously around, looking for the food they knew was coming. Salim snorted with derision. "She's one of my wife's relatives," he said.

I had not thought of a wife. "Were you married before you went off with Bethany?" I asked him as he drove me back to the hotel. It was a nice name and I had been waiting to use it.

"Yes," he said. We were driving down the ill-lit road that led to the loco-yard, but even in that light I could see the spite and anger in his face. "I was married to her a long time ago."

"Did you come back because of her?" I asked.

He chuckled. Then after a moment, with the car growling over the broken road, he spoke. "She gave me something in the end. That malaya. When I went with her, blood came out. I went to see the doctor she sent me to. He said it was nothing but she said I couldn't stay. I don't know what it is, but whenever I go with a woman blood comes out."

We drove in silence until the car stopped outside the hotel. "Have you seen a doctor since you've been back here?"

"What doctor? There are no doctors here," he said, staring ahead. Then he turned towards me with a coy, gentle smile. "Take me with you tomorrow. I'll see a doctor there. Take me. I'll do anything you want." He leant towards me, his smile now offering itself beseechingly in that grotesquely overwrought face.

He came for me the next day even though I had told him that I would make my own way to the airport. He talked with his usual malice and arrogance, scoffing at everything that crossed his sight. Even though I insisted that he drop me off and leave, he parked the car and strolled beside me with a rolled-up newspaper in his hand. "How much does a case like that cost? Bring me one next time. Or send one to me and I'll make sure you get your money back. Not that you'll need my money in the land of luxury. You'll soon stop playing and come back home, though," he said. "Everybody has to, otherwise they turn into a joke in some foreign place."

I shook hands with him and gave him all the local money I had. He looked at the fat bundle of notes with surprise. "I hope you get better," I said.

"What are you talking about?" he asked, grinning. He put the money in his pocket. "Next time you must stay," he said and then walked away, waving without looking back.

Barry Hannah

Midnight and I'm Not Famous Yet

(UNITED STATES)

I was walking around Gon one night, and this C-man—I saw him open the window, and there was a girl in back of him, so I thought it was all right— peeled down on me and shot the back heel off my boot. Nearest I came to getting mailed home when I was there. A jeep came by almost instantly with a thirty cal mounted, couple of allies in it. I pointed over to the window. They shot out about a box and a half on the apartment, just about burned out the dark slot up there. As if the dude was hanging around digging the weather after he shot at me. There were shrieks in the night, etc. But then a man opened the bottom door and started running in the street. This ARVN fellow knocked the shit out of his buddy's head turning the gun to zap the running man. Then I saw something as the dude hit a light: he was fat. I never saw a fat Cong. So I screamed out in Vietnamese. He didn't shoot. I took out my machine pistol and ran after the man, who was up the street by now, and I was hobbling without a heel on my left boot.

Some kind of warm nerve sparklers were getting all over me. I believe in magic, because, million-to-one odds, it was Ike "Tubby" Wooten, from Redwood, a town just north of Vicksburg. He was leaning on a rail, couldn't run anymore. He was wearing the uniform of our Army with a patch on it I didn't even know what was. Old Tubby would remember me. I was the joker at our school. I once pissed in a Dixie cup and eased three drops of it on the library radiator. But Tubby was so serious, reading some photo magazine. He peeped up and saw me do it, then looked down quickly. When the smell came over the place, he asked me, Why? What do you want? What profit is there in that? I guess I just giggled. Sometimes around midnight I'd wake up and think of his questions, and it disturbed me that there was no answer. I giggled my whole youth away. Then I joined the Army. So I thought it was fitting I'd play a Nelda on him now. A Nelda was invented by a corporal when they massacred a patrol up north on a mountain and he was the only one left. The NVA ran all around him and he had this empty rifle hanging on him. They spared him.

"I'm a virgin! Spare me!"

"You, holding the gun? Did you say you were a virgin?" said poor Tubby, trying to get air.

"I am a virgin," I said, which was true, but hoping to get a laugh, anyway.

"And a Southern virgin. A captain. Please to God, don't shoot me," that fat boy said. "I was cheating on my wife for the first time. The penalty shouldn't be death."

"Why'd you run from the house, Tubby?"

"You know me." Up the street they had searchlights moved up all over the apartment house. They shot about fifty rounds into the house. They were shooting tracers now. It must've lit up my face; then a spotlight went by us.

"Bobby Smith," said Tubby. "My God, I thought you were God."

"I'm not. But it seems holy. Here we are looking at each other."

"Aw, Bobby, they were three beautiful girls. I'd never have done the thing with one, but there were *three*." He was a man with a small pretty face laid around by three layers of jowl and chin. "I heard the machine gun and the guilt struck me. I had to get out. So I just ran."

"Why're you in Nam, anyway?"

"I joined. I wasn't getting anything done but being in love with my wife. That wasn't doing America any good."

"What's that patch on you?"

"Photography." He lifted his hands to hold an imaginary camera. "I'm with the Big Red. I've done a few things out of helicopters."

"You want to see a ground unit? With me. Or does Big Red own you?"

"I have no idea. There hasn't been much to shoot. Some smoking villages. A fire in a bamboo forest. I'd like to see a face."

"You got any pictures of Vicksburg?"

"Oh, well, a few I brought over."

The next day I found out he was doing idlework and Big Red didn't care where he was, so I got him over in my unit. I worried about his weight, etc., and the fact he might be killed. But the boys liked a movie-cameraist being along and I wanted to see the pictures from Vicksburg. It was nice to have Tubby alongside. He was hometown, such as he was. Before we flew out north, he showed me what he had. There was a fine touch in his pictures. There was a cute little Negro on roller skates, and an old woman on a porch, a little boy sleeping in a speedboat with the river in the background. Then there was a blurred picture of his wife naked, just moving through the kitchen, nothing sexy. The last picture was the best. It was John Whitelaw about to crack a golf ball. Tubby had taken it at Augusta, at the Masters. I used to live about five houses away from the Whitelaws. John had his mouth open and his arms, the forearm muscles, were bulked up plain as wires.

John was ten years older than me, but I knew about him. John Whitelaw was our only celebrity since the Civil War. In the picture he wore spectacles. It struck me as something deep, brave, mighty and, well, modern; he had to have the eyeglasses on him to see the mighty thing he was about to do. Maybe I sympathized too much, since I have to wear glasses too, but I thought this picture was worthy of a statue. Tubby had taken it in a striking gray-and-white grain. John seemed to be hitting under a heroic deficiency. You could see the sweat droplets on his neck. His eyes were in an agony. But the thing that got me was that John Whitelaw *cared* so much about what he was doing. It made me love America to know he was in it, and I hadn't loved anything for nigh three years then. Tubby was talking about all this "our country" eagle and stars mooky and had seen all the war movies coming over on the boat. I never saw a higher case of fresh and crazy in my life.

But the picture of John at Augusta, it moved me. It was a man at work and play at the same time, doing his damnedest. And Whitelaw was a beautiful man. They pass that term "beautiful" around like pennies nowadays, but I saw him in the flesh once. It was fall in Baton Rouge, around the campus of LSU. He was getting out of a car with a gypsyish girl on his hand. I was ten, I guess, and he was twenty. We were down for a ball game, Mississippi vs. Louisiana, a classic that makes you goo-goo eyed when you're a full-grown man if your heart's in Dixie, etc. At ten, it's Ozville. So in the middle of it, this feeling, I saw Whitelaw and his woman. My dad stopped the car.

"Wasn't that Johnny Whitelaw?" he asked my grandfather.

"You mean that little peacock who left football for golf? He ought to be quarterbacking Ole Miss right now. It wouldn't be no contest," said my grandfather.

I got my whole idea of what a woman should look like that day . . . and what a man should be. The way John Whitelaw looked, it sort of rebuked yourself ever hoping to call yourself a man. The girl he was with woke up my clammy little dreams about, not even sex, but the perfect thing—it was something like her. As for Whitelaw, his face was curled around by that wild hair the color of beer; his chest was deep, just about to bust out of that collar and bow tie.

"That girl he had, she had a drink in her hand. You could hardly see her for her hair," said my grandfather.

"Johnny got him something Cajun," said my father.

Then my grandfather turned around, looking at me like I was a crab who could say a couple of words. "You look like your mother, but you got gray eyes. What's wrong? You have to take a leak?"

Nothing was wrong with me. I'd just seen John Whitelaw and his girl, that was all.

Tubby had jumped a half-dozen times at Fort Bragg, but he had that heavy box harnessed on him now and I knew he was going down fast and better know how to hit. I explained to him. I went off the plane four behind him, cupping a joint. I didn't want Tubby seeing me smoking grass, but it's just about the only way to get down. If the Cong saw the plane, you'd fall into a barbecue. They've killed a whole unit before, using shotguns and flame bullets, just like your ducks floating in. You hear a lot of noise going in with a whole unit in the air like this. We start shooting about a hundred feet from ground. If you ever hear one bullet pass you, you get sick thinking there might be a lot of them. All you can do is point your gun down and shoot it all out. You can't reload. You never hit anything. There's a sharpshooter, McIntire, who killed a C shooting from his chute, but that's unlikely. They've got you like a gallery of rabbits if they're down there.

I saw Tubby sinking fast over the wrong part of the field. I had two chutes out, so I cut one off and dropped over toward him, pulling on the left lines so hard I almost didn't have a chute at all for a while. I got level with him and he looked over, pointing down. He was doing his arm up and down. Could have been farmers or just curious rubbernecks down in the field, but there were about ten of them grouped up together, holding things. They weren't shooting, though. I was carrying an experimental gun, me and about ten of my boys. It was a big, light thing; really, it was just a launcher. There were five shells in it, bigger than shotgun shells. If you shot one of them, it was supposed to explode on impact and burn out everything in a twenty-five-yard radius. It was a mean little mother of phosphorus, is what it was. I saw the boys shooting them down into the other side of the field. This stuff would take down a whole tree and you'd chute into a quiet smoking bare area.

I don't know. I don't like a group waiting on me when I jump out of a plane. I almost zapped them, but they weren't throwing anything up. Me and Tubby hit the ground about the same time. They were farmers. I talked to them. They said there were three Cong with them until we were about a hundred feet over. The Cong knew we had the phosphorus shotgun and showed ass, loping out to the woods fifty yards to the north when me and Tubby were coming in.

Tubby took some film of the farmers. All of them had thin chin beards and soft hands because their wives did most of the work. They essentially just lay around and were hung with philosophy, and actually were pretty happy. Nothing had happened around here till we jumped in. These were fresh people. I told them to get everybody out of the huts because we were going to have a thing in the field. It was a crisis point. A huge army of NVA was coming down and they just couldn't avoid us if they wanted to have any run of the valley five miles south. We were there to harass the front point of the army, whatever it was like.

"We're here to check their advance," Tubby told the farmers.

Then we all collected in the woods, five hundred and fifty souls, scared out of mind. What we had going was we knew the NVA general bringing them down was not too bright. He went to the Sorbonne and we had this report from his professor: "Li Dap speaks French very well and had studied Napoleon before he got to me. He knows Robert Lee and the strategy of Jeb Stuart, whose daring circles around an immense army captured his mind. Li Dap wants to be Jeb Stuart. I cannot imagine him in command of more than five hundred troops."

And what we knew stood up. Li Dap had tried to circle left with twenty thousand and got the hell kicked out of him by idle Navy guns sitting outside Gon. He just wasn't very bright. He had half his army climbing around these bluffs, no artillery or air force with them, and it was New Year's Eve for our side.

"So we're here just to kill the edge of their army?" said Tubby.

"That's what I'm here for, why I'm elected. We kill more C's than anybody else in the Army."

"But what if they take a big run at you, all of them?" said Tubby.

"There'll be lots of cooking."

We went out in the edge of the woods and I glassed the field. It was almost night. I saw two tanks come out of the other side and our pickets running back. Pock, pock, pock from the tanks. Then you saw this white glare on one tank where somebody on our team had laid on with one of the phosphorus shotguns. It got white and throbbing, like a little star, and the gun wilted off of it. The other tank ran off a gully into a hell of a cow pond. You wouldn't have known it was that deep. It went underwater over the gun, and they let off the cannon when they went under, raising the water in a spray. It was the silliest-looking thing. Some of them got out and a sergeant yelled for me to come up. It was about a quarter mile out there. Tubby got his camera, and we went out with about fifteen troops.

At the edge of the pond, looking into flashlights, two tank-men sat, one tiny, the other about my size. They were wet, and the big guy was mad. Lot of the troops were chortling, etc. It was awfully damned funny, if you didn't happen to be one of the C-men in the tank.

"Of all the fuck-ups. This is truly saddening." The big guy was saying something like that. I took a flashlight and looked him over. Then I didn't believe it. I told Tubby to get a shot of the big cursing one. Then they brought them on back. I told the boys to tie up the big one and carry him in.

I sat on the ground, talking to Tubby.

"It's so quiet. You'd think they'd be shelling us," he said.

"We're spread out too good. They don't have much ammo now. They really galloped down here. That's the way Li Dap does it. Their side's got big trouble now. And, Tubby, me and you are famous."

"Me, what?"

"You took his picture. You can get some more, more arty angles on him tomorrow."

"Him?"

"It's Li Dap himself. He was in the tank in the pond."

"No. Their general?"

"You want me to go prove it?"

We walked over. They had him tied around a tree. His hands were above his head and he was sitting down. I smelled some hash in the air. The guy who was blowing it was a boy from Detroit I really liked, and I hated to come down on him, but I really beat him up. He never got a lick in. I kicked his rump when he was crawling away and some friends picked him up. You can't have lighting up that shit at night on the ground. Li Dap was watching the fight, still cursing.

"Asshole of the mountains." He was saying something like that. "Fortune's ninny."

"Hi, General. My French isn't too good. You speak English. Honor us."

He wouldn't say anything.

"You have a lot of courage, running out front with the tanks." There were some snickers in the bush, but I cut them out quick. We had a real romantic here and I didn't want him laughed at. He wasn't hearing much, though. About that time two of their rockets flashed into the woods. They went off in the treetops and scattered.

"It was worthy of Patton," I said. "You had some bad luck. But we're glad you made it alive."

"Kiss my ass."

"You want your hands free? Oliver, get his ropes off the tree." The guy I beat up cut him off the tree.

"You scared us very deeply. How many tanks do you have over there?"

"Nonsense," he said.

"What do you have except for a few rockets?"

"I had no credence in the phosphorus gun."

"Your men saw us use them when we landed."

"I had no credence."

"So you just came out to see."

"I say to them never to fear the machine when the cause is just. To throw oneself past the technology tricks of the monsters and into his soft soul."

"And there you will win, huh?"

"Of course. It is our country." He smiled at me. "It's relative to your war in the nineteenth century. The South had slavery. The North must purge it so that it is a healthy region of our country."

"You were out in the tank as an example to your men?"

"Yes!"

All this hero needed was a plumed hat.

"Sleep well," I said, and told Oliver to get him a blanket and feed him, and feed the tiny gunner with him.

When we got back to my dump, I walked away for a while, not wanting to talk with Tubby. I started crying. It started with these hard sobs coming up like rocks in my throat. I started looking out at forever, across the field. They shot up three more rockets from the woods below the hill. I waited for the things to land on us. They fell on the tops of trees, nothing near me, but there was some howling off to the right. Somebody had got some shrapnel.

I'd killed so many gooks. I'd killed them with machine guns, mortars, howitzers, knives, wire, me and my boys. My boys loved me. They were lying all around me, laying this great cloud of trust on me. The picture of John Whitelaw about to hit that ball at Augusta was jammed in my head. There was such care in his eyes, and it was only a golf ball, a goddamned piece of nothing. But it was wonderful and peaceful. Nobody was being killed. Whitelaw had the right. He had the beloved American right to the pursuit of happiness. The tears were out of my jaws then. Here we shot each other up. All we had going was the pursuit of horror. It seemed to me my life had gone straight from teen-age giggling to horror. I had never had time to be but two things, a giggler and a killer.

Christ, I was crying for myself. I had nothing for the other side, understand that. North Vietnam was a land full of lousy little Commie robots, as far as I knew. A place of the worst propaganda and hypocrisy. You should have read some of their agitprop around Gon, talking about freedom and throwing off the yoke, etc. The gooks went for Communism because they were so ignorant and had nothing to lose. The South Vietnamese, too. I couldn't believe we had them as allies. They were such a pretty and uniformly indecent people. I once saw a little taxi boy, a kid is all, walk into a Medevac with one arm and a hand blown off by a mine he'd picked up. These housewives were walking behind him in the street, right in the middle of Gon. Know what they were doing? They were laughing. They thought it was the most hysterical misadventure they'd ever seen. These people were on our side. These were our friends and lovers. That happened early when I got there. I was a virgin when I got to Nam and stayed a virgin, through a horde of B-girls, the most base and luscious-lipped hustlers. Because I did not want to mingle with this race.

In an ARVN hospital tent you see the hurt officers lined up in front of a private who's holding in his guts with his hands. They'll treat the officer with a bad pimple before they treat the dying private. We're supposed to be shaking hands with these people. Why can't we be fighting for some place like England? When you train yourself to blow gooks away, like I did, something happens, some kind of popping returning dream of murder-with-a-smile.

I needed away. I was sick. In another three months I'd be zapping orphanages.

"Bobby, are you all right?" said Tubby, waddling out to the tree I was hanging on.

"I shouldn't ever've seen that picture of John Whitelaw. I shouldn't've."

"Do you really think we'll be famous?" Tubby got an enchanted look on him, sort of a dumb angel look in that small pretty face amid the fat rolls. It was about midnight. There was a fine Southern moon lighting up the field. You could see every piece of straw out there. Tubby, by my ass, had the high daze on him. He'd stepped out here in the boonies and put down his foot in Ozville.

"This'll get me Major, anyhow. Sure. Fame. Both of us," I said.

Tubby said: "I tried to get nice touches in with the light coming over his face. These pictures could turn out awfully interesting. I was thinking about the cover of *Time* or *Newsweek*."

"It'll change your whole life, Tubby," I said.

Tubby was just about to die for love of fate. He was shivering.

I started enjoying the field again. This time the straws were waving. It was covered with rushing little triangles, these sort of toiling dots. Our side opened up. All the boys came up to join within a minute and it was a sheet of lightning rolling back and forth along the outside of the woods. I could see it all while I was walking back to the radio. I mean humping low. Tubby must've been walking straight up. He took something big right in the square of his back. It rolled him up twenty feet in front of me. He was dead and smoking when I made it to him.

"C'mon, I've got to get the pictures," he said.

I think he was already dead.

I got my phosphorus shotgun. Couldn't think of anything but the radio and getting it over how we were being hit, so we could get dragons—helicopters with fifty cals—in quick. The dragons are nice. They've got searchlights, and you put two of them over a field like we were looking at, they'd clean it out in half an hour. So I made it to the radio and the boys had already called the dragons in, everything was fine. Only we had to hold them for an hour and a half until the dragons got there. I humped up front. Every now and then you'd see somebody use one of the experimental guns. The bad thing was that it lit up the gunner too much at night, too much shine out of the muzzle. I took note of that to tell them when we got back. But the gun really smacked the gook assault. It was good for about seventy-five yards and hit with a huge circle burn about the way they said it would. The gooks' first force was knocked off. You could see men who were still burning running back through the straw, hear them screaming.

I don't remember too well. I was just loitering near the radio, a few fires out in the field, everything mainly quiet. Copters on the way. I decided to go take a look at Li Dap. I thought it was our boys around him, though I didn't know why. They were wearing green and standing up plain as day. There was Oliver, smoking a joint. His rifle was on the ground. The NVA were all around him and he hadn't even noticed. There were so many of them—twenty or so—they were clanking rifles against each other. One of them was going up behind Oliver with a bayonet, just about on him. If I'd had a carbine like usual, I could've taken the bayoneteer off and at least five of the others. Oliver and Li Dap might've ducked and survived.

But I couldn't pick and choose. I hardly even thought. The barrel of the shotgun was up and I pulled on the trigger, aiming at the bayoneteer.

I burned them all up.

Nobody even made a squeak.

There was a flare and they were gone.

Some of my boys rushed over with guns. All they were good for was stomping out the little fires on the edges.

When we got back, I handed over Tubby's pictures. The old man was beside himself over my killing a general, a captured general. He couldn't understand what kind of laxity I'd allowed to let twenty gooks come up on us like that. They thought I might have a court-martial, and I was under arrest for a week. The story got out to UPI and they were saying things like "atrocity," with my name spelled all over the column.

But it was dropped and I was pulled out and went home a lieutenant.

That's all right. I've got four hundred and two boys out there—the ones that got back—who love me and know the truth, who love me *because* they know the truth.

It's Tubby's lost fame I dream about.

The Army confiscated the roll and all his pictures. I wrote the Pentagon a letter asking for a print and waited two years here in Vicksburg without even a statement they received the note. I see his wife, who's remarried and is fat herself now, at the discount drugstore every now and then. She has the look of a kind of hopeless cheer. I got a print from the Pentagon when the war was over and it didn't matter. Li Dap looked wonderful—strained, abused and wild, his hair flying over his eyes while he's making a statement full of conviction.

It made me start thinking of faces again.

Since I've been home I've crawled in bed with almost anything that would have me. I've slept with high-school teachers, Negroes and, the other night, my own aunt. It made her smile. All those years of keeping her body in trim came to something, the big naughty surprise that the other women look for in religion, God showing up and killing their neighbors, sparing them. But she knows a lot about things and I think I'll be in love with her.

We were at the John Whitelaw vs. Whitney Maxwell playoff together. It was a piece of wonder. I felt thankful to the wind or God or whoever who brought that fine contest near enough by. When they hit the ball, the sound traveled like a rifle snap out over the bluffs. When it was impossible to hit the ball, that is exactly when they hit it.

My aunt grabbed hold of my fingers when the tension was almost up to a roar. The last two holes. Ah, John lost. I looked over the despondency of the home crowd.

Fools! Fools! I thought. Love it! Love the loss as well as the gain. Go home and dig it. Nobody was killed. We saw victory and defeat, and they were both wonderful.

Peter Høeg
Portrait of the Avant-Garde

(DENMARK)

On an October day in 1939, the painter Simon Bering and his friend Nina sailed out to the island of Christiansø. They sailed from Svaneke harbor on his twenty-eighth birthday, by which time six years had elapsed since the major exhibition at which his paintings had first made a wide public catch their breath the way one does when stepping out into the cold, then caused their eyes to water as if in a stiff headwind, and thereafter—and ever since—moved them to part with their money for a share in his faith in the future.

Simon painted large-scale canvases across which the twentieth century progressed as an unrelenting cavalcade of machines and horses and military detachments and forest fires. Back then, these had raised a storm that had not yet died down and had gone so far as to blow them into the Reichskammer der bildenden Künste, to which only a very few foreigners of immaculate racial pedigree were ever admitted.

One March night ten years earlier, as if in a fever Simon had painted the first of these pictures, works that did not close up to form flat planes but instead opened up like gateways into the future, and on this day in October he felt as though what was now happening to him came as a direct result of that night a decade before, as though—on a new and higher plane, so to speak—he was reliving that first breakthrough to himself.

A weaker character might have been bowled over by such fame, but not Simon, who believed that he belonged to a generation and a race healthier than any before them had ever been. With the money that all at once began to pour in, he placed a hard-nosed agent between himself and the public and bought property in the center of Copenhagen, an old yellow house with a garden surrounded by high walls. Here he found the relative peace at the eye of the typhoon, here he was able to work, and here the gale that howled around his pictures and his person filtered through to him as no more than a gentle tailwind bringing congratulations and a soft rain of gold.

He could have chosen to live and work as a recluse. He could have had his vast paintings carted off through the gates of the yellow house and could have watched from a safe distance as they detonated like shells in the capitals of Europe, but he did not. For Simon was also a speech maker. He felt a powerful urge to use words to speed the truths contained in his paintings on their way, for the word is also a brush and with it he wished to stand up in front of an assembly, to feel the crowd seething, to look upon these weaker brethren as a white canvas set before him, to make electrifying contact, create awareness, and then lean forward and apply his own hectic flush of color to the white faces upturned to his like so many blank pages. Hence the fact that the huge locomotives that thundered across his pictures also conveyed him all over Europe, a young prophet of a new age and a new truth. To begin with, he addressed art lovers only, but later he also made speeches at political rallies, and in Berlin on August 2, 1934, he assured his listeners that the young artists of Europe were right behind Germany's new leader and chancellor. He told them there was only one God, and that was progress. His celebrity earned him a hearing and because he was young he got away with saying more than many others; thus Simon succeeded in giving clear and crystallized expression to ideas that at that time were still vague and diffuse, speaking always with the same fresh and forthright power as when in Berlin—at the joint opening of the Olympics and the art exhibition in 1936—he had raised his strong, pale face to a public gathering, looked out across that sea of humanity, and said fiercely, straight into the microphone, that while we are waiting for the great war we so fervently desire, we must arm ourselves with art that can cut to the quick of our souls, and this art must be painting. Books and music are for people beset by doubts; the war and the future decree that we must march and observe, not molder in theaters and reading rooms.

Nina came to him as simply as his fame or an idea for a picture. He advertised for a housekeeper, having need of a helpmate, and one day there she was, standing before him, younger than he but steady-voiced as she assured him that she was up to the job. She spoke a dialect new to him but true to his theories that the past is of no consequence he did not question her further. To his own surprise there came a day when he realized that he enjoyed having her around. Later he began to feel homesick for her when he traveled. And in the end he dreaded leaving her.

One day when things had reached this stage, he was standing behind her in a bright room. The sun dissolved her contours into a yellow haze and condensed her figure to a black silhouette. Rooted to the spot by some obscure expectation, Simon tried out an exercise he had resorted to on previous occasions when—faced with a white expanse of canvas—he had been overcome by doubt. He closed his eyes and made his mind go blank, then slowly opened his eyes once more, imagining as he did so that until then the world had not existed but that it was being created, like a painting, in the moment that he laid eyes on it. Now, too, this method brought relief. With eyes screwed up against the light, he could see that another figure stood alongside that of the girl, and by stretching his creative faculty slightly he saw that it was himself.

And then he kissed her.

In keeping with his conviction that all ancient rituals were absurd, marriage was never an option for Simon and he was secretly proud of the fact that he never presented his declarations of love to Nina as anything but casual remarks. He had long since told the public at large that the true essence of love lay in there being no strings attached and he had an agreeable feeling that this put him, historically speaking, in good company with the long string of artistic movements that, since the middle of the previous century, had underlined their own particular brand of the avant-garde by proclaiming the virtues of free love.

Between himself and Nina, therefore, he had naturally insisted on a distance befitting two modern individuals. Since he traveled a great deal and worked even more, this distance was something that grew up all unbidden and they had been living together for a year before he learned that she had been born on Christiansø, an island that, as far as the map of Denmark is concerned, is near enough the end of the world. On this same occasion she told him that she was pregnant.

It was then that Simon decided to take a break in his life to rediscover the peace he had lost in the course of the preceding six years. He made his decision known to the world at a party he gave for his friends at the restaurant Stephan à Porta in Copenhagen. The guest list was composed of young businessmen, politicians, artists, and army officers, who demonstrated their contempt for the past by smashing champagne glasses against the walls, eating beluga caviar and Russian peas with their fingers, and fighting with the waiters and one another. At one point only did they quiet down and that was when Simon made his speech, but then on the other hand you could have heard a pin drop in the large room.

"There are," said Simon, "three stages along the way to total control over life.

"The first leads out of the nursery. From infancy, the world bends over us in the form of a woman: mothers, wet nurses, maids, and governesses endeavor to block our path to life. The first prerequisite for freedom is, therefore, the ability to say: I will do as I please with my own person. It is to this point that we are attempting to bring the masses. A man cannot march if he is still lying in the cradle. There is no way the necessity of war can be discerned from a nursery.

"But then comes the next stage, on which stand the politician and the soldier"—and here Simon let his eye fall on those politicians and soldiers in attendance. "This is reached when we become capable of infecting others with our own enthusiasm and then steer them in the right direction, when we have dominion over life and death, when we can do as we please with other people.

"Then there is a third stage: for my own part, I have given the world six years of my life. I have quelled all wishy-washy deliberation and rolled light and dark into one and played my part in raising the waters that are now washing over Europe. I have given the world an art form that is akin to a slap in the face."

Here Simon paused and eyed every single member of the company, feeling that his words had gotten through to them like a sudden attack of sobriety and that it was no longer clear whether they were his guests or his victims.

"Now," he went on, "the world has become accustomed to this slap in the face. If I were to stop for a moment, the world would come crawling to me and grab me by the throat with one hand while begging me with the other to give it a sound beating. And so I have made up my mind that during this seventh year I will rest, and this I have decided to do in order to show that I can do with the world exactly as I please."

Three weeks later, Nina and Simon set sail from Svaneke harbor. It was the first day of winter; from the south there blew a wind so cold that it seemed to come straight off some icy waste. The town of Svaneke is built atop rocky cliffs that slope steeply down to the harbor, and the cauldron thus formed caught the chill winds and swept them over the quayside and the white mail boat and the reporters who had pursued Simon, all of whom felt it as a reminder of their own mortality. They had made the journey on behalf of their newspapers and their readers, to write a piece about Simon's departure and his birthday, but for the moment all of that was forgotten. By now they were chilled to the bone, worn out, and greatly preoccupied with the war in Europe. A number of them fully expected on their return to be fired for some unspecified reason or to be posted overnight to distant war zones, and every one of them feared for the future, every one of them was haunted by just one question: How will it all end? And suddenly, this morning on the quayside, it seemed to them that this celebrated, pale-faced agitator ought to be able to answer that question. But Simon waved them away, roughly shoving back one of their number who was rash enough to follow him up the gangplank. They have been sent, he thought to himself, by the life I am about to leave behind, to prolong the leavetaking, but for me, for the new man, taking leave of the old life is a pleasure. And he turned his back on them.

As they sailed out of the harbor the reporters followed them along the pier like lost children.

For as long as the town was still visible off the boat's stern, the sea was sluggish, menacing, and of the color of congealing pewter. Then Simon shut his eyes and made his mind go blank. Only now does the world come into being, he thought. Then he felt warm sunshine on his eyelids, as though the boat had sailed into summer. And to say that in especially hot summers the seas around Bornholm store up the warmth of the sun and create an unnatural postponement of winter would be a feeble rebuttal to the sense of omnipotence with which Simon was filled as he gradually opened his eyes, creating first the season and his own hands on the rail in front of him, then Nina's silhouette, then—with triumphant awareness of his sex as a mighty brush—the child in her belly, and finally the blue sea under the sun and, sitting on the horizon, the two tiny islands—Christiansø and the even-smaller Frederiksø—and, like a fine black thread, the bridge connecting them.

He noticed that Nina had her eyes shut. "You're dreaming," said Simon. "It's the way of the world: women dream and men act." Nina looked at him, sharp-eyed. "Don't you dream?" she asked. Simon thought fleetingly of his pictures. "Even my dreams are actions," he said and immediately felt that he ought to follow up such an astute remark. He glanced round at the other passengers, trying to judge whether this might be the right spot for an impromptu speech.

Suddenly Nina was standing very close to him and when she spoke she was as grave as he had ever seen her.

"We went to school on Frederiksø," she said softly, "and there we learned about Bjarke's dreams. During the battle at Lejre, Bjarke slept while a fearsome bear fought in his place. They tried to wake him but he said: 'Leave me to dream.' Nonetheless they forced him to come with them and at that the bear vanished. The bear was Bjarke's dream."

Full of incredulous wonder, Simon realized that, for the first time ever, Nina had given him a warning. But of what he could not tell.

"The dreams of women," he said coolly, "are not bears." And on that note he would have liked to end the conversation, but it stuck in his mind like a burr, like a prophecy he did not understand.

By their second day on the island, Simon was admitting to himself that everything around him was totally alien to him and that Nina had come home.

He had always thought of himself—and often painted himself—as some fiery natural phenomenon, as an uninterrupted volcanic eruption, setting light to everything around it without itself ever being touched by its surroundings. He had always been of the opinion that it was he who spoke to mankind while it, in turn, kept its mouth shut and listened. Now, for the first time in a long, long while, he found himself passing unrecognized in the street. Not only that, but on this little island, which one could stroll around in an hour, there was not so much as a street on which he might be recognized, only dirt paths. On these paths they bumped into people who remembered Nina. These people greeted him kindly and asked after his health without knowing or understanding that before them stood a world-famous painter and eminent philosopher. Then they turned to talking to and about Nina. In his unaccustomed role as listener to a story with a central character other than himself and as spectator to a day-to-day life in which he figured as a welcome but anonymous guest, Simon noticed that there was something wrong with the vision of the people around about him. Their life, he now saw, lacked perspective. The men were fishermen who would now and again stare into the deeps and now and again into the heavens but who more often than not kept their eyes on the tools in their hands. As for the women, as a rule they gazed into the cooking pots and occasionally up at the religious samplers on the walls and sometimes down at the children. But no one, thought Simon, neither man nor woman, ever looks straight ahead; here, he thought, the horizon wraps itself so closely around them that even their questions do not stretch beyond the bare necessities of the daily round they follow with such short strides that they have no hope of ever getting on in life. He felt very lonely, and in his loneliness he caught himself missing the upturned faces of his audiences and his picture in the newspaper and the feverish chatter of private viewings, and it occurred to him that possibly, just possibly *my public has given me something after all.*

While Nina, he realized, had come home. As soon as she set foot on land she had been transformed and become one with the island. She put away the clothes he had brought her from Kurfürstendamm and went around instead in a blue dress that he had never seen before and that, together with the scarf she tied around her head, made her look like any of the other island women. She seemed to remember everyone they met and everyone remembered her. Her stride shortened, her gait slackened as she led Simon around, showing him the places where she had played as a child, and she would sit quite still for hours on end on the sun-warmed granite boulders while Simon restlessly paced off his prison.

On the morning of the second day he announced to her that this was to be their last day on the island. He saw how her face fell, but she bowed her head in resignation and he had expected nothing less. It was no longer conceivable to Simon that anyone might contradict him.

That afternoon she asked him to take a walk with her. He sensed that she had something she wished to say to him, but they walked in silence along the water's edge. Beside the bridge to Frederiksø they sat down on a bench. On the other side of the narrow stretch of water separating the two islands stood a tall tree. In this tree perched two sea eagles, an adult and a fledgling, their backs to Simon and Nina. "That's the male bird, there in the tree," said Nina, pointing to where the female was but a distant, lazily wheeling pinprick far off in the sky. "That pair of sea eagles have been here always," she said. "My grandfather told me that once, when he was a boy, a visiting hunter caught one of the young in a bird trap. Grandfather said that when the trap snapped shut the adult birds were so far away they might never have been there at all. But just as the hunter bent over the young one to break its neck so as not to ruin its plumage, they plummeted out of the sky like a couple of stones. Before taking to his heels he fired a few shots at them, but the blood ran into his eyes and he didn't hit them. Ever since then, though, the adult eagles have been deaf." She fell silent for a moment, casting her mind back. Then she said, "Grandfather set the young one free. The adult birds knew him, so they didn't touch him."

Simon observed her from the side. She was wearing no shoes that day and sitting there next to him, her feet buried in the grass, there was no way of telling where the island left off and the girl began. Under other circumstances, Simon would have been enthralled by the story of the eagle, king of birds, which he regarded as a fitting and wholesome symbol of the new Europe. But on this particular day there was, it seemed to him, a depth to Nina's story that he could not plumb.

"It can't possibly be the same birds," he said. "A sea eagle can't live to be a hundred." And without warning he gave a loud, piercing whistle. Over on

Frederiksø the young sea eagle slowly turned its head, cocked it to one side, and looked at Simon. But the adult bird kept its eyes fixed on the sea as if it had not heard a thing.

After this they sat quietly for a while. "Time," said Nina finally, "is not the same here as in Copenhagen. You've done a lot of traveling and most of the people I've met there have been all around Denmark. With the possible exception of the more remote parts, places like this. But here . . . here you'll find only a handful of people who have ever seen Copenhagen.

"Oh yes," she went on, nodding at the island facing them, "some people spend their whole life over there, without ever crossing the bridge to this side.

"My grandmother," she said pensively, "never once crossed over to Christiansø and once, when someone asked her why not, she simply replied: 'What business would I have there?' "

Just then, seemingly as an extension of Nina's words, a young girl in a long green dress broke out of the shade of the tree and slowly started walking across to the windmill. Simon stood up and grasped the handrail of the bridge. This is what we are up against, he thought sourly, such resistance to change is precisely what stands in the way of the new era.

He shut his eyes, then eased them open again, and as he did so he was struck by an idea. I'll have an enormous canvas taken across that bridge, he thought, and I'll paint them a picture over there the likes of which they have never seen, the likes of which no one has ever seen; a painting depicting the history of man as a frenzy of longing; a painting containing the hiss of steam, the pounding of pistons and rifle shots; and finally, right in the foreground, with a flash of all-consuming white fire, a painting that reaches out and grabs the public by the throat. And for a public it will have that girl in green and those intransigent men and women, and this picture will change their lives. It will hurl them into the future and inject a substance into their veins, forcing them to run away, forcing them to pour across this bridge and off and away. It will be, he thought to himself, the ultimate painting, a work of art capable of depopulating an island.

Thrown into a fever of excitement by his idea, he took a pace backward, as if he were in fact working at his canvas, and in his mind's eye he began to paint, strong in the ecstatic conviction that he was the creator of the universe and in the service of a higher cause.

At that moment he became aware of some form of resistance somewhere in the universe and he realized that Nina had risen to her feet and was now standing directly in front of him. She eyed him very intently, then said: "Really?"

Initially the shock checked Simon. He knew that not one word had escaped his lips and yet the woman was now talking to him as surely as if she were inside his head. He bent over until his eyes were level with hers and in a soft, steady voice he replied: "Really!"

Just for an instant she seemed to recoil. Then she appeared to bring all her being to bear on one single point. "We could give it a try," she said.

Anger, unexpected and intense, welled up in Simon's mouth like warm blood, leaving him incapable of speech, but without a second's thought he nodded in assent.

"Remember," said Nina, her words coming now as a whisper, and she pressed her swollen belly into Simon until he felt as if the child and her joint heartbeat were forcing him backward. "Remember to say when you've had enough."

And she stepped away from him and things slid back into place. Against the blue lacquer setting of the sea, the red granite sparkled under a yellow sun, the scent of seaweed and grass hung all around them, and on the dark green bushes huge matte-black berries were ripening. Simon shook his head, not sure whether the conversation really had taken place and whether it could possibly be true that his Nina had challenged him to a duel.

"We're dreaming," he said and started back toward the inn.

But he did not take Nina's arm. Although he had no idea how it had come about, he knew that between her and him a battle such as he had never experienced before and for which as yet he had no words was now being waged.

That night, Simon slept heavily and fitfully. He dreamed that a bear was sitting on his chest and he woke up fighting for breath. At Nina's request, they slept in one of the small fisherman's cottages next door to the inn. The house consisted of just one room with one window and through this window the moonlight streamed, catching as it fell the streamers of seaweed that hung from the eaves and throwing their shadows across the floor like the rusty iron bars of a prison. His mind in turmoil, Simon set foot on the cool floor and crossed to the window. From far off in space the full moon viewed him with the impassive alertness of a card player. The world wants something of me, he thought, and the next moment he knew what it was: out of the blue, for the very first time, it dawned on him that the woman lying behind him was going to have his child, and the recognition of this fact made him rigid with fright.

Prior to this Simon had regarded his child—to the extent that he had given it any thought at all—as yet another work of art, as a mot juste that had fallen on fertile ground, as a parallel to the inspired frame of mind in which, on a night in March ten years earlier, he had painted his first picture. Now he looked at the woman in the bed and knew without any doubt that with this child an inscription would be etched into the universe that could not be painted over like a canvas or forgotten or rewritten like some unsatisfactory speech. From far away, from the woman's womb, the nethermost level of humanity cried out to him, calling him to account, and Simon staggered under this burden as though struck by a blow.

Only momentarily, though. Then he shrugged it off and got dressed. He reeled about like a drunkard, bumping into the furniture, but in the bed Nina slumbered on, all her being seeming to be focused on sleep. In the doorway he stopped for a moment and considered her. Nothing, he thought, can waken a woman.

The night was warm and perfectly still, and in the moonlight the dark rock acquired a luster, for all the world as if the island were one enormous black pearl.

Simon felt happiness surging through him, he was filled with power, he walked briskly, with no thought for where he might be headed, and when he found himself standing facing the bridge to Frederiksø he was of the impression that the world around him was shaping itself in accordance with his wishes and that the night would give him an answer.

A woman was crossing the bridge. Simon thought he recognized the slender figure of the girl he had seen walking toward the windmill. She moved slowly but purposefully and as she drew closer, in the moonlight that on this night was strong enough for him to make out colors, he saw that under her jacket she wore a green dress. She was carrying a suitcase and a bag and when she came face-to-face with Simon she set these down and looked him in the eye.

Even Simon, even the great Simon Bering—a man who had urged nations to act spontaneously—never failed to falter when confronted with a woman. But this night he felt himself in possession of all his best qualities and he caught her hand and kissed it. It was the first time in his life he had ever made such a gesture. Her hand was cold, but she looked at him intently and when she tilted her head to one side and smiled, Simon experienced a giddy sense of recognition, as if he had seen her before. As she walked past him, down to the water's edge, he was suddenly aware that this was the first time she had ever crossed the bridge, that she was leaving the island, and that it had to have been his presence that had prompted her departure. She's about to sail over on a fishing boat, to catch the morning ferry to Copenhagen, he thought, and somewhere on Zealand a job as a housemaid awaits her. All this he sensed, knowing it as surely as if he were inside her head and without a word's having escaped her lips.

He did not take the straight road back, choosing instead a path that crossed the island by another route, and as he walked the certitude of a moment before drained out of him.

One year earlier, in Berlin, Simon had been awarded that city's most prestigious art prize. To mark the occasion his portrait had been painted, the intention being that his motto should be added to this painting. The matter had been brought up by the chancellor himself and Simon, in no hurry to reply, had silently asked himself why he did not have a motto and he had answered himself by saying that it was because his aim in life had been so self-evident that he had no need of any such linguistic crutch. Having thought this far, he looked the Führer in the eye and declared out loud: "My motto is 'Ohne Zweifel!' "—without doubt—and the little man facing him had nodded and returned his gaze and said: "A fine motto for a painter!"

Nevertheless, on this night Simon was visited by doubt. As he was walking from the bridge, he suffered another attack of the breathlessness with which he had woken. Around him the universe seemed to stretch into infinity and yet he had no room, no Lebensraum. For the first time in a long while he felt fear in the form of a sense that something was lying in wait for him in the darkness; felt, too, that he did not have the answers to the riddle with which he was faced but would have to draw them from outside himself. He had the feeling that the black yet reflective granite surfaces were absorbing all his strength, so he took to giving them a wide berth. He looked up at the stars and wondered what it was that the chancellor had whispered to him that time in Berlin about his constellation; he focused his attention on the firmament above him in order perhaps to evoke an answer from up there, until it dawned on him that he was staggering along like a drunkard, that he was about to lose his dignity.

At this his anger returned and he stepped up onto a large flat rock, feeling as though he were in a boxing ring. He was struck by the certainty that on this night he was leaning against a force unlike anything he had ever before encountered, one that accorded him his self-assurance only to deprive him of it. But now he was going to fight back and, shoulders hunched, he shifted this way and that on the rock.

So smooth was it that it reflected both his own shadow and a blurred mirror image of the moon's face. Simon shut his eyes, then slowly opened them, wanting to come up with his own answer to his own future. The white face at his feet turned into that of the girl by the bridge and he realized that he missed her, her and his freedom, with a longing nothing could be allowed to stand in the way of. He began to run back to the harbor.

Out on the sea he thought he saw white sails moving away from the island, but the sight left him undaunted. For now that he had made up his mind, nothing could possibly go wrong. As he bounded down the steps to the quayside he spotted a boat. With just one small foresail hoisted, it came scudding across the water from Frederiksø, making for the mouth of the harbor. Simon laughed out loud. He had never doubted that this very boat would be right here. He waved, the boat swung in alongside the quay, and he leaped aboard. "Over to Bornholm," he said, still laughing, and fumbled in his jacket pocket for a wad of notes that he held out to the figure on the aft thwart. The boat pitched and headed out of the harbor, and it occurred to Simon that money, too, can be both palette and brush.

There was only one person on the boat and in the darkness Simon took him to be an elderly man. He sat with his hand on the rudder and a rug over his legs, so that there was no way of telling where the boat left off and the man began. Once out of the harbor he hoisted the mainsail and the vessel heeled over and shot forward like a bird over a calm sea and beneath an unfathomable star-studded sky. With one thought Simon embraced both the woman behind him and the woman ahead of him, and it seemed to him that he was running a silver thread from one to the other along which the boat was now sailing and he sensed that the time was right for making a speech.

"As a sailor," he said to the fisherman, "you'll surely agree with me that for anyone who has seen something of the world there are three joys that surpass all others. The first of these is the joy of departure, the pleasure inherent in finding that, for the free spirit, as for the birds, gravity does not apply.

"The second joy is that of arrival, of finding that we can go anywhere we please and say: At this moment—and perhaps only at this moment—I belong here, wherever I lay my head."

At this poin the fell silent for a moment and thought; What a pity that I have only this one stunted spectator and not a proper audience, or at the very least someone who could have taken this down in shorthand. At the same time he felt that above his head his words spiraled upward on broad wings toward the glittering stars, and he stood up, grabbed hold of the mast, waited till he had regained his balance, then flung his arm wide.

"The third and greatest joy," he said, "is to leave one's mark on the place to which one has come, to feel that one could, if one wished, drop down on the world with such tremendous force that one would never, ever be forgotten, either by people or by places."

He stood there for a while with his eyes closed. The fisherman remained silent but his silence did not bother Simon, who had learned long ago—with or without applause—to congratulate himself on a splendid solo. It did, however, cross his mind that the old man might be slow-witted. But in that, he said to himself with a wry little smile, he would be no different from every other member of the general public.

While making his speech, he had had his back to the direction in which they were sailing, something that did not altogether fit with his theory on the glories of departure and arrival but that had been necessary in order that he might be facing his audience. Now, as slowly he opened his eyes, he saw the Christiansø light flashing, not astern of the boat as it ought to have been, but a fair bit to starboard. "We're sailing the wrong way," he told the fisherman, dumbfounded.

This remark was followed by a lengthy silence, during which Simon felt bound to conclude that his traveling companion was a mute.

Then the fisherman spoke.

"My hearing's not so good," he said in a husky voice in which Simon recognized the origin of Nina's dialect. "Well, actually I can't hear a thing. But I get by with 'aye, aye,' that being what everybody would rather hear anyway.

"Tonight," he added, "we're going to catch salmon."

The rage with which Simon was now filled arose not from the fact that they were going the wrong way or from his being mistaken for an angler. It arose from the fact that the man opposite him had not heard a word he had said.

"Ashore," said Simon, bringing his face right down to the fisherman's and spitting the words at him. "I want to be put ashore."

The fisherman looked along Simon's outstretched arm and nodded. "Aye," he said, "it's the fog."

Simon raised his eyes in disbelief. Where before the Svaneke lighthouse had flashed, there was now darkness and over this darkness hung a luminous, milky band. Again he pointed frantically at the spot where Bornholm had been, but the fisherman shook his head. "There's no fish there," he said, "and besides, the wind drops when the fog comes down."

Simon thought of the girl in the green dress sailing on ahead of him, bound for land, and once more he felt as though the universe were barring his way. Just as he took a step to stern, intended to lay hands on the tiller, the mist descended. It enveloped the boat like a cloak falling over it; sky and sea disappeared, the wind died down, the air shone with an opalescent light, and just a few feet in front of Simon, the fisherman's silhouette grew hazy. A hush fell on the boat. It was, thought Simon, as if the two of them were sitting in a tiny room, as if the universe had wrapped itself so closely around them that they were now all alone in the world. Tonight, he said to himself, I am by turns liberated and confined.

Across from him the fisherman fed a line strung with an endless succession of hooks over the side. "Here, right under us," he explained, "the cliffs plunge straight down and the water's deep. The fish hover there—like birds," he added thoughtfully, "high above the seabed."

There ensued a long silence during which Simon strove to understand what had gone wrong. Then the fisherman spoke.

"It's mild the night," he said. "Me, I'm only a deaf creature but I felt that you were telling a story a while back. Well, now I'll tell you one, a story about a cold, cold night."

The thought crossed Simon's mind that, ever since he had set off to do as he pleased with the world, the world had been forcing him to listen as never before. And now to this old dodderer as well, he thought.

"Once I was stranded on an ice floe," said the fisherman. "I was on my way to Greenland—the how or the why of it is neither here nor there—and I traveled some of the way on the good ship *Ragna* of the Greenland Trading Company. But the ice blocked the sea lanes and in the end it forced the ship down and closed over it. There we sat, twenty men beside myself. Some were suffering from tuberculosis—we laid them off to one side, by themselves. The rest of us paced back and forth alongside the black waters, wondering whether our hour had come. I fell in with a man dressed partly in Greenlandic fashion who walked up and down and sang as though he were already off his head. We were joined by a young man who had caught my eye because of his sorry attempt at growing a full beard. Back then I still had my hearing so I heard both the madman's singing and the young man's story of how he was a scientist who had left his wife and children because, unlike the rest of the world, he did not believe that women and children were necessary to guarantee a man eternal life and because he had heard that anyone who comes to the polar regions has found his way both to heaven and to hell.

"He told us that when he prized most in life was solitude and silence. I have a notion that he came over to join us and told us all of this in the hope that together the three of us might prove to be three times as solitary and three times as silent. So I did not respond. And the madman burst into song once more.

"All that night and all the following day—which, by the way, in that part of the world at that time of year was but one long, dark hour—he stood there, singing out across the water. At one point I heard the young man ask him why he sang and he replied that, when an Eskimo prays for something, he sings a song in honor of the gods. 'Do you believe that?' the young man asked him incredulously. 'In that old wives' tale!' retorted the other. 'No, no, I just sing to keep warm.

" 'And,' he added, 'because you never can tell.' And he went back to his singing."

Here the fisherman took a break, during which he drew in the line, checked the hook, and threw it out again. "Much later," he said, "I don't remember how much later, but it was long after our supplies had run out and the sick were dead and the healthy now only half alive, I was walking back and forth along the edge of the floe again, not wanting to die lying down. Everyone else had fallen silent but the lunatic in the anorak was still standing there singing. The sky was so clear that I felt I could see every single star, and the northern lights swept down to the icy rim like bridges of frozen light. I put out a hand and passed it through the light and the beam broke asunder only, a moment later, to run together again. Just then, from somewhere out at sea, there came an answering song and minutes later a group of Eskimos were running a boat up onto the floe. They took the sick ashore first, and after them the elderly. I helped the madman down to the boat and just before climbing aboard he turned to the young man. 'In parting,' he said, 'I have three pieces of advice for you.

" 'The first is that you have to have damned good references to get into heaven.

" 'The second is that, as far as children are concerned, we don't have them so we can enter into eternal life. We have them to remind us that one day we shall die.

" 'And the third thing I have to say to you is not a word of advice but a prayer to God: tonight I will pray to him to bless your beard.' "

For a while after that the fisherman said nothing, then: "I never saw that man again, or at least I saw him only at a distance. But while I could still hear, I heard someone say that he was Knud Rasmussen, the great Arctic explorer."

The silence in the boat was now absolute. The fisherman had curled up on himself, seeming, with his tale, to have completed his mission. Even the fishing line hung motionless from his fingers. On the thwart between him and Simon lay a hefty fishing knife. The boat had no engine, but as if from somewhere beyond the mist, Simon caught a whiff of a faint breeze. And yet he knew that the deaf man sitting opposite him would not hoist the sail, that on this night when his luck waxed and waned as the tide ebbed and flowed, cooped up in this weird, minute, and fogbound cell with the fisherman and his yawn, he was encountering a resistance the depths of which he could not plumb. He shut his eyes, and when he opened them again they were fixed, full of joy and inspiration, on the knife. He picked it up, ran a tentative finger along the blade. He could see now that beneath the rug the fisherman was slight and sinewy as a bird.

With the knife in his hand, the wellsprings of life flowed freely within Simon once more and he felt certainty building up in his breast. Death had always figured in his painting but he had never witnessed it at close quarters. Even the great war that would supposedly give birth to the new era, the war that he had advocated so fervently and had in a sense played out in his paintings, was not something he had ever imagined would affect him in a more personal manner. Rather, he envisaged this apocalypse as a long, cold shower that, while it might well leave Europe in ruins, would also clear and purge the air and waft away the mist. And he would then descend from his railway compartment into the purged air, scent the new growth, and speak to the new man.

Now, all at once, he was standing on the battlefield himself. He looked at the knife in his hand and thought to himself, This is also a paintbrush and this will be the ultimate painting. He felt no fear, only a powerful sense of purpose and a vague feeling of regret because not even for this act would he have any spectators. Then he bade farewell to this objection, too, and was filled with the great joy experienced by those in whose lives words and action suddenly are as one, and with no petty qualms over the thought that his victim happened to be a deaf man, he wrapped one hand around the mast for support and flung out his free arm.

"This," he said, addressing the fisherman's sharp profile, "is a speech to one who is about to die.

"Not that long ago," he said, raising his voice in the hope of, nonetheless, penetrating the silence that confronted him, "I made another speech, in which I stated that there are three sorts of freedom. The first of these is the ability to go wherever one pleases, and this I experienced tonight when we sailed out of the harbor. You, too, are familiar with this feeling; you must have experienced it when you altered course as I was speaking—because that is what you have done. Without quite understanding how or why, I know that you have deliberately led me astray and taken me where you saw fit.

"Then there is the second freedom, the one we possess when we find ourselves capable of ending a life, and to that one we will both return in a moment.

"But there is also a third sort of freedom, which lies in the ability to cope with utter loneliness. It consists of being able to act not only with no regard for the world around us—since there are many of us who can do that—but with no regard for the world inside our heads, for what is known as our conscience. If one can do that, then one is utterly alone and utterly free."

Here Simon broke off and was conscious of his words winging their way out into the wide world. Then he stepped behind the old man, and even while totally engrossed in the moment and in his own actions, he was able, with one small corner of his mind, to note his kinship with the great self-sacrificing figures of history; to feel that he had now become the incarnation of Abraham and Hakon Jarl and Agamemnon and perhaps even God himself, who sacrifices his own son on the cross in order to present his followers and himself with that third form of freedom.

At that instant a gust of wind whisked away the mist as if a curtain were being pulled aside. The sun still dallied beneath the horizon, not yet ready to play its hand, but like an interim bid a bright violet glow spread across the sea and the score of fishing boats lying to either side of Simon and the old man—freeboard to freeboard, a little forest of masts, the closest of them only an oar's length from Simon, all hovering like birds over the same underwater abyss and fishing ground. And along the rails, faces, possibly hundreds of them, all devoid of expression, turned toward the voice in the mist.

Never had Simon had a more deeply intent, more completely attentive audience and never had he had less to say.

Now I am to be crushed, he thought, feeling as though he were in an arena, held there by a tension that would not even allow him to fall flat on his face. And yet at that moment it was not concern for his own person with which he was filled but the giddy sensation of an unfamiliar impotence, of a defeat that went beyond him personally, and without his either willing it or resisting it he heard himself, in a whisper so soft that only he could hear it, begging the world for mercy.

At that, a tension seemed to leave the boat, the fisherman across from him drew himself upright like someone who has been asleep, the knife slipped out of Simon's hand and over the side, and he saw it glint with a green light as it sank through the water, heading into nothingness.

On the way into Christiansø Simon did not look back once. He knew that there would be nothing to see. That as soon as he had begged for mercy, both the mist and the fishing boats had ceased to exist. That since he had left his sleeping woman he had been moving through a world dreamed up by someone else. And now, only now, did he recall the story of Bjarke's dream.

He did not even glance at the fisherman. But as they laid to and he clambered up onto the quayside, the birdlike profile was there at the corner of his eye, and a shiver ran down his spine. Walking away from the harbor he suddenly turned around, knowing what he would find: boat and man had vanished as if they had never been, and high above him the great sea eagle was soaring heavenward.

Outside the cottage Simon stopped for a moment. Then slowly he opened the door and braced himself against the doorpost to keep himself from falling. From the bed the woman stared at him with a wan and utterly exhausted face.

"I have," said Simon, "had enough."

Translated from the Danish by Barbara Haveland

Pawel Huelle

Moving House

(POLAND)

My father had hired Mr. Bieszke to come on Saturday, in the early afternoon, but Mr. Bieszke called it off. It turned out he had to attend a christening somewhere in the neighborhood of Kartuzy, so off he'd gone with his entire family and the move was postponed until Monday.

In the room upstairs, where we'd always lived, terrible things were going on: my mother was packing and repacking cardboard boxes and suitcases, and was cross at having to go on doing it for two more days; my father was cross because my mother was cross; and that meant they were cross with each other and with me in the bargain. I preferred to keep out of their way by spending most of my time in the garden. I can't remember if I was unhappy about that, and maybe I wasn't; until dinnertime I could do whatever I wanted. Only two things were forbidden: going beyond the garden gate into the park, and playing on the terrace, from where you could see through the French windows into the Great Room.

I knew the park well. Its greatest attractions were flowerbeds grown wild, a weed-choked pond, a miniature waterfall that had been out of action for years, never spouting a single drop of water, and a stone plinth on which once upon a time, very long ago, had stood a statue of a king, or perhaps of a prince. In the dense undergrowth of nettles lay various objects: here a rusty bathtub with a large hole in it, there a crank handle for starting up an engine, over there a broken armchair, its upholstery disemboweled and its springs exposed. There were other bits of junk besides, whose purpose was obscure, or else forgotten. But that afternoon the park didn't tempt me, somehow. The terrace and the Great Room were quite another matter. Mysterious and ethereal things went on in there, to which neither my father nor Mr. Skiski, our upstairs neighbor, had access.

In the Great Room lived Madam Greta, the former owner of the house. Mr. Skiski didn't seem to like the word "owner," because he always called her "the Heiress," cackling maliciously. My father simply called her Mrs. Hoffmann, but my mother always referred to her as "that old Kraut," which didn't sound too friendly. I very rarely saw her—she avoided us as much as possible, and we avoided her.

"You're not to go there," my mother would warn. "She doesn't know Polish."

"Yes," my father would add, "there's no need to disturb her."

Although I didn't see Madam Greta often, I heard her every day. Almost every afternoon she'd sit at the grand piano and for two or three hours the house would resound with music.

"The Heiress is rattling the ivories again," Mr. Skiski would say dismissively.

"German music again," my mother would sigh.

"She's just playing," my father would shrug. "What's wrong with that?"

I liked her music. I especially liked it before going to sleep, when my father put out the light and shadows filled the room. Then the sounds of the grand piano would melt on the air, and I could almost feel their velvet touch; when she stopped playing, I felt sad, as if something was missing.

No, I had no desire at all to get to know Madam Greta. What would we have to talk about? All I wanted to know was what it was like inside the Great Room, and that meant getting in there one day, to watch her as she played.

I started walking around the house very slowly. First I passed the old maple tree wreathed in mistletoe, then the boarded-up windows of the outhouse, until at last I was on the terrace, facing the broad, glazed doors. Sometimes Madam Greta would open them and, standing or else sitting at a little wooden table, have a look at the garden. She'd gaze down at the stone wall, the shoots of wild vine and the flowering wisteria, and in the gentle sunlight her small gray head made me think of a startled bird. But that only happened in the summer. Now the doors were shut, and on the terrace paving, patterned like a chessboard, yellow leaves rustled beneath my shoes.

I pressed my forehead to the glass. There wasn't much light in the Great Room, and I couldn't see very well. The only thing visible was a table standing next to the French windows, entirely covered in objects. As soon as my eyes had grown accustomed to the dusky light, they began to explore this wilderness, picking out various shapes. There were brass and silver candlesticks, piles of fat books and scores, loose sheets of paper, china boxes and figurines, glass bottles, bits of dress material, needles and thread, earthenware pots, a pair of gloves, a child's toy rake, ladies' hats, cups with saucers and without, paperweights of lacquer and of bronze, a small bust of a man, a silver sugar bowl, some photographs set in frames, and an alarm clock with large bells, a little clapper, and one hand broken off. The contours of these objects were blurred and their shapes merged together as if seen through an out-of-focus lens. But what there was most of were books and musical scores. Heaped up, they recalled a ruined city with ravine-like streets and narrow passageways between one wall and the next.

My initial curiosity satisfied, I stood there waiting for Madam Greta to appear, sit down at the piano, and play. If she wasn't in the Great Room she must be doing something in the kitchen, but I couldn't see in there. The windows were too high, and were covered with packing paper. Not even any of the grown-ups had seen the kitchen. Even on the rare occasions when they visited the Great Room briefly, they never crossed the threshold of the kitchen. The rest of her living quarters—two sitting rooms, a bedroom, and bathroom—

were padlocked shut like the ones upstairs, sealed by officials long ago. For as long as I could remember they'd never been opened. Their ceilings threatened to cave in. So Madam Greta must be sitting in the kitchen.

If the French windows onto the terrace hadn't been locked from the inside, I could have pushed them slightly open, then slipped into the Great Room. I could have had a good look at everything and then left without anybody noticing. But what if she caught me in the act? She'd think I was a thief. While I was weighing up whether Mrs. Hoffmann would complain to my father or not and wondering what the German word for "thief" sounded like, a light went on in the Great Room, and between the massive bed, the wardrobe, and the grand piano which loomed up suddenly out of the darkness, I caught sight of her diminutive, slightly stooping frame. She didn't go straight to the piano, as I'd thought she would. She placed a glass of tea on a small round table and sat down in a deep armchair beside it. Seconds later I felt a shiver up my spine. Something odd was going on in the Great Room, something I couldn't understand, and I don't mean just the German language.

As she sipped her tea, Madam Greta was talking to someone. It wasn't a monologue—she kept asking questions, making comments, shaking her head and gesticulating, maybe even arguing—a couple of times I heard her raise her voice. But who was she talking to? There was no one else in the Great Room. What normal person talks to thin air? I thought—perhaps she's mad. That wasn't impossible. I'd seen a mad woman once on Red Army Street; she spat at the passersby and threatened them; she was all ragged and dirty, with spit hanging from her lips. Mrs. Hoffmann, by contrast, was wearing a brightly colored blouse fastened at the neck with an amber brooch, and a black skirt; her shortish gray hair bore the visible imprint of a hairdresser, though she didn't go anywhere in town except to the market at Oliwa and the Cistercian church. After a while, I found that by pressing my ear to the window I could catch a few words, and new doubts came to me: What if she's talking to someone she can see but I cannot? The conversation was clearly growing more animated—Mrs. Hoffmann was waving her hands about, explaining something heatedly, as if there was something the other person couldn't understand. Or was she just play-acting? But for whom? And why? I didn't know what to think. Yet the sight of this old woman, speaking whole sentences in an unfamiliar language, the sight of Madam Greta sitting in her armchair chatting to someone only she could see was so odd that I was rooted to the spot—I couldn't look away.

Suddenly the conversation stopped. Without switching off the light, Madam Greta went to the kitchen with her glass, then quickly came back and sat at the piano. I don't know how she noticed me; outside, dusk was falling, and the light from the chandelier was pretty strong. She rose swiftly from her stool, came over to the French windows and briskly opened them.

"Und vot arr you doink heer?" she asked.

"Me?" I tried to say something. "I was just coming by this way."

"Arr you hunkry?"

"No thanks, Ma'am."

"You vont zum tea? You do!" she answered for me. "You're to vait heer, gut?" And out she went into the kitchen.

Her steps echoed down the long corridor, and there I was in the Great Room, where I discovered lots of unusual things. The pictures, for example: all of them were very dark and very old; most showed horses, droshkies, and horse-drawn trams around the church of Our Lady, by Neptune's Fountain and beneath the Prison Tower. Or the grand piano: in its walnut paneling were ornate letters forming an inscription which I had trouble deciphering: GERHARD RICHTER UND SOHNEN, DANZIG 1932. In the bookshelf stood row upon row of weighty tomes, the light gleaming across their gilded spines, but the stuffed birds—one white, the other fabulously colored—interested me more, along with a viper in a phial full of liquid. There was also a small collection of pipes and china pipestems with little pictures on them. Then my gaze fell on an open book which lay beside an empty vase. Two color illustrations depicted a woman and a man, but they were nothing like my mother and father. Instead of skin, or rather under the skin which wasn't there, there were swirling veins, entrails, arteries and joints, muscles and bones. They weren't exactly naked, and I didn't feel ashamed, but looking at them gave me a mixed feeling of curiosity and revulsion: if they were human beings, then I must look like that inside as well.

When Madam Greta came back, I shut the book; she set down a tray of tea, apple charlotte, and jam on the little table, and said, "Vee arr heving a Geburtstag. Zat iz a kind of zelebrashun. You undershtent?"

I answered that I did, and as I was eating a piece of charlotte she asked, "You like it ven I play, don't you?"

"Yes," I replied. "But how did you know that?"

"I kan zee it in your eyz?"

I was amazed. I'd never actually looked her straight in the eyes; I'd never even met her on the stairs or in the garden. As soon as she'd played the first chord, which rang out pure and strong across the Great Room, she turned around on her swiveling stool and asked, "Und vich tune do you like ze best?"

I didn't know what to answer. I didn't know any of the titles, and I wouldn't have been able to hum anything. All I could have said was, "Please play the good-night tune—the one I fall asleep so well to. Or the one you played when it was snowing, and my mother was standing by the window and called me over to come and watch the snowflakes slowly blanketing the park, the avenue, and garden. Or else the one I heard when my father was fixing the radio, which blended in with all the radio stations in the world." But most of all I was longing to hear the tune from an evening in June.

My father and mother were sure I was asleep. They were sitting in bed, covered by the sheets and drinking wine from slender glasses, laughing every now and then. When the bottle was empty, my father whistled gently down its hollow neck and they laughed again; the sound was like the horn of the transatlantic liner they'd planned to sail away on for their honeymoon, but they never had a honeymoon. That was the moment when the sounds of the piano began to drift in from the Great Room. Mrs. Hoffmann was playing a slow, sad tune. My father took my mother in his arms and they danced around the room on tiptoe, careful not to wake me. Through my half-closed eyelids I could see their whirling figures; I watched the white wings of the sheets as they slowly settled, until the light went out and I could no longer see anything, but the music went on wafting in through the open window of our room along with a strong scent of peonies from the garden.

"I don't know what it's called," I said at last. "You played it once, in the summer."

"Vell, all right. I'll play a bit, und you tell me ven you recognise it."

I nodded, and Mrs.Hoffmann began to play. Although it wasn't the tune from that night in June, I listened to it enraptured, and was sorry when it broke off as Madam Greta suddenly lifted her fingers from the keyboard.

"I kan zee zat's not ze vun you vonted. Do you know vot I voz playing just now?"

"No."

"*Tannhäuser*, ze overture."

"Tann-hoyzer?"

"Yes."

"Is that a composer?"

Madam Greta looked me in the eyes, then got up from the piano, took a book from the shelf and motioned me to bring up another stool. She opened the book at a picture of a castle: there were knights, fine ladies, minstrels, horses, banners, and turrets.

"Zat is ze castle of ze Landgraf of Thuringia," she said.

I turned the pages of the book as Mrs. Hoffmann explained each picture in turn, playing each successive movement of *Tannhäuser*.

When we were past the Grotto of Venus, the duel of songs and Elisabeth's lament, and had reached the pilgrims and the wooden staff that burst into green shoots, Madam Greta said, as her fingers raced across the keys, "Now vatch out, here come ze trumpets, und now ze horns und oboes!" and I really could hear the trumpets, horns, and oboes, though the only sounds were from Gerhard Richter's grand piano.

"Is it all true?" I asked, once silence fell. "Did it really happen?"

Madam Greta took out a photograph album, and I saw pictures that were similar but a little different. On a large stage among beech trees stood men dressed in historical costumes, holding flaming torches in their hands.

"*Die Kunst*," she said, "zat's just art. Zey used to sing vot I've just been playing: *Beglück darf du nicht, O Heimat!* Zey vere performances in ze Wald—opera, you undershtent? At Zopott. Und here iz my huzband."

The photograph was of a tall man in a light striped suit, standing beside another man in a black suit against the background of a little waterfall and a pond. Both were smiling into the camera, and they looked like old friends.

"That's our park!" I said. "There's the waterfall, and there are the steps. You can even see the roof behind the trees!"

"Yes," said Mrs. Hoffmann, "zat voz ze park. Und my husband voz a musician und composer. Ze ozer man is Max. He came here zat time from Vienna to sing *Tannhäuser.* Both of zem are no longer living now. Und zis," she said, showing me another picture, "is Erikson. He voz a Norvegian from Oslo, und ze season after he sang Hagen in *Götterdämmerung.* Vot a vonderful voice he had!"

"Where's Gerta Daymerung?" I asked. "Is it somewhere in Sopot?"

At that, Madam Greta brought out another book and showed me more pictures, then sat at the piano again and played Siegfried's funeral march, which sent shivers down my spine. Then she played more—*Steuermann lass die Wacht,* and *Gesegnet soll Sie schreiten,* and *Wach auf, es nahet gen der Tag,* until everything started to get mixed up in my head. Parsifal was walking in the park by the dried-up pond, Mrs. Hoffmann's husband was chasing Hagen around the stage of the forest opera at Sopot to the terrible wailing of the Valkyries and the Nibelungs, Erikson was standing on Madam Greta's terrace, holding a flaming torch and singing *"Beglück darf du nicht, O Heimat!"* while the sailors from the *Flying Dutchman* were on their way back from Oliwa on the road to Sopot, singing *"Heil! der Gnade Wunder Heil!"*

It was all strange and entrancing and beautiful, like the park in the old photograph. My cheeks were flushed as I listened to Madam Greta play on and on, a new piece every time, now without telling the story, or showing pictures from the books. We were both in an odd state, in a sort of trance, perhaps, because we didn't hear my father's footsteps or notice him standing behind us. He, too, seemed enchanted by the music, or else by the scene in Mrs. Hoffmann's room: she stooping over the grand piano and I staring at her or at her fingers as if hypnotized. Or maybe he was bewitched by something else entirely. In any case, he stood behind us for several minutes before putting a hand on my shoulder and gently saying, "We've got to go now."

Mrs. Hoffmann struck a mighty, crowning chord, turned toward my father, and said, "Oh, Mr. Schiffbaumeister! Ve're just making a little music togezer. You're not angry, I hope?"

"No, I'm not angry," my father said, "but we really have to go now. Good night, Mrs. Hoffmann."

"Guten Nacht, gut night, gentlemen, gut night."

Once we were back in our room upstairs, my mother couldn't seem to calm down. Why had I gone there? She'd told me so many times! And what had she been doing to me, that old Kraut?

My father tried to stand up for me.

"She was playing him Wagner. That's all."

But an evil spirit had entered her.

"Germans! Germans! Germans!" Louder and louder she shrieked. "It's always those Germans! Always building their highways and machinery. They've got the best planes in the world, and the best gas ovens for burning people up. Those Germans, they play Wagner, they always feel marvelous, they've always got hearty appetites!"

I'd never seen my mother in such a state before. She shrieked at my father, saying how pointless it was that he'd brought her to this city, how he'd only done it so she could spend five years living under the same roof as a German.

"Why didn't she leave? Why didn't she get out of here like the others?"

"Calm down," said my father. "The child shouldn't hear such things."

But the evil spirit wouldn't leave her alone.

"Why not? He's got to find out one day, hasn't he?"

She began to shout names, beloved names she knew well, spreading out one finger for each name, first on her left, then on her right hand; once the fingers were all outspread, she repeated the same thing many times in tears, for there were far more murdered people than fingers.

Unable to stand it any longer, my father asked her to stop, shouting at her that it wasn't he who'd caused the war, it wasn't he who'd moved the borders, it wasn't he who'd taken a city from one people and given it to another. I stood between them, torn in two. I could see their bodies; I could see the man and woman in the color illustration, like two pulsating, living wounds.

My father fell silent at last, then took some medicine from the cupboard and gave it to my mother with a glass of water. Finally she came to her senses and made up with him, but in spite of that, once we were all in bed, the word "Germans" hovered in the room like a bird aroused in the darkness.

On Monday morning Mr. Bieszke came. We loaded all our worldly goods onto the cart and the horses pricked up their ears, the way they always do before the open road. At last we moved off downhill, along the avenue, between the rows of ancient trees. I looked back at the dried-up pond, the waterfall that didn't spout a single drop of water, and the nettles where objects of obscure or forgotten purpose lay concealed. Mrs. Hoffmann's house grew smaller and smaller in the distance, until it vanished among the trees, a small brown speck with a red dot for a roof. Hooves clattered on the flagstones; Mr. Bieszke's horses snorted merrily, and he sang a Kashubian song that must have been running through his head ever since the christening: *"I fancy me a tiny drop, from this my darling little flask!"* We passed the bridge and the tram depot. The chestnut trees began at the top of St. Hubert's Street. The new house, still unplastered, was not far away. Entering my room, I smelled fresh paint, lime, and parquet flooring. Just then that tune came back to me; Madam Greta had not got around to playing it. It must have been a love song, but was it by Richard Wagner? On the other side of the wall, in the other room, they were moving furniture around. I realized that I'd never find out now, nor would I ever know who Mrs. Hoffmann was talking to on the day of the Geburtstag, when I spied on her through the French windows of the Great Room.

Translated from the Polish by Michael Kandel

Kazuo Ishiguro

A Family Supper

(ENGLAND)

Fugu is a fish caught off the Pacific shores of Japan. The fish has held a special significance for me ever since my mother died through eating one. The poison resides in the sexual glands of the fish, inside two fragile bags. When preparing the fish, these bags must be removed with caution, for any clumsiness will result in the poison leaking into the veins. Regrettably, it is not easy to tell whether or not this operation has been carried out successfully. The proof is, as it were, in the eating.

Fugu poisoning is hideously painful and almost always fatal. If the fish has been eaten during the evening, the victim is usually overtaken by pain during his sleep. He rolls about in agony for a few hours and is dead by morning. The fish became extremely popular in Japan after the war. Until stricter regulations were imposed, it was all the rage to perform the hazardous gutting operation in one's own kitchen, then to invite neighbours and friends round for the feast.

At the time of my mother's death, I was living in California. My relationship with my parents had become somewhat strained around that period, and consequently I did not learn of the circumstances surrounding her death until I returned to Tokyo two years later. Apparently, my mother had always refused to eat fugu, but on this particular occasion she had made an exception, having been invited by an old schoolfriend whom she was anxious not to offend. It was my father who supplied me with the details as we drove from the airport to his house in the Kamakura district. When we finally arrived, it was nearing the end of a sunny autumn day.

"Did you eat on the plane?" my father asked. We were sitting on the tatami floor of his tea-room.

"They gave me a light snack."

"You must be hungry. We'll eat as soon as Kikuko arrives."

My father was a formidable-looking man with a large stony jaw and furious black eyebrows. I think now in retrospect that he much resembled Chou En-lai, although he would not have cherished such a comparison, being particularly proud of the pure samurai blood that ran in the family. His general presence was not one which encouraged relaxed conversation; neither were things helped much by his odd way of stating each remark as if it were the concluding one. In fact, as I sat opposite him that afternoon, a boyhood memory came back to me of the time he had struck me several times around the head for "chattering like an old woman." Inevitably, our conversation since my arrival at the airport had been punctuated by long pauses.

"I'm sorry to hear about the firm," I said when neither of us had spoken for some time. He nodded gravely.

"In fact the story didn't end there," he said. "After the firm's collapse, Watanabe killed himself. He didn't wish to live with the disgrace."

"I see."

"We were partners for seventeen years. A man of principle and honour. I respected him very much."

"Will you go into business again?" I asked.

"I am—in retirement. I'm too old to involve myself in new ventures now. Business these days has become so different. Dealing with foreigners. Doing things their way. I don't understand how we've come to this. Neither did Watanabe." He sighed. "A fine man. A man of principle."

The tea-room looked out over the garden. From where I sat I could make out the ancient well which as a child I had believed haunted. It was just visible now through the thick foliage. The sun had sunk low and much of the garden had fallen into shadow.

"I'm glad in any case that you've decided to come back," my father said. "More than a short visit, I hope."

"I'm not sure what my plans will be."

"I for one am prepared to forget the past. Your mother too was always ready to welcome you back—upset as she was by your behaviour."

"I appreciate your sympathy. As I say, I'm not sure what my plans are."

"I've come to believe now that there were no evil intentions in your mind," my father continued. "You were swayed by certain—influences. Like so many others."

"Perhaps we should forget it, as you suggest."

"As you will. More tea?"

Just then a girl's voice came echoing through the house.

"At last." My father rose to his feet. "Kikuko has arrived."

Despite our difference in years, my sister and I had always been close. Seeing me again seemed to make her excessively excited and for a while she did nothing but giggle nervously. But she calmed down somewhat when my father started to question her about Osaka and her university. She answered him with short formal replies. She in turn asked me a few questions, but she seemed inhibited by the fear that her questions might lead to awkward topics. After a while, the conversation had become even sparser than prior to Kikuko's arrival. Then my father stood up, saying: "I must attend to the supper. Please excuse me for being burdened down by such matters. Kikuko will look after you."

My sister relaxed quite visibly once he had left the room. Within a few minutes, she was chatting freely about her friends in Osaka and about her classes at university. Then quite suddenly she decided we should walk in the garden and went striding out onto the veranda. We put on some straw sandals that had been left along the veranda rail and stepped out into the garden. The daylight had almost gone.

"I've been dying for a smoke for the last half-hour," she said, lighting a cigarette.

"Then why didn't you smoke?"

She made a furtive gesture back towards the house, then grinned mischievously.

"Oh I see," I said.

"Guess what? I've got a boyfriend now."

"Oh yes?"

"Except I'm wondering what to do. I haven't made up my mind yet."

"Quite understandable."

"You see, he's making plans to go to America. He wants me to go with him as soon as I finish studying."

"I see. And you want to go to America?"

"If we go, we're going to hitch-hike." Kikuko waved a thumb in front of my face. "People say it's dangerous, but I've done it in Osaka and it's fine."

"I see. So what is it you're unsure about?"

We were following a narrow path that wound through the shrubs and finished by the old well. As we walked, Kikuko persisted in taking unnecessarily theatrical puffs on her cigarette.

"Well. I've got lots of friends now in Osaka. I like it there. I'm not sure I want to leave them all behind just yet. And Suichi—I like him, but I'm not sure I want to spend so much time with him. Do you understand?"

"Oh perfectly."

She grinned again, then skipped on ahead of me until she had reached the well. "Do you remember," she said, as I came walking up to her, "how you used to say this well was haunted?"

"Yes, I remember."

We both peered over the side.

"Mother always told me it was the old woman from the vegetable store you'd seen that night," she said. "But I never believed her and never came out here alone."

"Mother used to tell me that too. She even told me once the old woman had confessed to being the ghost. Apparently she'd been taking a short cut through our garden. I imagine she had some trouble clambering over these walls."

Kikuko gave a giggle. She then turned her back to the well, casting her gaze about the garden.

"Mother never really blamed you, you know," she said, in a new voice. I remained silent. "She always used to say to me how it was their fault, hers and Father's, for not bringing you up correctly. She used to tell me how much more careful they'd been with me, and that's why I was so good." She looked up and the mischievous grin had returned to her face. "Poor Mother," she said.

"Yes. Poor Mother."

"Are you going back to California?"

"I don't know. I'll have to see."

"What happened to—to her? To Vicki?"

"That's all finished with," I said. "There's nothing much left for me now in California."

"Do you think I ought to go there?"

"Why not? I don't know. You'll probably like it." I glanced towards the house. "Perhaps we'd better go in soon. Father might need a hand with the supper."

But my sister was once more peering down into the well. "I can't see any ghosts," she said. Her voice echoed a little.

"Is Father very upset about his firm collapsing?"

"Don't know. You can never tell with Father." Then suddenly she straightened up and turned to me. "Did he tell you about old Watanabe? What he did?"

"I heard he committed suicide."

"Well, that wasn't all. He took his whole family with him. His wife and his two little girls."

"Oh yes?"

"Those two beautiful little girls. He turned on the gas while they were all asleep. Then he cut his stomach with a meat knife."

"Yes, Father was just telling me how Watanabe was a man of principle."

"Sick." My sister turned back to the well.

"Careful. You'll fall right in."

"I can't see any ghost," she said. "You were lying to me all that time."

"But I never said it lived down the well."

"Where is it, then?"

We both looked around at the trees and shrubs. The light in the garden had grown very dim. Eventually I pointed to a small clearing some ten yards away.

"Just there I saw it. Just there."

We stared at the spot.

"What did it look like?"

"I couldn't see very well. It was dark."

"But you must have seen something."

"It was an old woman. She was just standing there, watching me."

We kept staring at the spot as if mesmerized.

"She was wearing a white kimono," I said. "Some of her hair had come undone. It was blowing around a little."

Kikuko pushed her elbow against my arm. "Oh be quiet. You're trying to frighten me all over again." She trod on the remains of her cigarette, then for a brief moment stood regarding it with a perplexed expression. She kicked some pine needles over it, then once more displayed her grin. "Let's see if supper's ready," she said.

We found my father in the kitchen. He gave us a quick glance, then carried on with what he was doing.

"Father's become quite a chef since he's had to manage on his own," Kikuko said with a laugh. He turned and looked at my sister coldly.

"Hardly a skill I'm proud of," he said. "Kikuko, come here and help."

For some moments my sister did not move. Then she stepped forward and took an apron hanging from a drawer.

"Just these vegetables need cooking now," he said to her. "The rest just needs watching." Then he looked up and regarded me strangely for some seconds. "I expect you want to look around the house," he said eventually. He put down the chopsticks he had been holding. "It's a long time since you've seen it."

As we left the kitchen I glanced back towards Kikuko, but her back was turned.

"She's a good girl," my father said quietly.

I followed my father from room to room. I had forgotten how large the house was. A panel would slide open and another room would appear. But the rooms were all startlingly empty. In one of the rooms the lights did not come on, and we stared at the stark walls and tatami in the pale light that came from the windows.

"This house is too large for a man to live in alone," my father said. "I don't have much use for most of these rooms now."

But eventually my father opened the door to a room packed full of books and papers. There were flowers in vases and pictures on the walls. Then I noticed something on a low table in the corner of the room. I came nearer and saw it was a plastic model of a battleship, the kind constructed by children. It had been placed on some newspaper; scattered around it were assorted pieces of grey plastic.

My father gave a laugh. He came up to the table and picked up the model.

"Since the firm folded," he said, "I have a little more time on my hands." He laughed again, rather strangely. For a moment his face looked almost gentle. "A little more time."

"That seems odd," I said. "You were always so busy."

"Too busy perhaps." He looked at me with a small smile. "Perhaps I should have been a more attentive father."

I laughed. He went on contemplating his battleship. Then he looked up. "I hadn't meant to tell you this, but perhaps it's best that I do. It's my belief that your mother's death was no accident. She had many worries. And some disappointments."

We both gazed at the plastic battleship.

"Surely," I said eventually, "my mother didn't expect me to live here for ever."

"Obviously you don't see. You don't see how it is for some parents. Not only must they lose their children, they must lose them to things they don't understand." He spun the battleship in his fingers. "These little gunboats here could have been better glued, don't you think?"

"Perhaps. I think it looks fine."

"During the war I spent some time on a ship rather like this. But my ambition was always the air force. I figured it like this. If your ship was struck by the enemy, all you could do was struggle in the water hoping for a lifeline. But in an aeroplane—well—there was always the final weapon." He put the model back onto the table. "I don't suppose you believe in war."

"Not particularly."

He cast an eye around the room. "Supper should be ready by now," he said. "You must be hungry."

Supper was waiting in a dimly lit room next to the kitchen. The only source of light was a big lantern that hung over the table, casting the rest of the room into shadow. We bowed to each other before starting the meal.

There was little conversation. When I made some polite comment about the food, Kikuko giggled a little. Her earlier nervousness seemed to have returned to her. My father did not speak for several minutes. Finally he said:

"It must feel strange for you, being back in Japan."

"Yes, it is a little strange."

"Already, perhaps, you regret leaving America."

"A little. Not so much. I didn't leave behind much. Just some empty rooms."

"I see."

I glanced across the table. My father's face looked stony and forbidding in the half-light. We ate on in silence.

Then my eye caught something at the back of the room. At first I continued eating, then my hands became still. The others noticed and looked at me. I went on gazing into the darkness past my father's shoulder.

"Who is that? In that photograph there?"

"Which photograph?" My father turned slightly, trying to follow my gaze.

"The lowest one. The old woman in the white kimono."

My father put down his chopsticks. He looked first at the photograph, then at me.

"Your mother." His voice had become very hard. "Can't you recognize your own mother?"

"My mother. You see, it's dark. I can't see it very well."

No one spoke for a few seconds, then Kikuko rose to her feet. She took the photograph down from the wall, came back to the table and gave it to me.

"She looks a lot older," I said.

"It was taken shortly before her death," said my father.

"It was the dark. I couldn't see very well."

I looked up and noticed my father holding out a hand. I gave him the photograph. He looked at it intently, then held it towards Kikuko. Obediently, my sister rose to her feet once more and returned the picture to the wall.

There was a large pot left unopened at the centre of the table. When Kikuko had seated herself again, my father reached forward and lifted the lid. A cloud of steam rose up and curled towards the lantern. He pushed the pot a little towards me.

"You must be hungry," he said. One side of his face had fallen into shadow.

"Thank you." I reached forward with my chopsticks. The steam was almost scalding. "What is it?"

"Fish."

"It smells very good."

In amidst soup were strips of fish that had curled almost into balls. I picked one out and brought it to my bowl.

"Help yourself. There's plenty."

"Thank you." I took a little more, then pushed the pot towards my father. I watched him take several pieces to his bowl. Then we both watched as Kikuko served herself.

My father bowed slightly. "You must be hungry," he said again. He took some fish to his mouth and started to eat. Then I too chose a piece and put it in my mouth. It felt soft, quite fleshy against my tongue.

"Very good," I said. "What is it?"

"Just fish."

"It's very good."

The three of us ate on in silence. Several minutes went by.

"Some more?"

"Is there enough?"

"There's plenty for all of us." My father lifted the lid and once more steam rose up. We all reached forward and helped ourselves.

"Here," I said to my father, "you have this last piece."

"Thank you."

When we had finished the meal, my father stretched out his arms and yawned with an air of satisfaction. "Kikuko," he said. "Prepare a pot of tea, please."

My sister looked at him, then left the room without comment. My father stood up.

"Let's retire to the other room. It's rather warm in here."

I got to my feet and followed him into the tea-room. The large sliding windows had been left open, bringing in a breeze from the garden. For a while we sat in silence.

"Father," I said, finally.

"Yes?"

"Kikuko tells me Watanabe-San took his whole family with him."

My father lowered his eyes and nodded. For some moments he seemed deep in thought. "Watanabe was very devoted to his work," he said at last. "The collapse of the firm was a great blow to him. I fear it must have weakened his judgement."

"You think what he did—it was a mistake?"

"Why, of course. Do you see it otherwise?"

"No, no. Of course not."

"There are other things besides work."

"Yes."

We fell silent again. The sound of locusts came in from the garden. I looked out into the darkness. The well was no longer visible.

"What do you think you will do now?" my father asked. "Will you stay in Japan for a while?"

"To be honest, I hadn't thought that far ahead."

"If you wish to stay here, I mean here in this house, you would be very welcome. That is, if you don't mind living with an old man."

"Thank you. I'll have to think about it."

I gazed out once more into the darkness.

"But of course," said my father, "this house is so dreary now. You'll no doubt return to America before long."

"Perhaps. I don't know yet."

"No doubt you will."

For some time my father seemed to be studying the back of his hands. Then he looked up and sighed.

"Kikuko is due to complete her studies next spring," he said. "Perhaps she will want to come home then. She's a good girl."

"Perhaps she will."

"Things will improve then."

"Yes, I'm sure they will."

We fell silent once more, waiting for Kikuko to bring the tea.

Roy Jacobsen

Encounter

(N O R W A Y)

Arvid had delivered the fish to the packing plant and returned the boat to its moorings. It wasn't much of a catch, a half crate of cod, three big coalfish, and some rosefish—from forty nets! Still, it was no worse than expected. It was a bleak time, with bleak expectations.

He rowed ashore in the dinghy and put the coalfish in the wooden crate on his moped. He always kept the biggest coalfish for himself. You can't get much for it, and besides, it tasted better than cod. He walked the moped past the drying rack and up onto the road, brushed wet snow off the seat, and put on his driving goggles.

From the packing plant it was twelve kilometers home on a country road, straight across a flat swamp. It could be a tough trip in the winter, but Arvid just bent over the handlebars when the weather got too bad, didn't push down on the gas so hard, and made sure that he stayed in the middle of the road. He got up at five every morning and drove the twelve kilometers to take the fishing boat out to sea. In the evenings he drove back. It was a nice rhythm. His parents had been farmers, but Arvid was a fisherman. He liked the sea better than the soil.

He started the engine.

Up on the swamp he shifted into third gear and accelerated. It was a gray day with no wind, so he could drive fast. When nobody was looking he sometimes leaned forward over the handlebars even though it wasn't really necessary.

After driving a few minutes he caught sight of a small figure at the other end of the world. It was moving toward him on the narrow ribbon of road and resembled a man on a moped, his own mirror image almost. Arvid didn't understand what this could mean. There was only one moped on the island and that was his. Once in a while there was a warm mist over the swamp that distorted one's vision, but that was only in the summertime.

He gave it more gas and leaned even closer into the handlebars. The figure was getting larger. It really was a man on a moped. Arvid moved over to the right a bit, but not much, so that his opponent had to yield more than he did. They passed each other. The man on the other moped was a black man.

Arvid sat up straight. He drove 230 meters into the darkness before he managed to brake. He stopped and looked back. The black man continued driving as though nothing had happened, kept getting smaller and smaller and threatened to disappear completely.

Arvid pulled himself together, turned the cycle around and went after him as fast as the moped would go. Fortunately the black man wasn't going very fast—he was the type who sat upright and looked around at the scenery while he drove. And slowly but surely Arvid caught up with him, glided up next to him and looked at him. They looked at each other. The black man smiled. He, too, had a crate on his baggage rack. Arvid signaled that he should stop. They stopped.

Arvid got off his moped and walked right up to the man.

"What are you doing here?" he asked.

"I be selling books," said the black man and patted the crate.

Arvid couldn't imagine anything more meaningless. The man talked just the way the blacks talk in the Donald Duck comic books.

"I came by ship," he said. "Many be buying books here on the island."

"By *ferry*," Arvid corrected and was forced to laugh. "You came by ferry. This afternoon?"

"Ja, ja," the black man continued to smile. He said he was a student from Ghana and that he had to sell books to finance his studies.

Arvid had never seen a stranger man. He took off his goggles and moved even closer. The black man took off his goggles, too.

"What kind of books?" Arvid wanted to know and slapped the crate.

"You be interested?" asked the man cheerfully and got off his moped. "Fine books."

He opened the crate and paged through a book, since Arvid's hands were too dirty to touch it himself. The book was red on the outside. On the inside there was a lot of text and Arvid saw several pictures of Jesus. The book was called *Gleams of Light*. He wrinkled his nose. He didn't like Jesus. They had a church in the community, but it was only used for confirmations and funerals. The black man laughed at him and pulled out another book. It was green and much thicker. It was a cookbook. Arvid looked at the colored pictures of the various dishes. He didn't like cookbooks either. But he didn't want to abandon this mystery so soon.

"Will you manage to sell this stuff?" he wondered.

"Ja, ja," said the black man. "I be going over there now."

He pointed at the farm of Martin Grønli, which they could barely see smoke from at the other end of the swamp. Arvid thought that though Martin couldn't read, he was probably just dumb enough to buy a book.

"Don't you have anything else?" he asked.

The black man happily pulled out one more.

"This be a novel," he said and displayed a thick book with nothing but writing. It was called *Moby Dick*.

"I've heard of that," said Arvid and was suddenly embarrassed. Maybe it had something to do with the name Moby Dick, but maybe it was just that he felt sorry for this person from the other side of the world who didn't realize how ridiculous he was.

"I'll take it," he said.

"Buying?"

"Ja, ja, buying."

But it was a premature act of charity, for Arvid had only a wrinkled wharf invoice in his pocket and nothing else. The black man looked at him.

"Fish," he said and pointed at his crate. And Arvid could, of course, have offered him the coalfish, but it sounded as if the man said "fish" just to show that he knew the word.

"I don't have any money on me," he said. "But you can come to my house afterwards, and I'll pay you then."

He explained where he lived, but they weren't able to communicate well enough, so he had to draw a map on a piece of paper that the black man gave him. He wanted to give him the book right away, too. He could pay later.

"Take it," he said.

Arvid hesitated. He wiped off his hands and held the book with his fingertips. It was heavy and nice to hold. He stuck it under his overalls, closed the zipper and looked around. There wasn't really anything else to say.

"Ja, ja," he said and was on the verge of exploding with laughter. The black man was laughing, too. They got on their respective mopeds and started the motors. They put on their goggles, lifted their thumbs in greeting, and drove off their separate ways.

Arvid steered straight ahead in the middle of the road without leaning over the handlebars. He was stiff. After several hundred meters he stopped and looked back. The black man was just a little figure on the other end of the swamp. Arvid stood still and watched him disappear. The only thing left of him was Moby Dick, heavy against his chest.

Translated from the Norwegian by Frankie Shackelford

Edward P. Jones

The First Day

(UNITED STATES)

In an otherwise unremarkable September morning, long before I learned to be ashamed of my mother, she takes my hand and we set off down New Jersey Avenue to begin my very first day of school. I am wearing a checkeredlike blue-and-green cotton dress, and scattered about these colors are bits of yellow and white and brown. My mother has uncharacteristically spent nearly an hour on my hair that morning, plaiting and replaiting so that now my scalp tingles. Whenever I turn my head quickly, my nose fills with the faint smell of Dixie Peach hair grease. The smell is somehow a soothing one now and I will reach for it time and time again before the morning ends. All the plaits, each with a blue barrette near the tip and each twisted into an uncommon sturdiness, will last until I go to bed that night, something that has never happened before. My stomach is full of milk and oatmeal sweetened with brown sugar. Like everything else I have on, my pale green slip and underwear are new, the underwear having come three to a plastic package with a little girl on the front who appears to be dancing. Behind my ears, my mother, to stop my whining, has dabbed the stingiest bit of her gardenia perfume, the last present my father gave her before he disappeared into memory. Because I cannot smell it, I have only her word that the perfume is there. I am also wearing yellow socks trimmed with thin lines of black and white around the tops. My shoes are my greatest joy, black patent-leather miracles, and when one is nicked at the toe later that morning in class, my heart will break.

I am carrying a pencil, a pencil sharpener, and a small ten-cent tablet with a black-and-white speckled cover. My mother does not believe that a girl in kindergarten needs such things, so I am taking them only because of my insistent whining and because they are presents from our neighbors, Mary Keith and Blondelle Harris. Miss Mary and Miss Blondelle are watching my two younger sisters until my mother returns. The women are as precious to me as my mother and sisters. Out playing one day, I have overheard an older child, speaking to another child, call Miss Mary and Miss Blondelle a word that is brand new to me. This is my mother: When I say the word in fun to one of my sisters, my mother slaps me across the mouth and the word is lost for years and years.

All the way down New Jersey Avenue, the sidewalks are teeming with children. In my neighborhood, I have many friends, but I see none of them as my mother and I walk. We cross New York Avenue, we cross Pierce Street, and we cross L and K, and still I see no one who knows my name. At I Street, between New Jersey Avenue and Third Street, we enter Seaton Elementary School, a timeworn, sad-faced building across the street from my mother's church, Mt. Carmel Baptist.

Just inside the front door, women out of the advertisements in *Ebony* are greeting other parents and children. The woman who greets us has pearls thick as jumbo marbles that come down almost to her navel, and she acts as if she had known me all my life, touching my shoulder, cupping her hand under my chin. She is enveloped in a perfume that I only know is not gardenia. When, in answer to her question, my mother tells her that we live at 1227 New Jersey Avenue, the woman first seems to be picturing in her head where we live. Then she shakes her head and says that we are at the wrong school, that we should be at Walker-Jones.

My mother shakes her vigorously. "I want her to go here," my mother says. "If I'da wanted her someplace else, I'da took her there." The woman continues to act as if she has known me all my life, but she tells my mother that we live beyond the area that Seaton serves. My mother is not convinced and for several more minutes she questions the woman about why I cannot attend Seaton. For as many Sundays as I can remember, perhaps even Sundays when I was in her womb, my mother has pointed across I Street to Seaton as we come and go to Mt. Carmel. "You gonna go there and learn about the whole world." But one of the guardians of that place is saying no, and no again. I am learning this about my mother: The higher up on the scale of respectability a person is—and teachers are rather high up in her eyes—the less she is liable to let them push her around. But finally, I see in her eyes the closing gate, and she takes my hand and we leave the building. On the steps, she stops as people move past us on either side.

"Mama, I can't go to school?"

She says nothing at first, then takes my hand again and we are down the steps quickly and nearing New Jersey Avenue before I can blink. This is my mother: She says, "One monkey don't stop no show."

Walker-Jones is a larger, newer school and I immediately like it because of that. But it is not across the street from my mother's church, her rock, one of her connections to God, and I sense her doubts as she absently rubs her thumb over the back of her hand. We find our way to the crowded auditorium where gray metal chairs are set up in the middle of the room. Along the wall to the left are tables and other chairs. Every chair seems occupied by a child or adult. Somewhere in the room a child is crying, a cry that rises above the buzz-talk of so many people. Strewn about the floor are dozens and dozens of pieces of white paper, and people are walking over them without any thought of picking them up. And seeing this lack of concern, I am all of a sudden afraid.

"Is there where they register for school?" my mother asks a woman at one of the tables.

The woman looks up slowly as if she has heard this question once too often. She nods. She is tiny, almost as small as the girl standing beside her. The woman's hair is set in a mass of curlers and all of those curlers are made of paper money, here a dollar bill, there a five-dollar bill. The girl's hair is arrayed in curls, but some of them are beginning to droop and this makes me happy. On the table beside the woman's pocketbook is a large notebook, worthy of someone in high school, and looking at me looking at the notebook, the girl places her hand possessively on it. In her other hand she holds several pencils with thick crowns of additional erasers.

"These the forms you gotta use?" my mother asks the woman, picking up a few pieces of the paper from the table. "Is this what you have to fill out?"

The woman tells her yes, but that she need fill out only one.

"I see," my mother says, looking about the room. Then: "Would you help me with this form? That is, if you don't mind."

The woman asks my mother what she means.

"This form. Would you mind helpin me fill it out?"

The woman still seems not to understand.

"I can't read it. I don't know how to read or write, and I'm askin you to help me." My mother looks at me, then looks away. I know almost all of her looks, but this one is brand new to me. "Would you help me, then?"

The woman says Why sure, and suddenly she appears happier, so much more satisfied with everything. She finishes the form for her daughter and my mother and I step aside to wait for her. We find two chairs nearby and sit. My mother is now diseased, according to the girl's eyes, and until the moment her mother takes her and the form to the front of the auditorium, the girl never stops looking at my mother. I stare back at her. "Don't stare," my mother says to me. "You know better than that."

Another woman out of the *Ebony* ads takes the woman's child away. Now, the woman says upon returning, let's see what we can do for you two.

My mother answers the questions the woman reads off the form. They start with my last name, and then on to the first and middle names. This is school, I think. This is going to school. My mother slowly enunciates each word of my name. This is my mother: As the questions go on, she takes from her pocketbook document after document, as if they will support my right to attend school, as if she has been saving them up for just this moment. Indeed, she takes out more papers than I have ever seen her do in other places: my birth certificate, my baptismal record, a doctor's letter concerning my bout with chicken pox, rent receipts, records of immunization, a letter about our public assistance payments, even her marriage license—every single paper that has anything even remotely to do with my five-year-old life. Few of the papers are needed here, but it does not matter and my mother continues to pull out the documents with the purposefulness of a magician pulling out a long string of scarves. She has learned that money is the beginning and end of everything in this world, and when the woman finishes, my mother offers her fifty cents, and the woman accepts it without hesitation. My mother and I are just about the last parent and child in the room.

My mother presents the form to a woman sitting in front of the stage, and the woman looks at it and writes something on a white card, which she gives to my mother. Before long, the woman who has taken the girl with the drooping curls appears from behind us, speaks to the sitting woman, and introduces herself to my mother and me. She's to be my teacher, she tells my mother. My mother stares.

We go into the hall, where my mother kneels down to me. Her lips are quivering. "I'll be back to pick you up at twelve o'clock. I don't want you to go nowhere. You just wait right here. And listen to every word she say." I touch her lips and press them together. It is an old, old game between us. She puts my hand down at my side, which is not part of the game. She stands and looks a second at the teacher, then she turns and walks away. I see where she has darned one of her socks the night before. Her shoes make loud sounds in the hall. She passes through the doors and I can still hear the loud sounds of her shoes. And even when the teacher turns me toward the classrooms and I hear what must be the singing and talking of all the children in the world, I can still hear my mother's footsteps above it all.

James Kelman

Remember Young Cecil

(S C O T L A N D)

Young Cecil is medium-sized and retired. For years he has been undisputed champion of our hall. Nowadays that is not saying much. This pitch has fallen from grace lately. John Moir who runs the place has started letting some of the punters rent a table Friday and Saturday nights to play Pontoons, and as an old head pointed out the other day: that is it for any place, never mind Porter's.

In Young Cecil's day it had one of the best reputations in Glasgow. Not for its decoration or the rest of it. But for all-round ability Porter's regulars took some beating. Back in these days we won the "City" eight years running with Young Cecil Number 1 and Wee Danny backing up at Number 2. You could have picked any four from ten to make up the rest of the team. Between the two of them they took the lot three years running; snooker singles and doubles, and billiards the same. You never saw that done very often.

To let you know just how good we were, John Moir's big brother Tam could not even get into the team except if we were short though John Moir would look at you as if you were daft if you said it out loud. He used to make out Tam, Young Cecil and Wee Danny were the big three. Nonsense. One or two of us had to put a stop to that. We would have done it a hell of a lot sooner if Wee Danny was still living because Young Cecil has a habit of not talking. All he does is smile. And that not very often either. I have seen Frankie Sweeny's boy come all the way down here just to say hello; and what does Young Cecil do but give him a nod and at the most a how's it going without even a name nor nothing. But that was always his way and Frankie Sweeney's boy still drops in once or twice yet. The big noises remember Cecil. And some of the young ones. Tam!—never mind John Moir—Young Cecil could have gave Tam forty and potting only yellows still won looking round. How far.

Nowadays he can hardly be annoyed even saying hello. But he was never ignorant. Always the same.

I mind the first time we clapped eyes on him. Years ago it was. In those days he used to play up the YM, but we knew about him. A hall's regulars kind of keep themselves to themselves and yet we had still heard of this young fellow that could handle a stick. And with a first name like Cecil nobody needed to know what his last one was. Wee Danny was the Number 1 at the time. It is not so good as all that being Number 1 cause you have got to hand out big starts otherwise you are lucky to get playing, never mind for a few bob—though there are always the one or two who do not bother about losing a couple of bob just so long as they get a game with you.

Wee Danny was about twenty-seven or thirty in those days but no more than that. Well, this afternoon we were hanging around. None of us had a coin—at least not for playing with. During the week it was. One or two of us were knocking them about on Table 3, which has always been the table in Porter's. Even John Moir would not dream of letting anyone mess about on that one. There were maybe three other tables in use at the time but it was only mugs playing. Most of us were just chatting or studying form and sometimes one would carry a line up to Micky at the top of the street. And then the door opened and in comes this young fellow. He walks up and stands beside us for a wee while. Then: Anybody fancy a game? he says.

We all looks at one another but at Wee Danny in particular and then we bursts out laughing. None of you want a game then? he says.

Old Porter himself was running the place in those days. He was just leaning his elbows on the counter in his wee cubbyhole and sucking on that falling-to-bits pipe of his. But he was all eyes in case of bother.

For a couple of bob? says the young fellow.

Well, we all stopped laughing right away. I do not think Wee Danny had been laughing at all; he was just sitting up on the ledge dangling his feet. It went quiet for a minute then Hector Parker steps forward and says that he would give the young fellow a game. Hector was playing 4 stick at that time and hitting not a bad ball. But the young fellow just looks him up and down. Hector was a big fat kind of fellow. No, says the young yin. And he looks round at the rest of us. But before he can open his mouth Wee Danny is off the ledge and smartly across.

You Young Cecil from the YM?

Aye, says the young fellow.

Well I'm Danny Thompson. How much you wanting to play for?

Fiver.

Very good. Wee Danny turns and shouts: William . . .

Old Porter ducks beneath the counter right away and comes up with Danny's jar. He used to keep his money in a jam-jar in those days. And he had a good few quid in there at times. Right enough sometimes he had nothing.

Young Cecil took out two singles, a half quid, and made the rest up with a pile of smash. He stuck it on the shade above Table 3 and Wee Danny done the same with his fiver. Old Porter went over to where the mugs were playing and told them to get a move on. One or two of us were a bit put out with Wee Danny because usually when there was a game on we could get into it ourselves for a couple of bob. Sometimes with the other fellow's cronies but if there was none of them Wee Danny maybe just covered the bet and let us make up the rest. Once or twice I have seen him skint and having to play a money game for us. And when he won we would chip in to give him a wage.

Sometimes he liked the yellow stuff too much. When he got a right turn off he might go and you would be lucky to see him before he had bevied it all in; his money right enough. But he had to look to us a few times, a good few times— so you might have thought: Okay I'll take three quid and let the lads get a bet with the deuce that's left. . . .

But no. You were never too sure where you stood with the wee man. I have seen him giving some poor bastard a right sherricking for nothing any of us knew about. Aye, more than once. Not everybody liked him.

Meanwhile we were all settled along the ledge. Old Porter and Hector were applying the brush and the stone; Wee Danny was fiddling about with his cue. But Young Cecil just hung around looking at the photos and the shield and that, that Old Porter had on full view on the wall behind his counter. When the table was finally finished Old Porter began grumbling under his breath and goes over to the mugs who had still not ended their game. He tells them to fuck off and take up bools or something and locks the door after them. Back into his cubbyhole he went for his chair so he could have a sit-down to watch the game.

Hector was marking the board. He chips the coin. Young Cecil calls it and breaks without a word. Well, maybe he was a bit nervous, I do not know; but he made a right mess of it. His cue ball hit the blue after disturbing a good few reds out the pack on its way back up the table. Nobody could give the wee man a chance like that and expect him to stand back admiring the scenery. In he steps and bump bump bump—a break of fifty-six. One of the best he had ever had.

It was out of three they were playing. Some of us were looking daggers at Danny, not every day you could get into a fiver bet. He broke for the next and left a good safety. But the young fellow had got over whatever it was, and his safety was always good. It was close but he took it. A rare game. Then he broke for the decider and this time it was no contest. I have seen him play as well but I do not remember him playing better all things considered. And he was barely turned twenty at the time. He went right to town and Wee Danny wound up chucking it on the colors, and you never saw that very often.

Out came the jam-jar and he says: Same again son?

Double or clear if you like, says Young Cecil.

Well Wee Danny never had the full tenner in his jar so he gives us the nod and in we dived to Old Porter for a couple of bob till broo day because to tell the truth we thought it was a bit of a flash in the pan. And even yet when I think about it, you cannot blame us. These young fellows come and go. Even now. They do not change. Still think they are wide. Soon as they can pot a ball they are ready to hand out J.D. himself three blacks of a start. Throw their money at you. Usually we were there to take it, and we never had to call on Wee Danny much either. So how were we supposed to know it was going to be any different this time?

Hector racked them. Young Cecil won the toss again. He broke and this time left the cue ball nudging the green's arse. Perfect. Then on it was a procession. And he was not just a potter like most of these young ones. Course at the time it was his main thing just like the rest but the real difference was that Young Cecil never missed the easy pot. Never. He could take a chance like anybody else. But you never saw him miss the easy pot.

One or two of us had thought it might not be a flash in the pan but had still fancied Wee Danny to do the business because whatever else he was he was a money-player. Some fellows are world beaters till there is a bet bigger than the price of renting the table then that is them—all fingers and thumbs and miscueing all over the shop. I have seen it many a time. And after Young Cecil had messed his break in that first frame we had seen Wee Danny do the fifty-six so we knew he was on form. Also, the old heads reckoned on the young fellow cracking up with the tenner bet plus the fact that the rest of us were into it as well. Because Wee Danny could pot a ball with a headcase at his back all ready to set about his skull with a hatchet if he missed. Nothing could put the wee man off his game.

But he met his match that day.

And he did not ask for another double or clear either. In fact a while after the event I heard he never even fancied himself for the second game—just felt he had to play it for some reason.

After that Young Cecil moved into Porter's, and ever since it has been home. Him and Wee Danny got on well enough but they were never close friends or anything like that. Outside they ran around in different crowds. There was an age gap between them right enough. That might have had something to do with it. And Cecil never went in for the bevy the way the wee man did. In some ways he was more into the game as well. He could work up an interest even when there was no money attached whereas Wee Danny was the other way.

Of course after Young Cecil met his he could hardly be bothered playing the game at all.

But that happened a while later—when we were having the long run in the "City." Cleaning up everywhere we were. And one or two of us were making a nice few bob on the side. Once Cecil arrived Wee Danny had moved down to Number 2 stick, and within a year or so people started hearing about Young Cecil. But even then Wee Danny was making a good few bob more than him because when he was skint the wee man used to run about different pitches and sometimes one or two of us went along with him and picked up a couple of bob here and there. Aye, and a few times he landed us in bother because in some of these places it made no difference Wee Danny was Wee Danny. In fact it usually made things worse once they found out. He was hell of a lucky not to get a right good hiding a couple of times. Him and Young Cecil never played each other again for serious money. Although sometimes they had an exhibition for maybe a nicker or so, to make it look good for the mugs. But they both knew who the 1 stick was and it never changed. That might have been another reason for them not being close friends or anything like that.

Around then Young Cecil started playing in a private club up the town where Wee Danny had played once or twice but not very often. This was McGinley's place. The big money used to change hands there. Frankie

Sweeney was on his way up then and hung about the place with the French-man and one or two others. Young Cecil made his mark right away and a wee bit of a change came over him. But this was for the best as far as we were con-cerned because up till then he was just too quiet. Would not push himself or that. Then all of a sudden we did not have to tell him he was Young Cecil. He knew it himself. Not that he went about shouting it out because he never did that at any time. Not like some of them you see nicking about all gallus and sticking the chest out at you. Young Cecil was never like that and come to think about it neither was Wee Danny—though he always knew he was Wee Danny right enough. But now when Young Cecil talked to the one or two he did speak to it was him did the talking and we did not have to tell him.

Then I mind fine we were all sitting around having a couple of pints in the Crown and there at the other end of the bar was our 1 and 2 sticks. Now they had often had a drink together in the past but normally it was always in among other company. Never like this—by themselves right through till closing time. Something happened. Whenever Young Cecil went up McGinley's after that Wee Danny would be with him, as if he was partners or something. And they started winning a few quid. So did Sweeney and the Frenchman; they won a hell of a lot more. They were onto Young Cecil from the start.

Once or twice a couple of us got let into the club as well. McGinley's place was not like a hall. It was the basement of an office building up near George Square and it was a fair-sized pitch though there was only the one table. It was set aside in a room by itself with plenty of seats round about it, some of them built up so that everybody could see. The other room was a big one and had a wee bar and a place for snacks and that, with some card tables dotted about; and there was a big table for Chemmy. None of your Pontoons up there. I heard talk about a speaker wired up for commentaries and betting shows and that from the tracks, but I never saw it myself. Right enough I was never there during the day. The snooker room was kept shut all the time except if they were playing or somebody was in cleaning the place. They kept it well.

McGinley and them used to bring players through from Edinburgh and one or two up from England to play exhibitions and sometimes they would set up a big match and the money changing hands was something to see. Young Cecil told us there was a couple of Glasgow fellows down there hardly any-body had heard about who could really handle a stick. It was a right eye-opener for him because up till then he had only heard about people like Joe Hutchinson and Simpson and one or two others who went in for the "Scottish" regular, yet down in McGinley's there was two fellows playing who could hand out a start to the likes of Simpson. Any day of the week. It was just that about money-players and the rest.

So Young Cecil became a McGinley man and it was not long before he joined Jimmy Brown and Sandy from Dumfries in taking on the big sticks through from Edinburgh and England and that. Then Sweeney and the Frenchman set up a big match with Cecil and Jimmy Brown. And Cecil beat him. Beat him well. A couple of us got let in that night and we picked up a nice wage because Jimmy Brown had been around for a good while and had a fair support. In a way it was the same story as Cecil and Wee Danny, only this time Wee Danny and the rest of Porter's squad had our money down the right way and we were carrying a fair wad for some of us who were not let in. There was a good crowd watching because word travels, but it was not too bad; McGinley was hell of a strict about letting people in—in case too many would put the players off in any way. With just onlookers sitting on the seats and him and one or two others standing keeping an eye on things it usually went well and you did not see much funny business though you heard stories about a couple of people who had tried it on at one time or another. But if you ask me, any man who tried to pull a stroke down McGinley's place was needing his head examined.

Well, Young Cecil wound up the man in Glasgow they all had to beat, and it was a major upset when anybody did. Sometimes when the likes of Hutchinson came through we saw a fair battle but when the big money was being laid it was never on him if he was meeting Young Cecil. Trouble was you could hardly get a bet on Cecil less he was handing out starts. And then it was never easy to find a punter, and even when you did find one there was liable to be upsets because of the handicapping.

But it was good at that time. Porter's was always buzzing cause Young Cecil still played 1 stick for us with Wee Danny backing him up at Number 2. It was rare walking into an away game knowing everybody was waiting for Young Cecil and Porter's to arrive and the bevy used to flow. They were good days and one or two of us could have afforded to let our broo money lie over a week if we had wanted though none of us ever did. Obviously. Down in McGinley's we were seeing some rare tussles; Young Cecil was not always involved but since he was Number 1 more often than not he was in there somewhere at the windup.

It went well for a hell of a long while.

Then word went the rounds that McGinley and Sweeney were bringing up Cuddihy. He was known as the County Durham at that time. Well, nobody could wait for the day. It was not often you got the chance to see Cuddihy in action and when you did it was worth going a long way to see. He liked a punt and you want to see some of the bets he used to make at times—on individual shots and the rest of it. He might be about to attempt a long hard pot and then just before he lets fly he stands back from the table and cries: Okay. Who'll lay me six to four to a couple of quid?

And sometimes a mug would maybe lay him thirty quid to twenty. That is right, that was his style. A bit gallus but he was pure class. And he could take a drink. To be honest, even us in Porter's did not fancy Young Cecil for this one—and that includes Wee Danny. They said the County Durham was second only to the J.D. fellow though I never heard of them meeting seriously together. But I do not go along with them that said the J.D. fellow would have turned out second best if they had. But we will never know.

They were saying it would be the best game ever seen in Glasgow and that is something. All the daft rumors about it being staged at a football ground were going the rounds. That was nonsense. McGinley was a shrewdie and if he wanted he could have put it on at the Kelvin Hall or something, but the game took place in his club and as far as everybody was concerned that was the way it should be even though most of us from Porter's could not get in to see it at the death.

When the night finally arrived it was like an Old Firm game on New Year's Day. More people were in the cardroom than actually let in to see the game and in a way it was not right for some of the ones left out were McGinley regulars and they had been turned away to let in people we had never clapped eyes on before. And some of us were not even let into the place at all. Right enough a few of us had never been inside McGinley's before, just went to Porter's and thought that would do. So they could not grumble. But the one or two of us who would have been down McGinley's every night of the week if they had let us were classed as I do not know what and not let over the doorstep. That was definitely not fair. Even Wee Danny was lucky to get watching as he told us afterwards. He was carrying our money. And there was some size of a wad there.

Everybody who ever set foot in Porter's was onto Young Cecil that night. And some from down our way who had never set foot in a snooker hall in their lives were onto him as well, and you cannot blame them. The pawnshops ran riot. Everything hockable was hocked. We all went daft. But there was no panic about not finding a punter because everybody knew that Cuddihy would back himself right down to his last penny. A hell of a man. Aye, and he was worth a good few quid too. Wee Danny told us that just before the marker tossed the coin Cuddihy stepped back and shouts: Anybody still wanting a bet now's the time!

And there were still takers at that minute.

All right. We all knew how good the County Durham was; but it made no difference because everybody thought he had made a right bloomer. Like Young Cecil said to us when the news broke a week before the contest: Nobody, he says, can give me that sort of start. I mean it. Not even J.D. himself.

And we believed him. We agreed with him. It was impossible. No man alive could give Young Cecil thirty of a start in each of a five-frame match. It was nonsense. Wee Danny was the same.

Off of thirty I'd play him for everything I've got. I'd lay my weans on it. No danger, he says: Cuddihy's coming the cunt with us. Young Cecil'll sort him out proper. No danger!

And this was the way of it as far as the rest of us were concerned. Right enough on the day you got a few who bet the County Durham. Maybe they had seen him play and that, or heard about him and the rest of it. But reputations are made to be broke and apart from that few, Cuddihy and his mates, everybody else was onto Young Cecil. And they thought they were stonewall certainties.

How wrong we all were.

But what can you say? Young Cecil played well. After the event he said he could not have played better. Just that the County Durham was in a different class. His exact words. What a turn-up for the books. Cuddihy won the first two frames then Young Cecil got his chance in the next but Cuddihy came again and took the fourth for the best of five.

Easy. Easy easy.

What can you do? Wee Danny told us the Frenchman had called Cecil a good handicapper and nothing else.

Well, that was that and a hell of a lot of long faces were going about our side of the river—Porter's was like a cemetery for ages after it. Some of the old heads say it's been going downhill ever since. I do not know. Young Cecil was the best we ever had. Old Porter said there was none better in his day either. So, what do you do? Sweeney told Young Cecil it was no good comparing himself with the likes of Cuddihy but you could see it did not matter.

Young Cecil changed overnight. He got married just before the game anyway and so what with that and the rest of it he dropped out of things. He went on playing 1 stick for us for a while and still had the odd game down McGinley's once or twice. But slowly and surely he just stopped and then somebody spoke for him in Fairfield's and he wound up getting a start in there as a docker or something. But after he retired he started coming in again. Usually he plays billiards nowadays with the one or two of us that are still going about.

Mind you he is still awful good.

Hanif Kureishi

Intimacy

(E N G L A N D)

It is the saddest night, for I am leaving and not coming back. Tomorrow morning, when the woman I have lived with for six years has gone to work on her bicycle, and our children have been taken to the park with their ball, I will pack some things into a suitcase, slip out of my house, and take the tube to Victor's place. There I will sleep on the floor in a tiny room next to the kitchen. Each morning I will heave a thin single mattress back into the airing cupboard and stuff the musty duvet into a box and replace the cushions on the sofa.

I will not be returning to this life. I cannot. Perhaps I should leave a note. "Dear Susan, I am not coming back. . . ." Perhaps it would be better to ring tomorrow afternoon. Or I could visit at the weekend. The details I haven't decided. I will not tell her this evening. I will put it off. Why? Because words make things happen. Once they are out, you cannot put them back. I am trembling, and have been all afternoon, all day.

This, then, could be our last evening as an innocent, complete family; my last night with a woman I know almost everything about and want no more of. Soon we will be like strangers. No, we can never be that. Hurting someone is an act of reluctant intimacy. We will be dangerous acquaintances with a history.

I perch on the edge of the bath and watch my sons, aged five and three. Their toys float on the surface, and they chatter. They are ebullient and fierce, and people say what happy and affectionate children they are. This morning, before I set out for the day, the elder boy, insisting on another kiss before I closed the door, said, "Daddy, I love everyone."

Tomorrow I will damage and scar them.

The younger boy was wearing chinos, a gray shirt, blue braces, and a policeman's helmet. As I toss the clothes in the washing basket, I am disturbed by a sound outside. I hold my breath.

Already!

She is pushing her bicycle into the hall. She is removing the shopping bags from the basket.

During the last few days, I have been trying to convince myself that leaving someone isn't the worst thing you can do to a person. It doesn't have to be a tragedy. If you never left anything or anyone, there would be no room for the new. Naturally, to move on is an act of infidelity—to others, to the past, to old notions of yourself. Perhaps every day should contain at least one essential infidelity. It would be an optimistic, hopeful act, guaranteeing belief in the future—a declaration that things can be not only different but better.

Eight years ago my friend Victor left his wife. Since then he has had only unsatisfactory loves, including the Chinese prostitute who played the piano naked and brought all her belongings to their assignations. If the phone rings he does a kind of panicky dance, wondering what new opprobrium may be on the way. Victor has always given women hope, if not satisfaction.

Susan is in the room now.

She says, "Why don't you ever shut the bathroom door?"

"What?"

"Why don't you?"

I can't think of a reason.

She kisses the children. When we really talk, it is about them—something they said or did.

She presents her cheek a few inches from my lips, so that to kiss her I must lean forward. She smells of perfume and the street. She goes to change and returns in jeans and sweatshirt with a glass of wine for each of us.

"Hallo. How are you?"

She looks at me hard, in order to have me notice her. I feel my body contract. I smile. Does she notice anything different in my face today? Usually, before seeing her, I prepare two or three possible subjects, as if our conversations were examinations. Today I have been too feverish to rehearse. She accuses me of being silent. But silence, like darkness, can be an act of kindness; it, too, is a language.

The boys' bathwater drains away slowly—their toys impede the plughole. They won't move until the water is gone, and then they sit there making mustaches and hats with the remaining bubbles. Eventually, I lift the younger one out. Susan takes the other.

We wrap them in thick hooded towels. With damp hair and beads of water on their necks, the boys look like diminutive boxers after a fight. They argue about what pajamas they want to wear. The younger one will only wear a Batman T-shirt. They seem to have become self-conscious at an early age. They must have got it from us.

Susan gives the younger boy a bottle, which he holds up to his mouth two-handedly, like a trumpeter. I watch her caressing his hair, kissing his dimpled fingers, and rubbing his stomach. He giggles and squirms. What a quality of innocence people have when they don't expect to be harmed. Who could violate it without damaging himself?

We take the children downstairs, where they lie on cushions, nonchalantly sucking their pacifiers, watching "The Wizard of Oz" with their eyes half open. They look like a couple of swells smoking cigars in a field on a hot day. They demand ginger biscuits. I fetch them from the kitchen without Susan's noticing me. The boys extend their greedy fingers but don't look away from the TV. After a while, I pick up the crumbs and, having considered what to do with them, fling them into a corner.

Susan works in the kitchen, listening to the radio. Her own family life, like mine, has mostly been unpleasant. Now she goes to a lot of trouble to make good meals. Even if we're having a takeaway, she won't let us eat in a slew of newspapers and children's books. She puts out napkins and a bottle of wine, and lights candles, insisting we have a proper family meal, including nervy silences and severe arguments.

I sit on the floor near the boys and examine them, their feet, ears, eyes. This evening, when I am both here and not here—almost a ghost already—I want to be aware of everything, I want a mental picture that I can carry around and refer to when I am at Victor's place. It will be the first of the few things I must, tonight, choose to take with me.

The boys have fallen asleep. I carry them upstairs, one by one. They lie side by side under vivid duvets. I am about to kiss them when I notice their eyes are open. I dread a second wind.

"If you lie still I will read to you," I say.

They regard me suspiciously, but I find a book and make a place between them. They stretch out across me, occasionally kicking each other.

It is a cruel story, as most children's stories are, and it involves a woodcutter. But it also concerns a conventional family, from which the father has not fled. The boys know the story so well they can tell when I skip a bit or attempt to make something up. When they stop asking questions I put the book down, creep out of the room, and switch off the light, then return to find their faces in the covers and kiss them. Outside I listen for their breathing. If only I could stand here all night. Then I hear them whispering to one another and giggling.

Old wives; old story.

I always look at women—in shops, on the street, in the bus, at parties—and wonder what it might be like to be with one of them. I imagine that with each woman I could be a different person for a time. There would be no past. I could keep the world outside my skin, huddled up with a whispering woman who wanted me.

But now I am not sure that I can touch a woman as I used to—frivolously. After a certain age, sex is no longer casual. To lay your hand on another's body, or to put your mouth against another's—what a commitment that is! Your whole life is uncovered.

Maybe that is what happened with Nina. One day a girl walked past and I wanted her. I've examined the moment a score of times. She and I go over it repeatedly, in joy and puzzlement. I can remember how tall and slim she appeared; and then there was a jolt, a violent jolt, when we met. Something about her changed everything. She was from another world.

My young gay friend Ian liked to stand with me outside tube stations, where I would watch the flocks of girls in the summer and he would watch the boys. Looks would be exchanged between him and a stranger and off he would go, while I waited, having coffee somewhere. Sometimes he fucked five people in a day.

"I've never understood all the fuss you straights make about infidelity," he'd say. "It's only fucking."

Susan has already laid the table. I open the wine and pour it. The man in the off-license said it is an easy wine to drink. These days I find anything easy to drink.

Susan brings the food in and sets it down. I glance over the newspaper. As she eats, she turns on the TV, puts on her glasses, and leans forward to watch a soap opera.

"Oh my God," she says, as something happens.

The noise presses into my head. I have begun to hate television.

After we clear up, Susan sits at the table, writing invitations for the boys' party. Then, making a shopping list for next week, she says, "What meals do you fancy?"

"I don't want to think about it now."

"What's your favorite ice-cream flavor at the moment? Is it the nut crunch or the vanilla?"

"I don't know."

She says, "It's not like you to be unable to think of food."

"No."

I consider how well I know her. The way she puts her head to one side, and the grimace she makes when concentrating. She looks as she must have as an eleven-year-old taking an exam. No doubt she will have a similar look at seventy, her gestures unchanged, writing a letter to one of our sons.

I imagine her as a teen-ager, getting up early to study, and then preparing for school—making her sandwiches, leaving the house while her parents sleep. She got herself into Cambridge, where she insured that she knew the most luminous people. She is as deliberate in her friendships as she is in everything else.

She is effective and organized. Our fridges and freezers are full of soup, vegetables, wine, cheese, and ice cream; the flowers and bushes in the garden are labelled; the children's clothes are washed, ironed, and folded. Every day there are deliveries of newspapers, books, alcohol, food, and, often, of furniture. Our front path is a thoroughfare for the service industries.

There are also people who come to clean the house, tend the garden, and cut the trees, as well as nannies, baby-sitters, and au pairs, not to mention masseurs, decorators, acupuncturists, piano teachers, the occasional drug dealer, and people to organize all of the above. Chalked on a board are instructions for the week. Susan is always thinking of how to improve things. She will have strong, considered opinions on the latest films and music. In bed she reads cookbooks.

I am from the lower middle class and from the suburbs, where poverty and pretension go together, and so I can see now how good the middle class has it—their separate, sealed world. They keep quiet about it, with reason. They feel guilty, too, but they insure that they have the best of everything.

It wasn't Susan's wit or beauty that attracted me. There was never great passion—perhaps that was the point. I liked her humdrum dexterity and ability to cope. She wasn't helpless before the world. I envy her capability, and wish I had half of it.

At the office Susan is too prudent to want power, but she is clear and articulate, and it is not difficult for her to make less confident people feel ineffectual. After all, she is cleverer than her colleagues, and has worked harder. Like many girls brought up to be good and well behaved, she likes to please. Perhaps that is why young women are so suitable for the contemporary working world. They are welcome to it.

The range of her feeling is narrow; she would consider it shameful to give way to her moods. Therefore she keeps most of herself out of view. I would say this odd thing: Because she has never been disillusioned or disappointed, her life has never appalled her. She has never lapsed into inner chaos.

"Sorry?" I say.

Susan is speaking—asking me to get my diary.

"Why?" I say.

"Why? Just do it, if you don't mind."

"Don't speak to me like that."

"I'm too tired for negotiation. The children wake at six. I have to spend the day at work. What do you do in the afternoons? I expect you sleep then!"

I say, "You're not too tired to raise your voice."

"It's the only way I can get you to do anything."

"No, it's not."

"You exhaust me."

I could strike her. She would know then. I am about to say, "Susan, can't you see that, of all the nights we have spent together, this is the last one—the last one of all?"

My anger, usually contained, can be cruel and vengeful. But this should be satisfying: I don't want to discover tonight that Susan and I really are suited.

I murmur, "All right, all right, I'll do it."

"At last."

Sometimes I go along with what Susan wants, but in an absurd parodic way, hoping she will see how foolish I find her. But she doesn't see it and, much to my annoyance, my cooperation pleases her.

I sit in front of her with my diary, flipping through the pages. After today the pages are blank.

She says how much she is looking forward to the weekend away that we have planned. We will stay at the country hotel we visited several years ago, when she was first pregnant. The weather was warm. I rowed her on a lake. We ate mussels and read the papers on the beach. It will be just us, without the children.

"The rest will do us good," she says. "I know things have been fraught."

"Do you think so?"

"You are gloomy and don't try. But . . . we can discuss things."

"What things?"

She says, "All this." Her hands flail. "I think we need to." She controls herself. "You used to be such an affectionate man." She reminds me that there are historic walks and castles in the vicinity of the country hotel. "And, please," she says, "will you remember to take your camera this time?"

"I'll try to."

"You don't want any photographs of me, do you?"

"Sometimes I do."

"No you don't. You never offer."

"No, I don't offer."

"That's horrible. You should have one on your desk, as I do, of you."

I say, "I'm not interested in photography. And you're not as vain as I am."

"That's true."

I pace up and down with my drink, agitatedly. She takes no notice.

Fear is something I recognize. My childhood still tastes of fear. Fear of parents, aunts, and uncles, of vicars, police, and teachers, and of being kicked, abused, and insulted by other children. The fear of getting into trouble, of being discovered, castigated, smacked, ignored, locked in, locked out. There is, too, the fear of your own anger, of retaliation and of annihilation, as well as the fear of who you might become. It isn't surprising that you become accustomed to doing what you are told while making a safe place inside yourself and living a secret life.

"By the way," she says, "Victor rang."

"Oh yes? Any message?"

"He wanted to know when you are coming." She looks at me.

"O.K.," I say. "Thank you."

After a bit she says, "Why don't you see more people? I mean proper people, not just Victor."

"I can't bear the distraction," I say. "My internal life is too busy."

"I can't imagine what you have to think about," she says. Then she laughs. "You didn't eat much. Your trousers are baggy. They're always falling down."

"Sorry."

"Sorry? Don't say sorry. You sound pathetic." She grunts. After a few moments she gets up.

"Put the dishes in the machine," she says. "Don't just leave them on the side for me to clear up."

"I'll put them in the machine when I'm ready."

"That means never." Then she says, "Are you coming upstairs?"

I look at her searchingly and with interest, wondering if she means sex—it must be more than a month since we've fucked—or whether she intends us to read. I like books, but I don't want to get undressed for one.

"In a while," I say.

"You are so restless."

"Am I?"

"It's your age."

"It must be that."

I find myself thinking of the last time I saw Asif. He doesn't often come into the city; the rush and uproar make his head whirl. But when he and I have an "old friends" lunch I insist he meet me in the center of town. I take him to clamorous places where there will be fashionable young women in close-fitting items.

"What a picture gallery you have brought me to!" he says, rubbing his hands. "Is this how you spend your life?"

"Oh yes."

I indicate their attributes and inform him that they prefer mature men.

"Are you sure?" he says. "Have you tried them all?"

"I'm going to. Champagne?"

Our talk is of books and politics, and of mutual university friends. At university he was the brightest of our year, and was considered something of a martyr for becoming a teacher. Soon after finals he and Najma married.

I get him to confess that he wonders what another body might feel like. But then he imagines his wife's putting out flowers as she waits for him. He says he sees her across the bed in her negligee, three children sleeping between them.

I recall him describing how much he enjoys sucking her cunt, grunting and slurping down there for hours, after all this time. They massage each other's feet with coconut oil. In the conservatory their chairs face each other. When they are not discussing their children or questions of the day, they read Christina Rossetti aloud.

A few months ago I asked him to tell Susan that I had been with him when I had been with Nina.

He was dismayed.

"But don't ask me to do that."

"What?"

"Lie for you," he said.

"Aren't we friends?" I said. "It's a sensible lie. Susan doubts me. It is making her unhappy."

He shook his head. "You are too used to having your own way. You are making her unhappy."

"I am interested in someone else," I said.

I told him little of my relationships with women; he imagined such fabulous liaisons that I didn't want to disillusion him. He said to me once, "You remind me of someone who reads only the first chapter of a book. You never discover what happens next."

"How old is she?" he asked.

There was a discernible look of repulsion on his face, as if he were trying to swallow sour milk.

"It's only sex, then."

"There is that," I said.

"But marriage is a battle, a terrible journey, a season in Hell, and a reason for living. You need to be equipped in all areas, not just the sexual."

"Yes," I said, dully. "I know."

Oh to be equipped in all areas.

Asif's favorite opera is "Don Giovanni," and "Anna Karenina" and "Madame Bovary" are his favorite novels. Testaments of fire and betrayal. But people don't want you to have too much pleasure; you might start wanting it all the time. Desire is naughty. It mocks all human endeavor (and makes it worthwhile).

Once I tried out on Asif the idea of my leaving Susan.

"I can just about see why someone might leave their spouse," he said. "But I can't understand how someone could leave their children."

It is the men who must go. They are blamed for it, as I will be.

Comfortable chairs, old carpets, yards of books, many pictures, and piles of CDs: my study. I've always had a room like this. I take my weekend bag from the cupboard and open it. I stare into the bottom. What do you take when you're not coming back? I throw a book into the bag—something by Strindberg—and then replace the book on the shelf.

I stand here for ages. I am afraid of getting too comfortable in my own house, afraid that once I sit down I will lose my resolve. Above my desk is the shelf on which I keep my prizes and awards. Susan says it makes the place look like a dentist's waiting room.

An inventory, perhaps.

The desk—which my parents bought me when I was taking my A-levels—I have lugged around from shared houses to council flats, until it ended up here, the first property I have owned. A significant decision, getting a mortgage. It was as if you would never be able to move again.

I'll leave the desk for the boys. And the books?

Fuck it, I will leave everything here. My sons, wandering in this forsaken room, will discover, perhaps by mistake, the treasures they need.

After school or college, in my bedroom, I used to pile up Father's classical records on the spindle of my record-player, and the symphonies would clatter down, one by one, until supper. In those days it was rebellious for someone my age to like music that didn't sound better the louder it was played.

Then, surrounded by my father's books, I would reach up and pull down a few volumes. Father, like the other neighborhood men, spent most of his day in unsatisfying work. Time was precious and he had me fear its waste.

I will regret forfeiting this room.

I know how necessary fathers are for boys. I would hang on to Dad's hand as he toured the bookshops, climbing ladders to pull down rotting tomes. "Let's go, let's go," I'd say.

The writers Dad preferred are still my favorites, mostly nineteenth-century Europeans, the Russians in particular. The characters—Goriot, Vronsky, Mme Ranevskaya, Nana, Julien Sorel—feel part of me. It is Father's copies I will give to the boys. Father took me to see war films and cricket. Whenever I appeared in his room his face would brighten. He loved kissing me. He, more than anyone, was the person I wanted to marry. I wanted to walk, talk, laugh, and dress like him. My sons are the same with me, repeating my phrases in their tiny voices, staring admiringly at me and fighting to sit beside me. But I am leaving them. What would Father think of that?

Six years dead, he would have been horrified by my skulking off. It would have been undignified. Susan used to go to him when we fought and he would take her side, phoning me and saying, "Don't be cruel, boy." He said she had everything I could want. He didn't approve of leaving. He believed in loyalty.

Father was a civil servant who later worked as a clerk at Scotland Yard, for the police. In the mornings, he wrote novels. He must have completed five or six. A couple of them were admired by publishers, but none of them got into print. They weren't very bad and they weren't very good. He never gave up; it was all he ever wanted to do. The book on his bedside table had a picture of a middle-aged writer sitting on a pile of books, a portable typewriter on his knees. It was "Call It Experience," by Erskine Caldwell. Under the author's name it said, "Reveals the secrets of a great writer's private life and literary success." The writer did look experienced; he had been around. He was tough. That's what a writer was.

Failure strengthened Father's resolve. He was both brave and foolish. He wanted me to be a doctor, and I did consider it, but in the end he told me it was hopeless to take up something that wasn't going to please me. He was wise in that way. I was successful as a writer a couple of years after I left university. I could do it; I just could. Whether it was a knack or trick or talent, I didn't know. It puzzled both of us. Art is easy for those who can do it and impossible for those who can't.

What did Father's life show me? That life is a struggle, and that struggle gets you nowhere. That there is little pleasure in marriage; that it is like doing a job one hates. You can't leave and you can't enjoy it. Both he and Mother were frustrated, neither being able to find a way to get what they wanted. Nevertheless, they were loyal and faithful to each other. Disloyal and unfaithful to themselves. Or do I misunderstand?

Separation wouldn't have occurred to a lower-middle-class couple in the fifties. My parents remained in the same house all their lives. When we were older, money was short. Father refused to look for a better job and wouldn't move to a different part of the country. Nothing was allowed to happen until he "made it." Mother was forced to find employment. She was a school dinner lady; she worked in factories and offices; she worked in a shop.

The day I left home, my parents sat in separate armchairs, watching me carry out my records. What was there left for them to do?

But once I had gone my parents started going to art galleries, to the cinema, for walks, and on long holidays. They took a new interest in each other and couldn't get enough of life. Victor says that once the lights on a love have dimmed, you can never illuminate them again, any more than you can reheat a soufflé. But my parents went through the darkness and discovered a new intimacy.

I turn out the lights and find myself climbing the stairs to the bedroom. What am I doing? If this is my last night here, hadn't I better get packed and ready? I leave the light on in the hall. I step into our bedroom.

It's been weeks since we fucked. I've stopped approaching Susan in that way, to see if she desires me. I have waited for a flicker of interest. I am a dog under the table, hoping for a biscuit.

Without removing my clothes I lie down. Yellow light streaks the room from the street lamp opposite, a harsh, sickly color, reminding me of the smell of gas. I look at the ceiling where the roof has been leaking.

I am getting warm and dozy. The bed is comfortable. The house is silent; the children sheltered, healthy, and asleep.

Susan stirs.

I stroke her back. I am convinced she can feel my thoughts. If she wakes up, puts out her arms, and says she loves me, I will sink back into the pillow and never leave. But she has never done such a thing. Sensing my fingers on her, she moves away, pulling up the covers.

I rub myself through my jeans. I wish I had someone to do this. Not everything can be achieved alone. I won't do it here. Susan is offended by my solo efforts. She is of a disapproving generation of women. She thinks she's a feminist but she's just bad-tempered.

Nina encouraged me to masturbate on her back, stomach, or feet while she slept. She liked me to do it before she rushed off, to have me on her on the tube.

I want Nina, but then I always want Nina when I have an erection. I raise myself quietly and tiptoe to the bathroom.

I push down my trousers and look for a suitable lubricant. The last time I did this, when Susan had some friends round for dinner, I used my children's shampoo, and felt as if a wasp had been pushed into my urethra. I find a greenish cream in the cupboard. It's anti-aging unguent. God knows how much Susan has spent on this pig fat. Catching me once using it as hand cream, she became incensed. Maybe if I apply this every day to my prick it'll become fourteen again.

I stick my penis in it.

What if I met Susan now, for the first time, at a party? I would look at her twice, but not three times. It is likely that I would want to talk to her. Fearing those she can't seduce, she can be overattentive to certain men, looking at them with what I call "the enraptured gaze," until they wonder why she wants to appeal to their vanity rather than their intelligence. I should have gone out with her for six months. Or maybe a one-night stand. But I wasn't ruthless enough, and I didn't know what I wanted.

I sort through the laundry basket and extract a pair of Susan's knickers, pulling them from her tights and laying them on the sink. Here we go. No; the gray knickers lack the je ne sais quoi. The white might do the trick.

I run through my library of stimulating scenes. Which one will I replay—the time in Berlin or the middle-aged Italian who wept? What about the girl who rode her bicycle knickerless? In the old days I had possible scenes—scenes that might actually occur—which I used as an aid, rather than this nostalgia. And then, by mistake, I glance into the mirror and see a gray-haired, grimacing, mad-eyed monkey with a fist in front of him (his other hand placed delicately on his side because his back hurts from lifting the children). I suddenly feel that I am more likely to weep than ejaculate.

I will think of Nina. Nina's face; then the way she turns over and offers her arse to me. That should do it.

Suddenly I hear a noise. Quickly I close my pants. The bathroom door is pushed open, as if by a ghost. I watch and listen.

From the darkness of the hall, a child's luminous pacifier bobs into the room, a tiny circle of green light. The boy's eyes are shut as he stands there in his Batman T-shirt, pajama bottoms, and furry slippers, three years old. Actually, he is asleep. He staggers suddenly, and automatically raises his arms as if he has scored a goal. My hands fit under his arms, I pull him along my body, and smell and kiss his hair.

"What are you doing here, my beautiful boy?"

I carry him downstairs, lay him on the sofa, and pull off his bottoms and soggy nappy. The smell is unpleasantly sharp and familiar at the same time; it is him. He is willful and keeps trying to turn over, so I place one hand on the middle of his chest and push down while grasping his ankles with the other, as if I were about to hang him upside down from a hook. He thrashes and blinks as I wipe him. Then I shove and push to get the nappy in the right position. It is like trying to change the tire of a moving car. At last I replace his pajama bottoms.

"Have I been good enough to you, little boy?"

I didn't enjoy him as a baby, dreading the crying and whinging, the refusal to get dressed, eat, or go to sleep. I was astonished how whole days would pass when there was no time for anything but him, not even in the evenings. Having considered several books on the upbringing of children, often with feces or vomit on my fingers, I once threw him backward into his cot, hitting his head. I put brandy in his milk. I booted him hard up the nappy before he was even walking.

Susan cut me out, keeping the babies and the competence to herself, her female friends, and her mother. It has been only in the past few months that I've made myself useful. And only recently that I have fallen in love with my son. Now the boy and I talk ceaselessly. Where does the light go at night, what do spiders eat, why do women have "bosoms," where do people go when they die, and why do they have eyebrows? Where will he get the answers when I'm not here?

I am leaving this woman alone with two young children. My presence, however baleful, has perhaps reassured her. Now she will work, buy their clothes, feed them, tend them when they are sick. I'm sure she will ask herself, if she hasn't already, what men are for. Do they serve any useful function? They impregnate women. Occasionally they send money. What else could fathers be? It wasn't a question Dad asked himself. Being a father wasn't a question then. He was there to impose himself, to guide, exert discipline, and enjoy his children. We had to appreciate who he was and see things as he did.

I pick up my son. Holding his head with one hand and supporting his back with the other—his eyes are closed and his mouth open—I carry him to bed. But as I am about to lay him down I have a strange feeling. Sometimes you look into a mirror and can't always remember what age you are. Somehow you expect to see a twelve-year-old or an eighteen-year-old looking back at you. Now I feel as if I am looking at myself. He is me; I am him; both of us are part of one another but separate in the world. For now it is myself I am carrying in my arms.

I lay him down and cover him up.

I wonder when I will sleep beside him again. He has a vicious kick and a tendency, at unexpected moments, to vomit in my hair. But he can pat and stroke my face like a lover. His affectionate words and little voice are God's breath to me.

I creep down the stairs. I put my jacket on. I find my keys. I get to the door and open it. I step out of the house. It is dark and cold. The fresh wind sweeps through me. It invigorates me.

Go. You must go.

Torgny Lindgren
The Stump-Grubber

(S W E D E N)

It is an implement.

I tell you this so that you may understand that it is not a human being nor a monster, neither is it only wood, and bits of iron and cable and hook.

Three large sturdy legs made of wooden posts and on top the pulley, and then the cog-wheels, it is the cog-wheels and the pulley that do all the work, and on its side a winch of iron, and you put the cable round what is to be lifted, a stone or a stump, and you fasten the cable with the hook, and then you wind the winch round, and for each turn you make with the winch you lift the stone or the stump a fraction of an inch, your strength is multiplied a thousandfold. With a stump-grubber a poor weak creature can raise slaughtered horses and stones that are fast in the ground.

He needs help, though, to carry the stump-grubber and put it in place.

But if you lose your grip and if you have not locked the winch with the ratchet, then the object you have lifted falls back and all the power returns to the winch and that power is converted into speed and it whirls round so quickly that you cannot see it, and it crushes without mercy everything that comes in its way. Then the winch is like the hand of God's wrath.

Jacob Lundmark and Gerda, Jacob's Gerda, they lived on the smallholding in Inreliden. They had bought the partition in 1918. He had himself sawn the wood for the house and built it, and he had cleared and cultivated two fields so that they fed a cow; in the winter he was out in the timber-forest, and in summer he hewed charcoal-wood for the farmers. He had built the cowshed out of old timber that he had bought from Eric Markström in Bök. He was not a big stout man, Jacob, but tough and muscular; his nose had been crooked since his childhood, he had been kicked while helping to shoe a horse.

That was when he was ten, his job was to hold up the back legs, he stood just behind the horse. Then his mother, Alfrida, came out and saw him standing there—he was the apple of her eye—and she shouted to the men: "No, Jacob mustn't lift the hooves, it's dangerous."

And he abruptly straightened up to say that he was indeed not too small to give the blacksmith a hand, and the horse didn't like that and ever since then his nose had been crooked and he had a red mark just under his right eye.

Gerda, she was from Örträsk, so she didn't know anyone and no one knew anything about her for certain, so she was on her own. The only person she talked to occasionally was Isabella, Isabella Stenlund, the woman who had the illegitimate son. But that was only a few times a year. On the wall she had a hanging, it was one of the corduroy hangings, a blue one, and it said on it:

THE MYSTERY OF FAITH
IN A PURE CONSCIENCE

It was probably taken from the first Epistle of Timothy. She was plump but not fat.

Between the house and the cowshed at Inreliden Jacob had left a pine-tree, a huge pine which he thought could be a kind of good-luck tree; he had spared it. No one could embrace it though many had tried, not even Nylundius the preacher, though he could embrace seven feet; and the forester Nicolin had said that it might well be the largest pine in the Norsjö, and even in the area of Lycksele he did not know of a bigger one.

But Gerda was of the opinion that the big pine was as it were gloomy and depressing and that it kept out the light; she liked light, she delighted in it, so at last Jacob took it down and had it sawn up, and out of it he made a bed, a big wide bed, and a gate-legged table and six folding chairs, and a door for the small room—before they'd only had a piece of drapery there. That was in 1924, and their third girl Dagny, she was two years old.

But the stump was left.

And even the stump was enormous. A district forester came all the way from Ruskträsk just to see it, and to measure it and count its rings, and he said that the big pine had been like Methuselah, its days were like those of the sand.

And Jacob said that that stump was too much for him, its roots went out into the Vindel river to the south and out into the Skellefte river in the north, the big pine had certainly drunk from two rivers at the same time.

But to Gerda the stump was hateful, a human being sees what he has an eye for. It was in the way, she wanted to plant currant bushes there, or they could put in raspberries. Isabella could give them the plants, it was somehow a savage and ungodly thing on their farm where she wanted everything to be smooth and neat; it was a graven image.

So she said: "Dearest love, Jacob, can't you get rid of that stump?"

"I don't know whether I'm equal to it," said Jacob.

"You can burn it up, or bury it, or prize it loose with a crow-bar. It makes me feel ill, it is hateful and nasty."

"A stump like that has superhuman strength," said Jacob. "An ordinary human being was never meant to fight with a primitive monster like that."

But in the summer Jacob got hold of a ghastly stump-grubber, it was up for sale at the auction of the effects of Elis of Lillåberg; the legs were twenty feet long, it was the stump-grubber they had had when they made the Ajaur road. He got it cheap, it was a sort of monstrosity and a show-off, almost impossible to use—big men like Elis of Lillåberg don't exist these days. Jacob got it home on an open-sided wagon, as he had already borrowed Gabriel Israelsson's horse and was going in the direction of Svartlidlen.

By the last Saturday in July he had got in the hay and then he set the stump-grubber beside the stump of the great pine.

And he thought: "Men walk upon the earth like trees. And those who serve not He will tear out by their roots."

He exposed the thickest roots with a spade and with his axe he chopped off everything that he could get at for the moment, and then he dug deeper and took his pick-axe and even an iron bar; and he chopped and prized loose so that he could remove the small stones and moraine soil with his fingers; when the bark was cracked a smell of turpentine came from the stump; the earth smelt too; and he hewed off the tough roots with his axe, and it didn't worry him that it struck sparks out of the gravel and became blunt; it was for Gerda's sake he was doing this, and once he had started upon the stump there was no question of turning back and no mercy, he couldn't worry over the bluntness of his big axe, he could grind it on Monday.

He was dripping with sweat and he had to take off his blue smock, but he always sweated horribly when he became eager and was putting his back into it, and the gravel tore his cuticles and his knuckles so that they bled, but he took no notice; the roots were as thick as the thigh-bone of a horse and were just as many as the boughs had been on the pine itself while it was still alive; and when he stuck his crow-bar down into the ground he continually struck new roots that went in all directions in the depths; and he began to imagine that it was the pine that had held together his whole plot with its roots, and that if he were finally able to lift the stump the whole of Inreliden would crash together and be scattered; and when he dug and heaved and lifted the roots with his crow-bar, then he was aware that there was still life in that stump, the roots bent a trifle but only enough to make their strength and toughness apparent; and he said to that stump that, true enough, you are terrific, but a man too is tough and he has muscles and he can work out one thing and another that are beyond your powers of understanding, and moreover he has his stump-grubber.

At last he was forced to straighten up and go in to Gerda and drink some water.

"Aren't you going to take a rest soon?" she said. "It is Saturday after all."

"I'm only working on that stump," he said, "only by way of passing the time."

Then he went out and carried on.

When the time came for them to eat their evening porridge she came out and called him; he only ate one plate of barley-meal porridge. And she asked if she should not wash the small wounds on his knuckles and if he would not pull off his dirty clothes and put on his new trousers and his light-coloured shirt. It was after all the weekend, and the children wanted them to sing together and to read stories from the fairy-tale book.

But he heard from her voice that she had only one thing in her mind, that was the stump.

"It isn't really any sort of work," he said. "This job with the stump, I'm only trying to feel my way, and to reckon how I can best get it out."

He looked at her, her downy arms, her round chin, the little dimples in her cheeks, the grey-blue eyes that were sorrowful and happy at the same time—they were like some sort of warm spring—and on her forehead the little wrinkle that the parson had said meant deep thoughts.

And he suddenly felt almost happy to think that he might still be lucky enough to raise the stump and that when morning came she would be able to come out and view the big hole in the ground.

The earth was harder and harder the deeper he dug; the pebbles and gravel and clay were packed together so that they were almost like boulders, and he couldn't understand how the roots had penetrated them down in the depths, they might even have eaten their way into the rock; it was as if the pine had decided to stand for ever and ever.

But at last the largest roots were dug loose and chopped off and free.

Then he fetched the stump-grubber. He lifted first one leg then another, only a few feet at a time: if he hurried, the stump-grubber might get the upper hand and crash down—besides he had the whole night. He stood aside a few paces to see whether he had got it into the right position, and when he saw that the cog-wheel and pulley were right over the stump, he stamped it fast into the ground with his feet and his iron post.

Then he took the steel cable and pushed it in under the stump, under the roots that he could get at, and pulled it up in several places, under the worst of the thick roots, and finally fastened it firmly in place with the hook, the big iron hook, so that there could be no mistake, nothing could come loose, and the weight would be evenly balanced so that nothing could go wrong; now it was as it were an even contest between him and the stump.

And he sat down there on the grass and looked at the cable and the pulley and the winch, and the stump-grubber. And the stump.

"Now," he thought. "Now."

And he thought: "Gerda is standing behind the curtain watching me."

And he asked himself this too: "What is she thinking?" He had never been certain of what she was thinking—though no human being knows what love or hatred in others he has to deal with.

What were they thinking down in Örträsk?

First he wound the winch the number of turns needed to tense the cable, then he stopped to see that it had not gone slack under some root—it is important that the steel cable should always be stretched, that it is straight and that there is not any dislocation or weakness in it—then he made a few more turns so that the cable began to sing, it sounded as the ice on a lake does when it is going to break up.

When you use a stump-grubber you must not be in a hurry, you must stop from time to time, there is a ratchet that you can drop down against the cog-wheels to which the winch is fastened so that it does not unwind.

Then he made one turn at a time and rested a bit between each turn, it wasn't possible to make more than one turn at a time.

The half turn when the winch is going up is done with the muscles of a man's arms, back and legs; when the winch goes the half turn down, you lean on it with the upper part of your body and press it down with your weight.

In a little while the small roots began to give way, you could hear a snap far down in the earth when they broke, and Jacob thought: "All the same it is moving, it is not invincible."

That means half a turn at a time; and when the winch is going down one can lean against it and rest for a few breaths.

And he thought: "If it were not for the fact that this undertaking is mine, if this hadn't been put solely and only on me, then I would have spoken to Gerda and asked her to come out and help me, by leaning on the winch with the little bit of weight that she has after all."

It was the south side of the stump that gave way first, it snapped so much that at first he thought it was the cable that was being torn apart, but then when he got the winch down he saw that the stump had risen some half inch and that the earth had cracked round the roots where he had not dug and he said: "Dear God, let it give way on the north side too."

But he didn't want to let down the ratchet on the wheel yet, the ratchet of a stump-grubber ticks like a clock; if you use the ratchet you can't lift anything silently.

After yet a few more turns only the south side was moving: "I shall have to fasten it firm with the ratchet," he thought, "and dig and chop a bit on the north side, otherwise it will tilt over. And then I shall have to let it down once more and start again from the beginning. I'll do three turns more," he thought. "Only three turns. No more."

Now he had to exert himself to the full. And he could feel how the veins on the outside of his neck were swelling so that they pressed against the neck-band of his sweater, and what a strain it was on his thighs and arms so that it was almost like having cramp, and the red mark under his right eye throbbed, and the winch cut into his palms so they were on the way to being flayed. "Perhaps I ought to let down the ratchet, take a rest and put on my gloves," he thought.

Never before in his life had he exerted himself in this way. But neither was this work in the ordinary meaning of the word. It wasn't only that he had said: "I shall go at it and get up that stump before I take a rest day, that huge stump." No, he had a quite special sort of obligation and there was no mercy, and there behind the curtain in the living room Gerda was watching him.

"For the sake of that a man can give up everything," he thought. "For the sake of that a man can forget himself so that he is no longer aware of the blood and sinews of his own body."

And confirmation: there came a snap like a gun-shot on the north side and the whole stump shook like an animal wearing a slaughtering-mask and the south side sank down a fraction so that the north side should have room to rise.

"Gerda," thought Jacob. "Gerda."

"Now I'll take no more rests," he thought, "now I'll not drop the ratchet, now it's a matter of not giving up, now I have the better of it and I won't let it go, even if I have to fight until the morning."

The only question was: would the steel cable hold?

After each turn that he now took roots rose a half inch or so, they split there in the earth and cracked and groaned and broke as if they'd been strands of wool, and the little stones and the earth ran back into the hole, and the little roots that had not broken came up and were peeled; it almost felt as if the stump was giving up and blessed him. And he hardly took a rest when each turn was completed, if he had stopped the pain and ache in his hand might get the better of him; and he thought that no human being had ever pulled such a mighty stump out of the ground, there was almost something solemn about it, and Gerda is standing there and sees how calmly and firmly I wind the winch of the stump-grubber.

And very soon the stump hung almost free, it rocked and swayed a trifle on the cable and sometimes it tilted as if in its helplessness it were trying to shake itself loose; it was even larger and more horrible than Jacob had thought, you could clearly see that it was by nature infernal, it was as it were shaggy.

And the cable sang like the strings of a violin.

If he could only get it up high enough to be able to lift it to one side with a pole and lay it down on the edge of the hole then everything would be over, then he'd take a rest, then he would go in to Gerda and say: "I pulled up that stump, I got him up because I had the stump-grubber there."

At last there were only two roots holding the stump to the earth, they were half peeled and as stretched and tormented as the sinews of Jacob's body, they trembled as if they'd been alive. They were on the north side.

Jacob thought about his hands, he'd lost all feeling in them; "they are be-numbed, they are benumbed by pain," he thought, "perhaps the skin will fall off them like a pair of gloves; after this is over, and after I've had a rest, then I'll let my hands rest too, then I'll submerge them in cold water, and let them take a holiday and get back their strength, for one's hands are the body's crown."

And just then, just when it was all nearly over, Gerda came out on to the porch—he did not see her as he was standing at the back of the stump—and she was holding Dagny by one hand and in the other she had Dagny's doll, and she called with all the strength she had in her body.

"Dearest love Jacob! You must be careful!"

And that call, that was the most wonderful thing Jacob had been sensible of in the whole of his life, it was so inexpressibly warm and trembling, and so permeated with concern and love that he halted halfway through the winch, her call had made him quite weak and dazed, he felt that he must see her, and he turned his head and the upper part of his body so that she would perhaps be in sight, but he still held on to the winch, and he could really see her, she was standing in the porch and in her left hand she held the little girl and in her right hand the doll, and the evening sun lit her up from the side so that he could see how her apron clung to her stomach and thighs, and she had bound up her hair with a blue shawl, and her mouth was open, and her eyes were wide open with anxiety and fondness. No human being could seem more heavenly.

And she called to him once more: "Dearest love—Jacob, you must be careful!"

And just as she called for the second time, he got the feeling back in his hands, and he could feel that they couldn't do any more; his fingers began to straighten themselves out and he could not stop them, it felt as if there was no longer any mercy for them, and he tried to make the half turn that was wanting to bring the winch down to the bottom, but he had not the strength.

And then the last rootlets broke, they gave way suddenly and the stump, which was now hanging free, tipped over and swung round as if it were possessed by a frightful fit of rage, and Jacob was quite helpless, all he could hear was Gerda's voice within him, and the thickest root of the stump gave him a horrible blow on his hip-joint, just on the sinews of his hip, a tremendous blow on his hip so that he fell forwards and his fingers gave way altogether, and all the strength in the stump went back into the winch. But within him all he saw was Gerda, and he was bursting with her voice and her words, the eagerness and anxiety and warmth, her fondness for him that was so great that there were almost tears in her voice, so that when he fell headlong he did not grasp what it was that was happening, he did not realize what had befallen him. What it was that struck him like the hand of God's wrath and tore his breast open and killed him, if it was the winch, or if it was the almost unbearable heat of love, there are words that are like glowing coals, dearest love Jacob, you must be careful.

Translated from the Swedish by Mary Sandbach

Bobbie Ann Mason

Wish

(UNITED STATES)

Sam tried to hold his eyes open. The preacher, a fat-faced boy with a college degree, had a curious way of pronouncing his *r*'s. The sermon was about pollution of the soul and started with a news item about an oil spill. Sam drifted into a dream about a flock of chickens scratching up a bed of petunias. His sister Damson, beside him, knifed him in the ribs with her bony elbow. Snoring, she said with her eyes.

Every Sunday after church, Sam and Damson visited their other sister, Hortense, and her husband, Cecil. Ordinarily Sam drove his own car, but today Damson gave him a ride because his car was low on gas. Damson lived in town, but Hort and Cecil lived out in the country, not far from the old homeplace, which had been sold twenty years before, when Pap died. As they drove past the old place now, Sam saw Damson shudder. She had stopped saying "Trash" under her breath when they passed by and saw the junk cars that had accumulated around the old house. The yard was bare dirt now, and the large elm in front had split. Many times Sam and his sisters had wished the new interstate had gone through the homeplace instead. Sam knew he should have bought out his sisters and kept it.

"How are you, Sam?" Hort asked when he and Damson arrived. Damson's husband, Porter, had stayed home today with a bad back.

"About dead." Sam grinned and knuckled his chest, pretending heart trouble and exaggerating the arthritis in his hands.

"Not again!" Hort said, teasing him. "You just like to growl, Sam. You've been that way all your life."

"You ain't even knowed me that long! Why, I remember the night you was born. You come in mad at the world, with your stinger out, and you've been like that ever since."

Hort patted his arm. "Your barn door's open, Sam," she said as they went into the living room.

He zipped up his fly unself-consciously. At his age, he didn't care.

Hort steered Damson off into the kitchen, murmuring something about a blue dish, and Sam sat down with Cecil to discuss crops and the weather. It was their habit to review the week's weather, then their health, then local news—in that order. Cecil was a small amiable man who didn't like to argue.

A little later, at the dinner table, Cecil jokingly asked Sam, "Are you sending any money to Jimmy Swaggart?"

"Hell, no! I ain't sending a penny to that bastard."

"Sam never gave them preachers nothing," Hort said defensively as she sent a bowl of potatoes au gratin Sam's way. "That was Nova."

Nova, Sam's wife, had been dead eight and a half years. Nova was always buying chances on Heaven, Sam thought. There was something squirrelly in her, like the habit she had of saving out extra seed from the garden or putting up more preserves than they could use.

Hort said, "I still think Nova wanted to build on that ground she heired so she could have a house in her own name."

Damson nodded vigorously. "She didn't want you to have your name on the new house, Sam. She wanted it in her name."

"Didn't make no sense, did it?" Sam said, reflecting a moment on Nova. He could see her plainly, holding up a piece of fried chicken like a signal for attention. The impression was so vivid he almost asked her to pass the peas.

Hort said, "You already had a nice house with shade trees and a tobacco patch, and it was close to your kinfolks, but she just *had* to move toward town."

"She told me if she had to get to the hospital the ambulance would get there quicker," said Damson, taking a second biscuit. "Hort, these biscuits ain't as good as you usually make."

"I didn't use self-rising," said Hort.

"It wouldn't make much different, with that new highway," said Cecil, speaking of the ambulance.

On the day they moved to the new house, Sam stayed in bed with the covers pulled up around him and refused to budge. He was still there at four o'clock in the evening after his cousins had moved out all the furniture. Nova ignored him until they came for the bed. She laid his clothes on the bed and rattled the car keys in his face. She had never learned to drive. That was nearly fifteen years ago. Only a few years after that, Nova died and left him in that brick box she called a dream home. There wasn't a tree in the yard when they built the house. Now there were two flowering crab apples and a flimsy little oak.

After dinner, Hort and Cecil brought out new pictures of their great-grandchildren. The children had changed, and Sam couldn't keep straight which ones belonged to Linda and which ones belonged to Donald. He felt full. He made himself comfortable among the crocheted pillows on Hort's high-backed couch. For ten minutes, Hort talked on the telephone to Linda, in Louisiana, and when she hung up she reported that Linda had a new job at a finance company. Drowsily, Sam listened to the voices rise and fall. Their language was so familiar; his kinfolks never told stories or reminisced when they sat around on a Sunday. Instead, they discussed character. "He's the stingiest man alive." "She was nice to talk to on the street but *H* to work with." "He never would listen when you tried to tell him anything." "She'd do anything for you."

Now, as Sam stared at a picture of a child with a Depression-style bowl haircut, Damson was saying, "Old Will Stone always referred to himself as 'me.' '*Me* did this. *Me* wants that.'"

Hort said, "The Stones were always trying to get you to do something for them. Get around one of them and they'd think of something they wanted you to do." The Stones were their mother's people.

"I never would let 'em tell me what to do," Damson said with a laugh. "I'd say, 'I can't! I've got the nervous trembles.'"

Damson was little then, and her aunt Rue always complained of nervous trembles. Once, Damson had tried to get out of picking English peas by claiming that she had nervous trembles, too. Sam remembered that. He laughed— a hoot so sudden they thought he hadn't been listening and was laughing about something private.

Hort fixed a plate of fried chicken, potatoes, field peas, and stewed apples for Sam to take home. He set it on the back seat of Damson's car, along with fourteen eggs and a sack of biscuits. Damson spurted out of the driveway backward, scaring the hound dog back to his hole under a lilac bush.

"Hort and Cecil's having a time keeping up this place," Sam said, noticing the weed-clogged pen where they used to keep hogs.

Damson said, "Hort's house always smelled so good, but today it smelled bad. It smelled like fried fish."

"I never noticed it," said Sam, yawning.

"Ain't you sleeping good, Sam?"

"Yeah, but when my stomach sours I get to yawning."

"You ain't getting old on us, are you?"

"No, I ain't old. Old is in your head."

Damson invited herself into Sam's house, saying she wanted to help him put the food away. His sisters wouldn't leave him alone. They checked on his housekeeping, searched for ruined food, made sure his commode was flushed. They had fits when he took in a stray dog one day, and they would have taken her to the pound if she hadn't got hit on the road first.

Damson stored the food in the kitchen and snooped in his refrigerator. Sam was itching to get into his blue-jeans and watch something on Ted Turner's channel that he had meant to watch. He couldn't remember now what it was, but he knew it came on at four o'clock. Damson came into the living room and began to peer at all his pictures, exclaiming over each great-grandchild. All Sam's kids and grandkids were scattered around. His son worked in the tire industry in Akron, Ohio, and his oldest granddaughter operated a frozen-yogurt store in Florida. He didn't know why anybody would eat yogurt in any form. His grandson Bobby had arrived from Arizona last year with an Italian woman who spoke in a sharp accent. Sam had to hold himself stiff to keep from laughing. He wouldn't let her see him laugh, but her accent tickled him. Now Bobby had written that she'd gone back to Italy.

Damson paused over an old family portrait—Pap and Mammy and all six children, along with Uncle Clay and Uncle Thomas and their wives, Rosie and Zootie, and Aunt Rue. Sam's three brothers were dead now. Damson, a young girl in the picture, wore a lace collar, and Hort was in blond curls and a pinafore. Pap sat in the center on a chair with his legs set far apart, as if to anchor himself to hold the burden of this wild family. He looked mean and willful, as though he were about to whip somebody.

Suddenly Damson blurted out, "Pap ruined my life."

Sam was surprised. Damson hadn't said exactly that before, but he knew what she was talking about. There had always been a sadness about her, as though she had had the hope knocked out of her years ago.

She said, "He ruined my life—keeping me away from Lyle."

"That was near sixty years ago, Damson. That's don't still bother you now, does it?"

She held the picture close to her breast and said, "You know how you hear on television nowadays about little children getting beat up or treated nasty and it makes such a mark on them? Nowadays they know about that, but they didn't back then. They never knowed how something when you're young can hurt you so long."

"None of that happened to you."

"Not that, but it was just as bad."

"Lyle wouldn't have been good to you," said Sam.

"But I loved him, and Pap wouldn't let me see him."

"Lyle was a drunk and Pap didn't trust him no further than he could throw him."

"And then I married Porter, for pure spite," she went on. "You know good and well I never cared a thing about him."

"How come you've stayed married to him all these years then? Why don't you do like the kids do nowadays—like Bobby out in Arizona? Him and that Italian. They've done quit!"

"But she's a foreigner. I ain't surprised," said Damson, blowing her nose with a handkerchief from her pocketbook. She sat down on Sam's divan. He had towels spread on the upholstery to protect it, a habit of Nova's he couldn't get rid of. That woman was so practical she had even orchestrated her deathbed. She had picked out her burial clothes, arranged for his breakfast. He remembered holding up hangers of dresses from her closet for her to choose from.

"Damson," he said, "if you could do it over, you'd do it different, but it might not be no better. You're making Lyle out to be more than he would have been."

"He wouldn't have shot hisself," she said calmly.

"It was an accident."

She shook her head. "No, I think different."

Damson had always claimed he killed himself over her. That night, Lyle had come over to the homeplace near dark. Sam and his brothers had helped Pap put in a long day suckering tobacco. Sam was already courting Nova, and Damson was just out of high school. The neighborhood boys came over on Sundays after church like a pack of dogs after a bitch. Damson had an eye for Lyle because he was so daresome, more reckless than the rest. That Saturday night when Lyle came by for her, he had been into some moonshine, and he was frisky, like a young bull. Pap wouldn't let her go with him. Sam heard Damson in the attic, crying, and Lyle was outside, singing at the top of his lungs, calling her. "Damson! My fruit pie!" Pap stepped out onto the porch then, and Lyle slipped off into the darkness.

Damson set the family picture back on the shelf and said, "He was different from all the other boys. He knew a lot, and he'd been to Texas once with his daddy—for his daddy's asthma. He had a way about him."

"I remember when Lyle come back late that night," Sam said. "I heard him on the porch. I knowed it must be him. He was loud and acted like he was going to bust in the house after you."

"I heard him," she said. "From my pallet up there at the top. It was so hot I had a bucket of water and a washrag and I'd wet my face and stand in that little window and reach for a breeze. I heard him come, and I heard him thrashing around down there on the porch. There was loose board you always had to watch out for."

"I remember that!" Sam said. He hadn't thought of that warped plank in years.

"He fell over it," Damson said. "But then he got up and backed down the steps. I could hear him out in the yard. Then—" She clasped her arms around herself and bowed her head. "Then he yelled out, 'Damson!' I can still hear that."

A while later, they had heard the gunshot. Sam always remembered hearing a hollow thump and a sudden sound like cussing, then the explosion. He and his brother Bob rushed out in the dark, and then Pap brought a coal-oil lantern. They found Lyle sprawled behind the barn, with the shotgun kicked several feet away. There was a milk can turned over, and they figured that Lyle had stumbled over it when he went behind the barn. Sam had never forgotten Damson on the living-room floor, bawling. She lay there all the next day, screaming and beating her heavy work shoes against the floor, and people had to step around her. The women fussed over her, but none of the men could say anything.

Sam wanted to say something now. He glared at that big family in the picture. The day the photographer came, Sam's mother made everyone dress up, and they had to stand there as still as stumps for about an hour in that August heat. He remembered the kink in Damson's hair, the way she had fixed it so pretty for Lyle. A blurred chicken was cutting across the corner of the picture, and an old bird dog named Obadiah was stretched out in front, holding a pose better than the fidgety people. In the front row, next to her mother, Damson's bright, upturned face sparkled with a smile. Everyone had admired the way she could hold a smile for the camera.

Pointing to her face in the picture, he said, "Here you are, Damson—a young girl in love."

Frowning, she said, "I just wish life had been different."

He grabbed Damson's shoulders and stared into her eyes. To this day, she didn't even wear glasses and was still pretty, still herself in there, in that puffed-out old face. He said, "You wish! Well, wish in one hand and shit in the other one and see which one fills up the quickest!"

He got her. She laughed so hard she had to catch her tears with her hand-kerchief. "Sam, you old hound. Saying such as that—and on a Sunday."

She rose to go. He thought he'd said the right thing, because she seemed lighter on her feet now. "You've got enough eggs and bacon to last you all week," she said. "And I'm going to bring you some of that popcorn cake my neighbor makes. You'd never guess it had popcorn in it."

She had her keys in her hand, her pocketbook on her arm. She was wearing a pretty color of pink, the shade of baby pigs. She said, "I know why you've lived so long, Sam. You just see what you want to see. You're like Pap, just as hard and plain."

"That ain't the whole truth," he said, feeling a mist of tears come.

That night he couldn't get to sleep. He went to bed at eight-thirty, after a nature special on the television—grizzly bears. He lay in bed and replayed his life with Nova. The times he wanted to leave home. The time he went to a lawyer to inquire about a divorce. (It turned out to cost too much, and anyway he knew his folks would never forgive him.) The time she hauled him out of bed for the move to this house. He had loved their old place, a wood-frame house with a porch and a swing, looking out over tobacco fields and a strip of woods. He always had a dog then, a special dog, sitting on the porch with him. Here he had no porch, just some concrete steps where he would sit some-times and watch the traffic. At night, drunk drivers zoomed along, occasionally plowing into somebody's mailbox.

She had died at three-thirty in the morning, and toward the end she didn't want anything—no food, no talk, no news, nothing soft. No kittens to hold, no memories. He stayed up with her in case she needed him, but she went with-out needing him at all. And now he didn't need her. In the dim light of the street lamp, he surveyed the small room where he had chosen to sleep—the single bed, the bare walls, his jeans hanging up on a nail, his shoes on a shelf, the old washstand that had belonged to his grandmother, the little rag rug beside the bed. He was happy. His birthday was two months from today. He would be eighty-four. He thought of that bird dog, Obadiah, who had been with him on his way through the woods the night he set out to meet someone—the night he first made love to a girl. Her name was Nettie, and at first she had been reluctant to lie down with him, but he had brought a quilt, and he spread it out in the open pasture. The hay had been cut that week, and the grass was damp and sweet-smelling. He could still feel the clean, soft, cool cotton of that quilt, the stubble poking through and the patterns of the quilting pressing into his back. Nettie lay there beside him, her breath blowing on his shoulder as they studied the stars far above the field—little pinpoint holes punched through the night sky like the needle holes around the tiny stitches in the quilting. Nettie. Nettie Slade. Her dress had self-covered buttons, hard like seed corn.

Colum McCann

Everything in This Country Must

(I R E L A N D)

It was a summer flood when our draft horse was caught in the river and the river smashed against stones. The sound of it to me was like the turning of locks. It was silage time, and the water smelled of grass. The draft horse, Father's favorite, had stepped in the river for a sniff maybe, and she was caught, couldn't move, her foreleg trapped between rocks. Father found her and called, *Katie!* above the wailing of the rain. I was in the barn, waiting for drips on my tongue from the ceiling hole. I ran out past the farmhouse into the field. At the river the horse stared wild through the rain; maybe she remembered me. Father moved slow and scared, like someone traveling deep in snow except there was no snow, just flood, and Father was frightened of water, always frightened. Father told me, *Out on the rock there, girl.* He gave me the length of rope with the harness clip, and I knew what to do. I am taller than Father since my last birthday, fifteen. I stretched wide like love and put one foot on the rock in the river middle and one hand on the tree branch above it and swung out over the river flood.

Behind me Father said, *Careful now hai.* The water ran warm and fast, like girl blood, and I held the tree branch, still able to lean down from the rock and put the rope to the halter of the lovely draft horse.

The trees went down to the river in a whispering, and they hung their long branches over the water, and the horse jerked quick and sudden, and I felt there would be a dying, but I pulled the rope up to keep her neck above water.

Father was shouting, *Hold it, girl!* and I could see his teeth clenched and his eyes wide and all the traveling of veins in his neck, the same as when he walks the ditches of our farm, many cows, hedgerows, fences. Father is always full of ditches and fright for the losing of Mammy and Fiachra and now his horse, his favorite, a big Belgian mare that cut fields once in the peaceful dark soil of long ago.

The river split at the rock and jumped fast into sprays coming up above my feet into my dress. But I held tight to the rope, held it like Father sometimes holds his last Sweet Afton cigarette at mealtime before prayers. Father was shouting, *Keep it there, girl, good!* He was looking at the water as if Mammy was there, as if Fiachra was there, and he gulped air and down he went in the water and he was gone so long he made me wail to the sky for being alone. He kept a strong hold of one tree root but all the rest of his body went away under the quick brown water.

The night had started stars. They were up through the branches. The river was spraying in them.

Father came up splutter spluttering for air with his eyes all horsewild and his cap lost down the river. The rope was jumping in my hands and burning like oven rings, and he was shouting, *Hold it, girl, hold it, for the love of God hold it, please!*

Father went down in the water again but came up early, no longer enough in his lungs to keep down. He stayed in the river holding the root, and the water was hitting his shoulders and he was sad watching the draft horse die like everything does, but still I pulled on the halter rope so it would not, because Molly in the sweet shop told me it is not always so.

One more try, Father said in a sad voice like his voice over Mammy and Fiachra's coffins long ago.

Father dipped under and he stayed down as long as yesterday's yesterday, and then some headlights came sweeping up the town road. The lights made a painting of the rain way up high and they put shadows on the hedgerows and ditches. Father's head popped out of the water and he was breathing heavy, so he didn't see the light. His chest was wide and jumping. He looked at the draft horse and then at me. I pointed up the road and he turned in the flood and stared. Father smiled, maybe thinking it was Mack Devlin with his milk truck or Molly coming home from the sweet shop or someone come to help save his favorite horse. He dragged on the tree root and out-struggled from the river and stood on the bank, and his arms went up in the air like he was waving, shouting, *Over here over here hai!*

Father's shirt was wet under his overalls and it was very white when the headlights hit it. The lights got close close closer, and in the brightening we heard shouts and then the voices came clear. They sounded like they had swallowed things I never swallowed. I looked at Father and he looked at me all of a sudden with the strangest of faces, like he was lost, like he was punched, like he was the river cap floating, like he was a big alone tree desperate for forest. Someone shouted out, *Hey, mate, what's goin' on?* in a strange strange way, and Father said, *Nothing,* and his head dropped to his chest and he looked across the river at me and I think what he was telling me was *Drop the rope, girl,* but I didn't. I kept it tight, holding the draft horse's neck above the water, and all the time Father was saying but not saying, *Drop it, please, Katie, drop it, let her drown.*

They came right quick through the hedge, with no regard for the uniforms that hide them. One took off his helmet while he was running, and his hair was the color of winter ice. One had a moustache that looked like long grasses, and one had a scar on his cheek like the bottom end of Father's barn hay knife.

HayKnife was first to the edge of the river, and his rifle banged against his hip when he jumped out to the rock where I was halter-holding. *Okay, love, you're all right now*, he said to me, and his hand was rain-wet at my back, and he took the halter and shouted things to the other soldiers, what to do, where to stand. He kept ahold of the halter and passed me back to LongGrasses, who caught my hand and brought me safely to the riverbank. There were six of them now, all guns and helmets. Father didn't move. His eyes were steady looking at the river, maybe seeing Mammy and Fiachra in each eye of the draft horse, staring back.

One soldier was talking to him loud and fast, but Father was like a Derry shop-window dummy, and the soldier threw up his arms and turned away through the rain and spat a big spit into the wind.

HayKnife was all balance on the rock with the halter, and he didn't even hold the branch above his head. IceHair was taking off his boots and gun and shirt and he looked not like boys from town who come to the barn for love, he looked not like Father when Father cuts hay without his shirt, no, he looked not like anybody; he was very skinny and strong with ribs like sometimes a horse has after a long day in the field. He didn't dive like I think now I would have liked him to, he just stepped into the water very slow and not show-offy and began making his way across, arms high in the air getting lower. But the river got too deep and HayKnife shouted from the rock, saying, *Stay high, Stevie, stay high side, mate.*

And Stevie gave a thumb up to HayKnife and then he was down under the water and the last thing was the kick of the feet.

LongGrasses was standing beside me and he put Stevie's jacket on my shoulders to warm me, but then Father came over and pushed LongGrasses away. Father pushed hard. He was smaller than LongGrasses, but Long-Grasses bashed against the trunk of the tree. LongGrasses took a big breath and stared hard at him. Father said, *Leave her alone, can't you see she's just a child?* I covered my face for shame, like in school when they put me in class at a special desk bigger than the rest, not the wooden ones with lifting lids, except I don't go to school anymore since Mammy and Fiachra died. I felt shame like the shame of that day, and I covered my face and peeped through my fingers.

Father was giving a bad look to LongGrasses. LongGrasses stared at Father for a long time too and then shook his head and walked away to the riverbank where Stevie was still down in the water.

Father's hands were on my shoulders, keeping me warm, and he said, *It'll be all right now, love*, but I was only thinking about Stevie and how long he was under water. HayKnife was shouting at the top of his voice and staring down into the water, and I looked up and saw the big army truck coming through the hedgerow fence and the hedge was broken open with a big hole and Father screamed *No!* The extra lights of the truck were on and they were lighting up all the river. Father screamed again, *No!* but stopped when one of the soldiers stared at him. *Your horse or your bloody hedge, mate.*

Father sat down on the riverbank and said, *Sit down, Katie*, and I could hear in Father's voice more sadness than when he was over Mammy's and

Fiachra's coffins, more sadness than the day after they were hit by the army truck down near the Glen, more sadness than the day the judge said, *Nobody is guilty, it's just a tragedy,* more sadness than even that day and all the other days that follow.

Bastards, Father said in a whisper, *bastards,* and he put his arm around me and sat watching until Stevie came up from the water swimming against the current to stay in one place. He shouted up at HayKnife, *Her leg's trapped,* and then, *I'm gonna try and get the hoof out.* Stevie took four big gulps of air and HayKnife was pulling on the halter rope and the draft horse was screaming like I never heard a horse before or after. Father was quiet and I wanted to be back in the barn alone, waiting for drips on my tongue. I was wearing Stevie's jacket but I was shivering and wet and cold and scared, because Stevie and the draft horse were going to die, since everything in this country must.

Father likes his tea without bags, like Mammy used to make, and so there is a special way for me to make it. Put cold cold water in the kettle, and only cold, and boil it, and then put a little boiling water in the teapot and swish it around until the bottom of the teapot is warm. Then put in tea leaves, not bags, and then the boiling water, and stir it all very slowly and put on the tea cozy and let it stew on the stove for five minutes, making sure the flame is not too high so the tea cozy doesn't catch flame and burn. Then pour milk into the cups and then the tea, followed at last by the sugar all spooned around into a careful mixture.

My tea fuss made the soldiers smile, even Stevie, who had a head full of blood pouring down from where the draft horse kicked him above his eye. Father's face went white when Stevie smiled, but Stevie was very polite. He took a towel from me because he said he didn't want to get blood on the chair. He smiled at me two times when I put my head around the kitchen door, and held up one finger, meaning *One sugar, please,* and a big O from fingers for *No milk, please.* Some blood was drying in his hair, and his eyes were bright like the sky should be, and I could feel my belly sink way down until it was there like love in the barn, and he smiled at me number three.

Everyone felt good for saving a life, even a horse life, maybe even Father, but Father was silent in the corner. He was angry at me for asking the soldiers to tea, and his chin was long to his chest and there was a puddle at his feet. Everybody was towel-drying except Father and me, because we had not enough towels.

LongGrasses sat in the armchair and said, *Good thing ya had heat lamps, guvnor.*

Father just nodded.

How was it under the water, Stevie? LongGrasses said.

Wet, Stevie said, and everybody laughed but not Father. He stared at Stevie and then looked away.

The living room is always dark with Father grim, but it was brighter now. I liked the green of the uniforms and even the red of Stevie's blood. But Stevie's head from the horse kick must have been very sore. The other soldiers were talking about how maybe the army truck should take Stevie straight off to hospital and not get dry, just get stitches, and not get tea, just come back later to see about the draft horse if she survives under the heat lamps. But Stevie said, *I'm okay, guys, it's just a scrape. I'd kill for a cuppa.*

The tea was good-tasting from long brewing, and we had biscuits for special visitors. I fetched them from the pantry. I tasted one to make sure they were fresh-tasting and I carried out the tray.

I was sneezing but I was very careful to sneeze away from the tray so as to have politeness like Stevie. Stevie said, *God bless you* in his funny funny way, and we were all quiet as we sipped on the tea, but I sneezed again three four five times, and HayKnife said, *You should change out of them wet clothes, love.*

Father put down his teacup very heavy on the saucer and it was very quiet.

Everyone, even the soldiers, looked at the floor, and the mantelpiece clock was ticking and Mammy's picture was staring down from the wall, and Fiachra when he was playing football, and the soldiers didn't see them but Father did. The long silence was longer and longer until Father called me over, *Come here, Katie,* and he stood me by the window and he took the long curtain in his hands. He turned me around and wrapped the curtain around me and he took my hair and started rubbing not tender but hard. Father is good; he was just wanting to dry my hair because I was shivering even in Stevie's jacket. From under the curtain I could see the soldiers and I could see most of all Stevie. He sipped from his tea and smiled at me, and Father coughed real loud and the clock ticked some more until HayKnife said, *Here, guv, why don't you use my towel for her?*

Father said, *No, thanks.*

HayKnife said, *Go on, guv,* and he put the towel in a ball and made about to throw it.

Father said, *No!*

Stevie said, *Take it easy.*

Take it easy? HayKnife said.

Maybe you should all leave, Father said.

HayKnife changed his face and threw the towel on the ground at Father's feet, and HayKnife's cheeks were outpuffing and he was breathing hard and he was saying, *Fat lot of fuckin thanks we get from your sort, mister.*

HayKnife was up on his feet now and pointing at Father, and the light shone off his boots well polished, and his face was twitching so the scar looked like it was cutting his face. LongGrasses and Stevie stood up from the chairs and were holding HayKnife back, but HayKnife was saying, *Risk our fuckin lives and save your fuckin horse and that's all the thanks we get, eh?*

Father held me very tight with the curtain wrapped around me, and he seemed scared and small and trembly. HayKnife was shouting lots and his face was red and scrunched. Stevie kept him back. Stevie's face was long and sad and I knew he knew because he kept looking at Mammy and Fiachra on the mantelpiece beside the ticking clock. Stevie dragged HayKnife out from the living room and at the kitchen door he let go. HayKnife turned over Stevie's shoulder one last time and looked at Father with his face all twisted, but Stevie grabbed him again and said, *Forget it, mate.*

Stevie took HayKnife out through the kitchen door and into the yard toward the army truck, and still the rain was coming down outside, and then the living room was quiet except for the clock.

I heard the engine of the army truck start.

Father stood away from me and put his head on the mantelpiece near the photos. I stayed at the window still in Stevie's jacket, which Stevie forgot and hasn't come back for yet.

I watched the truck as it went down the laneway, and the red lights on the green gate as it stopped and then turned into the road past where the draft horse was lifted from the river. I didn't hear anything then, just Father starting low noises in his throat, and I didn't turn from the window because I knew he would be angry for me to see him. Father was sniff sniffling. Maybe he forgot I was there. It was going right down into him and it came in big gulps like I never heard before. I stayed still, but Father was trembling big and fast. He took out a handkerchief and moved away from the mantelpiece. I didn't watch him because I knew he would be shamed for his crying.

The army truck was near out of sight, red lights on the hedgerows.

I heard the living room door shut, then the kitchen door, then the pantry door where Father keeps his hunting rifle, then the front door, and I heard the sounds of the clicker on the rifle and him still crying going farther and farther away until they were gone, and he must have been in the courtyard standing in the rain.

The clock on the mantelpiece sounded very loud, so did the rain, so did my breathing, and I looked out the window.

It was all near empty on the outside road, and the soldiers were going around the corner when I heard the sounds, not like bullets, more like pops one two three and the echo of them came loud to me.

The clock still ticked.

It ticked and ticked and ticked.

The curtain was wet around me, but I pulled it tight. I was scared, I couldn't move. I waited it seemed like forever.

When Father came in from outside I knew what it was. His face was like it was cut from a stone and he was not crying anymore and he didn't even look at me, just went to sit in the chair. He picked up his teacup and it rattled in his fingers, so he put it down again and put his face in his hands and stayed like that. The ticking was gone from my mind, and all was quiet everywhere in the world, and I held the curtain like I held the sound of the bullets going into the draft horse's head, his favorite, in the barn, one two three, and I stood at the window in Stevie's jacket and looked and waited and still the rain kept coming down outside one two three one two three one two three and I was thinking oh, what a small sky for so much rain.

Ian McEwan

Pornography

(WALES)

O'Byrne walked through Soho market to his brother's shop in Brewer Street. A handful of customers leafing through the magazines and Harold watching them through pebble-thick lenses from his raised platform in the corner. Harold was barely five foot and wore built-up shoes. Before becoming his employee O'Byrne used to call him Little Runt. At Harold's elbow a miniature radio rasped details of race meetings for the afternoon. "So," said Harold with thin contempt, "the prodigal brother . . ." His magnified eyes fluttered at every consonant. He looked past O'Byrne's shoulder. "All the magazines are for sale, gentlemen." The readers stirred uneasily like troubled dreamers. One replaced a magazine and walked quickly from the shop. "Where d'you get to?" Harold said in a quieter voice. He stepped from the dais, put on his coat and glared up at O'Byrne, waiting for an answer. Little Runt. O'Byrne was ten years younger than his brother, detested him and his success but now, strangely, wanted his approbation. "I had an appointment, didn't I," he said quietly. "I got the clap." Harold was pleased. He reached up and punched O'Byrne's shoulder playfully. "Serves you," he said and cackled theatrically. Another customer edged out of the shop. From the doorway Harold called, "I'll be back at five." O'Byrne smiled as his brother left. He hooked his thumbs into his jeans and sauntered towards the tight knot of customers. "Can I help you gentlemen, the magazines are all for sale." They scattered before him like frightened fowl, and suddenly he was alone in the shop.

A plump woman of fifty or more stood in front of a plastic shower curtain, naked but for panties and gas mask. Her hands hung limply at her sides and in one of them a cigarette smoldered. Wife of the Month. Since gas masks and a thick rubber sheet on the bed, wrote J.N. of Andover, we've never looked back. O'Byrne played with the radio for a while then switched it off. Rhythmically he turned the pages of the magazine, and stopped to read the letters. An uncircumcised male virgin, without hygiene, forty-two next May, dared not peel back his foreskin now for fear of what he might see. I get these nightmares of worms. O'Byrne laughed and crossed his legs. He replaced the magazine, returned to the radio, switched it on and off rapidly and caught the unintelligible middle of a word. He walked about the shop straightening the magazines in the racks. He stood by the door and stared at the wet street intersected by the colored strips of the plastic walk-through. He whistled over and over a tune whose end immediately suggested its beginning. Then he returned to Harold's raised platform and made two telephone calls, both to the hospital, the first to Lucy. But Sister Drew was busy in the ward and could not come to the phone. O'Byrne left a message that he would not be able to see her that evening after all and would phone again tomorrow. He dialed the hospital switchboard and this time asked for Trainee Nurse Shepherd in the children's ward. "Hi," O'Byrne said when Pauline picked up the phone. "It's me." And he stretched and leaned against the wall. Pauline was a silent girl who once wept at a film about the effects of pesticides on butterflies, who wanted to redeem O'Byrne with her love. Now she laughed, "I've been phoning you all morning," she said. "Didn't your brother tell you?"

"Listen," said O'Byrne, "I'll be at your place about eight," and replaced the receiver.

Harold did not return till after six, and O'Byrne was almost asleep, his head pillowed on his forearm. There were no customers. O'Byrne's only sale was *American Bitch.* "Those American nags," said Harold as he emptied the till of £15 and a handful of silver, "are *good.*" Harold's new leather jacket. O'Byrne fingered it appreciatively. "Seventy-eight quid," said Harold and braced himself in front of the fish-eye mirror. His glasses flashed. "It's all right," said O'Byrne. "Fucking right it is," said Harold, and began to close up shop. "Never take much on Wednesday," he said wistfully as he reached up and switched on the burglar alarm. "Wednesday's a cunt of a day." Now O'Byrne was in front of the mirror, examining a small trail of acne that led from the corner of his mouth. "You're not fucking kidding," he agreed.

Harold's house lay at the foot of the Post Office Tower and O'Byrne rented a room from him. They walked along together without speaking. From time to time Harold glanced sideways into a dark shop window to catch the reflection of himself and his new leather jacket. Little Runt. O'Byrne said, "Cold, innit?" and Harold said nothing. Minutes later, when they were passing a pub, Harold steered O'Byrne into the dank, deserted public house saying, "Since you got the clap I'll buy you a drink." The publican heard the remark and regarded O'Byrne with interest. They drank three scotches apiece, and as O'Byrne was paying for the fourth round Harold said, "Oh yeah, one of those two nurses you've been knocking around with phoned." O'Byrne nodded and wiped his lips. After a pause Harold said, "You're well in there . . ." O'Byrne nodded again. "Yep." Harold's jacket shone. When he reached for his drink it creaked. O'Byrne was not going to tell him anything. He banged his hands together. "Yep," he said once more, and stared over his brother's head at the empty bar. Harold tried again. "She wanted to know where you'd been . . ." "I bet she did," O'Byrne muttered, and then smiled.

Pauline, short and untalkative, her face bloodlessly pale, intersected by a heavy black fringe, her eyes large, green and watchful, her flat small, damp and shared with a secretary who was never there. O'Byrne arrived after ten, a little drunk and in need of a bath to purge the faint purulent scent that lately had hung about his fingers. She sat on a small wooden stool to watch him luxuriate. Once she leaned forwards and touched his body where it broke the surface. O'Byrne's eyes were closed, his hands floating at his sides, the only sound the diminishing hiss of the cistern. Pauline rose quietly to bring a clean white towel from her bedroom, and O'Byrne did not hear her leave or return. She sat down again and ruffled, as far as it was possible, O'Byrne's damp, matted hair. "The food is ruined," she said without accusation. Beads of perspiration collected in the corners of O'Byrne's eyes and rolled down the line of his nose like tears. Pauline rested her hand on O'Byrne's knee where it jutted through the gray water. Steam turned to water on the cold walls, senseless minutes passed. "Never mind, love," said O'Byrne, and stood up.

Pauline went out to buy beer and pizzas, and O'Byrne lay down in her tiny bedroom to wait. Ten minutes passed. He dressed after cursory examination of his clean but swelling meatus, and wandered listlessly about the sitting room. Nothing interested him in Pauline's small collection of books. There were no magazines. He entered the kitchen in search of a drink. There was nothing but an overcooked meat pie. He picked around the burned bits and as he ate turned the pages of a picture calendar. When he finished he remembered again he was waiting for Pauline. He looked at his watch. She had been gone now almost half an hour. He stood up quickly, tipping the kitchen chair behind him to the floor. He paused in the sitting room and then walked decisively out of the flat and slammed the front door on his way. He hurried down the stairs, anxious not to meet her now he had decided to get out. But she was there. Halfway up the second flight, a little out of breath, her arms full of bottles and tinfoil parcels. "Where d'you get to?" said O'Byrne. Pauline stopped several steps down from him, her face tilted up awkwardly over her purchases, the whites of her eyes and the tinfoil vivid in the dark. "The usual place was closed. I had to walk miles . . . sorry." They stood. O'Byrne was not hungry. He wanted to go. He hitched his thumbs into the waist of his jeans and cocked his head towards the invisible ceiling, then he looked down at Pauline who waited. "Well," he said at last, "I was thinking of going." Pauline came up, and as she pushed past whispered, "Silly." O'Byrne turned and followed her, obscurely cheated.

He leaned in the doorway, she righted the chair. With a movement of his head O'Byrne indicated that he wanted none of the food Pauline was setting out on plates. She poured him a beer and knelt to gather a few black pastry droppings from the floor. They sat in the sitting room. O'Byrne drank, Pauline ate slowly, neither spoke. O'Byrne finished all the beer and placed his hand on Pauline's knee. She did not turn. He said cheerily, "What's wrong with you?" and she said, "Nothing." Alive with irritation O'Byrne moved closer and placed his arm protectively across her shoulders. "Tell you what," he half whispered. "Let's go to bed." Suddenly Pauline rose and went into the bedroom. O'Byrne sat with his hands clasped behind his head. He listened to Pauline undress, and he heard the creak of the bed. He got to his feet and, still without desire, entered the bedroom.

Pauline lay on her back and O'Byrne, having undressed quickly, lay beside her. She did not acknowledge him in her usual way, she did not move. O'Byrne raised his arm to stroke her shoulder, but instead let his hand fall back heavily against the sheet. They both lay on their backs in mounting silence, until O'Byrne decided to give her one last chance and with naked grunts hauled himself onto his elbow and arranged his face over hers. Her eyes, thick with tears, stared past him. "What's the matter?" he said in resignatory sing-song. The eyes budged a fraction and fixed into his own. "You," she said simply. O'Byrne returned to his side of the bed, and after a moment said threateningly, "I see." Then he was up, and on top of her, and then past her and on the far side of the room. "All right then . . ." he said. He wrenched his laces into a knot, and searched for his shirt. Pauline's back was to him. But as he crossed the sitting room her rising, accelerating wail of denial made him stop and turn. All white, in a cotton nightdress, she was there in the bedroom doorway and in the air, simultaneously at every point of arc in the intervening space, like the trick photographer's diver, she was on the far side of the room and she was at his lapels, knuckles in her mouth and shaking her head. O'Byrne smiled and put his arms around her shoulders. Forgiveness swept through him. Clinging to each other they returned to the bedroom. O'Byrne undressed and they lay down again, O'Byrne on his back, Pauline with her head pillowed on his shoulder.

O'Byrne said, "I never know what's going on in your mind," and deeply comforted by this thought, he fell asleep. Half an hour later he woke. Pauline, exhausted by a week of twelve-hour shifts, slept deeply on his arm. He shook her gently. "Hey," he said. He shook her firmly, and as the rhythm of her breathing broke and she began to stir, he said in a laconic parody of some unremembered film, "Hey, there's something we ain't done yet . . ."

Harold was excited. When O'Byrne walked into the shop towards noon the following day Harold took hold of his arm and waved in the air a sheet of paper. He was almost shouting. "I've worked it all out. I know what I want to do with the shop." "Oh, yeah," said O'Byrne dully, and put his fingers in his eyes and scratched till the intolerable itch there became a bearable pain. Harold rubbed his small pink hands together and explained rapidly. "I'm going All American. I spoke to their rep on the phone this morning and he'll be here in half an hour. I'm getting rid of all the quid a time piss-in-her-cunt letters. I'm gonna carry the whole of the House of Florence range at £4.50 a time."

O'Byrne walked across the shop to where Harold's jacket was spread across a chair. He tried it on. It was of course too small. "And I'm going to call it Transatlantic Books," Harold was saying. O'Byrne tossed the jacket onto the chair. It slid to the floor and deflated there like some reptilian air sac. Harold picked it up, and did not cease talking. "If I carry Florence exclusive

I get a special discount *and*"—he giggled—"they pay for the fucking neon sign."

O'Byrne sat down and interrupted his brother. "How many of those soddin' inflatable women did you unload? There's still twenty-five of the fuckers in the cellar." But Harold was pouring out scotch into two glasses. "He'll be here in half an hour," he repeated, and offered one glass to O'Byrne. "Big deal," said O'Byrne, and sipped. "I want you to take the van over to Norbury and collect the order this afternoon. I want to get into this straight away."

O'Byrne sat moodily with his drink while his brother whistled and was busy about the shop. A man came in and bought a magazine. "See," said O'Byrne sourly while the customer was still lingering over the tentacled condoms, "he bought English, didn't he?" The man turned guiltily and left. Harold came and crouched by O'Byrne's chair and spoke as one who explains copulation to an infant. "And what do I make? Forty per cent of 75p. Thirty p. Thirty fucking p. On House of Florence I'll make fifty percent of £4.50. And that"—he rested his hand briefly on O'Byrne's knee—"is what I call business."

O'Byrne wriggled his empty glass in front of Harold's face, and waited patiently for his brother to fill it . . . Little Runt.

The House of Florence warehouse was a disused church in a narrow terraced street on the Brixton side of Norbury. O'Byrne entered by the main porch. A crude plasterboard office and waiting room had been set up in the west end. The font was a large ashtray in the waiting room. An elderly woman with a blue rinse sat alone in the office typing. When O'Byrne tapped on the sliding window she ignored him, then she rose and slid aside the glass panel. She took the order form he pushed towards her, glancing at him with unconcealed distaste. She spoke primly. "You better wait there." O'Byrne tap-danced abstractedly about the font, and combed his hair, and whistled the tune that went in a circle. Suddenly a shriveled man with a brown coat and clipboard was at his side. "Transatlantic Books?" he said. O'Byrne shrugged and followed him. They moved together slowly down long aisles of bolted steel shelves, the old man pushing a large trolley and O'Byrne walking a little in front with his hands clasped behind his back. Every few yards the warehouseman stopped, and with bad-tempered gasps lifted a thick pile of magazines from the shelves. The load on the trolley grew. The old man's breath echoed hoarsely around the church. At the end of the first aisle he sat down on the trolley, between his neat piles, and coughed and hawked for a minute or so into a paper handkerchief. Then, carefully folding the tissue and its ponderous green contents back into his pocket, he said to O'Byrne, "Here, you're young. You push this thing." And O'Byrne said, "Push the fucker yourself. It's your job," and offered the man a cigarette and lit it for him.

O'Byrne nodded at the shelves. "You get some reading done here." The old man exhaled irritably. "It's all rubbish. It ought to be banned." They moved on. At the end, as he was signing the invoice, O'Byrne said, "Who you got lined up for tonight? Madam in the office there?" The warehouseman was pleased. His cackles rang out like bells, then tailed into another coughing fit. He leaned feebly against the wall, and when he had recovered sufficiently he raised his head and meaningfully winked his watery eye. But O'Byrne had turned and was wheeling the magazines out to the van.

Lucy was ten years older than Pauline, and a little plump. But her flat was large and comfortable. She was a sister and Pauline no more than a trainee nurse. They knew nothing of each other. At the underground station O'Byrne bought flowers for Lucy, and when she opened the door to him he presented them with a mock bow and the clicking of heels. "A peace offering?" she said contemptuously and took the daffodils away. She had led him into the bedroom. They sat down side by side on the bed. O'Byrne ran his hand up her leg in a perfunctory kind of way. She pushed away his arm and said, "Come on, then. Where have you been the past three days?" O'Byrne could barely remember. Two nights with Pauline, one night in the pub with friends of his brother.

He stretched back luxuriously on the pink candlewick. "You know . . . working late for Harold. Changing the shop around. That kind of thing."

"Those dirty books," said Lucy with a little high-pitched laugh.

O'Byrne stood up and kicked off his shoes. "Don't start that," he said, glad to be off the defensive. Lucy leaned forwards and gathered up his shoes. "You're going to ruin the backs of these," she said busily, "kicking them off like that."

They both undressed. Lucy hung her clothes neatly in the wardrobe. When O'Byrne stood almost naked before her she wrinkled her nose in disgust. "Is that you smelling?" O'Byrne was hurt. "I'll have a bath," he offered curtly.

Lucy stirred the bathwater with her hand, and spoke loudly over the thunder of the taps. "You should have brought me some clothes to wash." She hooked her fingers into the elastic of his shorts. "Give me these now and they'll be dry by the morning." O'Byrne laced his fingers into hers in a decoy of affection. "No, no," he shouted rapidly. "They were clean on this morning, they were." Playfully Lucy tried to get them off. They wrestled across the bathroom floor, Lucy shrieking with laughter, O'Byrne excited but determined.

Finally Lucy put on her dressing gown and went away. O'Byrne heard her in the kitchen. He sat in the bath and washed away the bright green stains. When Lucy returned his shorts were drying on the radiator. "Women's Lib, innit?" said O'Byrne from the bath. Lucy said, "I'm getting in too," and took off her dressing gown. O'Byrne made room for her. "Please yourself," he said with a smile as she settled herself in the gray water.

O'Byrne lay on his back on the clean white sheets, and Lucy eased herself onto his belly like a vast nesting bird. She would have it no other way, from the beginning she had said, "I'm in charge." O'Byrne had replied, "We'll see about that." He was horrified, sickened, that he could enjoy being overwhelmed, like one of those cripples in his brother's magazines. Lucy had spoken briskly, the kind of voice she used for difficult patients. "If you don't like it then don't come back." Imperceptibly O'Byrne was initiated into Lucy's wants. It was not simply that she wished to squat on him. She did not want him to move. "If you move again," she warned him once, "you've had it." From mere habit O'Byrne thrust upwards and deeper, and quick as the tongue of a snake she lashed his face several times with her open palm. On the instant she came, and afterwards lay across the bed, half sobbing, half laughing. O'Byrne, one side of his face swollen and pink, departed sulking. "You're a bloody pervert," he had shouted from the door.

Next day he was back, and Lucy agreed not to hit him again. Instead she abused him. "You pathetic, helpless little shit!" she would scream at the peak of her excitement. And she seemed to intuit O'Byrne's guilty thrill of pleasure, and wish to push it further. One time she had suddenly lifted herself clear of him and, with a far-away smile, urinated on his head and chest. O'Byrne had struggled to get clear, but Lucy held him down and seemed deeply satisfied by his unsought orgasm. This time O'Byrne left the flat enraged. Lucy's strong, chemical smell was with him for days, and it was during this time that he had met Pauline. But within the week he was back at Lucy's to collect, so he insisted, his razor, and Lucy was persuading him to try on her underwear. O'Byrne resisted with horror and excitement. "The trouble with you," said Lucy, "is that you're scared of what you like."

Now Lucy gripped his throat in one hand. "You dare move," she hissed, and closed her eyes. O'Byrne lay still. Above him Lucy swayed like a giant tree. Her lips were forming a word, but there was no sound. Many minutes later she opened her eyes and stared down, frowning a little as though struggling to place him. And all the while she eased backwards and forwards. Finally she spoke, more to herself than to him. "Worm . . ." O'Byrne moaned. Lucy's legs and thighs tightened and trembled. "Worm . . . worm . . . you little worm. I'm going to tread on you . . . dirty little worm." Once more her hand was closed about his throat. His eyes were sunk deep, and his word traveled a long way before it left his lips. "Yes," he whispered.

The following day O'Byrne attended the clinic. The doctor and his male assistant were matter-of-fact, unimpressed. The assistant filled out a form and wanted details of O'Byrne's recent sexual history. O'Byrne invented a whore at Ipswich bus station. For many days after that he kept to himself. Attending the clinic mornings and evenings, for injections, he was sapped of desire. When Pauline or Lucy phoned, Harold told them he did not know where O'Byrne was. "Probably taken off for somewhere," he said, winking across the shop at his brother. Both women phoned each day for three or four days, and then suddenly there were no calls from either.

O'Byrne paid no attention. The shop was taking in good money now. In the evenings he drank with his brother and his brother's friends. He felt himself to be both busy and ill. Ten days passed. With the extra cash Harold was giving him, he bought a leather jacket, like Harold's, but somehow better, sharper, lined with red imitation silk. It both shone and creaked. He spent many minutes in front of the fish-eye mirror, standing sideways on, admiring the manner in which his shoulders and biceps pulled the leather to a tight sheen. He wore his jacket between the shop and the clinic and sensed the glances of women in the street. He thought of Pauline and Lucy. He passed a day considering which to phone fist. He chose Pauline, and phoned her from the shop.

Trainee Nurse Shepherd was not available. O'Byrne was told after many minutes of waiting. She was taking an examination. O'Byrne had his call transferred to the other side of the hospital. "Hi," he said when Lucy picked up the phone. "It's me." Lucy was delighted. "When did you get back? Where have you been? When are you coming round?" He sat down. "How about tonight?" he said. Lucy whispered in sex-kitten French, "I can 'ardly wait . . ." O'Byrne laughed and pressed his thumb and forefinger against his forehead and heard other distant voices on the line. He heard Lucy giving instructions. Then she spoke rapidly to him. "I've got to go. They've just brought a case in. About eight tonight, then . . ." and she was gone.

O'Byrne prepared his story, but Lucy did not ask him where he had been. She was too happy. She laughed when she opened the door to him, she hugged him and laughed again. She looked different. O'Byrne could not remember her so beautiful. Her hair was shorter and a deeper brown, her nails were pale orange, she wore a short black dress with orange dots. There were candles and wine glasses on the dining table, music on the record player. She stood back, her eyes bright, almost wild, and admired his leather jacket. She ran her hands up the red lining. She pressed herself against it. "Very smooth," she said. "Reduced to sixty quid," O'Byrne said proudly, and tried to kiss her. But she laughed again and pushed him into a chair. "You wait there and I'll get something to drink."

O'Byrne lay back. From the corner a man sang of love in a restaurant with clean white tablecloths. Lucy brought an icy bottle of white wine. She sat on the arm of his chair and they drank and talked. Lucy told him recent stories of the ward, of nurses who fell in and out of love, patients who recovered or died. As she spoke she undid the top buttons of his shirt and pushed her hand down to his belly. And when O'Byrne turned in his chair and reached up for her she pushed him away, leaned down and kissed him on the nose. "Now, now," she said primly. O'Byrne exerted himself. He recounted anecdotes he had heard in the pub. Lucy laughed crazily at the end of each, and as he was beginning the third she let her hand drop lightly between his legs and rest there. O'Byrne closed his eyes. The hand was gone and Lucy was nudging him. "Go on," she said. "It was getting interesting." He caught her wrist and wanted to pull her onto his lap. With a little sigh she slipped away and returned with a second bottle. "We should have wine more often," she said, "if it makes you tell such funny stories."

Encouraged, O'Byrne told his story, something about a car and what a garage mechanic said to a vicar. Once again Lucy was fishing around his fly and laughing, laughing. It was a funnier story than he thought. The floor rose and fell beneath his feet. And Lucy so beautiful, scented, warm . . . her eyes glowed. He was paralyzed by her teasing. He loved her, and she laughed and robbed him of his will. Now he saw, he had come to live with her, and each night she teased him to the edge of madness. He pressed his face into her breasts. "I love you," he mumbled, and again Lucy was laughing, shaking, wiping the tears from her eyes. "Do . . . do you . . ." she kept trying to say. She emptied the bottle into his glass. "Here's a toast . . ." "Yeah," said O'Byrne. "To us." Lucy was holding down her laughter. "No, no," she squealed. "To *you*." All right," he said, and downed his wine in one swallow. Then Lucy was standing in front of him pulling his arm. "C'mon," she said. "C'mon." O'Byrne struggled out of the chair. "What about dinner, then?" he said. "You're the dinner," she said, and they giggled as they tottered towards the bedroom.

As they undressed Lucy said, "I've got a special little surprise for you so . . . no fuss." O'Byrne sat on the edge of Lucy's large bed and shivered. "I'm ready for anything," he said. "Good . . . good," and for the first time she kissed him deeply, and pushed him gently backwards onto the bed. She climbed forward and sat astride his chest. O'Byrne closed his eyes. Months ago he would have resisted furiously. Lucy lifted his left hand to her mouth and kissed each finger. "Hmmm . . . the first course." O'Byrne laughed. The bed and the room undulated softly about him. Lucy was pushing his hand towards the top corner of the bed. O'Byrne heard a distant jingle, like bells. Lucy knelt by his shoulder, holding down his wrist, buckling it to a leather strap. She had always said she would tie him up one day and fuck him. She bent low over his face and they kissed again. She was licking his eyes and whispering, "You're not going anywhere." O'Byrne gasped for air. He could not move his face to smile. Now she was tugging at his right arm, pulling it, stretching it to the far corner of the bed. With a dread thrill of compliance O'Byrne felt his arm die. Now that was secure and Lucy was running her hands along the inside of his thigh, and on down to his feet . . . He lay stretched almost to breaking, splitting, fixed to each corner, spread out against the white sheet. Lucy knelt at the apex of his legs. She stared down at him with a faint, objective smile, and fingered herself delicately. O'Byrne lay waiting for her to settle on him like a vast white nesting bird. She was tracing with the tip of one finger the curve of his excitement, and then with thumb and forefinger making a tight ring about its base. A sigh fled between his teeth. Lucy leaned forwards. Her eyes were wild. She whispered, "We're going to get you, me and Pauline are . . ."

Pauline. For an instant, syllables hollow of meaning. "What?" said O'Byrne, and as he spoke the word he remembered, and understood a threat. "Untie me," he said quickly. But Lucy's finger curled under her crotch and her eyes half closed. Her breathing was slow and deep. "Untie me," he shouted, and struggled hopelessly with his straps. Lucy's breath came now in light little gasps. As he struggled, so they accelerated. She was saying something . . . moaning something. What was she saying? He could not hear. "Lucy," he said, "please untie me." Suddenly she was silent, her eyes wide open and clear. She climbed off the bed. "Your friend Pauline will be here, soon," she said, and began to get dressed. She was different, her movements brisk and efficient, she no longer looked at him. O'Byrne tried to sound casual. His voice was a little high. "What's going on?" Lucy stood at the foot of the bed buttoning her dress. Her lip curled. "You're a bastard," she said. The doorbell rang and she smiled. "Now that's good timing, isn't it?"

"Yes, he went down very quietly," Lucy was saying as she showed Pauline into the bedroom. Pauline said nothing. She avoided looking at either O'Byrne or Lucy. And O'Byrne's eyes were fixed on the object she carried in her arms. It was large and silver, like an outsized electric toaster. "It can plug in just here," said Lucy. Pauline set it down on the bedside table. Lucy sat down at her dressing table and began to comb her hair. "I'll get some water for it in a minute," she said.

Pauline went and stood by the window. There was silence. Then O'Byrne said hoarsely, "What's that thing?" Lucy turned in her seat. "It's a sterilizer," she said breezily. "Sterilizer?" "You know, for sterilizing surgical instruments." The next question O'Byrne did not dare ask. He felt sick and dizzy. Lucy left the room. Pauline continued to stare out the window into the dark. O'Byrne felt the need to whisper. "Hey, Pauline, what's going on?" She turned to face him, and said nothing. O'Byrne discovered that the strap around his right wrist was slackening a little, the leather was stretching. His hand was concealed by pillows. He worked it backwards and forwards, and spoke urgently. "Look, let's get out of here. Undo these things."

For a moment she hesitated, then she walked around the side of the bed and stared down at him. She shook her head. "We're going to get you." The repetition terrified him. He thrashed from side to side. "It's not my idea of a fucking joke!" he shouted. Pauline turned away. "I hate you," he heard her say. The right-hand strap gave a little more. "I hate you. I hate you." He pulled till he thought his arm would break. His hand was too large still for the noose around his wrist. He gave up.

Now Lucy was at the bedside pouring water into the sterilizer. "This is a sick joke," said O'Byrne. Lucy lifted a flat black case onto the table. She snapped it open and began to take out long-handled scissors, scalpels and other bright, tapering silver objects. She lowered them carefully into the water. O'Byrne started to work his right hand again. Lucy removed the black case and set on the table two white kidney bowls with blue rims. In one lay two hypodermic needles, one large, one small. In the other was cotton wool. O'Byrne's voice shook. "What is all this?" Lucy rested her cool hand on his forehead. She enunciated with precision. "This is what they should have done for you at the clinic." "The clinic . . . ?" he echoed. He could see now that Pauline was leaning against the wall drinking from a bottle of scotch. "Yes," said Lucy, reaching down to take his pulse. "Stop you spreading round your secret little diseases." "And telling lies," said Pauline, her voice strained with indignation.

O'Byrne laughed uncontrollably. "Telling lies . . . telling lies," he spluttered. Lucy took the scotch from Pauline and raised it to her lips. O'Byrne recovered. His legs were shaking. "You're both out of your minds." Lucy tapped the sterilizer and said to Pauline, "This will take a few minutes yet. We'll scrub down in the kitchen." O'Byrne tried to raise his head. "Where are you going?" he called after them. "Pauline . . . Pauline."

But Pauline had nothing more to say. Lucy stopped in the bedroom doorway and smiled at him. "We'll leave you a pretty little stump to remember us by," she said, and she closed the door.

On the bedside table the sterilizer began to hiss. Shortly after, it gave out the low rumble of boiling water, and inside the instruments clinked together gently. In terror he pumped his hand. The leather was flaying the skin off his wrist. The noose was riding now around the base of his thumb. Timeless minutes passed. He whimpered and pulled, and the edge of the leather cut deep into his hand. He was almost free.

The door opened, and Lucy and Pauline carried in a small, low table. Through his fear O'Byrne felt excitement once more, horrified excitement. They arranged the table close to the bed. Lucy bent low over his erection. "Oh dear . . . oh dear," she murmured. With tongs Pauline lifted instruments from the boiling water and laid them out in neat silver rows on the starched white tablecloth she had spread across the table. The leather noose slipped forwards fractionally. Lucy sat on the edge of the bed and took the large hypodermic from the bowl. "This will make you a little sleepy," she promised. She held it upright and expelled a small jet of liquid. And as she reached for the cotton wool O'Byrne's arm pulled clear. Lucy smiled. She set aside the hypodermic. She leaned forwards once more . . . warm, scented . . . she was fixing him with wild red eyes . . . her fingers played over his tip . . . she held him still between her fingers. "Lie back, Michael, my sweet." She nodded briskly at Pauline. "If you'll secure that strap, Nurse Shepherd, then I think we can begin."

Steven Millhauser

Behind the Blue Curtain

(U N I T E D   S T A T E S)

On Saturday afternoons in summer my father took me to the movies. All morning long I waited for him to come down from his study, frowning at the bowl of his pipe and slapping the stairs with his slipper-moccasins, as though the glossy dark bowl, the slippers, the waiting itself were a necessary part of my long-drawn-out passage into the realm of dark. I savored every stage: the hot summer sunshine outside the ticket booth, the indoor sunlight of the entranceway with its glass-covered Coming Attractions and its velvet rope, the artificial glow of the red lobby, the mysterious dusk of the theater, the swift decisive darkening—and between the blue folds of the curtain, slowly parting, the sudden shining of the screen. Gravely my father had explained to me that the people on the screen were motionless photographs, passing quickly before my eyes. It was like my black-and-white flip-book from the candy store: a smiling mouse leaped from a diving board toward the water as a frowning shark rose up, opening its jaw wider and wider. And when you did it the other way, see!—the sinking jaws close, the upside-down mouse rises through the air and lands on his feet on the high board. My father was never wrong, but I felt he was trying to shield me from darker knowledge. The beings behind the curtain had nothing to do with childish flip-books or the long strips of gray negatives hanging in the kitchen from silver clips. They led their exalted lives beyond mine, in some other realm entirely, shining, desirable, impenetrable.

One Saturday afternoon when my father had to drive to the university on business, and my mother lay on two pillows in her darkened room, rasping with asthma, and my best friend was spending the day at his cousin Valerie's, it was decided that I could go to the movies alone. I knew that something forbidden was happening, but I greeted it with outward calm. After the second feature I was to go directly to the front of the theater and stand outside under the marquee, where my father would be waiting. I felt that the decision had been arrived at too hastily, that the careful, repeated instructions only revealed the danger in this sudden violation of the usual. I wondered whether I should warn my parents, but I remained silent and watchful. My father dropped me off at the ticket booth, where a short line had formed, and as I watched him drive away I felt an anxious exhilaration, as if in the pride of his knowledge he had failed to reckon with the powers of the dark.

Past the blue velvet rope on its silver post I stepped into the well-lit lobby with its red rug and glass-covered candy counter. The glossy wrappers brilliant under the counter lights, the high popcorn machine with its yellow glass that turned the popcorn butter-yellow, the crimson glow of a nearby exit sign, all these expressed the secret presence of the dark, which here made itself felt by the intensity of the effort to banish it. Behind me, through the open door leading back to the entranceway, I could see sunlight flashing on the glass of a Coming Attraction: in a green-black jungle a man in a pith helmet was taking aim with a rifle at something invisible in the blaze of obscuring light. I turned to the darkening corridor leading away from the candy counter. There the lights grew dim, as if they were candle-flames bending in the wind of the gathering dark, there the world was bathed in a reddish glow. I bought a box of popcorn and made my way along the glowing night of the corridor. The aisle surprised me: it sloped down more sharply than I had remembered. As I passed the arms of seats I felt a slight tugging at my calves, as if I were being pulled forward against my will. Impulsively I chose a row. I slipped past four chair-arms and pulled down a red, sagging seat. I leaned back eagerly, waiting for artificial night to fall, whispers of ushers, the cone of a flashlight beam in the darkened aisle.

Soon the lights went out, on the luminous curtain bright letters danced, the blue folds began to part; and sliding down, far down, I rested my popcorn on my stomach and pressed the back of my head against the fuzzy seat.

And suddenly it was over, the lights came on, people rose to go. Legs pushed past my knees, a coin clinked and someone bent over sharply, slapping at the floor. A foot kicked a popcorn box, a seat came up with a bang. Was it really over? The rolling coin struck something and stopped. A heaviness came over me—I could scarcely drag myself to my feet. Outside my father would be waiting under the marquee: one arm across his stomach, the elbow of the other arm in the palm of the first, the bowl of his pipe supported with thick fingers. I felt that I had let something slip away from me, that I had failed in some way, but my thoughts were sluggish and kept sinking out of sight.

At the top of the aisle I hesitated, looking with disappointment toward the band of sun streaming in through the open door. I went over to the drinking fountain and took a long swallow. At the darkening end of the corridor I noticed a sign that said REST ROOMS, with a red arrow pointing down. Perhaps my father had not arrived yet; the out-streaming crowd was dense, oppressive; I would only be two seconds. Slowly I descended the speckled stone steps, sliding my hand along the dark brass rail. In the men's room a teenager with slicked-back yellow hair and a black leather jacket stood wiping his hands on a soiled roller-towel. I slipped into a stall and listened with relief to the departing footsteps, the banging door. Two people entered without speaking and left one after the other. I felt weary and restless. I didn't know what I wanted. I did not move.

I must have fallen into a stupor or reverie, for I was startled by a clanking sound. I opened the door of the stall and saw an old man in droopy pants standing with his back to me beside a bucket of soapy water. He was slowly pushing a mop whose long gray strings moved first one way, then the other. The mop left glistening patches on the white-and-black tiles. I tiptoed out of the bathroom as if I had been guilty of something and began climbing the stairway, which seemed darker than before. It was very quiet. At the top of the stairs I came to the corridor, now empty and still. At the other end the darkened candy counter was lit by a single bulb. The theater appeared to be deserted. I was nervous and calm, nervous and calm. Nearby I saw the row of closed doors leading to the entranceway; under the doors I could see a disturbing line of sunlight. And clattering around a turn in the spookhouse, suddenly you see a sliver of light at the bottom of the black walls. My father would be striding up and down, up and down, looking at his sunny watch. He would talk to the girl in the ticket booth. All at once a desire erupted in me with such force that I felt as if I had been struck in both temples.

I stepped onto a downward-sloping aisle and plunged into the soothing half-dark, penetrated by the odor of old dark red seat cushions, butter-stained cardboard popcorn boxes, the sticky sweetness of spilled soda. On one seat I saw a fat rubber nose with a broken elastic string. At the end of the aisle I stepped over to the wall and reached up my hand, but the bottom of the great curtain was high above my straining fingers. It was set back, leaving a ledge. The thick dark folds looked heavy as marble. It seemed to me that if only I could touch that curtain, if only I could push it aside and stare for one second at the fearful blankness of the screen, and perhaps graze the magic whiteness with my fingers, then my deep restlessness would be stilled, my heart would grow calm, I could turn away from the theater and hurry back, quickly quickly, to my waiting father, who at any moment was going to burst through the doors or drive away forever. I walked along the wall, desperately searching for something to stand on, say a popcorn box or one of those tall ashtrays with white sand that I had seen near the blue velvet rope. I saw nothing but an empty, carefully folded silver gum-wrapper with its phantom stick of gum. High overhead the curtain stretched away. As I approached the end of the curtain the lower wall curved slightly and I saw a narrow flight of six steps going up. The stairs were cut into the wall. The top stair was half concealed by the final fold of the curtain.

With a glance over my shoulder I climbed swiftly and began to push at the velvety thick folds, which enveloped my arm and barely moved. I had the sense that the curtain was slowly waking, like some great, disturbed animal. Somehow I pushed the final, sluggish fold aside and found myself before a flaking wooden door with a dented metal knob. The door opened easily. I stepped into a small room, scarcely larger than a closet. I saw dark brooms, mops in buckets, dustpans, a bulging burlap sack in one corner, an usher's jacket hanging from a nail; in the back wall I made out part of a second door.

Stepping carefully over buckets, cans, and bottles I felt for the knob. The door opened onto a narrow corridor carpeted in red. Glass candle-flames glowed in brass sconces high on the walls. There were no doors. At the end of the passage I came to a flight of red-carpeted stairs going down. I descended to a landing; over the polished wooden rail I saw landings within landings, dropping away. At the bottom of the seventh landing I found myself in another corridor. Through high, open doorways I caught glimpses of festive rooms. I heard footsteps along the corridor and stepped through one of the tall doors.

In the uncanny light of reddish gas lamps, many-branched candelabra, and chandeliers with flaming candles, I saw them taking their ease. They were splendidly costumed, radiantly themselves, expressing their natures through grand and flawless gestures. They lolled against walls, strolled idly about, displayed themselves on great armchairs and couches. I wasn't surprised by their massiveness, which suited their extravagant natures, and I looked up at them as if gazing up at the screen from the second row. Even the furniture loomed; my head barely came over the cushions of armchairs.

They seemed to pay no attention to me as I made my way among the great chairs and couches and came to an open place with a high table. Beside it strode a figure with flowering black hair, a great crimson cape, and a glittering sword. He seized a gold goblet and took an immense swallow, while beside him a bearded figure with a leather helmet bearing two sharp silver horns burst into rich laughter, and a lady with high-piled hair and a hoop dress covered with ruffles turned to look over her rapidly fluttering fan. Passing under the table I came to a great couch where a queen with ink-black hair and blue eyelids lay on her side looking coldly before her as she stroked a white cat. Beside her stood a grim figure with a skull and crossbones on his three-cornered hat, a red scarf at his throat, a long-barreled pistol thrust through his belt, and loose pants plunging into thick, cracked boots. I passed the couch and saw on the other side a jungle girl dressed in a leopardskin loincloth and a vineleaf halter, standing with her hands on her hips and her head flung back haughtily as two gray-haired gentlemen in white dinner jackets bent forward to peer through monocles at a jewel in her navel. Farther away I saw a figure in green with a quiver of cloth yard arrows on his back and a stout quarterstaff in one hand, standing beside a tall, mournful ballerina whose shiny dark hair was pulled so tightly back that it looked like painted wood, and far across the room, through high, open doorways, I saw other rooms and other figures, stretching back and back.

Though shy of their glances, I soon realized I had nothing to fear from them. At first I thought they failed to notice me, or, noticing me, shrugged their shoulders and returned to their superior lives. But gradually I recognized that my presence, far from being ignored, inspired them to be more grandly themselves. For weren't they secretly in need of being watched, these lofty creatures, did they not become themselves through the act of being witnessed?

Through a wide doorway I wandered into another room, and then into a third—and always through open doorways I saw other figures, other rooms. The very abundance that drew me proved quickly tiring, and I looked for a quiet place to sit before returning to my father, who perhaps at this very moment was pushing open the glass doors and striding toward the blue velvet rope. He would step into the empty theater and stare at the dark seats, the closed curtain, the red-glowing exit signs. Downstairs in the rest room he would find an old man in droopy pants who would look up with red-rimmed eyes and shake his head slowly: no, no. On the rung of a tall wooden chair I sat down, hooking one arm around the thick leg. Almost at once I became aware of someone pacing up and down before me. She walked close to my chair in a great swirl of petticoats, her ruffled skirts shaking as she walked. She sighed deeply and petulantly, over and over again, and from time to time I caught snatches of muttered monologue: ". . . have to do something . . . impossible . . . unbearable . . ." Suddenly she sat down on a chair opposite; I saw a flowery burst of petticoats settling against white stockings, but she sprang up and continued her odd pantomime, gradually moving away so that I was able to catch a glimpse of her: a tumult of bouncing blond curls shaped like small tubes, a pouting red mouth and round blue eyes, a neckline that exposed the top third of high, very white breasts, which appeared to be pressed tightly upward. When she walked, all her curls shook like bells, the tops of her breasts shook, her skirts bounced up and down, her eyelids fluttered, her plump cheeks trembled; only her little nose was still. Sometimes she glanced in my direction, but not at me. All at once she stamped her foot, pushed out her bottom lip, and swished away, glancing for a moment over her shoulder. It was clear that she expected to be followed, that she always expected to be followed, and without hesitation I slipped from my rung.

She pushed open a door and I followed her into a red room brilliant with mirrors and the flames of many candles. I saw a high white armchair, a great dressing table with a soaring mirror. Smaller mirrors hung on each wall; the dark red wallpaper was patterned with little pale princesses leaning out of silver towers with their long flaxen hair. She stepped onto a stool before a swivel mirror and clapped her hands sharply twice. An elderly woman in a black dress appeared and began removing her ball gown with its flounced skirts and blue bows. Then she removed another skirt under that, and several petticoats, leaving a billowy, frilled petticoat and a satiny white corset with crisscross laces in back. "Thank you, Maria, now go away, go away, go away now . . ." For a while she stared at herself in the tall mirror, than hopped from the stool and began pacing about, glancing at herself in the swivel mirror, in the mirror over the dressing table, in the mirrors on the walls, in a silver bowl. The room filled with images of her, turning this way and that. As she paced and turned she heaved great sighs, and pushed out her bottom lip, and tossed her curls, and muttered to herself: "get away with . . . just who does he . . . can't breathe in here . . ." Though she paid not the slightest attention to me, I felt that my presence permitted her to display her petulance with the richness she required; and as she pranced and pouted she tugged at a fastening at the front of her corset, she kicked off her shoes, she unbound her high-piled hair, which spilled down her flame-lit shoulders and shook as she moved. And as she flickered and shook before me I felt a vague excitement, my skin began to tingle, as if she were brushing against me with her thick, shaking curls, her trembling skin, her white silk stockings. All at once the shaking stopped and I saw her raise the back of a hand to her forehead. Slowly, like a falling leaf, she swooned onto the dark red rug.

I had no thought of calling for help, for the swoon had been executed with such elegance that I felt certain she had intended it to be admired. She lay on the floor between the lion-paw legs of the chair and the red wallpaper. Her heavy yellow ringlets were strewn about her face and shoulders, her lips were partly open, her stomach moved gently up and down, the lines and bands of her corset went in and out, in and out. I stepped over to her and looked down. An unaccountable desire seized me: I wanted to feel the satiny material of her corset, I wanted to place my hand against the fire-lit white breathing cloth. In her white slip my mother had sat at the edge of the bed, drawing on a stocking. Slowly the corset bands went in and out. I bent over, careful not to touch the breathing form in any way; the skin of my palm prickled; I felt tense and anxious, as if I were about to transgress a law. And as I lowered my palm against the forbidden white cloth with its stretching and contracting bands I felt my hand sinking through melting barriers, as when, on a trip to New Hampshire with my parents, one morning I had walked through thick white cottony mist that lay heavy on the grass and parted like air as I passed. So my hand fell through the whiteness of that cloth. My sinking hand struck the velvety hard rug—I felt myself losing my balance—suddenly I was falling through her, plunging through her corset, her breasts, her bones, her blood. For a fearful instant I was inside her. I had a sensation of whiteness or darkness, a white darkness. On the sudden rug I rolled wildly through her, wildly out of her, and sprang up. Blood beat in my temples. She lay there drowsily. My whole body tingled, as if I had dried myself roughly with a towel.

I stared at my hands and shirt and pants as if fearing to see little pieces of cloth and flesh stuck to them, but I saw only myself.

A moment later she sat up, shook her headful of thick, springy curls, and pulled herself lightly to her feet. "Why I must have . . . fainted or . . . Maria! Oh, where is that woman?" She began pacing up and down, sighing, pouting, flinging back her hair; a corner of her flying petticoat rippled through my hand, which I snatched away; and in the many mirrors her many images appeared and reappeared, thrusting out their bottom lips, darting glances, fluttering their many eyelids.

I didn't know whether I was relieved or bitterly unhappy. Would I have guessed her secret? I knew only that I wanted to go.

In the doorway I stopped and half turned to look at her. Fiercely she paced, exuberantly she sulked, in the full radiance of her being. I was tempted to say something, to shout, to draw attention to myself in some way, but the desire drained swiftly out of me. A shout, a scream, a knife in the throat, a plunge to the death, all were quite useless here.

I stepped through the door and looked for the room I had come from, but found myself in an alien room filled with harsh laughter. I was careful not to touch any of them as I passed. Through a nearby doorway I emerged in a corridor that led to another room, another doorway, another room. I came to an upward-sloping corridor lined with shimmering mirrors; the sudden repetition of my anxious face gave me the sensation that my anxiety had increased in a burst. At the end of the corridor I climbed three steps to a closed door. I opened it and found myself in a dusky room I had never seen before, with many seats and a dark wall-hanging that resembled a curtain; gradually I recognized the theater.

I had entered by another door, beside one of the red-glowing exit signs. I hurried up the sloping aisle, stopped for a moment in the lobby to glance toward the sign that said REST ROOMS, then pushed open one of the metal doors and stepped into the sun-flooded entranceway.

A kneeling usher was sweeping a pile of candy wrappers and cigarette butts into a dustpan. In the white sand of a standing ashtray a slanting white straw cast a rippling shadow across a piece of bright yellow cellophane. The man in the pith helmet was taking aim at a tree concealing an orange tiger upon whose back sat a woman in a black fur loincloth. Through the brilliant glass doors I saw my father frowning at his watch. His look of stern surprise, when he saw me burst through the door into the late-afternoon sun, struck me as wildly funny, and I forgot to chasten my features into repentance as I seized his warm hand.

Lorrie Moore

Willing

(UNITED STATES)

How can I live my life without committing an act with a giant scissors?
— JOYCE CAROL OATES, "An Interior Monologue"

In her last picture, the camera had lingered at the hip, the naked hip, and even though it wasn't her hip, she acquired a reputation for being willing.

"You have the body," studio heads told her over lunch at Chasen's.

She looked away, "Habeas corpus," she said, not smiling.

"Pardon me?" A hip that knew Latin. Christ.

"Nothing," she said. They smiled at her and dropped names. Scorsese, Brando. Work was all playtime to them, playtime with gel in their hair. At times, she felt bad that it *wasn't* her hip. It should have been her hip. A mediocre picture, a picture queasy with pornography: these, she knew, eroticized the unavailable. The doctored and false. The stand-in. Unwittingly, she had participated. Let a hip come between. A false, unavailable, anonymous hip. She herself was true as a goddamn dairy product; available as lunch whenever.

But she was pushing forty.

She began to linger in juice bars. Sit for entire afternoons in places called I Love Juicy or Orange-U-Sweet. She drank juice and, outside, smoked a cigarette now and then. She'd been taken seriously—once—she knew that. Projects were discussed: Nina. Portia. Mother Courage with makeup. Now her hands trembled too much, even drinking juice, *especially* drinking juice, a Vantage wobbling between her fingers like a compass dial. She was sent scripts in which she was supposed to say lines she would never say, not wear clothes she would never not wear. She began to get obscene phone calls, and postcards signed, "Oh yeah, baby." Her boyfriend, a director with a growing reputation for expensive flops, a man who twice a week glowered at her Fancy Sunburst guppy and told it to get a job, became a Catholic and went back to his wife.

"Just when we were working out the bumps and chops and rocks," she said. Then she wept.

"I know," he said. "I know."

And so she left Hollywood. Phoned her agent and apologized. Went home to Chicago, rented a room by the week at the Days Inn, drank sherry, and grew a little plump. She let her life get dull—dull, but with Hostess cakes.

There were moments bristling with deadness, when she looked out at her life and went "*What?*" Or worse, feeling interrupted and tired, "Wha—?" It had taken on the shape of a terrible mistake. She hadn't been given the proper tools to make a real life with, she decided, that was it. She'd been given a can of gravy and a hairbrush and told, "There you go." She'd stood there for years, blinking and befuddled, brushing the can with the brush.

Still, she was a minor movie star, once nominated for a major award. Mail came to her indirectly. A notice. A bill. A Thanksgiving card. But there was never a party, a dinner, an opening, an iced tea. One of the problems with people in Chicago, she remembered, was that they were never lonely at the same time. Their sadnesses occurred in isolation, lurched and spazzed, sent them spinning fizzily back into empty, padded corners, disconnected and alone.

She watched cable and ordered in a lot from a pizza place. A life of obscurity and radical calm. She rented a piano and practiced scales. She invested in the stock market. She wrote down her dreams in the morning to locate clues as to what to trade. *Disney*, her dreams said once. *St. Jude's Medical.* She made a little extra money. She got obsessed. The words *cash cow* nestled in the side of her mouth like a cud. She tried to be original—not a good thing with stocks— and she began to lose. When a stock went down, she bought more of it, to catch it on the way back up. She got confused. She took to staring out the window at Lake Michigan, the rippled slate of it like a blackboard gone bad.

"Sidra, *what* are you doing there?" shrieked her friend Tommy long distance over the phone. "Where are you? You're living in some state that borders on North Dakota!" He was a screenwriter in Santa Monica and once, a long time ago and depressed on Ecstasy, they had slept together. He was gay, but they had liked each other very much.

"Maybe I'll get married," she said. She didn't mind Chicago. She thought of it as a cross between London and Queens, with a dash of Cleveland.

"Oh, *please*," he shrieked again. "What are you *really* doing?"

"Listening to seashore and self-esteem tapes," she said. She blew air into the mouth of the phone.

"Sounds like dust on the needle," he said. "Maybe you should get the squawking crickets tape. Have you *heard* the squawking crickets tape?"

"I got a bad perm today," she said. "When I was only halfway through with the rod part, the building the salon's in had a blackout. There were men drilling out front who'd struck a cable."

"How awful for you," he said. She could hear him tap his fingers. He had made himself the make-believe author of a make-believe book of essays called *One Man's Opinion*, and when he was bored or inspired, he quoted from it. "I was once in a rock band called Bad Perm," he said instead.

"Get out." She laughed.

His voice went hushed and worried. "What *are* you *doing* there?" he asked again.

Her room was a corner room where a piano was allowed. It was L-shaped, like a life veering off suddenly to become something else. It had a couch and two maple dressers and was never as neat as she might have wanted. She always had the DO NOT DISTURB sign on when the maids came by, and so things got a little out of hand. Wispy motes of dust and hair the size of small heads bumped around in the corners. Smudge began to darken the moldings and cloud the mirrors. The bathroom faucet dripped, and, too tired to phone anyone, she tied a string around the end of it, guiding the drip quietly into the drain, so it wouldn't bother her anymore. Her only plant, facing east in the window, hung over the popcorn popper and dried to a brown crunch. On the ledge, a jack-o'-lantern she had carved for Halloween had rotted, melted, froze, and now looked like a collapsed basketball—one she might have been saving for sentimental reasons, one from the *big game!* The man who brought her room service each morning—two poached eggs and a pot of coffee—reported her to the assistant manager, and she received a written warning slid under the door.

On Fridays, she visited her parents in Elmhurst. It was still hard for her father to look her in the eyes. He was seventy now. Ten years ago, he had gone to the first movie she had ever been in, saw her remove her clothes and dive into a pool. The movie was rated PG, but he never went to another one. Her mother went to all of them and searched later for encouraging things to say. Even something small. She refused to lie. "I liked the way you said the line about leaving home, your eyes wide and your hands fussing with your dress buttons," she wrote. "That red dress was so becoming. You should wear bright colors!"

"My father takes naps a lot when I visit," she said to Tommy.

"Naps?"

"I embarrass him. He thinks I'm a whore hippie. A hippie whore."

"That's ridiculous. As I said in *One Man's Opinion,* you're the most sexually conservative person I know."

"Yeah, well."

Her mother always greeted her warmly, puddle-eyed. These days, she was reading thin paperback books by a man named Robert Valleys, a man who said that after observing all the suffering in the world—war, starvation, greed—he had discovered the cure: hugs.

Hugs, hugs, hugs, hugs, hugs.

Her mother believed him. She squeezed so long and hard that Sidra, like an infant or a lover, became lost in the feel and smell of her—her sweet, dry skin, the gray peach fuzz on her neck. "I'm so glad you left that den of iniquity," her mother said softly.

But Sidra got calls from the den. At night, sometimes the director phoned from a phone booth, desiring to be forgiven as well as to direct. "I think of all the things you might be thinking, and I say, 'Oh, Christ.' I mean, do you think the things I sometimes think you do?"

"Of course," said Sidra. "Of course I think those things."

"*Of course! Of course* is a term that has no place in this conversation!"

When Tommy phoned, she often felt a pleasure so sudden and flooding, it startled her.

"God, I'm so glad it's you!"

"You have no right to abandon American filmmaking this way!" he would say affectionately, and she would laugh loudly, for minutes without stopping. She was starting to have two speeds: Coma and Hysteria. Two meals: breakfast and popcorn. Two friends: Charlotte Peveril and Tommy. She could hear the clink of his bourbon glass. "You are too gifted a person to be living in a state that borders on North Dakota."

"Iowa."

"Holy bejesus, it's worse than I thought. I'll bet they say that there. I'll bet they say 'Bejesus.' "

"I live downtown. They don't say that here."

"Are you anywhere near Champaign-Urbana?"

"No."

"I went there once. I thought from its name that it would be a different kind of place. I kept saying to myself, 'Champagne, ur*bah* na, *champagne,* ur*bah* na! Champagne! Urbana!' " He sighed. "It was just this thing in the middle of a field. I went to a Chinese restaurant there and ordered my entire dinner with *extra* MSG."

"I'm in Chicago. It's not so bad."

"Not so bad. There are no movie people there. Sidra, what about your *acting talent?*"

"I have no acting talent."

"Hello?"

"You heard me."

"I'm not sure. For a minute there, I thought maybe you had that dizziness thing again, that inner-ear imbalance."

"Talent. I don't have *talent.* I have willingness. What *talent?*" As a kid, she had always told the raunchiest jokes. As an adult, she could rip open a bone and speak out of it. Simple, clear. There was never anything to stop her. Why was there never anything to stop her? "I can stretch out the neck of a sweater to point at a freckle on my shoulder. Anyone who didn't get enough attention in nursery school can do that. Talent is something else."

"Excuse me, okay? I'm only a screenwriter. But someone's got you thinking you went from serious actress to aging bimbo. That's ridiculous. You just have to weather things a little out here. Besides. I think willing yourself to do a thing is brave, and the very essence of talent."

Sidra looked at her hands, already chapped and honeycombed with bad weather, bad soap, bad life. She needed to listen to the crickets tape. "But I *don't* will myself," she said. "I'm just already willing."

She began to go to blues bars at night. Sometimes she called Charlotte Peveril, her one friend left from high school.

"Siddy, how are you?" In Chicago, Sidra was thought of as a hillbilly name. But in L.A., people had thought it was beautiful and assumed she'd made it up.

"I'm fine. Let's go get drunk and listen to music."

Sometimes she just went by herself.

"Don't I know you from the movies?" a man might ask at one of the breaks, smiling, leering in a twinkly way.

"Maybe," she'd say, and he would look suddenly panicked and back away.

One night, a handsome man in a poncho, a bad poncho—though was there such a thing as a good poncho? asked Charlotte—sat down next to her with an extra glass of beer. "You look like you should be in the movies," he said. Sidra nodded wearily. "But I don't go to the movies. So if you *were* in the movies, I would never have gotten to set my eyes on you."

She turned her gaze from his poncho to her sherry, then back. Perhaps he had spent some time in Mexico or Peru. "What do you do?"

"I'm an auto mechanic." He looked at her carefully. "My name's Walter. Walt." He pushed the second beer her way. "The drinks here are okay as long as you don't ask them to mix anything. Just don't ask them to mix anything!"

She picked it up and took a sip. There was something about him she liked: something earthy beneath the act. In L.A., beneath the act you got nougat or Styrofoam. Or glass. Sidra's mouth was lined with sherry. Walt's lips shone with beer. "What's the last movie you saw?" she asked him.

"The last movie I saw. Let's see." He was thinking, but she could tell he wasn't good at it. She watched with curiosity the folded-in mouth, the tilted head: at last a guy who didn't go to the movies. His eyes rolled back like the casters on a clerk's chair, searching. "You know what I saw?"

"No. What?" She was getting drunk.

"It was this cartoon movie." Animation. She felt relieved. At least it wasn't one of those bad art films starring what's-her-name. "A man is asleep, having a dream about a beautiful little country full of little people." Walt sat back, looked around the room, as if that were all.

"*And?*" She was going to have to push and pull with this guy.

" 'And?' " he repeated. He leaned forward again. "And one day the people realize that they are only creatures in this man's dream. Dream people! And if the man wakes up, they will no longer exist!"

Now she hoped he wouldn't go on. She had changed her mind a little.

"So they all get together at a town meeting and devise a plan," he continued. Perhaps the band will be back soon. "They will burst into the man's bedroom and bring him back to a padded, insulated room in the town—the town of his own dream—and there they will keep watch over him to make sure he stays asleep. And they do just that. Forever and ever, everyone guarding him carefully, but apprehensively, making sure he never wakes up." He smiled. "I forget what the name of it was."

"And he never wakes up."

"Nope." He grinned at her. She liked him. She could tell he could tell. He took a sip of his beer. He looked around the bar, then back at her. "Is this a great country or what?" he said.

She smiled at him, with longing. "Where do you live," she asked, "and how do I get there?"

"I met a man," she told Tommy on the phone. "His name is Walter."

"A forced relationship. You're in a state of stress—you're in a *syndrome,* I can tell. You're going to force this romance. What does he do?"

"Something with cars." She sighed. "I want to sleep with someone. When I'm sleeping with someone, I'm less obsessed with the mail."

"But perhaps you should just be alone, be by yourself for a while."

"Like you've ever been alone," said Sidra. "I mean, have you *ever* been alone?"

"I've been alone."

"Yeah, and for how long?"

"Hours," said Tommy. He sighed. "At least it felt like hours."

"Right," she said. "so don't go lecturing me about inner resources."

"Okay. So I sold the mineral rights to my body years ago, but, hey, at least *I* got good money for mine."

"I got some money," said Sidra. "I got some."

Walter leaned her against his parked car. His mouth was slightly lopsided, paisley-shaped, his lips anneloid and full, and he kissed her hard. There was something numb and on hold in her. There were small dark pits of annihilation she discovered in her heart, in the loosening fist of it, and she threw herself into them, falling. She went home with him, slept with him. She told him who she was. A minor movie star once nominated for a major award. She told him she lived in the Days Inn. He had been there once, to the top, for a drink. But he did not seem to know her name.

"Never thought I'd sleep with a movie star," he did say. "I suppose that's every man's dream." He laughed—lightly, nervously.

"Just don't wake up," she said. Then she pulled the covers to her chin.

"Or change the dream," he added seriously. "I mean, in the movie I saw, everything is fine until the sleeping guy begins to dream about something else. I don't think he wills it or anything; it just happens."

"You didn't tell me about that part."

"That's right," he said. "You see, the guy starts dreaming about flamingos and then all the little people turn into flamingos and fly away."

"Really?" said Sidra.

"I *think* it was flamingos. I'm not too expert with birds."

"You're *not*?" She was trying to tease him, but it came out wrong, like a lizard with a little hat on.

"To tell you the truth, I really don't think I ever saw a single movie you were in."

"Good." She was drifting, indifferent, no longer paying attention.

He hitched his arm behind his head, wrist to nape. His chest heaved up and down. "I think I may of *heard* of you, though."

Django Reinhardt was on the radio. She listened, carefully. "Astonishing sounds came from that man's hands," Sidra murmured.

Walter tried to kiss her, tried to get her attention back. He wasn't that interested in music, though at times he tried to be. " 'Astonishing sounds'?" he said. "Like this?" He cupped his palms together, making little pops and suction noises.

"Yeah," she murmured. But she was elsewhere, letting a dry wind sweep across the plain of her to sleep. "Like that."

He began to realize, soon, that she did not respect him. A bug could sense it. A doorknob could figure it out. She never quite took him seriously. She would talk about films and film directors, then look at him and say, "Oh, never mind." She was part of some other world. A world she no longer liked.

And now she was somewhere else. Another world she no longer liked.

But she was willing. Willing to give it a whirl. Once in a while, though she tried not to, she asked him about children, about having children, about turning kith to kin. How did he feel about all that? It seemed to her that if she were ever going to have a life of children and lawn mowers and grass clippings, it would be best to have it with someone who was not demeaned or trivialized by discussions of them. Did he like those big fertilized lawns? How about a nice rock garden? How did he feel deep down about those combination storm windows with the built-in screens?

"Yeah, I like them all right," he said, and she would nod slyly and drink a little too much. She would try then not to think too strenuously about her *whole life.* She would try to live life one day at a time, like an alcoholic—drink, don't drink, drink. Perhaps she should take drugs.

"I always thought someday I would have a little girl and name her after my grandmother." Sidra sighed, peered wistfully into her sherry.

"What was your grandmother's name?"

Sidra looked at his paisley mouth. "Grandma. Her name was Grandma." Walter laughed in a honking sort of way. "Oh, thank you," murmured Sidra. "Thank you for laughing."

Walter had a subscription to *AutoWeek.* He flipped through it in bed. He also liked to read repair manuals for new cars, particularly the Toyotas. He knew a lot about control panels, light-up panels, side panels.

"You're so obviously wrong for each other," said Charlotte over tapas at a tapas bar.

"Hey, please," said Sidra. "I think my taste's a little subtler than that." The thing with tapas bars was that you just kept stuffing things into your mouth. "Obviously wrong is just the beginning. That's where *I always* begin. At obviously wrong." In theory, she liked the idea of mismatched couples, the wrangling and retangling, like a comedy by Shakespeare.

"I can't imagine you with someone like him. He's just not special." Charlotte had met him only once. But she had heard of him from a girlfriend of hers. He had slept around, she'd said. "Into the pudding" is how she phrased it, and there were some boring stories. "Just don't let him humiliate you. Don't mistake a lack of sophistication for sweetness," she added.

"I'm supposed to wait around for someone special, while every other girl in this town gets to have a life."

"I don't know, Sidra."

It was true. Men could be with whomever they pleased. But women had to date better, kinder, richer, and bright, bright, bright, or else people got embarrassed. It suggested sexual things. "I'm a very average person," she said desperately, somehow detecting that Charlotte already knew that, knew the deep, dark, wildly obvious secret of that, and how it made Sidra slightly pathetic, unseemly—*inferior,* when you got right down to it. Charlotte studied Sidra's face, headlights caught in the stare of a deer. Guns don't kill people, thought Sidra fizzily. Deer kill people.

"Maybe it's that we all used to envy you so much," Charlotte said a little bitterly. "You were so talented. You got all the lead parts in the plays. You were everyone's dream of what *they* wanted."

Sidra poked around at the appetizer in front of her, gardening it like a patch of land. She was unequal to anyone's wistfulness. She had made too little of her life. Its loneliness shamed her like a crime. "Envy," said Sidra. "That's a lot like hate, isn't it." But Charlotte didn't say anything. Probably she wanted Sidra to change the subject. Sidra stuffed her mouth full of feta cheese and onions, and looked up. "Well, all I can say is, I'm glad to be back." A piece of feta dropped from her lips.

Charlotte looked down at it and smiled. "I know what you mean," she said. She opened her mouth wide and let all the food inside fall out onto the table.

Charlotte could be funny like that. Sidra had forgotten that about her.

Walter had found some of her old movies in the video-rental place. She had a key. She went over one night and discovered him asleep in front of *Recluse with Roommate*. It was about a woman named Rose who rarely went out, because when she did, she was afraid of people. They seemed like alien life-forms—soulless, joyless, speaking asyntactically. Rose quickly became loosened from reality. Walter had it freeze-framed at the funny part, where Rose phones the psych ward to have them come take her away, but they refuse. She lay down next to him and tried to sleep, too, but began to cry a little. "What's wrong?" he asked.

"Nothing. You fell asleep. Watching me."

"I was tired," he said.

"I guess so."

"Let me kiss you. Let me find your panels." His eyes were closed. She could be anybody.

"Did you like the beginning part of the movie?" This need in her was new. Frightening. It made her hair curl. When had she ever needed so much?

"It was okay," he said.

"So what is this guy, a race-car driver?" asked Tommy.

"No, he's a mechanic."

"Ugh! Quit him like a music lesson!"

"Like *a music lesson*? What is this, *Similes from the Middle Class? One Man's Opinion*?" She was irritated.

"Sidra. This is not right! You need to go out with someone really smart for a change."

"I've been out with smart. I've been out with someone who had two Ph.D.'s. We spent all of our time in bed with the light on, proofreading his vita." She sighed. "Every little thing he'd ever done, every little, little, little. I mean, have you ever seen a vita?"

Tommy sighed, too. He had heard this story of Sidra's before. "Yes," he said. "I thought Patti LuPone was great."

"Besides," she said. "Who says he's not smart?"

The Japanese cars were the most interesting. Though the Americans were getting sexier, trying to keep up with them. *Those Japs!*

"Let's talk about my world," she said.

"What world?"

"Well, something *I'm* interested in. Something where there's something in it for me."

"Okay." He turned and dimmed the lights, romantically. "Got a stock tip for you," he said.

She was horrified, dispirited, interested.

He told her the name of a company somebody at work invested in. AutVis.

"What is it?"

"I don't know. But some guy at work said buy this week. They're going to make some announcement. If I had money, I'd buy."

She bought, the very next morning. A thousand shares. By the afternoon, the stock had plummeted 10 percent; by the following morning, 50. She watched the ticker tape go by on the bottom of the TV news channel. She had become the major stockholder. The major stockholder of a dying company! Soon they were going to be calling her, wearily, to ask what she wanted done with the forklift.

"You're a neater eater than I am," Walter said to her over dinner at the Palmer House.

She looked at him darkly. "What the hell were you thinking of, recommending that stock?" she asked. "How could you be such an irresponsible idiot?" She saw it now, how their life would be together. She would yell; then he would yell. He would have an affair; then she would have an affair. And then they would be gone and gone, and they would live in that gone.

"I got the name wrong," he said. "Sorry."

"You what?"

"It wasn't AutVis. It was AutDrive. I kept thinking it was vis for vision."

" 'Vis for vision,' " she repeated.

"I'm not that good with names," confessed Walter. "I do better with concepts."

" 'Concepts,' " she repeated as well.

The concept of anger. The concept of bills. The concept of flightless, dodo love.

Outside, there was a watery gust from the direction of the lake. "Chicago," said Walter. "The Windy City. Is this the Windy City or what?" He looked at her hopefully, which made her despise him more.

She shook her head. "I don't even know why we're together," she said. "I mean, why are we even together?"

He looked at her hard. "I can't answer that for you," he yelled. He took two steps back, away from her. "You've got to answer that for yourself!" And he hailed his own cab, got in, and rode away.

She walked back to the Days Inn alone. She played scales soundlessly, on the tops of the piano keys, her thin-jointed fingers lifting and falling quietly like the tines of a music box or the legs of a spider. When she tired, she turned on the television, moved through the channels, and discovered an old movie she'd been in, a love story–murder mystery called *Finishing Touches*. It was the kind of performance she had become, briefly, known for: a patched-together intimacy with the audience, half cartoon, half revelation; a cross between shyness and derision. She had not given a damn back then, sort of like now, only then it had been a style, a way of being, not a diagnosis or demise.

Perhaps she should have a baby.

In the morning, she went to visit her parents in Elmhurst. For winter, they had plastic-wrapped their home—the windows, the doors—so that it looked like a piece of avant-garde art. "Save on heating bills," they said.

They had taken to discussing her in front of her. "It was a movie, Don. It was a movie about adventure. Nudity can be art."

"That's not how I saw it! That's not how I saw it at all!" said her father, red-faced, leaving the room. Naptime.

"How are you doing?" asked her mother, with what seemed like concern but was really an opening for something else. She had made tea.

"I'm okay, really," said Sidra. Everything she said about herself now sounded like a lie. If she was bad, it sounded like a lie; if she was fine—also a lie.

Her mother fiddled with a spoon. "I was envious of you." Her mother sighed. "I was always so envious of you! My own daughter!" She was shrieking it, saying it softly at first and then shrieking. It was exactly like Sidra's childhood: just when she thought life had become simple again, her mother gave her a new portion of the world to organize.

"I have to go," said Sidra. She had only just gotten there, but she wanted to go. She didn't want to visit her parents anymore. She didn't want to look at their lives.

She went back to the Days Inn and phoned Tommy. She and Tommy understood each other. "I *get* you," he used to say. His childhood had been full of sisters. He'd spent large portions of it drawing pictures of women in bathing suits—Miss Kenya from Nairobi!—and then asking one of the sisters to pick the most beautiful. If he disagreed, he asked another sister.

The connection was bad, and suddenly she felt too tired. "Darling, are you okay?" he said faintly.

"I'm okay."

"I think I'm hard of hearing," he said.

"I think I'm hard of talking," she said. "I'll phone you tomorrow."

She phoned Walter instead. "I need to see you," she said.

"Oh, really?" he said skeptically, and then added, with a sweetness he seemed to have plucked expertly from the air like a fly, "Is this a great country or what?"

She felt grateful to be with him again. "Let's never be apart," she whispered, rubbing his stomach. He had the physical inclinations of a dog: he liked stomach, ears, excited greetings.

"Fine by me," he said.

"Tomorrow, let's go out to dinner somewhere really expensive. My treat."

"Uh," said Walter, "tomorrow's no good."

"Oh."

"How about Sunday?"

"What's wrong with tomorrow?"

"I've got. Well, I've gotta work and I'll be tired, first of all."

"What's second of all?"

"I'm getting together with this woman I know."

"Oh?"

"It's no big deal. It's nothing. It's not a date or anything."

"Who is she?"

"Someone whose car I fixed. Loose mountings in the exhaust system. She wants to get together and talk about it some more. She wants to know about catalytic converters. You know, women are afraid of getting taken advantage of."

"Really!"

"Yeah, well, so Sunday would be better."

"Is she attractive?"

Walter scrinched up his face and made a sound of unenthusiasm. "Enh," he said, and placed his hand laterally in the air, rotating it up and down a little.

Before he left in the morning, she said, "Just don't sleep with her."

"*Sidra*," he said, scolding her for lack of trust or for attempted supervision—she wasn't sure which.

That night, he didn't come home. She phoned and phoned and then drank a six-pack and fell asleep. In the morning, she phoned again. Finally, at eleven o'clock, he answered.

She hung up.

At 11:30, her phone rang. "Hi," he said cheerfully. He was in a good mood.

"So where were you all night?" asked Sidra. This was what she had become. She felt shorter and squatter and badly coiffed.

There was some silence. "What do you mean?" he said cautiously.

"You know what I mean."

More silence. "Look, I didn't call this morning to get into a heavy conversation."

"Well, then," said Sidra, "you certainly called the wrong number." She slammed down the phone.

She spent the day trembling and sad. She felt like a cross between Anna Karenina and Amy Liverhaus, who used to shout from the fourth-grade cloakroom, "I just don't feel *appreciated.*" She walked over to Marshall Field's to buy new makeup. "You're much more of a cream beige than an ivory," said the young woman working the cosmetics counter.

But Sidra clutched at the ivory. "People are always telling me that," she said, "and it makes me very cross."

She phoned him later that night and he was there. "We need to talk," she said.

"I want my key back," he said.

"Look. Can you just come over here so that we can talk?"

He arrived bearing flowers—white roses and irises. They seemed wilted and ironic; she leaned them against the wall in a dry glass, no water.

"All right, I admit it," he said. "I went out on a date. But I'm not saying I slept with her."

She could feel, suddenly, the promiscuity in him. It was a heat, a creature, a tenant twin. "I already know you slept with her."

"How can you know that?"

"Get a life! What am I, an idiot?" She glared at him and tried not to cry. She hadn't loved him enough and he had sensed it. She hadn't really loved him at all, not really.

But she had liked him a lot!

So it still seemed unfair. A bone in her opened up, gleaming and pale, and she held it to the light and spoke from it. "I want to know one thing." She paused, not really for effect, but it had one. "Did you have oral sex?"

He looked stunned. "What kind of question is that? I don't have to answer a question like that."

"*You don't have to answer a question like that.* You don't have any rights here!" she began to yell. She was dehydrated. "You're the one who did this. Now I want the truth. I just want to know. Yes or no!"

He threw his gloves across the room.

"Yes or no," she said.

He flung himself onto the couch, pounded the cushions with his fist, placed an arm up over his eyes.

"Yes or no," she repeated.

He breathed deeply into his shirtsleeve.

"Yes or no."

"Yes," he said.

She sat down on the piano bench. Something dark and coagulated moved through her, up from the feet. Something light and breathing fled through her head, the house of her plastic-wrapped and burned down to tar. She heard him give a moan, and some fleeing hope in her, surrounded but alive on the roof, said perhaps he would beg her forgiveness. Promise to be a new man. She might find him attractive as a new, begging man. Though at some point, he would have to stop begging. He would just have to be normal. And then she would dislike him again.

He stayed on the sofa, did not move to comfort or be comforted, and the darkness in her cleaned her out, hollowed her like acid or a wind.

"I don't know what to do," she said, something palsied in her voice. She felt cheated of all the simple things—the radical calm of obscurity, of routine, of blah domestic bliss. "I don't want to go back to L.A.," she said. She began to stroke the tops of the piano keys, pushing against one and finding it broken— thudding and pitchless, shiny and mocking like an opened bone. She hated, hated her life. Perhaps she had always hated it.

He sat up on the sofa, looked distraught and false—his face badly arranged. He should practice in a mirror, she thought. He did not know how to break up with a movie actress. It was boys' rules: don't break up with a movie actress. Not in Chicago. If *she* left *him,* he would be better able to explain it, to himself, in the future, to anyone who asked. His voice shifted into something meant to sound imploring. "I know" was what he said, in a tone approximating hope, faith, some charity or other. "I know you might not *want* to."

"For your own good," he was saying. "Might be willing . . ." he was saying. But she was already turning into something else, a bird—a flamingo, a hawk, a flamingo-hawk—and was flying up and away, toward the filmy pane of the window, then back again, circling, meanly, with a squint.

He began, suddenly, to cry—loudly at first, with lots of *ohs,* then tiredly, as if from a deep sleep, his face buried in the poncho he'd thrown over the couch arm, his body sinking into the plush of the cushions—a man held hostage by the anxious cast of his dream.

"What can I do?" he asked.

But his dream had now changed, and she was gone, gone out the window, gone, gone.

Mary Morris

The Lifeguard

(UNITED STATES)

The summer before I left for college, I was head lifeguard on the beach at Pirate's Point. I don't think real pirates ever landed there, but the name made me think that strange and mysterious things could happen right where I lived. I grew up on that peninsula, and it was my home. I never found it monotonous, staring across the sea, but instead I liked to think of what lay beyond, how someday perhaps, I'd sail to the other side.

The beach was a long strip of what had once been white sand but was now beginning to turn darker and less pristine. It was lined with striped umbrellas and beach chairs. I loved the gentle easing of the beach umbrellas into the sand, the smell of Coppertone on my skin, the way people looked up when I blew my whistle, their faces always with a slight look of terror that one of theirs had been swept up, ever since the drowning of Billy Mandel.

For four years of my youth I was the lifeguard there. I'd watched this beach, where I'd spent my summers as a boy, red bucket and shovel in hand, fill with more and more umbrellas. I had watched the boys who were lifeguards turn flabby. I had seen Ric Spencer, who had ruled this beach before me for half a decade, lose his hair, and I'd seen the slim bodies of women stretch with childbearing. I'd seen it all and it had not impressed me, but rather it flowed through me like a river, not stopping here.

I was eighteen then. I wore zinc oxide on my nose, a whistle around my neck. No. 4 Coppertone covered my body. I could lift a girl into the air with each arm, and I loved to walk the beach, a girl dangling from each bicep. Girls clung to my stand, like the shipwrecked to their raft, and I could do no wrong.

It would have been a perfect summer for me, were it not for Mrs. Lovenheim. Every day at the same time, about ten in the morning, Mrs. Lovenheim came. She never had to ask me to set up her red-and-white umbrella because she always came at the same time each day, so I was ready for her. Mrs. Lovenheim stretched out like a cat, opened a book, which she held open at almost the same page every day, and stayed like that for hours, then went away. She never went near the water or sat in the sun. She never walked to the hot-dog stand but instead just stayed beneath her umbrella, straw hat on her head.

That was all she did, except it seemed as though Mrs. Lovenheim never took her eyes off of me.

She was perhaps only thirty then but seemed very old. She had flaming red hair and a small, compact body. She'd been married to a real estate broker who'd dropped her, my mother told me, after she'd miscarried two babies. She could not hold them, my mother whispered to me one evening in a darkened corner of the den where my own father had drunk beer and watched TV sports, until he died suddenly during a winter storm, and this secret world of women seemed ever closed to me.

I did not care for such things—for women who could and could not hold babies, for women who had been left in the middle of their lives, alone. I had girls who loved me—the girls of summer, with their bronzed skin and naked unblemished bellies, and it would have been a perfect summer for me, this last summer of my youth, if I had not felt that at each moment my every move was being watched by Mrs. Lovenheim, who never spoke unless she wanted something or rose until it was time to go home. If I had not felt that while my eyes were on the water Mrs. Lovenheim's were on me.

Ric Spencer came on weekends with his wife, Sally, and their daughter, Becky. Sally used to babysit for me when I was a boy, and she'd make big vats of hot chocolate, which we'd sip in front of late movies. She liked the really scary movies in which giant pods swallowed people or where something came out of the muck, terrorizing a neighborhood, and Sally clutched my hand whenever the frightening thing appeared, making me feel, even though she was taking care of me, as if I were the one who was taking care of her.

Then she married Ric Spencer, and some say she had to. Becky was born not long after their marriage, and Sally's days in bikinis were done. On weekdays Sally and her mother, Mrs. Winston, who used to be our neighbor, came alone to the beach. But on the weekend Ric came as well, and I could see him, lying listlessly on the sand, bored within the confines of his family. And when he could get away from them, he'd plant himself beneath my stand.

He'd been on duty when the Mandel boy disappeared, and it was a story he liked to tell. The drowning of Billy Mandel was the only recorded drowning in the history of Pirate's Point, and the first time Ric told me about the Mandel boy it was like a warning to me, not that the drowning had been Ric's fault. But then over many Saturdays beneath my stand, the story grew and improved. "It was like this," Ric said, beads of sweat shimmering on the place where his hair used to be. In his glory Ric had had a taut swimmer's body and thick blond curls. "It was this quick thing." A split second when a child is playing with a bucket by the shore and the father looks up, distracted, by the call of a friend. Ric would make up dialogue for me. "Hey, Joe, how'ya doing? How about dinner with us next Saturday?" Or, "I see your wife's got you working."

Innocuous words like that, and when the father looked back, when he let his gaze turn to the place where the sea met the shore, where Billy had been digging just moments before, there was a blank space, a void where he'd been taken by a wave, not a very big wave, but big enough to pull him under. While my own eyes scanned the water, Ric loved to describe the search of the beach, the lifeguards' patrol. He'd describe himself, swimming endlessly along the shoreline, until the sea brought Billy Mandel back hours later, bloated and having strangely taken on the color of the sea.

That summer the girls would not stay away, and I'd have to hold them at bay. They'd offer to buy me things—Cokes, hot dogs—and rub cream on my back while I sat like an idol perched in my chair. I liked being above them because I could see down the front of their bathing suits, and even though they knew I was looking at their breasts, they did nothing to hide.

There was Cindy Hartwick, with her thick black hair, whom I dated sometimes on Saturday nights when my mom gave me the car. And Sara Clarkson, who would be beautiful as soon as her braces came off. And there was Peggy Mandel. Sometimes I'd look across the beach and see Mr. and Mrs. Mandel with their daughter, a girl almost my age now, their only child. Peggy, who was a sophomore and known to be fast, used to shout at her parents, who sat motionless, reading endless newspapers unless Peggy went for a swim. And then Mr. Mandel would stand in his sneakers, waves lapping at his feet, as if somehow, through his attentiveness, he could bring back what was gone.

I was above them all from my stand, where my eyes scanned the beach like a beacon. I could see the Spencers under their blue-and-yellow umbrella and watch Becky go toddling away. When Ric was there, Becky went naked and got to eat sand, but when it was just the women, Becky stayed dressed. And there was Mr. Potter, who'd had a heart attack and walked with small weights in his hands, up and down the shoreline. And there was Mrs. Lovenheim, always there watching my every move whenever the girls came around.

My dreams at night were like the dreams of other boys—I dreamed of the bodies of girls, dreams that woke me from my sleep, leaving me sweaty, the sheets twisted around me. Dreams that made me rise in the middle of the night and throw the window open, until my mother, who never slept well in the big bed after my father died, shouted, "Are you all right? Is anything wrong?" Those were most of my dreams, but there were others, dreams of water, and sometimes there was a nightmare that came to me. In it I see myself from a perspective that is high. I am a boy with a bucket in my hand playing in the setting of parents, umbrellas, buckets, and shovels. And then from behind me, always behind me, as I dig a hole in the sand, the sea is rising, black and surging against the sky.

All summer long, when he could sneak away, Ric Spencer came and sat at the base of my lifeguard stand and talked about the old days. Ric had been my teacher for Red Cross training and taught me what I know about riptides and undertows and sudden changes on the surface of the sea. He was only twenty-six that summer when I became head lifeguard, but he used to say, as bronzed girls handed me Cokes or asked if I needed more oil on my back, "Man, you don't know what it is. You don't know what you've got." He'd always say it in the same way, so finally one day I said to him, "What is it, Ric? What've I got?"

He extended his arms as if to encompass the beach. "You've got all this. It's yours."

I laughed, not understanding what he meant. "You know," he went on, "I've got this job, I sell computer parts. I go to these retail stores all over New England, even in the winter, when it's freezing cold, and I think to myself how I wish I were anywhere else doing anything else, but what can I do?"

He pointed over to Mrs. Lovenheim, who was looking our way, her novel lying flat on her blanket. "You know, I knew her when. Before she married that guy who dumped her." I looked over at Mrs. Lovenheim, and she did not look away. I couldn't imagine that anyone could have known her "when," whenever that was. "She was something," Ric said. He whistled between his teeth.

Just then Cindy Hartwick appeared, with a hot dog for me with everything on it, one I hadn't even asked for, and she handed it up. Then Peggy Mandel strutted by in a bikini, to her father's dismay. I tipped my visor, then Ric went on. "You don't know," he said, "how lucky you are."

I loved my body that summer. I loved its firmness and its bronzed skin. But mostly I loved the way it was admired. Girls I didn't know would come up and squeeze parts of me. Old people looked at me, their bodies covered with chicken skin and blue veins, as if I were an object in the museum that had become their lives. So I loved to stroll the beach among the girls who wanted to have me, old men who wanted to be me.

Sitting in my chair was harder, because the thing about being a lifeguard is that your eyes should be set on the sea. You watch for nothing, really, and sometimes you begin to see things. I've seen what I thought were the tidal waves of my dreams, heading straight for me, but it was only the meeting of a cloud and the sea. I've seen monsters rise from the belly of the deep when it's only a big fish leaping into the air. And then I've seen things that aren't there at all. I've seen people before my eyes disappear. And sometimes I've even heard cries for help from behind the waves. But these are all lifeguard mirages, and they happen to anyone who looks at one thing too long.

But at times it was hard for me to keep looking out, and so I welcomed the company of girls. Though I'd never intended to do this, one day I asked out Peggy Mandel. She had come to hand me a Coke, and I'd gazed down at her. Then I said, quite simply, "Would you like to go to a movie Saturday night?"

On Saturday night I picked up Peggy. She wore a pink cotton dress with spaghetti straps, and her parents stood at the door, despondent, as if I were taking her to live in another country, saying useless things like "Come back soon." I watched them curiously, these people whose life had been irrevocably altered with the sweep of a wave.

We went to a drive-in, where I let my arm dangle against the seat. She leaned her head into my arm, and I felt her breath against my chest. I pulled her closer to me, and she raised her head toward mine, bringing her lips to my lips. She was warm and alive, and I knew I could have almost anything I wanted with her. I leaned my own face close to hers. "Tell me about Billy," I heard myself say.

She pulled away slightly at first. "What?" she said. She was flushed and drowsy, like someone who has been asleep.

"About Billy. I want to know."

She sat back, tossing her dark brown hair. "Billy?"

"Your brother, the one who drowned," as if she didn't know. "Tell me about it."

Her face looked the way I've seen girls look, amazed and sickened, in biology labs when a rodent is about to be splayed. "You want to know about Billy? Why do you want to know about Billy? Why do you want to know about Billy?"

"I don't know. Tell me what happened." I couldn't explain why, but I wanted to know what it is like when you look at a patch of sand and a part of your life is gone. What does she imagine it felt like to be deep in the sea? Maybe it was because Ric Spencer had talked about it so much, but I wanted her to tell me what no one else could.

"What happened? You want to know what happened?"

I realized she thought my request was odd. "I'm the lifeguard," I said. "I don't want to make any mistakes."

"Okay, I'll tell you what happened." She was furious now and looked old for her years. "My dad looked away, and Billy drowned, and nobody's ever been the same. Is that what you want to know?"

"I want to know what he was like. Did you play with him when he was small?"

"I was four years old and my brother drowned." She flung her body to the opposite side of the car so that the door made a jangling sound, as if someone were trying to get in. "You're sick," she said under her breath. "Now take me home."

The day it happened was a day of particular calm. A Saturday when a gentle southwest wind blew. A day when the waves hardly lapped and it was almost hypnotic for me to keep my eyes fixed on the sea. It is easier to look at roughness and fast-breaking waves, and that day I was having trouble staying awake.

Ric Spencer stood beneath my lifeguard stand that morning. He stood there and said, "You know what, man, I've been thinking. I could do something else with my life. I mean, I could go to night school. Maybe become a coach. I don't have to do this door-to-door crap."

"Hey," I told him, "there's plenty you could do."

"That's just what I've been thinking. I've been thinking about opening a little retail store, maybe software. What d'ya think?" He seemed happy just having said this when Cindy Hartwick came by with a Coke; Ric winked and drifted away. "Catch you later," he said, heading back to his umbrella.

"Hey," Cindy said. "What're you doing after work?" I gazed down for a moment. Cindy wore a turquoise two-piece, and she had straight black hair and black eyes. She began climbing up my stand like a monkey, laughing, "Hey, so what are you doing?"

Then Peggy Mandel walked by. "He's a sicko," she shouted. "He's weird."

"Not as weird as you, Mandel," I called back. "Not like you."

"Oh, yeah? Go to a drive-in with him. You'll see."

"What's she talking about?" Cindy asked.

"Oh, it's nothing," I said. But Peggy had disturbed me. Now Cindy was reaching up, and I thought I'd take her out on Saturday night. I didn't have to look; I could feel Mrs. Lovenheim's eyes on me. Cindy kept reaching for me, and, as if I thought it would drive Mrs. Lovenheim wild, I pretended to pull Cindy up to my stand.

It was perhaps only an instant that I was distracted, but suddenly I was aware of the shouting, and it took me by surprise. At first I thought I was hearing things, but it was too loud and clear. Perhaps I'd had my eyes off the sea for one minute, maybe two. No more than that. Perhaps for the first time all summer I'd completely forgotten where I was. Now my instincts took over. I let go of Cindy and stood up straight in my chair. Grabbing my binoculars, I scanned the water for signs—the flailing arms, a bobbing head, the gathering of crowds, parents diving—but there was nothing, nothing at all. But still I heard the shouting, so I leaped to the sand and began to race up and down the shore.

That was when I saw Ric Spencer, running across the burning sand, waving his hands in an awkward way. He ran forward, then back, then forward again, like a dog wanting to play catch. He kept waving, shouting, then rushing back again. Then Mr. Potter, whose own failing heart kept him pacing the shore, came puffing to me. "A child," he said with surprising composure. "Over there," pointing to the Spencer umbrella.

I was amazed by this, taken off guard. While I had been searching ahead, what had happened was behind me. A crowd had gathered around the blue and yellow umbrella. The Mandels put their newspaper down and started walking, Mrs. Mandel clinging to her husband's arm. I saw a small frenzy of people moving up and down. I ran toward Ric. He caught me in his arms. "It's Becky." He shook me like a wet towel. "Get your kit. Get your damn kit."

I dashed back to my stand, grabbed the first-aid kit, and raced, my own feet searing on the sand. I made my way through where the crowd had gathered and saw Becky Spencer, her face puffed, her mouth open but no sound coming, her eyes in a fixed stare, turning as blue as the sea I'd set my sights on, and I knew this was the color of Billy Mandel when he'd been tossed back to the shore.

"She swallowed something," Ric said. He shook violently.

"Do something, man." Tears fell down his cheeks. "I've tried everything. God, please do something."

"You've killed her," Mrs. Winston, on her knees, shouted. "You've killed your daughter." And Sally, tears streaming down her face, kept banging her daughter on the back.

"Turn her over," I said, and I tipped Becky upside down, pounding on her back, but no breath came from her, no sound. I tipped her again, like an hour-glass, but still nothing came. Then I clutched the dying child in my arms.

"You've killed her," Mrs. Winston shrieked, pointing at Ric. "You'll live with this forever."

Sally Spencer, who'd once dug her nails into my arm during the horror movies of my youth, now did so again. "You're the lifeguard," she said matter-of-factly. "You're supposed to know what to do." But I'd done everything I'd been trained to do, and nothing could bring Becky Spencer, her mouth gaping in a silent, breathless hole, back to life.

It was then that I saw Mrs. Lovenheim close her book, take off her hat, and rise. I saw that woman, left and bereft, who had languished all summer be-neath her umbrella, coming toward us, her red hair wild in the breeze, and like Moses she parted the spectators, the advisers, the lookers-on. She pushed the screaming mother away, shoved the accusatory grandmother onto the hot sand. She thrust Ric into the background and plucked the dying child from my arms, forcing me to my knees. She held Becky, the child's face the shade of the deepest recesses of the sea, her body rigid and motionless. Then Mrs. Loven-heim wrapped her body around Becky's, folded the blue breathless body into her own.

I watched from my knees as the woman whose beach umbrella I had planted day after day, whose chairs I had arranged, who had tipped me poorly, whose face was beset by the grief of her own failed marriage, who nursed what I now recognize to be a broken heart, Mrs. Lovenheim, perhaps not more than thirty then, grappled the child into her arms, engulfed her as if bringing her back into her own womb, then pressed some place I had not found. She squeezed Becky above the navel three times with a force I'd never before seen in nature, until a perfect, unblemished green grape shot like a bullet from the child's mouth.

Becky gasped and spit as Mrs. Lovenheim handed the whimpering child to her mother, who sobbed in the sand. For the first time the grandmother was silent. Ric stood shaking, his life altered. Then Mrs. Lovenheim turned to me where I stood, first-aid kit dangling in my hand like a lunch box. I felt as if she were about to say or do something, but instead, without a word, she moved past me back to her umbrella, collected her things, and left.

That night I could not sleep. It was late, and I wasn't sure what was bothering me, so I went downstairs. I sat in my father's chair in the darkened den until I knew what I wanted to do. I found the address in the phone book. Then I got into the car and drove. I drove along the ocean road until I was a block short of her house, and I parked there.

It was a clear night at the end of August, and a salt breeze blew off the ocean. It was a nice night for a walk along the shore, so I took my time, suck-ing in my breath. Then I headed down the street until I reached the house where she lived. The lights were on upstairs, but I stood for a long time on the porch. Then I knocked on the door, softly at first, then louder.

At last she descended the stairs. She wore a yellow robe, tied around her waist, and her red hair fell to her shoulders. "Yes?" Mrs. Lovenheim said, her voice warm like a breeze.

"It's me," I said, "Josh Michaels."

She slowly opened the door, only partially at first. She looked at me oddly, as if trying to remember when she'd seen me before. "I'm the lifeguard," I said, not knowing what else to say. And it suddenly occurred to me that she had no idea who I was, that she'd never really seen me at all. So I added foolishly, "At the beach."

"Yes," she mumbled. "What is it?"

"I wanted to thank you," I said, not really knowing why I'd come. "I wanted to thank you for what you did. This afternoon."

She cocked her head. "Oh, it's just something I learned. I take silly courses sometimes."

"But I didn't know what to do," I mumbled. I was not aware as I said it that tears streamed down my face. But soon I found myself crying on Mrs. Lovenheim's porch, on the porch of the woman to whom I was, in fact, nothing at all. I dropped my shoulders and stood there, sobbing. "I didn't know what to do."

I don't know how long I stood there like that before she reached for me, pulled me to her, wrapped her arms around mine. She smelled of shampoo and oils, not the salt and sand I'd expected. It was the first time I felt what it was supposed to feel like to be in the arms of a woman, not the girls whose breath steamed my car on Saturday nights. But it was not her body I felt, though I liked the feel of it, it was not her sex, though I was aware of it. Rather, I felt myself longing for something I could never have, and I wanted her to take me back, fold me inside of herself as she'd folded Becky that afternoon.

But then she let me go. I grabbed at her, trying to hold on, as if her arms could save me from what came next. But without a word she went inside. "Wait," I said, "come back." I knew I would never want anyone or anything as much as I wanted Mrs. Lovenheim right then, and I found myself slipping into despair as she released me back into the world.

It was the last time I saw Mrs. Lovenheim that summer, or any other summer, for that matter. Or perhaps I saw her again, but we no longer recognized each other. It was my last summer on the beach, and after that the winds shifted, the weather changed, which would bring my departure for college. Years have passed since that day on Pirate's Point, and I am old now, perhaps as old as Mrs. Lovenheim was then, and I've never seen the water or the umbrellas of summer in the same way again.

Mohammed Mrabet

The Canebrake

(MOROCCO)

Kacem and Stito met every afternoon at a café. They were old friends. Kacem drank, and he had a wife whom he never allowed to go out of the house. No matter how much she entreated him and argued with him, he would not even let her go to the hammam to bathe. Stito had no troubles because he was a bachelor, and only smoked kif.

Kacem would come into the café with a bottle in his shopping bag, and soon both of them would go on to Kacem's house. On the way they would stop at the market to buy food, since Kacem would not permit his wife to go to market, either. Stito had no one to cook for him, and so he ate each night at Kacem's house, and always paid his share.

They would carry the food to Kacem's wife so she could prepare it. First, however, she would make tapas for Kacem's drinks, and tea for Stito's kif. Later when the food was cooking she would go in and sit with the two men.

Once when they were all sitting there together, Stito turned to Kacem and said: Sometimes I wonder how you can drink so much. Where do you store it all?

Kacem laughed. And you? You don't get anything but smoke out of your pipe. I get the alcohol right inside me, and it feels wonderful.

That's an empty idea you have, said Stito. Kif gives me more pleasure than alcohol could ever give anybody. And it makes me think straighter and talk better.

Kacem's wife decided that this was a good moment to say to her husband: Your friend's right. You drink too much.

Kacem was annoyed. Go and look at the food, he told her. It ought to be ready. We want to eat.

She brought the dinner in, and they set to work eating it. After they had finished, they talked for a half hour or so, and then Stito stood up. Until tomorrow, he told Kacem.

Yes, yes. Until tomorrow, said Kacem, who was drunk.

If Allah wills, Stito added.

Kacem's wife got up and opened the door for him.

Good night.

She shut the door, and then she and Kacem went to bed. Feeling full of love, she began to kiss her husband. But he only lay there, too drunk to notice her.

Soon she sat up and began to complain. From the day of our wedding you've never loved me, she said. You never pay me any attention at all unless you want to eat.

Go to sleep, woman, he told her.

She had started to cry, and it was a long time before she slept.

The next afternoon when he finished work, Kacem went to the café to meet Stito. They did the marketing and carried the food back to Kacem's house. The evening passed the same as always. Kacem was very drunk by the time Stito was ready to go home.

Kacem's wife opened the door for Stito and stepped outside. As he went through the doorway she whispered: Try and come alone tomorrow. Let him come by himself.

What do you mean? he said.

She pointed at the canebrake behind the garden. Hide there, she said.

Stito understood. But he'll be here, he whispered.

That's all right. Don't worry, she told him. Good night.

Good night.

The woman shut the door. Kacem was still sitting there drinking. She left him there and went to bed.

Again the following afternoon the two friends met in the café. Stito put away his pipe. How are you? he said.

Let's go, said Kacem. He was eager to get home and open his bottle.

I can't go right now, Stito told him. I've got to wait here and see somebody. I'll come later. Here's the money for the food.

Yes, said Kacem. I'll go on to the market, then.

Sit down with me a minute, said Stito.

No, no. I'll be going.

I'll see you later, Stito said.

Stito sat there in the café until dusk, and then he got up and went to the street where Kacem's house was. He waited until no one was passing by before he began to make his way through the canebrake. He was invisible in here. He peered between the canes and saw Kacem sitting in his room with a bottle on the table beside him, and a glass in his hand. And he saw the woman bring in the taifor.

Then she came outside carrying a large basin, and walked straight to the edge of the canebrake. She set the basin down and bent over it as if she were working. She was facing her husband and talking with him, and her garments reached to the ground in front of her. In the back, however, she was completely uncovered, and Stito saw everything he wanted to see. While she pretended to be washing something in the basin, she pushed her bare haunches back against the canes, and he pressed forward and began to enjoy himself with her.

When you're ready, she whispered, pull it out and let me catch it all in my hand.

That's no way, he said. How can I do that?

The woman moved forward suddenly and made it slip out, so that Stito understood that if he were to have anything at all with her, he would have to do as she wanted.

You can do it again afterwards and finish inside, if you like, she whispered.

She backed against the canes again, and he started once more. When he was almost ready he warned her, and she reached back with her hand, and got what she wanted. Keeping her fist shut, she waited so he could do it again the way he enjoyed it. He finished and went out of the canebrake into the street. No one saw him.

The woman walked into the house. She stood by the chair where Kacem sat, looking down at him. Can't I go to the hammam tomorrow?" she said.

Are you starting that all over again? cried Kacem. I've told you no a thousand times. No! You can't leave this house.

She reached out her hand, opened it, and let what she had been holding drip onto the taifor beside Kacem's glass.

Kacem stared. He had been drunk a moment before, and now he was no longer drunk. He did not even ask her from whom she had got it, or how. He stood up, leaving the bottle and glass, and went to bed without his dinner.

In the morning when he went out to work, Kacem left the door of his house wide open. All day he thought about his wife. When he had finished work, he went to the café to meet Stito.

His face was sad as he sat down. Fill me a pipe, he said.

What? Stito cried.

Yes.

Stito gave him his pipe. What's happened? It's the first time you've ever asked for kif.

I'm through with drinking, Kacem told him. I'm going to start smoking kif.

But why?

Kacem did not reply, and Stito did not ask again.

That evening the two friends arrived at Kacem's house laughing and joking, with their heads full of kif. Kacem was in a fine humor all evening. After Stito had gone, he said to his wife: You went to the hammam?

Yes, she said. Thank you for leaving the door open. I thought you'd forgotten to shut it when you went out.

I'm not going to lock it any more, he told her.

She kissed him and they went to bed. It was the first time in many nights that Kacem was not too drunk to play games with his wife. They made one another very happy, and finally they fell into a perfect sleep.

Translated from the Moghrebi by Paul Bowles

Bharati Mukherjee
The Management of Grief

(INDIA)

A woman I don't know is boiling tea the Indian way in my kitchen. There are a lot of women I don't know in my kitchen, whispering, and moving tactfully. They open doors, rummage through the pantry, and try not to ask me where things are kept. They remind me of when my sons were small, on Mother's Day or when Vikram and I were tired, and they would make big, sloppy omelets. I would lie in bed pretending I didn't hear them.

Dr. Sharma, the treasurer of the Indo-Canada Society, pulls me into the hallway. He wants to know if I am worried about money. His wife, who has just come up from the basement with a tray of empty cups and glasses, scolds him. "Don't bother Mrs. Bhave with mundane details." She looks so monstrously pregnant her baby must be days overdue. I tell her she shouldn't be carrying heavy things. "Shaila," she says, smiling, "this is the fifth." Then she grabs a teenager by his shirttails. He slips his Walkman off his head. He has to be one of her four children, they have the same doomed and dented foreheads. "What's the official word now?" she demands. The boy slips the headphones back on. "They're acting evasive, Ma. They're saying it could be an accident or a terrorist bomb."

All morning, the boys have been muttering, Sikh Bomb, Sikh Bomb. The men, not using the word, bow their heads in agreement. Mrs. Sharma touches her forehead at such a word. At least they've stopped talking about space debris and Russian lasers.

Two radios are going in the dining room. They are tuned to different stations. Someone must have brought the radios down from my boys' bedrooms. I haven't gone into their rooms since Kusum came running across the front lawn in her bathrobe. She looked so funny, I was laughing when I opened the door.

The big TV in the den is being whizzed through American networks and cable channels.

"Damn!" some man swears bitterly. "How can these preachers carry on like nothing's happened?" I want to tell him we're not that important. You look at the audience, and at the preacher in his blue robe with his beautiful white hair, the potted palm trees under a blue sky, and you know they care about nothing.

The phone rings and rings. Dr. Sharma's taken charge. "We're with her," he keeps saying. "Yes, yes, the doctor has given calming pills. Yes, yes, pills are having necessary effect." I wonder if pills alone explain this calm. Not peace, just a deadening quiet. I was always controlled, but never repressed. Sound can reach me, but my body is tensed, ready to scream. I hear their voices all around me. I hear my boys and Vikram cry, "Mommy, Shaila!" and their screams insulate me, like headphones.

The woman boiling water tells her story again and again. "I got the news first. My cousin called from Halifax before six A.M., can you imagine? He'd gotten up for prayers and his son was studying for medical exams and he heard on a rock channel that something had happened to a plane. They said first it had disappeared from the radar, like a giant eraser just reached out. His father called me, so I said to him, what do you mean, 'something bad'? You mean a hijacking? And he said, behn, there is no confirmation of anything yet, but check with your neighbors because a lot of them must be on that plane. So I called poor Kusum straightaway. I knew Kusum's husband and daughter were booked to go yesterday."

Kusum lives across the street from me. She and Satish had moved in less than a month ago. They said they needed a bigger place. All these people, the Sharmas and friends from the Indo-Canada Society, had been there for the housewarming. Satish and Kusum made homemade tandoori on their big gas grill and even the white neighbors piled their plates high with that luridly red, charred, juicy chicken. Their younger daughter had danced, and even our boys had broken away from the Stanley Cup telecast to put in a reluctant appearance. Everyone took pictures for their albums and for the community newspapers—another of our families had made it big in Toronto—and now I wonder how many of those happy faces are gone. "Why does God give us so much if all along He intends to take it away?" Kusum asks me.

I nod. We sit on carpeted stairs, holding hands like children. "I never once told him that I loved him," I say. I was too much the well brought up woman. I was so well brought up I never felt comfortable calling my husband by his first name.

"It's all right," Kusum says. "He knew. My husband knew. They felt it. Modern young girls have to say it because what they feel is fake."

Kusum's daughter, Pam, runs in with an overnight case. Pam's in her McDonald's uniform. "Mummy! You have to get dressed!" Panic makes her cranky. "A reporter's on his way here."

"Why?"

"You want to talk to him in your bathrobe?" She starts to brush her mother's long hair. She's the daughter who's always in trouble. She dates Canadian boys and hangs out in the mall, shopping for tight sweaters. The younger one, the goody-goody one according to Pam, the one with a voice so sweet that when she sang bhajans for Ethiopian relief even a frugal man like my husband wrote out a hundred dollar check, she was on that plane. She was going to spend July and August with grandparents because Pam wouldn't go. Pam said she'd rather waitress at McDonald's. "If it's a choice between Bombay and Wonderland, I'm picking Wonderland," she'd said.

"Leave me alone," Kusum yells. "You know what I want to do? If I didn't have to look after you now, I'd hang myself."

Pam's young face goes blotchy with pain. "Thanks," she says, "don't let me stop you."

"Hush," pregnant Mrs. Sharma scolds Pam. "Leave your mother alone. Mr. Sharma will tackle the reporters and fill out the forms. He'll say what has to be said."

Pam stands her ground. "You think I don't know what Mummy's thinking? *Why ever?* that's what. That's sick! Mummy wishes my little sister were alive and I were dead."

Kusum's hand in mine is trembly hot. We continue to sit on the stairs.

She calls before she arrives, wondering if there's anything I need. Her name is Judith Templeton and she's an appointee of the provincial government. "Multiculturalism?" I ask, and she says, "partially," but that her mandate is bigger. "I've been told you knew many of the people on the flight," she says. "Perhaps if you'd agree to help us reach the others . . . ?"

She gives me time at least to put on tea water and pick up the mess in the front room. I have a few *samosas* from Kusum's housewarming that I could fry up, but then I think, why prolong this visit?

Judith Templeton is much younger than she sounded. She wears a blue suit with a white blouse and a polka dot tie. Her blond hair is cut short, her only jewelry is pearl drop earrings. Her briefcase is new and expensive looking, a gleaming cordovan leather. She sits with it across her lap. When she looks out the front windows onto the street, her contact lenses seem to float in front of her light blue eyes.

"What sort of help do you want from me?" I ask. She has refused the tea, out of politeness, but I insist, along with some slightly stale biscuits.

"I have no experience," she admits. "That is, I have an MSW and I've worked in liaison with accident victims, but I mean I have no experience with a tragedy of this scale—"

"Who could?" I ask.

"—and with the complications of culture, language, and customs. Someone mentioned that Mrs. Bhave is a pillar—because you've taken it more calmly."

At this, perhaps, I frown, for she reaches forward, almost to take my hand. "I hope you understand my meaning, Mrs. Bhave. There are hundreds of people in Metro directly affected, like you, and some of them speak no English. There are some widows who've never handled money or gone on a bus, and there are old parents who still haven't eaten or gone outside their bedrooms. Some houses and apartments have been looted. Some wives are still hysterical. Some husbands are in shock and profound depression. We want to help, but our hands are tied in so many ways. We have to distribute money to some people, and there are legal documents—these things can be done. We have interpreters, but we don't always have the human touch, or maybe the right human touch. We don't want to make mistakes, Mrs. Bhave, and that's why we'd like to ask you to help us."

"More mistakes, you mean," I say.

"Police matters are not in my hands," she answers.

"Nothing I can do will make any difference," I say. "We must all grieve in our own way."

"But you are coping very well. All the people said, Mrs. Bhave is the strongest person of all. Perhaps if the others could see you, talk with you, it would help them."

"By the standards of the people you call hysterical, I am behaving very oddly and very badly, Miss Templeton." I want to say to her, *I wish I could scream, starve, walk into Lake Ontario, jump from a bridge.* "They would not see me as a model. I do not see myself as a model."

I am a freak. No one who has ever known me would think of me reacting this way. This terrible calm will not go away.

She asks me if she may call again, after I get back from a long trip that we all must make. "Of course," I say. "Feel free to call, anytime."

Four days later, I find Kusum squatting on a rock overlooking a bay in Ireland. It isn't a big rock, but it juts sharply out over water. This is as close as we'll ever get to them. June breezes balloon out her sari and unpin her knee-length hair. She has the bewildered look of a sea creature whom the tides have stranded.

It's been one hundred hours since Kusum came stumbling and screaming across my lawn. Waiting around the hospital, we've heard many stories. The police, the diplomats, they tell us things thinking that we're strong, that knowledge is helpful to the grieving, and maybe it is. Some, I know, prefer ignorance, or their own versions. The plane broke into two, they say. Unconsciousness was instantaneous. No one suffered. My boys must have just finished their breakfasts. They loved eating on planes, they loved the smallness of plates, knives, and forks. Last year they saved the airline salt and pepper shakers. Half an hour more and they would have made it to Heathrow.

Kusum says that we can't escape our fate. She says that all those people—our husbands, my boys, her girl with the nightingale voice, all those Hindus, Christians, Sikhs, Muslims, Parsis, and atheists on that plane—were fated to die together off this beautiful bay. She learned this from a swami in Toronto.

I have my Valium.

Six of us "relatives"—two widows and four widowers—chose to spend the day today by the waters instead of sitting in a hospital room and scanning photographs of the dead. That's what they call us now: relatives. I've looked through twenty-seven photos in two days. They're very kind to us, the Irish are very understanding. Sometimes understanding means freeing a tourist bus for this trip to the bay, so we can pretend to spy our loved ones through the glassiness of waves or in sunspeckled cloud shapes.

I could die here, too, and be content.

"What is that, out there?" She's standing and flapping her hands and for a moment I see a head shape bobbing in the waves. She's standing in the water, I, on the boulder. The tide is low, and a round, black, head-sized rock has just risen from the waves. She returns, her sari end dripping and ruined, and her face is a twisted remnant of hope, the way mine was a hundred hours ago, still laughing but inwardly knowing that nothing but the ultimate tragedy could bring two women together at six o'clock on a Sunday morning. I watch her face sag into blankness.

"That water felt warm, Shaila," she says at length.

"You can't, " I say. "We have to wait for our turn to come."

I haven't eaten in four days, haven't brushed my teeth.

"I know," she says. "I tell myself I have no right to grieve. They are in a better place than we are. My swami says I should be thrilled for them. My swami says depression is a sign of our selfishness."

Maybe I'm selfish. Selfishly I break away from Kusum and run, sandals slapping against stones, to the water's edge. What if my boys aren't lying pinned under the debris? What if they aren't stuck a mile below that innocent blue chop? What if, given the strong currents. . . .

Now I've ruined my sari, one of my best. Kusum has joined me, knee-deep in water that feels to me like a swimming pool. I could settle in the water, and my husband would take my hand and the boys would slap water in my face just to see me scream.

"Do you remember what good swimmers my boys were, Kusum?"

"I saw the medals," she says.

One of the widowers, Dr. Ranganathan from Montreal, walks out to us, carrying his shoes in one hand. He's an electrical engineer. Someone at the hotel mentioned his work is famous around the world, something about the place where physics and electricity come together. He has lost a huge family, something indescribable. "With some luck," Dr. Ranganathan suggests to me, "a good swimmer could make it safely to some island. It is quite possible that there may be many, many microscopic islets scattered around."

"You're not just saying that?" I tell Dr. Ranganathan about Vinod, my elder son. Last year he took diving as well.

"It's a parent's duty to hope," he says. "It is foolish to rule out possibilities that have not been tested. I myself have not surrendered hope."

Kusum is sobbing once again. "Dear lady," he says, laying his free hand on her arm, and she calms down.

"Vinod is how old?" he asks me. He's very careful, as we all are. *Is*, not was.

"Fourteen. Yesterday he was fourteen. His father and uncle were going to take him down to the Taj and give him a big birthday party. I couldn't go with them because I couldn't get two weeks off from my stupid job in June." I process bills for a travel agent. June is a big travel month.

Dr. Ranganathan whips the pockets of his suit jacket inside out. Squashed roses, in darkening shades of pink, float on the water. He tore the roses off creepers in somebody's garden. He didn't ask anyone if he could pluck the roses, but now there's been an article about it in the local papers. When you see an Indian person, it says, please give him or her flowers.

"A strong youth of fourteen," he says, "can very likely pull to safety a younger one."

My sons, though four years apart, were very close. Vinod wouldn't let Mithun drown. *Electrical engineering,* I think, foolishly perhaps: this man knows important secrets of the universe, things closed to me. Relief spins me lightheaded. No wonder my boys' photographs haven't turned up in the gallery of photos of the recovered dead. "Such pretty roses," I say.

"My wife loved pink roses. Every Friday I had to bring a bunch home. I used to say, why? After twenty odd years of marriage you're still needing proof positive of my love?" He has identified his wife and three of his children. Then others from Montreal, the lucky ones, intact families with no survivors. He chuckles as he wades back to shore. Then he swings around to ask me a question. "Mrs. Bhave, you are wanting to throw in some roses for your loved ones? I have two big ones left."

But I have other things to float: Vinod's pocket calculator; a half-painted model B-52 for my Mithun. They'd want them on their island. And for my husband? For him I let fall into the calm, glassy waters a poem I wrote in the hospital yesterday. Finally he'll know my feelings for him.

"Don't tumble, the rocks are slippery," Dr. Ranganathan cautions. He holds out a hand for me to grab.

Then it's time to get back on the bus, time to rush back to our waiting posts on hospital benches.

Kusum is one of the lucky ones. The lucky ones flew here, identified in multiplicate their loved ones, then will fly to India with the bodies for proper ceremonies. Satish is one of the few males who surfaced. The photos of faces we saw on the walls in an office at Heathrow and here in the hospital are mostly of women. Women have more body fat, a nun said to me matter-of-factly. They float better.

Today I was stopped by a young sailor on the street. He had loaded bodies, he'd gone into the water when—he checks my face for signs of strength—when the sharks were first spotted. I don't blush, and he breaks down. "It's all right," I say. "Thank you." I had heard about the sharks from Dr. Ranganathan. In his orderly mind, science brings understanding, it holds no terror. It is the shark's duty. For every deer there is a hunter, for every fish a fisherman.

The Irish are not shy; they rush to me and give me hugs and some are crying. I cannot imagine reactions like that on the streets of Toronto. Just strangers, and I am touched. Some carry flowers with them and give them to any Indian they see.

After lunch, a policeman I have gotten to know quite well catches hold of me. He says he thinks he has a match for Vinod. I explain what a good swimmer Vinod is.

"You want me with you when you look at photos?" Dr. Ranganathan walks ahead of me into the picture gallery. In these matters, he is a scientist, and I am grateful. It is a new perspective. "They have performed miracles," he says. "We are indebted to them."

The first day or two the policemen showed us relatives only one picture at a time; now they're in a hurry, they're eager to lay out the possibles, and even the probables.

The face on the photo is of a boy much like Vinod; the same intelligent eyes, the same thick brows dipping into a V. But this boy's features, even his cheeks, are puffier, wider, mushier.

"No." My gaze is pulled by other pictures. There are five other boys who look like Vinod.

The nun assigned to console me rubs the first picture with a fingertip. "When they've been in the water for a while, love, they look a little heavier." The bones under the skin are broken, they said on the first day—try to adjust your memories. It's important.

"It's not him. I'm his mother. I'd know."

"I know this one!" Dr. Ranganathan cries out suddenly from the back of the gallery. "And this one!" I think he senses that I don't want to find my boys. "They are the Kutty brothers. They were also from Montreal." I don't mean to be crying. On the contrary, I am ecstatic. My suitcase in the hotel is packed heavy with dry clothes for my boys.

The policeman starts to cry. "I am so sorry, I am so sorry, ma'am. I really thought we had a match."

With the nun ahead of us and the policeman behind, we, the unlucky ones without our children's bodies, file out of the makeshift gallery.

From Ireland most of us go on to India. Kusum and I take the same direct flight to Bombay, so I can help her clear customs quickly. But we have to argue with a man in uniform. He has large boils on his face. The boils swell and glow with sweat as we argue with him. He wants Kusum to wait in line and he refuses to take authority because his boss is on a tea break. But Kusum won't let her coffins out of sight, and I shan't desert her though I know that my parents, elderly and diabetic, must be waiting in a stuffy car in a scorching lot.

"You bastard!" I scream at the man with the popping boils. Other passengers press closer. "You think we're smuggling contraband in those coffins!"

Once upon a time we were well brought up women; we were dutiful wives who kept our heads veiled, our voices shy and sweet.

In India, I become, once again, an only child of rich, ailing parents. Old friends of the family come to pay their respects. Some are Sikh, and inwardly, involuntarily, I cringe. My parents are progressive people; they do not blame communities for a few individuals.

In Canada it is a different story now.

"Stay longer," my mother pleads. "Canada is a cold place. Why would you want to be all by yourself?" I stay.

Three months pass. Then another.

"Vikram wouldn't have wanted you to give up things!" they protest. They call my husband by the name he was born with. In Toronto he'd changed to Vik so the men he worked with at his office would find his name as easy as Rod or Chris. "You know, the dead aren't cut off from us!"

My grandmother, the spoiled daughter of a rich *zamindar,* shaved her head with rusty razor blades when she was widowed at sixteen. My grandfather died of childhood diabetes when he was nineteen, and she saw herself as the harbinger of bad luck. My mother grew up without parents, raised indifferently by an uncle, while her true mother slept in a hut behind the main estate house and took her food with the servants. She grew up a rationalist. My parents abhor mindless mortification.

The *zamindar's* daughter kept stubborn faith in Vedic rituals; my parents rebelled. I am trapped between two modes of knowledge. At thirty-six, I am too old to start over and too young to give up. Like my husband's spirit, I flutter between worlds.

Courting aphasia, we travel. We travel with our phalanx of servants and poor relatives. To hill stations and to beach resorts. We play contract bridge in dusty gymkhana clubs. We ride stubby ponies up crumbly mountain trails. At tea dances, we let ourselves be twirled twice round the ballroom. We hit the holy spots we hadn't made time for before. In Varanasi, Kalighat, Rishikesh, Hardwar, astrologers and palmists seek me out and for a fee offer me cosmic consolations.

Already the widowers among us are being shown new bride candidates. They cannot resist the call of custom, the authority of their parents and older brothers. They must marry; it is the duty of a man to look after a wife. The new wives will be young widows with children, destitute but of good family. They will make loving wives, but the men will shun them. I've had calls from the men over crackling Indian telephone lines. "Save me," they say, these substantial, educated, successful men of forty. "My parents are arranging a marriage for me." In a month they will have buried one family and returned to Canada with a new bride and partial family.

I am comparatively lucky. No one here thinks of arranging a husband for an unlucky widow.

Then, on the third day of the sixth month into this odyssey, in an abandoned temple in a tiny Himalayan village, as I make my offering of flowers and sweetmeats to the god of a tribe of animists, my husband descends to me. He is squatting next to a scrawny *sadhu* in moth-eaten robes. Vikram wears the vanilla suit he wore the last time I hugged him. The *sadhu* tosses petals on a butter-fed flame, reciting Sanskrit Mantras, and sweeps his face of flies. My husband takes my hands in his.

You're beautiful, he starts. Then, *What are you doing here?*

Shall I stay? I ask. He only smiles, but already the image is fading. *You must finish alone what we started together.* No seaweed wreathes his mouth. He speaks too fast just as he used to when we were an envied family in our pink split-level. He is gone.

In the windowless altar room, smoky with joss sticks and clarified butter lamps, a sweaty hand gropes for my blouse. I do not shriek. The *sadhu* arranges his robe. The lamps hiss and sputter out.

When we come out of the temple, my mother says, "Did you feel something weird in there?"

My mother has no patience with ghosts, prophetic dreams, holy men, and cults.

"No," I lie. "Nothing."

But she knows that she's lost me. She knows that in days I shall be leaving.

Kusum's put her house up for sale. She wants to live in an ashram in Hardwar. Moving to Hardwar was her swami's idea. Her swami runs two ashrams, the one in Hardwar and another here in Toronto.

"Don't run away," I tell her.

"I'm not running away," she says. "I'm pursuing inner peace. You think you or that Ranganathan fellow are better off?"

Pam's left for California. She wants to do some modelling, she says. She says when she comes into her share of the insurance money she'll open a yoga-cum-aerobics studio in Hollywood. She sends me postcards so naughty I daren't leave them on the coffee table. Her mother has withdrawn from her and the world.

The rest of us don't lose touch, that's the point. Talk is all we have, says Dr. Ranganathan, who has also resisted his relatives and returned to Montreal and to his job, alone. He says, whom better to talk with than other relatives? We've been melted down and recast as a new tribe.

He calls me twice a week from Montreal. Every Wednesday night and every Saturday afternoon. He is changing jobs, going to Ottawa. But Ottawa is over a hundred miles away, and he is forced to drive two hundred and twenty miles a day. He can't bring himself to sell his house. The house is a temple, he says; the king-sized bed in the master bedroom is a shrine. He sleeps on a folding cot. A devotee.

There are still some hysterical relatives. Judith Templeton's list of those needing help and those who've "accepted" is in nearly perfect balance. Acceptance means you speak of your family in the past tense and you make active plans for moving ahead with your life. There are courses at Seneca and Ryerson we could be taking. Her gleaming leather briefcase is full of college catalogues and lists of cultural societies that need our help. She has done impressive work, I tell her.

"In the textbooks on grief management," she replies—I am her confidante, I realize, one of the few whose grief has not sprung bizarre obsessions—"there are stages to pass through: rejection, depression, acceptance, reconstruction." She has compiled a chart and finds that six months after the tragedy, none of us still reject reality, but only a handful are reconstructing. "Depressed Acceptance" is the plateau we've reached. Remarriage is a major step in reconstruction (though she's a little surprised, even shocked, over *how* quickly some of the men have taken on new families). Selling one's house and changing jobs and cities is healthy.

How do I tell Judith Templeton that my family surrounds me, and that like creatures in epics, they've changed shapes? She sees me as calm and accepting but worries that I have no job, no career. My closest friends are worse off than I. I cannot tell her my days, even my nights, are thrilling.

She asks me to help with families she can't reach at all. An elderly couple in Agincourt whose sons were killed just weeks after they had brought their parents over from a village in Punjab. From their names, I know they are Sikh. Judith Templeton and a translator have visited them twice with offers of money for air fare to Ireland, with bank forms, power-of-attorney forms, but they have refused to sign, or to leave their tiny apartment. Their sons' money is frozen in the bank. Their sons' investment apartments have been trashed by tenants, the furnishings sold off. The parents fear that anything they sign or any money they receive will end the company's or the country's obligations to them. They fear they are selling their sons for two airline tickets to a place they've never seen.

The high-rise apartment is a tower of Indians and West Indians, with a sprinkling of Orientals. The nearest bus stop kiosk is lined with women in saris. Boys practice cricket in the parking lot. Inside the building, even I wince a bit from the ferocity of onion fumes, the distinctive and immediate Indianness of frying *ghee*, but Judith Templeton maintains a steady flow of information. These poor old people are in imminent danger of losing their place and all their services.

I say to her, "They are Sikh. They will not open up to a Hindu woman." And what I want to add is, as much as I try not to, I stiffen now at the sight of beards and turbans. I remember a time when we all trusted each other in this new country, it was only the new country we worried about.

The two rooms are dark and stuffy. The lights are off, and an oil lamp sputters on the coffee table. The bent old lady has let us in, and her husband is wrapping a white turban over his oiled, hip-length hair. She immediately goes to the kitchen, and I hear the most familiar sound of an Indian home, tap water hitting and filling a teapot.

They have not paid their utility bills, out of fear and the inability to write a check. The telephone is gone; electricity and gas and water are soon to follow. They have told Judith their sons will provide. They are good boys, and they have always earned and looked after their parents.

We converse a bit in Hindi. They do not ask about the crash and I wonder if I should bring it up. If they think I am here merely as a translator, then they may feel insulted. There are thousands of Punjabi-speakers, Sikhs, in Toronto to do a better job. And so I say to the old lady, "I too have lost my sons, and my husband, in the crash."

Her eyes immediately fill with tears. The man mutters a few words which sound like a blessing. "God provides and God takes away," he says.

I want to say, but only men destroy and give back nothing. "My boys and my husband are not coming back," I say. "We have to understand that."

Now the old woman responds. "But who is to say? Man alone does not decide these things." To this her husband adds his agreement.

Judith asks about the bank papers, the release forms. With a stroke of the pen, they will have a provincial trustee to pay their bills, invest their money, send them a monthly pension.

"Do you know this woman?" I ask them.

The man raises his hand from the table, turns it over and seems to regard each finger separately before he answers. "This young lady is always coming here, we make tea for her and she leaves papers for us to sign." His eyes scan a pile of papers in the corner of the room. "Soon we will be out of tea, then will she go away?"

The old lady adds, "I have asked my neighbors and no one else gets *angrezi* visitors. What have we done?"

"It's her job," I try to explain. "The government is worried. Soon you will have no place to stay, no lights, no gas, no water."

"Government will get its money. Tell her not to worry, we are honorable people."

I try to explain the government wishes to give money, not take. He raises his hand. "Let them take," he says. "We are accustomed to that. That is no problem."

"We are strong people," says the wife. "Tell her that."

"Who needs all this machinery?" demands the husband. "It is unhealthy, the bright lights, the cold air on a hot day, the cold food, the four gas rings. God will provide, not government."

"When our boys return," the mother says. Her husband sucks his teeth. "Enough talk," he says.

Judith breaks in. "Have you convinced them?" The snaps on her cordovan briefcase go off like firecrackers in that quiet apartment. She lays the sheaf of legal papers on the coffee table. "If they can't write their names, an X will do—I've told them that."

Now the old lady has shuffled to the kitchen and soon emerges with a pot of tea and two cups. "I think my bladder will go first on a job like this," Judith says to me, smiling. "If only there was some way of reaching them. Please thank her for the tea. Tell her she's very kind."

I nod in Judith's direction and tell them in Hindi, "She thanks you for the tea. She thinks you are being very hospitable but she doesn't have the slightest idea what it means."

I want to say, humor her. I want to say, my boys and my husband are with me too, more than ever. I look in the old man's eyes and I can read his stubborn, peasant's message: *I have protected this woman as best I can. She is the only person I have left. Give to me or take from me what you will, but I will not sign for it. I will not pretend that I accept.*

In the car, Judith says, "You see what I'm up against? I'm sure they're lovely people, but their stubbornness and ignorance are driving me crazy. They think signing a paper is signing their sons' death warrants, don't they?"

I am looking out the window. I want to say, *In our culture, it is a parent's duty to hope.*

"Now Shaila, this next woman is a real mess. She cries day and night, and she refuses all medical help. We may have to—"

"—Let me out at the subway," I say.

"I beg your pardon?" I can feel those blue eyes staring at me.

It would not be like her to disobey. She merely disapproves, and slows at a corner to let me out. Her voice is plaintive. "Is there anything I said? Anything I did?"

I could answer her suddenly in a dozen ways, but I choose not to. "Shaila? Let's talk about it," I hear, then slam the door.

A wife and mother begins her new life in a new country, and that life is cut short. Yet her husband tells her: Complete what we have started. We, who stayed out of politics and came halfway around the world to avoid religious and political feuding, have been the first in the New World to die from it. I no longer know what we started, nor how to complete it. I write letters to the editors of local papers and to members of Parliament. Now at least they admit it was a bomb. One MP answers back, with sympathy, but with a challenge. You want to make a difference? Work on a campaign. Work on mine. Politicize the Indian voter.

My husband's old lawyer helps me set up a trust. Vikram was a saver and a careful investor. He had saved the boys' boarding school and college fees. I sell the pink house at four times what we paid for it and take a small apartment downtown. I am looking for a charity to support.

We are deep in the Toronto winter, gray skies, icy pavements. I stay indoors, watching television. I have tried to assess my situation, how best to live my life, to complete what we began so many years ago. Kusum has written me from Hardwar that her life is now serene. She has seen Satish and has heard her daughter sing again. Kusum was on a pilgrimage, passing through a village, when she heard a young girl's voice, singing one of her daughter's favorite *bhajans*. She followed the music through the squalor of a Himalayan village, to a hut where a young girl, an exact replica of her daughter, was fanning coals under the kitchen fire. When she appeared, the girl cried out, "Ma!" and ran away. What did I think of that?

I think I can only envy her.

Pam didn't make it to California, but writes me from Vancouver. She works in a department store, giving make-up hints to Indian and Oriental girls. Dr. Ranganathan has given up his commute, given up his house and job, and accepted an academic position in Texas where no one knows his story and he has vowed not to tell it. He calls me now once a week.

I wait, I listen, and I pray, but Vikram has not returned to me. The voices and the shapes and the nights filled with visions ended abruptly several weeks ago.

I take it as a sign.

One rare, beautiful, sunny day last week, returning from a small errand on

Yonge Street, I was walking through the park from the subway to my apartment. I live equidistant from the Ontario Houses of Parliament and the University of Toronto. The day was not cold, but something in the bare trees caught my attention. I looked up from the gravel, into the branches and the clear blue sky beyond. I thought I heard the rustling of larger forms, and I waited a moment for voices. Nothing.

"What?" I asked.

Then as I stood in the path looking north to Queen's Park and west to the university, I heard the voices of my family one last time. *Your time has come,* they said. *Go, be brave.*

I do not know where this voyage I have begun will end. I do not know which direction I will take. I dropped the package on a park bench and started walking.

Murathan Mungan

Muradhan and Selvihan or
The Tale of the Crystal Kiosk

(T U R K E Y)

The Crystal Kiosk sat on that mountain top.

And what a mountain it was. Not just any old mountain. You know, there are mountains that embrace other mountains, as if dancing in a ring, standing side by side, barring passage. And still other mountains press their feet against other hills, other mountains,

and they rise and rise.

This was none like these.

It stood alone in the middle of a vast, desolate steppe. Its might was its solitude. Alone and mighty, it rose without embracing any mountain or hill, without leaning or pressing against any. Dignified, grave, self-confident, it rose slowly, with calm. As if in no hurry, as if it would stand there till the day of doom, as if even the flood couldn't touch it . . . It had no sharp cliffs, sudden and violent, that opened chasms in its midst. It rose slowly along its smooth hills and fitting slopes. In this manner, its awesome greatness assumed modesty.

Gazing at it, human beings thought that they could climb it easily, that they would make it to the top one day. The mountain was hope's safe.

It was grandiose, free of anger. Once upon a time, it had lived an angry, furious youth and spewed fires at its foot. Now youth had grown cold, petrified, turned into the ever-widening rings of small, fine-needled lacy hills. Everything had come to pass. Its fury had subsided. What used to be called wrath was no more than a youthful temper.

Its beauty was calm. Pure white clouds circled the pure white snow on its peak. The snow was the clouds' elusive threshold. The snow's color illuminated the clouds, the clouds' the snow. (When the sun came between them, the pure whiteness would dissipate, turning into a haze of vaporous colors.)

The mountain experienced all four seasons at once. (Human beings always dreamt of going there one day. They passed the time with dreams of the ascent, and many died before attaining this forever-deferred dream. Without ever climbing the mountain . . . Everything remained unfulfilled, the hope, the fancy, the journey.)

And at times they returned from half-finished journeys. Defeated, having discovered the mountain's truth. (It could not be climbed.) Having learned an important lesson for the remainder of their life. A wisdom they would not have been able to attain unless by daring the task, by attempting the journey. (The mountain and human beings had tested each other.)

From then on, their lives could no longer include the hope of climbing that mountain.

What you call mountain is an orb of fire, wrestling the sun, you'd think. Its flames the color of war. In early spring, fiery purple flowers swarm its surface. Down the slopes, all of nature is overshadowed, as if sheltered under a bird's wing. One side of the mountain is immersed in light, the other side in the clouds' shadow. The fog takes over the mountain, in ring after ring. One rising inside another, denser, narrowing rings reach the mountain's peak, climb layers upon layers, spiraling. In the end, a cloud of fog rests on the peak, hangs like a gentle tulle under the eternal veil of snow.

A never-lifting tulle.

The mountain is the native land of the flower.

Not only the flower, but the water, the springs, the myriad healing plants.

Leaving the mountain's heart, the brooks carry life to the river. They flow along the valleys, like thin silvery ropes. Without hurting or frightening anything, as if intent on remaining unnoticed. If you reached the springs replenishing the brooks, you'd be seized with wonderment. Dip your hand, it freezes, put a flower in the water, it stays fresh round the seasons. Delicate icy lace surrounds the mouth of each spring. Water embroidery, water filigree, laces of ice.

Gazelles descend to the foot of the mountain. Every time they pause, it's a sight. Magical.

These lakes are called winter lakes in the summer; you'd think they were clouds fallen on the grass. Every bird flying over a lake comes face-to-face with itself, descends, its wing touches the water. Motes of silver get caught in its plumes; ascending again, it draws a thin silvery flash in the sky.

In winter, ice sheets over the lakes. Silver has frozen. Fog descends. You'd think it was steam rising off of silver. The leaves get covered with clouds of snow, the evergreens and pine needles shawl themselves in tulle.

The birds' custom begins with the morning.

The sky awakens with the flutter of wings.

The nine lakes of mountains hold mirrors to the sky. The gazelles descending to the lakes fall in love with themselves.

On their return to the forest, they bear an absence in their hearts. An absence that would never leave them. Some aspect of their face and heart has stayed behind on the lake's icy surface. They search the forest in vain. They have lost a part of their face. The lakes make the gazelle a wanderer. The ice clouds the eyes of all gazelles—like fog, like mist. From then on, they would seek their hunter everywhere they looked.

In the summer, the ice thaws; yet the gazelles have long departed.

Love is a hallucination.

Green shows the seven provinces its seven thousand shades, proves it is the color of paradise. Flowers no one knows, no one has seen—native only to this mountain—cover the sides of the path without pretense, as if standing in salute.

And the path

is a snake that has shed its skin and becomes like the white marble. Giving ear to an Indian flute, it meanders coquettishly, with a thousand airs, climbs up the mountain and reaches the gates of the Crystal Kiosk.

there, it spreads as waves of white foam, becomes a waterfall on the stairs with long fine-chiseled stones.

the path ends at the stairs, the last surge of foam. the snake spent.

where the foam dies out, a night-blue crystal gate.

night blue.

The path is too awesome to welcome just any traveler. As if it would throw off its back the visitor it didn't like or deemed unfit for itself. As if it would stretch itself like the snake and shake the wanderer off. More than a path, it resembles a river coursing upward. As if it's cut in the stone. As if flowing end-lessly. As if frozen during the ascent.

Written on the mountain's forehead, the long path is like a promised journey.

It is such a destiny that only those marked with it are allowed passage.

It is like an ivy with myriad roots spun around the mountain. Its marble is veiny. Tempered in a thousand ovens, laid out painstakingly. The sound of hoofbeats leaves long echoes, announces the approaching traveler to the Crys-tal Kiosk.

Beauty speaks in a thousand tongues.

The mountain is a long fairy tale written in a thousand tongues.

One look and you'd think the kiosk was made of glass.

You'd think they carved it with the avalanches broken off the snowy peak. Look at its walls and you'd make out its chambers. Is it a fancy? a vision? it's uncertain. As if spirited away from a dream.

in sunlight, the kiosk seems ablaze,

at crimson dusk, it turns forest green,

you'd think it's a mighty plane tree in the forest, grafted from seven roots, sprawling itself out in seven thousand arms, its palm extending to the forest, to the heart of the forest, a beneficent and bountiful plane tree.

in the black of the night, it is the moon's teardrop. So when the mountain cold turned to frost, it froze like that,

when the moon calms down, so it does.

at sunrise, it is the sun's twin, the charmed mirror in which the sun sees itself. it stands witness to the sun's secret.

They say that thousands of workers toiled to build this kiosk; now no one knows their names. That awesome teardrop, it is said, is crystal cut from their labor's sweat.

with autumn comes the rain, the walls don't hold the water, as if the rain doesn't touch them—still there is a sense of relief, a feeling of beingcleansed—

the kiosk has tall, sharp towers (the moon hides behind them) tall towers scattered to four corners (the moon plays puss-in-the-corner among them) round, magical towers. (They hide echoes, secrets.) Long candles (pale, flickering) move about the arched windows. From one window to another, they move solitarily, as if wandering. The hands holding them are invisible.

Judas trees bleed the color of blood in the evenings; in the candles' trembling light, the lost scents of Judas trees . . .

All the villages, all the villagers are in love with the
mountain,
with this kiosk.

This kiosk is the farthest light, the most radiant.

So many clans, so many villages, so many tribes brighten their poverty by gazing endlessly at the kiosk. They migrate, see the kiosk once, and leave along their trajectory a bundle of fairy tales about the kiosk. The crystal kiosk is the fairy tale of night, day
the four seasons
the poor
the rich.

Time flows, even the Crystal Kiosk disappears.
let's say the moon has stopped crying
let's say the mirror cracks in the middle, turns to salt, unable to bear its own charm
let's say the plane tree collapses, rots and turns to soil

The Crystal Kiosk flows down the mountain (streams into the river, meets the sea, let's say) flows across the history (mixes in wars, in settlements, let's say)
its fairy tale remains.
and that tale, a thousand people hear, one understands.

The Crystal Kiosk remains to no one. (Poetry withers, legend is exhausted in those mountains. No poet climbs the mountains anymore.) Yet it leaves us a saying, a word. It leaves so that we can pass the word on to those who come after us, so we leave a story. Each story is in charge of its own moral, bound with it. (Each poet bears the seal of his own word)
to reach the path of the fairy tale,
life must be spent on the paths of truth.

Each morning, all the people of surrounding villages and clans used to wake up gazing at the kiosk.

The Crystal Kiosk was the morning star showing the day its way. The kiosk's chisel work used to blend in the mountain's panorama, in the gazelle's love,

and in those mornings, human beings used to think that they could, that they must, go to the mountain.

And that one day they would . . .

Translated from the Turkish by Aron R. Aji

Haruki Murakami

The Elephant Vanishes

(JAPAN)

When the elephant disappeared from our town's elephant house, I read about it in the newspaper. My alarm clock woke me that day, as always at 6:13. I went to the kitchen, made coffee and toast, turned on the radio, spread the paper out on the kitchen table, and proceeded to munch and read. I'm one of those people who read the paper from beginning to end, in order, so it took me awhile to get to the article about the vanishing elephant. The front page was filled with stories of SDI and the trade friction with America, after which I plowed through the national news, international politics, economics, letters to the editor, book reviews, real-estate ads, sports reports, and finally, the regional news.

The elephant article was the lead story in the regional section. The unusually large headline caught my eye: ELEPHANT MISSING IN TOKYO SUBURB, and, beneath that, in type one size smaller, CITIZENS' FEARS MOUNT. SOME CALL FOR PROBE. There was a photo of policemen in inspecting the empty elephant house. Without the elephant, something about the place seemed wrong. It looked bigger than it needed to be, blank and empty like some huge, dehydrated beast from which the innards had been plucked.

Brushing away my toast crumbs, I studied every line of the article. The elephant's absence had first been noticed at two o'clock on the afternoon of May 18—the day before—when men from the school-lunch company delivered their usual truckload of food (the elephant mostly ate leftovers from the lunches of children in the local elementary school). On the ground, still locked, lay the steel shackle that had been fastened to the elephant's hind leg, as though the elephant had slipped out of it. Nor was the elephant the only one missing. Also gone was its keeper, the man who had been in charge of the elephant's care and feeding from the start.

According to the article, the elephant and keeper had last been seen sometime after five o'clock the previous day (May 17) by a few pupils from the elementary school, who were visiting the elephant house, making crayon sketches. These pupils must have been the last to see the elephant, said the paper, since the keeper always closed the gate to the elephant enclosure when the six-o'clock siren blew.

There had been nothing unusual about either the elephant or its keeper at the time, according to the unanimous testimony of the pupils. The elephant had been standing where it always stood, in the middle of the enclosure, occasionally wagging its trunk from side to side or squinting its wrinkly eyes. It was such an awfully old elephant that its every move seemed a tremendous effort—so much so that people seeing it for the first time feared it might collapse at any moment and draw its final breath.

The elephant's age had led to its adoption by our town a year earlier. When financial problems caused the little private zoo on the edge of town to close its doors, a wildlife dealer found places for the other animals in zoos throughout the country. But all the zoos had plenty of elephants, apparently, and not one of them was willing to take in a feeble old thing that looked as if it might die of a heart attack at any moment. And so, after its companions were gone, the elephant stayed alone in the decaying zoo for nearly four months with nothing to do—not that it had had anything to do before.

This caused a lot of difficulty, both for the zoo and for the town. The zoo had sold its land to a developer, who was planning to put up a high-rise condo building, and the town had already issued him a permit. The longer the elephant problem remained unresolved, the more interest the developer had to pay for nothing. Still, simply killing the thing would have been out of the question. If it had been a spider monkey or a bat, they might have been able to get away with it, but the killing of an elephant would have been too hard to cover up, and if it ever came out afterward, the repercussions would have been tremendous. And so the various parties had met to deliberate on the matter, and they formulated an agreement on the disposition of the old elephant:

1. The town would take ownership of the elephant at no cost.

2. The developer would, without compensation, provide land for housing the elephant.

3. The zoo's former owners would be responsible for paying the keeper's wages.

I had had my own private interest in the elephant problem from the very outset, and I kept a scrapbook with every clipping I could find on it. I had even gone to hear the town council's debates on the matter, which is why I am able to give such a full and accurate account of the course of events. And while my account may prove somewhat lengthy, I have chosen to set it down here in case the handling of the elephant problem should bear directly upon the elephant's disappearance.

When the mayor finished negotiating the agreement—with its provision that the town would take charge of the elephant—a movement opposing the measure boiled up from within the ranks of the opposition party (whose very existence I had never imagined until then). "Why must the town take ownership of the elephant?" they demanded of the mayor, and they raised the following points (sorry for all these lists, but I use them to make things easier to understand):

1. The elephant problem was a question for private enterprise—the zoo and the developer; there was no reason for the town to become involved.

2. Care and feeding costs would be too high.

3. What did the mayor intend to do about the security problem?

4. What merit would there be in the town's having its own elephant?

"The town has any number of responsibilities it should be taking care of before it gets into the business of keeping an elephant—sewer repair, the purchase of a new fire engine, etcetera," the opposition group declared, and while they did not say it in so many words, they hinted at the possibility of some secret deal between the mayor and the developer.

In response, the mayor had this to say:

1. If the town permitted the construction of high-rise condos, its tax revenues would increase so dramatically that the cost of keeping an elephant would be insignificant by comparison; thus it made sense for the town to take on the care of this elephant.

2. The elephant was so old that it neither ate very much nor was likely to pose a danger to anyone.

3. When the elephant died, the town would take full possession of the land donated by the developer.

4. The elephant could become the town's symbol.

The long debate reached the conclusion that the town would take charge of the elephant after all. As an old, well-established residential suburb, the town boasted a relatively affluent citizenry, and its financial footing was sound. The adoption of a homeless elephant was a move that people could look upon favorably. People like old elephants better than sewers and fire engines.

I myself was all in favor of having the town care for the elephant. True, I was getting sick of high-rise condos, but I liked the idea of my town's owning an elephant.

A wooded area was cleared, and the elementary school's aging gym was moved there as an elephant house. The man who had served as the elephant's keeper for many years would come to live in the house with the elephant. The children's lunch scraps would serve as the elephant's feed. Finally, the elephant itself was carted in a trailer to its new home, there to live out its remaining years.

I joined the crowd at the elephant-house dedication ceremonies. Standing before the elephant, the mayor delivered a speech (on the town's development and the enrichment of its cultural facilities); one elementary-school pupil, representing the student body, stood up to read a composition ("Please live a long and healthy life, Mr. Elephant"); there was a sketch contest (sketching the elephant thereafter became an integral component of the pupils' artistic education); and each of two young women in swaying dresses (neither of whom was especially good-looking) fed the elephant a bunch of bananas. The elephant endured these virtually meaningless (for the elephant, entirely meaningless) formalities with hardly a twitch, and it chomped on the bananas with a vacant stare. When it finished eating the bananas, everyone applauded.

On its right rear leg, the elephant wore a solid, heavy-looking steel cuff from which there stretched a thick chain perhaps thirty feet long, and this in turn was securely fastened to a concrete slab. Anyone could see what a sturdy anchor held the beast in place: The elephant could have struggled with all its might for a hundred years and never broken the thing.

I couldn't tell if the elephant was bothered by its shackle. On the surface, at least, it seemed all but unconscious of the enormous chunk of metal wrapped around its leg. It kept its blank gaze fixed on some indeterminate point in space, its ears and a few white hairs on its body waving gently in the breeze.

The elephant's keeper was a small, bony old man. It was hard to guess his age; he could have been in his early sixties or late seventies. He was one of those people whose appearance is no longer influenced by their age after they pass a certain point in life. His skin had the same darkly ruddy, sunburned look both summer and winter, his hair was stiff and short, his eyes were small. His face had no distinguishing characteristics, but his almost perfectly circular ears stuck out on either side with disturbing prominence.

He was not an unfriendly man. If someone spoke to him, he would reply, and he expressed himself clearly. If he wanted to he could be almost charming— though you always knew he was somewhat ill at ease. Generally, he remained a reticent, lonely-looking old man. He seemed to like the children who visited the elephant house, and he worked at being nice to them, but the children never really warmed to him.

The only one who did that was the elephant. The keeper lived in a small prefab room attached to the elephant house, and all day long he stayed with the elephant, attending to its needs. They had been together for more than ten years, and you could sense their closeness in every gesture and look. Whenever the elephant was standing there blankly and the keeper wanted it to move, all he had to do was stand next to the elephant, tap it on a front leg, and whisper something in its ear. Then, swaying its huge bulk, the elephant would go exactly where the keeper had indicated, take up its new position, and continue staring at a point in space.

On weekends, I would drop by the elephant house and study these operations, but I could never figure out the principle on which the keeper-elephant communication was based. Maybe the elephant understood a few simple words (it had certainly been living long enough), or perhaps it received its information through variations in the taps on its leg. Or possibly it had some special power resembling mental telepathy and could read the keeper's mind. I once asked the keeper how he gave his orders to the elephant, but the old man just smiled and said, "We've been together a long time."

And so a year went by. Then, without warning, the elephant vanished. One day it was there, and the next it had ceased to be.

I poured myself a second cup of coffee and read the story again from beginning to end. Actually, it was a pretty strange article—the kind that might excite Sherlock Holmes. "Look at this, Watson," he'd say, tapping his pipe. "A very interesting article. Very interesting indeed."

What gave the article its air of strangeness was the obvious confusion and bewilderment of the reporter. And this confusion and bewilderment clearly came from the absurdity of the situation itself. You could see how the reporter had struggled to find clever ways around the absurdity in order to write a "normal" article. But the struggle had only driven his confusion and bewilderment to a hopeless extreme.

For example, the article used such expressions as "the elephant escaped," but if you looked at the entire piece it became obvious that the elephant had in no way "escaped." It had vanished into thin air. The reporter revealed his own conflicted state of mind by saying that a few "details" remained "unclear," but this was not a phenomenon that could be disposed of by using such ordinary terminology as "details" or "unclear," I felt.

First, there was the problem of the steel cuff that had been fastened to the elephant's leg. This had been found *still locked.* The most reasonable explanation for this would be that the keeper had unlocked the ring, removed it from the elephant's leg, *locked the ring again,* and run off with the elephant—a hypothesis to which the paper clung with desperate tenacity despite the fact that the keeper had no key! Only two keys existed, and they, for security's sake, were kept in locked safes, one in police headquarters and the other in the firehouse, both beyond the reach of the keeper—or of anyone else who might attempt to steal them. And even if someone had succeeded in stealing a key, there was no need whatever for that person to make a point of returning the key after using it. Yet the following morning both keys were found in their respective safes at the police and fire stations. Which brings us to the conclusion that the elephant pulled its leg out of that solid steel ring without the aid of a key—an absolute impossibility unless someone had sawed the foot off.

The second problem was the route of escape. The elephant house and grounds were surrounded by a massive fence nearly ten feet high. The question of security had been hotly debated in the town council, and the town had settled upon a system that might be considered somewhat excessive for keeping one old elephant. Heavy iron bars had been anchored in a thick concrete foundation (the cost of the fence was borne by the real-estate company), and there was only a single entrance, which was found locked from the inside. There was no way the elephant could have escaped from this fortresslike enclosure.

The third problem was elephant tracks. Directly behind the elephant enclosure was a steep hill, which the animal could not possibly have climbed, so even if we suppose that the elephant had somehow managed to pull its leg out of the steel ring and leap over the ten-foot-high fence, it would still have had to escape down the path to the front of the enclosure, and there was not a single mark anywhere in the soft earth of that path that could be seen as an elephant's footprint.

Riddled as it was with such perplexities and labored circumlocutions, the newspaper article as a whole left but one possible conclusion: The elephant had not escaped. It had vanished.

Needless to say, however, neither the newspaper nor the police nor the mayor was willing to admit—openly, at least—that the elephant had vanished. The police were continuing to investigate, their spokesman saying only that the elephant either "was taken or was allowed to escape in a clever, deliberately calculated move. Because of the difficulty involved in hiding an elephant, it is only a matter of time till we solve the case.' To this optimistic assessment he added that they were planning to search the woods in the area with the aid of local hunters' clubs and sharpshooters from the national Self-Defense Force.

The mayor had held a news conference, in which he apologized for the inadequacy of the town's police resources. At the same time, he declared, "Our elephant-security system is in no way inferior to similar facilities in any zoo in the country. Indeed, it is far stronger and far more fail-safe than the standard cage." He also observed, "This is a dangerous and senseless antisocial act of the most malicious kind, and we cannot allow it to go unpunished."

As they had the year before, the opposition-party members of the town council made accusations. "We intend to look into the political responsibility of the mayor; he has colluded with private enterprise in order to sell the townspeople a bill of goods on the solution of the elephant problem."

One "worried looking" mother, thirty-seven, was interviewed by the paper. "Now I'm afraid to let my children out to play," she said.

The coverage included a detailed summary of the steps leading to the town's decision to adopt the elephant, an aerial sketch of the elephant house and grounds, and brief histories of both the elephant and the keeper who had vanished with it. The man, Noboru Watanabe, sixty-three, was from Tateyama, in Chiba Prefecture. He had worked for many years as a keeper in the mammalian section of the zoo, and "had the complete trust of the zoo authorities, both for his abundant knowledge of these animals and for his warm sincere personality." The elephant had been sent from East Africa twenty-two years earlier, but little was known about its exact age or its "personality." The report concluded with a request from the police for citizens of the town to come forward with any information they might have regarding the elephant.

I thought about this request for a while as I drank my second cup of coffee, but I decided not to call the police—both because I preferred not to come into contact with them if I could help it and because I felt the police would not believe what I had to tell them. What good would it do to talk to people like that, who would not even consider the possibility that the elephant had simply vanished?

I took my scrapbook down from the shelf, cut out the elephant article, and pasted it in. Then I washed the dishes and left for the office.

I watched the search on the seven-o'clock news. There were hunters carrying large-bore rifles loaded with tranquilizer darts, Self-Defense Force troops, policemen, and firemen combing every square inch of the woods and hills in the immediate area as helicopters hovered overhead. Of course, we're talking about the kind of "woods" and "hills" you find in the suburbs outside Tokyo, so they didn't have an enormous area to cover. With that many people involved, a day should have been more than enough to do the job. And they weren't searching for some tiny homicidal maniac: They were after a huge African elephant. There was a limit to the number of places a thing like that could hide. But still they had not managed to find it. The chief of police appeared on the screen, saying, "We intend to continue the search." And the anchorman concluded the report, "Who released the elephant, and how? Where have they hidden it? What was their motive? Everything remains shrouded in mystery."

The search went on for several days, but the authorities were unable to discover a single clue to the elephant's whereabouts. I studied the newspaper reports, clipped them all, and pasted them in my scrapbook—including editorial cartoons on the subject. The album filled up quickly, and I had to buy another. Despite their enormous volume, the clippings contained not one fact of the kind that I was looking for. The reports were either pointless or off the mark: ELEPHANT STILL MISSING, GLOOM THICK IN SEARCH HQ, MOB BEHIND DISAPPEARANCE? And even articles like this became noticeably scarcer after a week had gone by, until there was virtually nothing. A few of the weekly magazines carried sensational stories—one even hired a psychic—but they had nothing to substantiate their wild headlines. It seemed that people were beginning to shove the elephant case into the large category of "unsolvable mysteries." The disappearance of one old elephant and one old elephant keeper would have no impact on the course of society. The earth would continue its monotonous rotations, politicians would continue issuing unreliable proclamations, people would continue yawning on their way to the office, children would continue studying for their college-entrance exams. Amid the endless surge and ebb of everyday life, interest in a missing elephant could not last forever. And so a number of unremarkable months went by, like a tired army marching past a window.

Whenever I had a spare moment, I would visit the house where the elephant no longer lived. A thick chain had been wrapped round and round the bars of the yard's iron gate, to keep people out. Peering inside, I could see that the elephant-house door had also been chained and locked, as though the police were trying to make up for having failed to find the elephant by multiplying the layers of security on the now-empty elephant house. The area was deserted, the previous crowds having been replaced by a flock of pigeons resting on the roof. No one took care of the grounds any longer, and thick green summer grass had sprung up there as if it had been waiting for this opportunity. The chain coiled around the door of the elephant house reminded me of a huge snake set to guard a ruined palace in a thick forest. A few short months without its elephant had given the place an air of doom and desolation that hung there like a huge, oppressive rain cloud.

I met her near the end of September. It had been raining that day from morning to night—the kind of soft, monotonous, misty rain that often falls at that time of year, washing away bit by bit the memories of summer burned into the earth. Coursing down the gutters, all those memories flowed into the sewers and rivers, to be carried to the deep, dark ocean.

We noticed each other at the party my company threw to launch its new advertising campaign. I work for the PR section of a major manufacturer of electrical appliances, and at the time I was in charge of publicity for a coordinated line of kitchen equipment, which was scheduled to go on the market in time for the autumn-wedding and winter-bonus seasons. My job was to negotiate with several women's magazines for tie-in articles—not the kind of work that takes a great deal of intelligence, but I had to see to it that the articles they wrote didn't smack of advertising. When magazines gave us publicity, we rewarded them by placing ads in their pages. They scratched our backs, we scratched theirs.

As an editor of a magazine for young housewives, she had come to the party for material for one of these "articles." I happened to be in charge of showing her around, pointing out the features of the colorful refrigerators and coffeemakers and microwave ovens and juicers that a famous Italian designer had done for us.

"The most important point is unity," I explained. "Even the most beautifully designed item dies if it is out of balance with its surroundings. Unity of design, unity of color, unity of function: This is what today's *kit-chin* needs above all else. Research tells us that a housewife spends the largest part of her day in the *kit-chin*. The *kit-chin* is her workplace, her study, her living room. Which is why she does all she can to make the *kit-chin* a pleasant place to be. It has nothing to do with size. Whether it's large or small, one fundamental principle governs every successful *kit-chin,* and that principle is unity. This is the concept underlying the design of our new series. Look at this cooktop, for example. . . ."

She nodded and scribbled things in a small notebook, but it was obvious that she had little interest in the material, nor did I have any personal stake in our new cooktop. Both of us were doing our jobs.

"You know a lot about kitchens," she said when I finished. She used the Japanese word, without picking up on *"kit-chin."*

"That's what I do for a living," I answered with a professional smile. "Aside from that, though, I do like to cook. Nothing fancy, but I cook for myself every day."

"Still, I wonder if unity is all that necessary for a kitchen."

"We say *'kit-chin,' "* I advised her. "No big deal, but the company wants us to use the English."

"Oh. Sorry. But still, I wonder. Is unity so important for a *kit-chin?* What do *you* think?"

"My personal opinion? That doesn't come out until I take my necktie off," I said with a grin. "But today I'll make an exception. A kitchen probably *does* need a few things more than it needs unity. But those other elements are things you can't sell. And in this pragmatic world of ours, things you can't sell don't count for much."

"*Is* the world such a pragmatic place?"

I took out a cigarette and lit it with my lighter.

"I don't know—the word just popped out," I said. "But it explains a lot. It makes work easier, too. You can play games with it, make up neat expressions: 'essentially pragmatic,' or 'pragmatic in essence.' If you look at things that way, you avoid all kinds of complicated problems."

"What an interesting view!"

"Not really. It's what everybody thinks. Oh, by the way, we've got some pretty good champagne. Care to have some?"

"Thanks. I'd love to."

As we chatted over champagne, we realized we had several mutual acquaintances. Since our part of the business world was not a very big pond, if you tossed in a few pebbles, one or two were bound to hit a mutual acquaintance. In addition, she and my kid sister happened to have graduated from the same university. With markers like this to follow, our conversation went along smoothly.

She was unmarried, and so was I. She was twenty-six, and I was thirty-one. She wore contact lenses, and I wore glasses. She praised my necktie, and I praised her jacket. We compared rents and complained about our jobs and salaries. In other words, we were beginning to like each other. She was an attractive woman, and not at all pushy. I stood there talking with her for a full twenty minutes, unable to discover a single reason not to think well of her.

As the party was breaking up, I invited her to join me in the hotel's cocktail lounge, where we settled in to continue our conversation. A soundless rain went on falling outside the lounge's panoramic window, the lights of the city sending blurry messages through the mist. A damp hush held sway over the nearly empty cocktail lounge. She ordered a frozen daiquiri and I had a scotch on the rocks.

Sipping our drinks, we carried on the kind of conversation that a man and woman have in a bar when they have just met and are beginning to like each other. We talked about our college days, our tastes in music, sports, our daily routines.

Then I told her about the elephant. Exactly how this happened, I can't recall. Maybe we were talking about something having to do with animals, and that was the connection. Or maybe, unconsciously, I had been looking for someone—a good listener—to whom I could present my own, unique view on the elephant's disappearance. Or, then again, it might have been the liquor that got me talking.

In any case, the second the words left my mouth, I knew that I had brought up one of the least suitable topics I could have found for this occasion. No, I should never have mentioned the elephant. The topic was—what?—too complete, too closed.

I tried to hurry on to something else, but as luck would have it she was more interested than most in the case of the vanishing elephant, and once I admitted that I had seen the elephant many times she showered me with questions—what kind of elephant was it, how did I think it had escaped, what did it eat, wasn't it a danger to the community, and so forth.

I told her nothing more than what everybody knew from the news, but she seemed to sense constraint in my tone of voice. I had never been good at telling lies.

As if she had not noticed anything strange about my behavior, she sipped her second daiquiri and asked, "Weren't you shocked when the elephant disappeared? It's not the kind of thing that somebody could have predicted."

"No, probably not," I said. I took a pretzel from the mound in the glass dish on our table, snapped it in two, and ate half. The waiter replaced our ashtray with an empty one.

She looked at me expectantly. I took out another cigarette and lit it. I had quit smoking three years earlier but had begun again when the elephant disappeared.

"Why 'probably not'? You mean you could have predicted it?"

"No, of course I couldn't have predicted it," I said with a smile. "For an elephant to disappear all of a sudden one day—there's no precedent, no need, for such a thing to happen. It doesn't make any logical sense."

"But still, your answer was very strange. When I said, 'It's not the kind of thing that somebody could have predicted,' you said, 'No, probably not.' Most people would have said, 'You're right,' or 'Yeah, it's weird,' or something. See what I mean?"

I sent a vague nod in her direction and raised my hand to call the waiter. A kind of tentative silence took hold as I waited for him to bring me my next scotch.

"I'm finding this a little hard to grasp," she said softly. "You were carrying on a perfectly normal conversation with me until a couple of minutes ago—at least until the subject of the elephant came up. Then something funny happened. I can't understand you anymore. Something's wrong. Is it the elephant? Or are my ears playing tricks on me?"

"There's nothing wrong with your ears," I said.

"So then it's you. The problem's with you."

I stuck my finger in my glass and stirred the ice. I like the sound of ice in a whiskey glass.

"I wouldn't call it a 'problem,' exactly. It's not that big a deal. I'm not hiding anything. I'm just not sure I can talk about it very well, so I'm trying not to say anything at all. But you're right—it's very strange."

"What do you mean?"

It was no use: I'd have to tell her the story. I took one gulp of whiskey and started.

"The thing is, I was probably the last one to see the elephant before it disappeared. I saw it after seven o'clock on the evening of May seventeenth, and they noticed it was gone on the afternoon of the eighteenth. Nobody saw it in between because they lock the elephant house at six."

"I don't get it. If they closed the house at six, how did you see it after seven?"

"There's a kind of cliff behind the elephant house. A steep hill on private property, with no real roads. There's one spot, on the back of the hill, where you can see into the elephant house. I'm probably the only one who knows about it."

I had found the spot purely by chance. Strolling through the area one Sunday afternoon, I had lost my way and come out at the top of the cliff. I found a little flat open patch, just big enough for a person to stretch out in, and when I looked down through the bushes, there was the elephant-house roof. Below the edge of the roof was a fairly large vent opening, and through it I had a clear view of the inside of the elephant house.

I made it a habit after that to visit the place every now and then to look at the elephant when it was inside the house. If anyone had asked me why I bothered doing such a thing, I wouldn't have had a decent answer. I simply enjoyed watching the elephant during its private time. There was nothing more to it than that. I couldn't see the elephant when the house was dark inside, of course, but in the early hours of the evening the keeper would have the lights on the whole time he was taking care of the elephant, which enabled me to study the scene in detail.

What struck me immediately when I saw the elephant and keeper alone together was the obvious liking they had for each other—something they never displayed when they were out before the public. Their affection was evident in every gesture. It almost seemed as if they stored away their emotions during the day, taking care not to let anyone notice them, and took them out at night when they could be alone. Which is not to say that they did anything different when they were by themselves inside. The elephant just stood there, as blank as ever, and the keeper would perform those tasks one would normally expect him to do as a keeper: scrubbing down the elephant with a deck broom, picking up the elephant's enormous droppings, cleaning up after the elephant ate. But there was no way to mistake the special warmth, the sense of trust, between them. While the keeper swept the floor, the elephant would wave its trunk and pat the keeper's back. I liked to watch the elephant doing that.

"Have you always been fond of elephants?" she asked. "I mean, not just that particular elephant?"

"Hmm . . . come to think of it, I do like elephants," I said. "There's something about them that excites me. I guess I've always liked them. I wonder why."

"And that day, too, after the sun went down, I suppose you were up on the hill by yourself, looking at the elephant. May—what day was it?"

"The seventeenth. May seventeenth at seven P.M. The days were already very long by then, and the sky had a reddish glow, but the lights were on in the elephant house."

"And was there anything unusual about the elephant or the keeper?"

"Well, there was and there wasn't. I can't say exactly. It's not as if they were standing right in front of me. I'm probably not the most reliable witness."

"What did happen, exactly?"

I took a swallow of my now somewhat watery scotch. The rain outside the windows was still coming down, no stronger or weaker than before, a static element in a landscape that would never change.

"Nothing happened, really. The elephant and the keeper were doing what they always did—cleaning, eating, playing around with each other in that friendly way of theirs. It wasn't what they *did* that was different. It's the way they looked. Something about the balance between them."

"The balance?"

"In size. Of their bodies. The elephant's and the keeper's. The balance seemed to have changed somewhat. I had the feeling that to some extent the difference between them had shrunk."

She kept her gaze fixed on her daiquiri glass for a time. I could see that the ice had melted and that the water was working its way through the cocktail like a tiny ocean current.

"Meaning that the elephant had gotten smaller?"

"Or the keeper had gotten bigger. Or both simultaneously."

"And you didn't tell this to the police?"

"No, of course not," I said. "I'm sure they wouldn't have believed me. And if I had told them I was watching the elephant from the cliff at a time like that, I'd have ended up as their number one suspect."

"Still, are you *certain* that the balance between them had changed?"

"Probably. I can only say 'probably.' I don't have any proof, and as I keep saying, I was looking at them through the air vent. But I had looked at them like that I don't know how many times before, so it's hard for me to believe that I could make a mistake about something as basic as the relation of their sizes."

In fact, I had wondered at the time whether my eyes were playing tricks on me. I had tried closing and opening them and shaking my head, but the elephant's size remained the same. It definitely looked as if it had shrunk—so much so that at first I thought the town might have got hold of a new, smaller elephant. But I hadn't heard anything to that effect, and I would never have missed any news reports about elephants. If this was not a new elephant, the only possible conclusion was that the old elephant had, for one reason or another, shrunk. As I watched, it became obvious to me that this smaller elephant had all the same gestures as the old one. It would stamp happily on the ground with its right foot while it was being washed, and with its now somewhat narrower trunk it would pat the keeper on the back.

It was a mysterious sight. Looking through the vent, I had the feeling that a different, chilling kind of time was flowing through the elephant house—but nowhere else. And it seemed to me, too, that the elephant and the keeper were gladly giving themselves over to this new order that was trying to envelop them—or that had already partially succeeded in enveloping them.

Altogether, I was probably watching the scene in the elephant house for less than a half hour. The lights went out at seven-thirty—much earlier than usual—and from that point on, everything was wrapped in darkness. I waited in my spot, hoping that the lights would go on again, but they never did. That was the last I saw of the elephant.

"So, then, you believe that the elephant kept shrinking until it was small enough to escape through the bars, or else that it simply dissolved into nothingness. Is that it?"

"I don't know," I said. "All I'm trying to do is recall what I saw with my own eyes, as accurately as possible. I'm hardly thinking about what happened after that. The visual image I have is so strong that, to be honest, it's practically impossible for me to go beyond it."

That was all I could say about the elephant's disappearance. And just as I had feared, the story of the elephant was too particular, too complete in itself, to work as a topic of conversation between a young man and woman who had just met. A silence descended upon us after I had finished my tale. What subject could either of us bring up after a story about an elephant that had vanished—a story that offered virtually no openings for further discussion? She ran her finger around the edge of her cocktail glass, and I sat there reading and rereading the words stamped on my coaster. I never should have told her about the elephant. It was not the kind of story you could tell freely to anyone.

"When I was a little girl, our cat disappeared," she offered after a long silence. "But still, for a cat to disappear and for an elephant to disappear—those are two different stories."

"Yeah, really. There's no comparison. Think of the size difference."

Thirty minutes later, we were saying good-bye outside the hotel. She suddenly remembered that she had left her umbrella in the cocktail lounge, so I went up in the elevator and brought it down to her. It was a brick-red umbrella with a large handle.

"Thanks," she said.

"Good night," I said.

That was the last time I saw her. We talked once on the phone after that, about some details in her tie-in article. While we spoke, I thought seriously about inviting her out for dinner, but I ended up not doing it. It just didn't seem to matter one way or the other.

I felt like this a lot after my experience with the vanishing elephant. I would begin to think I wanted to do something, but then I would become incapable of distinguishing between the probable results of doing it and of not doing it. I often get the feeling that things around me have lost their proper balance, though it could be that my perceptions are playing tricks on me. Some kind of balance inside me has broken down since the elephant affair, and maybe that causes external phenomena to strike my eye in a strange way. It's probably something in me.

I continue to sell refrigerators and toaster ovens and coffeemakers in the pragmatic world, based on afterimages of memories I retain from that world. The more pragmatic I try to become, the more successfully I sell—our campaign has succeeded beyond our most optimistic forecasts—and the more people I succeed in selling myself to. That's probably because people are looking for a kind of unity in this *kit-chin* we know as the world. Unity of design. Unity of color. Unity of function.

The papers print almost nothing about the elephant anymore. People seem to have forgotten that their town once owned an elephant. The grass that took over the elephant enclosure has withered now, and the area has the feel of winter.

The elephant and keeper have vanished completely. They will never be coming back.

Translated from the Japanese by Jay Rubin

Joyce Carol Oates

Mark of Satan

(UNITED STATES)

A woman had come to save his soul and he wasn't sure he was ready.

It isn't every afternoon in the dead heat of summer, cicadas screaming out of the trees like lunatics, the sun a soft, slow explosion in the sky, that a husky young woman comes on foot rapping shyly at the screen door of a house not even yours, a house in which you are a begrudged guest, to save your soul. And she'd brought an angel-child with her too.

Thelma McCord, or was it McCrae. And Magdalena who was a wisp of a child, perhaps four years old.

They were Church of the Holy Witness, headquarters Scranton, PA. They were God's own, and proud. Saved souls glowing like neon out of their identical eye sockets.

Thelma was an "ordained missionary" and this was her "first season of itinerary" and she apologized for disturbing his privacy but did he, would he, surrender but a few minutes of his time to the Teachings of the Holy Witness?

He'd been taken totally by surprise. He'd been dreaming a disagreeable churning-sinking dream and suddenly he'd been wakened, summoned, by a faint but persistent knocking at the front door. Tugging on wrinkled khaki shorts and yanking up the zipper in angry haste—he was already wearing a T-shirt frayed and tight in the shoulders—he'd padded barefoot to the screen door, blinking the way a mollusk might blink if it had eyes. In a house unfamiliar to you, it's like waking to somebody else's dream. And there on the front stoop out of a shimmering-hot August afternoon he'd wished to sleep through, this girlish-eager young female missionary. An angel of God sent special delivery to *him*.

Quickly, before he could change his mind, before *no! no!* intervened, he invited Thelma and little Magdalena inside. Out of the wicked hot sun—quick.

"Thank you," the young woman said, beaming with surprise and gratitude. "Isn't he a kind, thoughtful man, Magdalena!"

Mother and daughter were heat-dazed, clearly yearning for some measure of coolness and simple human hospitality. Thelma was carrying a bulky straw purse and a tote bag with a red plastic sheen that appeared to be heavy with books and pamphlets. The child's face was pinkened with sunburn, and her gaze was so downcast she stumbled on the threshold of the door and her mother murmured *Tsk!* and clutched her hand tighter, as if, already, before their visit had begun, Magdalena had brought them both embarrassment.

He led them inside and shut the door. The living room opened directly off the front door. The house was a small three-bedroom tract ranch with simulated redwood siding; it was sparsely furnished, the front room uncarpeted, with a butterscotch-vinyl sofa, twin butterfly chairs in fluorescent lime, and a coffee table that was a slab of weather-stained granite set atop cinder blocks. (The granite slab was in fact a grave marker, so old and worn by time that its name and dates were illegible. His sister Gracie, whose rented house this was, had been given the coffee table slab by a former boyfriend.) A stain the color of tea and the shape of an octopus disfigured a corner of the ceiling but the missionaries, seated with self-conscious murmurs of thanks on the sofa, would not see it.

He needed a name to offer to Thelma McCord, or McCrae, who had so freely offered her name to him. "Flash," he said, inspired, "my name is Flashman."

He was a man no longer young yet by no means old; nor even, to the eye of a compassionate observer, middle-aged. His ravaged looks, his blood-veined eyes, appeared healable. He was a man given, however, to the habit of irony, distasteful to him in execution but virtually impossible to resist. (Like masturbation, to which habit he was, out of irony too, given as well.) When he spoke to Thelma he heard a quaver in his voice that was his quickened, erratic pulse but might sound to another's ear like civility.

He indicated they should take the sofa, and he lowered himself into the nearest butterfly chair on shaky legs. When the damned contraption nearly overturned, the angel child Magdalena, fluffy pale-blonde hair and delicate features, jammed her thumb into her mouth to keep from giggling. But her eyes were narrowed, alarmed.

"Mr. Flashman, so pleased to make your acquaintance," Thelma said uncertainly. Smiling at him with worried eyes, possibly contemplating whether he was Jewish.

Contemplating the likelihood of a Jew, a descendant of God's chosen people, living in the scraggly foothills of southwestern Pennsylvania, in a derelict ranch house seven miles from Waynesburg with a front yard that looked as if motorcycles had torn it up. Would a Jew be three days' unshaven, jaws like sandpaper, knobbily barefoot and hairy-limbed as a gorilla? Would a Jew so readily welcome a Holy Witness into his house?

Offer them drinks, lemonade, but no, he was thinking, *no.*

This, an opportunity for him to confront goodness, to look innocence direct in the eye, should not be violated.

Thelma promised that her visit would not take many minutes of Mr. Flashman's time. For time, she said, smiling breathlessly, is of the utmost. "That is one of the reasons I am here today."

Reaching deep into the tote bag to remove, he saw with a sinking heart, a hefty black Bible with gilt-edged pages and a stack of pamphlets printed on pulp paper—THE WITNESS. Then easing like a brisk mechanical doll into her recitation.

The man who called himself Flash was making every effort to listen. He knew this was important, there are no accidents. Hadn't he wakened in the night to a pounding heart and a taste of bile with the premonition that something, one of *his things,* was to happen soon? Whether of his volition and calculation, or seemingly by accident (but there are no accidents), he could not know. Leaning forward, gazing at the young woman with an elbow on his bare knee, the pose of Rodin's Thinker, listening hard. Except the woman was a dazzlement of sweaty-fragrant female flesh. Speaking passionately of the love of God and the passion of Jesus Christ and the book of Revelation of St. John the Divine and the Testament of the Witness. Then eagerly opening her Bible on her knees and dipping her head toward it so that her sand-colored, limp-curly hair fell into her face and she had to brush it away repeatedly—he was fascinated by the contrapuntal gestures, the authority of the Bible and the meek dipping of the head and the way in which, with childlike unconscious persistence, she pushed her hair out of her face. Unconscious too of her grating singsong voice, an absurd voice in which no profound truth could ever reside, and of her heavy, young breasts straining against the filmy material of her lavender-print dress, her fattish-muscular calves and good, broad feet in what appeared to be white wicker ballerina slippers.

The grimy venetian blinds of the room were drawn against the glaring heat. It was above ninety degrees outside and there had been no soaking rains for weeks and in every visible tree hung ghostly bagworm nests. In his sister's bedroom a single-window-unit air conditioner vibrated noisily and it had been in this room, on top of, not in, the bed, that he'd been sleeping when the knocking came at the front door; the room that was his had no air conditioner. Hurrying out, he'd left the door to his sister's bedroom open and now a faint trail of cool-metallic air coiled out into the living room and so he fell to thinking that his visitors would notice the cool air and inquire about it and he would say, Yes, there *is* air conditioning in this house, in one of the bedrooms, shall we go into that room and be more comfortable?

Now the Bible verses were concluded. Thelma's fair, fine skin glowed with excitement. Like a girl who has shared her most intimate secret and expects you now to share yours, Thelma lifted her eyes to Flash's and asked, almost boldly, Was he aware of the fact that God loved him? He squirmed hearing such words. Momentarily unable to respond, he laughed, embarrassed, shook his head, ran his fingers over his sandpaper jaws, and mumbled, No, not really, he guessed that he was not aware of that fact, not really.

Thelma said that was why she was here, to bring the good news to him. That God loved him whether he knew of Him or acknowledged Him. And the Holy Witness was their mediator.

Flashman mumbled, Is that so. A genuine blush darkening his face.

Thelma insisted, Yes, it *is* so. A brimming in her close-set eyes, which were the bluest eyes Flash had ever glimpsed except in glamour photos of models, movie stars, naked centerfolds. He said apologetically that he wasn't one hundred percent sure how his credit stood with God these days. "God and me," he said, with a boyish, tucked-in smile, "have sort of lost contact over the years."

Which was *the* answer the young female missionary was primed to expect. Turning to the little girl, she whispered in her ear, "Tell Mr. Flashman the good, good news, Magdalena!" and like a wind-up doll, the blonde child began to recite in a breathy, high-pitched voice, "We can lose God but God never loses *us*. We can despair of God but God never despairs of *us*. The Holy Witness records, 'He that overcometh shall not be hurt by the second death.' " As abruptly as she'd begun, the child ceased, her mouth going slack on the word *death*.

It was an impressive performance. Yet there was something chilling about it. Flash grinned and winked at the child in his uneasiness and said, "Second death, eh? What about the first?" But Magdalena just gaped at him. Her left eye losing its focus as if coming unmoored.

The more practiced Thelma quickly intervened. She took up both her daughter's hands in hers and in a brisk patty-cake rhythm chanted, "As the Witness records, 'God shall wipe away all tears from their eyes; and there *will be* no more death.' "

Maybe it was so? So simple? *No more death.*

He was bemused by the simplicity of fate. In this house unknown to him as recently as last week, in this rural no-man's-land where his older sister Gracie had wound up a county social worker toiling long grueling hours five days a week and forced to be grateful for the shitty job, he'd heard a rapping like a summons to his secret blood padding barefoot to the dream doorway that's shimmering with light and there she *is*.

"Excuse me, Thelma—would you and Magdalena like some lemonade?"

Thelma immediately demurred out of countrybred politeness as he'd expected, so he asked Magdalena, who appeared to be parched with thirst, poor exploited child, but, annoyingly, she was too shy to even nod her head yes, please. Flash, stimulated by challenge, apologized for not having fresh-squeezed lemonade—calculating that Thelma would have to accept to prove she wasn't offended by his offer—adding that he was about to get some lemonade for himself, icy-cold, and would they please join him, so Thelma, lowering her eyes, said yes. As if he'd reached out to touch her and she hadn't dared draw back.

In the kitchen, out of sight, he moved swiftly—which was why his name was Flash. For a man distracted, a giant, black-feathered eagle tearing out his liver, he moved with surprising alacrity. But that had always been his way.

Opening the fridge, nostrils pinching against the stale stink inside, trying his best to ignore his sister Gracie's depressed housekeeping, he took out the stained Tupperware pitcher of Bird's Eye lemonade—thank God, there was some. Tart chemical taste he'd have to mollify, in his own glass, with an ounce or two of Gordon's gin. For his missionary visitors he ducked into his bedroom and located his stash and returned to the kitchen counter, crumbling swiftly between his palms several chalky-white pills, six milligrams each of barbiturate, enough to fell a healthy horse, reducing them to gritty powder to dissolve in the greenish lemonade he poured into two glasses: the taller for Thelma, the smaller for Magdalena. He wondered what the little girl weighed—forty pounds? Thirty? Fifty? He had no idea, children were mysteries to him. His own childhood was a mystery to him. But he wouldn't want Magdalena's heart to stop beating.

He'd seen a full-sized man go glassy-eyed and clutch at his heart and topple over stone dead overdosing on—what? Heroin. It was a clean death, so far as deaths go, but it came out of the corner of your eye, you couldn't prepare.

Carefully setting the three glasses of lemonade, two tall and slim for the adults, the other roly-poly for sweet little Magdalena, on a laminated tray. Returning then, humming cheerfully, to the airless living room where his visitors were sitting primly on the battered sofa as if, in his absence, they hadn't moved an inch. Shyly yet with trembling hands, both reached for their glasses. "Say 'thankyou, sir,'" Thelma whispered to Magdalena, who whispered, "Thankyou, sir," and lifted her glass to her lips.

Thelma disappointed him by taking only a ladylike sip, then dabbing at her lips with a tissue. "Delicious," she murmured. But setting the glass down as if it were a temptation. Poor Magdalena was holding her glass in both hands taking quick swallows, but at a sidelong glance from her mother, she too set her glass down on the tray.

Flash said, as if hurt, "There's lots more sugar if it isn't sweet enough."

But Thelma insisted, No, it was fine. Taking up, with the look of a woman choosing among several rare gems, one of the pulp-printed pamphlets. Now, Flash guessed, she'd be getting down to business. Enlisting him to join the Church of the Holy Ghost, or whatever it was—Holy Witness?

She named names and cited dates that flew past him—except for the date Easter Sunday, 1899, when, apparently, there'd been a "shower from the heavens" north of Scranton, PA—and he nodded to encourage her though she hardly needed encouraging, taking deep, thirsty sips from his lemonade to encourage her too. Out of politeness Thelma did lift her glass and take a chaste swallow but no more. Maybe there was a cult prescription against frozen foods, chemical drinks? The way the Christian Scientists, unless it was the Seventh Day Adventists, forbade blood transfusions because such was "eating blood," which was outlawed by the Bible.

Minutes passed. The faint trickle of metallic-cool air touched the side of his feverish face. He tried not to show his impatience with Thelma, fixing instead on the amazing fact of her: a woman not known to him an hour before, now sitting less than a yard away addressing him as if, out of all of the universe, *he mattered.* Loving how she sat wide-hipped and settled into the vinyl cushions like a partridge in a nest. Knees and ankles together, chunky farmgirl feet in the discount-mart wicker flats, half-moons of perspiration darkening the underarms of her floral-print dress. It was a Sunday school kind of dress, lavender rayon with a wide, white collar and an awkward flared skirt and cloth-covered buttons the size of half-dollars. Beneath it the woman would be wearing a full slip, no half-slip for her. Damp from her warm, pulsing body. No doubt a white brassiere—D cups—and white cotton panties, the waist and legs of which left red rings in her flesh. Undies damp, too. And the crotch of the panties, damp. Just possibly stained. She was bare-legged, no stockings, a concession to the heat: just raw, female leg, reddish-blond transparent hairs on the calves, for she was not a woman to shave her body hair. Nor did she wear makeup. No such vanity. Her cheeks were flushed as if rouged and her lips were naturally moist and rosy. Her skin would be hot to the touch. She was twenty-eight or -nine years old and probably Magdalena was not her first child, but her youngest. She had the sort of female body mature by early adolescence, beginning to go flaccid by thirty-five. That fair, thin skin that wears out from too much smiling and aiming to please. Suggestion of a double chin. Hips would be spongy and cellulite-puckered. Kneaded like white bread, squeezed, banged, and bruised. Moist heat of a big bush of curly pubic hair. Secret crevices of pearl drops of moisture he'd lick away with his tongue.

Another woman would have been aware of Flash's calculating eyes on her like ants swarming over sugar, but not this impassioned missionary for the Church of the Holy Witness. Had an adder risen quivering with desire before her, she would have taken no heed. She was reading from one of THE WIT-NESS pamphlets and her gaze was shining and inward as she evoked in a hushed, little-girl voice a vision of bearded prophets raving in the deserts of Smyrna and covenants made by Jesus Christ to generations of sinners up to this very hour. Jesus Christ was the most spectacular of the prophets, it seemed, for out of his mouth came a sharp, two-edged sword casting terror into all who beheld. Yet he was a poet, his words had undeniable power, for here was Flash the man squirming in his butterfly chair as Thelma recited tremulously, " 'And Jesus spake: I am he that liveth, and was death; and, behold, I am alive for evermore; and have the keys of hell and death.' "

There was a pause. A short distance away a neighbor was running a chain saw, and out on the highway cars, trucks, thunderous diesel vehicles passed in an erratic whooshing stream, and on all sides beyond the house's walls the air buzzed, quivered, vibrated, rang with the insects of late summer but otherwise it was quiet, it was silent. Like a vacuum waiting to be filled.

The child Magdalena, unobserved by her mother, had drained her glass of lemonade and licked her lips with a flicking pink tongue and was beginning to be drowsy. She wore a pink rayon dress like a nightie with a machine-stamped lace collar, she had tiny feet in white socks and shiny white plastic shoes. Flash saw, yes, the child's left eye had a cast in it. The right eye perceived you head-on but the left drifted outward like a sly, wayward moon.

A defect in an eye of so beautiful a child would not dampen Flash's ardor. He was certain of that.

Ten minutes, fifteen. By now it was apparent that Thelma did not intend to drink her lemonade though Flash had drained his own glass and wiped his mouth with gusto. Did she suspect? Did she sense something wrong? But she'd taken no notice of Magdalena, who had drifted off into a light doze, her angel-head drooping and a thread of saliva shining on her chin. Surely a suspicious

Christian mother would not have allowed her little girl to drink spiked lemonade handed her by a barefoot, bare-legged pervert, possibly a Jew, with eyes like the yanked-up roots of thistles—that was encouraging.

"Your lemonade, Thelma," Flash said, with a host's frown, "it will be getting warm if you don't—"

Thelma seemed not to hear. With a bright smile she was asking, "Have you been baptized, Mr. Flashman?"

For a moment he could not think who Mr. Flashman was. The gin coursing through his veins, which ordinarily buoyed him up like debris riding the crest of a flood and provided him with an acute clarity of mind, had had a dulling, downward sort of effect. He was frightened of the possibility of one of *his things* veering out of his control, for in the past when this had happened the consequences were always very bad. For him as for others.

His face burned. "I'm afraid that's my private business, Thelma. I don't bare my heart to any stranger who walks in off the road."

Thelma blinked, startled. Yet was immediately repentant. "Oh, I know! I have overstepped myself, please forgive me, Mr. Flashman!"

Such passion quickened the air between them. Flash felt a stab of excitement. But ducking his head, boyish-repentant too, he murmured, "No, it's okay, I'm just embarrassed, I guess. I don't truly *know* if I was baptized. I was an orphan discarded at birth, set out with the trash. There's a multitude of us scorned by man and God. What happened to me before the age of twelve is lost to me. Just a whirlwind. A whirlpool of oblivion."

Should have left his sister's bedroom door shut, though. To keep the room cool. If he had to carry or drag this woman any distance—the child wouldn't be much trouble—he'd be miserable by the time he got to where he wanted to go.

Thelma all but exploded with solicitude, leaning forward as if about to gather him up in her arms.

"Oh, that's the saddest thing I have ever heard, Mr. Flashman! I wish one of our elders was here right now to counsel you as I cannot! 'Set out with the trash'—can it be? Can any human mother have been so cruel?"

"If it was a cruel mother, which I don't contest, it was a cruel God guiding her hand, Thelma—wasn't it?"

Thelma blinked rapidly. This was a proposition not entirely new to her, Flash surmised, but one which required a moment's careful and conscious reflection. She said, uncertainly at first and then with gathering momentum, "The wickedness of the world is Satan's hand, and the ways of Satan, as with the ways of God, are not to be comprehended by man."

"What's Satan got to do with this? I thought we were talking about the good guys."

"Our Savior Jesus Christ—"

"*Our* Savior? Who says? On my trash heap I looked up, and He looked down, and He said, 'Fuck you, kid. Life *is* unfair.' "

Thelma's expression was one of absolute astonishment. Like a cow, Flash thought ungallantly, in the instant the sledgehammer comes crashing down on her head.

Flash added, quick to make amends, "I thought this was about me, Thelma, about my soul. I thought the Holy Witness or whoever had something special to say to *me*."

Thelma was sitting stiff, her hands clasping her knees. One of THE WIT-NESS pamphlets had fallen to the floor and the hefty Bible too would have slipped had she not caught it. Her eyes now were alert and wary and she knew herself to be in the presence of an enemy, yet did not know that more than theology was at stake. "The Holy Witness does have something special to say to you, Mr. Flashman. Which is why I am here. There is a growing pestilence in the land, flooding the Midwest with the waters of the wrathful Mississippi, last year razing the Sodom and Gomorrah of Florida. Everywhere there are droughts and famines and earthquakes and volcanic eruptions and plagues—all signs that the old world is nearing its end. As the Witness proclaimed in the Book of Revelation that is our sacred scripture, 'There will be a new heaven and a new earth, as the first heaven and the first earth pass away. And the Father on His throne declaring, Behold I make all things new—' "

Flash interrupted, "None of this *is* new! It's been around for how many millenia, Thelma, and what good's it done for anybody?"

"—'I am Alpha and Omega, the beginning and the end,' " Thelma continued, unheeding, rising from the sofa like a fleshy angel of wrath in her lavender dress that stuck to her belly and legs, fumbling to gather up her Bible, her pamphlets, her dazed child, " '—I will give unto him that is a thirst of the fountain of life freely but the fearful, and unbelieving, and the abominable, and murderers, and all liars, shall sink into the lake which burneth with fire and brimstone: which is the second death.' " Her voice rose jubilantly on the word *death*.

Flash struggled to disentangle himself from the butterfly chair. The gin had done something weird to his legs—they were numb, and rubbery. Cursing, he fell to the floor, the rock-hard carpetless floor, as Thelma roused Magdalena and lifted her to her feet and half-carried her to the door. Flash tried to raise himself by gripping the granite coffee table but this too collapsed, the cinder blocks giving way and the heavy slab crashing down on his right hand. Three fingers were broken at once, but in the excitement he seemed not to notice. "Wait! You can't leave me now! I need you!"

At the door Thelma called back, panting, "Help *is* needed here. There is Satan in this house."

Flash stumbled to his feet and followed the woman to the door, calling after her, "What do you mean, 'Satan in this house'—there is no Satan, there is no Devil, it's all in the heads of people like you. You're religious maniacs! You're mad! Wait—"

He could not believe the woman was escaping so easily. That *his thing* was no thing of *his* at all.

Hauling purse and bulky tote bag, her sleep-dazed daughter on her hip,

Thelma was striding in her white wicker ballerina flats swiftly yet without apparent haste or panic out to the gravel driveway. There was a terrible quivering of the sun-struck air. Cicadas screamed like fire sirens. Flash tried to follow after, propelling himself on his rubbery legs which were remote from his head which was too small for his body and at the end of a swaying stalk. He was laughing, crying, "You're a joke, people like you! You're tragic victims of ignorance and superstition! You don't belong in the twentieth century with the rest of us! You're the losers of the world! You can't cope! *You* need salvation!"

He stared amazed at the rapidly departing young woman—at the dignity in her body, the high-held head, and the very arch of the backbone. Her indignation was not fear, an indignation possibly too primitive to concede to fear, like nothing in his experience nor even in his imagination. If this was a movie, he was thinking, panicked, the missionary would be *walking out of the frame,* leaving him behind—just him.

"Help! Wait! Don't leave me here alone!"

He was screaming, terrified. He perceived that his life was of no more substance than a cicada's shriek. He'd stumbled as far as the driveway when a blinding light struck him like a sword piercing his eyes and brain.

He'd fallen to his knees then in the driveway, amid sharp gravel and broken glass, and he was bawling like a child beyond all pride, beyond all human shame. His head was bowed, sun beating down on the balding crown of his head. His very soul wept through his eyes for he knew he would die, and nothing would save him, not even irony. *Don't flatter yourself you matter enough even to be grieved! Asshole!*—no, not even his wickedness would save him. Yet seeing him stricken, the young Christian woman could not walk away. He cried, "Satan *is* here! In me! He speaks through me! It isn't me! Please help me, don't leave me to die!" His limbs shook as if palsied and his teeth chattered despite the heat. Where the young woman stood wavering there was a blurry, shimmering figure of light and he pleaded with it, tore open his chest, belly, to expose the putrescent tumor of Satan choking his entrails, he begged for mercy, for help, for Christ's love, until at last the young woman cautiously approached him to a distance of about three feet, knelt too, though not in the gravel driveway but in the grass, and by degrees put aside her distrust. Seeing the sickness in this sinner howling to be saved, she bowed her head and clasped her hands to her breasts and began to pray loudly, triumphantly. "O Heavenly Father, help this tormented sinner to repent of his sins and to be saved by Your Only Begotten Son that he might stand by the throne of Your righteousness, help all sinners to be saved by the Testament of the Holy Witness—"

How many minutes the missionary prayed over the man who had in jest called himself Flashman he would not afterward know. For there seemed to be a fissure in time itself. The two were locked in ecstasy as in the most intimate of embraces in the fierce heat of the sun, and in the impulsive generosity of her spirit the young woman reached out to clasp his trembling hands in hers and to squeeze them tight. Admonishing him, "Pray! Pray to Jesus Christ!

Every hour of every day pray to Him in your heart!" She was weeping too and her face was flushed and swollen and shining with tears. He pleaded with her not to leave him, for Satan was still with him, he feared Satan's grip on his soul, but there was a car at the end of the driveway toward which the child Magdalena had made her unsteady way and now a man's voice called, "Thelma! Thel-ma!" and at once the young woman rose to her full height, brushing her damp hair out of her face, and with a final admonition to him to love God and Christ and abhor Satan and all his ways, she was gone, vanished into the light out of which she had come.

Alone, he remained kneeling, too weak to stand. Rocking and swaying in the sun. His parched lips moved, uttering babble. In a frenzy of self-abnegation he ground his bare knees in the gravel and shattered glass, deep and deeper into the pain so that he might bleed more freely, bleeding all impurity from him or at least mutilating his flesh, so that in the arid stretch of years before him that would constitute the remainder of his life he would possess a living memory of this hour, scars he might touch, read like Braille.

When Gracie Shuttle returned home hours later, she found her brother Harvey in the bathroom dabbing at his wounded knees with a blood-soaked towel, picking bits of gravel and glass out of his flesh with a tweezers. And his hand—several fingers of his right hand were as swollen as sausages and grotesquely bruised. Gracie was a tall, lank, sardonic woman of forty-one with deep-socketed eyes that rarely acknowledged surprise; yet, seeing Harvey in this remarkable posture, sitting hunched on the toilet seat, a sink of blood-tinged water beside him, she let out a long, high whistle. "What the hell happened to *you*?" she asked.

Harvey raised his eyes to hers. He did not appear to be drunk or drugged; his eyes were terribly bloodshot, as if he'd had one of his crying jags, but his manner was unnervingly composed. His face was ravaged and sunburnt in uneven splotches as if it had been baked. He said, "I've been on my knees to Gethsemane and back. It's too private to speak of."

From years ago, when by an accident of birth they'd shared a household with two hapless adults who were their parents, Gracie knew that her younger brother in such a state was probably telling the truth, or a kind of truth; she knew also that he would never reveal it to her. She waved in his face a pulp religious pamphlet she'd found on the living room floor beside the collapsed granite marker. "And what the hell is *this*? she demanded.

But again with that look of maddening calm, Harvey said, "It's my private business, Gracie. Please shut the door on your way out."

Gracie slammed the door in Harvey's face and charged through the house to the rear where wild, straggly bamboo was choking the yard. Since she'd moved in three years before, the damned bamboo had spread everywhere, marching from the marshy part of the property where the cesspool was located too close to the surface of the soil. Just her luck! And her with a master's degree in social work from the University of Pennsylvania! She'd hoped, she'd expected more from her education, as from life. She lit a cigarette and rapidly smoked it, exhaling luxuriant streams of smoke through her nostrils. "Well, fuck you," she said, laughing. She frequently laughed when she was angry, and she laughed a good deal these days.

It *was* funny. Whatever it was, it *was* funny—her parolee kid brother, once an honors student, now a balding, middle-aged man picking tenderly at his knees that looked as if somebody had slashed them with a razor. That blasted-sober look in the poor guy's eyes she hadn't seen in twelve years—since one of his junkie buddies in Philly had dropped over dead mainlining heroin.

Some of the bamboo stalks were brown and desiccated but most of the god-damned stuff was still greenly erect, seven feet tall and healthy. Gracie flicked her cigarette butt out into it. Waiting, bored, to see if it caught fire, if there'd be a little excitement out here on Route 71 tonight, the Waynesburg Volunteer Firemen exercising their shiny red equipment and every yokel for miles around hopping in his pickup to come gape—but it didn't, and there wasn't.

Ben Okri

In the Shadow of War

(NIGERIA)

That afternoon three soldiers came to the village. They scattered the goats and chickens. They went to the palm-frond bar and ordered a calabash of palm-wine. They drank amidst the flies.

Omovo watched them from the window as he waited for his father to go out. They both listened to the radio. His father had bought the old Grundig cheaply from a family that had to escape the city when the war broke out. He had covered the radio with a white cloth and made it look like a household fetish. They listened to the news of bombings and air raids in the interior of the country. His father combed his hair, parted it carefully, and slapped some aftershave on his unshaven face. Then he struggled into the shabby coat that he had long outgrown.

Omovo stared out of the window, irritated with his father. At that hour, for the past seven days, a strange woman with a black veil over her head had been going past the house. She went up the village paths, crossed the Express road, and disappeared into the forest. Omovo waited for her to appear.

The main news was over. The radio announcer said an eclipse of the moon was expected that night. Omovo's father wiped the sweat off his face with his palm and said, with some bitterness:

"As if an eclipse will stop this war."

"What is an eclipse?" Omovo asked.

"That's when the world goes dark and strange things happen."

"Like what?"

His father lit a cigarette.

"The dead start to walk about and sing. So don't stay out late, eh."

Omovo nodded.

"Heclipses hate children. They eat them."

Omovo didn't believe him. His father smiled, gave Omovo his ten kobo allowance, and said:

"Turn off the radio. It's bad for a child to listen to news of war."

Omovo turned it off. His father poured a libation at the doorway and then prayed to his ancestors. When he had finished he picked up his briefcase and strutted out briskly. Omovo watched him as he threaded his way up the path to the bus-stop at the main road. When a danfo bus came, and his father went with it, Omovo turned the radio back on. He sat on the window-sill and waited for the woman. The last time he saw her she had glided past with agitated flutters of her yellow smock. The children stopped what they were doing and stared at her. They had said that she had no shadow. They had said that her feet never touched the ground. As she went past, the children began to throw things at her. She didn't flinch, didn't quicken her pace, and didn't look back.

The heat was stupefying. Noises dimmed and lost their edges. The villagers stumbled about their various tasks as if they were sleep-walking. The three soldiers drank palm-wine and played draughts beneath the sun's oppressive glare. Omovo noticed that whenever children went past the bar the soldiers called them, talked to them, and gave them some money. Omovo ran down the stairs and slowly walked past the bar. The soldiers stared at him. On his way back one of them called him.

"What's your name?" he asked.

Omovo hesitated, smiled mischievously, and said:

"Heclipse."

The soldier laughed, spraying Omovo's face with spit. He had a face crowded with veins. His companions seemed uninterested. They swiped flies and concentrated on their game. Their guns were on the table. Omovo noticed that they had numbers on them. The man said:

"Did your father give you that name because you have big lips?"

His companions looked at Omovo and laughed. Omovo nodded.

"You are a good boy," the man said. He paused. Then he asked, in a different voice:

"Have you seen that woman who covers her face with a black cloth?"

"No."

The man gave Omovo ten kobo and said:

"She is a spy. She helps our enemies. If you see her come and tell us at once, you hear?"

Omovo refused the money and went back upstairs. He re-positioned himself on the window-sill. The soldiers occasionally looked at him. The heat got to him and soon he fell asleep in a sitting position. The cocks, crowing dispiritedly, woke him up. He could feel the afternoon softening into evening. The soldiers dozed in the bar. The hourly news came on. Omovo listened without comprehension to the day's casualties. The announcer succumbed to the stupor, yawned, apologized, and gave further details of the fighting.

Omovo looked up and saw that the woman had already gone past. The men had left the bar. He saw them weaving between the eaves of the thatch houses, stumbling through the heat-mists. The woman was further up the path. Omovo ran downstairs and followed the men. One of them had taken off his uniform top. The soldier behind had buttocks so big they had begun to split his pants. Omovo followed them across the Express road. When they got into the forest the men stopped following the woman, and took a different route. They seemed to know what they were doing. Omovo hurried to keep the woman in view.

He followed her through the dense vegetation. She wore faded wrappers and a grey shawl, with the black veil covering her face. She had a red basket on her head. He completely forgot to determine if she had a shadow, or whether her feet touched the ground.

He passed unfinished estates, with their flaking ostentatious signboards and their collapsing fences. He passed an empty cement factory: blocks lay crumbled in heaps and the workers' sheds were deserted. He passed a baobab tree, under which was the intact skeleton of a large animal. A snake dropped from a branch and slithered through the undergrowth. In the distance, over the cliff edge, he heard loud music and people singing war slogans above the noise.

He followed the woman till they came to a rough camp on the plain below. Shadowy figures moved about in the half-light of the cave. The woman went to them. The figures surrounded her and touched her and led her into the cave. He heard their weary voices thanking her. When the woman reappeared she was without the basket. Children with kwashiorkor stomachs and women wearing rags led her half-way up the hill. Then, reluctantly, touching her as if they might not see her again, they went back.

He followed her till they came to a muddied river. She moved as if an invisible force were trying to blow her away. Omovo saw capsized canoes and trailing waterlogged clothes on the dark water. He saw floating items of sacrifice: loaves of bread in polythene wrappings, gourds of food, Coca-Cola cans. When he looked at the canoes again they had changed into the shapes of swollen dead animals. He saw outdated currencies on the riverbank. He noticed the terrible smell in the air. Then he heard the sound of heavy breathing from behind him, then someone coughing and spitting. He recognized the voice of one of the soldiers urging the others to move faster. Omovo crouched in the shadow of a tree. The soldiers strode past. Not long afterwards he heard a scream. The men had caught up with the woman. They crowded round her.

"Where are the others?" shouted one of them.

The woman was silent.

"You dis witch! You want to die, eh? Where are they?"

She stayed silent. Her head was bowed. One of the soldiers coughed and spat towards the river.

"Talk! Talk!" he said, slapping her.

The fat soldier tore off her veil and threw it to the ground. She bent down to pick it up and stopped in the attitude of kneeling, her head still bowed. Her head was bald, and disfigured with a deep corrugation. There was a livid gash along the side of her face. The bare-chested soldier pushed her. She fell on her face and lay still. The lights changed over the forest and for the first time Omovo saw that the dead animals on the river were in fact the corpses of grown men. Their bodies were tangled with river-weed and their eyes were bloated. Before he could react, he heard another scream. The woman was getting up, with the veil in her hand. She turned to the fat soldier, drew herself to her fullest height, and spat in his face. Waving the veil in the air, she began to howl dementedly. The two other soldiers backed away. The fat soldier wiped his face and lifted the gun to the level of her stomach. A moment before

Omovo heard the shot a violent beating of wings just above him scared him from his hiding place. He ran through the forest screaming. The soldiers tramped after him. He ran through a mist which seemed to have risen from the rocks. As he ran he saw an owl staring at him from a canopy of leaves. He tripped over the roots of a tree and blacked out when his head hit the ground.

When he woke up it was very dark. He waved his fingers in front of his face and saw nothing. Mistaking the darkness for blindness he screamed, thrashed around, and ran into a door. When he recovered from his shock he heard voices outside and the radio crackling on about the war. He found his way to the balcony, full of wonder that his sight had returned. But when he got there he was surprised to find his father sitting on the sunken cane chair, drinking palm-wine with the three soldiers. Omovo rushed to his father and pointed frantically at the three men.

"You must thank them," his father said. "They brought you back from the forest."

Omovo, overcome with delirium, began to tell his father what he had seen. But his father, smiling apologetically at the soldiers, picked up his son and carried him off to bed.

Amos Oz

Where the Jackals Howl

(ISRAEL)

1.

At last the heat wave abated.

A blast of wind from the sea pierced the massive density of the *khamsin*, opening up cracks to let in the cold. First came light, hesitant breezes, and the tops of the cypresses shuddered lasciviously, as if a current had passed through them, rising from the roots and shaking the trunk.

Toward evening the wind freshened from the west. The *khamsin* fled eastward, from the coastal plain to the Judean hills and from the Judean hills to the rift of Jericho, from there to the deserts of the scorpion that lie to the east of Jordan. It seemed that we had seen the last *khamsin*. Autumn was drawing near.

Yelling stridently, the children of the kibbutz came streaming out onto the lawns. Their parents carried deck chairs from the verandas to the gardens. "It is the exception that proves the rule," Sashka is fond of saying. This time it was Sashka who made himself the exception, sitting alone in his room and adding a new chapter to his book about problems facing the kibbutz in times of change.

Sashka is one of the founders of our kibbutz and an active, prominent member. Squarely built, florid and bespectacled, with a handsome and sensitive face and an expression of fatherly assurance. A man of bustling energy. So fresh was the evening breeze passing through the room that he was obliged to lay a heavy ashtray on a pile of rebellious papers. A spirited straightforwardness animated him, giving a trim edge to his sentences. Changing times, said Sashka to himself, changing times require changing ideas. Above all, let us not mark time, let us not turn back upon ourselves, let us be vigorous and alert.

The walls of the houses, the tin roofs of the huts, the stack of steel pipes beside the smithy, all began to exhale the heat accumulated in them during the days of the *khamsin*.

Galila, daughter of Sashka and Tanya, stood under the cold shower, her hands clasped behind her neck, her elbows pushed back. It was dark in the shower room. Even the blond hair lying wet and heavy on her shoulders looked dark. If there was a big mirror here, I could stand in front of it and look myself over. Slowly, calmly. Like watching the sea wind that's blowing outside.

But the cubicle was small, like a square cell, and there was no big mirror, nor could there have been. So her movements were hasty and irritable. Impatiently she dried herself and put on clean clothes. What does Matityahu Damkov want of me? He asked me to go to his room after supper. When we were children we used to love watching him and his horses. But to waste the evening in some sweaty bachelor's room, that's asking too much. True, he did promise to give me some paints from abroad. On the other hand, the evening is short and we don't have any other free time. We are working girls.

How awkward and confused Matityahu Damkov looked when he stopped me on the path and told me I should come to his room after supper. And that hand in the air, waving, gesticulating, trying to pluck words out of the hot wind, gasping like a fish out of water, not finding the words he was looking for. "This evening. Worth your while to drop in for a few minutes," he said. "Just wait and see, it will be interesting. Just for a while. And quite . . . er . . . important. You won't regret it. Real canvases and the kind of paints professional artists use, as well. Actually, I got all these things from my cousin Leon who lives in South America. I don't need paints or canvases. I . . . er . . . and there's a pattern as well. It's all for you, just make sure that you come."

As she remembered these words, Galila was filled with nausea and amusement. She thought of the fascinating ugliness of Matityahu Damkov, who had chosen to order canvases and paints for her. Well, I suppose I should go along and see what happens and discover why I am the one. But I won't stay in his room more than five minutes.

2.

In the mountains the sunset is sudden and decisive. Our kibbutz lies on the plain, and the plain reduces the sunset, lessens its impact. Slowly, like a tired bird of passage, darkness descends on the land surface. First to grow dark are the barns and the windowless storerooms. The coming of the darkness does not hurt them, for it has never really left them. Next it is the turn of the houses. A timer sets the generator in motion. Its throbbing echoes down the slope like a beating heart, a distant drum. Veins of electricity awake into life and a hidden current passes through our thin walls. At that moment the lights spring up in all the windows of the veterans' quarters. The metal fittings on the top of the water tower catch the fading rays of daylight, hold them for a long moment. Last to be hidden in the darkness is the iron rod of the lightning conductor on the summit of the tower.

The old people of the kibbutz are still at rest in their deck chairs. They are like lifeless objects, allowing the darkness to cover them and offering no resistance.

Shortly before seven o'clock the kibbutz begins to stir, a slow movement toward the dining hall. Some are discussing what has happened today, others discuss what is to be done tomorrow, and there are a few who are silent. It is time for Matityahu Damkov to emerge from his lair and become a part of society. He locks the door of his room, leaving behind him the sterile silence, and goes to join the bustling life of the dining hall.

3.

Matityahu Damkov is a small man, thin and dark, all bone and sinew. His eyes are narrow and sunken, his cheekbones slightly curved, an expression of "I told you so" is fixed upon his face. He joined our kibbutz immediately after World War II. Originally he was from Bulgaria. Where he has been and what he has done, Damkov does not tell. And we do not demand chapter and verse. However, we know that he has spent some time in South America. He has a mustache as well.

Matityahu Damkov's body is a cunning piece of craftsmanship. His torso is lean, boyish, strong, almost unnaturally agile. What impression does such a body make on women? In men it arouses a sense of nervous discomfort.

His left hand shows a thumb and a little finger. Between them is an empty space. "In time of war," said Matityahu Damkov, "men have suffered greater losses than three fingers."

In the daytime he works in the smithy, stripped to the waist and gleaming with sweat, muscles dancing beneath the taut skin like steel springs. He solders together metal fittings, welds pipes, hammers out bent tools, beats worn-out implements into scrap metal. His right hand or his left, each by itself is strong enough to lift the heavy sledgehammer and bring it down with controlled ferocity on the face of the unprotesting metal.

Many years ago Matityahu Damkov used to shoe the kibbutz horses, with fascinating skill. When he lived in Bulgaria it seems that his business was horsebreeding. Sometimes he would speak solemnly of some hazy distinction between stud horses and work horses, and tell the children gathered around him that he and his partner or his cousin Leon used to raise the most valuable horses between the Danube and the Aegean.

Once the kibbutz stopped using horses, Matityahu Damkov's craftsmanship was forgotten. Some of the girls collected redundant horseshoes and used them to decorate their rooms. Only the children who used to watch the shoeing, only they remember sometimes. The skill. The pain. The intoxicating smell. The agility. Galila used to chew a lock of blond hair and stare at him from a distance with gray, wide-open eyes, her mother's eyes, not her father's.

She won't come.

I don't believe her promises.

She's afraid of me. She's as wary as her father and as clever as her mother. She won't come. And if she does come, I won't tell her. If I tell her, she won't believe me. She'll go and tell Sashka everything. Words achieve nothing. But here there are people and light: supper time.

On every table gleamed cutlery, steel jugs and trays of bread.

"This knife needs sharpening," Matityahu Damkov said to his neighbors at the table. He cut his onions and tomatoes into thin slices and sprinkled them with salt, vinegar and olive oil. "In the winter, when there's not so much work to be done, I shall sharpen all the dining-room knives and repair the gutter as well. In fact, the winter isn't so far away. This *khamsin* was the last, I think. So there it is. The winter will catch us this year before we're ready for it."

At the end of the dining room, next to the boiler room and the kitchen, a group of bony veterans, some bald, some white-haired, are gathered around an evening paper. The paper is taken apart and the sections passed around in turn to the readers who have "reserved" them. Meanwhile there are some who offer interpretations of their own and there are others who stare at the pundits with the eyes of weary, good-humored old age. And there are those who listen in silence, with quiet sadness on their faces. These, according to Sashka, are the truest of the true. It is they who have endured the true suffering of the labor movement.

While the men are gathered around the paper discussing politics, the women are besieging the work organizer's table. Tanya is raising her voice in protest. Her face is wrinkled, her eyes harassed and weary. She is clutching a tin ashtray, beating it against the table to the rhythm of her complaints. She leans over the work sheets as if bending beneath the burden of injustice that has been laid or is about to be laid on her. Her hair is gray. Matityahu Damkov hears her voice but misses her words. Apparently the work organizer is trying to retreat with dignity in the face of Tanya's anger. And now she casually picks up the fruits of victory, straightens up and makes her way to Matityahu Damkov's table.

"Now it's your turn. You know I've got a lot of patience, but there are limits to everything. And if that lock isn't welded by ten o'clock tomorrow morning, I shall raise the roof. There is a limit, Matityahu Damkov. Well?"

The man contorted the muscles of his face so that his ugliness intensified and became repulsive beyond bearing, like a clown's mask, a nightmare figure.

"Really," he said mildly, "there's no need to get so excited. Your lock has been welded for days now, and you haven't come to collect it. Come tomorrow. Come whenever you like. There's no need to hurry me along."

"Hurry you? Never in my life have I dared harass a working man. Forgive me. I'm sure you're not offended."

"I'm not offended," said Matityahu. "On the contrary. I'm an easygoing type. Good night to you."

With these words the business of the dining room is concluded. Time to go back to the room, to put on the light, to sit on the bed and wait quietly And what else do I need? Yes. Cigarettes. Matches. Ashtray.

4.

The electric current pulses in twining veins and sheds a weary light upon everything: our little red-roofed houses, our gardens, the pitted concrete paths, the fences and the scrap iron, the silence. Dim, weak puddles of light. An elderly light.

Searchlights are mounted on wooden posts set out at regular intervals along the perimeter fence. These beacons strive to light up the fields and the valleys that stretch away to the foothills of the mountains. A small circle of plowed land is swamped by the lights on the fence. Beyond this circle lies the night and the silence. Autumn nights are not black. Not here. Our nights are gray. A gray radiance rising over the fields, the plantations, and the orchards. The orchards have already begun to turn yellow. The soft gray light embraces the treetops with great tenderness, blurring their sharp edges, bridging the gap between lifeless and living. It is the way of the night light to distort the appearance of inanimate things and to infuse them with life, cold and sinister, vibrant with venom. At the same time it slows down the living things of the night, softening their movements, disguising their elusive presence. Thus it is that we cannot see the jackals as they spring out from their hiding places. Inevitably we miss the sight of their soft noses sniffing the air, their paws gliding over the turf, scarcely touching the ground.

The dogs of the kibbutz, they alone understand this enchanted motion. That is why they howl at night in jealousy, menace, and rage. That is why they paw at the ground, straining at their chains till their necks are on the point of breaking.

An adult jackal would have kept clear of the trap. This one was a cub, sleek, soft, and bristling, and he was drawn to the smell of blood and flesh. True, it was not outright folly that led him into the trap. He simply followed the scent and glided to his destruction with careful, mincing steps. As times he stopped, feeling some obscure warning signal in his veins. Beside the snare he paused, froze where he stood, silent, as gray as the earth and as patient. He pricked up his ears in vague apprehension and heard not a sound. The smells got the better of him.

Was it really a matter of chance? It is commonly said that chance is blind; we say that chance peers out at us with a thousand eyes. The jackal was young, and if he felt the thousand eyes fixed upon him, he could not understand their meaning.

A wall of old, dusty cypresses surrounds the plantation. What is it, the hidden thread that joins the lifeless to the living? In despair, rage, and contortion we search for the end of this thread, biting lips till we draw blood, eyes contorted in frenzy. The jackals know this thread. Sensuous, pulsating currents are alive in it, flowing from body to body, being to being, vibration to vibration. And rest and peace are there.

At last the creature bowed his head and brought his nose close to the flesh of the bait. There was the smell of blood and the smell of sap. The tip of his muzzle was moist and twitching, his saliva was running, his hide bristling, his delicate sinews throbbed. Soft as a vapor, his paw approached the forbidden fruit.

Then came the moment of cold steel. With a metallic click, light and precise, the trap snapped shut.

The animal froze like stone. Perhaps he thought he could outwit the trap, pretending to be lifeless. No sound, no movement. For a long moment jackal and trap lay still, testing each other's strength. Slowly, painfully, the living awoke and came back to life.

And silently the cypresses swayed, bowing and rising, bending and floating. He opened his muzzle wide, baring little teeth that dripped foam.

Suddenly despair seized him.

With a a frantic leap he tried to tear himself free, to cheat the hangman.

Pain ripped through his body.

He lay flat upon the earth and panted.

Then the child opened his mouth and began to cry. The sound of his wailing rose and filled the night.

5.

At this twilight hour our world is made up of circles within circles. On the outside is the circle of the autumn darkness, far from here, in the mountains and the great deserts. Sealed and enclosed within it is the circle of our night landscape, vineyards and orchards and plantations. A dim lake astir with whispering voices. Our lands betray us in the night. Now they are no longer familiar and submissive, crisscrossed with irrigation pipes and dirt tracks. Now our fields have gone over to the enemy's camp. They send out to us waves of alien scents. At night we see them bristling in a miasma of threat and hostility and returning to their former state, as they were before we came to this place.

The inner circle, the circle of lights, keeps guard over our houses and over us, against the accumulated menace outside. But it is an inffective wall, it cannot keep out the smells of the foe and his voices. At night the voices and the smells touch our skin like tooth and claw.

And inside, in the innermost circle of all, in the heart of our illuminated world, stands Sashka's writing desk. The table lamp sheds a calm circle of brightness and banishes the shadows from the stacks of papers. The pen in his hand darts to and fro and the words take shape. "There is no stand more noble than that of the few against the many," Sashka is fond of saying. His daughter stares wide-eyed and curious at the face of Matityahu Damkov. You're ugly and you're not one of us. It's good that you have no children and one day those dull mongoloid eyes will close and you'll be dead. And you won't leave behind anyone like you. I wish I wasn't here, but before I go I want to know what it is you want of me and why you told me to come. It's so stuffy in your room and there's an old bachelor smell that's like the smell of oil used for frying too many times.

"You may sit down," said Matityahu from the shadows. The shabby stillness that filled the room deepened his voice and made it sound remote.

"I'm in a bit of a hurry."

"There'll be coffee as well. The real thing. From Brazil. My cousin Leon sends me coffee too, he seems to think a kibbutz is a kind of kolkhoz. A kolkhoz labor camp. A collective farm in Russia, that's what a kolkhoz is."

"Black without sugar for me, please," said Galila, and these words surprised even her.

What is this ugly man doing to me? What does he want of me?

"You said you were going to show me some canvases, and some paints, didn't you?"

"All in good time."

"I didn't expect you to go to the trouble of getting coffee and cakes, I thought I'd only be here for a moment."

"You are fair," the man said, breathing heavily, "you are fair-haired, but I'm not mistaken. There is doubt. There has to be. But it is so. What I mean is, you'll drink your coffee, nice and slow, and I'll give you a cigarette too, an American one, from Virginia. In the meantime, have a look at this box. The brushes. The special oil too. And the canvases. And all the tubes. It's all for you. First of all drink. Take your time."

"But I still don't understand," said Galila.

A man pacing about his room in an undershirt on a summer night is not a strange sight. But the monkeylike body of Matityahu Damkov set something stirring inside her. Panic seized her. She put down the coffee cup on the brass tray, jumped up from the chair and stood behind it, clutching the chair as if it were a barricade.

The transparent, frightened gesture delighted her host. He spoke patiently, almost mockingly:

"Just like your mother. I have something to tell you when the moment's right, something that I'm positive you don't know, about your mother's wickedness."

Now, at the scent of danger, Galila was filled with cold malice:

"You're mad, Matityahu Damkov. Everybody says that you're mad."

There was tender austerity in her face, an expression both secretive and passionate.

"You're mad, and get out of my way and let me pass. I want to get out of here. Yes. Now. Out of my way."

The man retreated a little, still staring at her intently. Suddenly he sprang onto his bed and sat there, his back to the wall, and laughed a long, happy laugh.

"Steady, daughter, why all the haste? Steady. We've only just begun. Patience. Don't get so excited. Don't waste your energy."

Galila hastily weighed up the two possibilities, the safe and the fascinating, and said:

"Please tell me what you want of me."

"Actually," said Matityahu Damkov, "actually, the kettle's boiling again. Let's take a short break and have some more coffee. You won't deny, I'm sure, that you've never drunk coffee like this."

"Without milk or sugar for me. I told you before."

6.

The smell of coffee drove away all other smells: a strong, sharp, pleasant smell, almost piercing. Galila watched Matityahu Damkov closely, observing his manners, the docile muscles beneath his string shirt, his sterile ugliness. When he spoke again, she clutched the cup tightly between her fingers and a momentary peace descended on her.

"If you like, I can tell you something in the meantime. About horses. About the farm that we used to have in Bulgaria, maybe fifty-seven kilometers from the port of Varna, a stud farm. It belonged to me and my cousin Leon. There were two branches that we specialized in: work horses and stud horses, in other words, castration and covering. Which would you like to hear about first?"

Galila relaxed, leaning back in the chair and crossing her legs, ready to hear a story. In her childhood she had always loved the moments before the start of a bedtime story.

"I remember," she said, "how when we were children we used to come and watch you shoeing the horses. It was beautiful and strange and so . . . were you."

"Preparing for successful mating," said Matityahu, passing her a plate of crackers, "is a job for professionals. It takes expertise and intuition as well. First, the stallion must be kept in confinement for a long time. To drive him mad. It improves his seed. He's kept apart from the mares for several months, from the stallions too. In his frustration he may even attack another male. Not every stallion is suitable for stud, perhaps one in a hundred. One stud horse to a hundred work horses. You need a lot of experience and keen observation to pick out the right horse. A stupid, unruly horse is the best. But it isn't all that easy to find the most stupid horse."

"Why must he be stupid?" asked Galila, swallowing spittle.

"It's a question of madness. It isn't always the biggest, most handsome stallion that produces the best foals. In fact a mediocre horse can be full of energy and have the right kind of nervous temperament. After the candidate had been kept in confinement for a few months, we used to put wine in his trough, half a bottle. That was my cousin Leon's idea. To get the horse a bit drunk. Then we'd fix it so he could take a look at the mares through the bars and get a whiff of their smell. Then he starts going mad. Butting like a bull. Rolling on his back and kicking his legs in the air. Scratching himself, rubbing himself, trying desperately to ejaculate. He screams and starts biting in all directions. When the stallion starts to bite, then we know that the time has come. We open the gate. The mare is waiting for him. And just for a moment, the stallion hesitates. Trembling and panting. Like a coiled spring."

Galila winced, staring entranced at Matityahu Damkov's lips.

"Yes," she said.

"And then it happens. As if the law of gravity had suddenly been revoked. The stallion doesn't run, he flies through the air. Like a cannon ball. Like a spring suddenly released. The mare bows and lowers her head and he thrusts into her, blow after blow. His eyes are full of blood. There's not enough air for him to breathe and he gasps and chokes as if he's dying. His mouth hangs open and he pours saliva and foam on her head. Suddenly he starts to roar and howl. Like a dog. Like a wolf. Writhing and screaming. In that moment there is no telling pleasure from pain. And mating is very much like castration."

"Enough, Matityahu, for God's sake, enough."

"Now let's relax. Or perhaps you'd like to hear how a horse is castrated?"

"Please, enough, no more," Galila pleaded.

Slowly Matityahu raised his maimed hand. The compassion in his voice was strange, almost fatherly:

"Just like your mother. About that," he said, "about the fingers and about castration as well, we'll talk some other time. Enough now. Don't be afraid now. Now we can rest and relax. I've got a drop of cognac somewhere. No? No. Vermouth then. There's vermouth too. Here's to my cousin Leon. Drink. Relax. Enough."

7.

The cold light of the distant stars spreads a reddish crust upon the fields. In the last weeks of the summer the land has all been turned over. Now it stands ready for the winter sowing. Twisting dirt tracks cross the plain, here and there are the dark masses of plantations, fenced in by walls of cypress trees.

For the first time in many months our lands feel the first tentative fingers of the cold. The irrigation pipes, the taps, the metal fittings, they are the first to capitulate to any conqueror, summer's heat or autumn's chill. And now they are the first to surrender to the cool moisture.

In the past, forty years ago, the founders of the kibbutz entrenched themselves in this land, digging their pale fingernails into the earth. Some were fair-haired, like Sashka, others, like Tanya, were brazen and scowling. In the long, burning hours of the day they used to curse the earth scorched by the fires of the sun, curse it in despair, in anger, in longing for rivers and forests. But in the darkness, when night fell, they composed sweet love songs to the earth, forgetful of time and place. At night forgetfulness gave taste to life. In the angry darkness oblivion enfolded them in a mother's embrace. "There," they used to sing, not "Here."

> *There in the land our fathers loved,*
> *There all our hopes shall be fulfilled.*
> *There we shall live and there a life*
> *Of health and freedom we shall build. . . .*

People like Sashka were forged in fury, in longing and in dedication. Matityahu Damkov, and the latter-day fugitives like him, know nothing of the longing that burns and the dedication that draws blood from the lips. That is why they seek to break into the inner circle. They make advances to the women. They use words similar to ours. But theirs is a different sorrow, they do not belong to us, they are extras, on the outside, and so they shall be until the day they die.

The captive jackal cub was seized by weariness. The tip of his right paw was held fast in the teeth of the trap. He sprawled flat on the turf as if reconciled to his fate.

First he licked his fur, slowly, like a cat. Then he stretched out his neck and began licking the smooth, shining metal. As if lavishing warmth and love upon the silent foe. Love and hate, they both breed surrender. He threaded his free paw beneath the trap, groped slowly for the meat of the bait, withdrew the paw carefully and licked off the savor that had clung to it.

Finally, the others appeared.

Jackals, huge, emaciated, filthy and swollen-bellied. Some with running sores, others stinking of putrid carrion. One by one they came together from all their distant hiding places, summoned to the gruesome ritual. They formed themselves into a circle and fixed pitying eyes upon the captive innocent. Malicious joy striving hard to disguise itself as compassion, triumphant evil breaking through the mask of mourning. The unseen signal was given, the marauders of the night began slowly moving in a circle as in a dance, with mincing, gliding steps. When the excitement exploded into mirth the rhythm was shattered, the ritual broken, and the jackals cavorted madly like rabid dogs. Then the despairing voices rose into the night, sorrow and rage and envy and triumph, bestial laughter and a choking wail of supplication, angry, threatening, rising to a scream of terror and fading again into submission, lament, and silence.

After midnight they ceased. Perhaps the jackals despaired of their helpless child. Quietly they dispersed to their own sorrows. Night, the patient gatherer, took them up in his arms and wiped away all the traces.

8.

Matityahu Damkov was enjoying the interlude. Nor did Galila try to hasten the course of events. It was night. The girl unfolded the canvases that Matityahu Damkov had received from his cousin Leon and examined the tubes of paint. It was good quality material, the type used by professionals. Until now she had painted on oiled sackcloth or cheap mass-produced canvases with paints borrowed from the kindergarten. She's so young, thought Matityahu Damkov, she's a little girl, slender and spoiled. I'm going to smash her to pieces. Slowly. For a moment he was tempted to tell her the truth outright, like a bolt from the blue, but he thought better of it. The night was slow.

In oblivion and delight, compulsively, Galila fingered the fine brush, lightly touching the orange paint, lightly stroking the canvas with the hairs of the brush, an unconscious caress, like fingertips on the hairs of the neck. Innocence flowed from her body to his, his body responded with waves of desire.

Afterward Galila lay without moving, as if asleep, on the oily, paint-splashed tiles, canvases and tubes of paint scattered about her. Matityahu lay back on his single bed, closed his eyes and summoned a dream.

At his bidding they come to him, quiet dreams and wild drams. They come and play before him. This time he chose to summon the dream of the flood, one of the severest in his repertoire.

First to appear is a mass of ravines descending the mountain slopes, scores of teeming watercourses, crisscrossing and zigzagging.

In a flash the throngs of tiny people appear in the gullies. Like little black ants they swarm and trickle from their hiding places in the crevices of the mountain, sweeping down like a cataract. Hordes of thin dark people streaming down the slopes, rolling like an avalanche of stone and plunging in a headlong torrent to the levels of the plain. Here they split into a thousand columns, racing westward in furious spate. Now they are so close that their shapes can be seen: a dark, disgusting, emaciated mass, crawling with lice and fleas, stinking. Hunger and hatred distort their faces. Their eyes blaze with madness. In full flood they swoop upon the fertile valleys, racing over the ruins of deserted villages without a moment's check. In their rush toward the sea they drag with them all that lies in their path, uprooting posts, ravaging fields, mowing down fences, trampling the gardens and stripping the orchards, pillaging homesteads, crawling through huts and stables, clambering over walls like demented apes, onward, westward, to the sands of the sea.

And suddenly you too are surrounded, besieged, paralyzed with fear. You see their eyes ablaze with primeval hatred, mouths hanging open, teeth yellow and rotten, curved daggers gleaming in their hands. They curse you in clipped tones, voices choking with rage or with dark desire. Now their hands are groping at your flesh. A knife and a scream. With the last spark of your life you extinguish the vision and almost breathe freely again.

"Come on," said Matityahu Damkov, shaking the girl with his right hand, while the maimed hand, his left, caressed her neck. "Come on. Let's get away from here. Tonight. In the morning. I shall save you. We'll run away together to South America, to my cousin Leon. I'll take care of you. I'll always take care of you."

"Leave me alone, don't touch me," she said.

He clasped her in a powerful and silent embrace.

"My father will kill you tomorrow. I told you to leave me alone."

"Your father will take care of you now and he'll always take care of you." Matityahu Damkov replied softly. He let her go. The girl stood up, buttoning her skirt, smoothing back her blond hair.

"That isn't what I want. I didn't want to come here at all. You're taking advantage of me and doing things to me that I don't want and saying all kinds of things because you're mad and everyone knows you're mad, ask anyone you like."

Matityahu Damkov's lips broadened into a smile.

"I won't come to you again, not ever. And I don't want your paints. You're dangerous. You're as ugly as a monkey. And you're mad."

"I can tell you about your mother, if you want to hear. And if you want to hate and curse, then it's her you should hate, not me."

The girl turned hurriedly to the window, flung it open with a desperate movement and leaned out into the empty night. Now she's going to scream, thought Matityahu Damkov in alarm, she'll scream and the opportunity won't come again. Blood filled his eyes. He swooped upon her, clapped his hand over her mouth, dragged her back inside the room, buried his lips in her hair, probed with his lips for her ear, found it, and told her.

9.

Sharp waves of chill autumn air clung to the outer walls of the houses, seeking entry. From the yard on the slope of the hill came the sounds of cattle lowing and herdsmen cursing. A cow having difficulty giving birth perhaps, the big torch throwing light on the blood and the mire. Matityahu Damkov knelt on the floor and gathered up the paints and the brushes that his guest had left scattered there. Galila still stood beside the open window, her back to the room and her face to the darkness. Then she spoke, still with her back to the man.

"It's doubtful," she said. "it's almost impossible, it isn't even logical, it can't be proved, and it's crazy. Absolutely."

Matityahu Damkov stared at her back with his mongoloid eyes. Now his ugliness was complete, a concentrated, penetrating ugliness.

"I won't force you. Please. I shall say nothing. Perhaps just laugh to myself quietly. For all I care you can be Sashka's daughter or even Ben-Gurion's daughter. I shall say nothing. Like my cousin Leon I shall say nothing. He loved his Christian son and never said I love you, only when this son of his had killed eleven policemen and himself did he remember to tell him in his grave, I love you. Please."

Suddenly, without warning, Galila burst into laughter:

"You fool, you little fool, look at me, I'm blond, look!"

Matityahu said nothing.

"I'm not yours, I'm sure of it because I'm blond, I'm not yours or Leon's either, I'm blond and it's all right! Come on!"

The man leaped at her, panting, groaning, groping his way blindly. In his rush he overturned the coffee table, he shuddered violently and the girl shuddered with him.

And then she recoiled from him, fled to the far wall. He pushed aside the coffee table. He kicked it. His eyes were shot with blood, and a sound like gargling came from his lips. She suddenly remembered her mother's face and the trembling of her lips and her tears, and she pushed the man from her with a dreamy hand. As if struck, they both retreated, staring at each other, eyes wide open.

"Father," said Galila in surprise, as if waking on the first morning of winter at the end of a long summer, looking outside and saying, rain.

10.

The sun rises without dignity in our part of the world. With a cheap sentimentality it appears over the peaks of the eastern mountains and touches our lands with tentative rays. No glory, no complicated tricks of light. A purely conventional beauty, more like a picture postcard than a real landscape.

But this will be one of the last sunrises. Autumn will soon be here. A few more days and we shall wake in the morning to the sound of rain. There may be hail too. The sun will rise behind a screen of dirty gray clouds. Early risers will wrap themselves in overcoats and emerge from their houses fortified against the daggers of the wind.

The path of the seasons is well trodden. Autumn, winter, spring, summer, autumn. Things are as they have always been. Whoever seeks a fixed point in the current of time and the seasons would do well to listen to the sounds of the night that never change. They come to us from out there.

Translated from the Hebrew by Nicholas de Lange and Philip Simpson

Victor Pelevin

The Life and Adventures of Shed Number XII

(RUSSIA)

In the beginning was the word, and maybe not even just one, but what could he know about that? What he discovered at his point of origin was a stack of planks on wet grass, smelling of fresh resin and soaking up the sun with their yellow surfaces: he found nails in a plywood box, hammers, saws, and so forth—but visualizing all this, he observed that he was thinking the picture into existence rather than just seeing it. Only later did a weak sense of self emerge, when the bicycles already stood inside him and three shelves one above the other covered his right wall. He wasn't really Number XII then; he was merely a new configuration of the stack of planks. But those were the times that had left the most pure and enduring impression. All around lay the wide incomprehensible world, and it seemed as though he had merely interrupted his journey through it, making a halt here, at this spot, for a while.

Certainly the spot could have been better—out behind the low five-storey prefabs, alongside the vegetable gardens and the garbage dump. But why feel upset about something like that? He wasn't going to spend his entire life here, after all. Of course, if he'd really thought about it, he would have been forced to admit that that was precisely what he was going to do—that's the way it is for sheds—but the charm of life's earliest beginnings consists in the absence of such thoughts. He simply stood there in the sunshine, rejoicing in the wind whistling through his cracks if it blew from the woods, or falling into a slight depression if it blew in from over the dump. The depression passed as soon as the wind changed direction, without leaving any long-term effect on a soul that was still only partially formed.

One day he was approached by a man naked to the waist in a pair of red tracksuit pants, holding a brush and a huge can of paint. The shed was already beginning to recognize this man, who was different from all the other people because he could get inside, to the bicycles and the shelves. He stopped by the wall, dipped the brush into the can, and traced a bright crimson line on the planks. An hour later the hut was crimson all over. This was the first real landmark in his memory—everything that came before it was still cloaked in a sense of distant and unreal happiness.

The night after the painting (when he had been given his Roman numeral, his name—the other sheds around him all had ordinary numbers), he held up his tar-papered roof to the moon as he dried. "Where am I?" he thought. "Who am I?"

Above him was the dark sky and inside him stood the brand-new bicycles. A beam of light from the lamp in the yard shone on them through a crack, and the bells on their handlebars gleamed and twinkled more mysteriously than the stars. Higher up, a plastic hoop hung on the wall, and with the very thinnest of his planks Number XII recognized it as a symbol of the eternal riddle of creation which was also represented—so very wonderfully—in his own soul. On the shelves lay all sorts of stupid trifles that lent variety and uniqueness to his inner world. Dill and scented herbs hung drying on a thread stretched from one wall to another, reminding him of something that never ever happens to sheds—but since they reminded him of it anyway, sometimes it seemed that he once must have been not a mere shed, but a dacha, or at the very least a garage.

He became aware of himself, and realized that what he was aware of, that is himself, was made up of numerous small individual features: of the unearthly personalities of machines for conquering distance, which smelled of rubber and steel; of the mystical introspection of the self-enclosed hoop; of the squeaking in the souls of the small items, such as the nails and nuts which were scattered along the shelves; and of other things. Within each of these existences there was an infinity of subtle variation, but still for him each was linked with one important thing, some decisive feeling—and fusing together, these feelings gave rise to a new unity, defined in space by the freshly painted planks, but not actually limited by anything. That was him, Number XII, and above his head the moon was his equal as it rushed through the mist and the clouds. . . . That night was when his life really began.

Soon Number XII realized that he liked most of all the sensation which was derived from or transmitted by the bicycles. Sometimes on a hot summer day, when the world around him grew quiet, he would secretly identify himself in turn with the "Sputnik" and the folding "Kama" and experience two different kinds of happiness.

In this state he might easily find himself forty miles away from his real location, perhaps rolling across a deserted bridge over a canal bounded by concrete banks, or along the violet border of the sun-baked highway, turning into the tunnels formed by the high bushes lining a narrow dirt track and then hurtling along it until he emerged onto another road leading to the forest, through the forest, through the open fields, straight up into the orange sky above the horizon: he could probably have carried on riding along the road till the end of his life, but he didn't want to, because what brought him happiness was the possibility itself. He might find himself in the city, in some yard where long stems grew out of the pavement cracks, and spend the evening there—in fact he could do almost anything.

When he tried to share some of his experiences with the occult-minded garage that stood beside him, the answer he received was that in fact there is only one higher happiness: the ecstatic union with the archetypal garage. So how could he tell his neighbor about two different kinds of perfect happiness, one of which folded away, while the other had three-speed gears?

"You mean I should try to feel like a garage too?" he asked one day.

"There is no other path," replied the garage. "Of course, you're not likely to succeed, but your chances are better than those of a kennel or a tobacco kiosk."

"And what if I like feeling like a bicycle?" asked Number XII, revealing his cherished secret.

"By all means, feel like one. I can't say you mustn't," said the garage. "For some of us feelings of the lower kind are the limit, and there's nothing to be done about it."

"What's that written in chalk on your side?" Number XII inquired.

"None of your business, you cheap piece of plywood shit," the garage replied with unexpected malice.

Of course, Number XII had only made the remark because he felt offended—who wouldn't by having his aspirations termed "lower"? After this incident there could be no question of associating with the garage, but Number XII didn't regret it. One morning the garage was demolished, and Number XII was left alone.

Actually, there were two other sheds quite close, to his left, but he tried not to think about them. Not because they were built differently and painted a dull, indefinite color—he could have reconciled himself with that. The problem was something else: on the ground floor of the five-storey prefab where Number XII's owners lived there was a big vegetable shop and these sheds served as its warehouses. They were used for storing carrots, potatoes, beets, and cucumbers, but the factor absolutely dominating every aspect of Number 13 and Number 14 was the pickled cabbage in two huge barrels covered with plastic. Number XII had often seen their great hollow bodies girt with steel hoops surrounded by a retinue of emaciated workmen who were rolling them out at an angle into the yard. At these times he felt afraid and he recalled one of the favorite maxims of the deceased garage, whom he often remembered with sadness, "There are some things in life which you must simply turn your back on as quickly as possible." And no sooner did he recall the maxim than he applied it. The dark and obscure life of his neighbors, their sour exhalations, and obtuse grip on life were a threat to Number XII: the very existence of these squat structures was enough to negate everything else. Every drop of brine in their barrels declared that Number XII's existence in the universe was entirely unnecessary: that, at least, that was how he interpreted the vibrations radiating from their consciousness of the world.

But the day came to an end, the light grew thick, Number XII was a bicycle rushing along a deserted highway and any memories of the horrors of the day seemed simply ridiculous.

It was the middle of the summer when the lock clanked, the hasp was thrown back, and two people entered Number XII: his owner and a woman. Number XII did not like her—somehow she reminded him of everything that he simply could not stand. Not that this impression sprang from the fact that she smelled of pickled cabbage—rather the opposite: it was the smell of pickled cabbage that conveyed some information about this woman, that somehow or other she was the very embodiment of the fermentation and the oppressive force of will to which Numbers 13 and 14 owed their present existence.

Number XII began to think, while the two people went on talking:

"Well, if we take down the shelves it'll do fine, just fine. . . ."

"This is a first-class shed," replied his owner, wheeling the bicycles outside. "No leaks or any other problems. And what a color!"

After wheeling out the bicycles and leaning them against the wall, he began untidily gathering together everything lying on the shelves. It was then that Number XII began to feel upset.

Of course, the bicycles had often disappeared for certain periods of time, and he knew how to use his memory to fill in the gap. Afterwards, when the bicycles were returned to their places, he was always amazed how inadequate the image his memory created was in comparison with the actual beauty that the bicycles simply radiated into space. Whenever they disappeared the bicycles always returned, and these short separations from the most important part of his own soul lent Number XII's life its unpredictable charm. But this time everything was different—the bicycles were being taken away forever.

He realized this from the unceremonious way that the man in the red pants was wreaking total devastation in him—nothing like this had ever happened before. The woman in the white coat had left long ago, but his owner was still rummaging around, raking tools into a bag, and taking down the old cans and patched inner tubes from the wall. Then a truck backed up to his door, and both bicycles dived obediently after the overfilled bags into its gaping tarpaulin maw.

Number XII was empty, and his door stood wide open.

Despite everything he continued to be himself. The souls of all that life had taken away continued to dwell in him, and although they had become shadows of themselves they still fused together to make him Number XII: but it now required all the willpower he could muster to maintain his individuality.

In the morning he noticed a change in himself. No longer interested in the world around him, his attention was focused exclusively on the past, moving in concentric rings of memory. He could explain this: when he left, his owner had forgotten the hoop, and now it was the only real part of his otherwise phantom soul, which was why Number XII felt like a closed circle. But he didn't have enough strength to feel really anything about this, or wonder if it was good or bad. A dreary, colorless yearning overlay every other feeling. A month passed like that.

One day workmen arrived, entered his defenseless open door, and in the space of a few minutes broke down the shelves. Number XII wasn't even fully aware of his new condition before his feelings overwhelmed him—which incidentally demonstrates that he still had enough vital energy left in him to experience fear.

They were rolling a barrel towards him across the yard. Towards him! In his great depths of nostalgic self-pity, he'd never dreamed anything could be worse than what had already happened—that this could be possible!

The barrel was a fearful sight. Huge and potbellied, it was very old, and its sides were impregnated with something hideous which gave out such a powerful stench that even the workers angling it along, who were certainly no strangers to the seamy side of life, turned their faces away and swore. And Number XII could also see something that the men couldn't: the barrel exuded an aura of cold attention as it viewed the world through the damp likeness of an eye. Number XII did not see them roll it inside and circle it around on the floor to set it at his very center—he had fainted.

Suffering maims. Two days passed before Number XII began to recover his thoughts and his feelings. Now he was different, and everything in him was different. At the very center of his soul, at the spot once occupied by the bicycles' windswept frames, there was pulsating repulsive living death, concentrated in the slow existence of the barrel and its equally slow thoughts, which were now Number XII's thoughts. He could feel the fermentation of the rotten brine, and the bubbles rose in him to burst on the surface, leaving holes in the layer of green mold. The swollen corpses of the cucumbers were shifted about by the gas, and the slime-impregnated boards strained against their rusty iron hoops inside him. All of it was him.

Numbers 13 and 14 no longer frightened him—on the contrary, he rapidly fell into a half-unconscious state of comradery with them. But the past had not totally disappeared; it had simply been pushed aside, squashed into a corner. Number XII's new life was a double one. On the one hand, he felt himself the equal of Numbers 13 and 14, and yet on the other hand, buried somewhere deep inside him, there remained a sense of terrible injustice about what had happened to him. But his new existence's center was located in the barrel, which emitted the constant gurgling and crackling sounds that had replaced the imagined whooshing of tires over concrete.

Numbers 13 and 14 explained to him that all he had gone through was just a normal life change that comes with age.

"The entry into the real world, with its real difficulties and concerns, always involves certain difficulties," Number 13 would say. "One's soul is occupied with entirely new problems."

And he would add some words of encouragement: "Never mind, you'll get used to it. It's only hard at the beginning."

Number 14 was a shed with a rather philosophical turn of mind. He often spoke of spiritual matters, and soon managed to convince his new comrade that if the beautiful consisted of harmony ("That's for one," he would say) and inside you—objectively speaking now—you had pickled cucumbers or pickled cabbage ("That's for two"), then the beauty of life consisted in achieving harmony with the contents of the barrel and removing all obstacles hindering that. An old dictionary of philosophical terms had been wedged under his own barrel to keep it from overflowing, and he often quoted from it. It helped him explain to Number XII how he should live his life. Number 14 never did feel complete confidence in the novice, however, sensing something in him that Number 14 no longer sensed in himself.

But gradually Number XII became genuinely resigned to the situation. Sometimes he even experienced a certain inspiration, an upsurge of the will to live this new life. But his new friends' mistrust was well founded. On several occasions Number XII caught glimpses of something forgotten, like a gleam of light through a keyhole, and then he would be overwhelmed by a feeling of intense contempt for himself—and he simply hated the other two.

Naturally, all of this was suppressed by the cucumber barrel's invincible worldview, and Number XII soon began to wonder what it was he'd been getting so upset about. He became simpler and the past gradually bothered him less because it was growing hard for him to keep up with the fleeting flashes of memory. More and more often the barrel seemed like a guarantee of stability and peace, like the ballast of a ship, and sometimes Number XII imagined himself like that, like a ship sailing out into tomorrow.

He began to feel the barrel's innate good nature, but only after he had finally opened his own soul to it. Now the cucumbers seemed almost like children to him.

Numbers 13 and 14 weren't bad comrades—and most importantly, they lent him support in his new existence. Sometimes in the evening the three of them would silently classify the objects of the world, imbuing everything around them with an all-embracing spirit of understanding, and when one of the new little huts that had recently been built nearby shuddered he would look at it and think: "How stupid, but never mind, it'll sow its wild oats and then it'll come to understand. . . ." He saw several such transformations take place before his own eyes, and each one served to confirm the correctness of his opinion yet again. He also experienced a feeling of hatred when anything unnecessary appeared in the world, but thank God, that didn't happen often. The days and the years passed, and it seemed that nothing would change again.

One summer evening, glancing around inside himself, Number XII came across an incomprehensible object, a plastic hoop draped with cobwebs. At first he couldn't make out what it was or what it might be for, and then suddenly he recalled that there were so many things that once used to be connected with this item. The barrel inside him was dozing, and some other part of him cautiously pulled in the threads of memory, but all of them were broken and they led nowhere. But there was something once, wasn't there? Or was there? He concentrated and tried to understand what it was he couldn't remember, and for a moment he stopped feeling the barrel and was somehow separate from it.

At that very moment a bicycle entered the yard and for no reason at all the rider rang the bell on his handlebars twice. It was enough—Number XII remembered:

A bicycle. A highway. A sunset. A bridge over a river.

He remembered who he really was and at last became himself, really himself. Everything connected with the barrel dropped off like a dry scab. He suddenly smelt the repulsive stench of the brine and saw his comrades of yesterday, Numbers 13 and 14, for what they really were. But there was no time to think about all this, he had to hurry: he knew that if he didn't do what he had to do now, the hateful barrel would overpower him again and turn him into itself.

Meanwhile the barrel had woken up and realized that something was happening. Number XII felt the familiar current of cold obtuseness he'd been used to thinking was his own. The barrel was awake and starting to fill him—there was only one answer he could make.

Two electric wires ran under his eaves. While the barrel was still getting its bearings and working out exactly what was wrong, he did the only thing he could. He squeezed the wires together with all his might, using some new power born of despair. A moment later he was overwhelmed by the invincible force emanating from the cucumber barrel, and for a while he simply ceased to exist.

But the deed was done: torn from their insulation, the wires touched, and where they met a purplish-white flame sprang into life. A second later a fuse blew and the current disappeared from the wires, but a narrow ribbon of smoke was already snaking up the dry planking. Then more flames appeared, and meeting no resistance they began to spread and creep towards the roof.

Number XII came round after the first blow and realized that the barrel had decided to annihilate him totally. Compressing his entire being into one of the upper planks in his ceiling, he could feel that the barrel was not alone—it was being helped by Number 13 and 14, who were directing their thoughts at him from outside.

"Obviously," Number XII thought with a strange sense of detachment, "what they are doing now must seem to them like restraining a madman, or perhaps they see an enemy spy whose cunning pretence to be one of them has now been exposed—"

He never finished the thought, because at that moment the barrel threw all its rottenness against the boundaries of his existence with redoubled force. He withstood the blow, but realized that the next one would finish him, and he prepared to die. But time passed, and no new blow came. He expanded his boundaries a little and felt two things—first, the barrel's fear, as cold and sluggish as every sensation it manifested; and second, the flames blazing all around, which were already closing in on the ceiling plank animated by Number XII. The walls were ablaze, the tar-paper roof was weeping fiery tears, and the plastic bottles of sunflower oil were burning on the floor. Some of them were bursting, and the brine was boiling in the barrel, which for all its ponderous might was obviously dying. Number XII extended himself over to the section of the roof that was still left, and summoned up the memory of the day he was painted, and more importantly, of that night: he wanted to die with that thought. Beside him he saw Number 13 was already ablaze, and that was the last thing he noticed. Yet death still didn't come, and when his final splinter burst into flames, something quite unexpected happened.

The director of Vegetable Shop 17, the same woman who had visited Number XII with his owner, was walking home in a foul mood. That evening, at six o'-clock, the shed where the oil and cucumbers were stored had suddenly caught fire. The spilled oil had spread the fire to the other sheds—in short, every-thing that could burn had burned. All that was left of hut Number XII were the keys, and huts Number 13 and 14 were now no more than a few scorched planks.

While the repots were being drawn up and the explanations were being made to the firemen, darkness had fallen, and now the director felt afraid as she walked along the empty road with the trees standing on each side like ban-dits. She stopped and looked back to make sure no one was following her. There didn't seem to be anyone there. She took a few more steps, then glanced round again, and she thought she could see something twinkling in the distance. Just in case, she went to the edge of the road and stood behind a tree. Staring intently into the darkness, she waited to see what would happen. At the most distant visible point of the road a bright spot came into view. "A motorcycle!" thought the director, pressing hard against the tree trunk. But there was no sound of an engine.

The bright spot moved closer, until she could see that it was not moving on the surface of the road but flying along above it. A moment later, and the spot of light was transformed into something totally unreal—a bicycle without a rider, flying at a height of ten or twelve feet. It was strangely made; it some-how looked at though it had been crudely nailed together out of planks. But strangest of all was that it glowed and flickered and changed color, sometimes turning transparent and then blazing with an unbearably intense brightness. Completely entranced, the director walked out into the middle of the road, and to her appearance the bicycle quite clearly responded. Reducing its height and speed, it turned a few circles in the air above the dazed woman's head. Then it rose higher and hung motionless before swinging round stiffly above the road like a weather vane. It hung there for another moment or two and then finally began to move, gathering speed at an incredible rate until it was no more than a bright dot in the sky. Then that disappeared as well.

When she recovered her senses, the director found herself sitting in the middle of the road. She stood up, shook herself off, completely forgetting. . . . But then, she's of no interest to us.

Translated from the Russian by Andrew Bromfield

Francine Prose

Talking Dog

(UNITED STATES)

The dog was going to Florida. The dog knew all the best sleeping places along the side of the highway, and if my sister wanted to come along, the dog would be glad to pace himself so my sister could keep up. My sister told our family this when she came back to the dinner table from which Mother and I had watched her kneeling in the snowy garden, crouched beside the large shaggy white dog, her ear against its mouth.

My sister's chair faced the window, and when the dog first appeared in our yard, she'd said, "Oh, I know that dog," and jumped up and ran out the door. I thought she'd meant whose dog it was, not that she knew it to talk to.

"What dog?" My father slowly turned his head.

"A dog, dear," Mother said.

That year it came as a great surprise how many sad things could happen at once. At first you might think the odds are that one grief might exempt you, but that year I learned the odds are that nothing can keep you safe. So many concurrent painful events altered our sense of each one, just as a color appears to change when another color is placed beside it.

That year my father was going blind from a disease of the retina, a condition we knew a lot about because my father was a scientist and used to lecture us on it at dinner with the glittery detached fascination he'd once had for research gossip and new developments in the lab. Yet as his condition worsened he'd stopped talking about it; he could still read but had trouble with stairs and had begun to touch the furniture. Out in daylight he needed special glasses, like twin tiny antique cameras, and he ducked his head as he put them on, as if burrowing under a cloth. I was ashamed for anyone to see and ashamed of being embarrassed.

My father still consulted part-time for a lab that used dogs in experiments, and at night he worked at home with a microscope and a tape recorder. "Slide 109," he'd say. "Liver condition normal." My sister had always loved animals, but no one yet saw a connection between my father dissecting dogs and my sister talking to them.

For several weeks before that night when the white dog came through our yard, my sister lay in bed with the curtains drawn and got up only at mealtime. Mother told the high school that my sister had bronchitis. At first my sister's friends telephoned, but only once, Marcy, still called. I'd hear Mother telling Marcy that my sister was much better, being friendlier to Marcy than she'd ever been before. Marcy had cracked a girl's front tooth and been sent to a special school. Each time Marcy telephoned, Mother called my sister's name and, when she didn't answer, said she must be sleeping. I believed my sister was faking it but even I'd begun to have the sickish, panicky feeling you get when someone playing dead takes too long getting up.

One night at dinner my sister told us that every culture but ours believed that ordinary household pets were the messengers of the dead.

"I don't know about that," my father said. "I don't know about *every* culture."

After that it was just a matter of time till she met the dog with a message. And we all knew who it was that my sister was waiting to hear from.

Her boyfriend, Jimmy Kowalchuk, had just been killed in Vietnam.

Mother had gone with my sister to Jimmy Kowalchuk's funeral. I was not allowed to attend, though I'd been in love with him, too. All day in school all I could think of was how many hours, how many minutes till they lowered him in the ground. It was a little like the time they executed Caryl Chessman and the whole school counted down the minutes till he died. The difference was that with Jimmy I was the only one counting, and I had to keep reminding myself that he was already dead.

Mother came home from the funeral in a bubbly, talkative mood. After my sister drifted off, Mother sat on the arm of my father's chair. She said, "They call this country a melting pot but if you ask me there's still a few lumps. Believe it or not, they had two priests—one Polish and one Puerto Rican. The minute I saw them I said to myself: This will take twice as long."

Mother had never liked it that Jimmy was half Polish, half Puerto Rican—if he couldn't be white Protestant, better Puerto Rican completely. She never liked it that our family knew someone named Jimmy Kowalchuk, and she liked it least of all that we knew someone fighting in Vietnam. Every Wednesday night Mother counseled draft resisters, and it made her livid that Jimmy had volunteered.

"Guess what?" Mother told us. "His name wasn't even Jimmy. It was Hymie. That's what the priests and the relatives kept saying. Hymie. Hymie. Hymie. Do you think she would have gone out with him if she had known that?"

"J pronounced Y," my father said. "J-A-I-M-E."

"Pedant," mumbled Mother, so softly only I heard.

"Excuse me?" my father said.

"Nothing," Mother said. "Maybe we should have got her that pony she nagged us about in junior high. Maybe we should have let her keep that falcon that needed a home."

To me she said, "This does not mean you, dear. You cannot have a bird or a pony."

But I didn't want a bird or a pony. I still wanted Jimmy Kowalchuk. And I alone knew that he and my sister had had a great love, a tragic love. For unlike my parents I had seen what Jimmy had gone through to win it.

The first time was on a wet gray day, winter twilight, after school. My parents were in the city, seeing one of my father's doctors, my sister was taking care of me, we were supposed to stay home. Jimmy came to take my sister out in his lemon-yellow '65 Malibu. My sister must have decided it was safer to bring me along—better an accomplice than a potential snitch. I felt like a criminal, like the Barrow Gang on the Jericho Turnpike, ready to hit the floor if I saw Mother's car in the opposite lane.

As Jimmy left the highway for smaller and smaller roads, I felt safer from my parents but more nervous about Jimmy. He was slight and tense and Latin with a wispy beard, dangerous and pretty, like Jesus with an earring. We drove past black trees, marshy scrub-pine lots, perfect for dumping bodies, not far from a famous spot where the Mafia often did. The light was fading and scraps of fog clung regretfully to the windshield.

Jimmy pulled off on the side of the road beside the bank of a frozen lake. "Ladies," he said, "I'll have to ask you to step outside for a minute." Leaning across my sister, he opened the door on her side and then arched back over the seat and opened mine for me.

A wet mist prickled our faces—tiny sharp needles of ice.

"I'm freezing," said my sister.

I said, "Do you think he'd leave us here?"

She said, "Stupid, why would my boyfriend leave us in the middle of nowhere?" I hadn't known for certain till then that Jimmy was her boyfriend. He hadn't even touched her leg when he'd reached down to shift gears.

Jimmy rammed the car in gear and pointed it at the lake and sped out onto the ice and hit the brake and spun. It was thrilling and terrifying to see a car whip around like a snake, and there was also a grace in it, the weightless skimming of a skater. The yellow car gathered the last of the light and cast a faint lemon glow on the ice.

Suddenly we heard the ice crack—first with a squeak, then a groan. My sister grabbed my upper arm and dug her fingers in.

Jimmy must have heard it, too, because the car glided to a stop and he gingerly turned it around and drove back in our direction. I stood up on tiptoe though I could see perfectly well. Then I looked at my sister as if she knew what was going to happen.

I was shocked by my sister's expression: not a trace of fear or concern, but an unreadable concentration and the sullen fixed anger I saw sometimes when we fought. She was very careful not to look like that out in the world, except if she saw a pet she thought was being mistreated. It was like watching a simmering pot, lid rattling, about to boil over, but her lids were halfway down and you couldn't see what was cooking. At the moment I understood that men would always like her better, prefer her smoky opacity to a transparent face like mine.

On the drive home Jimmy elaborated on his theory of danger. He said it was important for males to regularly test themselves against potentially fatal risks. He said it was like a checkup or maybe a vacation—you did it regularly for your health and for a hit on how you were doing.

"That's bullshit," my sister said.

"She thinks it's bullshit," Jimmy told me. "Do you think it's bullshit, kid?"

I knew he was inviting me to contradict my sister; it made me feel like a younger brother instead of an eighth-grade girl. I knew that if I agreed with him I might get to come along again. But that wasn't my reason for saying no. At that moment I believed him.

"The kid knows," Jimmy said, and I whispered: The kid. The kid. The kid.

"This danger thing," Jimmy told us, "is only about yourself. It would be criminal to take chances with somebody else's life. I would never go over the speed limit with you ladies in the car." I hunched my shoulders and burrowed into the fragrant back seat. I felt—and I think my sister felt—supremely taken care of.

My parents were often in the city with my father's doctors, occasionally staying over for tests, not returning till the next day. They told my sister to take care of me, though I didn't need taking care of.

Jimmy would drive over when he got through at Babylon Roofing and Siding. He loved his job and sometimes stopped to show us roofs he'd done. His plan was to have his own company and retire to Florida young and get a little house with grapefruit and mango trees in the yard. He said this to my sister. He wanted her to want it, too.

My sister said, "Mangoes in Florida? You're thinking about Puerto Rico."

One night Jimmy parked in front of a furniture store and told us to slouch down and keep our eye on the dark front window. My sister and I were alone for so long I began to get frightened.

A light flickered on inside the store, the flame from Jimmy's lighter, bright enough to see Jimmy smiling and waving, reclining in a lounger.

When Jimmy talked about testing himself, he said he did it sometimes, but I began to wonder if he thought about it always. Just sitting in a diner, waiting for his coffee, he'd take the pointiest knife he could find and dance it between his fingers. I wondered what our role in it was. I wondered if he and my sister were playing a game of chicken: all she had to do was cry "Stop!" and Jimmy would have won. Once he ate a cigarette filter. Once he jumped off a building.

One evening Jimmy drove me and my sister over to his apartment. He lived in a basement apartment of a brick private house. It struck me as extraordinary: people lived in basement apartments. But it wasn't a shock to my sister, who knew where everything was and confidently got two beers from Jimmy's refrigerator.

Jimmy turned on the six o'clock news and the three of us sat on his bed. There was the usual Vietnam report: helicopters, gunfire. A sequence showed American troops filing through the jungle. The camera moved in for a close-up of soldier's faces, faces that I recognize now as the faces of frightened boys but that I mistook then for cruel grown men, happy in what they were doing.

My sister said, "Wow. Any one of those suckers could just get blown off that trail." On her face was that combustible mix of sympathy and smoldering anger, and in her voice rage and contempt combined with admiration. I could tell Jimmy was jealous that she looked like that because of the soldiers, and he desperately wanted her to look that way for him. I knew, even if he didn't, that she already had, and that she looked like that if she saw a dog in a parked car, in the heat.

Jimmy had a high draft number but he went down and enlisted. He said he couldn't sit back and let other men do the dying, an argument I secretly thought was crazy and brave and terrific. Mother said it was ridiculous, no one had to die, every kid she counseled wound up with a psychiatric 1-Y. And when Jimmy died she seemed confirmed; he had proved her right.

On the night of the funeral, Mother told us how Jimmy died. The friend who'd accompanied his body home had given a little speech. He said often at night Jimmy sneaked out to where they weren't supposed to be; once a flare went off and they saw him freaking around in the jungle. He said they felt better knowing that crazy Kowalchuk was out there fucking around.

Mother said, "That's what he said at the service. 'Out there fucking around.'"

But I was too hurt to listen, I was feeling so stupid for having imagined that Jimmy's stunts were about my sister and me.

Mother said, "Of course I think it's terrible that the boy got killed. But I have to say I don't hate it that now the two of them can't get married."

After that it was just a matter of time till my sister met the white dog that Jimmy had sent from the other world to take her to Florida.

My sister didn't go to Florida, or anyway not yet. Eventually she recovered—recovered or stopped pretending. Every night after dinner Mother said, "She's eating well. She's improving." Talking to strange dogs in the yard was apparently not a problem. Father's problem was a real problem; my sister's would improve. I knew that Mother felt this way, and once more she was right.

One night Marcy telephoned, Mother called my sister, and my sister came out of her room. She took the phone and told Marcy, "Sure, great. See you. Bye."

"Marcy knows about a party," she said.

Mother said, "Wonderful, dear," though in the past there were always fights about going to parties with Marcy.

We all stayed up till my sister came home, though we all pretended to sleep. My window was over the front door and I watched her on the front step, struggling to unlock the door, holding something bulky pressed against her belly. At last she disappeared inside. Something hit the floor with a thud. I heard my sister running. There was so much commotion we all felt justified rushing downstairs. Mother helped my father down, they came along rather quickly.

We found my sister in the kitchen. It was quiet and very dark. The refrigerator was open, not for food but for light. Bathed in its glow, my sister was rhythmically stroking a large iguana that stood poised, alert, its head slightly raised, on the butcher block by the stove.

In the equalizing darkness my father saw almost as well as we did. "Jesus Christ," he said.

My sister said, "He was a little freaked. You can try turning the light on."

Only then did we notice that the lizard's foot was bandaged. My sister said, "This drunken jerk bit off one of his toes. He got all the guys at the party to bet that he wouldn't do it. I just waded in and took the poor thing and the guy just gave it up. The asshole couldn't have cared very much if he was going to bite its toes off."

"Watch your language," Mother said. "What a cruel thing to do! Is this the kind of teenager you're going to parties with?"

"Animals," my father said. After that there was a silence, during which all of us thought that once my father would have unwrapped the bandage and taken a look at that foot.

"His name's Reynaldo," my sister said.

"Sounds Puerto Rican," said Mother.

Once there would have been a fight about her keeping the iguana, but like some brilliant general, my sister had retreated and recouped and emerged from her bedroom, victorious and in control. At that moment I hated her for always getting her way, for always outlasting everyone and being so weird and dramatic and never letting you know for sure what was real and what she was faking.

Reynaldo had the run of my sister's room, no one dared open the door. After school she'd lie belly down on her bed, cheek to cheek with Reynaldo. And in a way it was lucky that my father couldn't see that.

One night the phone rang. Mother covered the receiver and said, "Thank you, Lord. It's a boy."

It was a boy who had been at the party and seen my sister rescue Reynaldo. His name was Greg; he was a college student, studying for a business degree.

After he and my sister went out a few times, Mother invited Greg to dinner. I ate roast beef and watched him charm everyone but me. He described my sister grabbing the iguana out of its torturer's hands. He said, "When I saw her do that, I thought, This is someone I want to know better." He and my parents talked about her like some distant mutual friend. I stared hard at my sister, wanting her to miss Jimmy, too, but she was playing with her food, I couldn't tell what she was thinking.

Greg had a widowed mother and two younger sisters; he'd gotten out of the draft by being their sole support. He said he wouldn't go anyway, he'd go to Canada first. No one mentioned Reynaldo, though we could hear him scrabbling jealously around my sister's room.

Reynaldo wasn't invited on their dates and neither, obviously, was I. I knew Greg didn't drive onto the ice or break into furniture stores. He took my sister to Godard movies and told us how much she liked them.

One Saturday my sister and Greg took Reynaldo out for a drive. And when they returned—I waited up—the iguana wasn't with them.

"Where's Reynaldo?" I asked.

"A really nice pet shop," she said. And then for the first time I understood that Jimmy was really dead.

Not long after that my father died. His doctors had made a mistake. It was not a disease of the retina but a tumor of the brain. You'd think they would have known that, checked for that right away, but he was a scientist, they saw themselves in him and didn't want to know. Before he died he disappeared, one piece at a time. My sister and I slowly turned away so as not to see what was missing.

Greg was very helpful throughout this terrible time. Six months after my father died, Greg and my sister got married. By then he'd graduated and got a marketing job with a potato-chip company. Mother and I lived alone in the house—as we'd had, really, for some time. My father and sister had left so gradually that the door hardly swung shut behind them. Father's Buick sat in the garage, as it had since he'd lost his vision, and every time we saw it we thought about all that had happened.

My sister and Greg bought a house nearby; sometimes Mother and I went for dinner. Greg told us about his work and the interesting things he found out. In the Northeast they liked the burnt chips, the lumpy misshapen ones, but down South every chip had to be pale and thin and perfect.

"A racial thing, no doubt," I said, but no one seemed to hear, though one of Mother's favorite subjects was race relations down South. I'd thought my sister might laugh or get angry, but she was a different person. A slower, solid, heavier person who was eating a lot of chips.

One afternoon the doorbell rang, and it was Jimmy Kowalchuk. It took me a while to recognize him; he didn't have his beard. For a second—just a second—I was afraid to open the door. He was otherwise unchanged except that he'd got even thinner, and looked even less Polish and even more Puerto Rican.

He was wearing army fatigues. I was glad Mother wasn't home. He gave me a hug, my first ever from him, and lifted me off the ground. He said no, he was never dead, never even missing.

He said, "Some army computer glitch, some creep's clerical error." My father's death had made it easier to believe that people made such mistakes, and for one dizzying moment I allowed myself to imagine that maybe Jimmy's being alive meant my father was, too.

"You got older," Jimmy said. "This is like *The Twilight Zone*." And he must have thought so—that time had stopped in his absence. I invited him in, made him sit down, and then told him about my sister.

Jimmy got up and left the house. He didn't ask whom she'd married. He didn't ask where they lived, though I knew he was going to find her.

Once again I waited, counting down the hours. This time, although weeks passed, it was like counting one two three. Four—the phone rang. It was Greg. He had come home from the office and found my sister packed and gone.

A week later my sister called collect from St. Petersburg, Florida. She said Jimmy knew a guy, a buddy from Vietnam, he had found Jimmy a rental house and a job with a roofing company. They had hurricanes down there that would rip the top of your house off. She emphasized the hurricane part, as if that made it all make sense. In fact, she seemed so sure about the sensibleness of her situation that she made me promise to tell Mother and Greg she'd called and that she was fine.

Mother had less trouble believing that my sister had been kidnapped than that she'd left Greg and taken off with her dead boyfriend from Vietnam. It was a lot to process at once; she'd seen Jimmy buried. Greg had never heard of Jimmy, which made me wonder about my sister. I thought about Reynaldo, how forcefully she had seized him, how easily she'd let him go.

My sister had called from a pay phone. All she'd said was "St. Petersburg." Mother telephoned Mrs. Kowalchuk and got Jimmy's address from her. Afterwards Mother said, "The woman thinks it's a miracle. The army loses her son, she goes through hell, and she think it's the will of God."

Mother wrote my sister a letter. A month passed. There was no answer. By now Greg was in permanent shock, though he still went to work. One night he told us about a dipless chip now in the blueprint stage. Then even Mother knew we were alone, and her eyes filled with tears. She said, "Florida! It's warm there. When is your Easter vacation?"

We took my father's Buick, a decision that almost convinced us that some reason besides paralysis explained its still being in our garage. I sat up front beside Mother, scrunched low in the spongy seat. States went by. The highway was always the same. There was nothing to watch except Mother, staring furiously at the road. Though the temperature rose steadily, Mother wouldn't turn off the heat and by Florida I was riding with my head out the window, for air, and also working on a tan for Jimmy.

It was easy finding the address we got from Mrs. Kowalchuk. They were living in a shack, but newly painted white, and with stubby marigolds lining the cracked front walk.

"Tobacco Road," said Mother.

Then Mother and I saw Jimmy working out in the yard. His back was smooth and golden and muscles churned under his skin as he swayed from side to side, planing something—a door. Behind him a tree with shiny leaves sagged under its great weight of grapefruit, and sunlight dappled the round yellow fruit and the down on Jimmy's shoulders.

Jimmy stopped working and turned and smiled. He didn't seem surprised to see us. As he came toward us a large dog roused itself from the ground at his feet, a long-haired white dog so much like the one my sister spoke to in our yard that for a moment I felt faint and had to lean on Mother.

Mother shook me off. She hardly noticed the dog. She was advancing on Jimmy.

"I wasn't dead, it was a mistake." Jimmy sounded apologetic.

"Obviously," said Mother. Then she told me not to move and went into the house.

I couldn't have moved if I'd wanted. Every muscle had fused, every tiny flutter and tic felt grossly magnified and disgusting. I had never seen Jimmy without a shirt. I wanted to touch his back. He said, "I got my grapefruit tree."

"Obviously," I said in Mother's voice, and Jimmy grinned and we laughed. On the table lay a pile of tools. He wasn't stabbing them between his fingers. He must have gotten that out of his system, dying and coming back.

Even though it was Jimmy's house, we felt we couldn't go in. Every inch of space was taken up by what my mother and sister were saying. Where was Jimmy's Malibu? We walked to a cafeteria and stood in a line of elderly couples deciding between the baked fish and the chicken. Jimmy couldn't be served there, he wasn't wearing a shirt. The manager was sorry, it was a Florida law. Jimmy had gone to Vietnam and been lost in a computer and now couldn't even get a cup of cafeteria coffee. But I couldn't say that, my head was ringing with things I couldn't say—for example, that I had waited for him, and my sister hadn't.

Half a block from Jimmy's house, we saw an upsetting sight—my mother and sister in Mother's car with the engine running.

"Going for lunch?" Jimmy said. But we all knew they weren't.

Mother told me to get in back. Jimmy looked in and I saw him notice my sister's suitcase. He did nothing to stop us—that was the strangest part. He let me get in and let us take off and stood there and watched us go.

I never knew, I never found out what Mother said to my sister. Or maybe it wasn't what Mother said, perhaps it was all about Jimmy. Once again I thought of Reynaldo and my sister's giving him up. If I never knew what had happened with that, how could I ask about Jimmy? You assume you will ask the important questions, you will get to them sooner or later, an idea that ignores two things: the power of shyness, the fact of death.

That should have been the last time I saw Jimmy Kowalchuk—a wounded young god glowing with sun in a firmament of grapefruit. But there was one more time, nearer home, in the dead of winter.

Before that, Greg took my sister back. They went on as if nothing had happened. Greg got a promotion. They moved to a nicer house. I saw my sister sometimes. Jimmy was not a subject. I never asked about him, his name never came up. I would talk about school sometimes, but she never seemed to be listening. Once she said, out of nowhere, "I guess people want different things at different times in their lives."

I was a senior in high school when my sister was killed. Her car jumped a divider on the Sunrise Highway. It was a new car Greg kept well maintained, so it was nobody's fault.

On the way to the funeral Mother sat between me and Greg. When my sister went back to Greg, Mother had gone back to him, too. But that day, in the funeral car, she was talking to me.

"What was I doing?" Mother said. "I knew I couldn't make you girls happy.

I was just trying to give you the chance to be happy if you wanted. I thought that life was a corridor with doors that opened and shut as you passed, and I was just trying to keep them from slamming on you."

The reality of my sister's death hadn't come home to me yet, and though my father's dying had taught me that death was final, perhaps Jimmy's reappearance had put that in some doubt. Guiltily, I wondered if Jimmy would be at my sister's funeral, as if it were a party at which he might show up.

Jimmy came with his mother, a tiny woman in black. He was gritty, unshaven, tragically handsome in a wrinkled suit and dark glasses. He looked as if he'd hitchhiked or rode up on the Greyhound.

I went and stood beside Jimmy. No one expected that. After the service I left with him. Not even I could believe it. All the relatives watched me leave, Mother and Greg and my sister's friend Marcy. I wondered if this was how Jimmy felt, driving out onto the ice.

Jimmy was driving a cousin's rusted Chevy Nova. We dropped his mother at her house. Jimmy and I kept going. I could tell he'd been drinking. He must have given up on his rule about endangering other people. Finally I was alone with him, but it wasn't what I'd pictured. I wondered which friend I could call if I needed someone to pick me up.

I was starting college in the fall. I had some place I had to be. A new life was expecting me with its eye on the clock and no time and no patience for me to run away with Jimmy.

Jimmy drove to a crowded strip somewhere off Hempstead Turnpike. We stopped at the Shamrock, a dark, beery-smelling bar. Jimmy and I sat at a table. The bartender took our order. The regulars seemed too relaxed to pay any special attention to a Charlie Mansonesque Puerto Rican and a girl, below the drinking age, nervously sipping her beer.

Jimmy put away several boilermakers. He was getting drunker and drunker. He kept talking about my sister. He said some very unlikely things but nothing too strange to believe, especially when he repeated it, each time exactly the same.

He told me that the white dog had shown up the first day they moved to Florida. It ran up to my sister in the yard; they seemed to know each other. The dog, said my sister, had come to her after Jimmy died and personally guaranteed it that Jimmy was alive. Jimmy said, "I had to wonder how the goddamn dog found out our Florida address."

The light in the Shamrock was fading. Jimmy blamed the war. He said, "*I* died and got through it halfway all right. But it gets you no matter what. I came back but it was too late. Your sister was talking to dogs."

I pictured Mother setting out silver platters of roast beef for the relatives who would be coming back after the funeral. I saw light wink off her coffee urn and the plates of little iced cakes and for one shaming moment a bright bubble shone and popped in the dusty fermented air of the bar.

It hadn't scared Mother but it had scared Jimmy, my sister talking to dogs. I remembered how unresistingly Jimmy had let Mother take her, as easily as my sister had let Reynaldo go. I had a vision of people pulling at each other, and of the people who loved them letting them slip through their hands and almost liking the silky feel of them sliding through their fingers.

Jimmy said my sister blamed herself for my father's death. She'd told Jimmy that when she realized he was looking at slides of dead dogs, she wished for something to happen so he would have to stop it. No matter how much my father told us about his disease, my sister believed that somehow she had caused it, and she had this pet iguana that was the only one she could tell. She told Jimmy the iguana had died in her arms and she blamed herself for that, too.

Tears welled up in Jimmy's eyes. He said, "The woman had powers."

For a fraction of a second I thought I might still want him. But I didn't want him. I just didn't want her to have him forever. I was shocked to be so jealous when death meant it could never be fixed. I didn't want it to be that way, but that was how it was.

I wanted to tell Jimmy that my sister didn't have powers. I wanted to say that her only power was the power to make everyone look, she'd had nothing, nothing to do with my father going blind, and she had lied to one of us about what happened to that iguana. I wanted to say she'd lied to us all, she'd faked it about the dog, as if it mattered whether the animal spoke, as if love were about the truth, as if he would love her less—and not more—for pretending to talk to a dog.

Salman Rushdie

The Free Radio

(E N G L A N D)

We all knew nothing good would happen to him while the thief's widow had her claws dug into his flesh, but the boy was an innocent, a real donkey's child, you can't teach such people.

That boy could have had a good life. God had blessed him with God's own looks, and his father had gone to the grave for him, but didn't he leave the boy a brand-new first-class cycle rickshaw with plastic covered seats and all? So: looks he had, his own trade he had, there would have been a good wife in time, he should just have taken out some years to save some rupees; but no, he must fall for a thief's widow before the hairs had time to come out on his chin, before his milk-teeth had split, one might say.

We felt bad for him, but who listens to the wisdom of the old today?

I say: who listens?

Exactly; nobody, certainly not a stone-head like Ramani the rickshaw-wallah. But I blame the widow. I saw it happen, you know, I saw most of it until I couldn't stand any more. I sat under this very banyan, smoking this self-same hookah, and not much escaped my notice.

And at one time I tried to save him from his fate, but it was no go . . .

The widow was certainly attractive, no point denying, in a sort of hard vicious way she was all right, but it is her mentality that was rotten. Ten years older than Ramani she must have been, five children alive and two dead, what that thief did besides robbing and making babies God only knows, but he left her not one new paisa, so of course she would be interested in Ramani. I'm not saying a rickshaw-wallah makes much in this town but two mouthfuls are better to eat than wind. And not many people will look twice at the widow of a good-for-nothing.

They met right here.

One day Ramani rode into town without a passenger, but grinning as usual as if someone had given him a ten-chip tip, singing some playback music from the radio, his hair greased like for a wedding. He was not such a fool that he didn't know how the girls watched him all the time and passed remarks about his long and well-muscled legs.

The thief's widow had gone to the bania shop to buy some three grains of dal and I won't say where the money came from, but people saw men at night near her rutputty shack, even the bania himself they were telling me but I personally will not comment.

She had all her five brats with her and then and there, cool as a fan, she called out: *"Hey! Rickshaaa!"* Loud, you know, like a truly cheap type. Showing us she can afford to ride in rickshaws, as if anyone was interested. Her children must have gone hungry to pay for the ride but in my opinion it was an investment for her, because must-be she had decided already to put her hooks into Ramani. So they all poured into the rickshaw and he took her away, and with the five kiddies as well as the widow there was quite a weight, so he was puffing hard, and the veins were standing out on his legs, and I thought, careful, my son, or you will have this burden to pull for all of your life.

But after that Ramani and the thief's widow were seen everywhere, shamelessly, in public places, and I was glad his mother was dead because if she had lived to see this her face would have fallen off from shame.

Sometimes in those days Ramani came into this street in the evenings to meet some friends, and they thought they were very smart because they would go into the back room of the Irani's canteen and drink illegal liquor, only of course everybody knew, but who would do anything, if boys ruin their lives let their relations worry.

I was sad to see Ramani fall into this bad company. His parents were known to me when alive. But when I told Ramani to keep away from those hot-shots he grinned like a sheep and said I was wrong, nothing bad was taking place.

Let it go, I thought.

I knew those cronies of his. They all wore the armbands of the new Youth Movement. This was the time of the State of Emergency, and these friends were not peaceful persons, there were stories of beatings-up, so I sat quiet under my tree. Ramani wore no armband but he went with them because they impressed him, the fool.

These armband youths were always flattering Ramani. Such a handsome chap, they told him, compared to you Shashi Kapoor and Amitabh are like lepers only, you should go to Bombay and be put in the motion pictures.

They flattered him with dreams because they knew they could take money from him at cards and he would buy them drink while they did it, though he was no richer than they. So now Ramani's head became filled with these movie dreams, because there was nothing else inside to take up any space, and this is another reason why I blame the widow woman, because she had more years and should have had more sense. In two ticks she could have made him forget all about it, but no, I heard her telling him one day for all to hear, "Truly you have the looks of Lord Krishna himself, except you are not blue all over." In the street! So all would know they were lovers! From that day on I was sure a disaster would happen.

The next time the thief's widow came into the street to visit the bania shop I decided to act. Not for my own sake but for the boy's dead parents. I risked being shamed by a . . . no, I will not call her the name, she is elsewhere now and they will know what she is like.

"Thief's widow!" I called out.

She stopped dead, jerking her face in an ugly way, as if I had hit her with a whip.

"Come here and speak," I told her.

Now she could not refuse because I am not without importance in the town and maybe she calculated that if people saw us talking they would stop ignoring her when she passed, so she came as I knew she would.

"I have to say this thing only," I told her with dignity. "Ramani the rickshaw boy is dear to me, and you must find some person of your own age, or, better still, go to the widows' ashrams in Benares and spend the rest of your life there in holy prayer, thanking God that widow-burning is now illegal."

So at this point she tried to shame me by screaming out and calling me curses and saying that I was a poisonous old man who should have died years ago, and then she said, "Let me tell you, mister teacher sahib *retired,* that your Ramani has asked to marry me and I have said no, because I wish no more children, and he is a young man and should have his own. So tell that to the whole world and stop your cobra poison."

For a time after that I closed my eyes to this affair of Ramani and the thief's widow, because I had done all I could and there were many other things in the town to interest a person like myself. For instance, the local health officer had brought a big white caravan into the street and was given permission to park it out of the way under the banyan tree; and every night men were taken into his van for a while and things were done to them.

I did not care to be in the vicinity at these times, because the youths with armbands were always in attendance, so I took my hookah and sat in another place. I heard rumours of what was happening in the caravan but I closed my ears.

But it was while this caravan, which smelled of ether, was in town that the extent of the widow's wickedness became plain; because at this time Ramani suddenly began to talk about his new fantasy, telling everyone he could find that very shortly he was to receive a highly special and personalised gift from the Central Government in Delhi itself, and this gift was to be a brand-new first-class battery-operated transistor radio.

Now then: we had always believed that our Ramani was a little soft in the head, with his notions of being a film star and what all; so most of us just nodded tolerantly and said, "Yes, Ram, that is nice for you," and, "What a fine, generous Government it is that gives radios to persons who are so keen on popular music."

But Ramani insisted it was true, and seemed happier than at any time in his life, a happiness which could not be explained simply by the supposed imminence of the transistor.

Soon after the dream-radio was first mentioned, Ramani and the thief's widow were married, and then I understood everything. I did not attend the nuptials—it was a poor affair by all accounts—but not long afterwards I spoke to Ram when he came past the banyan with an empty rickshaw one day.

He came to sit by me and I asked, "My child, did you go to the caravan? What have you let them do to you?"

"Don't worry," he replied. "Everything is tremendously wonderful. I am in love, teacher sahib, and I have made it possible for me to marry my woman."

I confess I became angry; indeed, I almost wept as I realised that Ramani had gone voluntarily to subject himself to a humiliation which was being forced upon the other men who were taken to the caravan. I reproved him bitterly. "My idiot child, you have not let that woman deprive you of your manhood."

"It is not so bad," Ram said, meaning the *nasbandi*. "It does not stop love-making or anything, excuse me, teacher sahib, for speaking of such a thing. It stops babies only and my woman did not want children any more, so now all is hundred per cent OK. Also it is in national interest," he pointed out. "And soon the free radio will arrive."

"The free radio," I repeated.

"Yes, remember, teacher sahib," Ram said confidentially, "some years back, in my kiddie days, when Laxman the tailor had this operation? In no time the radio came and from all over town people gathered to listen to it. It is how the Government says thank you. It will be excellent to have."

"Go away, get away from me," I cried out in despair, and did not have the heart to tell him what everyone else in the country already knew, which was that the free radio scheme was a dead duck, long gone, long forgotten. It had been over—*funtoosh!*—for years.

After these events the thief's widow, who was now Ram's wife, did not come into town very often, no doubt being too ashamed of what she had made him do, but Ramani worked longer hours than ever before, and every time he saw any of the dozens of people he'd told about the radio he would put one hand up to his ear as if he were already holding the blasted machine in it, and he would mimic broadcasts with a certain energetic skill.

"*Yé Akashvani hai,*" he announced to the streets. "This is All-India Radio. Here is the news. A Government spokesman today announced that Ramani rickshaw-wallah's radio was on its way and would be delivered at any moment. And now some playback music." After which he would sing songs by Asha Bhonsle or Lata Mangeshkar in a high, ridiculous falsetto.

Ram always had the rare quality of total belief in his dreams, and there were times when his faith in the imaginary radio almost took us in, so that we half-believed it was really on its way, or even that it was already there, cupped invisibly against his ear as he rode his rickshaw around the streets of the town. We began to expect to hear Ramani, around a corner or at the far end of a lane, ringing his bell and yelling cheerfully:

"All-India Radio! This is All-India Radio!"

Time passed. Ram continued to carry the invisible radio around town. One year passed. Still his caricatures of the radio channel filled the air in the streets. But when I saw him now, there was a new thing in his face, a strained thing, as if he were having to make a phenomenal effort, which was much more tiring than driving a rickshaw, more tiring even than pulling a rickshaw containing a thief's widow and her five living children and the ghosts of two dead ones; as if all the energy of his young body was being poured into that fictional space between his ear and his hand, and he was trying to bring the radio into existence by a mighty, and possibly fatal, act of will.

I felt most helpless, I can tell you, because I had divined that Ram had poured into the idea of the radio all his worries and regrets about what he had done, that if the dream were to die he would be forced to face the full gravity of his crime against his own body, to understand that the thief's widow had turned him, before she married him, into a thief of a stupid and terrible kind, because she had made him rob himself.

And then the white caravan came back to its place under the banyan tree and I knew there was nothing to be done, because Ram would certainly come to get his gift.

He did not come for one day, then for two, and I learned afterwards that he had not wished to seem greedy; he didn't want the health officer to think he was desperate for the radio. Besides, he was half hoping they would come over and give it to him at his place, perhaps with some kind of small, formal presentation ceremony. A fool is a fool and there is no accounting for his notions.

On the third day he came. Ringing his bicycle-bell and imitating weather forecasts, ear cupped as usual, he arrived at the caravan. And in the rickshaw behind him sat the thief's widow, the witch, who had not been able to resist coming along to watch her companion's destruction.

It did not take very long.

Ram went into the caravan gaily, waving at his armbanded cronies who were guarding it against the anger of the people, and I am told—for I had left the scene to spare myself the pain—that his hair was well-oiled and his clothes were freshly starched. The thief's widow did not move from the rickshaw, but sat there with a black sari pulled over her head, clutching at her children as if they were straws.

After a short time there were sounds of disagreement inside the caravan, and then louder noises still, and finally the youths in armbands went in to see what was becoming, and soon after that Ram was frogmarched out by his drinking-chums, and his hair-grease was smudged on to his face and there was blood coming from his mouth. His hand was no longer cupped by his ear.

And still—they tell me—the thief's black widow did not move from her place in the rickshaw, although they dumped her husband in the dust.

Yes, I know, I'm an old man, my ideas are wrinkled with age, and these days they tell me sterilisation and God knows what is necessary, and maybe I'm wrong to blame the widow as well—why not? Maybe all the views of the old can be discounted now, and if that's so, let it be. But I'm telling this story and I haven't finished yet.

Some days after the incident at the caravan I saw Ramani selling his rickshaw to the old Muslim crook who runs the bicycle-repair shop. When he saw me watching, Ram came to me and said, "Goodbye, teacher sahib, I am off to Bombay, where I will become a bigger film star than Shashi Kapoor or Amitabh Bachchan even."

" 'I am off,' you say?" I asked him. "Are you perhaps travelling alone?"

He stiffened. The thief's widow had already taught him not to be humble in the presence of elders.

"My wife and children will come also," he said. It was the last time we spoke. They left that same day on the down train.

After some months had passed I got his first letter, which was not written by himself, of course, since in spite of all my long-ago efforts he barely knew how to write. He had paid a professional letter-writer, which must have cost him many rupees, because everything in life costs money and in Bombay it costs twice as much. Don't ask me why he wrote to me, but he did. I have the letters and can give you proof positive, so maybe there are some uses for old people still, or maybe he knew I was the only one who would be interested in his news.

Anyhow: the letters were full of his new career, they told me how he'd been discovered at once, a big studio had given him a test, now they were grooming him for stardom, he spent his days at the Sun'n'Sand Hotel at Juhu beach in the company of top lady artistes, he was buying a big house at Pali Hill, built in the split-level mode and incorporating the latest security equipment to protect him from the movie fans, the thief's widow was well and happy and getting fat, and life was filled with light and success and no-questions-asked alcohol.

They were wonderful letters, brimming with confidence, but whenever I read them, and sometimes I read them still, I remember the expression which came over his face in the days just before he learned the truth about his radio, and the huge mad energy which he had poured into the act of conjuring reality, by an act of magnificent faith, out of the hot thin air between his cupped hand and his ear.

Ken Saro-Wiwa

Africa Kills Her Sun

(NIGERIA)

Dear Zole,

You'll be surprised, no doubt, to receive this letter. But I couldn't leave your beautiful world without saying goodbye to you who are condemned to live in it. I know that some might consider my gesture somewhat pathetic, as my colleagues, Sazan and Jimba, do, our finest moments having been achieved two or three weeks ago. However, for me, this letter is a celebration, a final act of love, a quality which, in spite of my career, in spite of tomorrow morning, I do possess in abundance, and cherish. For I've always treasured the many moments of pleasure we spent together in our youth when the world was new and fishes flew in golden ponds. In the love we then shared have I found happiness, a true resting place, a shelter from the many storms that have buffeted my brief life. Whenever I've been most alone, whenever I've been torn by conflict and pain, I've turned to that love for the resolution which has sustained and seen me through. This may surprise you, considering that this love was never consummated and that you may possibly have forgotten me, not having seen me these ten years gone. I still remember you, have always remembered you, and it's logical that on the night before tomorrow, I should write you to ask a small favor of you. But more important, the knowledge that I have unburdened myself to you will make tomorrow morning's event as pleasant and desirable to me as to the thousands of spectators who will witness it.

   I know this will get to you because the prison guard's been heavily bribed to deliver it. He should rightly be with us before the firing squad tomorrow. But he's condemned, like most others, to live, to play out his assigned role in your hell of a world. I see him burning out his dull, uncomprehending life, doing his menial job for a pittance and a bribe for the next so many years. I pity his ignorance and cannot envy his complacency. Tomorrow morning, with this letter and our bribe in his pocket, he'll call us out, Sazan, Jimba and I. As usual, he'll have all our names mixed up: he always calls Sazan "Sajim" and Jimba "Samba." But that won't matter. We'll obey him, and as we walk to our death, we'll laugh at his gaucherie, his plain stupidity. As we laughed at that other thief, the High Court Judge.

You must've seen that in the papers too. We saw it, thanks to our bribe-taking friend, the prison guard, who sent us a copy of the newspaper in which it was reported. Were it not in an unfeeling nation, among a people inured to evil and taking sadistic pleasure in the loss of life, some questions might have been asked. No doubt, many will ask the questions, but they will do it in the safety and comfort of their homes, over the interminable bottles of beer, un-comprehendingly watching their boring, cheap television programs, the re-jects of Europe and America, imported to fill their vacuity. They will salve their conscience with more bottles of beer, wash the answers down their gul-lets and pass question, conscience and answer out as waste into their open sewers choking with concentrated filth and murk. And they will forget.

I bet, though, the High Court Judge himself will never forget. He must re-member it the rest of his life. Because I watched him closely that first morn-ing. And I can't describe the shock and disbelief which I saw registered on his face. His spectacles fell to his table and it was with difficulty he regained com-posure. It must have been the first time in all his experience that he found persons arraigned on a charge for which the punishment upon conviction is death, entering a plea of guilty and demanding that they be sentenced and shot without further delay.

Sazan, Jimba and I had rehearsed it carefully. During the months we'd been remanded in prison custody while the prosecutors prepared their case, we'd agreed we weren't going to allow a long trial, or any possibility that they might impose differing sentences upon us: freeing one, sentencing another to life imprisonment and the third to death by firing squad.

Nor did we want to give the lawyers in their funny black funeral robes an opportunity to clown around, making arguments for pleasure, engaging in worthless casuistry. No. We voted for death. After all, we were armed robbers, bandits. We knew it. We didn't want to give the law a chance to prove itself the proverbial ass. We were being honest to ourselves, to our vocation, to our country and to mankind.

"Sentence us to death immediately and send us before the firing squad without further delay," we yelled in unison. The Judge, after he had recovered from his initial shock, asked us to be taken away that day, "for disturbing my court." I suppose he wanted to see if we'd sleep things over and change our plea. We didn't. When they brought us back the next day, we said the same thing in louder voice. We said we had robbed and killed. We were guilty. Cool. The Judge was bound hand and foot and did what he had to. We'd forced him to be honest to his vocation, to the laws of the country and to the course of jus-tice. It was no mean achievement. The court hall was stunned; our guards were utterly amazed as we walked out of court, smiling. "Hardened crimi-nals." "Bandits," I heard them say as we trooped out of the court. One specta-tor actually spat at us as we walked into the waiting Black Maria!

And now that I've confessed to banditry, you'll ask why I did it. I'll answer that question by retelling the story of the young, beautiful prostitute I met in

St. Pauli in Hamburg when our ship berthed there years back. I've told my friends the story several times. I did ask her, after the event, why she was in that place. She replied that some girls chose to be secretaries in offices, others to be nurses. She had chosen prostitution as a career. Cool. I was struck by her candor. And she set me thinking. Was I in the Merchant Navy by choice or because it was the first job that presented itself to me when I left school? When we returned home, I skipped ship, thanks to the prostitute of St. Pauli, and took a situation as a clerk in the Ministry of Defense.

It was there I came face-to-face with the open looting of the national treasury, the manner of which I cannot describe without arousing in myself the deepest, basest emotions. Everyone was busy at it and there was no one to complain to. Everyone to whom I complained said to me: "If you can't beat them, join them." I was not about to join anyone; I wanted to beat them and took it upon myself to wage a war against them. In no time they had gotten rid of me. Dismissed me. I had no option but to join them then. I had to make a choice. I became an armed robber, a bandit. It was my choice, my answer. And I don't regret it.

Did I know it was dangerous? Some girls are secretaries, others choose to be prostitutes. Some men choose to be soldiers and policemen, others doctors and lawyers; I chose to be a robber. Every occupation has its hazards. A taxi driver may meet his death on the road; a businessman may die in an air crash; a robber dies before a firing squad. It's no big deal. If you ask me, the death I've chosen is possibly more dramatic, more qualitative, more eloquent than dying in bed of a ruptured liver from overindulgence in alcohol. Yes? But robbery is antisocial, you say? A proven determination to break the law. I don't want to provide an alibi. But just you think of the many men and women who are busy breaking or bending the law in all coasts and climes. Look for a copy of *The Guardian* of 19th September. That is the edition in which our plea to the Judge was reported. You'll find there the story of the Government official who stole over seven million naira. Seven million. Cool. He was antisocial, right? How many of this type do you know? And how many more go undetected? I say, if my avocation was antisocial, I'm in good company. And that company consists of Presidents of countries, transnational organizations, public servants high and low, men and women. The only difference is that while I'm prepared to pay the price for it all, the others are not. See?

I'm not asking for your understanding or sympathy. I need neither, not now nor hereafter. I'm saying it as it is. Right? Cool. I expect you'll say that armed robbery should be the special preserve of the scum of society. That no man of my education has any business being a bandit. To that I'll answer that it's about time well-endowed and well-trained people took to it. They'll bring to the profession a romantic quality, a proficiency which will ultimately conduce to the benefit of society. No, I'm not mad. Truly. Time was when the running and ruining of African nations was in the hands of half-literate politicians. Today, well-endowed and better-trained people have taken over the task. And look how well they're doing it. So that even upon that score, my conscience sleeps easy. Understand?

Talking about sleep, you should see Sazan and Jimba on the cold, hard prison floor, snoring away as if life itself depends on a good snore. It's impossible, seeing them this way, to believe that they'll be facing the firing squad tomorrow. They're men of courage. Worthy lieutenants. It's a pity their abilities will be lost to society forever, come tomorrow morning. Sazan would have made a good Army General any day, possibly a President of our country in the mold of Idi Amin or Bokassa. The Europeans and Americans would have found in him a useful ally in the progressive degradation of Africa. Jimba'd have made an excellent Inspector-General of Police, so versed is he in the ways of the Police! You know, of course, that Sazan is a dismissed Sergeant of our nation's proud army. And Jimba was once a Corporal in the Police Force. When we met, we had similar reasons for pooling our talents. And a great team we did make. Now here we all are in the death cell of a maximum security prison and they snoring away the last hours of their lives on the cold, smelly floor. It's exhilarating to find them so disdainful of life. Their style is the stuff of which history is made. In another time and in another country, they'd be Sir Francis Drake, Cortés or Sir Walter Raleigh. They'd have made empires and earned national honors. But here, our life is one big disaster, an endless tragedy. Heroism is not in our star. We are millipedes crawling on the floor of a dank, wet forest. So Sazan and Jimba will die unsung. See?

One thing, though. We swore never to kill. And we never did. Indeed, we didn't take part in the particular "operation" for which we were held, Sazan, Jimba and I. That operation would've gone quite well if the Superintendent of Police had fulfilled his part of the bargain. Because he was in it with us. The Police are involved in every single robbery that happens. They know the entire gang, the gangs. We'd not succeed if we didn't collaborate with them. Sazan, Jimba and I were the bosses. We didn't go out on "operations." The boys normally did. And they were out on that occasion. The Superintendent of Police was supposed to keep away the police escorts from the vehicle carrying workers' salaries that day. For some reason, he failed to do so. And the policeman shot at our boys. The boys responded and shot and killed him and the Security Company guards. The boys got the money all right. But the killing was contrary to our agreement with the Police. We had to pay. The Police won't stand for any of their men being killed. They took all the money from us and then they went after the boys. We said no. The boys had acted on orders. We volunteered to take their place. The Police took us in and made a lot of public noises about it. The boys, I know, will make their decisions later. I don't know what will happen to the Superintendent of Police. But he'll have to look to himself. So, if that is any comfort to you, you may rest in the knowledge that I spilt no blood. No, I wouldn't. Nor have I kept the loot. Somehow, whatever we took from people—the rich ones—always was shared by the gang, who were almost always on the bread line. Sazan, Jimba and I are not wealthy.

Many will therefore accuse us of recklessness, or of being careless with our lives. And well they might. I think I speak for my sleeping comrades when I say we went into our career because we didn't see any basic difference between what we were doing and what most others are doing throughout the land today. In every facet of our lives—in politics, in commerce and in the professions—robbery is the base line. And it's been so from time. In the early days, our forebears sold their kinsmen into slavery for minor items such as beads, mirrors, alcohol and tobacco. These days, the tune is the same, only the articles have changed into cars, transistor radios and bank accounts. Nothing else has changed, and nothing will change in the foreseeable future. But that's the problem of those of you who will live beyond tomorrow, Zole.

The cock crows now and I know dawn is about to break. I'm not speaking figuratively. In the cell here, the darkness is still all-pervasive, except for the flickering light of the candle by which I write. Sazan and Jimba remain fast asleep. So is the prison guard. He sleeps all night and is no trouble to us. We could, if we wanted, escape from here, so lax are the guards. But we consider that unnecessary, as what is going to happen later this morning is welcome relief from burdens too heavy to bear. It's the guard and you the living who are in prison, the ultimate prison from which you cannot escape because you do not know that you are incarcerated. Your happiness is the happiness of ignorance and your ignorance is it that keeps you in the prison, which is your life. As this night dissolves into day, Sazan, Jimba and I shall be free. Sazan and Jimba will have left nothing behind. I shall leave at least this letter, which, please, keep for posterity.

Zole, do I rant? Do I pour out myself to you in bitter tones? Do not lay it to the fact that I'm about to be shot by firing squad. On second thoughts, you could, you know. After all, seeing death so clearly before me might possibly have made me more perspicacious? And yet I've always seen these things clearly in my mind's eye. I never did speak about them, never discussed them. I preferred to let them weigh me down. See?

So, then, in a few hours we shall be called out. We shall clamber with others into the miserable lorry which they still call the Black Maria. Notice how everything miserable is associated with us. Black Sheep. Black Maria. Black Death. Black Leg. The Black Hole of Calcutta. The Black Maria will take us to the Beach or to the Stadium. I bet it will be the Stadium. I'd prefer the Beach. So at least to see the ocean once more. For I've still this fond regard for the sea which dates from my time in the Merchant Navy. I love its wide expanse, its anonymity, its strength, its unfathomable depth. And maybe after shooting us, they might decide to throw our bodies into the ocean. We'd then be eaten up by sharks which would in turn be caught by Japanese and Russian fishermen, be refrigerated, packaged in cartons and sold to Indian merchants and then for a handsome profit to our people. That way, I'd have helped keep people alive a bit longer. But they won't do us that favor. I'm sure they'll take us to the Stadium. To provide a true spectacle for the fun-loving unemployed. To keep them out of trouble. To keep them from thinking. To keep them laughing. And dancing.

We'll be there in the dirty clothes which we now wear. We've not had any of our things washed this past month. They will tie us to the stakes, as though that were necessary. For even if we were minded to escape, where'd we run to? I expect they'll also want to blindfold us. Sazan and Jimba have said they'll not allow themselves to be blindfolded. I agree with them. I should want to see my executors, stare the nozzles of their guns bravely in the face, see the open sky, the sun, daylight. See and hear my countrymen as they cheer us to our death. To liberation and freedom.

The Stadium will fill to capacity. And many will not find a place. They will climb trees and hang about the balconies of surrounding houses to get a clear view of us. To enjoy the free show. Cool.

And then the priest will come to us, either to pray or to ask if we have any last wishes. Sazan says he will ask for a cigarette. I'm sure they'll give it to him. I can see him puffing hard at it before the bullets cut him down. He says he's going to enjoy that cigarette more than anything he's had in life. Jimba says he'll maintain a sullen silence as a mark of his contempt. I'm going to yell at the priest. I will say, "Go to hell, you hypocrite, fornicator and adulterer." I will yell at the top of my voice in the hope that the spectators will hear me. How I wish there'd be a microphone that will reverberate through the Stadium, nay, through the country as a whole! Then the laugh would be on the priest and those who sent him!

The priest will pray for our souls. But it's not us he should be praying for. He should pray for the living, for those whose lives are a daily torment. Between his prayer and when the shots ring out, there will be dead silence. The silence of the graveyard. The transition between life and death. And it shall be seen that the distinction between them both is narrow as the neck of a calabash. The divide between us breathing like everyone else in the Stadium and us as meat for worms is, oh, so slim, it makes life a walking death! But I should be glad to be rid of the world, of a meaningless existence that grows more dreary by the day. I should miss Sazan and Jimba, though. It'll be a shame to see these elegant gentlemen cut down and destroyed. And I'll miss you, too, my dear girl. But that will be of no consequence to the spectators.

They will troop out of the Stadium, clamber down the trees and the balconies of the houses, as though they'd just returned from another football match. They will march to their ratholes on empty stomachs, with tales enough to fill a Saturday evening. Miserable wretches!

The men who shall have eased us out of life will then untie our bodies and dump them into a lorry and thence to some open general grave. That must be a most distasteful task. I'd not do it for a million dollars. Yet some miserable fellows will do it for a miserable salary at the end of the month. A salary which will not feed them and their families till the next payday. A salary which they will have to augment with a bribe, if they are to keep body and soul together. I say, I do feel sorry for them. See?

The newspapers will faithfully record the fact of our shooting. If they have space, they'll probably carry a photograph of us to garnish your breakfasts.

I remember once long ago reading in a newspaper of a man whose one request to the priest was that he be buried along with his walking stick—his faithful companion over the years. He was pictured slumping in death, devotedly clutching his beloved walking stick. True friendship, that. Well, Zole, if ever you see such a photograph of me, make a cutting. Give it to a sculptor and ask him to make a stone sculpture of me as I appear in the photograph. He must make as faithful a representation of me as possible. I must be hard of feature and relentless in aspect. I have a small sum of money in the bank and have already instructed the bank to pay it to you for the purpose of the sculpture I have spoken about . . .

Time is running out, Zole. Sazan and Jimba are awake now. And they're surprised I haven't slept all night. Sazan says I ought at least to have done myself the favor of sound sleep on my last night on earth. I ask him if I'm not going to sleep soundly, eternally, in a few hours? This, I argue, should be our most wakeful night. Sazan doesn't appreciate that. Nor does Jimba. They stand up, yawn, stretch and rub their eyes. Then they sit down, crowding round me. They ask me to read out to them what I've written. I can't do that, I tell them. It's a love letter. And they burst out laughing. A love letter! And at the point of death! Sazan says I'm gone crazy. Jimba says he's sure I'm afraid of death and looks hard and long at me to justify his suspicion. I say I'm neither crazy nor afraid of death. I'm just telling my childhood girlfriend how I feel this special night. And sending her on an important errand. Jimba says I never told them I had a girlfriend. I reply that she was not important before this moment.

I haven't even seen her in ten years, I repeat. The really compelling need to write her is that on this very special night I have felt a need to be close to a living being, someone who can relate to others why we did what we did in and out of court.

Sazan says he agrees completely with me. He says he too would like to write his thoughts down. Do I have some paper to lend him? I say no. Besides, time is up. Day has dawned and I haven't even finished my letter. Do they mind leaving me to myself for a few minutes? I'd very much like to end the letter, envelope it and pass it on to the prison guard before he rouses himself fully from sleep and remembers to assume his official harsh role.

They're nice chaps, are Jimba and Sazan. Sazan says to tell my girl not to bear any children because it's pointless bringing new life into the harsh life of her world. Jimba says to ask my girl to shed him a tear if she can so honor a complete stranger. They both chuckle and withdraw to a corner of the cell and I'm left alone to end my letter.

Now, I was telling you about my statue. My corpse will not be available to you. You will make a grave for me, nonetheless. And place the statue on the gravestone. And now I come to what I consider the most important part of this letter. My epitaph.

I have thought a lot about it, you know. Really. What do you say about a robber shot in a stadium before a cheering crowd? That he was a good man who strayed? That he deserved his end? That he was a scallywag? A ragamuffin? A murderer whose punishment was not heavy enough? "Here lies X, who was shot in public by firing squad for robbing a van and shooting the guards in broad daylight. He serves as an example to all thieves and would-be thieves!"

Who'd care for such an epitaph? They'd probably think it was a joke. No.

That wouldn't carry. I'll settle for something different. Something plain and commonsensical. Or something truly cryptic and worthy of a man shot by choice in public by firing squad.

Not that I care. To die the way I'm going to die in the next hour or two is really nothing to worry about. I'm in excellent company. I should find myself recorded in the annals of our history. A history of violence, of murder, of disregard for life. Pleasure in inflicting pain—sadism. Is that the word for it? It's a world I should be pleased to leave. But not without an epitaph.

I recall, many years ago as a young child, reading in a newspaper of an African leader who stood on the grave of a dead lieutenant and through his tears said, "Africa kills her sons." I don't know what he meant by that, and though I've thought about it long enough, I've not been able to unravel the full mystery of those words. Now, today, this moment, they come flooding back to me. And I want to borrow from him. I'd like you to put this on my gravestone, as my epitaph: "Africa Kills Her Sun." A good epitaph, eh? Cryptic. Definite. A stroke of genius, I should say, I'm sure you'll agree with me. "Africa Kills Her Sun!" That's why she's been described as the Dark Continent? Yes?

So, now, dear girl, I'm done. My heart is light as the daylight which seeps stealthily into our dark cell. I hear the prison guard jangle his keys, put them into the keyhole. Soon he'll turn it and call us out. Our time is up. My time here expires and I must send you all my love. Goodbye.

Yours forever,

Bana

Ingo Schulze

The Ring

(G E R M A N Y)

I had figured it was merely a matter of time, that is, of the right moment, before I got a yes out of her for an evening or a weekend, maybe even longer.
But she held up her hand to me like a photograph with just one significant detail, a narrow gold band—as if I weren't already on intimate terms with her
fingers, didn't love the gentle arch bedding each nail and all the little wrinkles
on her knuckles. Her ring with the pearl had suited her much better. Splaying
her fingers, she picked up three glasses at once, held them clustered as she
put them on her tray, and left.

I came here only for her sake. If the window tables she served were occupied, I would wait outside the door or at the bar. During the day the restaurant was full of tourists and their children scattering toys about, but in the
evening it was crowded with businessmen, who laid their cellular phones on
the table between the glasses and bottles. You ate well here: Kamchatka crabs
for four dollars, Weiner schnitzel, stroganoff or a seafood platter for eight,
beer and vodka for two. If she had a little break between orders, I would
watch as she stood temple to temple with the head waitress, yet never taking
her eyes off the room as she talked. Straight-backed but at seemingly perfect
ease, she would stand at the buffet table, where the ashtrays and baskets of
silverware in napkins were kept. I needed only to raise a finger above the table
and she was at my side. She would immediately unclasp her hands held folded
before her and nudge the napkin up her forearm. Her skirt was tight, which
made her take short steps. Under the taut fabric, first one leg showed, then
the other. A strand of her smooth black hair swayed between chin and neck.
With her last step to my table she would toss her head back, but then her hair
would fall into place around her face.

How I hated guests who asked her for her name, laid an arm around her
waist and gave her a tip without it ever occurring to them that a man could be
lost without that smile. Her smile—revealing a minute gap between two front
teeth and promising that she was ready for anything, capable of anything, right
here, in front of the guests and the head waitress. I wanted to lean my head
against her, against that spot where she held her pad to the gentle swell of her
waistband. She thanked me for the order. I had to control myself when she

bent her knee slightly and picked up her tray! With every step, her foot trembled for the tiniest moment on its high heel and each time created that special line between shin and calf. I sucked in the air that she had walked through.

I have divulged my passion to no one. Not one of my coworkers would have suspected it had he ever chanced to spot me through the window, since the blinds were never closed at night. Anyone who wanted to could observe the black tables and chairs, the blue and red settees, the bar with its glistening taps and tropical plants, plus the festive lighting and the well-dressed people eating and drinking, talking and laughing.

If old women weren't leaning with their backs to the windows and blocking the view as they hawked their wares of dolls and scarves, records and egg warmers, you could gaze across Nevsky Prospekt to the City Duma, with artists hawking their works on the steps. At the bus stop in front of me, buses burst open, emptied out and sank back askew under the boarding throng. Next came beggars crouching on the stairs to the subway. And everywhere children—whose magic trick was to cover their hands with a kerchief and stick them in other people's pockets and who suddenly came to a halt for you to stumble over them. The staffs at the hotels shooed them from the entrances. You were safe here inside.

Anyone peeping in the window would never have guessed my yearning to awaken next to her, to stand beside her while she washed and brushed her teeth, to talk with her while she crooked up a leg and cut her toenails.

She set the beer down in front of me—not a hand-breadth separated her head from my brow—picked up my empty glass, laid the bill down in its place and was already looking for change, but she must have misheard the figure I mentioned and instead gave back the full amount, down to the last ruble note. I neither contradicted her nor looked up.

Then—yes, she had only been waiting for me to raise my head as if it were all just a misunderstanding—she smiled at me, her lips moving as if for a kiss, and vanished. I closed my eyes in happiness.

And yet only three, four minutes later, when I had taken up my post beside the entrance, I was tormented by the notion that I might have missed her. Despite my assumption that she would have to punch out for the day and change clothes, the temptation grew to ask the doormen in their gray suits. Not only did they have an eye and a nose for quality in shoes, excellence in coat fabrics and the latest model in glasses—"You are welcome"—but they also had good memories.

"A woman, a woman, he wants a woman!"

A few steps away, at the corner of Nevsky, several passersby were standing around a lanky guy flailing his arms. For a few moments, as the west wind ripped open the clouds, you were blinded by the bright, clear light that was an announcement of spring and filled the endless Prospekt with sea air.

"A woman, a woman!" the tall guy repeated.

Even if she had taken another exit, she would have to come past here on her way to the subway—and past that little group gathered at the entrance to the subway stairs near the corner of the building. The tall guy's excitement was echoed in the uneasy movements of coats, necks and handbags all around him.

She appeared in the doorway, alone and with a red wide-brimmed hat. The men in gray greeted her. Without looking around, she walked off in the direction of the Pushkin Monument. Her high heels must have been audible from the topmost stories. The tips of my shoes almost touched the hem of her cream-colored coat. I tried to breathe normally. She wore the hat at such an angle that it hid her hair entirely on the left side. At the hotel entrance she slowed down, her coat fell around her ankles. Then she stopped to search her handbag. For the first time I could smell her perfume. I waited. Her fingers moved as if typing on a midget keyboard. She pulled out a dollar, closed the handbag and—my God! "*Nyet, nyet,*" she scolded. Between her front teeth— not the tiniest gap.

When I looked up again, the only evidence of her presence was the bowing liveried hotel doorman and the green dollar bill in his hand.

I didn't run back. I didn't ask anyone, didn't bribe the men in gray. With no will of my own, I stared at the red carpet at the entrance until some instinct for the path of least resistance led me back to my previous post, which saved me from the catcalls of taxi drivers and children.

The crowd had grown larger around the tall guy, who looked to me to be not quite right in the head. Chin jutted forward, he was staring at something I couldn't make out, even when I stood on tiptoe behind the last row of backs. I asked why people had gathered here. Instead of giving an answer, a man whose elbow was digging into my chest tapped the woman ahead of him, who, with a quick exchange of glances, signaled the shoulder ahead of her. And so on. I assured them that I merely wanted to know why people were standing here. My accent betrayed me. And so they urged me to make use of the path that with some effort had now been cleared for me.

The crazy guy eyed me—the cause of this disturbance—from head to toe. I shrugged, he looked away. "Go on, do it, go on!" the woman ahead of me scolded in an almost toneless voice, and I made my way to the center of it all.

An old man in rags and with an open wound above his right eyebrow lay on the sidewalk, gazing up at those around him. A woman knelt at his side. She was just raising his head to shove a cap underneath. He wrenched his toothless mouth in a truly mad way. Threads of mucus between his lips broke, and his pale blue eyes danced to and fro. An old woman bowed to him several times and made the sign of the cross with broad gestures, as if wrapping herself in a long cloth. Others followed her example, including some young men. But no one helped, except the woman—a doctor, presumably—holding the old man's head. Holding one hand to his cheek, the doctor undid the knot of her head scarf and, wrapping it around two fingers, pulled it from her hair. She put an ear to his lips. What he said was inaudible. She kissed him on the brow.

"God bless you, girl!" Like most of these people, the man with disheveled hair next to me was here by himself. His gray scarf, neatly crossed at his chest, lent him a certain elegance despite his threadbare coat and unshaven chin.

"What a girl!" "A real Russian!" people whispered. A large, broad-shouldered policeman forced his way into the circle, demanded to know what was going on and cast the old man a quick glance. A hulk who towered above the rows of people, he kept both hands hooked at his wide belt, his billy club dangling from his left wrist.

The doctor calmly took off her cape and handed it and her scarf to the redheaded woman next to her. Paying no attention to the gawkers or the policeman, she opened the few buttons of her blouse and undid the ribbons gathering the sleeves at her wrists.

"A beauty!" The disheveled man bowed low and crossed himself along with many others. I was touched by a round vaccination mark on her upper arm. I would gladly have assisted her, yet she seemed neither to expect nor to need any help.

When the zipper got stuck, she literally ripped her skirt from her body, rolled down her panty hose and slipped out of her shoes at the same time.

"Hallelujah!" the policeman boomed, never taking his massive hands off his belt or his eyes off the doctor.

"Little dove, don't stop halfway! Don't you know anything about men?" I heard the tiny old lady across from me ask. Yet the woman she had addressed had eyes and ears only for the man whose cheek she was patting, wiping blood from his brow.

"Quiet!" a man admonished, and swiped a thumb across his fogged spectacles.

His face frozen in a grimace, the old man fixed his little eyes on every motion of her hands. She unhooked her bra and slipped the straps off. The old man let out a faint "Ahh" as she pulled her panties down and flung them with her right foot—to the disheveled man. He kissed them hungrily and tossed them to the redhead.

The doctor was now straddling the old man. Carefully she squatted down, placing her left knee on the pavement, followed by the right.

"God be with you, what a saint!"

"You're Russia's redemption!"

"A saint!" Many voices took up the cry.

"Your name, girl, tell us your name!"

A woman sobbed. The doctor grabbed the old man's hands, which had been lying lifelessly beside him, raised them to her shoulders, led them gently down over her body and pressed them to her breasts.

An elbow in my side turned me around. The woman I had bumped against offered me a bouquet of thin, honey-colored candles that she was having trouble holding together.

"Take one," she muttered. I had barely touched a candle when she demanded a hundred rubles, then bent confidentially closer. "Two for a hundred and fifty."

While I looked for money, the disheveled man wrapped a scrap of newspaper around the base of his lit candle. Wax dripped on his hand and up his sleeve. I was the only one standing erect amid a bowing crowd. But when the same fellow held his candle out for me to light mine, I no longer felt alone. A few women had begun to sing. Voice after voice joined in. The tall crazy guy timidly beat out the rhythm.

Before I realized it, I was weeping. Not since childhood had my tears flowed so freely. How long had it been since I had heard music like this.

"Your name, girl, your name!" Women held handkerchiefs to their mouths or dabbed their eyes. Prayers and hymns vied in competition. With goose bumps down to my thighs, I luxuriated in the crescendo, hummed along with the melody, sang what words I understood, and would have loved to cross myself and bow low. Yes, I wanted to kiss the ground, wanted to kneel down to keep this singing from ever stopping, and wanted this doctor never to leave our midst again—and resting now on the old man's legs, she opened his fly, nestled his skinny penis in her hand and concealed it in her mouth.

"The snake, the divine snake!"

"Everything, everything will change!"

And now the first voices bawled: "He is risen!"

"Yes, he is risen indeed!" others replied.

Cars along the Nevsky honked. Even the policeman accepted kisses, but then he tugged his uniform jacket taut under his belt and swallowed hard. Like a child, he smeared a tear on his cheek with the flat of his hand.

As the crowd cheered, the doctor released the old man's shaft, squatted quickly atop it and lowered herself—head thrown back, mouth a soundless scream.

At the same moment the old man's pale blue eyes went rigid, a shudder flitted across his face. Little bubbles formed at his lips, and burst. The singing broke off, the prayer dwindled to a murmur. People craned their necks, stood on tiptoe, edged closer together. The doctor looked stupefied. Gradually, however, her mouth relaxed. She began to smile and the spectators' faces grew radiant.

She kissed him. There was a sound like falling raindrops in the fervor with which her lips touched his brow, cheeks and mouth. She stretched farther forward. The tips of her breasts covered his eyes, the nipples brushing the lids three times. And with that she pulled her lower body from his member. It was all so still that this could have been the start of a swoon. Finally, however, she raised herself up from his head. The old man lay there in our midst, his penis festively erect, his eyes closed.

"Closed them with her breasts!" people whispered. "A saint, truly, with her breasts!"

Slowly she passed her hand between her legs, nodded, looked up, raised her arm, stretching it higher and higher and finally spreading her wet fingers in token of victory.

What a cry of jubilation pierced the air, what happiness, what thundering applause. And they all wanted to touch her, kiss her feet, press a cheek to her knees, stroke her black hair, moisten it with their tears. I couldn't tell if these were fierce embraces or pokes and shoves that pushed me forward now, causing me to stumble. But I did not fall, there was no room.

People stormed the redhead, tearing the doctor's clothes out of her hands in seconds. She managed to save only a scrap of panties for herself. As the first blows from the policeman's billy club landed, people incited him to really lay it on, others cursed him and provoked him with obscenities and grabbed his club away. Once he blew his whistle, however, several men rallied to him and with linked arms formed a phalanx of backs, shoulders and necks, pushing us back until only the policeman, the doctor and the body of the old man were left inside the circle.

The woman, who had not been left with so much as shoes for her feet, awkwardly covered her breasts and genitals. The tall crazy guy, however, who was still part of the cordon, stepped up to her like a lord chamberlain, bowed, kissed her hand and spread his coat out before her, the lining showing. From his pants pocket he pulled a sack, smoothed it out and proclaimed, "For our saint! For our good lady!" and cast a few rubles of his own into it, as if we were monkeys who needed to be shown how.

In a crush of backs, necks and shoulders, we waved at him with our money, as if placing bets. Those in the back rows balled their money up and threw it into the circle. "Here! Here's mine! Here!" they called to the crazy guy, a hundred voices shouting orders to him all at once. He did what he could, leaping here and there amid the applause, bending like a giraffe and raising his skinny arms in protest when instead of rubles people began to throw bundles of chives and butter, bags of farmer cheese and sausages, garlic, bananas and bread. They also took aim at the policeman and the doctor with eggs, kohlrabis, herring and their homemade maxims: "Honor she paid him, with her body she weighed him, in a warm grave she laid him." As best she could, she attempted to escape the hail of gifts, dodging and ducking the heaviest pieces, but finally crouched down, exhausted, as she was struck by cucumbers, tomatoes and cabbages. But even then they did not leave off. "Down her sweet young twat run juices from that old sot!" The crazy guy kept bounding about like a gouty old goat. But his limbs were obviously flagging. "Her cheeks are pale, her hole's a mess, the brat'll be born fatherless!'

The policeman, his face beet-red, rushed the crowd and blindly opened a breach in the dam that had been protecting him as well. The next moment he was grabbed by a dozen arms and lifted up. The crazy guy was soon caught and shouldered, too, but turned out to be so weakened already that he had to be propped up on all sides with canes and crutches. The sack of balled-up money was dumped out over the doctor, whereupon she willingly climbed on the shoulders of a kneeling Goliath. She now headed the procession that spread out over the pavement, inundating traffic. The light of several thousand candles bobbed back and forth, illuminating faces.

The doctor waved at us, blowing kisses in all directions, and suddenly burst into bright laughter. Only now did I spot a tiny gap between her front teeth and notice the ring on her hand, which she turned until a pearl appeared on top again. Then all I saw was the cloud cover moving in over the city, thick and grayish blue. Only to the northwest was there a sharp burst of yellowish green light, directly above the Admiralty, whose spire towered heavenward, showing us the way.

Translated from the German by John E. Woods

Graham Swift

Learning to Swim

(ENGLAND)

Mrs. Singleton had three times thought of leaving her husband. The first time was before they were married, on a charter plane coming back from a holiday in Greece. They were students who had just graduated. They had rucksacks and faded jeans. In Greece they had stayed part of the time by a beach on an island. The island was dry and rocky with great grey and vermilion coloured rocks and when you lay on the beach it seemed that you too became a hot, basking rock. Behind the beach there were eucalyptus trees like dry, leafy bones, old men with mules and gold teeth, a fragrance of thyme, and a café with melon pips on the floor and a jukebox which played bouzouki music and songs by Cliff Richard. All this Mr. Singleton failed to appreciate. He'd only liked the milk-warm, clear-blue sea, in which he'd stayed most of the time as if afraid of foreign soil. On the plane she'd thought: he hadn't enjoyed the holiday, hadn't liked Greece at all. All that sunshine. Then she'd thought she ought not to marry him.

Though she had, a year later.

The second time was about a year after Mr. Singleton, who was a civil engineer, had begun his first big job. He became a junior partner in a firm with a growing reputation. She ought to have been pleased by this. It brought money and comfort; it enabled them to move to a house with a large garden, to live well, to think about raising a family. They spent weekends in country hotels. But Mr. Singleton seemed untouched by this. He became withdrawn and incommunicative. He went to his work austere-faced. She thought: he likes his bridges and tunnels better than me.

The third time, which was really a phase; not a single moment, was when she began to calculate how often Mr. Singleton made love to her. When she started this it was about once every fortnight on average. Then it became every three weeks. The interval had been widening for some time. This was not a predicament Mrs. Singleton viewed selfishly. Love-making had been a problem before, in their earliest days together, which, thanks to her patience and initiative, had been overcome. It was Mr. Singleton's unhappiness, not her own, that she saw in their present plight. He was distrustful of happiness as some people fear heights or open spaces. She would reassure him, encourage him again. But the averages seemed to defy her personal effort: once every three weeks, once every month ... She thought: things go back to as they were.

But then, by sheer chance, she became pregnant.

Now she lay on her back, eyes closed, on the coarse sand of the beach in Cornwall. It was hot and, if she opened her eyes, the sky was clear blue. This and the previous summer had been fine enough to make her husband's refusal to go abroad for holidays tolerable. If you kept your eyes closed it could be Greece or Italy or Ibiza. She wore a chocolate-brown bikini, sun-glasses, and her skin, which seldom suffered from sunburn, was already beginning to tan. She let her arms trail idly by her side, scooping up little handfuls of sand. If she turned her head to the right and looked towards the sea she could see Mr. Singleton and their son Paul standing in the shallow water. Mr. Singleton was teaching Paul to swim. "Kick!" he was saying. From here, against the gentle waves, they looked like no more than two rippling silhouettes.

"Kick!" said Mr. Singleton, "Kick!" He was like a punisher, administering lashes.

She turned her head away to face upwards. If you shut your eyes you could imagine you were the only one on the beach; if you held them shut you could be part of the beach. Mrs. Singleton imagined that in order to acquire a tan you had to let the sun make love to you.

She dug her heels in the sand and smiled involuntarily.

When she was a thin, flat-chested, studious girl in a grey school uniform Mrs. Singleton had assuaged her fear and desperation about sex with fantasies which took away from men the brute physicality she expected of them. All her lovers would be artists. Poets would write poems to her, composers would dedicate their works to her. She would even pose, naked and immaculate, for painters, who having committed her true, her eternal form to canvas, would make love to her in an impalpable, ethereal way, under the power of which her bodily and temporal self would melt away, perhaps for ever. These fantasies (for she had never entirely renounced them) had crystallized for her in the image of a sculptor, who from a cold intractable piece of stone would fashion her very essence—which would be vibrant and full of sunlight, like the statues they had seen in Greece.

At university she had worked on the assumption that all men lusted uncontrollably and insatiably after women. She had not yet encountered a man who, whilst prone to the usual instincts, possessing moreover a magnificent body with which to fulfil them, yet had scruples about doing so, seemed ashamed of his own capacities. It did not matter that Mr. Singleton was reading engineering, was scarcely artistic at all, or that his powerful physique was unlike the nebulous creatures of her dreams. She found she loved this solid man-flesh. Mrs. Singleton had thought she was the shy, inexperienced timid girl. Overnight she discovered that she wasn't this at all. He wore tough denim shirts, spoke and smiled very little and had a way of standing very straight and upright as if he didn't need any help from anyone. She had to educate him into moments of passion, of self-forgetfulness which made her glow with her own achievement. She was happy because she had not thought she was happy and she believed she could make someone else happy. At the university girls were starting to wear jeans, record-players played the Rolling Stones and in the hush of the Modern Languages Library she read Leopardi and Verlaine. She seemed to float with confidence in a swirling, buoyant element she had never suspected would be her own.

"Kick!" she heard again from the water.

Mr. Singleton had twice thought of leaving his wife. Once was after a symphony concert they had gone to in London when they had not known each other very long and she still tried to get him to read books, to listen to music, to take an interest in art. She would buy concert or theatre tickets, and he had to seem pleased. At this concert a visiting orchestra was playing some titanic, large-scale work by a late nineteenth-century composer. A note in the programme said it represented the triumph of life over death. He had sat on his plush seat amidst the swirling barrage of sound. He had no idea what he had to do with it or the triumph of life over death. He had thought the same thought about the rapt girl on his left, the future Mrs. Singleton, who now and then bobbed, swayed or rose in her seat as if the music physically lifted her. There were at least seventy musicians on the platform. As the piece worked to its final crescendo the conductor, whose arms were flailing frantically so that his white shirt back appeared under his flying tails, looked so absurd Mr. Singleton thought he would laugh. When the music stopped and was immediately supplanted by wild cheering and clapping he thought the world had gone mad. He had struck his own hands together so as to appear to be sharing the ecstasy. Then, as they filed out, he had almost wept because he felt like an insect. He even thought she had arranged the whole business so as to humiliate him.

He thought he would not marry her.

The second time was after they had been married some years. He was one of a team of engineers working on a suspension bridge over an estuary in Ireland. They took it in turns to stay on the site and to inspect the construction work personally. Once he had to go to the very top of one of the two piers of the bridge to examine work on the bearings and housing for the main overhead cables. A lift ran up between the twin towers of the pier amidst a network of scaffolding and power cables to where a working platform was positioned. The engineer, with the supervisor and the foreman, had only to stay on the platform where all the main features of construction were visible. The men at work on the upper sections of the towers, specialists in their trade, earning up to two hundred pounds a week—who balanced on precarious cat-walks and walked along exposed reinforcing girders—often jibed at the engineers who never left the platform. He thought he would show them. He walked out on to one of the cat-walks on the outer face of the pier where they were fitting huge grip-bolts. This was quite safe if you held on to the rails but still took some nerve. He wore a check cheese-cloth shirt and his white safety helmet. It was a grey, humid August day. The cat-walk hung over greyness. The water of the estuary was the colour of dead fish. A dredger was chugging near the base of the pier. He thought, I could swim the estuary; but there is a bridge. Below him the yellow helmets of workers moved over the girders for the roadway like beetles. He took his hands from the rail. He wasn't at all afraid. He had been away from his wife all week. He thought: she knows nothing of this. If he were to step out now into the grey air he would be quite by himself, no harm would come to him . . .

Now Mr. Singleton stood in the water, teaching his son to swim. They were doing the water-wings exercise. The boy wore a pair of water-wings, red underneath, yellow on top, which ballooned up under his arms and chin. With this to support him, he would splutter and splash towards his father who stood facing him some feet away. After a while at this they would try the same procedure, his father moving a little nearer, but without the water-wings, and this the boy dreaded. "Kick!" said Mr Singleton, "Use your legs!" He watched his son draw painfully towards him. The boy had not yet grasped that the boy naturally floated and that if you added to this certain mechanical effects, you swam. He thought that in order to swim you had to make as much frantic movement as possible. As he struggled towards Mr. Singleton his head, which was too high out of the water, jerked messily from side to side, and his eyes which were half closed swivelled in every direction but straight ahead. "Towards me!" shouted Mr. Singleton. He held out his arms in front of him for Paul to grasp. As his son was on the point of clutching them he would step back a little, pulling his hands away, in the hope that the last desperate lunge to reach his father might really teach the boy the art of propelling himself in water. But he sometimes wondered if this were his only motive.

"Good boy. Now again."

At school Mr. Singleton had been an excellent swimmer. He had won various school titles, broken numerous records and competed successfully in ASA championships. There was a period between the age of about thirteen and seventeen which he remembered as the happiest in his life. It wasn't the medals and trophies that made him glad, but the knowledge that he didn't have to bother about anything else. Swimming vindicated him. He would get up every morning at six and train for two hours in the baths, and again before lunch; and when he fell asleep, exhausted, in French and English periods in the afternoon, he didn't have to bother about the indignation of the masters— lank, ill-conditioned creatures—for he had his excuse. He didn't have to bother about the physics teacher who complained to the headmaster that he would never get the exam results he needed if he didn't cut down his swimming, for the headmaster (who was an advocate of sport) came to his aid and told the physics teacher not to interfere with a boy who was a credit to the school. Nor did he have to bother about a host of other things which were supposed to be going on inside him, which made the question of what to do in the evening, at week-ends, fraught and tantalizing, which drove other boys to moodiness and recklessness. For once in the cool water of the baths, his arms reaching, his eyes fixed on the blue marker line on the bottom, his ears full so that he could hear nothing around him, he would feel quite by himself, quite sufficient. At the end of races, when for one brief instant he clung panting alone like a survivor to the finishing rail which his rivals had yet to touch, he felt an infinite peace. He went to bed early, slept soundly, kept to his training regimen; and he enjoyed this Spartan purity which disdained pleasure and disorder. Some of his school mates mocked him—for not going to dances on Saturdays or to pubs, under age, or the Expresso after school. But he did not mind. He didn't need them. He knew they were weak. None of them could hold out, depend on themselves, spurn comfort if they had to. Some of them would go under in life. And none of them could cleave the water as he did or possessed a hard, streamlined, perfectly tuned body like he did.

Then, when he was nearly seventeen all this changed. His father, who was an engineer, though proud of his son's trophies, suddenly pressed him to different forms of success. The headmaster no longer shielded him from the physics master. He said: "You can't swim into your future." Out of spite perhaps or an odd consistency of self-denial, he dropped swimming altogether rather than cut it down. For a year and a half he worked at his maths and physics with the same single-mindedness with which he had perfected his sport. He knew about mechanics and engineering because he knew how to make his body move through water. His work was not merely competent but good. He got to university where he might have had the leisure, if he wished, to resume his swimming. But he did not. Two years are a long gap in a swimmer's training; two years when you are near your peak can mean you will never get back to your true form. Sometimes he went for a dip in the university pool and swam slowly up and down amongst practising members of the university team, whom perhaps he could still have beaten, as a kind of relief.

Often, Mr. Singleton dreamt about swimming. He would be moving through vast expanses of water, an ocean. As he moved it did not require any effort at all. Sometimes he would go for long distances under water, but he did not have to bother about breathing. The water would be silvery-grey. And always it seemed that as he swam he was really trying to get beyond the water, to put it behind him, as if it were a veil he were parting and he would emerge on the other side of it at last, on to some pristine shore, where he would step where no one else had stepped before.

When he made love to his wife her body got in the way; he wanted to swim through her.

Mrs. Singleton raised herself, pushed her sun-glasses up over her dark hair and sat with her arms stretched straight behind her back. A trickle of sweat ran between her breasts. They had developed to a good size since her schoolgirl days. Her skinniness in youth had stood her in good stead against the filling out of middle age, and her body was probably more mellow, more lithe and better proportioned now than it had ever been. She looked at Paul and Mr. Singleton half immersed in the shallows. It seemed to her that her husband was the real boy, standing stubbornly upright with his hands before him, and that Paul was some toy being pulled and swung relentlessly around him and towards him as though on some string. They had seen her sit up. Her husband waved, holding the boy's hand, as though for the two of them. Paul did not wave; he seemed more concerned with the water in his eyes. Mrs. Singleton did not wave back. She would have done if her son had waved. When they had left for their holiday Mr. Singleton had said to Paul, "You'll learn to swim this time. In salt water, you know, it's easier." Mrs. Singleton hoped her son wouldn't swim; so that she could wrap him, still, in the big yellow towel when he came out, rub him dry and warm, and watch her husband stand apart, his hands empty.

She watched Mr. Singleton drop his arm back to his side. "If you wouldn't splash it wouldn't go in your eyes," she just caught him say.

The night before, in their hotel room, they had argued. They always argued about half way through their holiday. It was symbolic, perhaps, of that first trip to Greece, when he had somehow refused to enjoy himself. They had to incur injuries so that they could then appreciate their leisure, like convalescents. For the first four days or so of their holiday Mr. Singleton would tend to be moody, on edge. He would excuse this as "winding down," the not-to-be-hurried process of dispelling the pressures of work. Mrs. Singleton would be patient. On about the fifth day Mrs. Singleton would begin to suspect that the winding down would never end and indeed (which she had known all along) that it was not winding down at all—he was clinging, as to a defence, to his bridges and tunnels; and she would show her resentment. At this point Mr. Singleton would retaliate by an attack upon her indolence.

Last night he had called her "flabby." He could not mean, of course, "flabby-bodied" (she could glance down, now, at her still flat belly), though such a sensual attack would have been simpler, almost heartening, from him. He meant "flabby of attitude," And what he meant by this, or what he wanted to mean, was that *he* was not flabby; that he worked, facing the real world, erecting great solid things on the face of the land, and that, whilst he worked, he disdained work's rewards—money, pleasure, rich food, holidays abroad—that he hadn't "gone soft," as she had done since they graduated eleven years ago, with their credentials for the future and their plane tickets to Greece. She knew this toughness of her husband was only a cover for his own failure to relax and his need to keep his distance. She knew that he found no particular virtue in his bridges and tunnels (it was the last thing he wanted to do really—build); it didn't matter if they were right or wrong, they were there, he could point to them as if it vindicated him—just as when he made his infrequent, if seismic love to her it was not a case of enjoyment or satisfaction; he just did it.

It was hot in their hotel room. Mr. Singleton stood in his blue pyjama bottoms, feet apart, like a PT instructor.

"Flabby? What do you mean—'flabby'!?" she had said, looking daunted.

But Mrs. Singleton had the advantage whenever Mr. Singleton accused her in this way of complacency, of weakness. She knew he only did it to hurt her, and so to feel guilty, and so to feel the remorse which would release his own affection for her, his vulnerability, his own need to be loved. Mrs. Singleton was used to this process, to the tenderness that was the tenderness of successively opened and reopened wounds. And she was used to being the nurse who took care of the healing scars. For though Mr. Singleton inflicted the first blow he would always make himself more guilty than he made her suffer, and

Mrs. Singleton, though in pain herself, could not resist wanting to clasp and cherish her husband, wanting to wrap him up safe when his own weakness and submissiveness showed and his body became liquid and soft against her; could not resist the old spur that her husband was unhappy and it was for her to make him happy. Mr. Singleton was extraordinarily lovable when he was guilty. She would even have yielded indefinitely, foregoing her own grievance, to this extreme of comforting him for the pain he caused her, had she not discovered, in time, that this only pushed the process a stage further. Her forgiveness of him became only another level of comfort, of softness he must reject. His flesh shrank from her restoring touch.

She thought: men go round in circles, women don't move.

She kept to her side of the hotel bed, he, with his face turned, to his. He lay like a person washed up on a beach. She reached out her hand and stroked the nape of his neck. She felt him tense. All this was a pattern.

"I'm sorry," he said. "I didn't mean—"

"It's all right, it doesn't matter."

"Doesn't it matter?" he said.

When they reached this point they were like miners racing each other for deeper and deeper seams of guilt and recrimination.

But Mrs. Singleton had given up delving to rock bottom. Perhaps it was five years ago when she had thought for the third time of leaving her husband, perhaps long before that. When they were students she'd made allowances for his constraints, his reluctances. An unhappy childhood perhaps, a strict upbringing. She thought his inhibition might be lifted by the sanction of marriage. She'd thought, after all, it would be a good thing if he married her. She had not thought what would be good for her. They stood outside Gatwick Airport, back from Greece, in the grey, wet August light. Their tanned skin had seemed to glow. Yet she'd known this mood of promise would pass. She watched him kick against contentment, against ease, against the long, glittering life-line she threw to him; and, after a while, she ceased to try to haul him in. She began to imagine again her phantom artists. She thought: people slip off the shores of the real world, back into dreams. She hadn't "gone soft," only gone back to herself. Hidden inside her like treasure there were lines of Leopardi, of Verlaine her husband would never appreciate. She thought, he doesn't need me, things run off him, like water. She even thought that her husband's neglect in making love to her was not a problem he had but a deliberate scheme to deny her. When Mrs. Singleton desired her husband she could not help herself. She would stretch back on the bed with the sheets pulled off like a blissful nude in a Modigliani. She thought this ought to gladden a man. Mr. Singleton would stand at the foot of the bed and gaze down at her. He looked like some strong, chaste knight in the legend of the Grail. He would respond to her invitation, but before he did so there would be this expression that good men in books and films are supposed to make to prostitutes. It would ensure that their love making was marred and that afterwards it would seem as if he had performed something out of duty that only she wanted. Her body would feel like stone. It was at such times, when she felt the cold, dead-weight feel of abused happiness, that Mrs. Singleton most thought she was through with Mr. Singleton. She would watch his strong, compact torso already lifting itself off the bed. She would think: he thinks he is tough, contained in himself, but he won't see what I offer him, he doesn't see how it is I who can help him.

Mrs. Singleton lay back on her striped towel on the sand. Once again she became part of the beach. The careless sounds of the seaside, of excited children's voices, of languid grownups', of wooden bats on balls, fluttered over her as she shut her eyes. She thought: it is the sort of day on which someone suddenly shouts, "Someone is drowning."

When Mrs. Singleton became pregnant she felt she had outmanoeuvred her husband. He did not really want a child (it was the last thing he wanted, Mrs. Singleton thought, a child), but he was jealous of her condition, as of some achievement he himself could attain. He was excluded from the little circle of herself and her womb, and, as though to puncture it, he began for the first time to make love to her of a kind where he took the insistent initiative. Mrs. Singleton was not greatly pleased. She seemed buoyed up by her own bigness. She noticed that her husband began to do exercises in the morning, in his underpants, press-ups, squat-jumps, as if he were getting in training for something. He was like a boy. He even became, as the term of her pregnancy drew near its end, resilient and detached again, the virile father waiting to receive the son (Mr. Singleton knew it would be a son, so did Mrs. Singleton) that she, at the appointed time, would deliver him. When the moment arrived he insisted on being present so as to prove he wasn't squeamish and to make sure he wouldn't be tricked in the transaction. Mrs. Singleton was not daunted. When the pains became frequent she wasn't at all afraid. There were big, water lights clawing down from the ceiling of the delivery room like the lights in dentists' surgeries. She could just see her husband looking down at her. His face was white and clammy. It was his fault for wanting to be there. She had to push, as though away from him. Then she knew it was happening. She stretched back. She was a great surface of warm, splitting rock and Paul was struggling bravely up into the sunlight. She had to coax him with her cries. She felt him emerge like a trapped survivor. The doctor groped with rubber gloves. "There we are," he said. She managed to look at Mr. Singleton. She wanted suddenly to put him back inside for good where Paul had come from. With a fleeting pity she saw that this was what Mr. Singleton wanted too. His eyes were half closed. She kept hers on him. He seemed to wilt under her gaze. All his toughness and control were draining from him and she was glad. She lay back triumphant and glad. The doctor was holding Paul; but she looked, beyond, at Mr. Singleton. He was far away like an insect. She knew he couldn't hold out. He was going to faint. He was looking where her legs were spread. His eyes went out of focus. He was going to faint, keel over, right there on the spot.

Mrs. Singleton grew restless, though she lay unmoving on the beach. Wasps were buzzing close to her head, round their picnic bag. She thought that Mr. Singleton and Paul had been too long at their swimming lesson. They should come out. It never struck her, hot as she was, to get up and join her husband and son in the sea. Whenever Mrs. Singleton wanted a swim she would wait until there was an opportunity to go in by herself; then she would wade out, dip her shoulders under suddenly and paddle about contentedly, keeping her hair dry, as though she were soaking herself in a large bath. They did not bathe as a family; nor did Mrs. Singleton swim with Mr. Singleton—who now and then, too, would get up by himself and enter the sea, swim at once about fifty yards out, then cruise for long stretches, with a powerful crawl or butterfly, back and forth across the bay. When this happened Mrs. Singleton would engage her son in talk so he would not watch his father. Mrs. Singleton did not swim with Paul either. He was too old, now, to cradle between her knees in the very shallow water, and she was somehow afraid that while Paul splashed and kicked around her he would suddenly learn how to swim. She had this feeling that Paul would only swim while she was in the sea, too. She did not want this to happen, but it reassured her and gave her sufficient confidence to let Mr. Singleton continue his swimming lessons with Paul. These lessons were obsessive, indefatigable. Every Sunday morning at seven, when they were at home, Mr. Singleton would take Paul to the baths for yet another attempt. Part of this, of course, was that Mr. Singleton was determined that his son should swim; but it enabled him also to avoid the Sunday morning languor: extra hours in bed, leisurely love-making.

Once, in a room at college, Mr. Singleton had told Mrs. Singleton about his swimming, about his training sessions, races; about what it felt like when you could really swim well. She had run her fingers over his long, naked back.

Mrs. Singleton sat up and rubbed sun-tan lotion on to her thighs. Down near the water's edge, Mr. Singleton was standing about waist deep, supporting Paul who, gripped by his father's hands, water-wings still on, was flailing, face down, at the surface. Mr. Singleton kept saying, "No, keep still." He was trying to get Paul to hold his body straight and relaxed so he would float. But each time as Paul nearly succeeded he would panic, fearing his father would let go, and thrash wildly. When he calmed down and Mr Singleton held him, Mrs. Singleton could see the water running off his face like tears.

Mrs. Singleton did not alarm herself at this distress of her son. It was a guarantee against Mr. Singleton's influence, an assurance that Paul was not going to swim; nor was he to be imbued with any of his father's sullen hardiness. When Mrs. Singleton saw her son suffer, it pleased her and she felt loving towards him. She felt that an invisible thread ran between her and the boy which commanded him not to swim, and she felt that Mr. Singleton knew that it was because of her that his efforts with Paul were in vain. Even now, as Mr. Singleton prepared for another attempt, the boy was looking at her smoothing the sun-tan oil on to her legs.

"Come on, Paul," said Mr. Singleton. His wet shoulders shone like metal.

When Paul was born it seemed to Mrs. Singleton that her life with her husband was dissolved, as a mirage dissolves, and that she could return again to what she was before she knew him. She let her staved-off hunger for happiness and her old suppressed dreams revive. But then they were not dreams, because they had a physical object and she knew she needed them in order to live. She did not disguise from herself what she needed. She knew that she wanted the kind of close, even erotic relationship with her son that women who have rejected their husbands have been known to have. The kind of relationship in which the son must hurt the mother, the mother the son. But she willed it, as if there would be no pain. Mrs. Singleton waited for her son to grow. She trembled when she thought of him at eighteen or twenty. When he was grown he would be slim and light and slender, like a boy even though he was a man. He would not need a strong body because all his power would be inside. He would be all fire and life in essence. He would become an artist, a sculptor. She would pose for him naked (she would keep her body trim for this), and he would sculpt her. He would hold the chisel. His hands would guide the cold metal over the stone and its blows would strike sunlight.

Mrs. Singleton thought: all the best statues they had seen in Greece seemed to have been dredged up from the sea.

She finished rubbing the lotion on to her insteps and put the cap back on the tube. As she did so she heard something that made her truly alarmed. It was Mr. Singleton saying, "That's it, that's the way! At last! Now keep it going!" She looked up. Paul was in the same position as before but he had learnt to make slower, regular motions with his limbs and his body no longer sagged in the middle. Though he still wore the water-wings he was moving, somewhat laboriously, forwards so that Mr. Singleton had to walk along with him; and at one point Mr. Singleton removed one of his hands from under the boy's ribs and simultaneously looked at his wife and smiled. His shoulders flashed. It was not a smile meant for her. She could see that. And it was not one of her husband's usual, infrequent, rather mechanical smiles. It was the smile a person makes about some joy inside, hidden and incommunicable.

"That's enough," thought Mrs. Singleton, getting to her feet, pretending not to have noticed, behind her sun-glasses, what had happened in the water. It *was* enough: they had been in the water for what seemed like an hour. He was only doing it because of their row last night, to make her feel he was not outmatched by using the reserve weapon of Paul. And, she added with relief to herself, Paul still had the water-wings and one hand to support him.

"That's enough now!" she shouted aloud, as if she were slightly, but not ill-humouredly, peeved at being neglected. "Come on in now!" She had picked up her purse as a quickly conceived ruse as she got up and as she walked towards the water's edge she waved it above her head. "Who wants an ice-cream?"

Mr. Singleton ignored his wife. "Well done, Paul," he said. "Let's try that again."

Mrs. Singleton knew he would do this. She stood on the little ridge of sand just above where the beach, becoming fine shingle, shelved into the sea. She replaced a loose strap of her bikini over her shoulder and with a finger of each hand pulled the bottom half down over her buttocks. She stood feet apart, slightly on her toes, like a gymnast. She knew other eyes on the beach would be on her. It flattered her that she—and her husband, too—received admiring glances from those around. She thought, with relish for the irony: perhaps they think we are happy, beautiful people. For all her girlhood diffidence, Mrs. Singleton enjoyed displaying her attractions, and she liked to see other people's pleasure. When she lay sunbathing she imagined making love to all the moody, pubescent boys on holiday with their parents, with their slim waists and their quick heels.

"See if you can do it without me holding you," said Mr. Singleton. "I'll help you at first." He stooped over Paul. He looked like a mechanic making final adjustments to some prototype machine.

"Don't you want an ice-cream then, Paul?" said Mrs. Singleton. "They've got those chocolate ones."

Paul looked up. His short wet hair stood up in spikes. He looked like a prisoner offered a chance of escape, but the plastic water-wings, like some absurd pillory, kept him fixed.

Mrs. Singleton thought: he crawled out of me; now I have to lure him back with ice-cream.

"Can't you see he was getting the hang of it?" Mr. Singleton said. "If he comes out now he'll—"

"Hang of it! It was you. You were holding him all the time."

She thought: perhaps I am hurting my son.

Mr. Singleton glared at Mrs. Singleton. He gripped Paul's shoulders. "You don't want to get out now, do you Paul?" He looked suddenly as if he really might drown Paul rather than let him come out.

Mrs. Singleton's heart raced. She wasn't good at rescues, at resuscitations. She knew this because of her life with her husband.

"Come on, you can go back in later," she said.

Paul was a hostage. She was playing for time, not wanting to harm the innocent.

She stood on the sand like a marooned woman watching for ships. The sea, in the sheltered bay, was almost flat calm. A few, glassy waves idled in but were smoothed out before they could break. On the headlands there were outcrops of scaly rocks like basking lizards. The island in Greece had been where Theseus left Ariadne. Out over the blue water, beyond the heads of bobbing swimmers, seagulls flapped like scraps of paper.

Mr. Singleton looked at Mrs. Singleton. She was a fussy mother daubed with Ambre Solaire, trying to bribe her son with silly ice-creams; though if you forgot this she was a beautiful, tanned girl, like the girls men imagine on desert islands. But then, in Mr. Singleton's dreams, there was no one else on the untouched shore he ceaselessly swam to.

He thought, if Paul could swim, then I could leave her.

Mrs. Singleton looked at her husband. She felt afraid. The water's edge was like a dividing line between them which marked off the territory in which each existed. Perhaps they could never cross over.

"Well, I'm getting the ice-creams: you'd better get out."

She turned and paced up the sand. Behind the beach was an ice-cream van painted like a fairground.

Paul Singleton looked at his mother. He thought: she is deserting me—or I am deserting her. He wanted to get out to follow her. Her feet made puffs of sand which stuck to her ankles, and you could see all her body as she strode up the beach. But he was afraid of his father and his gripping hands. And he was afraid of his mother, too. How she would wrap him, if he came out, in the big yellow towel like egg yolk, how she would want him to get close to her smooth, sticky body, like a mouth that would swallow him. He thought: the yellow towel humiliated him, his father's hands humiliated him. The water-wings humiliated him: you put them on and became a puppet. So much of life is humiliation. It was how you won love. His father was taking off the water-wings like a man unlocking a chastity belt. He said: "Now try the same, coming towards me." His father stood some feet away from him. He was a huge, straight man, like the pier of a bridge. "Try." Paul Singleton was six. He was terrified of water. Every time he entered it he had to fight down fear. His father never realized this. He thought it was simple; you said: "Only water, no need to be afraid." His father did not know what fear was; the same as he did not know what fun was. Paul Singleton hated water. He hated it in his mouth and in his eyes. He hated the chlorine smell of the swimming baths, the wet, slippery tiles, the echoing whoops and screams. He hated it when his father read to him from *The Water Babies*. It was the only story his father read, because, since he didn't know fear or fun, he was really sentimental. His mother read lots of stories. "Come on then. I'll catch you." Paul Singleton held out his arms and raised one leg. This was the worst moment. Perhaps having no help was most humiliating. If you did not swim you sank like a statue. They would drag him out, his skin streaming. His father would say: "I didn't mean . . ." But if he swam his mother would be forsaken. She would stand on the beach with chocolate ice-cream running down her arm. There was no way out; there were all these things to be afraid of and no weapons. But then, perhaps he was not afraid of his mother nor his father, nor of water, but of something else. He had felt it just now—when he'd struck out with rhythmic, reaching strokes and his feet had come off the bottom and his father's hand had slipped from under his chest: as if he had mistaken what his fear was; as if he had been unconsciously pretending, even to himself, so as to execute some plan. He lowered his chin into the water. "Come on!" said Mr. Singleton. He launched himself forward and felt the sand leave his feet and his legs wriggle like cut ropes. "There," said his father as he realized. "There!" His father stood like a man waiting to clasp a lover; there was a gleam on his face. "Towards me! Towards me!" said his father suddenly. But he kicked and struck, half in panic, half in pride, away from his father, away from the shore, away, in this strange new element that seemed all his own.

Antonio Tabucchi

A Riddle

(ITALY)

Last night I dreamed of Miriam. She was wearing a long white dress which, from a distance, seemed like a nightgown. She was walking along the beach; the waves were dangerously high and breaking in silence; it must have been the beach at Biarritz, but it was totally deserted. I was sitting on the first of an interminable line of empty deck chairs, but perhaps it was another beach because at Biarritz I don't remember deck chairs like those; it was just an imaginary beach. I waved to her, inviting her to sit down, but she went on walking, as if she didn't know me, looking straight ahead and, when she passed close by, I was struck by a gust of cold air, like an aura which she carried behind her: and then, with the unsurprised amazement of a dream, I realized that she was dead.

Sometimes it's only in a dream that we glimpse a plausible solution. Perhaps because reason is fearful; it can't fill in the gaps and achieve completeness, which is a form of simplicity; it prefers complexity, with all its gaps, and so the will entrusts the solution to dreams. But then tomorrow, or some other day, I'll dream that Miriam's alive, that she'll walk close to the sea, respond to my call and sit down on a deck chair belonging to the beach at Biarritz or to an imaginary beach. With her usual languid, sensual gesture she'll push back her hair, look out to sea, point to a sailing boat or a cloud, and laugh. And we'll laugh together because here we are, we've made it, we've kept our appointment.

Life's an appointment—what I'm saying is very banal, Monsieur, I realize; the only thing is that we don't know when, where, how, and with whom. Then we think: if I'd said this instead of that or that instead of this, if I'd got up late instead of early, today I'd be imperceptibly different from what I am, and perhaps the world would be imperceptibly different, too. Or else it would be the same and I couldn't know it. For instance, I shouldn't be here telling a story, proposing a riddle that has no solution or else that has always had an inevitable solution, only I don't know about it and so, every now and then, rarely, when I'm having a drink with a friend, I say: Here's a riddle for you, let's see how you solve it. But then, why do you care about riddles? Do you go in for puzzles and the like, or is it just the sterile curiosity with which you observe other people's lives?

An appointment and a journey, this too is banal, I mean as a definition of life; it's been said any number of times, and then in the great journey there are other journeys, our insignificant trips over the crust of this planet, which is journeying also, but where to? It's all a riddle; perhaps you find me a bit odd. But, at that time, I had come to a standstill; I was stuck in a morass of boredom, in the lethargic mood of a man who is no longer very young, but not completely an adult, who is simply waiting for life.

And instead Miriam came on the scene. "I'm the Countess of Terrail, and I have to get to Biarritz." "And I'm the Marquis of Carabas, but I seldom leave my estate." That's exactly how it began, with this exchange. We were at Chez Albert, near the Porte Saint-Denis, not exactly a stamping ground for countesses. In the afternoon, after I'd closed the shop, I went to this bistro for a drink. It's gone now and, in its place, there's one of those establishments that sell human flesh on film—it's the times. Albert would have liked to be buried at Père-Lachaise, because Proust is there, but I think he wound up in the cemetery at Ivry, another sign of the times. The old days—I don't mean to hark back to the past—but they were different, they really were. Take today's motor cars: the engine's all squeezed in—you could wrap it up in a handkerchief—and there's not even room to take the carburettor apart. Albert wasn't exactly my partner, but he might just as well have been because he got hold of many of the cars. He'd been a racing driver before there were macadam roads, when drivers wore special goggles to keep out the dust. He was a wee slip of a man, grown melancholy from standing behind the bar, who laughed only when he'd had a glass too many. At such moments he drew off some Alsatian beer and put a pitcher of it on the bar, just like in a cowboy film, exclaiming: "Speed!" Speed had done him in, but not too much; he was lame in one leg and his left hand had lost its grip. He was the one to get hold of the car that had belonged to Agostinelli, that is, to Proust. Lord knows how he did it. Agostinelli was Proust's chauffeur, and a good fellow; together they visited all the Gothic cathedrals of Normandy. I don't know if there was anything between them, and it doesn't really matter. Proust, as you know, had his particular tastes. Anyhow, to go back to what I was saying, during my first year of Literature at the university I'd written a paper that I thought I might turn into a thesis, but then I dropped out; the Sorbonne and its professors seemed pointless to me. My thesis was to be entitled *What Proust Saw from a Car.* Obviously the car, not Proust, was what interested me. One fine day I made up my mind and sold the piece for publication in two instalments in a third-class magazine, a feeble imitation of *Harper's Bazaar* (I'm not telling you the name, so you won't find it) and, God knows how, it fell into Albert's hands. He took that for granted; everything fell into his hands. And then, you know how life is, like a woven fabric in which all the threads cross, and what I want one day is to see the whole pattern. That's why, one evening, I went to Chez Albert with a copy of the magazine under my arm and ordered a drink. I was wandering about Saint-Denis because I'd been told that, in the area, there was a body shop owned by an old man who repaired vintage cars. I was a proper mechanic, because I grew up in a garage at Meudon, the town where Céline lived. Not that I knew him; he was a bad egg, they say, but a good doctor, apparently, especially to the poor. Albert saw the magazine under my arm. "There's a piece in there about Proust's car," he said, "by a lunatic who signs himself the Marquis of Carabas." "I'm the Marquis of Carabas," I said, "but for the moment I'm what they call fallen on hard times. I'm looking for the Pegasus body shop, where I hear there's a job." Albert looked at me hard, as if to see whether I was joking, but I wasn't; I was in low spirits. "Don't take it so hard, my boy; the shop's in that courtyard over there, and so is Agostinelli's car, which I brought in last Sunday. I bought it at a junkyard in Suresnes, where they didn't have the foggiest idea what it was. Now it's only a matter of putting it back into working order."

And that's what we spent the summer doing. "This one's not for sale," said Albert. "It's the car in which I want to run my last race, destination Père-Lachaise, with a little band behind, playing *En passant par la Lorraine*." Lorraine is where he came from, of course. I don't know if you can visualize Proust's car, but probably you've seen a photograph of it. It was a monument, with headlights like searchlights, which served, on the trip through Normandy, to light up the facades of the various cathedrals. When Proust and Agostinelli arrived in a town after dark, they drove through the empty streets up to the cathedral square, stopping on a slight incline so that the headlights would point upwards and illuminate the tympanum. "Agostinelli . . ." Proust would say, and open the volume of Ruskin, which was his bible. This is all true: he wrote it up in the *Le Figaro* of 1907 under the title *Impressions de route en automobile*. Of course, I was never quite sure that our car really had been Proust's. In the junkyard where Albert had bought it there was no registration paper and it was impossible to trace the original owner. But, in the glove compartment, there was a pair of gloves, which Albert insisted were the real thing. If he liked the idea, what was wrong with it? Only the car wasn't used for his funeral; but that's another story.

When the owner of the repair shop died, I took over. For some time I had been a silent partner. Monsieur Gélin had given me a free hand and I had made a pile of money, partly thanks to Albert, who found the vintage cars. Sales were my affair; I created a mid-city headquarters for public relations because we couldn't receive prospective buyers at the shop. It was a microscopic but handsome set-up on the fashionable Avenue Foch: a waiting room and a paneled office with two leather-upholstered chairs and a brass plate on the door: PEGASUS. DE-LUXE VINTAGE CARS. I received customers twice a week—Saturday afternoon and Sunday morning—as advertised. Most of the time I was bored to death because there was seldom more than one buyer a month. But seven or eight sales a year yielded all the money I wanted. Albert managed to find old wrecks that cost him a song and he had made connections with a repair shop in Marseilles which sold us museum pieces for a pittance. All we had to do was fix them up, but that was quite a job. I enjoyed it, and I took on a bright, nimble-fingered young assistant, the son of one of Albert's cousins, called Jacob who, like him, came from Lorraine. For three of four years we restored a bit of everything: Delages, Aston Martins, a Hispano-

Suiza, an Isotta Fraschini, and even a 1922 Fiat Mefistofele, the most beautiful racing car in the world. That one wasn't a car, really; it was a torpedo, a copy of the 1908 original, and in 1924 it set a world speed record. The customers were usually Americans, rolling in money, mad about Europe, with an abominable accent and a craving for vintage cars. They pictured themselves as so many Fitzgeralds, geniuses and wastrels, drunk on champagne, Montmartre, and *Sous le ciel de Paris*. Those, too, were the days. People had been scared by bombs and the slaughter in the trenches and they wanted to celebrate and feel themselves alive: let's laugh and have fun; life's a gift to be enjoyed; we don't want to be like the foolish virgins. There was an Egyptian, one of our best customers, a jovial, fat fellow; he wanted a car every three months, one for every season, he said, laughing like a child. He drank like a sponge and wrecked the cars, one after another. Eventually he came to a bad end; the French police arrested him, I never knew why; for political reasons, they said, but your guess is as good as mine. Albert wanted me to get married. "Get yourself a wife, Carabas," he used to say. "You're over thirty and you need the right kind of woman. What's a man to do, in the house, after he's spent the day fixing a hood? Time slips by, without our noticing, and you'll be an old man before you know it." Albert was a bit of a philosopher, like every good mechanic. You may not believe it, Monsieur, but the study of automobiles is very instructive: life's a gearbox, a wheel here, a pump here and then the transmission, which links it all up and turns power into movement, yes, just the way it is in life. Some day I'd like to understand the workings of the transmission that ties the components of my life together. It's the same idea; just open up the hood and study the humming motor, then tie up all the minutes, people, and events and say: here's the engine block (that stage of my life); here's Albert (the starter); here am I (the pistons with their valves) and here's the spark plug that sets off the spark and gives the word to go. The spark was Miriam, of course, as you probably realize, but what was the transmission? Not the obvious one, as I told Albert, which was a Bugatti Royale, but the real, hidden one, which ties all the components together and causes a car to move just the way this one moved, with its rhythm, pulse, acceleration, speed and final slow-down.

"There's no resisting a Bugatti Royale," I said to Albert. "I'm going." He looked up from wiping the bar and I thought I saw a shadow of melancholy cross his eyes. "It'll give you problems," he said, "you know that better than I do, but I understand. It's your race. You've always been stuck between the starting line and the track and now you're in a position to run. You're too young and the fascination of risk is too strong."

But first I must go back, because that isn't where our conversation ended, I mean the conversation between Miriam and myself, when I told her I was the Marquis of Carabas but I had no mind to leave my estate. "Don't joke, please," she said. "I'm not joking," I replied. Then she repeated: "Don't joke, *please*." And picking up her glass, distractedly, as if what she was about to say were the most natural thing in the world, "They want to kill me," she added. She said it with the voice of a woman who has seen, drunk, and loved too much and so was beyond lying. I stared at her, like a fool, not knowing what to answer and then I objected, ignobly, "What's in it for me?" She emptied her glass, hurriedly, with the melancholy smile of disillusionment. "Very little," she said; "you're quite right, practically nothing." She left some change on the table and wearily pushed back her hair. "Excuse me," she said, and went away. Besides her glass she had left a matchbox with Miriam written on it, and a telephone number. I didn't call; better pass it up, I said to myself. But the following Saturday, I met the Count. I was in my office on the Avenue Foch, summer was at hand and through the window I could see the new green leaves on the trees. I was reading a book by an Italian dandy who drove to Peking at the turn of the century—I don't remember his name—when the Count came in. Of course, I didn't know at first who he was. He was a stout man, no longer young, with a short reddish beard, wearing a navy-blue blazer, light-coloured trousers, and old-fashioned sunglasses and carrying a newspaper and a cane, a rich banker or lawyer type of fellow. He introduced himself and sat down, crossing his legs awkwardly because of his weight. "I believe my wife contacted you about a job proposal," he said deliberately, "and I'd like to clarify the terms." His tone of voice was flat and bored, as if the matter did not concern him and he wanted to get rid of it with a cheque. "We have an old car," he went on, "A 1927 Bugatti Royale, and my wife has got it into her head to take it to Biarritz, to take part in a rally at San Sebastion." As I had foreseen, he pulled out a chequebook and signed a cheque for an amount more than the price of the car. His expression was more and more bored; as for me, I was sparked up, but I tried to keep cool. There are plenty of drivers around, I nearly said. If you put an ad in the paper there'll be a flock of applicants; as for me, right now, I'm sorry, but I'm very busy. Instead, he got in first: "I want you to turn down my wife's offer." And he held out the cheque. It stayed in his hand, because I was staring at him stupidly, taken by surprise. At the same time I had a feeling that there was something fishy about the whole story; it was too vague and contradictory. I don't know why, perhaps just instinctively, I said: "I don't know your wife or anything about a job proposal. I don't know what you're talking about." It was his turn to be taken aback, I was sure of it, but he didn't flinch. He tore up the cheque and threw it into the wastepaper basket. "If that's so," he said, "please excuse the interruption. My secretary must have made a mistake; goodbye." As soon as he'd left, I called the number Miriam had left me. The Hôtel de Paris answered: "The Count and Countess have gone out. Do you want to leave a message?" "Yes, its a personal message for the Countess; tell her that the Marquis de Carabas called, that's all."

It was a genuine Bugatti Royale, a *coupé de ville*. I don't know if that means anything to you, Monsieur; it's quite understandable if it doesn't. Albert and I went to fetch it, in a little garage on the Quai d'Anjou, behind a wooden door opening onto a courtyard as musky as an English house, with the Seine running below. Albert couldn't believe his eyes. "It's impossible," he said, "impossible," caressing the long, tapering fenders; I don't know whether you get the idea, but the Bugatti has something of a woman's body about it, a woman lying on her back with her legs out in front of her. It was a superb specimen, the body in excellent condition, the damask velvet upholstery in fairly good shape aside from a few moth holes and a single tear. The main problem—at least at first sight—lay in the wheels and the exhaust pipes. The engine seemed unaffected by its long idleness and in need only of being roused from its slumber. We roused it successfully and drove it to the shop. The elephant on the hood was missing, and this was an unpleasant surprise, because you can't take a Bugatti Royale to a rally without its elephant. Perhaps you didn't know, but at the top of the radiator the Royale had a silver elephant sculpted by Ettore Bugatti's brother, Rembrandt. It wasn't just a trademark like the Rolls Royce's Spirit of Ecstasy or the Packard swan, it was a symbol, undecipherable, like all symbols; an elephant standing on his hind legs, with his trunk upraised and trumpeting, in a gesture of attack or mating. Is it too glib to say that these two go together? Perhaps so. But just imagine this: A Bugatti Royale on its haunches, climbing a slight incline, with fenders flared, ready to gather speed and intoxication, with power throbbing behind a fabulous radiator grille and, atop it, an elephant with upraised trunk.

I wanted to stay on the sidelines. Albert called the Countess at the Hôtel de Paris to find out if she knew what had become of the elephant. It had simply disappeared; in any case, it was lost, he reported. The car had been standing too long; she says to make a copy. And so we had three weeks to do something about it, while we were touching up the engine and the upholstery. One cylinder needed adjusting, but that was not a big job. The upholsterer was a wily young fellow with a shop on the Rue Le Peletier, who sent antique fabrics to be repaired by the nuns of a certain convent. There's nobody like a nun for a painstaking job, believe me, and their mending was invisible; it was all done on the reverse side, where it left a network of threads like a telephone exchange. The worst thing was the elephant. A sculptor of sorts offered to make a clay copy to be covered with metal, but bumps and jolts would soon have caused it to crack. Finally Albert thought of a cabinetmaker from Lorraine—this story is full of Lorrainers—who had a shop in the Marais, an old fellow who carved wood in naturalistic style. It was easy enough to find a photograph of the elephant, which we took to the old man, together with the exact measurements, telling him to make an identical copy. After that we had to see to the chrome plating, and that came out satisfactorily. Of course, if you looked at the figure when the car was standing still you could see that it was a fake, but in motion it seemed like the real thing.

The morning of our departure was quite an event. Albert had fallen completely into the role of father, and kept asking whether I needed this or had forgotten that. The day before I'd bought a leather suitcase—the car and the trip deserved nothing less—as well a cream-colored linen jacket and another in leather and an Italian silk scarf. When I got to the Hôtel de Paris a liveried doorman opened the car, and, feeling like the Marquis of Carabas, I told him to call the Countess. A porter came with a valise and a vanity case; she arrived, on her husband's arm, greeted me distractedly and got into the back seat. Here was the first surprise of the day. I had been fearful of seeing the Count again because I didn't exactly like him, but he spoke to me as if we'd never met, playing the part to perfection. It was a Monday towards the end of

June. "We'll meet in Biarritz a week from today," he said affably to his wife. "If you like you can send your driver to pick me up at the station—my train gets in at eight thirty-five in the evening; otherwise we'll meet at the Hôtel des Palais." I went into first gear, and she gave a brief wave of her hand through the open window.

The second surprise was her telling me to take the Route Nationale 6, and her tone of voice, a dry, decisive tone which seemed to reflect a strong will or else some sort of phobia. I objected that this wasn't the shortest way to Biarritz. "I want to take another route," she said sharply, "I'd appreciate it if you didn't argue the point." And there was a third surprise as well. When I first met her at Chez Albert she was so defenceless and such an open book that I thought I could read her whole life on her face; now, instead, she had withdrawn behind a mask of distance and reserve, like a real countess. She was beautiful, and that was no surprise, but now she seemed to me of an absolute beauty, because I understood that no beauty in the world is greater than that of a woman, and this, you'll understand, Monsieur, put me into a sort of a frenzy. Meanwhile the Bugatti glided over the gentle, inviting roads of France, up and down and along level stretches, the way our roads go, bordered by plane trees on either side. Behind me the road retreated, before me it opened up, and I thought of my life and the boredom of it, and of what Albert had said to me, and I felt ashamed that I'd never known love. I don't mean physical love, of course, I'd had that, but real love, the kind that blazes up inside and breaks out and spins like a motor while the wheels speed over the ground. It was like that, a sort of remorse, an awareness of mediocrity or cowardice. Up to now my wheels had turned slowly and tediously over a long, long road, and I couldn't remember a single landscape along the way. Now I was travelling another road, which led nowhere, with a beautiful and distant woman who was escaping or fleeing from I knew not what. It was a useless race across France, I felt quite sure, on a road as empty as those that had gone before. Those were my exact thoughts at that particular moment. Limoges was not far, we were deep in the countryside, where farmers were working among their fruit trees. Limoges, I thought, what does Limoges have to do with my life? I drew the car over to the side of the road and stopped. Turning towards her, I said: "Look here. . . ." Before I could say any more she laid a finger gently across my lips and murmured: "Don't be a fool, Carabas." Without another word she got out and came to sit beside me. "Go on," she said, "I know that we're taking an absurd route, but perhaps everything's absurd, and I have my reasons."

It's a curious sensation to arrive in a strange city, knowing that there you'll love with a love you've never experienced before. That's how it was. We stopped at a little hotel on the river—I don't remember the name of the river that runs by Limoges. The room had faded wallpaper and very ordinary furniture; in those years many hotels were like that; you've only to look at the films of Jean Gabin. Miriam asked me to say that she was my wife, she didn't want to identify herself and the hotel didn't ask for the papers of both members of a couple. From the room we could see the river, bordered by willows; it was a fine night and we fell asleep at dawn. "Who is it you're running away from,

Miriam," I asked her. "What's wrong in your life?" But she laid a finger across my lips.

An absurd route, as I said before. We went down to Rodez and then towards Albi and its vineyards, because of a landscape she wanted to see. I thought it was an outdoor view but it was a painting, and we found it. We skipped Toulouse and made for Pau, because her mother had spent her childhood there, and I lingered over the idea of her mother as a child, in a boarding school which we couldn't locate. It was the first time I'd thought of the childhood of a woman companion's mother, a new and strange sensation. We looked at the splendid square and at the houses, with their white attic windows suspended from tile roofs, and I imagined a winter in Pau, behind one of those windows. I was tempted say: Listen, Miriam, let's forget about everything else and spend the winter behind one of these windows, in this city where nobody knows us.

When we got to Biarritz it was Saturday; the rally was to be the next day. I thought we'd go to the Hôtel des Palais and take two rooms there, but she chose to go elsewhere, to the Hôtel d'Angleterre, and she signed the register in my name. In luxury hotels, too, they don't ask to see a woman's papers. She was hiding out, obviously, and I was haunted by the strange sentence she had pronounced on the day of our first meeting, a subject to which she refused to return. I put my hands on her shoulders and looked into her eyes—we had gone down to the beach at sunset, seagulls were standing around, a sign of bad weather, they say, and some children were playing in the sand. "I want to know," I told her, and she said: "Tomorrow you'll know everything. Tomorrow evening, after the rally, we'll meet here on the beach and go for a drive in the car. Don't insist, please."

The rally rules demanded that every driver be dressed in the style of the period of his car. I had bought a pair of baggy Zouave-style trousers and a tan cloth cap with a visor. "This is a show," I said to Miriam; "it's not a race, it's a fashion parade." But she said no, I'd see. Competition wasn't the order of the day, but almost. The course ran along the ocean, a road riddled with curves hanging over the water: Bidart, Saint-Jean-de-Luz, Donibane and, finally, San Sebastian. We set out three by three, our names drawn by lot, regardless of the type of car. The time was to be clocked and calculated according to each car's horsepower. And so we started out with a 1928 Hispano-Suiza, called La Boulogne, and a bright red 1922 Lambda, a superb creation (suffice it to say that Mussolini had one). Not that the Hispano-Suiza was to be sneezed at; it was definitely elegant, with its bottle-green coupé body and long chrome hood. We were among the first to take off, at ten o'clock in the morning. It was a fine typically Atlantic day, with a cool breeze and clouds flitting across the sun. The Hispano-Suiza took off like a shot. "We'll let it go," I said to Miriam; "I refuse to let others set the pace; we'll catch up when I feel like it." The Lambda stayed quietly behind. It was driven by a fellow with a black moustache, accompanied by a young girl, probably rich Italians, who smiled at us and every now and then called out *ciao*. They remained behind us on all the curves until Saint-Jean-de-Luz, then they passed us at Hendaye, the border town, and began to slow up on the straight, flat road to Donibane. I thought it was strange that they should linger at this particular point. We had passed the Hispano-Suiza before arriving at Irun; now I meant to step on the accelerator and I expected the driver of the Lambda to do likewise. Instead, he let us pass with the greatest of ease. For a hundred yards or so we were side by side; the girl waved and laughed. "They're out for a good time," I said to Miriam. They caught up with us at the end of the straight, at which point there were two nasty curves in rapid succession. We'd tried them out the evening before, and they were imprinted on my memory. Miriam cried out when she saw them coming at us, pushing us towards the precipice. Instinctively I braked and then accelerated, managing to hit the Lambda. It was a hard, quick blow, enough to throw the Lambda off the road, to the left, where it slithered along the inside embankment for about twenty yards. I was following the scene in the rear-view mirror as the Lambda lost a fender against a pole, skidded towards the centre of the road and then back to the left where, having run out of all impetus, it bogged down in a pile of dirt. Plainly the passengers were not injured. I was drenched with cold sweat. Miriam clasped my arm. "Don't stay," she said, "please, please don't stay," and I drove on. San Sebastian was directly below us; no one had witnessed the incident. After passing the finish line I made for the improvised, open-air garage, but I didn't get out of the car. "It was intentional," I said; "they did it on purpose." Miriam was very pale, and speechless, as if petrified. "I'm going to the police to report it," I said. "Please," she murmured. "But don't you see that they did it on purpose?" I shouted. "That they were trying to kill us?" She looked at me, with an expression half troubled, half imploring. "You can take care of the car," I said; "get the bumper straightened while I walk around." And I got out, slamming the door; there was nothing seriously wrong with the car and the whole thing could have been just a bad dream. I wandered around San Sebastian, especially along the sea. It's a fine city, with those white late nineteenth-century buildings. Then I went into an enourmous café—the sort you find only in Spain, the walls lined with mirrors and a restaurant attached to it—and ate some fried fish.

Miriam was waiting in the car, near the garage. She had put on make-up and regained her composure and the fear was gone. Mechanics straightened the bumper, the rally was over and people were streaming away. I asked her if we'd won anything. "I don't know," she answered, "it doesn't matter, let's go back to the hotel." I didn't notice the time; it must have been around three. As far as Irun we didn't say a word. At the border, when they saw that we'd taken part in the rally they waved us by, and we were back in France. It was only then that I noticed. I noticed by pure chance, because we had the sun at our backs and its reflection on the radiator ornament bothered me, as if it were sparkling in a mirror. Coming the other way, that morning, it hadn't been a bother because the wood had to some extent absorbed the chrome, leaving it opaque. I stopped the car, but I didn't get out and look more closely because I already knew. "They've changed the elephant," I said. "This one is in metal, steel or silver, I don't know which, but it's not the same." Then I thought of something else, something absurd, but I voiced it: "I want to see what's inside." Miriam looked at me and paled. Once more she was ashen grey, as at the time of the incident, and seemed to be trembling. "I'll tell you about it this evening," she said; "please, my husband will be here in a few hours and I want to go." "Is he the one you're afraid of?" I asked. "When I first met you, you told me something, do you remember? Is he the one?" She squeezed my hand, trembling. "Let's go, please," she said, "don't let's waste any more time. I want to go back to the hotel."

We made love intensely, almost convulsively, as if it were a last act, dictated by an impulse of survival. I lay, dazed, between the sheets, without sleeping, in the sort of drowsy state that allows the mind to wander from image to image. Before my eyes there paraded Albert and the Pegasus body shop, the attic on the square in Pau, a small metal elephant, a ribbonlike road along a cliff overhanging the ocean, with Miriam standing at the edge of the precipice until the Count noiselessly crept up on her and pushed her over, and she fell, hugging the handbag which she never let go. That's how my mind was working when Miriam got up and went into the bathroom. My right arm travelled down the side of the bed to the floor, searching for the bag, my hand delicately opened it and felt the butt of a revolver. Unconsciously I took it, got quickly out of bed and dressed. I looked at my watch; there was plenty of time. When Miriam came out of the bathroom she grasped the situation but did not object. I told her to pack and wait for me. "No," she said, "I'll wait for you on the beach; I'm afraid to stay alone in a hotel room." "At half-past nine," I said. "Leave the car with me," she said; "It's wiser for you to go in a taxi." I went down to pay the bill and caught a cab. Mist was falling. I got out near the station and wandered about, wondering what I was going to do and knowing perfectly well that I hadn't the slightest notion. It seemed perfectly ridiculous to wait for a man I'd seen twice in my life, and what for? To threaten him, to say that I knew he meant to kill his wife? And what if he wouldn't give up the idea? What would I do if he reacted? I turned the little toylike revolver over and over in my pocket. There were a few people in the station, the loudspeaker announced the arrival of the train and I hid, trying to look casual, behind a column on the platform. After all, he already knew me. Shall I face up to him there, I wondered, or follow him along the street? The hand gripping the revolver was sweaty. At this point people began getting off the train: a group of carefree Spaniards, a nursemaid with two blond children, a newly-wed couple, a few tourists. Finally the railway attendants opened all the train doors and, armed with brooms and suction pumps, began to clean up. A few seconds went by before I realized that he hadn't been on the train at all. Suddenly I was stricken with panic; not exactly panic but tremendous anxiety. I raced through the station, hailed a taxi, and made for the Hôtel des Palais. I could have gone on foot, but I was in a hurry. The hotel was magnificent, one of the oldest in the city, a majestic yet airy white structure. The receptionist examined the register from start to finish and from finish to start, running his finger down the list of guests. "No," he said, "we've no guest by that name." "Perhaps he hasn't arrived yet; look at the reservations, will you?" He took his list and examined it with the same care. "No, sir, I'm sorry, but there's nothing." I asked for the telephone and called the Hôtel d'Angleterre. "The lady left shortly after you," said the desk clerk. "Are you sure?" "Yes, she handed in the key and went off in the car; the porter loaded the luggage." I left the Hôtel des Palais and walked to the beach, which was only a few steps away. I went down the steps and walked slowly over the sand. It was half-past nine, a mist had fallen and the waves were high; summer nights at Biarritz can be chilly. At the place where we were to meet there was a bathhouse with a row of deck chairs. I sat down on one and looked out to sea. I heard a church bell ring out ten o'clock, then eleven and twelve. The revolver was still in my pocket; I was tempted to throw it into the ocean, but I couldn't do it, I don't know why.

Do you know, once I put an advertisement in *Le Figaro:* "Lost elephant looking for 1927 Bugatti." That's a good one, isn't it? But you've made me drink too much, Monsieur, although when it comes to drinking you're good company. Sometimes, when you've drunk a bit, reality is simplified; the gaps between one thing and another are closed, everything hangs together and you say to yourself: I've got it. Just like a dream.

But why are you interested in other people's stories? You too must be unable to fill in the gaps. Can't you be satisfied with your own dreams?

Translated from the Italian by Frances Frenaye

Ngugi wa Thiong'o
Minutes of Glory

(KENYA)

Her name was Wanjiru. But she liked better her Christian one, Beatrice. It sounded more pure and more beautiful. Not that she was ugly; but she could not be called beautiful either. Her body, dark and full fleshed, had the form, yes, but it was as if it waited to be filled by the spirit. She worked in beer halls where sons of women came to drown their inner lives in beer cans and froth. Nobody seemed to notice her. Except, perhaps, when a proprietor or an impatient customer called out her name, Beatrice; then other customers would raise their heads briefly, a few seconds, as if to behold the bearer of such a beautiful name, but not finding anybody there, they would resume their drinking, their ribald jokes, their laughter and play with the other serving girls. She was like a wounded bird in flight: a forced landing now and then but nevertheless wobbling from place to place so that she would variously be found in Alaska, Paradise, The Modern, Thome and other beer-halls all over Limuru. Sometimes it was because an irate proprietor found she was not attracting enough customers; he would sack her without notice and without a salary. She would wobble to the next bar. But sometimes she was simply tired of nesting in one place, a daily witness of familiar scenes; girls even more decidedly ugly than she were fought over by numerous claimants at closing hours. What do they have that I don't have? she would ask herself, depressed. She longed for a bar-kingdom where she would be at least one of the rulers, where petitioners would bring their gifts of beer, frustrated smiles and often curses that hid more lust and love than hate.

She left Limuru town proper and tried the mushrooming townlets around. She worked at Ngarariga, Kamiritho, Rironi and even Tiekunu and everywhere the story was the same. Oh, yes, occasionally she would get a client; but none cared for her as she would have liked, none really wanted her enough to fight for her. She was always a hard-up customer's last resort. No make-believe even, not for her that sweet pretence that men indulged in after their fifth bottle of Tusker. The following night or during a pay-day, the same client would pretend not to know her; he would be trying his money-power over girls who already had more than a fair share of admirers.

She resented this. She saw in every girl a rival and adopted a sullen attitude. Nyagũthĩ especially was the thorn that always pricked her wounded flesh. Nyagũthĩ, arrogant and aloof, but men always in her courtyard; Nyagũthĩ, fighting with men, and to her they would bring propitiating gifts which she accepted as of right. Nyagũthĩ could look bored, impatient, or downright contemptuous and still men would cling to her as if they enjoyed being whipped with biting words, curled lips and the indifferent eyes of a free woman. Nyagũthĩ was also a bird in flight, never really able to settle in one place, but in her case it was because she hungered for change and excitement: new faces and new territories for her conquest. Beatrice resented her very shadow. She saw in her the girl she would have liked to be, a girl who was both totally immersed in and yet completely above the underworld of bar violence and sex. Wherever Beatrice went the long shadow of Nyagũthĩ would sooner or later follow her.

She fled Limuru for Ilmorog in Chiri District. Ilmororg had once been a ghost village, but had been resurrected to life by that legendary woman, Nyang'endo, to whom every pop group had paid their tribute. It was of her that the young dancing Muthuu and Muchun g' wa sang:

> When I left Nairobi for Ilmorog
> Never did I know
> I would bear this wonder-child of mine
> Nyang'endo.

As a result, Ilmorog was always seen as a town of hope where the weary and the down-trodden would find their rest and fresh water. But again Nyagũthĩ followed her.

She found that Ilmorog, despite the legend, despite the songs and dances, was not different from Limuru. She tried various tricks. Clothes? But even here she never earned enough to buy herself glittering robes. What was seventy-five shillings a month without house allowance, *posho*, without salaried boy-friends? By that time, Ambi had reached Ilmorog, and Beatrice thought that this would be the answer. Had she not, in Limuru, seen girls blacker than herself transformed overnight from ugly sins into white stars by a touch of skin-lightening creams? And men would ogle them, would even talk with exaggerated pride of their newborn girl friends. Men were strange creatures, Beatrice thought in moments of searching analysis. They talked heatedly against Ambi, Butone, Firesnow, Moonsnow, wigs, straightened hair; but they always went for a girl with an Ambi-lightened skin and head covered with a wig made in imitation of European or Indian hair. Beatrice never tried to find the root cause of this black self-hatred, she simply accepted the contradiction and applied herself to Ambi with a vengeance. She had to rub out her black shame. But even Ambi she could not afford in abundance; she could only apply it to her face and to her arms so that her legs and her neck retained their blackness. Besides there were parts of her face she could not readily reach—behind the ears and above the eyelashes, for instance—and these were a constant source of shame and irritation to her Ambi-self.

She would always remember this Ambi period as one of her deepest humiliation before her later minutes of glory. She worked in Ilmorog Starlight Bar and Lodging. Nyagũthĩĩ, with her bangled hands, her huge earrings, served behind the counter. The owner was a good Christian soul who regularly went to church and paid all his dues to *Harambee* projects. Pot-belly. Grey hairs. Soft-spoken. A respectable family man, well known in Ilmorog. Hardworking even, for he would not leave the bar until the closing hours, or more precisely, until Nyagũthĩĩ left. He had no eyes for any other girl; he hung around her, and surreptitiously brought her gifts of clothes without receiving gratitude in kind. Only the promise. Only the hope for tomorrow. Other girls he gave eighty shillings a month. Nyagũthĩĩ had a room to herself. Nyagũthĩĩ woke up whenever she liked to take the stock. But Beatrice and the other girls had to wake up at five or so, make tea for the lodgers, clean up the bar and wash dishes and glasses. Then they would hang around the bar in shifts until two o'clock when they would go for a small break. At five o'clock, they had to be in again, ready for customers whom they would now serve with frothy beers and smiles until twelve o'clock or for as long as there were customers thirsty for more Tuskers and Pilsners. What often galled Beatrice, although in her case it did not matter one way or another, was the owner's insistence that the girls should sleep in Starlight. They would otherwise be late for work, he said. But what he really wanted was for the girls to use their bodies to attract more lodgers in Starlight. Most of the girls, led by Nyagũthĩĩ, defied the rule and bribed the watchman to let them out and in. They wanted to meet their regular or one-night boy-friends in places where they would be free and where they would be treated as not just barmaids. Beatrice always slept in. Her occasional one-night patrons wanted to spend the minimum. Came a night when the owner, refused by Nyagũthĩĩ, approached her. He started by finding fault with her work; he called her names, then as suddenly he started praising her, although in a grudging almost contemptuous manner. He grabbed her, struggled with her, pot-belly, grey hairs, and everything. Beatrice felt an unusual revulsion for the man. She could not, she would not bring herself to accept that which had so recently been cast aside by Nyagũthĩĩ. My God, she wept inside, what does Nyagũthĩĩ have that I don't have? The man now humiliated himself before her. He implored. He promised her gifts. But she would not yield. That night she too defied the rule. She jumped through a window; she sought a bed in another bar and only came back at six. The proprietor called her in front of all the others and dismissed her. But Beatrice was rather surprised at herself.

She stayed a month without a job. She lived from room to room at the capricious mercy of the other girls. She did not have the heart to leave Ilmorog and start all over again in a new town. The wound hurt. She was tired of wandering. She stopped using Ambi. No money. She looked at herself in the mirror. She had so aged, hardly a year after she had fallen from grace. Why then was she scrupulous, she would ask herself. But somehow she had a horror of soliciting lovers or directly bartering her body for hard cash. What she wanted was decent work and a man or several men who cared for her. Perhaps she took that need for a man, for a home and for a child with her to bed. Perhaps it was this genuine need that scared off men who wanted other things from barmaids. She wept late at nights and remembered home. At such moments, her mother's village in Nyeri seemed the sweetest place on God's earth. She would invest the life of her peasant mother and father with romantic illusions of immeasurable peace and harmony. She longed to go back home to see them. But how could she go back with empty hands? In any case the place was now a distant landscape in the memory. Her life was here in the bar among this crowd of lost strangers. Fallen from grace, fallen from grace. She was part of a generation which would never again be one with the soil, the crops, the wind and the moon. Not for them that whispering in dark hedges, not for her that dance and love-making under the glare of the moon, with the hills of TumuTumu rising to touch the sky. She remembered that girl from her home village who, despite a life of apparent glamour being the kept mistress of one rich man after another in Limuru, had gassed herself to death. This generation was not awed by the mystery of death, just as it was callous to the mystery of life; for how many unmarried mothers had thrown their babies into latrines rather than lose that glamour? The girl's death became the subject of jokes. She had gone metric—without pains, they said. Thereafter, for a week, Beatrice thought of going metric. But she could not bring herself to do it.

She wanted love; she wanted life.

A new bar was opened in Ilmorog. Treetop Bar, Lodging and Restaurant. Why Treetop, Beatrice could not understand unless because it was a storied building: tea-shop on the ground floor and beer-shop in a room at the top. The rest were rooms for five-minute or one-night lodgers. The owner was a retired civil servant but one who still played at politics. He was enormously wealthy with business sites and enterprises in every major town in Kenya. Big shots from all over the country came to his bar. Big men in Mercedeses. Big men in their Bentleys. Big men in their Jaguars and Daimlers. Big men with uniformed chauffeurs drowsing with boredom in cars waiting outside. There were others not so big who came to pay respects to the great. They talked politics mostly. And about their work. Gossip was rife. Didn't you know? Indeed so and so has been promoted. Really? And so and so has been sacked. Embezzlement of public funds. So foolish you know. Not clever about it at all. They argued, they quarrelled, sometimes they fought it out with fists, especially during the elections campaign. The only point on which they were all agreed was that the Luo community was the root cause of all the trouble in Kenya; that intellectuals and University students were living in an ivory tower of privilege and arrogance; that Kiambu had more than a lion's share of developments; that men from Nyeri and Muranga had acquired all the big business in Nairobi and were even encroaching on Chiri District; that African workers, especially those on the farms, were lazy and jealous of "us" who had sweated ourselves to sudden prosperity. Otherwise each would hymn his own praises or return compliments. Occasionally in moments of drunken ebullience and self-praise, one would order two rounds of beer for each man present in the bar. Even the poor from Ilmorog would come to Treetop to dine at the gates of the *nouveaux riches.*

Here Beatrice got a job as a sweeper and bedmaker. Here for a few weeks she felt closer to greatness. Now she made beds for men she had previously known as names. She watched how even the poor tried to drink and act big in front of the big. But soon fate caught up with her. Girls flocked to Treetop from other bars. Girls she had known at Limuru, girls she had known at Ilmorog. And most had attached themselves to one or several big men, often playing a hide-and-not-to-be-found game with their numerous lovers. And Nyagūthiī was there behind the counter, with the eyes of the rich and the poor fixed on her. And she, with her big eyes, bangled hands and earrings, maintained the same air of bored indifference. Beatrice as a sweeper and bedmaker became even more invisible. Girls who had fallen into good fortune looked down upon her.

She fought life with dreams. In between putting clean sheets on beds that had just witnessed a five-minute struggle that ended in a half-strangled cry and a pool, she would stand by the window and watch the cars and the chauffeurs, so that soon she knew all the owners by the number plates of their cars and the uniforms of their chauffeurs. She dreamt of lovers who would come for her in sleek Mercedes sports cars made for two. She saw herself linking hands with such a lover, walking in the streets of Nairobi and Mombasa, tapping the ground with high heels, quick, quick short steps. And suddenly she would stop in front of a display glass window, exclaiming at the same time; Oh darling, won't you buy me those . . . ? Those what, he would ask, affecting anger. Those stockings, darling. It was as an owner of several stockings, ladderless and holeless, that she thought of her well-being. Never again would she mend torn things. Never, never, never. Do you understand? Never. She was the next proud owner of different coloured wigs, blonde wigs, brunette wigs, Redhead wigs, Afro wigs, wigs, wigs, all the wigs in the world. Only then would the whole earth sing hallelujah to the one Beatrice. At such moments, she would feel exalted, lifted out of her murky self, no longer a floor sweeper and bedmaker for a five-minute instant love, but Beatrice, descendant of Wangu Makeri who made men tremble with desire at her naked body bathed in moonlight, daughter of Nyang'endo, the founder of modern Ilmorog, of whom they often sang that she had worked several lovers into impotence.

Then she noticed him and he was the opposite of the lover of her dreams. He came on Saturday afternoon driving a big five-ton lorry. He carefully parked it beside the Benzes, the Jaguars and the Daimlers, not as a lorry, but as one of those sleek cream-bodied frames, so proud of it he seemed to be. He dressed in a baggy grey suit over which he wore a heavy khaki military overcoat. He removed his overcoat, folded it with care, and put it in the front seat. He locked all the doors, dusted himself a little, then walked round the lorry as if inspecting it for damage. A few steps before he entered Treetop, he turned round for a final glance at his lorry dwarfing the other things. At Treetops he sat in a corner and, with a rather loud defiant voice, ordered a Kenya one. He drank it with relish, looking around at the same time for a face he might recognize. He indeed did recognize one of the big ones and he immediately ordered him a quarter bottle of Vat 69. This was accepted with a bare nod of the head and a patronizing smile; but when he tried to follow his generosity with a conversation, he was firmly ignored. He froze, sank into his Muratina. But only for a time. He tried again: he was met with frowning faces. More pathetic were his attempts to join in jokes; he would laugh rather too loudly, which would make the big ones stop, leaving him in the air alone. Later in the evening he stood up, counted several crisp hundred shilling notes and handed them to Nyagūthī behind the counter ostensibly for safekeeping. People whispered; murmured; a few laughed, rather derisively, though they were rather impressed. But this act did not win him immediate recognition. He staggered towards room no. 7 which he had hired. Beatrice brought him the keys. He glanced at her, briefly, then lost all interest.

Thereafter he came every Saturday. At five when most of the big shots were already seated. He repeated the same ritual, except the money act, and always met with defeat. He nearly always sat in the same corner and always rented room 7. Beatrice grew to anticipate his visits and, without being conscious of it, kept the room ready for him. Often after he had been badly humiliated by the big company, he would detain Beatrice and talk to her, or rather he talked to himself in her presence. For him, it had been a life of struggles. He had never been to school although getting an education had been his ambition. He never had a chance. His father was a squatter in the European settled area in the Rift Valley. That meant a lot in those colonial days. It meant among other things a man and his children were doomed to a future of sweat and toil for the white devils and their children. He had joined the freedom struggle and like the others had been sent to detention. He came from detention the same as his mother had brought him to this world. Nothing. With independence he found he did not possess the kind of education which would have placed him in one of the vacancies at the top. He started as a charcoal burner, then a butcher, gradually working his own way to become a big transporter of vegetables and potatoes from the Rift Valley and Chiri districts to Nairobi. He was proud of his achievement. But he resented that others, who had climbed to their present wealth through loans and a subsidized education, would not recognize his like. He would rumble on like this, dwelling on education he would never have, and talking of better chances for his children. Then he would carefully count the money, put it under the pillow, and then dismiss Beatrice. Occasionally he would buy her a beer but he was clearly suspicious of women, whom he saw as money-eaters of men. He had not yet married.

One night he slept with her. In the morning he scratched for a twenty shilling note and gave it to her. She accepted the money with an odd feeling of guilt. He did this for several weeks. She did not mind the money. It was useful. But he paid for her body as he would pay for a bag of potatoes or a sack of cabbages. With the one pound, he had paid for her services as a listener, a vessel of his complaints against those above, and as a one-night receptacle of his man's burden. She was becoming bored with his ego, with his stories that never varied in content, but somehow, in him, deep inside, she felt that something had been there, a fire, a seed, a flower which was being smothered. In him she saw a fellow victim and looked forward to his visits. She too longed to talk to someone. She too longed to confide in a human being who would understand.

And she did it one Saturday night, suddenly interrupting the story of his difficult climb to the top. She did not know why she did it. Maybe it was the rain outside. It was softly drumming the corrugated iron sheets, bringing with the drumming a warm and drowsy indifference. He would listen. He had to listen. She came from Karatina in Nyeri. Her two brothers had been gunned down by the British soldiers. Another one had died in detention. She was, so to speak, an only child. Her parents were poor. But they worked hard on their bare strip of land and managed to pay her fees in primary school. For the first six years she had worked hard. In the seventh year, she must have relaxed a little. She did not pass with a good grade. Of course she knew many with similar grades who had been called to good government secondary schools. She knew a few others with lesser grades who had gone to very top schools on the strength of their connections. But she was not called to any high school with reasonable fees. Her parents could not afford fees in a Harambee school. And she would not hear of repeating standard seven. She stayed at home with her parents. Occasionally she would help them in the shamba and with house chores. But imagine: for the past six years she had led a life with a different rhythm from that of her parents. Life in the village was dull. She would often go to Karatina and to Nyeri in search of work. In every office, they would ask her the same questions: what work do you want? What do you know? Can you type? Can you take shorthand? She was desperate. It was in Nyeri, drinking Fanta in a shop, tears in her eyes, that she met a young man in a dark suit and sun-glasses. He saw her plight and talked to her. He came from Nairobi. Looking for work? That's easy; in a big city there would be no difficulty with jobs. He would certainly help. Transport? He had a car—a cream-white Peugeot. Heaven. It was a beautiful ride, with the promise of dawn. Nairobi. He drove her to Terrace Bar. They drank beer and talked about Nairobi. Through the window she could see the neon-lit city and knew that here was hope. That night she gave herself to him, with the promise of dawn making her feel light and gay. She had a very deep sleep. When she woke in the morning, the man in the cream-white Peugeot was not there. She never saw him again. That's how she had started the life of a barmaid. And for one and a half years now she had not been once to see her parents. Beatrice started weeping. Huge sobs of self-pity. Her humiliation and constant flight were fresh in her mind. She had never been able to take to bar culture, she always thought that something better would come her way. But she was trapped, it was the only life she now knew, although she had never really learnt all its laws and norms. Again she heaved out and in, tears tossing out with every sob. Then suddenly she froze. Her sobbing was arrested in the air. The man had long covered himself. His snores were huge and unmistakable.

She felt a strange hollowness. Then a bile of bitterness spilt inside her. She wanted to cry at her new failure. She had met several men who had treated her cruelly, who had laughed at her scruples, at what they thought was an ill-disguised attempt at innocence. She had accepted. But not this, Lord, not this. Was this man not a fellow victim? Had he not, Saturday after Saturday, unburdened himself to her? He had paid for her human services; he had paid away his responsibility with his bottle of Tuskers and hard cash in the morning. Her innermost turmoil had been his lullaby. And suddenly something in her snapped. All the anger of a year and a half, all the bitterness against her humiliation were now directed at this man.

What she did later had the mechanical precision of an experienced hand.

She touched his eyes. He was sound asleep. She raised his head. She let it fall. Her tearless eyes were now cold and set. She removed the pillow from under him. She rummaged through it. She took out his money. She counted five crisp pink notes. She put the money inside her brassiere.

She went out of room no. 7. Outside it was still raining. She did not want to go to her usual place. She could not now stand the tiny cupboard room or the superior chatter of her roommate. She walked through mud and rain. She found herself walking towards Nyagūthiī's sleepy voice above the drumming rain.

"Who is that?"

"It is me. Please open."

"Who?"

"Beatrice."

"At this hour of the night?"

"Please."

Lights were put on. Bolts unfastened. The door opened. Beatrice stepped inside. She and Nyagūthiī stood there face to face. Nyagūthiī was in a see-through nightdress: on her shoulders she had a green pullover.

"Beatrice, is there anything wrong?" she at last asked, a note of concern in her voice.

"Can I rest here for a while? I am tired. And I want to talk to you." Beatrice's voice carried assurance and power.

"But what has happened?"

"I only want to ask you a question, Nyagūthiī."

They were still standing. Then, without a word, they both sat on the bed.

"Why did you leave home, Nyagūthiī?" Beatrice asked. Another silent moment. Nyagūthiī seemed to be thinking about the question. Beatrice waited. Nyagūthiī's voice when at last it came was slightly tremulous, unsteady.

"It is a long story, Beatrice. My father and mother were fairly wealthy. They were also good Christians. We lived under regulations. You must never walk with the heathen. You must not attend their pagan customs—dances and circumcision rites, for instance. There were rules about what, how and when to eat. You must even walk like a Christian lady. You must never be seen with boys. Rules, rules all the way. One day instead of returning home from school, I and another girl from a similar home ran away to Eastleigh. I have never been home once this last four years. That's all."

Another silence. Then they looked at one another in mutual recognition.

"One more question, Nyagũthĩĩ. You need not answer it. But I have always thought that you hated me, you despised me."

"No, no, Beatrice, I have never hated you. I have never hated anybody. It is just that nothing interests me. Even men do not move me now. Yet I want, I need instant excitement. I need the attention of those false flattering eyes to make me feel myself, myself. But you, you seemed above all this—somehow you had something inside you that I did not have."

Beatrice tried to hold her tears with difficulty.

Early the next day, she boarded a bus bound for Nairobi. She walked down Bazaar street looking at the shops. Then down Government Road, right into Kenyatta Avenue, and Kimathi street. She went into a shop near Hussein Suleman's street and bought several stockings. She put on a pair. She next bought herself a new dress. Again she changed into it. In a Bata Shoe-shop, she bought high heeled shoes, put them on and discarded her old flat ones. On to an Akamba kiosk, and she fitted herself with earrings. She went to a mirror and looked at her new self. Suddenly she felt enormous hunger as if she had been hungry all her life. She hesitated in front of Moti Mahal. Then she walked on, eventually entering Fransae. There was a glint in her eyes that made men's eyes turn to her. This thrilled her. She chose a table in a corner and ordered Indian curry. A man left his table and joined her. She looked at him. Her eyes were merry. He was dressed in a dark suit and his eyes spoke of lust. He bought her a drink. He tried to engage her in conversation. But she ate in silence. He put his hand under the table and felt her knees. She let him do it. The hand went up and up her thigh. Then suddenly she left her unfinished food and her untouched drink and walked out. She felt good. He followed her. She knew this without once turning her eyes. He walked beside her for a few yards. She smiled at herself but did not look at him. He lost his confidence. She left him standing sheepishly looking at a glass window outside Gino's. In the bus back to Ilmorog, men gave her seats. She accepted this out of right. At Treetops bar she went straight to the counter. The usual crowd of big men was there. Their conversations stopped for a few seconds at her entry. Their lascivious eyes were turned to her. The girls stared at her. Even Nyagũthĩĩ could not maintain her bored indifference. Beatrice bought them drinks. The manager came to her, rather unsure. He tried a conversation. Why had she left work? Where had she been? Would she like to work in the bar, helping Nyagũthĩĩ behind the counter? Now and then? A barmaid brought her a note. More notes came from different big quarters with one question; would she be free tonight? A trip to Nairobi even. She did not leave her place at the counter. But she accepted their drinks as of right. She felt a new power, confidence even.

She took out a shilling, put it in the slot and the juke box boomed with the voice of Robinson Mwangi singing Hũnyũ wa Mashambani. He sang of those despised girls who worked on farms and contrasted them with urban girls. Then she played a Kamaru and a D.K. Men wanted to dance with her. She ignored them, but enjoyed their flutter around her. She twisted her hips to the sound of yet another D.K. Her body was free. She was free. She sucked in the excitement and tension in the air.

Then suddenly at around six, the man with the five-ton lorry stormed into the bar. This time he had on his military overcoat. Behind him was a policeman. He looked around. Everybody's eyes were raised to him. But Beatrice went on swaying her hips. At first he could not recognize Beatrice in the girl celebrating her few minutes of glory by the juke box. Then he shouted in triumph. "That is the girl! Thief! Thief!"

People melted back to their seats. The policeman went and handcuffed her. She did not resist. Only at the door she turned her head and spat. Then she went out followed by the policeman.

In the bar the stunned silence broke into hilarious laughter when someone made a joke about sweetened robbery without violence. They discussed her. Some said she should have been beaten. Others talked contemptuously about "these bar girls." Yet others talked with a concern noticeable in unbelieving shakes of their heads about the rising rate of crime. Shouldn't the Hanging Bill be extended to all thefts of property? And without anybody being aware of it the man with the five-ton lorry had become a hero. They now surrounded him with questions and demanded the whole story. Some even bought him drinks. More remarkable, they listened, their attentive silence punctuated by appreciative laughter. The averted threat to property had temporarily knit them into one family. And the man, accepted for the first time, told the story with relish.

But behind the counter Nyagũthĩ wept.

Tatyana Tolstaya

On the Golden Porch

(RUSSIA)

FOR MY SISTER, SHURA
On the golden porch sat:
Tsar, tsarevich, king, prince,
Cobbler, tailor.
Who are you?
Tell me fast, don't hold us up.

—CHILDREN'S COUNTING RHYME

In the beginning was the garden. Childhood was a garden. Without end or limit, without borders and fences, in noises and rustling, golden in the sun, pale green in the shade, a thousand layers thick—from heather to the crowns of the pines: to the south, the well with toads, to the north, white roses and mushrooms, to the west, the mosquitoed raspberry patch, to the east, the huckleberry patch, wasps, the cliff, the lake, the bridges. They say that early in the morning they saw a *completely* naked man at the lake. Honest. Don't tell Mother. Do you know who it was?—It can't be.—Honest, it was. He thought he was alone. We were in the bushes.—What did you see?—*Everything.*

Now, that was luck. That happens once every hundred years. Because the only available naked man—in the anatomy textbook—isn't real. Having torn off his skin for the occasion, brazen, meaty, and red, he shows off his clavicular-sternum-nipple muscles (all dirty words!) to the students of his eighth grade. When we're promoted (in a hundred years) to the eighth grade, he'll show us all that too.

The old woman, Anna Ilyinichna, feeds her tabby cat, Memeka, with red meat like that. Memeka was born after the war and she has no respect for food. Digging her four paws into the pine tree trunk, high above the ground, Memeka is frozen in immobile despair.

"Memeka, meat, meat!"

The old woman shakes the dish of steaks, lifts it higher for the cat to see better.

"Just look at that meat!"

The cat and the old woman regard each other drearily. "Take it away," thinks Memeka.

"*Meat*, Memeka."

In the suffocating undergrowths of Persian red lilac, the cat mauls sparrows. We found a sparrow like that. Someone had scalped its toy head. A naked fragile skull like a gooseberry. A martyred sparrow face. We made it a cap of lace scraps, made it a white shroud, and buried it in a chocolate box. Life is eternal. Only birds die.

Four carefree dachas stood without fences—go wherever you want. The fifth was a privately owned house. The black log framework spread sideways from beneath the damp overhang of maples and larches and growing brighter, multiplying its windows, thinning out into sun porches, pushing aside nasturtiums, jostling lilacs, avoiding hundred-year-old firs, it ran out laughing onto the southern side and stopped above the smooth strawberry-dahlia slope *down-down-down* where warm air trembles and the sun breaks up on the open glass lids of magical boxes filled with cucumber babies inside rosettes of orange flowers.

By the house (and what was inside?), having flung open all the windows of the July-pierced veranda, Veronika Vikentievna, a huge white beauty, weighs strawberries: for jam and for sale to neighbors. Luxurious, golden, applelike beauty! White hens cluck at her heavy feet, turkey-cocks stick their indecent faces out of the burdock, a red-and-green rooster cocks his head and looks at us: what do you want, girls? "We'd like some strawberries." The beautiful merchant's wife's fingers in berry blood. Burdock, scales, basket.

Tsaritsa! The greediest woman in the world:

> They pour foreign wines for her,
> She eats iced gingerbread,
> Terrifying guards surround her. . . .

Once she came out of the dark shed with red hands like that, smiling. "I killed a calf . . ."

> Axes over their shoulders. . . .

Aargh! Let's get out of here, run, it's horrible—an icy horror—shed, damp, death. . . .

And Uncle Pasha is the husband of this scary woman. Uncle Pasha is small, meek, henpecked. An old man: he's fifty. He works as an accountant in Leningrad; he gets up at five in the morning and runs over hill and dale to make the commuter train. Seven kilometers at a run, ninety minutes on the train, ten minutes on the trolley, then put on black cuff protectors and sit down on a hard yellow chair. Oilcloth-covered doors, a smoky half-basement, weak light, safes, overhead costs—that's Uncle Pasha's job. And when the cheerful light blue day has rushed past, its noise done, Uncle Pasha climbs out of the basement and runs back: the postwar clatter of trolleys, the smoky rush-hour station, coal smells, fences, beggars, baskets; the wind chases crumpled paper along the emptied platform. Wearing sandals in summer and patched felt boots in winter, Uncle Pasha hurries to his Garden, his Paradise, where evening peace comes from the lake, to the House where the huge, golden-haired Tsaritsa lies waiting on a bed with four glass legs. But we didn't see the glass legs until later. Veronika Vikentievna had been feuding a long time with Mother.

The thing was that one summer she sold Mother an egg. There was an iron-clad condition: the egg had to be boiled and eaten immediately. But light-hearted Mother gave the egg to the dacha's owner. The crime was revealed. The consequences could have been monstrous: the landlady could have let her hen sit on the egg, and in its chicken ignorance it could have incubated a copy of the unique breed of chicken that ran in Veronika Vikentievna's yard. It's a good thing nothing happened. The egg was eaten. But Veronika Vikentievna could not forgive Mother's treachery. She stopped selling us strawberries and milk, and Uncle Pasha smiled guiltily as he ran past. The neighbors shut themselves in; they reinforced the wire fence on metal posts, sprinkled broken glass in strategic points, stretched barbed wire and got a scary yellow dog. Of course, that wasn't enough.

After all, couldn't Mother still climb over the fence in the dead of night, kill the dog, crawl over the glass, her stomach shredded by barbed wire and bleeding, and with weakening hands steal a runner from the rare variety of strawberries in order to graft it onto her puny ones? After all, couldn't she still run to the fence with her booty and with her last ounce of strength, groaning and gasping, toss the strawberry runner to Father hiding in the bushes, his round eyeglasses glinting in the moonlight?

From May to September, Veronika Vikentievna, who suffered from insomnia, came out into the garden at night, stood in her long white nightgown holding a pitchfork like Neptune, listening to the nocturnal birds, breathing jasmine. Of late her hearing had grown more acute: Veronika Vikentievna could hear Mother and Father three hundred yards away in our dacha, with the camel's hair blanket over their heads, plotting in a whisper to get Veronika Vikentievna: they would dig a tunnel to the greenhouse with her early parsley.

The night moved on, and the house loomed black behind her. Somewhere in the dark warmth, deep in the house, lost in the bowels of their connubial bed, little Uncle Pasha lay still as a mouse. High above his head swam the oak ceiling, and even higher swam the garrets, trunks of expensive black coats sleeping in mothballs, even higher the attic with pitchforks, clumps of hay, and old magazines, and even higher the roof, the chimney, the weather vane, the moon—across the garden, through dreams, they swam, swaying, carrying Uncle Pasha into the land of lost youth, the land of hopes come true, and the chilled Veronika Vikentievna, white and heavy, would return, stepping on his small warm feet.

Hey, wake up, Uncle Pasha! Veronika is going to die soon.

You will wander around the empty house, not a thought in your head, and then you will straighten, blossom, look around, remember, push away memories and desire, and bring—to help with the housekeeping—Veronika's younger sister, Margarita, just as pale, large, and beautiful. And in June she'll be laughing in the bright window, bending over the rain barrel, passing among the maples on the sunny lake.

Oh, in our declining years. . . .

But we didn't even notice, we forgot Veronika, we had spent a winter, a whole winter, a winter of mumps and measles, flooding and warts and a Christmas tree blazing with tangerines, and they made a fur coat for me, and a lady in the yard touched it and said: "Mouton."

In the winter the yardmen glued golden stars onto the black sky, sprinkled ground diamonds into the connecting courtyards of the Petrograd side of town and, clambering up the frosty air ladders to our windows, prepared morning surprises: with fine brushes they painted the silver tails of firebirds.

And when everyone got sick of winter, they took it out of town in trucks, shoving the skinny snowbanks into underground passages protected by gratings, and smeared perfumed mush with yellow seedlings around the parks. And for several days the city was pink, stone, and noisy.

And from over there, beyond the distant horizon, laughing and rumbling, waving a motley flag, the green summer came running with ants and daisies.

Uncle Pasha got rid of the yellow dog—he put it in a trunk and sprinkled it with mothballs; he let summer renters onto the second floor—a strange, dark woman and her fat granddaughter; and he invited kids into the house and fed them jam.

We hung on the fence and watched the strange grandmother fling open the second-story windows every hour and, illuminated by the harlequin rhomboids of the ancient panes, call out:

"Want milkandcookies?"

"No."

"Want potty?"

"No."

We hopped on one leg, healed scrapes with spit, buried treasures, cut worms in half with scissors, watched the old woman wash pink underpants in the lake, and found a photograph under the owner's buffet: a surprised, big-eared family with the caption, "Don't forget us. 1908."

Let's go to Uncle Pasha's. You go first. No, you. Careful, watch the sill. I can't see in the dark. Hold on to me. Will he show us *the room*. He will, but first we have to have tea.

Ornate spoons, ornate crystal holders. Cherry jam. Silly Margarita laughs in the orange light of the lamp shade. Hurry up and drink! Uncle Pasha knows, he's waiting, holding open the sacred door to Aladdin's cave. O room! O children's dreams! O Uncle Pasha, you are King Solomon! You hold the Horn of Plenty in your mighty arms. A caravan of camels passed with spectral tread through your house and dropped its Baghdad wares in the summer twilight. A waterfall of velvet, ostrich feathers of lace, a shower of porcelain, golden columns of frames, precious tables on bent legs, locked glass cases of mounds where fragile yellow glasses are entwined by black grapes, where Negroes in golden skirts hide in the deep darkness, where something bends, transparent, silvery . . . Look, a precious clock with foreign numbers and snakelike hands. And this one, with forget-me-nots. Ah, but look, look at that one! There's a glass room over the face and in it a golden Chevalier seated at a golden table, a golden sandwich in his hand. And next to him, a Lady with a goblet: and when the clock strikes, she strikes the goblet on the table—*six, seven, eight*. . . . The lilacs are jealous, they peek through the window, and Uncle Pasha sits down at the piano and plays the *Moonlight* Sonata. Who are you, Uncle Pasha?

There it is, the bed on glass legs. Semitransparent in the twilight, invisible and powerful, they raise on high the tangle of lace, the Babylon towers of pillows, the moonlit, lilac scent of the divine music. Uncle Pasha's noble white head is thrown back, a Mona Lisa smile on Margarita's golden face as she appears silently in the doorway, the lace curtains sway, the lilacs sway, the waves of dahlias sway on the slope right to the horizon, to the evening lake, to the beam of moonlight.

Play, play, Uncle Pasha! Caliph for an hour, enchanted prince, starry youth, who gave you this power over us, to enchant us, who gave you those white winds on your back, who carried your silvery head to the evening skies, crowned you with roses, illuminated you with mountain light, surrounded you with lunar wind?

> *O Milky Way, light brother*
> *Of Canaan's milky rivers,*
> *Should we swim through the starry fall*
> *To the fogs, where entwined*
> *The bodies of lovers fly?*

. . . Well, enough. Time to go home. It doesn't seem right to use the ordinary word "Thanks" with Uncle Pasha. Have to be more ornamental: "I am grateful." "It's not worthy of gratitude."

"Did you notice they have only one bed in the house?"

"Where does Margarita sleep, then? In the attic?"

"Maybe. But that's where the renters are."

"Well, then she must sleep on the porch, on a bench."

"What if they sleep in the same bed, head to foot?"

"Stupid. They're strangers."

"You're stupid. What if they're lovers?"

"But they only have lovers in France."

She's right, of course, I forgot.

. . . Life changed the slides ever faster in the magic lantern. With Mother's help we penetrated into the mirrored corners of the grownups' atelier, where the bald tubby tailor took our embarrassing measurements, muttering *excuse me's;* we envied girls in nylon stockings, with pierced ears, we drew in our textbooks: glasses on Pushkin, a mustache on Mayakovsky, a large white chest on Chekhov, who was otherwise normally endowed. And we were recognized immediately and welcomed joyfully by the patient and defective nude model from the anatomy course generously offering his numbered innards; but the poor fellow no longer excited anyone. And, looking back once, with unbelieving fingers we felt the smoked glass behind which our garden waved a hankie before going down for the last time. But we didn't feel the loss yet.

Autumn came into Uncle Pasha's house and struck him on the face. Autumn, what do you want? Wait; are you kidding? . . . The leaves fell, the days grew dark, Margarita grew stooped. The white chickens died, the turkey flew off to warmer climes, the yellow dog climbed out of the trunk and, embracing Uncle Pasha, listened to the north wind howl at night. Girls, someone, bring Uncle Pasha some India tea. How you've grown. How old you've gotten, Uncle Pasha. Your hands are spotted, your knees bent. Why do you wheeze like that? I know, I can guess; in the daytime, vaguely, and at night, clearly, you hear the clang of metal locks. The chain is wearing out.

What are you bustling about for? You want to show me your treasures? Well, all right, I have five minutes for you. It's so long since I was here! I'm getting old. So that's *it*, *that's* what enchanted us? All this secondhand rubbish, these chipped painted night tables, these tacky oilcloth paintings, these brocade curtains, the worn plush velvet, the darned lace, the clumsy fakes from the peasant market, the cheap beads? This sang and glittered, burned and beckoned? What mean jokes you play, life! Dust, ashes, rot. Surfacing from the magical bottom of childhood, from the warm, radiant depths, we open our chilled fist in the cold wind—and what have we brought up with us besides sand? But just a quarter century ago Uncle Pasha wound the golden clock with trembling hands. Above the face, in the glass room, the little inhabitants huddle—the Lady and the Chevalier, masters of Time. The Lady strikes the table with her goblet, and the thin ringing sound tries to break through the shell of decades. *Eight, nine, ten.* No. Excuse me, Uncle Pasha. I have to go.

. . . Uncle Pasha froze to death on the porch. He could not reach the metal ring of the door and fell face down in the snow. White snow daisies grew between his stiff fingers. The yellow dog gently closed his eyes and left through the snowflakes up the starry ladder to the black heights, carrying away the trembling living flame.

The new owner—Margarita's elderly daughter—poured Uncle Pasha's ashes into a metal can and set it on a shelf in the empty chicken house; it was too much trouble to bury him.

Bent in half by the years, her face turned to the ground, Margarita wanders through the chilled, drafty garden, as if seeing lost footsteps on the silent paths.

"You're cruel! Bury him!"

But her daughter smokes indifferently on the porch. The nights are cold. Let's turn on the lights early. And the golden Lady of Time, drinking bottoms up from the goblet of life, will strike a final midnight on the table for Uncle Pasha.

Translated from the Russian by Antonina W. Bouis

Rose Tremain

John-Jin

(ENGLAND)

When I was a child, the pier was a promising place.

You walked along and along and along it, with all its grey sea underneath, and at the end of it was the Pavilion.

"Now," my father used to say, "here we are." He was a person who enjoyed destinations. Inside the Pier Pavilion were far more things going on than you could imagine from the outside; it was like a human mind in this one respect. You could drink tea or rum or 7-Up in there. You could play the fruit machines or buy a doll made of varnished shells. You could shoot at a line of tin hens to win a goldfish. You could talk about your life to a fortune teller or ride a ghost train. There was a section of the great glass roof from which flamenco music came down. And under the music was a Miniature Golf track.

My father and I used to play. Our two miniature golf balls followed each other over bridges and through castle gates and round little slalom arrangements until they reached their destination. This destination was a wishing well and every time we played both of us had to make a wish, no matter who won the game. My wishes changed with time, but I know now that my father's did not. I wished for a pair of wings and a trampoline and a pet reptile and flamenco dancing lessons. My father wished for John-Jin.

Then, when I was ten, the Pavilion detached itself from the pier in a storm and moved five inches out to sea.

I remember saying: "Five inches isn't much." My father replied: "Don't be silly, Susan." My mother took my hand and said: "It's a building, pet. Imagine if this house were to move."

They closed the whole pier. Things separated from their destinations can become unsafe. When we went down to the beach, I used to walk to the locked pier gates, on which the word "Danger" hung like an advertisement for an old red car, and watch the tugs and cranes dismantling the Pavilion bit by bit. They towed it all away and stacked it on a car park. Their idea was to raise all the money it would cost to bring it back and rebuild it and join it onto the pier again, but no one said when this would be.

It was the year 1971. It was the year I got my flamenco shoes and began my Spanish dancing lessons. It was the year that John-Jin arrived.

He was Chinese.

He'd been left wrapped in a football scarf in a woman's toilet in Wetherby. He'd been found and taken to a hospital and christened John-Jin by the nurses there. How he came to be ours was a story nobody told me then. No one seemed to remember, either, what colour the football scarf was or if it had a team name on it. "The details don't matter, love," said my mother, changing John-Jin's nappy on her lap; "what matters is that he's with us now. We've waited for him for ten years and here he is."

"Do you mean," I said, "that you *knew* he was going to come?"

"Oh, yes."

"So you had someone waiting in that toilet all that time?"

"No, no, pet! We didn't know *where* he was going to come from. We never thought of him being Chinese necessarily. We were just certain that he'd arrive one day."

He was as beautiful as a flower. His eyes were like two little fluttering creatures that had landed on the flower. If I'd been an ogress in a story, I would have eaten John-Jin. I used to put his flat face against mine and kiss it. And I entertained him when my parents were busy. They'd put him in a baby-bouncer that hung from a door lintel and I'd get out my castanets and put on my flamenco shoes and dance for him. The first word he ever said was *olé*. When he learned to stand up, he went stamp, stamp, stamp in his red bootees.

"Don't wear him out, Susan," said my mother. "He's only one."

"I'm not," I said. "I'm helping him get strong."

When he was in bed sometimes, with his gnome night-light on, I'd creep into his room and tell him about the world. I told him about the building of a gigantic wall in China and about the strike of the school dinner ladies. I told him about the Miniature Golf and the wishing well. I said: "The Pier Pavilion was there and then not. There and then not. And that happens to certain things and I don't know why."

Making the pier safe took two years. People in our town were asked to "sponsor a girder." You could have your name cast in the girder and then you would be able to imagine the waves breaking against it. I liked the idea of the sea breaking against my name, but my parents decided that it was John-Jin who needed his own girder more. They said: "You never know, Susan. Doing this might help in some way."

We needed help now for John-Jin. Something was going wrong. He could do everything he was meant to do—talk, bounce, walk, laugh, eat and sing—except grow. He just did not grow. Nobody explained why. Our doctor said: "Remember his origins. He's going to be a very small person, that's all." But we thought that was a poor answer.

We kept on and on measuring him. He grew in minute little bursts and stopped again. When he was three, he could still fit into the baby-bouncer. I wanted to buy him his first pair of flamenco shoes, but his feet were too small. At his nursery school, he was seven inches shorter than the shortest girl. The little tables and chair were too high for him and the steps going up to the slide too far apart. The nursery teacher said to my mother: "Are you seeking advice from the right quarters?" And that night, my parents sat up talking until it got light and I went down and found them both asleep in their armchairs, like old people.

The next day, we all went out in an eel boat to see John-Jin's girder bolted onto the pier. John-Jin kept trying to reach down into the eel tank to stroke the eels; he wasn't very interested in his girder. My mother and father looked exhausted. It was a bright day and they kept trying to shade their eyes with their fingers. I thought the girder was beautiful—as if it had been made in Spain. It was curved and black and John-Jin's name stood out in the sunlight. This was one of the last girders to be put in place. Our eel boat was anchored right where the pavilion used to be. And so I said to John-Jin: "Pay attention. Look. Without your girder, they couldn't have finished mending the pier." He blinked up at it, his straight, thick eyelashes fluttering in the bright light. Then he turned back to the eels.

"Where are they going?" he asked.

My parents took John-Jin to a specialist doctor in Manchester. Every part of his body was measured, including his penis and his ears. My mother said: "Don't worry, Susan, he's far too young to feel embarrassed."

A course of injections was prescribed for him. He had to go to the surgery every week to get one. I said: "What are they injecting you *with*, John-Jin?"

"Something," he said.

"Just a growth hormone, dear," said my mother.

I was going to ask, what is a "growth hormone?" Where does it come from? But a time in my life had come when I couldn't carry on a conversation of any length without my thoughts being interrupted. The person who interrupted them was my flamenco dancing partner, Barry. He was fifteen. He wore an earring and a spangled matador jacket. When I danced with Barry, I wore a scarlet flamenco skirt with black frills and a flower from Woolworths in my hair. And so, instead of asking more about John-Jin's growth hormones, I went dancing with Barry in my mind. I replaced the subject of growth hormones with the smell of Barry's underarm deodorant and the sight of his shining teeth. I knew my mind was a vast pavilion, capable of storing an unimaginable quantity of knowledge, but all that was in it—at this moment in my life—was a single item.

And then, John-Jin began growing.

We measured him against the kitchen door. When he got to three feet, we gave a party, to which Barry came minus his earring and danced with John-Jin on his shoulders. John-Jin had a laugh like a wind chime. Barry said when he left. "That kid. He's so sweet. In't he?"

"Now we can stop worrying," said my mother. "Everything's going to be

OK. He'll never be tall because his parents almost certainly weren't tall, but he'll be much nearer a normal size. And that's all we were asking for."

I know something important now. Don't ask for a thing unless you know precisely and absolutely what it is you're going to get and how you're going to get it. Don't ask for the old Pier Pavilion back. There's no such thing as the old Pier Pavilion. There will only be the *new* Pier Pavilion and it will be different. It will not be what you wanted in your imagination. My parents asked for something to make John-Jin grow. They didn't ask what that "something" was and nor did I. And together we allowed in the unknown.

It took some time to show itself. It took ten years exactly.

I had become a dance student in London when I first learned about it. In a cold phone box, I heard my father say: "We waited so long for another child. I used to wish for John-Jin at the end of every game of Miniature Golf. Remember that?"

I said: "Yes, Dad. Except you never told me what it was you were wishing for."

"Didn't I? Well, never mind. But . . . after all that . . . I never, Susan . . . I mean I never thought about the possibility of losing him."

"Shall I come home?" I said.

It was near to Christmas. John-Jin was twelve years old. He lay in bed without moving. His curtains were drawn, to rest his eyes, and he had his old gnome night-light on. He said it reminded him of being happy. His speech was beginning to go, but he wanted to talk and talk, while he could still remember enough words. He said: "Suze, I can't hardly move a toe, but I can still chat, *olé!* Tell me about the world."

I said: "Here's some news, then. Remember Barry?"

"Yes."

"Well, he's in prison. I went to visit him. He stole a van. He remembers you. He sent—"

"If you don't love him any more, it doesn't matter," said John-Jin.

"No, it doesn't," I said, "but he was a good dancer."

I sat in a chair by John-Jin's bed and he stared up at me. His face-like-a-flower was smooth and creamy and undamaged. After a while, he said: "I've had it, Suze. Did they tell you?"

I took his hand, which felt cold and heavy in mine. "Not necessarily," I said, but he ignored this. He knew every detail about his disease, which had been named after two German scientists called Creutzfeldt and Jacob. It was called CJD for short. It had been there in the growth hormones and had lain dormant in John-Jin for ten years.

He explained: "The hormones come from human glands. The chief source of pituitaries used to be the mental hospitals—the cadavers no one minded about—and some of these died of CJD. Mum and Dad are going to sue, but it's much too late. Someone should have known, shouldn't they?"

"Why didn't they?"

John-Jin shook his head. He said: "I can still move my neck, see? I can turn it and look at the room. So why don't you get a flamenco tape and dance while I can still see you. You could become a star, and I would have missed it all."

I found the music and an old pair of castanets. I put on a black skirt and fixed a bit of tinsel to my hair. I was ready to begin when I looked down and saw that John-Jin was crying. "Sorry, Suze," he said. "Get Mum to come and clean me first. I've no control over anything now. I live in a fucking toilet."

In the dark December afternoon, I walked out along the pier on my own, along and along it to where it ended at the deep water.

I imagined John-Jin's girder underneath me. I wondered, in my rage, if you took that one piece away, would everything fall?

Luisa Valenzuela

Who, Me a Bum?

(ARGENTINA)

When I'm in front of my bowl of lentils and I count them one by one, I tell myself that we've seen better days—right, kid? And I pat myself on the shoulder a bit, gently of course, not like before when a hearty slap on the back didn't bother me any. Not now though, the old mechanism is breaking down what with food being so scarce. Get out of here, they shout at me, you have to make room for somebody else, and I put my violin in its case, that is to say I tuck my head between my shoulders—the only thing that belongs to me—and go to the subway station to get warm.

There's a great ruckus in the station and, remembering the old saying that there's much to be gained from confusion, I take advantage of it to slip in free through the entrance for those with commuter tickets. Nobody says a word to me, they're all yelling and running around. Somebody complains:

"Damn it, he would choose this time of day to jump under the train, disgraceful, committing suicide when everybody's on the way to work, no one has the right to do that, what's the boss going to say, you've always got some excuse he's going to say, why did that guy have to choose my train, I'll be late and what can I say, it's all that imbecile's fault."

I immediately identify, but I'd be hard put to tell with which of the two: the guy that's complaining or the suicide. A few years ago I'd have identified with the grouch, but now it's with the suicide. Perhaps I'm wrong. Perhaps I should have committed suicide when I was called teacher and wore a suit and tie and was eager to get to the classroom on time, whereas now I can allow myself the luxury of complaining since I've nothing to lose. Not any more. When you're risking something your protest is weaker, it becomes hollow and you don't allow yourself to take it too seriously for fear it might boomerang, as everyone knows. But now—why not?—a punch in the nose for the sake of protest might do me some good since I was such a coward in the past. Protesting would be like being born again, I'd be again on the alert, so here I go:

A suicide, gentlemen? What a disgrace, what a scandal. He has no consideration for those of us who have to be at work on time. He must have been somebody who didn't know what it was like to work, to have to earn a living by the sweat of one's brow. A brow that's none too noble or full of ideas but nevertheless—beg your pardon, I shouldn't digress. A suicide, gentlemen, ladies—you women who must be working in this time of starvation when a husband's salary isn't enough to pay for food. And now the subways aren't running and we must be above ground and find some other means of transportation, and so we lose more time and money. A suicide who doesn't appreciate the harm he's doing us by choosing this early morning hour instead of throwing himself under a train at ten at night, say, when only idlers are riding the subway. And all that just to call attention to himself.

"And what do you think you're doing? Stop yelling—you're under arrest."

"I was protesting like a good citizen—"

"Yeah, yeah."

Obviously, protesting isn't for me. But here behind bars I at least have my own place and it's not as cold as they say. I've already written my name on the wall and an almost illegible comment on the police in general and Corporal Figueras in particular. Apart from that, I can only note that the shouting bothers me a lot—the moaning and groaning and those swear words in the night when one doesn't know where they come from or why.

In the past I was a Spanish teacher in high school and so I know what I'm saying, or rather I know how to say what I'm saying. The screams in the night wake me up, and I feel the same healthy indignation as the man who protested the suicide in the subway. I want to protest now too, but my mind is distracted by these grotesque drunks who share my lodgings but not my humiliation. The cries send shivers up my spine every night and it's getting worse; I demand to be transferred to a penal institution like everybody else. Get me out of this infernal police station.

They're finally letting me go. Yes. They've pushed me out in the street: good-by to food that's awful but regular, good-by to a flea-ridden blanket but a blanket nonetheless. Back to seeing where I can get a little dough for eats, back to the daily grind, to this city that's more and more impossible, where I can't even get in a little morning snooze because the 8:37 A.M. suicide comes then and interferes with my rest.

Translated from the Spanish by Helen Lane

Edmund White

Cinnamon Skin

(UNITED STATES)

When I was a kid, I was a Buddhist and an atheist, but I kept making bargains with God: if he'd fulfill a particular wish, I'd agree to believe in him. He always came through, but I still withheld my faith, which shows, perhaps, how unreasonable rationality can be.

One of God's miracles occurred when I was thirteen. I was spending most of that year with my father in Cincinnati; my mother, a psychologist, thought I needed the promixity of a man, even though my father then ignored me and was uninterested in teaching me baseball or tennis, sports in which he excelled. My father and stepmother were going to Mexico for a winter holiday that would not, alas, fall during my Christmas school break, although it was unlikely that he would have invited me even if I had been free, since the divorce agreement specified nothing about winter vacations. One long weekend, I returned to Chicago to see my mother and sister, and fell on my knees beside my bed in the dark and prayed that I'd be invited to come along anyway. The next morning my mother received a telegram from my father asking me to join him in Cincinnati the following day for a three-week car trip to Acapulco. He'd already obtained advance assignments from my teachers; he would supervise my homework.

My mother had a phobia about speaking to my father, and spent thirty-five years without ever hearing his voice. If vocal communication was forbidden, the exchange of cordial but brief tactical notes or telegrams was acceptable, provided it didn't occur regularly. My mother's generation believed in something called *character,* and it was established through self-discipline. Anyway, my mother suggested that I phone my father, since court etiquette prevented her from doing so.

The next day I took the train to Cincinnati; it was the James Whitcomb Riley, named after the Hoosier Poet ("When the frost is on the punkin," one of his odes begins). At the end of each car, there were not scenes of rural Indiana, as one might have expected, but, instead, large reproductions of French Impressionist paintings—hayricks, water lilies. Notre-Dame, mothers and children *en fleurs* ... This train, which I took twice a month to visit my dad when I was living with my mom, or to visit Mom when I was living with Dad, was the great forcing shed of my imagination: no one knew me; I was free to become anyone. I told one startled neighbor that I was English and in America for the first time, affecting an accent so obviously fabricated and snobbish that it eventually provoked a smile. I told another I had leukemia but was in remission. Another time I said that both my parents had just died in a car crash, and I was going to live with a bachelor uncle. Once I chatted up a handsome young farmer, his face stiff under its burn, his T-shirt incapable of containing the black hair sprouting up from under it; he inspired a tragic opera that I started writing the next week; it was called "Orville."

On this trip, my imagination was busy with a thick guidebook on Mexico I'd checked out of the public library. I read everything I could about Toltecs, Aztecs, and Mayans; but the astrology bored me, as did the bloody attacks and counterattacks, and one century blended into another without a single individual's emerging out of the plumed hordes—until the tragic Montezuma (a new opera subject, even more heartrending than Orville, whose principal attribute had been a smell of Vitalis hair tonic and, more subtly, of starch and ironing, a quality difficult to render musically).

The year was 1953; my father and stepmother rode in the front of his new, massive Cadillac—shiny pale-blue metal and chrome and, inside, an oiled, dark-blue leather with shag carpet—and I had so much space in the back seat that I could stretch out full length, slightly nauseated from the cigars that my father chain-smoked and his interminable monologues about the difference between stocks and bonds. While in the States, he listened to broadcasts of the news, the stock reports, and sporting events, three forms of impersonal entertainment that I considered to be as tedious as the Toltecs' battles.

I lay in the back seat, knocking my legs together in an agony of unreleased desire. My head filled with vague daydreams, as randomly rotating as the clouds I could see up above through the back window. In those days, the speed limit was higher than now and the roads were just two-lane meanders; there was no radar and no computers, and if a cop stopped us for speeding my father tucked a five-dollar bill under his license and instantly we were urged on our way with a cheerful wave and a "Y'all come back, yuh heah?" My father then resumed his murderous speed, lunging and turning and braking and swearing, and I hid so I wouldn't witness, white-knuckled, the near-disasters. As night fell, the same popular song, the theme song from the film *Moulin Rouge,* was played over and over again on station after station, like a flame being passed feebly from torch to torch in a casual marathon.

We stopped in Austin, Texas, to see my grandfather, who was retired and living alone in a small wooden house he rented. He was famous locally for his "nigger" jokes, which he collected in self-published books with titles such as *Let's Laugh, Senegambian Sizzles, Folks Are Funny,* and *Chocolate Drops from the South,* and he made fun of me for saying "Cue" Klux Klan instead of "Koo"—an organization he'd once belonged to, and accepted as a harmless if stern fraternity. He was dull, like my father, though my father was different: whereas my grandfather was gregarious but disgustingly self-absorbed, my

father was all facts, all business, misanthropic, his racism genial and condescending, though his anti-Semitism was virulent and reeked of hate. He
wanted as little contact as possible with other people. And while he liked
women, he regarded them as silly and flighty and easy to seduce; they excited
men but weren't themselves sexual, although easily tricked into bed. Men he
despised, even boys.

My stepmother, Kay, was "cockeyed and harelipped," according to my mother,
although the truth was she simply had a lazy eye that wandered in and out of
focus and an everted upper lip that rose on one side like Judy Garland's whenever she hit a high note. Kay read constantly, anything at all; she'd put down
Forever Amber to pick up *War and Peace,* trade in *Désirée* for *Madame Bovary,* but the next day she couldn't remember a thing about what she'd been
reading. My father, who never finished a book, always said, when the subject
of literature came up, "You'll have to ask Kay about that. She's the reader in
this family." He thought novels were useless, even corrupting; if he caught me
reading he'd find me a chore to do, such as raking the lawn.
  My father liked long-legged redheads in high heels and short nighties, if his
addiction to *Esquire* and its illustrations was any indication, but my stepmother was short and dumpy, like my mother, though less intelligent. She'd
been brought up on a farm in northern Ohio by a scrawny father in bib overalls and a pretty, calm, roundfaced mother from Pennsylvania Dutch country,
who said "mind" for "remember." ("Do you mind that time we went to the
caves in Kentucky?") Kay had done well in elocution class, and even now she
could recite mindless doggerel with ringing authority—and with the sort of
steely diction and hearty projection that are impossible to tune out. She could
paint—watercolors of little Japanese maidens all in a row, or kittens or pretty
flowers—and her love of art led her to be a volunteer at the art museum,
where she worked three hours a week in the gift shop run by the Ladies' Aux-
iliary. Oh, she had lots of activities and belonged to plenty of clubs—the
Ladies' Luncheon Club and the Queen City Club and the Keyboard Club.
  Kay had spent her twenties and thirties being a shrewd, feisty office "gal"
who let herself be picked up by big bored businessmen out for a few laughs
and a roll in the hay with a good sport. She always had a joke or a wisecrack to
dish up, she'd learned how to defend herself against a grabby drunk, and she
always knew the score. I'm not sure how I acquired this information about
her early life. Probably from my mother, who branded Kay a Jezebel, an unattractive woman with secret sexual power, someone like Wallis Simpson. After Kay married my father, however, and moved up a whole lot of social
rungs, she pretended to be shocked by the very jokes she used to deliver. She
adopted the endearingly dopey manner of the society matron immortalized
in Helen E. Hokinson's *New Yorker* cartoons. Dad gave her an expensive
watch that dangled upside down from a brooch (so that only Kay could read
it), which she pinned to her lapel: a bow of white and yellow gold studded
with beautiful lapis lazuli. Her skirts became longer, her voice softer, her hair

grayer, and she replaced her native sassiness with an acquired innocence. She'd always been cunning rather than intelligent, but now she appeared to become naïve as well, which in our milieu was a sign of wealth: only rich women were sheltered; only the overprotected were unworldly. As my real mother learned to fend for herself, my stepmother learned to feign incompetence.

Such astute naïveté, of course, was only for public performance. At home, Kay was as crafty as ever. She speculated out loud about other people's motives and pieced together highly unflattering scenarios based on the slimmest evidence. Every act of kindness was considered secretly manipulative, any sign of generosity profoundly selfish. She quizzed me for hours about my mother's finances (turbulent) and love life (usually nonexistent, sometimes disastrous). She was, of course, hoping that Mother would remarry so Dad wouldn't have to pay out the monthly alimony. My sister was disgusted that I'd betray our mother's secrets, but Kay bewitched me. We had few entertainments and spent long, tedious hours together in the stifling Cincinnati summer heat, and I'd been so carefully sworn to silence by my mother that, finally, when one thing came out, I told all. I was thrilled to have a promise to break.

Kay and my father fought all the time. She'd pester him to do something or challenge him over a trivial question of fact until he exploded: "God damn it, Kay, shut your goddam mouth, you don't know what the hell you're talking about, and I don't want to hear one more goddam word out of your mouth! I'm warning you to shut it and shut it now. Got it?"

"Oh, E. V.," she wailed (his nickname; his middle name was Valentine), "you don't have to talk to me that way, you're making me sick, physically sick, my heart is pounding, and, look, I'm sweating freely, I'm soaked right through, my underarms are drenched, and you know—my high *blood* pressure." Here she'd break off and begin blubbering. She had only to invoke her blood pressure ("Two hundred and fifty over a hundred and ten," she'd mysteriously confide) in order to win the argument and subdue my red-faced father. I pictured the two of them as thermometers in which the mounting mercury was about to explode through the upper tip. Kay constantly referred to her imminent death, often adding, "Well, I won't be around much longer to irritate you with my remarks, which you find so *stupid* and *ignorant.*"

My father filled his big house with Mahler, and played it throughout the night; he went to sleep at dawn. And the more socially successful Kay became the less she conformed to his hours. They scarcely saw each other. During the hot Cincinnati days, while Daddy slept in his air-conditioned room, Kay and I spent the idle hours talking to each other. I bit my nails; she paid me a dollar a nail to let them grow. When they came in, I decided I wanted them longer and longer and shaped like a woman's; Kay promised to cut them as I desired, but each time she tricked me and trimmed them short while I whined my feeble protests: "C'mon. I want them long and *pointy.* . . . Kay! You *promised!*" I danced for her in my underpants; once I did an elaborate (and very girly) striptease. As I became more and more feminine; she became increasingly masculine. She put one leg up and planted her foot on the chair seat, hugging her knee to her chest as a guy might. I felt I was dancing for a man.

Perhaps she watched me because she was bored and had nothing else to do. Or perhaps she knew these games attached me to her with thrilling, erotic bonds; in the rivalry with my mother for my affections, she was winning.

Or perhaps she got off on me. I remember that she gave me long massages with baby oil as I lay on the Formica kitchen table in my underpants, and I sprang a boner. Her black maid watched us and smiled benignly. Her name was Naomi and she'd worked for Kay one day a week ironing before Kay married; afterward she moved in as a full-time, live-in employee in my father's big house. She knew Kay's earlier incarnation as a roaring girl and no doubt wondered how far she'd go now.

In fact, she went very far. Once when I told her I was constipated she had me mount the Formica table on all fours and administered a hot-water enema out of a blue rubber pear she filled and emptied three times before permitting me to go to the toilet and squirt it out.

My whole family was awash with incestuous desires. When my real mother was drunk (as she was most nights), she'd call out from her bed and beg me to rub her back, then moan with pleasure as I kneaded the cool, sweating dough. My sister was repulsed by our mother's body, but I once walked in on her and my father in his study in Cincinnati. She must have been fourteen or fifteen. She was sitting in a chair and he stood behind her, brushing her long blond hair and quietly crying. (It as the only time I ever saw him cry.) Later she claimed she and Daddy had made love. She said she and I'd done it in an upper berth on the night train from Chicago to Cincinnati once, but I can't quite be sure I remember it.

When I was twelve, Kay was out of town once and Daddy took me to dinner at the Gourmet Room, a glass-walled dome on top of the Terrace Hilton. The restaurant had a mural by Miró and French food. Daddy drank a lot of wine and told me I had my mother's big brown eyes. He said boys my age were rather like girls. He said there wasn't much difference between boys and girls my age. I was thrilled. I tried to be warm and intuitive and seductive.

Now, as we approached the Mexican border, Kay started teasing me: "I hope you have on very clean underpants, Eddie, because the Mexican police strip-search every tourist and if they find skid marks in your Jockey shorts they may not let you in."

My father thought this was a terrific joke and with his thin-lipped smile nodded slowly and muttered, "She's serious, and she's a hundred percent right."

Although I worried about my panties, I half hoped that a brown-skinned, mustachioed guard in a sweat-soaked uniform would look into them, and at my frail, naked body: even though I was convinced that I'd never been uglier. I had a brush cut Kay had forced on me ("You'll be hot if you don't get all that old hair out of your face"), and my white scalp showed through it. I wore glasses with enormous black frames and looked like an unappealing quiz kid, without the budding intellectual's redeeming brashness. I was ashamed of my recently acquired height, cracking voice, and first pubic hairs, and I posed in front of the foggy bathroom mirror with a towel turban around my head and my penis pushed back and concealed between my legs. In public, I'd fold into myself like a Swiss Army knife, hoping to occupy as little space as possible.

But at the border the guards merely waved us through after querying my father about the ten cartons of Cuban cigars in the trunk (Dad had to grease a few palms to convince them the cigars were for his own use, not for resale). We drove down the two-lane Pan-American Highway from the Rio Grande through an endless flat cactus desert into the mountains. Kay encouraged me to wave at the tiny, barefoot Indians walking along the highway in their bright costumes, their raven-black hair hanging straight down to their shoulders. Sometimes they'd shake their fists at our retreating fins, but I seemed to be the only one who noticed.

From the highway, we seldom saw villages or even houses, although from time to time we noticed a red flag that had been tossed into the top of a mesquite tree. Daddy said the flag signified that a cow had just been slaugh-tered. "Since they don't have refrigeration," he informed us through a cloud of cigar smoke, his tiny yellow teeth revealed in a rare smile, "they must sell all the edible parts of the animal and cook them within a few hours." I don't know how he knew that, although he had grown up in Texas, worked summers as a cowboy, and must have known many Mexicans. I was struck by his equanimity in contemplating such shameful poverty, which would have disgusted him had we still been in the States; in Mexico, he smiled benignly at it, as though it were an integral part of a harmonious whole.

My father had a passion for travelling long hours and making record time. He also had ironclad kidneys. Kay had to stop to pee every hour. Perhaps her blood-pressure medicine was a diuretic. "Anyway," she whined, "I don't understand why we have to rush like this. What's the hurry? For Pete's sake, E. V., we're in a foreign country and we should take a gander at it. *No es problema?*"

Before her marriage, when she was still just my father's secretary and "mis-tress" (my mother's lurid, old-fashioned word), Kay would have said, "For Christ's sake." If she now replaced "Christ with "Pete, she did so as part of her social beatification. She might actually have said "take a gander" when she was a farm girl in northern Ohio, but now it was placed between gently inverted commas to suggest that she was citing, with mild merriment but without con-tempt, an endearingly rural but outdated Americanism. Like many English-speaking North Americans, she thought foreign languages were funny, as though no one would ordinarily speak one except as a joke. *"No es problema?"* was her comic contribution to the mishap of being in Mexico, the verbal equivalent of a jumping bean.

Halfway to Mexico City we stopped at a beautiful old colonial-style hotel that had what it advertised as the world's largest porch, wrapped around it on all four sides. Meek Indian women were eternally on all fours scrubbing tiles the garnet color of fresh scabs still seeping blood. That night, Kay and Dad and I walked past banana trees spotlit orange and yellow and a glowing swimming pool that smelled of sulfur. *"Pee-you,"* Kay said, holding her little nose with her swollen, red-nailed fingers.

It's a sulfur spa, Kay," Dad explained. "The Mexicans think it has curative powers."

We entered a roomy, high-ceilinged cave in which a band was playing so-phisticated rumbas. The headwaiter, broad and tall as a wardrobe, wore a double-breasted jacket.

"Uno whiskey," Dad said once we were seated, showing off for our benefit. "*Y* two Coca-Cola *por favorita."*

"Sí, señor!" the headwaiter shouted before he reclaimed his dignity by palming the order off with lofty disdain on a passing Indian busboy in a collar-less blue jacket.

All the other guests at the hotel appeared to be rich Mexicans. No one around us was speaking English. The most attractive people I'd ever seen were dancing an intricate samba, chatting and smiling to each other casually while their slender hips swivelled into and out of provocative postures, and their small, expensively shod feet shuffled back and forth in a well-rehearsed, syncopated trot.

Daddy was decked out in a pleated jacket with side tabs that opened up to accommodate extra girth; I think it was called a Havana shirt. Suddenly both he and Kay looked impossibly sexless in their pale, perspiring bodies. In my blood the marimbas had lit a crackling fire, a fiery longing for the Mexican couple before me, their bodies expert and sensual, their manner light and sophisticated—a vision of a civilized sexuality I'd never glimpsed before. Out-side, however, the heavy sulfur smell somehow suggested an animal in rut, just as the miles of unlit rural night around the cave made me jumpy. There was no-where to go, and the air was pungent with smoke from hearths and filled with the cry of cocks; in the distance were only the shadowy forms of the mountains.

In Mexico City, we stayed in a nineteen-thirties hotel on the Reforma. There were then only two million people in "México," as the citizens called their beautiful city, with a proud use of synecdoche. People swarmed over our car at each stoplight, proferring lottery tickets, but we kept our windows closed and sailed down the spacious boulevards. We saw the Ciudad Universitaria under construction outside town, with its bold mural by Diego Rivera—a lien on a bright future, a harbinger of progress. We visited the Museum of Modern Art and ate in a French restaurant, Normandie, a few blocks away. We as-cended the hill to the fortress castle of Chapultepec, where the Austrian rulers, the lean Maximilian, the pale Carlota, had lived. We were poled in bar-ques through floating gardens and climbed the Aztecs' step pyramids.

We were accompanied everywhere by one of Daddy's business associates and his wife. After I corrected this man ("Not the eighteenth century," I snapped, "that was in the *sixteenth*"), Daddy drew me aside and said, "Never contradict another person like that, especially someone older. Just say 'I may be wrong but I thought I read somewhere . . .' or 'What do I know, but it seems . . .' Got it? Best to let it just go by, but if you must correct him do it that way. And by the way, don't say you *love* things. Women say that. Rather, say you *like* things."

I had always been proud of noticing the fatuous remarks made by adults. Now I was appalled to learn that my father had been vexed by things I said. I was half flattered by his attention (he was looking at me, after all) but also half irritated at how he wanted me to conform to his idea of a man.

We went to Cuernavaca and saw the flower-heavy walls of its mansions, then to Taxco, where Kay bought a very thin silver bracelet worked into interlocking flowers. The heat made her heavy perfume, Shalimar, smell all the stronger; its muskiness competed with my father's cigar smoke. Only I had no smell at all. Daddy warned us to look for tarantulas in our shoes before we put them on.

We arrived at Acapulco, still a chic beach resort, not the paved-over fast-food hellhole it would become, and stayed at the Club de Pesca. I had a room to myself on a floor above my father and Kay's. The manager had delivered baskets of soft and slightly overripe fruit to our rooms; after a day, the pineapple smelled pungent.

One night we went to a restaurant in a hotel on top of a cliff and watched teen-age boys in swimsuits shed their silk capes and kneel before a spotlit statue of the Virgin, then plunge a hundred and fifty feet down into the waves flowing into and out of a chasm. Their timing had to be exact or they'd be dashed on the rocks. They had superb, muscled bodies, tan skin, glinting religious medals, and long black hair slicked back behind their ears. Afterward, the divers walked among the crowd, passing a hat for coins, their feet huge, their faces pale behind their tans, their haughty smiles at odds with the look of shock in their eyes.

The popular song that year in Mexico was "Piel Canela" ("Cinnamon Skin"), an ode to a beautiful mulatto girl. In the States, reference to color was considered impolite, although everyone told racist jokes in private; here, apparently, a warm brown color was an attribute of beauty. In the afternoons on the beach, young water-ski instructors stretched their long brown arms and legs, adjusting themselves inside their swimsuits, offering to give lessons to pale tourists, both male and female. We gringos had a lot to learn from them.

A singer and movie star from Argentina, Libertad Lamarque, was staying in our hotel. When we rode up in the elevator with her, she was wearing a tailored white linen suit and had a clipped, snowy-white Chihuahua on a leash. It turned out that her room was next to mine. I became friendly with her daughter—I don't remember how we met. Although Libertad was in exile from Perón's Argentina, her daughter still lived most of the time in Buenos Aires, where she sang American ballads in a night club. One night she volunteered to sing "You Go to My Head" at the Club de Pesca—yes, that must be how I met her. I went up to congratulate her and was surprised to discover she scarcely spoke English, though she sang it without an accent.

Libertad's daughter must have found me amusing, or perhaps docile, or a convenient alibi for her midday mid-ocean pastimes. She invited me to go out on her speedboat late the next morning; after dropping anchor, she and the handsome Indian driver kissed and embraced for an hour. I didn't know what to do with my eyes, so I watched. The sun was hot but the breeze constant. That night I was so burned Kay had to wrap me in sheets drenched in cold water.

I moaned and turned for two days and nights in wet sheets. A local doctor came and went. My fever soared. In my confused, feverish thoughts I imagined that I'd been burned by the vision of that man and woman clawing at each other on the varnished doors that folded down over the speedboat's powerful motor.

The man who had accompanied Libertad's daughter on the piano was a jowly Indian in his late thirties. Perhaps he smiled at me knowingly or held my hand a second too long when we were introduced, but I honestly can't remember his giving me the slightest sign of being interested in me. And yet I became determined to seduce him. My skin was peeling in strips, like long white gauze, revealing patches of a cooked-shrimp pink underneath. My mirror told me the effect wasn't displeasing; in fact the burn brought out my freckles and gave me a certain raffishness. Perhaps soon I, too, would have cinnamon skin. Until now, I'd resembled a newly shorn sheep.

One night at ten, my well-sauced father, atypically genial, sent me off to bed with a pat on the shoulder. But, instead of undressing and going to sleep, I prepared myself for a midnight sortie. I showered in the tepid water that smelled of chlorine and pressed my wet brush-cut hair flat against my skull. From my chest I coaxed off another strip of dead skin; I felt I was unwinding a mummy. I soaked myself in a cheap aftershave made by Mennen and redolent of the barbershop (witch hazel and limes). I sprinkled the toilet water onto the sheets. I put on a fresh pair of white Jockey underpants and posed in front of the mirror. I rolled the waistband down until it revealed just a tuft of newly sprouting pubic hair. I danced my version of the samba toward the mirror and back again. I wriggled out of my undershorts, turned, and examined my buttocks. I kissed my shoulder, then stood on tiptoe and looked at my chest, belly button, penis.

At last, my watch told me it was midnight. I dressed in shorts and a pale-green shirt and new sandals and headed down toward the bar. My legs looked as long and silky as those of Dad's pinups. I stood beside the piano and stared holes through the musician; I hoped he could smell my aftershave. He didn't glance up at me once, but I felt he was aware of my presence.

He took his break between sets and asked me if I wanted to walk to the end of the dock. When we got there we sat on a high-backed bench, which hid us from view. We looked out across the harbor at the few lights on the farther shore, one of them moving. A one-eyed car or a motor scooter climbed the road and vanished over the crest of a hill. A soft warm breeze blew in over the Pacific.

Some people lived their whole lives beside the restless, changeable motions of the ocean, rocked by warm breezes night and day, their only clothing the merest concession to decency, their bodies constantly licked by water and wind. I who had known the cold Chicago winters, whose nose turned red and hands blue in the arctic temperatures, whose scrotum shrank and feet went numb, who could scarcely guess the gender, much less discern the degree of beauty, under those moving gray haystacks of bonnets, mittens, overcoats, and scarves—here, in Mexico, I felt my body, browned and peeled into purity, expand and relax.

The pianist and I held hands. He said, "I could come up to your room after I get off at four in the morning."

"I'm in Room 612," I said.

I looked over my shoulder and saw my very drunk father weaving his way toward me. When he was halfway out the dock, I stood up and hailed him.

"Hi, Daddy," I said. "I just couldn't sleep. I decided to come down and relax. Do you know Pablo, the pianist from the bar?" I made up the name out of thin air.

"Hello, Pablo," They shook hands. "Now you better get to bed, young man."

"O.K. Good night, Daddy. Good night, Pablo."

Back in my room, I looked at the luminescent dial on my watch as it crept toward two, then three. I had no idea what sex would be like; in truth, I had never thought about it. I just imagined our first embrace would be as though we were in a small wooden boat floating down a river by moonlight. Pablo and I would live here by the sea; I'd learn to make tortillas.

I woke to the sound of shouts in the hall. Oh, no! I'd given Pablo not my room number, 610, but that of Libertad Lamarque, 612. I could hear her angry denunciations in Spanish and Pablo's timid murmurs. At last, she slammed her door shut and I opened mine. I hissed for him to come in. He pushed past me, I shut the door, and he whispered curses in Spanish against me. He sat on the edge of the bed, a mountain that had become a volcano. I knelt on the floor before him and looked up with meek eyes, pleading for forgiveness.

I was appalled by the mistake in room numbers. In my fantasies love was easy, a costume drama, a blessed state that required neither skill nor aptitude but was conferred—well, on *me*, simply because I wanted it so much and because, even if I wasn't exactly worthy of it, I would become so once love elected me. Now my hideous error showed me that I wasn't above mishaps and that a condition of cinematic bliss wasn't automatic.

Pablo undressed. He didn't kiss me. He pulled my underpants down, spit on his wide, stubby cock, and pushed it up my ass. He didn't hold me in his arms. My ass hurt like hell. I wondered if I'd get blood or shit on the sheets. He was lying on top of me, pushing my face and chest into the mattress. He plunged in and out. It felt like I was going to shit, and I hoped I would be able to hold it in. I was afraid I'd smell and repulse him. He smelled of old sweat.

His fat belly felt cold as it pressed against my back. He breathed a bit harder, then abruptly stopped his movements. He pulled out and stood up. He must have ejaculated. It was in me now. He headed for the bathroom, switched on the harsh light, washed his penis in the bowl, and dried it off with one of the two small white towels that the maid brought every day. He had to stand on tiptoe to wash his cock properly in the bowl.

I sat on the edge of the bed and put my underpants back on. The Indian dressed and put one finger to his lips as he pulled open the door and stuck his head out to see if all was clear. Then he was gone.

A couple of years later, when my dad found out I was gay, he said, "It's all your mother's fault, I bet. When did it first happen?" He was obsessed with such technicalities.

"I was with *you,* Daddy," I said, triumphant. "It was in Acapulco that time, with the Indian who played the piano in the Club de Pesca."

A year later, after he'd made another trip with Kay to Acapulco, he told me he'd asked a few questions and learned that the pianist had been caught molesting two young boys in the hotel and had been shot dead by the kids' father, a rich Mexican from Mexico City. I never knew whether the story was true or just a cautionary tale dreamed up by Daddy. Not that he ever had much imagination.

Recently I was in Mexico City to interview Maria Felix, an old Mexican movie star. She kept me waiting a full twenty-four hours while she washed her hair (as she explained). I wandered around the city, still in ruins from a recent earthquake. The beautiful town of two million had grown into a filthy urban sprawl of slums where twenty-four million people now lived and milled around and starved.

I returned to my hotel. My room was on the fifteenth floor of a shoddy tower. I had an overwhelming desire—no, not a desire, a compulsion—to jump from the balcony. It was the closest I ever came to suicide. I sealed the glass doors and drew the curtains, but still I could feel the pull. I left the room, convinced that I'd jump if I stayed there another moment.

I walked and walked, and I cried as I went, my body streaked by passing headlights. I felt that we'd been idiots back then, Dad and Kay and I, but we'd been full of hope and we'd come to a beautiful Art Deco hotel, the Palacio Nacional, and we'd admired the castle in Chapultepec Park and the fashionable people strolling up and down the Reforma. We'd been driving in Daddy's big Cadillac, Kay was outfitted in her wonderfully tailored Hattie Carnegie suit, with the lapel watch Daddy had given her dangling from the braided white and yellow gold brooch studded with lapis lazuli.

Now they were both dead, and the city was dirty and crumbling, and the man I was travelling with was sero-positive, and so was I. Mexico's hopes seemed as dashed as mine, and all the goofy innocence of that first thrilling trip abroad had died, my boyhood hopes for love and romance faded, just as the blue in Kay's lapis had lost its intensity year after year, until it ended up as white and small as a blind eye.

Zoë Wicomb

You Can't Get Lost in Cape Town

(SOUTH AFRICA)

In my right hand resting on the base of my handbag I clutch a brown leather purse. My knuckles ride to and fro, rubbing against the lining . . . surely cardboard . . . and I am surprised that the material has not revealed itself to me before. I have worn this bag for months. I would have said with a dismissive wave of the hand, "Felt, that is what the base of this bag is lined with."

Then, Michael had said, "It looks cheap, unsightly," and lowering his voice to my look of surprise, "Can't you tell?" But he was speaking of the exterior, the way it looks.

The purse fits neatly into the palm of my hand. A man's purse. The handbag gapes. With my elbow I press it against my hip but that will not avert suspicion. The bus is moving fast, too fast, surely exceeding the speed limit, so that I bob on my seat and my grip on the purse tightens as the springs suck at my womb, slurping it down through the plush of the red upholstery. I press my buttocks into the seat to ease the discomfort.

I should count out the fare for the conductor. Perhaps not; he is still at the front of the bus. We are now travelling through Rondebosch so that he will be fully occupied with white passengers at the front. Women with blue-rinsed heads tilted will go on telling their stories while fishing leisurely for their coins and just lengthen a vowel to tide over the moment of paying their fares.

"Don't be so anxious," Michael said. "It will be all right." I withdrew the hand he tried to pat.

I have always been anxious and things are not all right; things may never be all right again. I must not cry. My eyes travel to and fro along the grooves of the floor. I do not look at the faces that surround me but I believe that they are lifted speculatively at me. Is someone constructing a history for this hand resting foolishly in a gaping handbag? Do these faces expect me to whip out an amputated stump dripping with blood? Do they wince at the thought of a hand, cold and waxen, left on the pavement where it was severed? I draw my hand out of the bag and shake my fingers ostentatiously. No point in inviting conjecture, in attracting attention. The bus brakes loudly to conceal the sound of breath drawn in sharply at the exhibited hand.

Two women pant like dogs as they swing themselves on to the bus. The conductor has already pressed the bell and they propel their bodies expertly along the swaying aisle. They fall into seats opposite me—one fat, the other thin—and simultaneously pull off the starched servants' caps which they scrunch into their laps. They light cigarettes and I bite my lip. Would I have to vomit into this bag with its cardboard lining? I wish I had brought a plastic bag; this bag is empty save for the purse. I breathe deeply to stem the nausea that rises to meet the curling bands of smoke and fix on the bulging bags they grip between their feet. They make no attempt to get their fares ready; they surely misjudge the intentions of the conductor. He knows that they will get off at Mowbray to catch the Golden Arrow buses to the townships. He will not allow them to avoid paying; not he who presses the button with such promptness.

I watch him at the front of the bus. His right thumb strums an impatient jingle on the silver levers, the leather bag is cradled in the hand into which the coins tumble. He chants a barely audible accompaniment to the clatter of coins, a recitation of the newly decimalised currency. Like times tables at school and I see the fingers grow soft, bending boyish as they strum an ink-stained abacus; the boy learning to count, leaning earnestly with propped elbows over a desk. And I find the image unaccountably sad and tears are about to well up when I hear an impatient empty clatter of thumb-play on the coin dispenser as he demands, "All fares please" from a sleepy white youth. My hand flies into my handbag once again and I take out the purse. A man's leather purse.

Michael too is boyish. His hair falls in a straight blond fringe into his eyes. When he considers a reply he wipes it away impatiently, as if the hair impedes thought. I cannot imagine this purse ever having belonged to him. It is small, U-shaped and devoid of ornament, therefore a man's purse. It has an extending tongue that could be tucked into the mouth or be threaded through the narrow band across the base of the U. I take out the smallest note stuffed into this plump purse, a five-rand note. Why had I not thought about the busfare? The conductor will be angry if my note should exhaust his supply of coins although the leather bag would have a concealed pouch for notes. But this thought does not comfort me. I feel angry with Michael. He has probably never travelled by bus. How would he know of the fear of missing the unfamiliar stop, the fear of keeping an impatient conductor waiting, the fear of saying fluently, "Seventeen cents please," when you are not sure of the fare and produce a five-rand note? But this is my journey and I must not expect Michael to take responsibility for everything. Or rather, I cannot expect Michael to take responsibility for more than half the things. Michael is scrupulous about this division; I am not always sure of how to arrive at half. I was never good at arithmetic, especially this instant mental arithmetic that is sprung on me.

How foolish I must look sitting here clutching my five-rand note. I slip it back into the purse and turn to the solidity of the smoking women. They have still made no attempt to find their fares. The bus is going fast and I am surprised that we have not yet reached Mowbray. Perhaps I am mistaken, perhaps we have already passed Mowbray and the women are going to Sea Point to serve a nightshift at the Pavilion.

Marge, Aunt Trudie's eldest daughter, works as a waitress at the Pavilion but she is rarely mentioned in our family. "A disgrace," they say. "She should know better than to go with white men."

"Poor whites," Aunt Trudie hisses. 'She can't even find a nice rich man to go steady with. Such a pretty girl too. I won't have her back in this house. There's no place in this house for a girl who's been used by white trash."

Her eyes flash as she spits out a cherished vision of a blond young man sitting on her new vinyl sofa to whom she serves gingerbeer and koeksisters, because it is not against the law to have a respectable drink in a Coloured home. "Mrs. Holman," he would say, "Mrs Holman, this is the best gingerbeer I've had for years."

The family do not know of Michael even though he is a steady young man who would sit out such a Sunday afternoon with infinite grace. I wince at the thought of Father creaking in a suit and the unconcealed pleasure in Michael's successful academic career.

Perhaps this is Mowbray after all. The building that zooms past on the right seems familiar. I ought to know it but I am lost, hopelessly lost, and as my mind gropes for recognition I feel a feathery flutter in my womb, so slight I cannot be sure, and again, so soft, the brush of a butterfly, and under cover of my handbag I spread my left hand to hold my belly. The shaft of light falling across my shoulder, travelling this route with me, is the eye of God. God will never forgive me.

I must anchor my mind to the words of the women on the long seat opposite me. But they fall silent as if to protect their secrets from me. One of them bends down heavily, holding on to the jaws of her shopping bag as if to relieve pressure on her spine, and I submit to the ache of my own by swaying gently while I protect my belly with both hands. But having eyed the contents of her full bag carefully, her hand becomes the beak of a bird dipping purposefully into the left-hand corner and rises triumphantly with a brown paper bag on which grease has oozed light-sucking patterns. She opens the bag and her friend looks on in silence. Three chunks of cooked chicken lie on a piece of greaseproof paper. She deftly halves a piece and passes it to her thin friend. The women munch in silence, their mouths glossy with pleasure.

"These are for the children," she says, her mouth still full as she wraps the rest up and places it carelessly at the top of the bag.

"It's the spiced chicken recipe you told me about." She nudges her friend. "Lekker hey!"

The friend frowns and says, "I like to taste a bit more cardamom. It's nice to find a whole cardamom in the food and crush it between your teeth. A cardamom seed will never give up all its flavour to the pot. You'll still find it there in the chewing."

I note the gaps in her teeth and fear for the slipping through of cardamom seeds. The girls at school who had their two top incisors extracted in a fashion that raged through Cape Town said that it was better for kissing. Then I, fat and innocent, nodded. How would I have known the demands of kissing?

The large woman refuses to be thwarted by criticism of her cooking. The chicken stimulates a story so that she twitches with an irrepressible desire to tell.

"To think," she finally bursts out, "that I cook them this nice surprise and say what you like, spiced chicken can make any mouth water. Just think, it was yesterday when I say to that one as she stands with her hands on her hips against the stove saying, 'I don't know what to give them today, I've just got too much organising to do to bother with food.' And I say, feeling sorry for her, I say, 'Don't you worry about a thing, Marram, just leave it all in cook's hands (wouldn't it be nice to work for really grand people where you cook and do nothing else, no bladdy scrubbing and shopping and all that) . . . in cook's hands,' I said," and she crows merrily before reciting: "And I'll dish up a surprise / For Master Georgie's blue eyes.

"That's Miss Lucy's young man. He was coming last night. Engaged, you know. Well there I was on my feet all day starching linen, making roeties and spiced lentils and sweet potato and all the lekker things you must mos have with cardamom chicken. And what do you think she says?"

She pauses and lifts her face as if expecting a reply, but the other stares grimly ahead. Undefeated she continues, "She says to me, 'Tiena,' because she can't keep out of my pots, you know, always opening my lids and sniffing like a brakhond she says, 'Tiena,' and waits for me to say, 'Yes Marram,' so I know she has a wicked plan up her sleeve and I look her straight in the eye. She smile that one, always smile to put me off the track, and she say looking into the fridge, 'You can have this nice bean soup for your dinner so I can have the remains of the chicken tomorrow when you're off.' So I say to her, 'That's what I had for lunch today,' and she say to me, 'Yes I know but me and Miss Lucy will be on our own for dinner tomorrow,' and she pull a face, 'Ugh, how I hate reheated food.' Then she draws up her shoulders as if to say, That's that.

"Cheek hey! And it was a great big fowl." She nudges her friend. "You know for yourself how much better food tastes the next day when the spices are drawn right into the meat and anyway you just switch on the electric and there's no chopping and crying over onions, you just wait for the pot to dance on the stove. Of course she wouldn't know about that. Anyway, a cheek, that's what I call it, so before I even dished up the chicken for the table, I took this," and she points triumphantly to her bag, "and to hell with them."

The thin one opens her mouth, once, twice, winding herself up to speak.

"They never notice anyway. There's so much food in their pantries, in the fridge and on the tables; they don't know what's there and what isn't." The other looks pityingly at her.

"Don't you believe that. My marram was as cross as a bear by the time I brought in the pudding, a very nice apricot ice it was, but she didn't even look at it. She know it was a healthy grown fowl and she count one leg, and she know what's going on. She know right away. Didn't even say, 'Thank you

Tiena.' She won't speak to me for days but what can she do?" Her voice softens into genuine sympathy for her madam's dilemma.

"She'll just have to speak to me." And she mimics, putting on a stern horse face. " 'We'll want dinner by seven tonight,' then 'Tiena the curtains need washing,' then, 'Please, Tiena, will you fix this zip for me, I've got absolutely nothing else to wear today.' And so on the third day she'll smile and think she's smiling forgiveness at me."

She straightens her face. "No," she sighs, "the more you have, the more you have to keep your head and count and check up because you know you won't notice or remember. No, if you got a lot you must keep snaps in your mind of the insides of all the cupboards. And every day, click, click, new snaps of the larder. That's why that one is so tired, always thinking, always reciting to herself the lists of what's in the cupboards. I never know what's in my cupboard at home but I know my Sammie's a thieving bastard, can't keep his hands in his pockets."

The thin woman stares out of the window as if she had heard it all before. She has finished her chicken while the other, with all the talking, still holds a half-eaten drumstick daintily in her right hand. Her eyes rove over the shopping bag and she licks her fingers abstractedly as she stares out of the window.

"Lekker hey!" the large one repeats, "the children will have such a party."

"Did Master George enjoy it?" the other asks.

"Oh he's a gentleman all right. Shouted after me, 'Well done, Tiena. When we're married we'll have to steal you from madam.' Dressed to kill he was, such a smart young man, you know. Mind you, so's Miss Lucy. Not a prettier girl in our avenue and the best-dressed too. But then she has mos to be smart to keep her man. Been on the pill for nearly a year now; I shouldn't wonder if he don't feel funny about the white wedding. Ooh, you must see her blush over the pictures of the wedding gowns, so pure and innocent she think I can't read the packet. 'Get me my headache pills out of that drawer Tiena,' she say sometimes when I take her cup of cocoa at night. But she play her cards right with Master George; she have to 'cause who'd have what another man has pushed to the side of his plate. A bay leaf and a bone!" and moved by the alliteration the image materialises in her hand. "Like this bone," and she waves it under the nose of the other, who starts. I wonder whether with guilt, fear or a debilitating desire for more chicken.

"This bone," she repeats grimly, "picked bare and only wanted by a dog." Her friend recovers and deliberately misunderstands, "Or like yesterday's bean soup, but we women mos know that food put aside and left to stand till tomorrow always has a better flavour. Men don't know that hey. They should get down to some cooking and find out a thing or two."

But the other is not deterred. "A bone," she insists, waving her visual aid, "a bone."

It is true that her bone is a matt grey that betrays no trace of the meat or fat that only a minute ago adhered to it. Master George's bone would certainly look nothing like that when he pushes it aside. With his fork he would coax off the fibres ready to fall from the bone. Then he would turn over the whole, deftly, using a knife, and frown at the sinewy meat clinging to the joint before pushing it aside towards the discarded bits of skin.

This bone, it is true, will not tempt anyone. A dog might want to bury it only for a silly game of hide and seek.

The large woman waves the bone as if it would burst into prophecy. My eyes follow the movement until the bone blurs and emerges as the Cross where the head of Jesus lolls sadly, his lovely feet anointed by sad hands, folded together under the driven nail. Look, Mamma says, look at those eyes molten with love and pain, the body curved with suffering for our sins, and together we weep for the beauty and sadness of Jesus in his white loincloth. The Roman soldiers stand grimly erect in their tunics, their spears gleam in the light, their dark beards are clipped and their lips curl. At midday Judas turns his face to the fading sun and bays, howls like a dog for its return as the darkness grows around him and swallows him whole with the money still jingling in the folds of his saffron robes. In a concealed leather purse, a pouch devoid of ornament.

The buildings on this side of the road grow taller but oh, I do not know where I am and I think of asking the woman, the thin one, but when I look up the stern one's eyes already rest on me while the bone in her hand points idly at the advertisement just above my head. My hands, still cradling my belly, slide guiltily down my thighs and fall on my knees. But the foetus betrays me with another flutter, a sigh. I have heard of books flying off the laps of gentle mothers-to-be as their foetuses lash out. I will not be bullied. I jump up and press the bell.

There are voices behind me. The large woman's "Oi, I say" thunders over the conductor's cross "Tickets please." I will not speak to anyone. Shall I throw myself on the grooved floor of this bus and with knees drawn up, hands over my head, wait for my demise? I do not in any case expect to be alive tomorrow. But I must resist; I must harden my heart against the sad, complaining eyes of Jesus.

"I say, Miss," she shouts and her tone sounds familiar. Her voice compels like the insistence of Father's guttural commands. But the conductor's hand falls on my shoulder, the barrel of his ticket dispenser digs into my ribs, the buttons of his uniform gleam as I dip into my bag for my purse. Then the large woman spills out of her seat as she leans forward. Her friend, reconciled, holds the bar of an arm across her as she leans forward shouting, "Here, I say, your purse." I try to look grateful. Her eyes blaze with scorn as she proclaims to the bus, "Stupid these young people. Dressed to kill maybe, but still so stupid."

She is right. Not about my clothes, of course, and I check to see what I am wearing. I have not been alerted to my own stupidity before. No doubt I will sail through my final examinations at the end of this year and still not know how I dared to pluck a fluttering foetus out of my womb. That is if I survive tonight.

I sit on the steps of this large building and squint up at the marble facade.

My elbows rest on my knees flung comfortably apart. I ought to know where I am; it is clearly a public building of some importance. For the first time I long for the veld of my childhood. There the red sand rolls for miles, and if you stand on the koppie behind the house the landmarks blaze their permanence: the river points downward, runs its dry course from north to south; the geel-bos crowds its banks in near straight lines. On either side of the path winding westward plump little buttocks of cacti squat as if lifting the skirts to pee, and the swollen fingers of vygies burst in clusters out of the stone, pointing the way. In the veld you can always find your way home.

I am anxious about meeting Michael. We have planned this so carefully for the rush hour when people storming home crossly will not notice us together in the crush.

"It's simple," Michael said. "The bus carries along the main roads through the suburbs to the City, and as you reach the Post Office you get off and I'll be there to meet you. At five."

A look at my anxious face compelled him to say, "You can't get lost in Cape Town. There," and he pointed over his shoulder, "is Table Mountain and there is Devil's Peak and there Lion's Head, so how in heaven's name could you get lost?" The words shot out unexpectedly, like the fine arc of brown spittle from between the teeth of an old man who no longer savours the tobacco he has been chewing all day. There are, I suppose, things that even a loved one can-not overlook.

Am I a loved one?

I ought to rise from these steps and walk towards the City. Fortunately I al-ways take the precaution of setting out early, so that I should still be in time to meet Michael who will drive me along de Waal Drive into the slopes of Table Mountain where Mrs. Coetzee waits with her tongs.

Am I a loved one? No. I am dull, ugly and bad-tempered. My hair has grown greasy, I am forgetful and I have no sense of direction. Michael, he has long since stopped loving me. He watched me hugging the lavatory bowl, retching, and recoiled at my first display of bad temper. There is a faraway look in his eyes as he plans his retreat. But he is well brought up, honourable. When the first doubts gripped the corners of his mouth, he grinned madly and said, "We must marry," showing a row of perfect teeth.

"There are laws against that," I said unnecessarily.

But gripped by the idyll of an English landscape of painted greens, he saw my head once more held high, my lettuce-luscious skirts crisp on a camomile lawn and the willow drooping over the red mouth of a suckling infant.

"Come on," he urged. "Don't do it. We'll get to England and marry. It will work out all right," and betraying the source of his vision, "and we'll be happy for ever, thousands of miles from all this mess."

I would have explained if I could. But I could not account for this vision: the slow shower of ashes over yards of diaphanous tulle, the moth wings tucked back with delight as their tongues whisked the froth of white lace. For two years I have loved Michael, have wanted to marry him. Duped by a dream I merely shook my head.

"But you love babies, you want babies some time or other, so why not accept God's holy plan? Anyway, you're a Christian and you believe it's a sin, don't you?"

God is not a good listener. Like Father, he expects obedience and withdraws peevishly if his demands are not met. Explanations of my point of view infuriate him so that he quivers with silent rage. For once I do not plead and capitulate; I find it quite easy to ignore these men.

"You're not even listening," Michael accused. "I don't know how you can do it." There is revulsion in his voice.

For two short years I have adored Michael.

Once, perched perilously on the rocks, we laughed fondly at the thought of a child. At Capt Point where the oceans meet and part. The Indian and the Atlantic, fighting for their separate identities, roared and thrashed fiercely so that we huddled together, his hand on my belly. It is said that if you shut one eye and focus the other carefully, the line separating the two oceans may rear drunkenly but remains ever clear and hair-fine. But I did not look. In the mischievous wind I struggled with the flapping ends of a scarf I tried to wrap around my hair. Later that day on the silver sands of a deserted beach he wrote solemnly: Will you marry me? and my trembling fingers traced a huge heart around the words. Ahead the sun danced on the waves, flecking them with gold.

I wrote a poem about that day and showed Michael. "Surely that was not what Logiesbaai was about," he frowned, and read aloud the lines about warriors charging out of the sea, assegais gleaming in the sun, the beat of tom-toms riding the waters, the throb in the carious cavities of rocks.

"It's good," he said, nodding thoughtfully, "I like the title, 'Love at Logiesbaai (White Only),' though I expect much of the subtlety escapes me. Sounds good," he encouraged, "you should write more often."

I flushed. I wrote poems all the time. And he was wrong; it was not a good poem. It was puzzling and I wondered why I had shown him this poem that did not even make sense to me. I tore it into little bits.

Love, love, love, I sigh as I shake each ankle in turn and examine the swelling.

Michael's hair falls boyishly over his eyes. His eyes narrow merrily when he smiles and the left corner of his mouth shoots up so that the row of teeth forms a queer diagonal line above his chin. He flicks his head so that the fringe of hair lifts from his eyes for a second, then falls, so fast, like the tongue of a lizard retracted at the very moment of exposure.

"We'll find somewhere," he would say, "a place where we'd be quite alone." This country is vast and he has an instinctive sense of direction. He discovers the armpits of valleys that invite us into their shadows. Dangerous climbs led by the roar of the sea take us to blue bays into which we drop from impossible cliffs. The sun lowers herself on to us. We do not fear the police with their torches. They come only by night in search of offenders. We have the immunity of love. They cannot find us because they do not know we exist. One day they will find out about lovers who steal whole days, round as gloves.

There has always been a terrible thrill in that thought.

I ease my feet back into my shoes and the tears splash on to my dress with such wanton abandon that I cannot believe they are mine. From the punctured globes of stolen days these fragments sag and squint. I hold, hold these pictures I have summoned. I will not recognise them for much longer.

With tilted head I watch the shoes and sawn-off legs ascend and descend the marble steps, altering course to avoid me. Perhaps someone will ask the police to remove me.

Love, love, love, I sigh. Another flutter in my womb. I think of moth wings struggling against a window pane and I rise.

The smell of sea unfurls towards me as I approach Adderley Street. There is no wind but the brine hangs in an atomised mist, silver over a thwarted sun. In answer to my hunger, Wellingtons looms on my left. The dried-fruit palace which I cannot resist. The artificial light dries my tears, makes me blink, and the trays of fruit, of Cape sunlight twice trapped, shimmer and threaten to burst out of their forms. Rows of pineapple are the infinite divisions of the sun, the cores lost in the amber discs of mebos arranged in arcs. Prunes are the wrinkled backs of aged goggas beside the bloodshot eyes of cherries. Dark green figs sit pertly on their bottoms peeping over trays. And I too am not myself, hoping for refuge in a metaphor that will contain it all. I buy the figs and mebos. Desire is a Tsafendas tapeworm in my belly that cannot be satisfied and as I pop the first fig into my mouth I feel the danger fountain with the jets of saliva. Will I stop at one death?

I have walked too far along this road and must turn back to the Post Office. I break into a trot as I see Michael in the distance, drumming with his nails on the side of the car. His sunburnt elbow juts out of the window. He taps with anxiety or impatience and I grow cold with fear as I jump into the passenger seat and say merrily, "Let's go," as if we are setting off for a picnic.

Michael will wait in the car on the next street. She had said that it would take only ten minutes. He takes my hand and so prevents me from getting out. Perhaps he thinks that I will bolt, run off into the mountain, revert to savagery. His hand is heavy on my forearm and his eyes are those of a wounded dog, pale with pain.

"It will be all right." I try to comfort and wonder whether he hears his own voice in mine. My voice is thin, a tinsel thread that springs out of my mouth and flutters straight out of the window.

"I must go." I lift the heavy hand off my forearm and it falls inertly across the gearstick.

The room is dark. The curtains are drawn and a lace-shaded electric light casts shadows in the corners of the rectangle. The doorway in which I stand divides the room into sleeping and eating quarters. On the left there is a table against which a servant girl leans, her eyes fixed on the blank wall ahead. On the right a middle-aged white woman rises with a hostess smile from a divan which serves as sofa, and pats the single pink-flowered cushion to assert homeliness. There is a narrow dark wardrobe in the corner.

I say haltingly, "You are expecting me. I spoke to you on the telephone yesterday. Sally Smit." I can see no telephone in the room. She frowns.

"You're not Coloured, are you?" It is an absurd question. I look at my brown arms that I have kept folded across my chest, and watch the gooseflesh sprout. Her eyes are fixed on me. Is she blind? How will she perform the operation with such defective sight? Then I realise: the educated voice, the accent has blinded her. I have drunk deeply of Michael, swallowed his voice as I drank from his tongue. Has he swallowed mine? I do not think so.

I say "No," and wait for all the cockerels in Cape Town to crow simultaneously. Instead the servant starts from her trance and stares at me with undisguised admiration.

"Good," the woman smiles, showing yellow teeth. "One must check nowadays. These Coloured girls, you know, are very forward, terrible types. What do they think of me, as if I would do every Tom, Dick and Harry. Not me you know; this is a respectable concern and I try to help decent women, educated you know. No, you can trust me. No Coloured girl's ever been on this sofa."

The girl coughs, winks at me and turns to stir a pot simmering on a primus stove on the table. The smell of offal escapes from the pot and nausea rises in my throat, feeding the fear. I would like to run but my feet are lashed with fear to the linoleum. Only my eyes move, across the room where she pulls a newspaper from a wad wedged between the wall and the wardrobe. She spreads the paper on the divan and smooths with her hand while the girl shuts the door and turns the key. A cat crawls lazily from under the table and stares at me until the green jewels of its eyes shrink to crystal points.

She points me to the sofa. From behind the wardrobe she pulls her instrument and holds it against the baby-pink crimplene of her skirt.

"Down, shut your eyes now," she says as I raise my head to look. Their movements are carefully orchestrated, the manoeuvres practised. Their eyes signal and they move. The girl stations herself by my head and her mistress moves to my feet. She pushes my knees apart and whips out her instrument from a pocket. A piece of plastic tubing dangles for a second. My knees jerk and my mouth opens wide but they are in control. A brown hand falls on my mouth and smothers the cry; the white hands wrench the knees apart and she hisses, "Don't you dare. Do you want the bladdy police here? I'll kill you if you scream."

The brown hand over my mouth relaxes. She looks into my face and says. "She won't." I am a child who needs reassurance. I am surprised by the softness of her voice. The brown hand moves along the side of my face and pushes back my hair. I long to hold the other hand; I do not care what happens below. A black line of terror separates it from my torso. Blood spurts from between my legs and for a second the two halves of my body make contact through the pain.

So it is done. Deflowered by yellow hands wielding a catheter. Fear and hypocrisy, mine, my deserts spread in a dark stain on the newspaper.

"OK," she says, "get yourself decent." I dress and wait for her to explain. "You go home now and wait for the birth. Do you have a pad?"

I shake my head uncomprehendingly. Her face tightens for a moment but then she smiles and pulls a sanitary towel out of the wardrobe.

"Won't cost you anything lovey." She does not try to conceal the glow of her generosity. She holds out her hand and I place the purse in her palm. She counts, satisfied, but I wave away the purse which she reluctantly puts on the table.

"You're a good girl," she says and puts both hands on my shoulders. I hold my breath; I will not inhale the foetid air from the mouth of this my grotesque bridegroom with yellow teeth. She plants the kiss of complicity on my cheek and I turn to go, repelled by her touch. But have I the right to be fastidious? I cannot deny feeling grateful, so that I turn back to claim the purse after all. The girl winks at me. The purse fits snugly in my hand; there would be no point in giving it back to Michael.

Michael's face is drawn with fear. He is as ignorant of the process as I am. I am brisk, efficient and rattle off the plan. "It'll happen tonight so I'll go home and wait and call you in the morning. By then it will be all over." He looks relieved.

He drives me right to the door and my landlady waves merrily from the stoep where she sits with her embroidery among the potted ferns.

"Don't look," she says anxiously. "It's a present for you, for your trousseau," and smiling slyly, "I can tell when a couple just can't wait any longer. There's no catching me out, you know."

Tonight in her room next to mine she will turn in her chaste bed, tracing the tendrils from pink and orange flowers, searching for the needle lost in endless folds of white linen.

Semi-detached houses with red-polished stoeps line the west side of Trevelyan Road. On the east is the Cape Flats line where electric trains rattle reliably according to timetable. Trevelyan Road runs into the elbow of a severely curved Main Road which nevertheless has all the amenities one would expect: butcher, baker, hairdresser, chemist, library, liquor store. There is a fish and chips shop on that corner, on the funny bone of that elbow, and by the side, strictly speaking in Trevelyan Road, a dustbin leans against the trunk of a young palm tree. A newspaper parcel dropped into this dustbin would absorb the vinegary smell of discarded fish and chips wrappings in no time.

The wrapped parcel settles in the bin. I do not know what has happened to God. He is fastidious. He fled at the moment that I smoothed the wet black hair before wrapping it up. I do not think he will come back. It is 6 A.M. Light pricks at the shroud of Table Mountain. The streets are deserted and, relieved, I remember that the next train will pass at precisely 6.22.

John Edgar Wideman

Doc's Story

(UNITED STATES)

He thinks of her small, white hands, blue veined, gaunt, awkwardly knuckled. He'd teased her about the smallness of her hands, hers lost in the shadow of his when they pressed them together palm to palm to measure. The heavy drops of color on her nails barely reached the middle joints of his fingers. He'd teased her about her dwarf's hands but he'd also said to her one night when the wind was rattling the windows of the apartment on Cedar and they lay listening and shivering though it was summer on the brass bed she'd found in a junk store on Haverford Avenue, near the Woolworth's five-and-dime they'd picketed for two years, that God made little things closer to perfect than he ever made big things. Small, compact women like her could be perfectly formed, proportioned, and he'd smiled out loud running his hand up and down the just-right fine lines of her body, celebrating how good she felt to him.

She'd left him in May, when the shadows and green of the park had started to deepen. Hanging out, becoming a regular at the basketball court across the street in Regent Park was how he'd coped. No questions asked. Just the circle of stories. If you didn't want to miss anything good you came early and stayed late. He learned to wait, be patient. Long hours waiting were not time lost but time doing nothing because there was nothing better to do. Basking in sunshine on a stone bench, too beat to play any longer, nowhere to go but an empty apartment, he'd watch the afternoon traffic in Regent Park, dog strollers, baby carriages, winos, kids, gays, students with blankets they'd spread out on the grassy banks of the hollow and books they'd pretend to read, the black men from the neighborhood who'd search the park for braless young mothers and white girls on blankets who didn't care or didn't know any better than to sit with their crotches exposed. When he'd sit for hours like that, cooking like that, he'd feel himself empty out, see himself seep away and hover in the air, a fine mist, a little flattened-out gray cloud of something wavering in the heat, a presence as visible as the steam on the window as he stares for hours at winter.

He's waiting for summer. For the guys to begin gathering on the court again. They'll sit in the shade with their backs against the Cyclone fencing or lean on cars parked at the roller-coaster curb or lounge in the sun on low, stone benches catty-corner from the basketball court. Some older ones still drink wine, but most everybody cools out on reefer, when there's reefer passed along, while they bullshit and wait for winners. He collects the stories they tell. He needs a story now. The right one now to get him through this long winter because she's gone and won't leave him alone.

In summer fine grit hangs in the air. Five minutes on the court and you're coughing. City dirt and park dust blowing off bald patches from which green is long gone, and deadly ash blowing over from New Jersey. You can taste it some days, bitter in your spit. Chunks pepper your skin, burn your eyes. Early fall while it's still warm enough to run outdoors the worst time of all. Leaves pile up against the fence, higher and higher, piles that explode and jitterbug across the court in the middle of a game, then sweep up again, slamming back where they blew from. After a while the leaves are ground into coarse, choking powder. You eat leaf trying to get in a little hoop before the weather turns, before those days when nobody's home from work yet but it's dark already and too cold to run again till spring. Fall's the only time sweet syrupy wine beats reefer. Ripple, Manischewitz, Taylor's Tawny Port coat your throat. He takes a hit when the jug comes round. He licks the sweetness from his lips, listens for his favorite stories one more time before everybody gives it up till next season.

His favorite stories made him giggle and laugh and hug the others, like they hugged him when a story got so good nobody's legs could hold them up. Some stories got under his skin peculiar ways. Some he liked to hear because they made the one performing them do crazy stuff with his voice and body. He learned to be patient, learned his favorites would be repeated, get a turn just like he got a turn on the joints and wine bottles circulating the edges of the court.

Of all the stories, the one about Doc had bothered him most. Its orbit was unpredictable. Twice in one week, then only once more last summer. He'd only heard Doc's story three times, but that was enough to establish Doc behind and between the words of all the other stories. In a strange way Doc presided over the court. You didn't need to mention him. He was just there. Regent Park stories began with Doc and ended with Doc and everything in between was preparation, proof the circle was unbroken.

They say Doc lived on Regent Square, one of the streets like Cedar, deadending at the park. On the hottest afternoons the guys from the court would head for Doc's stoop. Jars of ice water, the good feeling and good talk they'd share in the shade of Doc's little front yard was what drew them. Sometimes they'd spray Doc's hose on one another. Get drenched like when they were kids and the city used to turn on fire hydrants in the summer. Some of Doc's neighbors would give them dirty looks. Didn't like a whole bunch of loud, sweaty, half-naked niggers backed up in their nice street where Doc was the only colored on the block. They say Doc didn't care. He was just out there like everybody else having a good time.

Doc had played at the University. Same one where Doc taught for a while. They say Doc used to laugh when white people asked him if he was in the Athletic Department. No reason for niggers to be at the University if they weren't playing ball or coaching ball. At least that's what white people thought, and since they thought that way, that's the way it was. Never more than a sprinkle of black faces in the white sea of the University. Doc used to laugh till the joke got old. People freedom-marching and freedom-dying, Doc said, but some dumb stuff never changed.

He first heard Doc's story late one day, after the yellow streetlights had popped on. Pooner was finishing the one about gang warring in North Philly: Yeah. They sure nuff lynched this dude they caught on their turf. Hung him up on the goddamn poles behind the backboard. Little kids found the sucker in the morning with his tongue all black and shit down his legs, and the cops had to come cut him down. Worst part is them little kids finding a dead body swinging up there. Kids don't be needing to find nothing like that. But those North Philly gangs don't play. They don't even let the dead rest in peace. Run in a funeral parlor and fuck up the funeral. Dumping over the casket and tearing up the flowers. Scaring people and turning the joint out. It's some mean shit. But them gangs don't play. They kill you they ain't finished yet. Mess with your people, your house, your sorry-ass dead body to get even. Pooner finished telling it and he looked round at the fellows and people were shaking their heads and then there was a chorus of You got that right, man. It's a bitch out there, man. Them niggers crazy, boy, and Pooner holds out his hand and somebody passes the joint. Pooner pinches it in two fingers and takes a deep drag. Everybody knows he's finished, it's somebody else's turn.

One of the fellows says, I wonder what happened to old Doc. I always be thinking about Doc, wondering where the cat is, what he be doing now . . .

Don't nobody know why Doc's eyes start to going bad. It just happen. Doc never even wore glasses. Eyes good as anybody's far as anybody knew till one day he come round he got goggles on. Like Kareem. And people kinda joking, you know. Doc got him some goggles. Watch out, youall. Doc be skyhooking youall to death today. Funning, you know. Cause Doc like to joke and play. Doc one the fellas like I said, so when he come round in goggles he subject to some teasing and one another thing like that cause nobody thought nothing serious wrong. Doc's eyes just as good as yours or mine, far as anybody knew.

Doc been playing all his life. That's why you could stand him on the foul line and point him at the hoop and more times than not, Doc could sink it. See he be remembering. His muscles know just what to do. You get his feet aimed right, line him up so he's on target, and Doc would swish one for you. Was a game kinda. Sometimes you get a sucker and Doc win you some money. Swish. Then the cat lost the dough start crying. He ain't blind. Can't no blind man shoot no pill. Is you really blind, brother? You niggers trying to steal my money, trying to play me for a fool. When a dude start crying the blues like that Doc wouldn't like it. He'd walk away. Wouldn't answer.

Leave the man lone. You lost fair and square. Doc made the basket so shut up and pay up, chump.

Doc practiced. Remember how you'd hear him out here at night when people sleeping. It's dark but what dark mean to Doc? Blacker than the rentman's heart but don't make no nevermind to Doc, he be steady shooting fouls. Al-

ways be somebody out there to chase the ball and throw it back. But shit, man.
When Doc into his rhythm, didn't need nobody chase the ball. Ball be swish-
ing with that good backspin, that good arch bring it back blip, blip, blip, three
bounces and it's coming right back to Doc's hands like he got a string on the
pill. Spooky if you didn't know Doc or know about foul shooting and understand when you got your shit together don't matter if you blindfolded. You put
the motherfucker up and you know it's spozed to come running back just like a
dog with a stick in his mouth.

Doc always be hanging at the court. Blind as wood but you couldn't fool
Doc. Eyes in his ears. Know you by your walk. He could tell if you wearing
new sneaks, tell you if your old ones is laced or not. Know you by your breath.
The holes you make in the air when you jump. Doc was hip to who fucking
who and who was getting fucked. Who could play ball and who was jiving. Doc
use to be out here every weekend, steady rapping with the fellows and doing
his foul-shot thing between games. Every once in a while somebody tease
him, Hey, Doc. You want to run winners next go? Doc laugh and say, No,
Dupree . . . I'm tired today, Dupree. Besides which you ain't been on a winning team in a week have you, Du? And everybody laugh. You know, just funning cause Doc one the fellas.

But one Sunday the shit got stone serious. Sunday I'm telling youall about,
the action was real nice. If you wasn't ready, get back cause the brothers was
cooking. Sixteen points, rise and fly. Next. Who got next? . . . Come on out
here and take your ass kicking. One them good days when it's hot and everybody's juices is high and you feel you could play till next week. One them kind
of days and a run's just over. Doc gets up and he goes with Billy Moon to the
foul line. Fellas hanging under the basket for the rebound. Ain't hardly gon be
a rebound Doc get hisself lined up right. But see, when the ball drop through
the net you want to be the one grab it and throw it back to Billy. You want to
be out there part of Doc shooting fouls just like you want to run when the running's good.

Doc bounce the ball, one, two, three times like he does. Then he raise it.
Sift it in his fingers. You know he's a ballplayer, a shooter already way the ball
spin in them long fingers way he raises it and cocks his wrist. You know Doc
can't see a damn thing through his sunglasses but swear to God you'd think he
was looking at the hoop way he study and measure. Then he shoots and ain't a
sound in whole Johnson. Seems like everybody's heart stops. Everybody's
breath behind that ball pushing it and steadying it so it drops through clean as
new money.

But that Sunday something went wrong. Couldna been wind cause wasn't
no wind. I was there. I know. Maybe Doc had playing on his mind. Couldn't
help have playing on his mind cause it was one those days wasn't nothing better to do in the world than play. Whatever it was, soon as the ball left his
hands, you could see Doc was missing, missing real bad. Way short and way
off to the left. Might hit the backboard if everybody blew on it real hard.

A young boy, one them skinny, jumping-jack young boys got pogo sticks for
legs, one them kids go up and don't come back down till they ready, he was

standing on the left side the lane and leap up all the sudden catch the pill out the air and jams it through. Blam. A monster dunk and everybody break out in Goddamn. Do it, Sky, and Did you see that nigger get up? People slapping five and all that mess. Then Sky, the young boy they call Sky, grinning like a Chessy cat and strutting out with the ball squeezed in one hand to give it to Doc. In his story. Grinning and strutting.

Gave you a little help, Doc.

Didn't ask for no help, Sky. Why'd you fuck with my shot, Sky?

Well, up jumped the Devil. The joint gets real quiet again real quick. Doc ain't cracked smile the first. He ain't playing.

Sorry, Doc. Didn't mean no harm, Doc.

You must think I'm some kind of chump fucking with my shot that way.

People start to feeling bad. Doc is steady getting on Sky's case. Sky just a young, light-in-the-ass kid. Jump to the moon but he's just a silly kid. Don't mean no harm. He just out there like everybody else trying to do his thing. No harm in Sky but Doc ain't playing and nobody else says shit. It's quiet like when Doc's shooting. Quiet as death and Sky don't know what to do. Can't wipe that lame look off his face and can't back off and can't hand the pill to Doc neither. He just stands there with his arm stretched out and his rusty fingers wrapped round the ball. Can't hold it much longer, can't let it go.

Seems like I coulda strolled over to Doc's stoop for a drinka water and strolled back and those two still be standing there. Doc and Sky. Billy Moon off to one side so it's just Doc and Sky.

Everybody holding they breath. Everybody want it over with and finally Doc says, Forget it, Sky. Just don't play with my shots anymore. And then Doc say, Who has next winners?

If Doc was joking nobody took it for no joke. His voice still hard. Doc ain't kidding around.

Who's next? I want to run.

Now Doc knows who's next. Leroy got next winners and Doc knows Leroy always saves a spot so he can pick up a big man from the losers. Leroy tell you to your face, I got my five, man, but everybody know Leroy saving a place so he can build him a winner and stay on the court. Leroy's a cold dude that way, been that way since he first started coming round and ain't never gon change and Doc knows that, everybody knows that but even Leroy ain't cold enough to say no to Doc.

I got it, Doc.

You get your five yet?

You know you got a spot with me, Doc. Always did.

Then I'ma run.

Say to myself, Shit . . . Good God Almighty. Great Googa-Mooga. What is happening here? Doc can't see shit. Doc blind as this bench I'm sitting on. What Doc gon do out there?

Well, it ain't my game. If it was, I'd a lied and said I had five. Or maybe not. Don't know what I'da done, to tell the truth. But Leroy didn't have no choice. Doc caught him good. Course Doc knew all that before he asked.

Did Doc play? What kinda question is that? What you think I been talking about all this time, man? Course he played. Why the fuck he be asking for winners less he was gon play? Helluva run as I remember. Overtime and shit. Don't remember who won. Somebody did, sure nuff. Leroy had him a strong unit. You know how he is. And Doc? Doc ain't been out on the court for a while but Doc is Doc, you know. Held his own . . .

If he had tried to tell her about Doc, would it have made a difference? Would the idea of a blind man playing basketball get her attention or would she have listened the way she listened when he told her stories he'd read about slavery days when Africans could fly, change themselves to cats and humming-birds, when black hoodoo priests and conjure queens were feared by powerful whites even though ordinary black lives weren't worth a penny. To her it was folklore, superstition. Interesting because it revealed the psychology, the pa-thology of the oppressed. She listened intently, not because she thought she'd hear truth. For her, belief in magic was like belief in God. Nice work if you could get it. Her skepticism, her hardheaded practicality, like the smallness of her hands, appealed to him. Opposites attracting. But more and more as the years went by, he'd wanted her with him, wanted them to be together . . .

They were walking in Regent park. It was clear to both of them that things weren't going to work out. He'd never seen her so beautiful, perfect.

There should have been stars. Stars at least, and perhaps a sickle moon. In-stead the edge of the world was on fire. They were walking in Regent park and dusk had turned the tree trunks black. Beyond them in the distance, below the fading blue of sky, the colors of sunset were pinched into a narrow, radiant band. Perhaps he had listened too long. Perhaps he had listened too intently for his own voice to fill the emptiness. When he turned back to her, his eyes were glazed, stinging. Grit, chemicals, whatever it was coloring, poisoning the sky, blurred his vision. Before he could blink her into focus, before he could speak, she was gone.

If he'd known Doc's story he would have said: *There's still a chance. There's always a chance. I mean this guy, Doc. Christ. He was stone blind. But he got out on the court and played. Over there. Right over there. On that very court across the hollow from us. It happened. I've talked to people about it many times. If Doc could do that, then anything's possible. We're possible . . .*

If a blind man could play basketball, surely we . . . If he had known Doc's story, would it have saved them? He hears himself saying the words. The ball arches from Doc's fingertips, the miracle of it sinking. Would she have be-lieved any of it?

Joy Williams

The Farm

(UNITED STATES)

It was a dark night in August. Sarah and Tommy were going to their third party that night, the party where they would actually sit down to dinner. They were driving down Mixtuxet Avenue, a long black avenue of trees that led out of the village, away from the shore and the coastal homes into the country. Tommy had been drinking only soda that night. Every other weekend, Tommy wouldn't drink. He did it, he said, to keep trim. He did it because he could.

Sarah was telling a long story as she drove. She kept asking Tommy if she had told it to him before, but he was noncommittal. When Tommy didn't drink, Sarah talked and talked. She was telling him a terrible story that she had read in the newspaper about an alligator at a jungle farm attraction in Florida. The alligator had eaten a child who had crawled into its pen. The alligator's name was Cookie. Its owner had shot it immediately. The owner was sad about everything, the child, the parents' grief, Cookie. He was quoted in the paper as saying that shooting Cookie was not an act of revenge.

When Tommy didn't drink, Sarah felt cold. She was shivering in the car. There were goosepimples on her tanned, thin arms. Tommy sat beside her smoking, saying nothing.

There had been words between them earlier. The parties here had an undercurrent of sexuality. All the parties here did. Sarah could almost hear it, flowing around them all, carrying them all along. In the car, on the night of the accident, Sarah was at that point in the evening when she felt guilty. She wanted to make things better, make things nice. She had gone through her elated stage, her jealous stage, her stubbornly resigned stage and now she felt guilty. Had they talked about divorce that night, or had that been before, on other evenings? There was a flavor she remembered in their talks about divorce, a scent. It was hot, as Italy had been hot when they had been there. Dust, bread, sun, a burning at the back of the throat from too much drinking.

They hadn't been talking about divorce that night. The parties had been crowded. Sarah had hardly seen Tommy. Then, on her way to the bathroom, she had seen him sitting with a girl on a bed in one of the back rooms. He was telling the girl about condors, about hunting for condors in small, light planes.

"Oh, but you didn't hurt them, did you?" the girl asked. She was someone's daughter, a little overweight but with beautiful skin and large green eyes.

"Oh no," Tommy assured her, "we weren't hunting to hurt."

Condors. Sarah looked at them sitting on the bed. When they noticed her, the girl blushed. Tommy smiled. Sarah imagined what she looked like, standing in the doorway. She wished that they had shut the door.

That had been at the Steadmans'. The first party had been at the Perrys'. The Perrys never served food. Sarah had had two or three drinks there. The bar had been set up beneath the grape arbor and everyone stood outside. It had still been light at the Perrys' but at the Steadmans' it was dark and people drank inside. Everyone spoke about the end of summer as though it were a bewildering and unnatural event.

They had stayed at the Steadmans' longer than they should have and they were going to be late for dinner. Nevertheless, they were driving at a moderate speed, through a familiar landscape, passing houses that they had been entertained in many times. There were the Salts and the Hollands and the Greys and the Dodsons. The Dodsons kept their gin in the freezer and owned two large and dappled crotch-sniffing dogs. The Greys imported Southerners for their parties. The women all had lovely voices and knew how to make spoon bread and pickled tomatoes and artillery punch. The men had smiles when they'd say to Sarah, "Why, let me get you another. You don't have a thing in that glass, ah swear." The Hollands gave the kind of dinner party where the shot was still in the duck and the silver should have been in a vault. Little whiskey was served but there was always excellent wine. The Salts were a high-strung couple who often quarreled. Jenny Salt was on some type of medication for tension and often dropped the canapés she attempted to serve. Jenny and her husband, Pete, had a room in which there was nothing but a large doll house where witty mâché figures carried on assignations beneath tiny clocks and crystal chandeliers. Once, when Sarah was examining the doll house's library where two figures were hunched over a chess game which was just about to be won, Pete had always said, on the twenty-second move, Pete told Sarah that she had pretty eyes. She had moved away from him immediately. She had closed her eyes. In another room, with the other guests, she had talked about the end of summer.

On that night, at the end of summer, the night of the accident, Sarah was still talking as they passed the Salts' house. She was talking about Venice. She and Tommy had been there once. They had drunk in the Plaza and listened to the orchestras. Sarah quoted D. H. Lawrence on Venice . . . "Abhorrent green and slippery city . . ." But she and Tommy had liked Venice. They drank standing up at little bars. Sarah had had a cold and she drank grappa and the cold had disappeared for the rest of her life.

After the Salts' house, the road swerved north and became very dark. There were no lights, no houses for several miles. There were stone walls, an orchard of sickly peach trees, a cider mill. There was St. James Episcopal Church where Tommy took their daughter, Martha, to Sunday School. The Sunday

School was highly fundamental. There were many arguments among the children and their teachers as to the correct interpretation of Bible Story favorites. For example, when Lazarus rose from the dead, was he still sick? Martha liked the fervor at St. James. Each week, her dinner graces were becoming more impassioned and fantastic. Martha was seven.

Each Sunday, Tommy takes Martha to her little classes at St. James. Sarah can imagine the child sitting there at a low table with her jars of colors. Tommy doesn't go to church himself and Martha's classes are two hours long. Sarah doesn't know where Tommy goes. She suspects he is seeing someone. When they come home on Sundays, Tommy is sleek, exhilarated. The three of them sit down to the dinner Sarah has prepared.

Over the years, Sarah suspects, Tommy has floated to the surface of her. They are swimmers now, far apart, on the top of the sea.

Sarah at last fell silent. The road seemed endless as in a dream. They seemed to be slowing down. She could not feel her foot on the accelerator. She could not feel her hands on the wheel. Her mind was an untidy cupboard filled with shining bottles. The road was dark and silvery and straight. In the space ahead of her, there seemed to be something. It beckoned, glittering. Sarah's mind cleared a little. She saw Martha with her hair cut oddly short. Sarah gently nibbled on the inside of her mouth to keep alert. She saw Tommy choosing a succession of houses, examining the plaster, the floorboards, the fireplaces, deciding where windows should be placed, walls knocked down. She saw herself taking curtains down from a window so that there would be a better view of the sea. The curtains knocked her glass from the sill and it shattered. The sea was white and flat. It did not command her to change her life. It demanded of her, nothing. She saw Martha sleeping, her paint-smudged fingers curled. She saw Tommy in the city with a woman, riding in a cab. The woman wore a short fur jacket and Tommy stroked it as he spoke. She saw a figure in the road ahead, its arms raised before its face as though to block out the sight of her. The figure was a boy who wore dark clothing, but his hair was bright, his face was shining. She saw her car leap forward and run him down where he stood.

Tommy had taken responsibility for the accident. He had told the police he was driving. The boy apparently had been hitchhiking and had stepped out into the road. At the autopsy, traces of a hallucinogen were found in the boy's system. The boy was fifteen years old and his name was Stevie Bettencourt. No charges were filed.

"My wife," Tommy told the police, "was not feeling well. My wife," Tommy said. "was in the passenger seat."

Sarah stopped drinking immediately after the accident. She felt nauseous much of the time. She slept poorly. Her hands hurt her. The bones in her hands ached. She remembered that this was the way she felt the last time she had stopped drinking. It had been two years before. She remembered why she had stopped and she remembered why she had started again. She had stopped because she had done a cruel thing to her little Martha. It was spring and she and Tommy were giving a dinner party. Sarah had two martinis in the late afternoon when she was preparing dinner and then she had two more martinis with her guests. Martha had come downstairs to say a polite good-night to everyone as she had been taught. She had put on her nightie and brushed her teeth. Sarah poured a little more gin in her glass and went up-stairs with her to brush out her hair and put her to bed. Martha had long, thick blonde hair of which she was very proud. On that night she wore it in a pony tail secured by an elasticized holder with two small colored balls on the end. Sarah's fingers were clumsy and she could not get it off without pulling Martha's hair and making her cry. She got a pair of scissors and carefully began snipping at the stubborn elastic. The scissors were large, like shears, and they had been difficult to handle. A foot of Martha's gathered hair had abruptly fallen to the floor. Sarah remembered trying to pat it back into place on the child's head.

So Sarah had stopped drinking the first time. She did not feel renewed. She felt exhausted and wary. She read and cooked. She realized how little she and Tommy had to talk about. Tommy drank Scotch when he talked to her at night. Sometimes Sarah would silently count as he spoke to see how long the words took. When he was away and he telephoned her, she could hear the ice tinkling in the glass. She loved him.

Tommy was in the city four days a week. He often changed hotels. He would bring Martha little bars of soap wrapped in the different colored papers of the hotels. Martha's drawers were full of the soaps scenting her clothes. When Tommy came home on the weekends he would work on the house and they would give parties at which Tommy was charming. Tommy had a talent for holding his liquor and for buying old houses, restoring them and selling them for three times what he had paid for them. Tommy and Sarah had moved six times in eleven years. All their homes had been fine old homes in excellent locations two or three hours from New York. Sarah would stay in the country while Tommy worked in the city. Sarah did not know her way around New York.

For three weeks, Sarah did not drink. Then it was her birthday. Tommy gave her a slim gold necklace and fastened it around her neck. He wanted her to come to New York with him, to have dinner, see a play, spend the night with him in the fine suite the company had given him at the hotel. They had got a baby-sitter for Martha, a marvelous woman who polished the silver in the afternoon when Martha napped. Sarah drove. Tommy had never cared for driving. His hand rested on her thigh. Occasionally, he would slip his hand be-neath her skirt. Sarah was sick with the thought that this was the way he touched other women.

By the time they were in Manhattan, they were arguing. They had been married for eleven years. Both had had brief marriages before. They could ar-gue about anything. In midtown, Tommy stormed out of the car as Sarah braked for a light. He took his suitcase and disappeared.

Sarah drove carefully for many blocks. When she had the opportunity, she would pull to the curb and ask someone how to get to Connecticut. No one seemed to know. Sarah thought she was probably phrasing the question poorly but she didn't know how else to present it. After half an hour, she made her way back to the hotel where Tommy was staying. The doorman parked the car and she went into the lobby. She looked into the hotel bar and saw Tommy in the dimness, sitting at a small table. He jumped up and kissed her passionately. He rubbed his hands up and down her sides. "Darling, darling," he said, "I want you to have a happy birthday."

Tommy ordered drinks for both of them. Sarah sipped hers slowly at first but then she drank it and he ordered others. The bar was subdued. There was a piano player who sang about the lord of the dance. The words seemed like those of a hymn. The hymn made her sad but she laughed. Tommy spoke to her urgently and gaily about little things. They laughed together like they had when they were first married. They had always drunk a lot together then and fallen asleep, comfortably and lovingly entwined on white sheets.

They went to their room to change for the theater. The maid had turned back the beds. There was a fresh rose in a bud vase on the writing desk. They had another drink in the room and got undressed. Sarah awoke the next morning curled up on the floor with the bedspread tangled around her. Her mouth was sore. There was a bruise on her leg. The television set was on with no sound. The room was a mess although Sarah could see that nothing had been really damaged. She stared at the television where black-backed gulls were dive-bombing on terrified and doomed cygnets in a documentary about swans. Sarah crept into the bathroom and turned on the shower. She sat in the tub while the water beat upon her. Pinned to the outside of the shower curtain was a note from Tommy who had gone to work. "Darling," the note said, "we had a *good* time on your birthday. I can't say I'm sorry we never got out. I'll call you for lunch. Love."

Sarah turned the note inward until the water made the writing illegible. When the phone rang just before noon, she did not answer it.

There is a certain type of conversation one hears only when one is drunk and it is like a dream, full of humor and threat and significance, deep significance. And the way one witnesses things when one is drunk is different as well. It is like putting a face mask against the surface of the sea and looking into things, into their baffled and guileless hearts.

When Sarah had been a drinker, she felt that she had a fundamental and inventive grasp of situations, but now that she drank no longer, she found herself in the midst of a great and impenetrable silence which she could in no way interpret.

It was a small village. Many of the people who lived there did not even own cars. The demands of life were easily met in the village and it was pretty there besides. It was divided between those who always lived there and who owned fishing boats and restaurants and the city people who had more recently discovered the area as a summer place and winter weekend investment. On the weekends, the New Yorkers would come up with their houseguests and their pâté and cheeses and build fires and go cross-country skiing. Tommy came home to Sarah on weekends. They did things together. They agreed on where to go. During the week she was on her own.

Once, alone, she saw a helicopter carrying a tree in a sling across the sound. The wealthy could afford to leave nothing behind.

Once, with the rest of the town, she saw five boats burning in their storage shrouds. Each summer resort has its winter pyromaniac.

Sarah did not read any more. Her eyes hurt when she read and her hands ached all the time. During the week, she marketed and walked and cared for Martha.

It was three months after Stevie Bettencourt was killed when his mother visited Sarah. She came to the door and knocked on it and Sarah let her in.

Genevieve Bettencourt was a woman Sarah's age although she looked rather younger. She had been divorced almost from the day that Stevie was born. She had another son named Bruce who lived with his father in Nova Scotia. She had an old powder-blue Buick parked on the street before Sarah's house. The Buick had one white door.

The two women sat in Sarah's handsome, sunny living room. It was very calm, very peculiar, almost thrilling. Genevieve looked all around the room. Off the living room were the bedrooms. The door to Sarah's and Tommy's was closed but Martha's door was open. She had a little hanging garden against the window. She had a hamster in a cage. She had an enormous bookcase filled with dolls and books.

Genevieve said to Sarah, "That room wasn't there before. This used to be a lobster pound. I know a great deal about this town. People like you have nothing to do with what I know about this town. Do you remember the way things were, ever?"

"No," Sarah said.

Genevieve sighed. "Does your daughter look like you or your husband?"

"No one's ever told me she looked like me," Sarah said quietly.

On the glass-topped table before them there was a little wooden sculpture cutout that Tommy had bought. A man and woman sat on a park bench. Each wore a startled and ambiguous expression. Each had a terrier on the end of a string. The dogs were a puzzle. One fit on top of the other. Sarah was embarrassed about it being there. Tommy had put it on the table during the weekend and Sarah hadn't moved it. Genevieve didn't touch it.

"I did not want my life to know you," Genevieve said. She removed a hair from the front of her white blouse and dropped it to the floor. She looked out the window at the sun. The floor was of a very light and varnished pine. Sarah could see the hair upon it.

"I'm so sorry," Sarah said. "I'm so very, very sorry." She stretched her neck and put her head back. She looked as though she were choking.

"Stevie was a mixed-up boy," Genevieve said. "They threw him off the basketball team. He took pills. He had bad friends. He didn't study and he got a D in geometry and they wouldn't let him play basketball."

She got up and wandered around the room. She wore green rubber boots, dirty jeans and a beautiful, hand-knit sweater. "I once bought all my fish here," she said. "The O'Malleys owned it. There were practically no windows. Just narrow high ones over the tanks. Now it's all windows, isn't it? Don't you feel exposed?"

"No, I . . ." Sarah began. "There are drapes," she said.

"Off to the side, where you have your garden, there are whale bones if you dig deep enough. I can tell you a lot about this town."

"My husband wants to move," Sarah said.

"I can understand that, but you're the real drinker, after all, aren't you, not him."

"I don't drink any more," Sarah said. She looked at the woman dizzily.

Genevieve was not pretty but she had a clear, strong face. She sat down on the opposite side of the room. "I guess I would like something," she said. "A glass of water." Sarah went to the kitchen and poured a glass of Vichy for them both. Her hands shook.

"We are not strangers to one another," Genevieve said. "We could be friends."

"My first husband always wanted to be friends with my second husband," Sarah said after a moment. "I could never understand it." This had somehow seemed analogous when she was saying it but now it did not. "It is not appropriate that we be friends," she said.

Genevieve continued to sit and talk. Sarah found herself concentrating desperately on her articulate, one-sided conversation. She suspected that the words Genevieve was using were codes for other words, terrible words. Genevieve spoke thoughtlessly, dispassionately, with erratic flourishes of language. Sarah couldn't believe that they were chatting about food, men, the red clouds massed above the sea.

"I have a friend who is a designer," Genevieve said. "She hopes to make a great deal of money someday. Her work has completely altered her perceptions. Every time she looks at a view, she thinks of sheets. 'Take out those mountains,' she will say, 'lighten that cloud a bit and it would make a great sheet.' When she looks at the sky, she thinks of lingerie. Now when I look at the sky, I think of earlier times, happier times when I looked at the sky. I have never been in love, have you?"

"Yes," Sarah said, "I'm in love."

"It's not a lucky thing, you know, to be in love."

There was a soft scuffling at the door and Martha came in. "Hello," she said. "School was good today. I'm hungry."

"Hello, dear," Genevieve said. To Sarah, she said, "Perhaps we can have lunch sometime."

"Who is that?" Martha asked Sarah after Genevieve had left.

"A neighbor," Sarah said, "one of Mommy's friends."

When Sarah told Tommy about Genevieve coming to visit her, he said, "It's harassment. It can be stopped."

It was Sunday morning. They had just finished breakfast and Tommy and Martha were drying the silver and putting it away. Martha was wearing her church-school clothes and she was singing a song she had learned the Sunday before.

"... I'm going to the Mansion on the Happy Days' Express ..." she sang.

Tommy squeezed Martha's shoulders. "Go get your coat, sweetie," he said. When the child had gone, he said to Sarah, "Don't speak to this woman. Don't allow it to happen again."

"We didn't talk about that."

"What else could you talk about? It's weird."

"No one talks about that. No one, ever."

Tommy was wearing a corduroy suit and a tie Sarah had never seen before. Sarah looked at the pattern in the tie. It was random and bright.

"Are you having an affair?" Sarah asked.

"No," he said easily. "I don't understand you, Sarah. I've done everything I could to protect you, to help you straighten yourself out. It was a terrible thing but it's over. You have to get over it. Now, just don't see her again. There's no way that she can cause trouble if you don't speak to her."

Sarah stopped looking at Tommy's tie. She moved her eyes to the potatoes she had peeled and put in a bowl of water.

Martha came into the kitchen and held on to her father's leg. Her hair was long and thick, but it was getting darker. It was as though it had never been cut.

After they left, Sarah put the roast in the oven and went into the living room. The large window was full of the day, a colorless windy day without birds. Sarah sat on the floor and ran her fingers across the smooth, varnished wood. Beneath the expensive flooring was cold cement. Tanks had once lined the walls. Lobsters had crept back and forth across the mossy glass. The phone rang. Sarah didn't look at it, suspecting it was Genevieve. Then she picked it up.

"Hello," said Genevieve, "I thought I might drop by. It's a bleak day, isn't it. Cold. Is your family at home?"

"They go out on Sunday," Sarah said. "It gives me time to think. They go to church."

"What do you think about?" The woman's voice seemed far away. Sarah strained to hear her.

"I'm supposed to cook dinner. When they come back we eat dinner."

"I can prepare clams in forty-three different ways," Genevieve said.

"This is a roast. A roast pork."

"Well, may I come over?"

"All right," Sarah said.

She continued to sit on the floor, waiting for Genevieve, looking at the water beneath the sky. The water on the horizon was a wide, satin ribbon. She wished that she had the courage to swim on such a bitter, winter day. To swim far out and rest, to hesitate and then to return. Her life was dark, unexplored. Her abstinence had drained her. She felt sluggish, robbed. Her body had no freedom.

She sat, seeing nothing, the terrible calm light of the day around her. The things she remembered were so far away, bathed in a different light. Her life seemed so remote to her. She had sought happiness in someone, knowing she could not find it in herself and now her heart was strangely hard. She rubbed her head with her hands.

Her life with Tommy was broken, irreparable. Her life with him was over. His infidelities kept getting mixed up in her mind with the death of the boy, with Tommy's false admission that he had been driving when the boy died. Sarah couldn't understand anything. Her life seemed so random, so needlessly constructed and now threatened in a way which did not interest her.

"Hello," Genevieve called. She had opened the front door and was standing in the hall. "You didn't hear my knock."

Sarah got up. She was to entertain this woman. She felt anxious, adulterous. The cold rose from Genevieve's skin and hair. Sarah took her coat and hung it in the closet. The fresh cold smell lingered on her hands. She found herself staring at her hands as though they were predatory animals.

Sarah moved into the kitchen. She took a package of rolls out of the freezer.

"Does your little girl like church?" Genevieve asked.

"Yes, very much."

"It's a stage," said Genevieve. "I'm Catholic myself. As a child, I used to be fascinated by the martyrs. I remember a picture of St. Lucy, carrying her eyes like a plate of eggs, and St. Agatha. She carried her breasts on a plate."

Sarah said, "I don't understand what we're talking about. I know you're just using these words, that they mean other words, I . . ."

"Perhaps we could take your little girl to a movie sometime, a matinee, after she gets out of school."

"Her name is Martha," Sarah said. She saw Martha grown up, her hair cut short once more, taking rolls out of the freezer, waiting.

"Martha, yes," Genevieve said. "Have you wanted more children?"

"No," Sarah said. Their conversation was illegal, unspeakable. Sarah couldn't imagine it ever ending. Her fingers tapped against the ice-cube trays. "Would you care for a drink?"

"A very tall glass of vermouth," Genevieve said. She was looking at a little picture Martha had made, that Sarah had tacked to the wall. It was a very badly drawn horse. "I wanted children. I wanted to fulfill myself. One can never fulfill oneself. I think it is an impossibility."

Sarah made Genevieve's drink very slowly. She did not make one for herself.

"When Stevie was Martha's age, he knew everything about whales. He kept notebooks. Once, on his birthday, I took him to the whaling museum in New Bedford." She sipped her drink. "It all goes wrong somewhere," she said. She turned her back on Sarah and went into the other room. Sarah followed her.

"There are so many phrases for 'dead,' you know," Genevieve was saying. "The kids think them up. Stevie had one. He was a slangy kid. He'd use it for dead animals and rock stars. He'd say they'd 'bought the farm.' "

Sarah nodded. She was pulling and peeling at the nails of her hands.

"I think it's pretty creepy. A dark farm, you know. Weedy. Run-down. Broken machinery everywhere. A real job."

Sarah raised her head. "You want us to share Martha, don't you," she said. "It's only right, isn't it?"

". . . the paint blown away, acres and acres of tangled, black land, a broken shutter over the well."

Sarah lowered her head again. Her heart was cold, horrified. The reality of the two women, placed by hazard in this room, this bright functional tasteful room that Tommy had created, was being tested. Reality would resist, for days, perhaps weeks, but then it would yield. It would yield to this guest, this visitor, for whom Sarah had made room.

"Would you join me in another drink?" Genevieve asked. "Then I'll go."

"I mustn't drink," Sarah said.

"You don't forget," Genevieve said, "that's just an old saw." She went into the kitchen and poured more vermouth for herself. Sarah could smell the meat cooking. From another room, the clock chimed.

"You must come to my home soon," Genevieve said. She did not sit down. Sarah looked at the pale green liquid in the glass.

"Yes," Sarah said, "soon."

"We must not greet one another on the street, however. People are quick to gossip."

"Yes," Sarah said. "They would condemn us." She looked heavily at Genevieve, full of misery and submission.

There was knocking on the door. "Sarah," Tommy's voice called, "why is the door locked?" She could see his dark head at the window.

"I must have thrown the bolt," Genevieve said. "It's best to lock your house in winter, you know. It's the kids mostly. They get bored. Stevie was a robber once or twice, I'm sure." She put down her glass, took her coat from the closet and went out. Sarah heard Martha say, "That's Mommy's friend."

Tommy stood in the doorway and stared at Sarah. "Why did you lock the door?" he asked again.

Sarah imagined seeing herself, naked. She said, "There are robbers."

Tommy said, "If you don't feel safe here, we'll move. I've been looking at a wonderful place about twenty miles from here, on a cove. It only needs a little work. It will give us more room. There's a barn, some fence. Martha could have a horse."

Sarah looked at him with an intent, halted expression, as though she were listening to a dialogue no one present was engaged in. Finally, she said, "There are robbers. Everything has changed."

Jeanne Wilmot

Dirt Angel

(U N I T E D   S T A T E S)

It is the time of year the gypsies come out of hibernation. The ochre-faced children make an altar of plastic roses when they see me heading up Broadway straight to Said's. I recognize the little ones who are new to the marketplace even though the willful charcoal eyes and the con are familiar. They learn to spit at grace young here. Immediately after returning from the hospital I changed into a red two-piece halter and shawl that match the first spring air. When I enter the club, Mario is holding court from his usual corner, speaking in chants that are in keeping with the cadence of his gang days, stabbing down into the air with his fingers, floating high on the hawk with the dust of an angel. I haven't been to Said's for a while. Haven't seen Mario for longer. Tonight I needed to be back home. I like my life now all right. I work a professional day job. I get up, have morning coffee and am at the hospital by nine. But this place, Mario, and the people here manage to sustain something close to the sense of silent commotion I associate with home—there is no routine, crisis is our energy and the silence is just the waiting for something to happen.

Mario glances at me quick as I rock into the center of the club, swivel-headed and a little coked up. A beautiful sandy-haired womanchild straddling a stool at the bar fixes on my small breasts. She looks as white as I look black, and for all her sexual smugness, I can smell the captive in her. Tall ferns and palms sway to a breeze propelled by a wind machine that rocks the third-sex lovers lined up against the street windows. Instead of looking out onto the fantastical tropics of Macao, they see a homeland of yellow cabs and Midwestern boys with swollen hormonal breasts. I rhyme with the chants until the music starts playing and Mario strolls over to kiss my ear, aiming intuitively through burnt red eyes. In '59 we'd been kids together on John R and Brush in Detroit, playing *bobo-bedetton-dotton* games with sticks, balls and jump ropes. Half the snowfiends in the club are from blocks like mine, and although some might say I fucked destiny standing up, I could still catch the disease. The sandy-haired girl with the translucent skin was probably destined for the Henderson, North Carolina Junior League and she's caught it. Mario calls her Pandy.

I look more closely at this girl Pandy. She wants me to watch her, and for a moment it's as if I'm in the presence of royalty, the red and blue lights of Said's reaching through her rich blonde curls and across the tiny features placed perfectly upon her Anglo-Saxon face. However, there is a trapped expression in Pandy's eyes as they embrace mine. She stands up and immediately I see that she is pregnant. Probably close to seven months. She is surrounded by the sycophants and true admirers of her court. The French silk and sequin shirt she wears covers her filled belly. She gracefully strides over to the dance floor. Her transition from empress to royal mother is effortless. It could humble the barren. She has engaged me without having to say a word. Mario says she always wears sequins. That she is referred to as the Sequin.

My eyes follow the Sequin's stride to the middle of the neon room where she automatically demands center spot. Her competition plays fierce and violent around her for a few minutes until it is absorbed into her dance. Joyfully the other dancers join the girl, not puzzled in the slightest by her grace and agility. She has two partners, likewise her partners, seven in all trading off girl for boy, boy for girl—little ambidextrous babies riding high on the mania of pills and madness. They dance fast. Jerky to the beat, step to step on sparkling shoes with stilt-heels, dervish turns Latin style, calling out high-pitched expletives meant to dot the same place in each skull. I watch the naked backs of the dancing boys, their greased spines like healthy roots, my eyes clinging tenuously to their ancient strength. Go down, go down on your boy, hump him from the back, hump him in the front—girl to girl, belly to belly, boy to boy up to down—fast now—not Latin erotic-smooth—fast bumping here and there, fast computer motions clicking on the upstroke, a slighter downbeat, bent knees, flamboyant male arms, rigid but cool female arms.

Pandy's earthbound body compels her partners to remain fixed. The floor chants, *She's so cool, she's icebox cool.* Little thirteen-year-old girls undulate involuntarily on the sidelines, their firm young bodies seasonally in need of the bizarre, calling back *I'm so cool, I'm icebox cool,* while their boys move next to them—each forsaking the other with the fantasy of making it with this sequined mothergirl and her androgynous entourage. I smirk at her glitter but its blood-color takes me captive. I fight her glory, yet her urgency wins. It might be the coke, or it might be that we each know about stepping out of one world into others, being watched as travelers always in between, claiming a love or a hate for some recent home whose legacy we daily tangle into more lie than truth. Or it might be that our lives intersect at a place beyond the gypsies, who, afoot for the spring thaw, remind us both that rebirth applies to all things. Whatever it is, she's taken my night from me, and maybe more.

A little girl painted head-to-toe in white paint over her dark skin, wearing a black hood over her hair, pasties over her breasts and a g-string-like facade over her tiny cunt, grabs my hand suddenly and pulls me out to the dance floor. She doesn't belong here. Someone must have brought her as a mascot, a cruel joke. She belongs downtown. Mario grins as she highsteps smoothly around me, softly leading me into a sensual counterpoint to the erratic moves of the dancers around us. We dance a slow hypnotic grind at first, half-time to the chant. Only our knees move, deliberately and in unison. The Sequin struts out and stands opposite us. Her stomach is thrust forward and proud. The seven-headed Dancing Machine stops to watch their girl come on cold. She is the star here. The Sequin turns her misshapen body to me, grasps me around the waist, and pulls me against her groin. I initiate a gesture of contempt, but knowing he has to get Pandy away from me fast, Mario slithers up laughing. He grabs Pandy around her waist and flips her toward him, twirling her the way a father would his child, gleefully offering a moment's different reality in the sweeping motion of a top, then releases her on the sideline before returning to me. Mario's attention has short-circuited the tension and the Sequin becomes no more than one of the sweet dancing girls I grew up with. The touch of a man has lessened the weight of her child so that she laughs as if through liquid. I continue to dance, waiting patiently while Mario slides down off his sloppy high. He holds me close as the song comes to its end.

Mario had been my first and I float along with that memory. He is tall and light-skinned. Almost pretty. Considered one of the lucky ones in those days. But he didn't deal in lucky. He had a brutal and facile mind. He chose me. I had style, no great beauty, but I could go toe-to-toe with him on any scheme. None of us thought he'd ever get hooked.

We dance until his eyes return to the bright they used to be after he'd beat me at stickball, and at the very moment this nostalgic mist could have turned into regret and accusation, Pandy touches me on the shoulder. Dugie takes you up and dugie takes you down, and part of the glitter of a sequin is the artificiality of its evanescence. I choose to sleep the tragedy of what has made me one thing and Mario a junkie, and decide instead to caress those blazing eyes that seem to leap from the dark rims set into Pandy's face. Drug solitude is common here, so I let her hold me from behind and dance with us.

I smell the rot of Pandy's imminent death. Someone else might miss the agony of her exile and sensationalize the choices she must have made, but I imagine that within Pandy's doom there is something pure and hyperbolic. There are separate, individual pains that are more vile in their means to exile than exile itself. It is an organic condition, not metaphor, and I want to flee from it. I want to walk right out of Said's and out of New York, out of the universe for that matter.

But instead, I take Pandy home with me that night, passing through streets littered with pigeon bone and bottle caps. My place is between Ninth and Tenth Avenues in the fifties. As soon as we arrive Pandy uses my egg poacher as a cooker and shoots up at the kitchen table while we talk about setting the styles with rags, bandannas and secondhand acetate that Gucci later redesigns for the weary rich. As Pandy speaks, she plucks the air with her long fingers, drawing bows and barrettes and ankle bracelets on the air. I soon tire of her meanderings.

"Why are you having this baby? You're doing everything you possibly can to harm it."

She looks straight at me, not at all surprised by my brash change of subject.

"I'm not really a junkie. I just like to get high sometimes."

"All the time looks like to me."

"No, that's not really true. I go a day or two without nothin."

"Why do you say *nothin*? Was that the way you were taught to talk?"

"Don't be so hard on me. I'd like to be your friend."

"Sorry, I don't make friends easily. And they never make me."

I turn on her. She can't hold her head up any longer. She nods onto the table so I carry her to the chair and try to make her as comfortable as possible, surrounding her with old clothes I shape into pillows. I put a blanket my mother had left in the project when she died over Pandy's birdlike ankles and legs—they could have been my mother's. Pandy half dozes as I rinse out the dishes in the sink and prepare for bed. I'm angry with myself for finding her so compelling.

She startles me when she speaks out.

"Why did you cover my legs with the blanket and tuck me into a bed you made if you hate me?"

"I don't hate you, I just don't know what you want from me, and I know it's something."

The twilight color of predawn lights up one square foot of the rug in my first-floor room. Pandy leaves the nest I made her, twists her hair up into a little knot on top of her head and angles around the room. I light a joint and sit on the edge of my bed, following her transit across the floor. She watches me a minute. I don't say anything. Finally she does.

"You know, I used to be a cheerleader."

"So did I."

I can visualize Pandy's light hair in a flip and her lithe body wrapped in a red uniform as a highlight to the Henderson, North Carolina School Yearbook.

I am hooked by her vulnerability and decay in the same way I was by my mother's in the days before her death. But their decay is also my anger and defense. My mother's swollen alcoholic belly pressing against an organ that eventually turned her yellow and filled her tissues with the excrement of a body gone mad was my ticket out.

I decide to get ready for bed. I go first into the little room that holds the toilet, strip and grab a towel from the closet, then out to the screened-in area around the sink and bathtub. I stay behind the matchstick curtains for an unusually long time. Still, Pandy is not asleep when I pull the blanket back on my bed.

She whispers into the stale air, "I'll take you home with me tomorrow night."

Her unpredictability is as engaging as her vulnerability. Again, reminiscent. I would pay a lot of money if this were not the case. If I could resist.

In the morning I leave at my usual time, tired, but this isn't the first time. I trust Pandy to be there with nothing missing when I return in the evening. Our intimacy is automatic and, for me, uncomfortable. That night when I come home, she is dressed up in a plaid pleated skirt designed in such a way that she barely looks pregnant. She is a very small woman anyway. Her baby looks like it might be as well. She has cleaned my apartment, probably shot up for the day, been to her own place and gone shopping.

"You're coming over for dinner."

I'm not wild about the idea but decide to go anyway. We take the IRT express up to '25th and then walk crosstown. I don't know East Harlem all that well and the further east we go, the more uneasy I become. We don't talk much. We zigzag uptown, turn off the avenue and onto an unpaved, muddy street, heading toward the East River. We could be anywhere. Empty lots filled with city weeds and brick dust shroud the uneven boundaries of the street. I notice the wild dogs snarling in harmony when we pass them in the brush.

We leave the path, abandoned totally now by the city's compass of light. Pandy strikes a match and pokes her foot into the familiar earth as we continue to walk. Eventually we hit metal. I assume it is the old tracks from trains that used to carry the rich out of the city. Along the tracks a cement slab interrupted by periodic holes covered with gratings gives Pandy the direction she needs. The only peculiarity that makes these openings different from sewer covers is the large padlocks evidently holding sections of the gratings together. Pandy takes out a cylindrical key and opens one of these locks. She does it with a brief finesse that claims it as her home.

Pandy lifts the city grate up and drops it against the cement, then unlocks another padlock and shoves something heavy and metal inward. A gaslight globe lights our way down a flight of cement steps which opens onto a cave charmed only slightly by the touch of humanity. I notice the lamp immediately. The floor is packed mud, the walls cinder block, and in the center a small generator Pandy has switched on offers a glitter to the room. There is no bathroom. The generator seems also to hype up an hydraulic pump that brings water to a tiny sink Pandy uses to wash her hands and to pee in. The lamp possesses one corner, a bentwood rocker belonging in a young married's apartment another, a pile of neatly folded clothing the third; and finally, standing on an orange crate is a bowl filled with goldfish floating in scummy water. Her winter pets. The bed is swung up against the wall exposing bits and pieces of fabric draped onto the wire tapestry at odd intervals. Between the aquarium and the clothes, a metal door covered with posters of dark, dead jazz musicians stands ajar.

"Come and see the neighborhood."

"Is this where you live all the time?"

"It's my home, if that's what you mean."

The doorway leads out to the old subway tracks unused by the city since the twenties. The backs of an entire community of these part-mud, part-cement huts, all with doorways leading out to the tracks, line the ledge that eventually falls off into the pit of dead rails. From the stench it is obvious that this area is used for all forms of refuse, consumed daily by the rats that now slink around our legs.

I know rats. I move cautiously, remembering their feel on my face babied with milk, back in Detroit. Here the constant motion their squat bodies create imprisons me. In fact, the tracks themselves are fur-lined with the backs of these Norwegian city squirrels used to eating babies' faces and the mothers' arms that hold them. The numbing calm of shock allowed me a moment to adjust, yet even as I stand paralyzed, I can see that the rats are like pets in this neighborhood. Doglike in their sensibility, the rats know if they don't graze on the flesh of their strange life-fellows, they will be fed a daily menu of garbage and human feces. Whirring armies of flying beetles the size of small mice stop just short of attacking my head. I sense in their kingdom the same peculiar fear and curiosity the families of a small village might experience when confronted by a stranger. Although the insects don't bite, Pandy runs into her home and brings out a foul-smelling root that she smears over my head and hair. With the odor signaling my rite of passage into their ranks, they move away to sit happily on the backs of the rats dozing on the forgotten tracks. In this symbiotic hell of the cryptozoa, the bugs live off the maggots that spontaneously appear in the garbage the rats leave behind, and although my fascination impoverishes my fear, there exists a dread far beneath the surface that has to do with Pandy and her comfort at my being here with her.

Halfway down the tracks I can see a bonfire being fed rags by a man with thick dreadlocks. Pandy tentatively explains that the groups of people I now begin to see around other bonfires strung along the edge of the pit as it curves to the left would be outlawed up on the streets. The people in the nicer homes living within the cinder and mud igloos provide these people with food and necessities, even though the longer the outlaws remain, the less they desire anything but their own sludge fires, their own conversation and a meal every so often.

For several moments there is silence between Pandy and me. Pandy moves from foot to foot restlessly. It is a graceful gesture. Her limbs sway to a silent chorus. Then,

"You shocked by where I live?"

"Is that what you want me to be? Is that why you live here?"

Her glow fades as I continue.

"Look, I know you don't have to live like this—that dress you wore last night cost more than a year's rent on my apartment. You have antiques in your mud hut. What kind of joke are you playing on yourself and the people who have to live here?"

Pandy spreads her hands out in all directions.

"Why shouldn't I live like this if they do?"

I am not amused by martyrs—their innocence a luxury I could never afford.

"Come on, we're going to have a talk. All you are is a kid."

Narcotized though she is, she stands her ground. "But why? Why shouldn't I live like they do?" She won't budge.

I lose patience and shout, "What about that baby in your belly?"

I grab her by the hand, expecting resistance, and find that she has gone limp. Her acquiescence to me seems total, so I lead her back to her hut. The usual distance and tension the drugs maintain are gone, and within seconds it is as if she has entered a fugue state interrupted only slightly by confusion, not wanting to submit or admit to anything, but reticently allowing me to move her about.

When she starts to cry uncontrollably as I pack a few things in her hut, I can't understand the words she is trying to form. This abrupt shift in mood is all too sudden for me, yet I suspect she has been moving toward this crescendo since before we met. Meeting me was mere serendipity. Now it all fits.

I lock the door to her home and we take a subway back to my house. I hold her in the back of one of the cars. When I finally get to my apartment I stick her in the bathtub. Her full stomach looks hard and mottled, as if her own flesh is all that can protect the jewel lying hidden inside. I consider shooting her up with an I.V. of valium and demerol from the hospital, but the bath seems to be calming her down. She calls to me that she has to return to get her lamp, she never travels without it; and then she dopes herself. Finally I get her into my bed to rest.

She must have left after I went to buy food at the Ninth Avenue markets. When I come back and can't find her, I call Mario. If I have to return to her hut, I don't want to go alone. I tell him to meet me at 125th and First, we can walk from there.

Mario is drugged to a fine tuning and in complete control.

I don't have a landmark or a key so when I find the gratings, I start knocking. The silence beyond each padlock does not unnerve me. I walk five blocks and, like a machine programmed for solution, I keep knocking and screaming Pandy's name. Mario follows me. We cross a patch that looks familiar. There is a stark sapling standing cold, new, out of place and memorable for its solitude—and the bricks some caretaker has built around it—in the middle of the path. I wait. I think I hear the tinny sound of a transistor radio.

Mario sucks the wind through his teeth as I holler, the matches burning in my fist illuminating the ground around us and one of the padlocked grates. All at once the noise stops and the grate is thrown open so suddenly that the only thing I glimpse is a dark head as it descends some steps into a pit below. Words pierce the darkness.

"All right. All right. My baby is me."

I follow the hysterical cries down the steps, turning around three times to beckon Mario to follow. He stands riveted to the clammy slab of cement, as if he is a watchdog bred in the bushes with the other wild dogs. He tells me to wait for him, but instead I continue into the deep black room at the bottom of the steps. I light another match and glance quickly around to get my bearings. The room is empty except for a sink like the one at Pandy's and a cot shoved up against the wall. The person who opened the door squats in the middle of the floor, cuddling what I presume to be an infant and screeching a lullaby in that high-pitched voice I mistook for a small radio.

The blanket swaddling the infant looks familiar. It takes a few minutes for my eyes to adjust to the lack of light, but gradually I can discern color and detail. An orange glow shines under the bottom and through the sides of the back door, stippling the mud floor around the woman. Pandy's neighbor holds a light brown child mottled from new birth. I feel very afraid. The neighbor is an old black-skinned woman with a goiter that hangs down to her breast where she is trying to suckle the child. The taunting shriek announces her insanity less vividly than the look in her eyes. "It's my baby see, it's my baby, please, you can't have my baby, my baby is me."

The old woman repeats the singsong over and over again. She pulls at the extra skin hanging from beneath her chin as the rhyme becomes a hymnal refrain. I step back and glance up to see if Mario is still at the top of the stairs, but he has already begun his slow descent. Obviously the sounds from below have both alerted and disoriented him. Like a night animal, once his eyes can make use of the available light, he adjusts to the situation. He sees my fear. In a guttural voice pitched against the noise of the old woman, he speaks to me.

"Get the fuck outta here. I'll help her. Get the fuck outta here!"

"Ask her about Pandy, please ask her."

I hear Mario from the twilight.

"If you don't get outta here, I'll walk right out and leave you *and* Pandy."

Mario stalks the distance between this creature and myself with an exorbitant hatred toward me for getting him into the mess. Out of habit, he begins rolling up his sleeves. When he is certain that the poor woman is reasonably harmless, although unpredictable, he very calmly addresses her.

"*Por favor, dónde está su amiga Pandy?*"

I hadn't heard the Latin accent in her song. Mario stares kindly and repeats his sentence. I try to focus.

"*Por favor, dónde está su amiga Pandy?*"

Without missing a beat or altering her expression, the old woman drops the baby and jumps back, hissing the words of the hymn in Spanish. I run to the baby and discover it is very recently stillborn. The goiter flaps as the old woman takes off around the room. When she races to her sink in the corner, sticking first one leg and then the other into the bowl, I run out the back door which leads to the tracks. Mario follows. Without thinking, I run deep into the city behind the huts and don't stop until I feel safe. Mario grabs me. My fever makes me a dangerous friend. It matches the heat of the sludge fires warming the dreadlocked men.

"Cut it out. What's happening to you? We're on a mission. Don't go *saditty* on me now."

Mario has reached far back into our past to criticize my fear of this place. I stare at him. In the glow of a hundred different bonfires I fight the demon that drives me to embrace a stranger's pain. Mario doesn't respond to my stillness. He is watching something over my shoulder. I twist around so fast I am thrown off balance and fall. The palms of my hands touch a thin layer of mud before sinking with the weight of my body into the hideous rat food. The immediate impact of the odor makes me cry out, just as a voice above me begins to speak. Squatting there, arms thrown back for support, vulnerable to the dungeon and its recent history, I begin to weep.

The voice offers me a rag. I feel a need to be proper.

"Oh, thank you."

I stand up and peer into the face of a man who could have been the shadow with the thick dreadlocks I saw yesterday down near the main bonfire. He nods to me and watches peacefully as I primly clean off my hands. He repeats the words he has spoken before, and this time I hear what he means.

"She left you a note."

"What do you mean—left?"

"She's dead. Do you want me to take you to her?"

"How do you know who I am?"

"She said you would be coming. She expected you."

"What about the old woman? She's got Pandy's baby."

"We'll take care of that here."

We follow the man through the tunnel, past clots of people, their yellow fire lighting our way and the activity of the nether world, past the old woman's screams, down to Pandy's house which I can now see is in a cul-de-sac where the direction of the old train track takes a sharp turn to the right. All of the houses on the same line with Pandy's have colorful flowerpots filled with plastic flowers outside their doors. Mario follows the rats with his eyes. He never stops and never asks a question. The bugs are clustered in halos over Mario's head and my own. Mario does not try to brush them away. He keeps his fists clenched and his arms free to swing. Pandy's back door is open. Inside, the single Murphy bed is suspended halfway to the floor, swinging gently to the rock of the subway rumble. The material covering the springs and legs is eaten away by rats. Earlier in the day Pandy told me that wherever she goes to stay she carries with her the bronze lamp given her by her grandmother. Here the piece is more a touch of art in a room made barren by deliberate poverty. The base is broad—and carved out in bronze, against the light shining through a red Tiffany glass, is a small lady carrying a parasol as she descends a flight of steps into a Japanese garden. It is the little red light that now illuminates Pandy hanging in the center of the room. A gnarl of veins bulges through her needle-pocked skin like a blue worm reappearing in the nape of her neck, in her arms and in her legs. Even the femoral artery in her groin is swollen.

Mario's nose begins to run as we three stand. Pandy's commotion is mostly over. The roar of a subway crossing town to head up to the Bronx echoes in another part of the catacombs. The immediate stillness is interrupted each time Mario sniffs. I shake a little, never taking my eyes from Pandy and the homely afterbirth which hangs from her.

The man is the first to speak, and he speaks to Mario.

"If you want to leave, I'll watch over your friend."

"No, there's no more either of us can do. I think we should both leave."

I know I have many things to do yet. "You leave. Don't worry. I'm not frightened."

"I can't just leave you."

"Please. I'd rather. And besides," I gesture to our guide, "he'll make sure nothing happens."

Mario nods to the man, walks up the cement steps with the keys to the padlocks the man has handed him, unclasps the lock to the metal door, then the one for the grating covering the door. He throws the keys back down to me at the bottom of the steps and climbs out, leaving the door open but closing the top grate. The man walks out the back door and stations himself next to it. I close that door and look again at Pandy. I stand on the orange crate that has held the dead goldfish and lift Pandy out of her noose. I pull the bed down and lay her on it. Her pink sheets are covered with little rosebuds.

Then, finally, I look at the note underneath the lamp. She bequeathed me her grandmother's lamp. She had believed we had a preordained connection so strong that the force of her death would make itself known to me through a means beyond logic and information. What kind of ritual execution had been in her mind I can only crudely imagine; however, she probably had made peace in her final bargain: if the baby survived, it was meant to and she had protected and nurtured it as far as she could; if the baby died, then it was meant to because her poison had already begun to enter it. Understanding this primitive gesture binds me to Pandy in a way she would have wanted. Yet seeing that she could go no further into motherhood than expectancy does not surprise me. The Dancing Machine could come to life for a night in the afterglow of medicine, but it could not share a life with her. She wouldn't have wanted it to become her language. She was alone. And she had chosen it that way.

Touched briefly by clarity earlier today, she had seemed to understand what her choices meant. While Pandy was taking her bath in my apartment, after she calmed down a bit, she began talking about things she had read back in the days when she kept books. I tried to encourage her to confide in me but before I could stop her she shot up right in the bathtub and what might have become an explanation turned into babble. Instead of speech she spoke in tongues made feathery by the legs of spiders she claimed to feel spilling and prancing through her veins. It was frustration that precipitated my leaving for the market. Yet now as I stand next to her nearly alive body, I remember from the rubble of her monologue that there was an intaglio engraved upon her life, and that it is in a similar design to mine.

I ask the subway man to take me down to the old woman's home. He explains to her for me that she will have to give the baby back. That we have come for the baby. A group of people gathers outside her door merely to overhear our conversation. They lean into each other for comfort in the way old ladies might hold hands on the street. The woman hides in a corner and begins to sing the hymn again as she performs the ritual of wrapping the dead infant in the blanket, rolling the baby this way and that, murmuring her refrain until all of the blanket is tucked and folded around the infant. It is a boy. His little body stiffened into permanent innocence. I take him down to his mother's bed and fit him neatly inside the curve of her elbow.

I nod to the subway man and close the door to the rats. I put the groceries over my arm that Pandy bought earlier, pick up the lamp and climb the stairs. There is a picture of Stevie Wonder I hadn't noticed before, on the wall leading to the street. The photo is a familiar one—from the days when Yolanda beaded and wove his hair. Mario is waiting near the little sapling down the mud from me. I slam the street door onto the darkness inside and we decide to walk home. On Broadway a little gypsy girl comes up to us and offers Mario a plastic rose. I cook dinner with Pandy's groceries and Mario stays with me until I tell him to go. I put the lamp in the closet where my mother's blanket had been, and that is the end of it.

Mario is in the hospital today. Watershedding. He decided two days ago. He hadn't shot up for thirty-six hours and the pain was ripping his gut to hell. I went with him to the hospital and I'll see him again tonight. He'll be in a cell, screaming maybe, or perhaps silent. Then he'll get out. He's my homeboy.

Jeanette Winterson

The Green Man

(ENGLAND)

To honour. To mock. To fear. To hate. To be fascinated. To laugh out loud.

The gypsies come here every year once a year. Come living. Come memory. Half dream. Half danger. Half man half beast. Satyr them, satire us; safe, good, time keeping, clean, for a day dragged in front of their silvered mirrors.

Get my fortune told. Buy a pony. Sharpen my knives to their murder edge. I wear my pants baggy but pass their glass and I look like a stag in rut. Down Sir! Oh cool comfort on a sunny day that my embarrassment is mine alone. The river is wide where they camp either side and I am clothed but my reflection is naked.

They breed horses. That is they breed themselves and sell off their children of the nether parts, piebald rascals all mane and tail, to set a swag at a girl. Well known it is that young girls love horses, loving the wild underside of themselves, loving the long neck and hot ears of animal seduction.

Buy the young lady a pony and the trap is thrown in free. These round-bellied glint-eyed horses are Trojan horses. Truant, feckless, anarchic, unsaddled and munching to bare earth the ordered weekends of Daddy's life; the lawn.

Didn't Daddy save up to move out of the city? Didn't he save for a painted house and a picket fence? Didn't he save for wife and daughter? And after one long satisfactory shower of sperm hasn't his wife bottled him like a genie and taught him to spend his lust on the lawn?

Oh the suburban weekend oh!

On Friday Daddy cuts the lawn. On Saturday Daddy waters it. On Sunday Daddy barbeques on the lawn. On Monday Daddy leaves it and looks with half regret on his close-cropped green-eyed doll. His manhood is buried there and next weekend he'll spike it.

But the gypsies are coming and his daughter is thirteen.

Talk of the town is that the fair should be banned. This time could be the last time if the Mayor has his way. Time is gone when folks needed travelling play, when the bright band of gypsy caravans looping down the hill made a gold ring of holiday fire. What the gypsies sell you can buy any place and better. No one keeps their pans to copper. This town is stainless steel.

Why am I frightened by the scissor man? Why does my heart curl? The noise of the blacksmith hurts my feet and the knife grinder whets my backbone. The red-head trull selling silk will deck me in a beaded scarf. She would make me her Corn King if she could and take what little I have left. The Green Man on the green lawn sprouting ears of wheat.

My daughter came back from school and said "Daddy, in the Olden Days the Queen married the King and after a year she killed him."

I said "I know that sweetheart."

She said "It was to make the crops grow," and I went out and worked on the lawn.

The gypsies are coming, Gutsy from the North. Open faced from the West. Beguiling from the East. South and Sexy. In less than a day's march, less than a night's scheming, by compass and constellation they will be here. Spread out the map and pinpoint me. I am voodooed head to foot.

My wife said "What are those punctures in your chest?"

I said "I fell on the spiker."

I have taken great pains to neaten the garden. It is a triumph of restraint. Although it is summer and clematis and rose would garland my head if I let them I have clipped their easy virtue into something finer. They climb, they decorate, they do not spread. My wife admires this from her bedroom. Meanwhile, our inner and outer spheres have met at a point of mutuality. It is our daughter's birthday and the day of the fair.

When a horse pisses it locks its front legs raises its tail and drops a shaft of vast dimensions that shoots a fireman's douse. This was the first thing we saw, the three of us, as we walked hand in hand in the field.

"Daddy, look," said my daughter and gripped my finger. The grass turned liquid. I thought "We shall have to swim for it." My wife was wearing peep-toes.

A Hispanic came by selling ice creams.

"You want one?" he said, looking at the trunk of piss.

My wife paid, while my daughter and I stood helplessly together and I thought, "She wants to touch it. Oh God."

She broke from my hand and went up and patted the horse, dry now, shrinking up into himself. The green pool winked at us.

We walked on, a normal three way family, eating our ice creams. I tried to win at the shooting gallery but they screw the guns. There was a woman behind me, the kind I don't like, big boots and jeans, and a slender body and a stare. She slung a gun and massacred the target. The stall keeper laughed and said something to her in their own tongue. She chose her prize and strode away with it, another girl at her arm.

"Ciao Reina," shouted the stall keeper and I told my wife it was a put up job to fake an even chance and pull a sucker after his luck.

He gestured to me. "Try again."

I said, "You screw the guns."

He shrugged and picked up a glass rolling pin. "Maybe your wife would like this?"

They were blowing glass at the next stall. There were men in leather aprons, their skin as thick and dark, playing on their soundless trumpets and forcing a ball of glass into the fire-shot air.

"See your future in it," said the hag who took the money. "Quick, now, as it comes."

I turned away. My wife wanted to buy a witch ball for her display cabinet. I said I thought it was a mistake, "They are just cheap stuff." But she liked the way the colours caught in the lacunae of the surface. Reluctantly I gave the hag the money.

She caught my hand as I did so. Instinctively I closed it into a fist but she twisted it like a door knob and my fingers fell open, palm up under her greasy stare. My one hand was much bigger than both of hers together and if I were a quick bite horror writer I suppose I would call them claws. With her hooked nail she scored my heart line and laughed out loud.

"The heart stops," she said.

"You mean I'm going to die?"

"Only your heart."

I pulled away from her and put my hand up to my chest. My ironed cotton chest. My heart was still beating time. The two glass blowers were looking at me with open contempt, as though I were the one filthy, scarred, vagrant. I stepped backwards and collided with one of their women selling bracelets from a basket. My force spilled some of them and I bent down with her to pick them up, saying, "Sorry, sorry," all the while. I was conscious of the others watching me. Where was my wife?

I concentrated on scooping up the last of the fakey sliding gold and raised my head. Her breasts were by my mouth. Her breasts falling out of her man's loose shirt. Her breasts, tan, taut. Her breasts, unharnessed.

She pulled my head forward and even while I was pulling away I had her skin against my upper lip and my cheeks were burning with shame and I was worrying that I hadn't shaved enough and hating myself and hating this. . . .

To honour. To mock. To fear. To hate. To laugh out loud. To be fascinated.

Where was my wife?

They were laughing at me, all of them, as I scrambled off the grass and blundered away. My wife and daughter were up ahead moving at the same mesmerised pace as everyone else. I shoved through the tranced crowds and caught up with them both, their backs to me, hand in hand, my wife and daughter. I smoothed myself down and put my arms round their shoulders.

My wife turned and smiled and together we watched the jugglers and my heart paced back to its normal metronome and I breathed again, not too shallow, not too deep. I began to think about a beer.

"What happened to your trousers?"

My hand went straight to my crotch but my wife did not notice. She was glaring at my knees. I let my eyes travel downwards and there were two green splotches neatly capping my white ducks.

Yes I know we have only just bought me these trousers. These trousers were expensive. These trousers are blatant in their whiteness. Sassy as a virgin courting a stain. These are bachelor trousers not gelded chinos. These are touch trousers in fourteen ounce linen and we had a fight in the shop.

Now we shall have a fight in the field and our raised voices have sawn out a circle in the crowds around us. Our daughter is embarrassed and walks away. My wife says "Ruined." "Stupid." "Specialist cleaning." "Grass." "How could you?" and gradually her words break up, out of their sentences, verbs and objects falling away, leaving the subject, me, me, failed again. Failure.

I could no longer hear her. Could see the words forming in glass bubbles out of the crazy trumpet of her mouth. My cartoon wife. Her cartoon husband. Waving their arms and blowing bubbles at the crowd.

Till death us do part. Nothing in the marriage service about a pair of stained trousers. Let me pass. A man can still have a drink can't he? I went into the beer tent where there was a pianola and a long trestle table, a merciful place to hide my knees and prop my elbows. I don't go out to bars. I'm a family man and proud of it. We like to eat together and share a bottle of wine. My wife buys it from the Family Wine Club. We usually get the Mystery Mix and it's always the same. I would prefer beer but I don't do the shopping.

Sometimes, when I leave for work early in the morning and my wife and daughter are still asleep, I truly believe that I will never come back. I love them both, sincerely I do, and I can't explain how you can love a thing and want to be parted from it forever. Sometimes I wish she would kill me, collect the insurance, go on with her life and free me from the guilt of staying, the guilt of going.

A friend of mine did go and now he lives in a rented place in the city, two rooms and no responsibilities and he is about as miserable as before. Change your life, they tell me, in those popular New Age Bibles, and my wife and I both understand the importance of speaking the truth and we have learned about quality time. Yet when I look at her and when she looks at me our eyes are pale.

What's in your eyes darling? What do I see? The daily calculations of money and sex. How much of one, how little of the other, the see-saw of married life, keep the balance just. Keep the balance, just. I am a heterosexual male. My wife is a heterosexual female. Are we too normal to enjoy our bed?

Normal male to Norman Mailer: Please tell me how.

Have you ever had a boy? I'd like to but I can't do it.

Listen to me. A man will try anything or thinks he will. I talk like a tomcat but I act like a worm. What happened to youth and glory? What happened to those bright days when the sun was still rising? Soon it will be Midsummer and the light beginning to die back, imperceptibly at first, a few minutes a day, and then the gradual forcing back indoors earlier and earlier, helpless against the dark.

Midsummer used to be a fire festival. They used to light the bonfires on Midsummer night and burn them through June 24, Midsummer Day. Maybe they thought they could prop up the sun in his luminary ride. Hold him in the heavens at his peak. It was a night of visions and strange dreams. A night of lawlessness, for the Corn King, the Green Man, could copulate with whomsoever he pleased. For a spell time stopped. At the moment of decline, accelerate. Call it a wild perversity or a wild optimism, but they were right, our ancestors, to celebrate what they feared. What I fear, I avoid. What I fear, I pretend does not exist. What I fear is quietly killing me. Would there were a festival for my fears, a ritual burning of what is coward in me, what is lost in me. Let the light in before it is too late.

The gypsies have come down the hill, their eyes in burning hoops. Come pony tail, come pony. Come highwater, come Hell. The river has risen with summer rain, rain in steam clouds above their fires. Fires infernal, fires illegal, bursts of water, bursts of flame.

The Mayor says it will have to be stopped. This is a Conservation Area. No dumping. No overnight camping. No fishing. No fires. No hawking. No begging. No talking after lights out. No sickness without medical insurance. No travel without passports. No status without a bank account. No welfare without a job. No flirting. No slacking. No drugs. No Queers (maybe rich ones). No foreigners (maybe rich ones or cheap ones).

The gypsies are here. Eyes the colour of stars. Dressed in history. Dressed in rainbows. Some wear jerkins, some wear knee breeches, some wear swami robes, some wear cowhide coats. All wear gold and not the kind they sell. The men look like pirates. The women look like whores. Tall women, heads back, bold stare, easy hips. What right have they to walk as if they have never known pain? Do you watch the way people walk? I do. I look for the disappointments in their shoulders and the stress in their hips. Look for the slight limp that betrays their vulnerable side. What kind of man or woman they are is in their gait. I never give a man a job until I've seen the way he walks. I courted my wife because when she moved she seemed to take the earth with her.

What happened to us holding hands side by side? Somewhere in the fourteen years of our married life I seem to have had a sex change and converted to Islam. How else to explain the twenty paces I lag behind?

When I come home caught in the cobwebs of my day, my wife has been planning our next holiday or working out the finance for a new car. I am still building the extension she designed two years ago. I have to fit it in with my job and the garden and time for my daughter who loves me. My wife strides us on into prosperity and fulfilment and I shuffle behind clutching the bills and a tool box. She was right to make me drain the lawn. All our friends admire its rollered curves. I admire my wife. Admire our success. We were nothing and she has coaxed out the grit in me and held me to my job. Why do I wish we were young again and she would hold me in her arms?

Listen to me. I sound like the fool I am. Fortunately I am alone.

At that moment I looked up out of the comforting opacity of my beer and down the trestle table. Tightly packed, like rowers in a slave ship, were a couple of hundred men, heads on their fists, staring into their beer as if it were a crystal ball. And the table seemed to infinitely extend through the candy striped canvas and out over the hills into the city and to be forever lined with men.

I got to my feet and left through an open flap at the back of the tent. I was away from the bustle of the fair and out by a few caravans, their fires pushing up smoke. Sitting beside one of the fires was the woman I had met already.

She said, "Take off your trousers."

"What?"

"I'll clean them for you."

She turned back and went up the wooden steps into a caravan. I was about twenty paces behind.

When I finally hesitated myself inside she was pouring blue powder into a copper pot. The caravan was one of those old barrel types with a pair of long shafts for the horse to draw it. Inside it was panelled, carved, sprung, beautiful, clean. She had a feather eiderdown on the bed and the bed was how a bed should be. Not too hygienic, not too hospital, not a showroom bed with matching sheets and pillow cases.

She held out her hand for my trousers and I wondered how her hair seemed so red that when she leaned over the copper there was no distinction between the soft metal and her soft hair.

She smiled and looked down at me. Not at my knees. I had my shirt tails but it was obvious how things stood. I suppose it was obvious how things were going to be but when I bucked into her it was with the same surprise as all those years ago when Alison and I had walked in the woods and made love among the bluebells. I had the perfect freedom of loving her and although we have never given up sex we never have found those woods again.

I felt the trees closing over me and I slept.

It was dark when I woke up. I was alone in the bed. I sat up and grabbed the cover around me. Gradually I could make out the shapes in the caravan and I found an oil lamp with its wick just burning under the brass cover. I turned it up and on the chair beside it were my trousers neatly folded and dry.

I inspected the knees. The accusing stains had disappeared but was it a trick of the light or were the trousers all over now hued invisible green? I dressed as quickly as I could and let myself out of the caravan.

What time was it? I checked my wrist and found my watch had gone. Should I go back in? I couldn't. I wanted to be away, be home, not be noticed, not be caught. I still had my wallet.

As I set off through the fields towards the empty stalls I saw by the firelight a group of men leading a horse up and down. There was a girl on it, clinging to the mane, slithering a bit on the bare back. I changed direction to avoid them but then I heard the girl shout "Daddy! Daddy!" I started running towards her voice and forgetting everything that had happened I burst though the blanks of the men to the only thing that mattered and swept my daughter off the horse and into my arms. The men were laughing.

"What are you doing here?" I said. "Where's Mommy?"

"The young lady has bought a horse" said one of the men.

My daughter kissed me and said something about her birthday and in my swimming head drowned in horse piss and laundry blue, another woman's body and my own tears, I thought, "I have to get us out of here, I must get us home." I took her hand and we walked slowly away, me as cautious as a cat but unfollowed. One of the men shouted, "We will bring him tomorrow."

And I didn't care because they didn't know me or where we lived and the fair would move on and my daughter would forget and I would forget.

My wife was watching late night TV.

She said "Do you know what time it is?"

My daughter and I, hand in hand, looked at each other and each sheltered secrets the other half shared but could not betray.

The nights are short at this time of year; a reluctant darkness and a terrace of stars near enough to walk upon, as the gods used to do, before the light rinses the sky.

At dawn, around four o'clock, I was dozing, still dressed on the green lawn, my wife and daughter sound asleep upstairs, when I heard a clip clopping coming down the road in front of the house. Shiny noise of shod horse. I thought the hooves were going through my heart. I jumped up and took a short cut through the tool shed round to the front garden.

"Don't wake up please don't wake up," I prayed to the motionless windows.

The sky was turning laundry blue and the copper sun through it. She was standing quite still, smiling at me, holding the horse by its halter. A bright Bay the colour of her. I thought "I could leave now and not come back. Grow a pony tail and wear a cowhide coat," and my mind bucked into hers with the force of the morning unworn by any but ourselves. There was a noise behind me and my daughter came up beside me in her old dressing gown. She put her hand in mine just as the horse braced its forelegs and serenely shot its piss onto the clipped verge.

The gypsy woman named her sum, an amount as extravagant as unaffordable, and I shooed my daughter back inside with me while I fetched the cash. I had drawn it out on Friday as down payment on my wife's new car. The woman had tethered the horse to the fence post, and I on one side, she on the other, exchanged the money. I noticed she was wearing my watch. Then, as she counted the last notes and I withdrew my hand, she took it swiftly, put it on her breast where her heart beat and kissed me.

My own heart stopped as she turned and walked away up the empty road.

Tobias Wolff

The Night in Question

(UNITED STATES)

Frances had come to her brother's apartment to hold his hand over a disappointment in love, but Frank ate his way through half the cherry pie she'd brought him and barely mentioned the woman. He was in an exalted state over a sermon he'd heard that afternoon. Dr. Violet had outdone himself, Frank said. This was his best; this was the gold standard. Frank wanted to repeat it to Frances, the way he used to act out movie scenes for her when they were young.

"Gotta run, Franky."

"It's not that long," Frank said. "Five minutes. Ten—at the outside."

Three years earlier he had driven Frances' car into a highway abutment and almost died, then almost died again, in detox, of a *grand mal* seizure. Now he wanted to preach sermons at her. She supposed she was grateful. She said she'd give him ten minutes.

It was a muggy night, but as always Frank wore a long-sleeved shirt to hide the weird tattoos he woke up with one morning when he was stationed in Manila. The shirt was white, starched and crisply ironed. The tie he'd worn to church was still cinched up hard under his prominent Adam's apple. A big man in a small room, he paced in front of the couch as he gathered himself to speak. He favored his left leg, whose knee had been shattered in the crash; every time his right foot came down, the dishes clinked in the cupboards.

"Okay, here goes," he said. "I'll have to fill in here and there, but I've got most of it." He continued to walk, slowly, deliberately, hands behind his back, head bent at an angle that suggested meditation. "My dear friends," he said, "you may have read in the paper not long ago of a man of our state, a parent like many of yourselves here today . . . but a parent with a terrible choice to make. His name is Mike Bolling. He's a railroad man, Mike, a switchman, been with the railroad ever since he finished high school, same as his father and grandfather before him. He and Janice've been married ten years now. They were hoping for a whole houseful of kids, but the Lord decided to give them one instead, a very special one. That was nine years ago. Benny, they named him—after Janice's father. He died when she was just a youngster, but she remembered his big lopsided grin and the way he threw back his head when he laughed, and she was hoping some of her dad's spirit would rub off on his name. Well, it turned out she got all the spirit she could handle, and then some.

"Benny. He came out in high gear and never shifted down. Mike liked to say you could run a train off him, the energy he had. Good student, natural athlete, but his big thing was mechanics. One of those boys, you put him in the same room with a clock and he's got it in pieces before you can turn around. By the time he was in second grade he could put the clocks back together, not to mention the vacuum cleaner and the TV and the engine of Mike's old lawn mower."

This didn't sound like Frank. Frank was plain in his speech, neither formal nor folksy, so spare and sometimes harsh that his jokes sounded like challenges, or insults. Frances was about the only one who got them. This tone was putting her on edge. Something terrible was going to happen in the story, something Frances would regret having heard. She knew that. But she didn't stop him. Frank was her little brother, and she would deny him nothing.

When Frank was still a baby, not even walking yet, Frank Senior, their father, had set out to teach his son the meaning of the word no. At dinner he'd dangle his wristwatch before Frank's eyes, then say *no!* and jerk it back just as Frank grabbed for it. When Frank persisted, Frank Senior would slap his hand until he was howling with fury and desire. This happened night after night. Frank would not take the lesson to heart; as soon as the watch was offered, he snatched at it. Frances followed her mother's example and said nothing. She was eight years old, and while she feared her father's attention she also missed it, and resented Frank's obstinacy and the disturbance it caused. Why couldn't he learn? Then her father slapped Frank's face. This was on New Year's Eve. Frances still remembered the stupid tasseled hats they were all wearing when her father slapped her baby brother. In the void of time after the slap there was no sound but the long rush of air into Frank's lungs as, red-faced, twisting in his chair, he gathered himself to scream. Frank Senior lowered his head. Frances saw that he'd surprised himself and was afraid of what would follow. She looked at her mother, whose eyes were closed. In later years Frances tried to think of a moment when their lives might have turned by even a degree, turned and gone some other way, and she always came back to this instant when her father knew the wrong he had done, was shaken and open to rebuke. What might have happened if her mother had come flying out of her chair and stood over him and told him to stop, now and forever? Or if she had only *looked* at him, confirming his shame? But her eyes were closed, and stayed closed until Frank blasted them with his despair and Frank Senior left the room. As Frances knew even then, her mother could not allow herself to see what she had no strength to oppose. Her heart was bad. Three years later she reached for a bottle of ammonia, said "Oh," sat down on the floor and died.

Frances did oppose her father. In defiance of his orders, she brought food to Frank's room when he was banished, stood up for him and told him he was right to stand up for himself. Frank Senior had decided that his son needed to be broken, and Frank would not break. He went after everything his father said no to, with Frances egging him on and mothering him when he got caught. In time their father ceased to give reasons for his displeasure. As his silence grew heavier, so did his hand. One night Frances grabbed her father's belt as he started after Frank, and when he flung her aside Frank head-rammed him in the stomach. Frances jumped on her father's back and the three of them crashed around the room. When it was over Frances was flat on the floor with a split lip and a ringing sound in her ears, laughing like a madwoman. Frank was crying. That was the first time.

Frank Senior said no to his son in everything, and Frances would say no to him in nothing. Frank was aware of her reluctance and learned to exploit it, most shamelessly in the months before his accident. He'd invaded her home, caused her trouble at work, nearly destroyed her marriage. To this day her husband had not forgiven Frances for what he called her complicity in that nightmare. But her husband had never been thrown across a room, or kicked, or slammed headfirst into a door. No one had ever spoken to him as her father had spoken to Frank. He did not understand what it was to be helpless and alone. No one should be alone in this world. Everyone should have someone who kept faith, no matter what, all the way.

"On the night in question," Frank said, "Mike's foreman called up and asked him to take another fellow's shift at the drawbridge station where he'd been working. A Monday night it was, mid-January, bitter cold. Janice was at a PTA meeting when Mike got the call, so he had no choice but to bring Benny along with him. It was against the rules, strictly speaking, but he needed the overtime and he'd done it before, more than once. Nobody ever said anything. Benny always behaved himself, and it was a good chance for him and Mike to buddy up, batch it a little. They'd talk and kid around, heat up some franks, then Mike would set Benny up with a sleeping bag and air mattress. A regular adventure.

"A bitter night, like I said. There was a furnace at the station, but it wasn't working. The guy Mike relieved had on his parka and a pair of mittens. Mike ribbed him about it, but pretty soon he and Benny put their own hats and gloves back on. Mike brewed up some hot chocolate, and they played gin rummy, or tried to—it's not that easy with gloves on. But they weren't thinking about winning or losing. It was good enough just being together, the two of them, with the cold wind blowing up against the windows. Father and son: what could be better than that? Then Mike had to raise the bridge for a couple of boats, and things got pretty tense because one of them steered too close to the bank and almost ran aground. The skipper had to reverse engines and go back downriver and take another turn at it. The whole business went on a lot longer than it should have, and by the time the second boat got clear Mike was running way behind schedule and under pressure to get the bridge down for the express train out of Portland. That was when he noticed Benny was missing."

Frank stopped by the window and looked out in an unseeing way. He seemed to be contemplating whether to go on. But then he turned away from the window and started in again, and Frances understood that this little moment of reflection was just another part of the sermon.

"Mike calls Benny's name. No answer. He calls him again, and he doesn't spare the volume. You have to understand the position Mike is in. He has to get the bridge down for that train and he's got just about enough time to do it. He doesn't know where Benny is, but he has a pretty good idea. Just where he isn't supposed to be. Down below, in the engine room.

"The engine room. The mill, as Mike and the other operators call it. You can imagine the kind of power that's needed to raise and lower a drawbridge, aside from the engine itself—all the winches and levers, pulleys and axles and wheels and so on. Massive machinery. Gigantic screws turning everywhere, gears with teeth like file cabinets. They've got catwalks and little crawlways through the works for the mechanics, but nobody goes down there unless they know what they're doing. You have to know what you're doing. You have to know exactly where to put your feet, and you've got to keep your hands in close and wear all the right clothes. And even if you know what you're doing, you never go down there when the bridge is being moved. Never. There's just too much going on, too many ways of getting snagged and pulled into the works. Mike has told Benny a hundred times, stay out of the mill. That's the iron rule when Benny comes out to the station. But Mike made the mistake of taking him down for a quick look one day when the engine was being serviced, and he saw how Benny lit up at the sight of all that steel, all that machinery. Benny was just dying to get his hands on those wheels and gears, see how everything fit together. Mike could feel it pulling at Benny like a big magnet. He always kept a close eye on him after that, until this one night, when he got distracted. And now Benny's down in there. Mike knows it as sure as he knows his own name."

Frances said, "I don't want to hear this story."

Frank gave no sign that he'd heard her. She was going to say something else, but made a sour face and let him go on.

"To get to the engine room, Mike would have to go through the passageway to the back of the station and either wait for the elevator or climb down the emergency ladder. He doesn't have time to do the one or the other. He doesn't have time for anything but lowering the bridge, and just barely enough time for that. He's got to get that bridge down now or the train is going into the river with everyone on board. This is the position he's in; this is the choice he has to make. His son, his Benjamin, or the people on that train.

"Now, let's take a minute to think about the people on that train. Mike's never met any of them, but he's lived long enough to know what they're like. They're like the rest of us. There are some who know the Lord, and love their neighbors, and live in the light. And there are the others. On this train are men who whisper over cunning papers and take from the widow even her mean portion. On this train is the man whose factories kill and maim his workers. There are thieves on this train, and liars, and hypocrites. There is the man whose wife is not enough for him, who cannot be happy until he possesses every woman who walks the earth. There is the false witness. There is the bribe-taker. There is the woman who abandons her husband and children for her own pleasure. There is the seller of spoiled goods, the coward, and the usurer, and there is the man who lives for his drug, who will do anything for that false promise—steal from those who give him work, from his friends, his family, yes, even from his own family, scheming for their pity, borrowing in bad faith, breaking into their very homes. All these are on the train, awake and hungry as wolves, and also on the train are the sleepers, the sleepers with open eyes who sleepwalk through their days, neither doing evil nor resisting it, like soldiers who lie down as if dead and will not join the battle, not for their cities and homes, not even for their wives and children. For such people, how can Mike give up his son, his Benjamin, who is guilty of nothing?

"He can't. Of course he can't, not on his own. But Mike isn't on his own. He knows what we all know, even when we try to forget it: we are never alone, ever. We are in our Father's presence in the light of day and in the dark of night, even in that darkness where we run from Him, hiding our faces like fearful children. He will not leave us. No. He will never leave us alone. Though we lock every window and bar every door, still He will enter. Though we empty our hearts and turn them to stone, yet shall He make His home there.

"He will not leave us alone. He is with all of you, as He is with me. He is with Mike, and also with the bribe-taker on the train, and the woman who needs her friend's husband, and the man who needs a drink. He knows their needs better than they do. He knows that what they truly need is Him, and though they flee His voice He never stops telling them that He is there. And at this moment, when Mike has nowhere to hide and nothing left to tell himself, then he can hear, and he knows that he is not alone, and he knows what it is that he must do. It has been done before, even by Him who speaks, the Father of All, who gave His own son, His beloved, that others might be saved."

"No!" Frances said.

Frank stopped and looked at Frances as if he couldn't remember who she was.

"That's it," she said. "That's my quota of holiness for the year."

"But there's more."

"I know, I can see it coming. The guy kills his kid, right? I have to tell you, Frank, that's a crummy story. What're we supposed to get from a story like that—we should kill our own kid to save some stranger?"

"There's more to it than that."

"Okay, then, make it a trainload of strangers, make it *ten* trainloads of strangers. I should do this because the so-called Father of All did it? Is that the point? How do people think up stuff like this, anyway? It's an awful story."

"It's true."

"*True?* Franky. Please, you're not a moron."

"Dr. Violet knows a man who was on that train."

"I'll just bet he does. Let me guess." Frances screwed her eyes shut, then popped them open. "The drug addict! Yes, and he reformed afterward and worked with street kids in Brazil and showed everybody that Mike's sacrifice was not in vain. Is that how it goes?"

"You're missing the point, Frances. It isn't about that. Let me finish."

"No. It's a terrible story, Frank. People don't act like that. I sure as hell wouldn't."

"You haven't been asked. He doesn't ask us to do what we can't do."

"I don't care what He asks. Where'd you learn to talk like that, anyway? You don't even sound like yourself."

"I had to change. I had to change the way I thought about things. Maybe I sound a little different too."

"Yeah, well you sounded better when you were drunk."

Frank seemed about to say something, but didn't. He backed up a step and lowered himself into a hideous plaid La-Z-Boy left behind by the previous tenant. It was stuck in the upright position.

"I don't care if the Almighty poked a gun in my ear, I would never do that," Frances said. "Not in a million years. Neither would you. Honest, now, little brother, would you grind me up if I was the one down in the mill, would you push the Francesburger button?"

"It isn't a choice I have to make."

"Yeah, yeah, I know. But say you did."

"I don't. He doesn't hold guns to our heads."

"Oh, really? What about hell, huh? What do you call that? But so what. Screw hell, I don't care about hell. Do I get crunched or not?"

"Don't put me to the test, Frances. It's not your place."

"I'm down in the mill, Frank. I'm stuck in the gears and here comes the train with Mother Teresa and five hundred sinners on board, *whoo whoo, whoo whoo.* Who, Frank, who? Who's it going to be?"

Frances wanted to laugh. Glumly erect in the chair, hands gripping the armrests, Frank looked like he was about to take off into a hurricane. But she kept that little reflection to herself. Frank was thinking, and she had to let him. She knew what his answer would be—in the end there could be no other answer—but he couldn't just say *she's my sister* and let it go at that. No, he'd have to noodle up some righteous, high-sounding reasons for choosing her. And maybe he wouldn't, at first, maybe he'd chicken out and come up with the Bible-school answer. Frances was ready for that, she was up for a fight; she could bring him around. Frances didn't mind a fight, and she especially didn't mind fighting for her brother. For her brother she'd fought neighborhood punks, snotty teachers and unappreciative coaches, loan sharks, landlords, bouncers. From the time she was a scabby-kneed girl she'd taken on her own father, and if push came to shove she'd take on the Father of All, that incomprehensible bully. She was ready. It would be like old times, the two of them waiting in her room upstairs while Frank Senior worked himself into a rage below, muttering, slamming doors, stinking up the house with the cigars he puffed when he was on a tear. She remembered it all—the tremor in her legs, the hammering pulse in her neck as the smell of smoke grew stronger. She could still taste that smoke and hear her father's steps on the stairs, Frank panting beside her, moving closer, his voice whispering her name and her own voice answering as fear gave way to ferocity and unaccountable joy, *It's okay, Franky. I'm here.*

Can Xue

The Child Who Raised Poisonous Snakes

(CHINA)

Sha-yuan—one might call him Sandy Plain—was a child with an ordinary face, lacking any notable features. When he was not talking, his face was a dead blank. But of course this is somewhat different from being a corpse.

"He has been a well-behaved child," his mother explained to me. "The only trouble with him is that he should never be allowed outdoors. There wouldn't have been any trouble if he had stayed at home. We discovered his problem when he was only six. Once he sneaked away without the notice of his father and me. I looked for him everywhere. Finally we found him sleeping among the rosebushes in the park. He was lying on his back, with his limbs stretched out in a casual way. He told us later that he had not seen any roses, but many snake heads. He said he could even see the bones inside the snakes. Then, as one snake bit him, he had fallen asleep. To tell the truth, Sha-yuan hadn't seen a single snake in his life up to that point. He only saw snakes on TV. His father and I were terrified, and we were more cautious than ever not to let him out."

While we were talking, Sha-yuan was sitting in the room facing a cupboard door covered with paper resembling wood grain, absolutely still and motionless. In my astonishment, I kept peering at him.

"Don't pay any attention to him. He long ago acquired the ability not to listen whenever he doesn't want to. Once a doctor suggested that we take the child to a resort and let him socialize with other people. According to the doctor, this would improve his condition. So we went to the seashore. Sha-yuan often played with the kind of unruly children one finds at the seaside during the day. But he felt tired very easily. We had been observing him because we couldn't help feeling anxious about the child. Whenever he felt tired, he simply lay down no matter where and fell asleep. He became so languid that he could sleep while washing his feet in the evening. We thought he was washing, but it was no more than a mechanical movement—his brain was at rest.

"The third day after our arrival at the seaside, a fisherman's son ran in with a bleeding finger, telling us that Sha-yuan had bitten him. We questioned Sha-yuan afterward about the incident. He smiled absentmindedly and claimed that the finger was the head of a snake. If he had not bitten it, it would have bitten him. We stayed at the shore for a month. Apparently the beautiful scenery had no positive influence on Sha-yuan. That year he turned nine.

"After that, we traveled somewhere every year—to the desert or the lakes, to the forest or the plains. But Sha-yuan was completely indifferent. Sitting in the train, he behaved exactly as he did at home, never looking out the window, never talking to anybody. It was possible that he did not even know he was traveling. But his father and I knew that the child had been too carefree ever since he was young. He never paid attention to his surroundings. He might have been a little cold. I don't know how to put it, but he lacked sensitivity toward new things.

"It culminated last year when we discovered that his right arm was covered with wounds. Questioning him closely, we were led to a pitch-dark air-raid shelter where he squatted down with a flashlight. We found a box of little flowery snakes. His father asked him with horror where those snakes had come from. Sha-yuan replied: 'I caught them one after another.' This was very odd because he had been with us every day. Hadn't we watched him with care? 'I was not always with you. Don't be fooled by superficial appearances,' he said in his casual tone. After his father coaxed him away, I found a hoe and exterminated those little vipers.

"When we got home, we stayed up nights to prevent his sneaking away again. Yet after two days, fresh wounds had appeared on his arms—like pairs of red spots from snakebites. He said to us, 'Why bother to tire yourselves out. You simply can't understand that I'm only sitting with you in appearance. But there's no place I can't go even while I seem to be sitting with you. There are so many snakes, and they lose their way often. So I gather them from here and there, so they won't feel lonely. Of course you can't see them, but yesterday I found one over there under the bookshelf. I can always find snakes if I look around. I was afraid of them when I was young. I even bit a snake's head once. I can't help laughing at myself when I think of it now.' He kept talking to us like this."

One day, while sitting with his back to us, Sha-yuan suddenly patted his head with his hand. We walked over, and Sha-yuan's mother turned him around so he was facing us. His facial expression was calm and relaxed. Cautiously choosing my words, I asked him what he was thinking about while sitting here, and if he was feeling lonely.

"Listen," he replied briefly.

"What do you hear?"

"Nothing, very quiet. But the situation will change completely after nine o'clock in the evening."

"How can you possibly dare to desert us like that? How can we live without you?" Sha-yuan's mother started her lament.

"You can't call it desertion," Sha-yuan said gently. "I was born to catch snakes."

I advised Sha-yuan's mother not to worry too much about her son. In my opinion, her boy, odd as he was, appeared to be a genius, who might one day turn out to be somebody.

"We don't care if he will be somebody," the mother said. "Both his father and I are only ordinary people. How is it that we should have a son who is involved in such shameful business? Raising poisonous snakes, that's frightening. What does he want to do? I might as well have given birth to a poisonous snake! We simply can't stop worrying about him. We're completely worn out by him. The worst thing is that now he can do strange things even without going outdoors. He always has a way to achieve what he wants."

One day I saw Sha-yuan's mother coming out of the air-raid shelter with a hoe in her hand. She looked wan and sallow. She told me she had just exterminated another nest of little snakes, eight altogether. She was almost bald, and she walked like an aged woman. Behind her appeared Sha-yuan's father, an old man who couldn't stop blinking one eye. Finally Sha-yuan himself emerged. His back was bent, and he appeared calm. When he saw me, he nodded and started talking: "I created this scene of slaughter on purpose. It might even be described as spectacular—eight lives destroyed once and for all. To them, it was not a matter of any particular terror. I was only surprised by the firmness and confidence of the hands that raised the hoe."

When asked if he was the one who took his parents to the shelter, he said yes. As soon as they asked, he took them there. He had always maintained a kind of curiosity about his parents' behavior. While he was talking, his mother stared at the sky with her empty eyes, and his father mumbled repeatedly: "Extreme views can cause tremendous difficulty in a person's life, but beautiful scenery can open one's mind."

I found that the slaughterer, the mother, was the most crestfallen among the three, but Sha-yuan remained detached. All at once it dawned on me that there existed a subtle relationship among these three, a peculiar mutual check. What had just happened was a proof. He didn't have to take his parents to the shelter; instead, he could have led them somewhere else. Was this only the result of his easygoing personality?

Then I recalled Sha-yuan's infancy. No doubt, he had been an extraordinarily sensitive baby, with extremely rich facial expressions. The mother had been very proud of him, yet she was nervous. She told me privately that she found the child got tired very easily, particularly when others were talking. As soon as a person started talking to him, he would lower his eyelids and fall into a sound sleep. "He's just like one of those sensitive mimosa plants whose leaves fold up when you touch them, though he's not as shy." Sha-yuan kept his habit until he was five. Then he learned to control himself, though purely for the sake of courtesy. When others talked to him a little bit too long, he would start yawning, then doze off without any consideration for the speaker.

At that time, he did not hate traveling. On the contrary, he appeared to like it somewhat, because he did not need to listen to others while traveling. While his parents were enjoying the beauty of nature, he would sit down to the side and listen attentively to any smallest sound made by little animals. He could always point out accurately where a field vole had just dug a hole, or in which direction a banded krait was advancing quietly. It was possible he had been training his unique listening ability ever since he was born. It seems, however, that this talent has never been tuned to the human voice. After several years' practice, he could make certain movements just by activating his mental will. On the surface, he was a soft and obedient kid. Such a child very easily makes people lose their vigilance. The fisherman's child was bitten under such circumstances. Now Sha-yuan's parents were getting hurt. It was a profound puzzle how he considered the people and objects surrounding him. On the one hand, he seemed to pity those little snakes, but on the other hand, he instigated his parents to slaughter them. Nobody can figure out such contradictory actions. I can't say that beautiful scenery did not affect him. It may have been the beautiful scenery that cultivated his temperament. After all, different people can appreciate scenery very differently. By the same token, his parents' painstaking efforts to control the child could only lead to the opposite result.

Then suddenly there came a day when Sha-yuan stopped meditating facing the wall, and his attitude toward his parents also turned warmer. Whenever I went for a visit, I always saw the threesome living in harmony. The smile had returned to his mother's face. In the past decade or so, the old lady had been completely tied down by her son. But now, even the wrinkles on her face had smoothed out. She said to me happily, "My child Sha-yuan is getting sensible. Just think how many poisonous snakes I have killed for his sake!" As she was talking, Sha-yuan in the background was nodding his head in agreement.

I did not believe the matter was as simple as that. I felt vaguely the falseness in Sha-yuan's smile. Though he was no longer raising poisonous snakes, who could guess what new trick he might be up to? I decided to talk to him seriously.

"Now I don't need a place to raise snakes," Sha-yuan answered. "They are in my belly. They don't stay inside all the time, of course. They come out whenever I want them to. The little flowery snake is my favorite."

Staring at his body, which was getting thinner daily, I asked if his mother knew about all of this. But Sha-yuan said that it was not necessary to let her know. Since the little snakes did not really occupy space, the matter need not be considered to exist so long as he did not mention it. Just let everybody be happy. My next question was whether this would affect his health.

He gave me an attentive look, then he suddenly appeared sleepy. Yawning hard, he said, "Who doesn't have something like that in his belly? They just don't know, that's all. That's why they're healthy. I'm always sleepy. You've talked so much. I rarely talk so much. You're weird."

Despite my efforts to ask for more, he dropped his head down and fell into a sound sleep while standing by the table.

Sha-yuan's mother got really excited, and she looked much younger now. While packing, she said, "It seems that travel is necessary." Sha-yuan joined her with joy in packing. But after a while, he turned aside and started vomiting. "Nothing serious." He wiped his pale lips and muttered almost secretly, "It was some mischief from the little flowery snake."

Quickly they started their journey on a northwest-bound train. It was a windy day.

They did not come back until two years later. The three looked the same as they had been, harmonious and peaceful. Nothing unusual could be detected. Sha-yuan obviously had gained some weight, and his face looked healthier than before. When I asked him quietly about the snakes, he said they were still in his belly. But he had learned how to adjust, so that even running and doing the high jump would not cause him any harm. Sometimes, having snakes in his belly was even beneficial to his health. I asked him what benefit it could bring to the body, and Sha-yuan's yawns started again. He complained that it was painful to listen to others. Sha-yuan's mother invited me for dinner. While eating, the old lady, who used to grumble, was now silent. She did not appear as confident as before. Sha-yuan's father only said one sentence: "No more travel." Then everybody was quiet.

After that they kept their front gate open. The parents stopped watching Sha-yuan's behavior as if they had lost interest and become oblivious. But they appeared anxious and from morning till night they checked their watches constantly. Obviously they were waiting for something. "Waiting for their deaths," Sha-yuan said. He tapped his belly, which was flat. There was no sign of anything inside. According to Sha-yuan, it had worked out fine. Nobody suspected that he raised snakes anymore. But in fact, the leopard can't change its spots.

The fall wind was whistling across the plain. It sounded musical from morning to night. This mysterious family was baffling me more and more. I remembered that the mother was only fifty, and the father, fifty-five. But just see how old they looked. Both were suffering from cardiac arteriosclerosis and their slow movements worried me. "He has destroyed us," the father said suddenly one day. His facial expression revealed his confusion. "We are dying so fast." After the remark, his face relaxed instantly. His glance lingered on the skinny shoulder of Sha-yuan. The glance was both kind and loving. The three certainly had a tacit understanding.

The parents had different explanations about the disappearance of the child. According to the father, the boy had mentioned going to the air-raid shelter after supper, because he hadn't been there for a long time, and he was curious about any new changes there. Neither of the parents had paid any attention to their son's remark. They were too tired. The son then stood up and walked toward the door with staggering steps. Recently he had become all bony. He did not return that whole night, and nobody bothered looking for him. "It's too troublesome," the father said, his eyes fixed on the windowpane.

Sha-yuan's mother never admitted that her son had walked out on her. "The child was never reliable. For more than a decade, we had both kept our eyes wide open in watching, without any obvious effect. What can I say? He could still wander around at will without our seeing him. Now I've given up. Who knows whether or not he was my child to start with, or even if he had been living with us at all? I don't think he left yesterday. I've never even been able to confirm his existence."

Listening to them, I became perplexed also. What was Sha-yuan, after all? I pondered hard, but in my mind there were only some miscellaneous fragments, some odd remarks. When I tried to concentrate, even the remarks faded away. As a result, I could not think of anything about Sha-yuan except his name.

Just when everybody believed that he had vanished, however, Sha-yuan came back. He resumed his quiet and friendly life at home. His behavior once again contributed to the indifferent attitude of his parents. They no longer cared at all if the boy existed or not. They were simply worn out.

"Where did you get the name Sha-yuan?" I asked abruptly.

"I've been wondering about it myself. Nobody ever gave him that name. Where *did* it come from?" the mother said, looking confused.

Translated from the Chinese by Ronald R. Janssen and Jian Zhang

Banana Yoshimoto

Helix

(JAPAN)

I make my living as a writer, but I had a terrible hangover that day and hadn't done a bit of work the whole afternoon. I was supposed to be working on a rush job, finishing up the captions for a volume of photographs by an artist I knew. My throbbing head, though, left me totally uninterested in her pictures of crashing ocean waves.

I'm fond of collaborating with artists whose work I like, but sometimes I get the strangest feeling, almost as if we're peeking inside each other's brains, saying, Hey, do you remember that promise we made?

But that day, I hadn't promised anyone anything, or at least I was acting as though I hadn't. I just lay there in bed, staring at the clear blue autumn sky. It looked so impossibly clear that I somehow felt betrayed.

From next door, I could hear a little girl practicing the violin, and the screeching brought tears to my eyes. The tones, as she clumsily drew her bow across the strings, spread through the blue sky filling my mind. The more wrong notes she hit, the worse she sounded, the more the sound perfectly matched the shade of brilliant blue, which I could see even with my eyes shut.

As I listened, the image of the blue sky faded into another image, that of the eyelashes of a woman friend of mine. When she was at a loss for words, she would always stammer—"Uh, you know"—while, at the same time, closing her eyes. I could then see the fringe of her jet black eyelashes below the white half-moons of her eyelids, and recognize a mix of anxiety and calm in her ever-so-slightly wrinkled brow. I had the unusual sensation of having grasped her entire personality in that single expression.

Those moments of comprehension always trouble me. I feel as if my heart will stop beating, because once I know that much about a woman, it can never work out between us. And with that particular girlfriend, I was further alarmed by the way she closed her eyes like that. She screwed them shut and searched for just the right word, and finally (in fact, it probably didn't take more than a second or two), her eyes would open up wide, and she'd be her usual lucid self again. She'd say something like "Understanding is a wonderful thing."

You can't get much more straightforward than that, I'd think, but I didn't hold it against her. In fact, I considered her simplicity a great merit, and despaired my lack of similar virtues.

She called that day and said she wanted to see me. I agreed, but privately felt a bit annoyed, because I knew she had something on her mind, and was probably planning to spill her guts to me that night.

On the phone, she said, "I'll be at our favorite spot at nine." I knew, in fact, that the place she had chosen closed at eight. She was always messing with my mind.

I called to tell her that I couldn't make it, but her answering machine pleasantly reminded me that she was nowhere to be found. I had no idea where she'd be when she wasn't at work. So I had no choice but to get out of bed and go meet her.

There was not a soul on the dark streets, save the autumn wind. I encountered this emptiness at every moonlit corner I turned. Considering how clear and brisk the air was, time had slowed down drastically, but at least the cool wind purged my mind of aimless thoughts.

When I reached the cafe, it was indeed closed, and she was nowhere to be seen. A boutique of imported goods occupied half of the shop, and then there was an area by the front window with a few tables, where you could sit and get something to drink.

I liked places like that where one thing runs into another, blurring the boundaries. Night and day; the sauce on a plate; the things they're selling in the shop right up near the cafe tables. I think that came from my love for her. She was like an evening moon, her white light almost swallowed up by the gradations of pale blue sky.

I decided to go see whether she was waiting in the entranceway by the stairs leading up to the shop, but she wasn't there either. Just then, I heard her voice, oddly muffled, calling my name, as if she were speaking from the clouds far above.

I looked up and there she stood, just inside the window of the boutique. The white chairs and tables floated up in the darkness behind her. She smiled and motioned for me to join her. I climbed the stairs and found her holding the heavy glass door open for me.

"How did you get in?" I asked.

"The manager lent me the key."

She led me inside. It felt somewhat like being in a museum, with objects on display, and our footsteps and voices echoing through the space. It seemed like a completely different place from the cafe where we always met, but it wasn't. Like ghosts of the daytime crowd, we crept in and found ourselves a table.

She went over to the counter and found some clean glasses and a bottle of apple juice in the refrigerator.

"Are you allowed to raid the refrigerator, too?" I asked.

"Sure, she told me to help myself," she answered from the other side of the counter.

"Can't we turn the lights on?" I asked, a bit uneasy in the darkness.

"Oh, no. People would think the store was open and start coming in. Then what would we do?"

"I guess you're right. So we'll just sit here in the dark."

"Oh, I like it. Don't you think it's kind of fun?" she exclaimed, setting the glasses of apple juice on a tray, just like a waitress.

"Don't you have any beer?"

"But you've got a hangover, so I thought you wouldn't want any."

"How did you know?" I asked with surprise. "I don't remember telling you."

"Yes, you did, on the message on my answering machine," she said, giggling. I felt relieved.

"It's after nine at night, for heaven's sake. I feel fine."

"Whatever you want," she said, and went over to the refrigerator to get a bottle of beer.

I could tell that something was up, though I didn't know what. She was a bit too cheerful, and the sound of her footsteps as she had walked over to get the beer sounded like someone leaving. That made me nervous.

Plus, I was having a hard time enjoying my beer in that dark room. I felt for all the world like I was having a drink at the North Pole, sparkling with ice and frigid. Maybe it was the alcohol in my body from the night before, or the dim moonscape of the cafe, but I felt a buzz before I finished the first glass.

"I wanted to tell you about this seminar I'm going to next week," she said.

"What kind of seminar?"

"One of my girlfriend's having some personal problems, and then someone told her about this seminar. It's supposed to be really radical, so she wanted me to go with her."

"Radical? What's that supposed to mean?"

"She said that they completely clear your mind. It's not one of those mental development things or meditation. They take you down to zero, so you can start all over again. They told her that most of the thoughts and memories crowding our minds are totally unnecessary. Doesn't that sound good?"

"No, it sounds awful. And besides, who decides what is necessary and what isn't?"

"I guess that's the chance you take if you go to one of these sessions. You might even end up forgetting things that seemed really important to you, things you don't want to forget."

"Like stuff you're obsessing about?"

"That, too. My girlfriend is really depressed about her divorce, and I think that's what she wants to forget. I bet she won't be able to, though."

"Don't go," I told her, insistently.

"But I can't let her go by herself She's counting on me," she said. "And, besides, I want to see what it's like. How can I tell if it's right for her if I don't go myself?"

"I don't trust those kinds of places. Who wants to forget everything anyway?"

"It's okay to get rid of your bad memories, don't you think? What's wrong with that?"

"But you can do that on your own. At least then you get to choose what you forget, right?"

She closed her eyes and searched for the right words. Then she opened her eyes and said, "Well, no matter what happens, I know that I won't forget you."

"How do you know you won't?"

"I just do. Don't get so uptight," she said with a grin. I knew full well that privately, deep inside, she was worried. I could almost hear her voice.

"I'd like to forget about the part of me who wants to forget you."

I knew that there was no more point in trying to talk her out of it. I was bummed.

"You might forget all about our relationship, for all I know," I said, grinning.

"All thousand years of it?" she asked, also with a smile. Sometimes when she'd say something like that, it seemed real. Just for an instant, but still, very true. Maybe it was the cheerful, deep sound of her voice—I could almost believe that we'd been together for a thousand years.

"Do you think I'd forget the first time we went on a trip together?"

"We were so young then. Nineteen."

"Yeah, remember how the maid at that inn said to me, 'Your wife is so young!'? I can't believe how people stick their noses into other people's business!"

"Yeah, especially since I wasn't any older than you."

"No, but you looked older. Remember how big that room was? It was so spooky. Yeah, full of dark shadows."

"But then we went out into the garden, and looked at the stars. I couldn't believe how bright they were."

"The grass smelled so fresh. That's one of the things I love about summer."

"You had your hair cut short then."

"And we put our futons right next to each other."

"Yeah."

"Then you kept telling me ghost stories, and I got too scared to go to the spa alone."

"So I went with you."

"And we made love in that mineral bath outside, near the garden."

"Right, it was like doing it in a jungle."

"The stars were gorgeous. . . . That was so much fun, wasn't it?"

"It would be like dying."

"What are you talking about?"

"If you lost your memory."

"Oh, stop being so morose."

"Maybe they do something to you like in *One Flew over the Cuckoo's Nest*."

"Like a lobotomy? Are you kidding? Of course not." She shut her eyes. "They just make you forget memories you don't need anymore."

"Like me?"

"No! But, you know, to tell you the truth, I'm not sure which ones are necessary and which aren't."

"Let's get out of here. It's too quiet. I feel like I'm at a summit conference or something."

"Yeah, doesn't the echo in here make you feel like you're saying something profound? Wait a sec. I want to check out the store."

We strolled around, glancing at the imported items on the glass display shelves. The crystal glasses, stacked one on top of another, sparkled like prisms, looking much more elegant than in broad daylight.

We went out the front door, and locked it, just as if we were leaving our own apartment. Outside, we were greeted by a gust of cold wind, and, with that, the clock started ticking once again.

"Let's have a drink somewhere before we go home."

"Good idea." I was feeling a lot happier.

"I promise that I'll be able to recover all my memories of you," she said, all of a sudden, as we were walking along. "Even if I forget them at first."

"Every single one?"

"Of course. We've done so much together, wherever I go and whatever I see, I think of you. Newborn babies; the pattern on the plate that you can see under a paper-thin slice of sashimi; fireworks in August. The moon hidden behind clouds over the ocean at night. When I'm sitting down someplace, inadvertently step on someone's toes, and have to apologize. And when someone picks up something I've dropped, and I thank him. When I see an elderly man tottering along, and wonder how much longer he has to live. Dogs and cats peeking out from alleyways. A beautiful view from a tall building. The warm blast of air you feel when you go down into a subway station. The phone ringing in the middle of the night. Even when I have crushes on other men, I always see you in the curve of their eyebrows."

"So, does that mean every single thing on earth reminds you of me?"

Once again, she closed her eyes, and then, opening them, looked directly at me, her eyes shining like glass.

"No, just everything in my heart."

"So, you mean, your love for me?" I said, somewhat surprised.

At that moment, I saw a bright flash and, a split second later, heard a loud rumble, like thunder. At first I didn't know what had happened. We looked up and saw a glow from the top of the building across the way, and then flames flared up. And there was a dull boom, accompanied by splinters of glass raining down in slow motion through the darkness.

In a matter of seconds, people, awakened from sleep by the noise, started pouring into the street from every doorway. Over the din of voices, we could hear ambulances and police cars approaching the scene, sirens wailing.

"It must have been a bomb!" I said, excited by the spectacle.

"And we were the only witnesses, don't you think? I hope no one got hurt."

"I doubt it. It's an office building, and there weren't any lights on. Besides, we were the only people on the street. I bet it was just some kids."

"I hope so. It looked really pretty, though, didn't it? This might sound silly, but it looked like fireworks to me."

"Yeah, I've never seen anything like it."

"Fantastic."

She looked up toward the sky again. I gazed at her profile, and thought about the two of us.

Your love is different from mine. What I mean is, when you close your eyes, for that moment, the center of the universe comes to reside within you. And you become a small figure within that vastness, which spreads without limit behind you, and continues to expand at tremendous speed, to engulf all of my past, even before I was born, and every word I've ever written, and each view I've seen, and all the constellations, and the darkness of outer space that surrounds the small blue ball that is earth. Then, when you open your eyes, all that disappears.

I anticipate the next time you are troubled and must close your eyes again.

The way we think may be completely different, but you and I are an ancient, archetypal couple, the original man and woman. We are the model for Adam and Eve. For all couples in love, there comes a moment when a man gazes at a woman with the very same kind of realization. It is an infinite helix, the dance of two souls resonating, like the twist of DNA, like the vast universe.

Oddly, at that moment, she looked over at me and smiled. As if in response to what I'd been thinking, she said, "That was beautiful. I'll never forget it."

Translated from the Japanese by Ann Sherif

BIOGRAPHICAL NOTES

Ama Ata Aidoo (1940, Ghana) Aidoo, who teaches at Brandeis University, has received the Commonwealth Writers Prize, Africa Division. She has written plays, poetry, two novels, and *No Sweetness Here*, a collection of short stories.

Hanan Al-Shaykh (1945, Lebanon) Al-Shaykh was raised in Beirut and educated in Cairo. When she returned home, she pursued a successful career in journalism at the daily *Al-Nahar*. She has now settled in London. *I Sweep the Sun Off Rooftops*, a collection of her stories, was published in 1998.

Julia Alvarez (1950, United States) Though she was born in New York City, Alvarez spent the first ten years of her life in the Dominican Republic, the setting for many of her stories and poems. She attended Middlebury College, where she teaches today, and Syracuse University for graduate work. Her fiction, much praised and anthologized, has been recognized by PEN with two awards for excellence.

Martin Amis (1949, England) Amis lives in London but is read widely in America and Europe. A frequent contributor to *Vanity Fair*, the *Observer*, and the *New Statesman*, he has written numerous novels, a collection of articles, and *Einstein's Monsters*, a collection of short stories.

Reinaldo Arenas (1943–1990, Cuba) Born near Holguín, Arenas studied in Havana and taught at Florida International University, Miami, and Cornell University. Because his second novel was viewed as counterrevolutionary by the Cuban government, he was sent to perform forced labor on a sugarcane plantation, where he published two more novels that were smuggled out of Havana. He escaped to the United States in 1980. His stories are collected in *The Glass Tower* and *Adiós a Mamá*.

Margaret Atwood (1939, Canada) Born in Ottawa, Atwood studied at Victoria and Radcliffe Colleges and lives now in Toronto. She is the celebrated author of over twenty-five books of fiction, poetry, and criticism. Her stories are collected in *Dancing Girls, Bluebeard's Egg, Good Bones and Simple Murders,* and *Wilderness Tips.*

Toni Cade Bambara (1939–1995, United States) Born in New York, Bambara attended Queens College and City College–CUNY, with additional study in linguistics, dance, and film. She was an unflagging civil rights activist, respected professor and story gatherer, and acclaimed author. Her first book was the short story collection *Gorilla, My Love,* followed by *The Sea Birds Are Still Alive,* also stories. In 1981 her novel *The Salt Eaters* won the American Book Award. In the mid-1980s, Bambara became deeply involved in film and documentary.

Russell Banks (1940, United States) Born in Newton, Massachusetts, Banks grew up in New Hampshire and graduated from the University of North Carolina, Chapel Hill. Having taught for nearly thirty years, Banks is now professor emeritus at Princeton University and lives and writes in the Adirondacks. His stories are collected in *Searching for Survivors, The New World, Trailerpark, Success Stories,* and the forthcoming *Just Don't Touch Anything: New and Selected Stories.*

Nicola Barker (1966, England) Barker lives in Hackney, a suburb of London. Winner of the David Higham Prize and joint winner of the Macmillan Silver Pen Award, she is the author of two novels and the collections of stories *Love Your Enemies, Heading Inland,* and *Three Button Trick.*

Julian Barnes (1946, England) Born in Leicester, Barnes was educated at Oxford and lives in London. He was first recognized for sharp television reviews and literary criticism; by the time he joined the *New Yorker* as London correspondent, his novels were getting favorable notice. A nominee for the Booker Prize, Barnes has written thirteen books, which include *Flaubert's Parrot, Letters from London,* a series of mysteries under the pseudonym Dan Kavanagh, and the short story collection *Cross Channel.*

Richard Bausch (1939, United States) Bausch, who now lives in Fauquier County, Virginia, is the author of four novels and two collections of stories, *Spirits* and *Rare and Endangered Species.* He has twice been nominated for the PEN/Faulkner Award in fiction, and won the National Magazine Award in 1988 and in 1990. His stories have appeared in *Best American Short Stories, O. Henry Prize Stories,* and *New Stories from the South.*

Ann Beattie (1947, United States) Born in Washington, D.C., and now living in Key West, Florida, and Maine, Beattie has taught at Harvard College and the University of Virginia. She has published six novels and six collections of short stories: *Distortions, Secrets and Surprises, The Burning House, Where You'll Find Me, What Was Mine,* and *Park City.*

T. Coraghessan Boyle (1948, United States) A native of New York City who now lives in Los Angeles, Boyle is a novelist and short story writer with two collections, *Descent of Man* and *Greasy Lake*. His stories appear regularly in *Esquire*, the *Paris Review*, the *Atlantic*, and elsewhere.

Robert Olen Butler (1945, United States) A novelist and short story writer, Butler teaches at McNeese State University in Lake Charles, Louisiana. He has won a Guggenheim Fellowship, the Rosenthal Foundation Award, and the 1993 Pulitzer Prize for his volume of short stories, *A Good Scent from a Strange Mountain*. In 1995 he published the collection *Tabloid Dreams*.

Peter Carey (1943, Australia) Carey lives in New York. He has won the prestigious Booker Prize, and his novel *Oscar and Lucinda* was made into a critically acclaimed film in 1995. *Collected Stories* is his first published collection.

Angela Carter (1940–1992, England) Carter taught at Sheffield University and Brown University, among others, and lived mainly in London. She won prestigious awards for her fiction, which includes nine novels and five short story collections, *The Bloody Chamber*, *Fireworks: Nine Profane Pieces*, *Saints and Strangers*, *American Ghosts and Old World Wonders*, and *Burning Your Boats*. Carter also translated and edited several collections of fairy and folk tales.

Raymond Carver (1939–1988, United States) Born in Clatskanie, Oregon, Carver was a poet and short story writer who had an enormous influence on American short fiction. His stories are collected in numerous volumes, including *Where I'm Calling From*, *Cathedral*, *What We Talk About When We Talk About Love*, and *Will You Please Be Quiet, Please?* A National Book Award nominee, Carver received the prestigious Mildred and Harold Strauss Living Award as well as numerous other grants.

Patrick Chamoiseau (1953, Martinique) Born in Fort-de-France, in the French West Indies, Chamoiseau is a leader of literary efforts to advance Creole language and culture. His significant contributions to French Caribbean literature include three novels, several memoirs and works of literary criticism, and *Creole Folktales*, a collection of short stories. His novel *Texaco* (1997) won the prestigious Prix de Goncourt.

Vikram Chandra (1961, India) Born in Delhi, Chandra divides his time between Bombay and Washington, D.C., where he teaches at George Washington University. He earned degrees from Johns Hopkins and the University of Houston, and his work has garnered such laurels as the David Higham Prize and the Commonwealth Prize. *Love and Longing in Bombay*, his first collection of stories, was published in 1997.

Sandra Cisneros (1954, United States) Born in Chicago to Mexican parents, Cisneros earned degrees from Loyola University and the University of Iowa Writer's Workshop. She's been a high school teacher and a visiting writer at many universities. Her novels, poetry, and a collection of short stories, *Woman Hollering Creek*, have received NEA fellowships and the Lannan Foundation Literary Award. She is best known for *The House on Mango Street*, a series of vignettes described as being like stories and prose poems combined. San Antonio, Texas, is her home.

Jim Crace (1946, England) Crace was born in Lemsford, Hertfordshire, and now lives in Birmingham, England. He graduated with honors from the Birmingham College of Commerce and soon after worked in Khartoum as a producer for Sudanese educational television, then in Botswana as an English teacher. For two decades Crace was a journalist and scriptwriter for the BBC. His collection of stories, *Continent*, won the David Higham Award. Other laurels include the Whitbread First Novel Award and the *Guardian* Fiction Prize.

Edwidge Danticat (1969, Haiti) Danticat came to the United States at age twelve and was published in English two years later. She holds degrees from Barnard College and Brown University and lives in Brooklyn, New York. After her first novel, Danticat was picked as one of *Granta*'s Best Young American Novelists. Her recent collection of short stories, *Krik? Krak!*, was nominated for the 1995 National Book Award.

Lydia Davis (1947, United States) Davis lives in upstate New York and teaches at Bard College. She is a noted translator, from the French, of works by Maurice Blanchot, Michel Foucault, Jean-Paul Sartre, and others. Davis has received fellowships for her fiction from the NEA and the Ingram Merrill Foundation, as well as a Whiting Writer's Award for Fiction. Her stories are collected in *Almost No Memory*.

Daniele del Giudice (1949, Italy) Living now in Venice, Del Giudice is the author of many novels and the much-praised *Takeoff*, which won Italy's Bagutta Prize, Flaiano International Prize, and Campiello Prize.

Junot Díaz (1968, Dominican Republic) Born in Santo Domingo, Diaz attended Rutgers University and Cornell University. *Drown* is his highly acclaimed first collection; his stories can also be found in the *New Yorker*, *Story*, and *Paris Review*. Diaz is at work in New York on his second novel.

Patricia Duncker (1951, England) A novelist and short story writer, Duncker was born in the West Indies and educated at Oxford and Cambridge. She teaches at the University of Wales and lives part of the year in France. *Hallucinating Foucault* won Britain's McKitterick Prize for the best first novel of

1996; *Monsieur Shoushana's Lemon Trees*, Duncker's collection of short stories, was published in 1998.

Duong Thu Huong (1947, Vietnam) Born in Thai Binh, Huong served for seven years in a Communist Youth Brigade during the Vietnam War, and during the 1979 war with China she was the first female combatant/reporter at the front. Huong is author of four novels and the story collection *Night Again*.

Deborah Eisenberg (1945, United States) Born in Chicago, Eisenberg now lives in New York City and is a professor in the MFA Creative Writing Program at the University of Virginia. She has received accolades including the American Academy of Arts and Letters Award in Literature, a Guggenheim Fellowship, and three O. Henry Awards. Her stories are published in *Transactions in a Foreign Currency*, *Under the 82nd Airborne*, *The Stories (So Far) of Deborah Eisenberg*, and most recently, *All Around Atlantis*.

Nathan Englander (1970, United States) Born in New York, Englander studied at the Hebrew University in Jerusalem, Binghamton University, and the Iowa Writers' Workshop; at home in Jerusalem, he is presently at work on a novel. His stories have appeared in *Story* and *American Short Fiction*. *For the Relief of Unbearable Urges* is Englander's first collection.

Victor Erofeyev (1947, Russia) Born in Moscow, with part of his childhood spent in Paris, Erofeyev studied at Moscow State University and the Institute of World Literature. Because he was expelled from the Soviet Union of Writers, Erofeyev's fiction was not published until the late 1980s. He regularly contributes from Moscow to the *Times Literary Supplement* and the *New York Review of Books*. His short story collection, *Life with Idiot*, was published in 1999.

Péter Esterházy (1950, Hungary) Trained as a mathematician, Esterházy is a prolific essayist, playwright, and fiction writer. *The Book of Hrabal* was named by the *New York Times Book Review* as one of the Notable Books of 1994. He has written a number of books, including *She Loves Me*, *A Little Hungarian Pornography*, and *The Glance of Countess Hahn-Hahn (Down the Danube)*.

Nuruddin Farah (1945, Somalia) Born in the Italian Somaliland in Baidoa, Farah grew up in Kallafo under Egyptian rule and was educated in India and London. He has been a professor and lecturer at universities throughout Europe, Africa, and the United States, writing many plays and novels that champion the oppressed in his homeland. *Sweet and Sour Milk* won the English-Speaking Union Literary Award but also created political enemies, forcing Farah into exile for nearly twenty years.

Richard Ford (1944, United States) Born in Jackson, Mississippi, Ford attended Michigan State University and taught at Princeton University for several years. Ford's novels and short stories have been heaped with literary honors, from the Rea Award for the Short Story in 1993 to the Pulitzer Prize and the PEN/Faulkner Award for Fiction in 1996, for *Independence Day*. His stories are collected in *Rock Springs* and *Women and Men: Three Stories*. He divides his time between New Orleans; Paris; Missoula, Montana; and rural Mississippi.

Eduardo Galeano (1940, Uruguay) Born in Montevideo, Galeano has long been a journalist, editor, historian, and political activist. In the 1970s he was imprisoned and forced into exile by a right-wing military coup; he did not return to Uruguay until 1984. His trilogy *Memory of Fire* won the American Book Award. Galeano has written many other books, though few have been translated into English; his collection *Ameristories* is forthcoming.

Hervé Guibert (1955–1991, France) A celebrated author and journalist for *Le Monde*, Guibert was also a photographer whose prints have been shown in Paris, New York, Buenos Aires, Berlin, and Brussels. Only a handful of the twenty books Guibert published in his short life, including *To the Friend Who Did Not Save My Life*, *The Man in the Red Hat*, *My Parents*, and *The Compassion Protocol*, have been translated into English.

Abdulrazak Gurnah (1948, Tanzania) Born in Zanzibar, Gurnah teaches literature at the University of Kent at Canterbury, England. He has written five novels, one of which, *Paradise*, was short-listed for the 1994 Booker Prize.

Barry Hannah (1942, United States) Hannah lives in Oxford, Mississippi. Lauded for his novels and short stories, he has won the William Faulkner Prize, a National Book Award nomination, and an American Book Award nomination. His collections of short stories include *Airships* and *High Lonesome*.

Peter Høeg (1957, Denmark) Having worked variously as an actor, dancer, drama teacher, and sailor, Høeg now writes full-time in Copenhagen. His first novel, translated into English after a year on Denmark's best-seller list, was *Smilla's Sense of Snow*, which was eventually turned into a celebrated film. He has written six books, including the short story collection *Tales of the Night*.

Pawel Huelle (1957, Poland) Born in Gdańsk, Huelle has worked as critic, editor, and journalist. His first novel was short-listed for England's *Independent* Foreign Fiction Award. His short story collection *Moving House* was published in 1995.

Kazuo Ishiguro (1954, England) Born in Nagasaki, Ishiguro has been a resident of Great Britain since 1960, working as a grouse beater for the Queen Mother in Scotland, and as a social worker in London. His four novels have garnered much critical recognition: *Artist of the Floating World* won the 1986 Whitbread Book of the Year Award, and *The Remains of the Day* won the

1989 Booker Prize, later becoming an award-winning Merchant Ivory feature film.

Roy Jacobsen (1954, Norway) Jacobsen has written four novels, and his stories have been collected in *Prison Life* (1982) and *Somebody Might Come* (1989), which won the Norwegian Critics' Prize.

Edward P. Jones (1950, United States) Born and raised in Washington, D.C., Jones attended Holy Cross College and the University of Virginia. His first book, *Lost in the City*, was greeted with much critical and popular acclaim, and was nominated for the National Book Award in 1992—the first time in six years that a collection of stories was so honored.

James Kelman (1946, Scotland) Born in Glasgow, where he lives to this day, Kelman is both novelist and short story writer. His many books include the short story collections *The Good Times* and *Busted Scotch*. His novel *How Late It Was, How Late* won the Booker Prize in 1994.

Hanif Kureishi (1954, England) Kureishi lives in London, where he studied philosophy at the University of London and began writing plays for the Royal Court when he was twenty-one. His numerous screenplays have received critical praise; one, *My Beautiful Launderette*, was nominated for an Academy Award. Kureishi's novels *The Buddha of Suburbia*, winner of the Whitbread Prize, and *The Black Album* have been translated into fifteen languages.

Torgny Lindgren (1938, Sweden) Born in Norsjö, Lindgren is a member of the Swedish Academy and has written two novels, *The Way of a Serpent*, winner of the National Book Award, and *Bathsheba*, winner of the French Prix Fémina Etranger. His collection *Merab's Beauty and Other Stories* was published in 1993.

Bobbie Ann Mason (1940, United States) Born in Kentucky, where she lives today, Mason has received the PEN/Hemingway Award for her fiction. She is the author of several novels and the short story collection *Midnight Magic*.

Colum McCann (1965, Ireland) Born in Dublin, McCann has worked as a journalist, teacher, rancher, and wilderness guide. He has written a novel, and his short story collection *Fishing the Sloe-Black River* (1996) won high praise and the Rooney Award for Irish Literature. He now lives part of the year in New York City.

Ian McEwan (1938, Wales) Born in Wales, McEwan lives in Oxford. His work has twice been short-listed for the Booker Prize, and his novel *A Child in Time* won the Whitbread Novel of the Year award. He has written five novels and two collections of short stories: *First Love, Last Rites*, winner of the Somerset Maugham Award, and *In Between the Sheets*.

Steven Millhauser (1943, United States) Born in New York City and raised in Connecticut, Millhauser now lives in Mamaroneck, New York. He has written seven books, including *Edwin Mullhouse: The Life and Death of an American Writer* (winner of the Prix Médicis Etranger) and *Portrait of a Romantic*. Millhauser has won the Pulitzer Prize and an Award in Literature from the American Academy and Institute of Arts and Letters. His collection *The Barnum Museum* was published in 1999.

Lorrie Moore (1957, United States) Recipient of prized fellowships from the NEA, the Guggenheim Foundation, and the Ingram Merrill Foundation, Moore has published two novels and three collections of stories, *Self-Help*, *Like Life*, and *Birds of America*. She teaches at the University of Wisconsin in Madison.

Mary Morris (1947, United States) Born in Chicago, Morris attended Tufts College and Columbia University. She has taught at Princeton, New York University, the University of California, and American University, and is now at Sarah Lawrence. Her stories are published in *Vanishing Animals*, *The Bus of Dreams*, and *The Lifeguard*.

Mohammed Mrabet (1940, Morocco) Born in Tangier of Riffian parentage, Mrabet made his first of three trips to the United States in 1960. In 1965 he met Paul Bowles, who taped and translated his legends and tales. These appear in a number of books, including *M'Hashish* and *The Boy Who Set the Fire*.

Bharati Mukherjee (1940, India) Born in Calcutta, Mukherjee lived in Canada before settling in the United States. She attended college in India and earned her doctorate from the University of Iowa. She has taught at Columbia, New York University, and Queens College, and presently teaches at Berkeley. *The Middleman and Other Stories* is her collection of short stories; Mukherjee has also published numerous novels.

Murathan Mungan (1955, Turkey) Born in Istanbul, Mungan grew up in Mardin and holds a master's degree in drama from Ankara University. Winner of the 1989 Best Author of the Year Award from the Turkish weekly *Nokta*, he has written prolifically in prose and has published thirteen books of poetry. He has also published six volumes of short stories: *The Last Istanbul*, *Battle Stories*, *Forty Rooms*, *Silent Tales*, *This Side of Legends*, and *The Djinns of Money*.

Haruki Murakami (1949, Japan) Murakami grew up in Kobe and lives in Cambridge, Massachusetts. He has published many books, including the short story collections *A Day in the Life* and *The Elephant Vanishes*, and translated works by Raymond Carver, F. Scott Fitzgerald, Truman Capote, Tim O'Brien, and Tobias Wolff into Japanese. His work has generally been characterized as disenchanted with traditional culture, but of late Murakami says, "The most important thing is to face our history."

Joyce Carol Oates (1938, United States) Born in Lockport, New York, Oates graduated from Syracuse University. Her honors include numerous O. Henry Awards, publications in *The Best American Short Stories*, the 1990 Rea Award for the Short Story, and the National Book Award. Oates is a professor at Princeton University. Her collections of stories include *Night-Side, Marriages and Infidelities, Wheel of Love, Upon the Sweeping Flood, By the North Gate, A Sentimental Education*, and *Last Days*.

Ben Okri (1959, Nigeria) Living now in London, Okri has worked as poetry editor *(West Africa)* and broadcaster with the BBC. For his writing, he has been awarded the Commonwealth Writers' Prize for Africa and the Booker Prize. Okri has written two novels and two short story collections, *Incidents at the Shrine* and *Stars of the New Curfew*.

Amos Oz (1939, Israel) Born in Jerusalem, Oz studied at the Hebrew University and received a master of arts degree from Oxford University. In 1973 he served with the Israeli tank force on the Golan Heights, and he now lives on Kibbutz Hulda, where he teaches and farms. Oz writes in Hebrew and has won several of Israel's most prestigious literary awards. His stories are collected in *The Hill of Evil Counsel* and *Where the Jackals Howl*.

Victor Pelevin (1962, Russia) Born in Moscow, Pelevin is one of a new wave of Russian writers. His work has been translated into French, Dutch, German, and Japanese, and his short story collection *The Blue Lantern* won the Little Russian Booker Prize in 1993. A second collection will be published soon.

Francine Prose (1947, United States) Prose lives in upstate New York and New York City. Her essays, reviews, and stories have appeared in *Harper's*, the *New Yorker*, and the *New York Times Book Review*. She is the author of eight novels and two collections of short stories, *Women and Children First* and *Peaceable Kingdom*.

Salman Rushdie (1947, England) A novelist and story writer, Rushdie has written ten books, including *Midnight's Children*, which was judged the "Booker of all Bookers." *East, West*, a collection of his short stories, was published in 1996.

Ken Saro-Wiwa (1941–1995, Nigeria) Before becoming a writer and a champion of the cause of his people, the Ogoni, Saro-Wiwa was a schoolteacher and businessman. He started writing for newspapers and a popular soap opera, but it was his experiences in the 1960s in Nigeria's civil war that compelled him to write the novel *Sozaboy*. For his belief that writers must play an interventionist role he was imprisoned for two years and finally hung.

Ingo Schulze (1962, Germany) Born in Dresden, Schulze studied classical philology at the University of Jena, working as a dramaturg and then as a newspaper editor in St. Petersburg. He lives in Berlin. His volume of short stories *33 Moments of Happiness: St. Petersburg Stories* won the Döblin Prize and the Willner Prize for Literature.

Graham Swift (1949, England) Born in London, Swift has written six novels, winning prestigious awards throughout Europe, including the *Guardian* Fiction Award, the Italian Premio Grinzane Cavour, and the French Prix du Meilleur Livre Etranger. His stories are collected in *Learning to Swim* (1992).

Antonio Tabucchi (1943, Italy) Born in Pisa, Tabucchi studied at the University of Pisa and now teaches at the University of Genoa. He lives in the Tuscan countryside but spends long periods in Lisbon. Though he has written six books, the short story collections *Little Misunderstandings of No Importance* and *Letter from Casablanca* are his first to be translated into English.

Ngugi wa Thiong'o (1938, Kenya) Educated at the University of Leeds in England, Thiong'o returned to Africa as an intellectual leader of the pan-African, anti-imperialist movement. He has taught at Northwestern University and is now head of the department of literature at Nairobi University, as well as an editor, playwright, novelist, and short story writer. *Secret Lives* is his collection of stories.

Tatyana Tolstaya (1951, Russia) Born in Leningrad, Tolstaya is the great-grandniece of Leo Tolstoy and the granddaughter of Alexei Tolstoy. She graduated from Leningrad University and has taught at the University of Richmond, Virginia. Her stories appear frequently in Soviet literary journals. *On the Golden Porch* is a volume of her short stories.

Rose Tremain (1943, England) Dividing her time between Norfolk and London, Tremain is a fellow of the Royal Society of Literature. Her novels have been highly praised and widely read: *Restoration* was short-listed for the Booker Prize, and *Sacred Country* won the Prix Fémina Etranger and the James Tait Black Memorial Prize. Her collection *The Colonel's Daughter* won the Dylan Thomas Short Story Award. *Evangelista's Fan* is Tremain's other story collection.

Luisa Valenzuela (1938, Argentina) Born in Buenos Aires, Valenzuela is one of Argentina's foremost writers and journalists. She is currently correspondent of *La Nacion* and an editor of *Crisis*, a magazine of literature, sociology, and politics. Her works of fiction include several volumes of short stories, *Clara: Thirteen Short Stories and a Novel*, *Strange Things Happen Here*, and *Other Weapons*.

Edmund White (1940, United States) Born in Cincinnati and now living in Paris and New York City, White, who has taught at Yale, Johns Hopkins, New

York University, Columbia, and Brown, is teaching currently at Princeton. His fiction and nonfiction have been honored in France and the United States, and his biography of Jean Genet won the National Book Critics Circle Award. *Skinned Alive* is a collection of White's short stories.

Zoë Wicomb (1948, South Africa) Born in the Cape Province, Wicomb resides in Scotland today. She taught for fifteen years and published her first book, *You Can't Get Lost in Cape Town*, in 1987.

John Edgar Wideman (1941, United States) Wideman lives in Amherst, Massachusetts. His excellence as a novelist and short story writer has been recognized with two PEN/Faulkner Awards, the Lannan Literary Fellowship for Fiction, a MacArthur Fellowship, and the Rea Award for the Short Story. He has written eight novels, and his short stories are collected in *Damballah*, *Fever*, *The Stories of John Edgar Wideman*, and *All Stories Are True*.

Joy Williams (1944, United States) Born in Chelmsford, Massachusetts, Williams studied at the University of Iowa and has taught in numerous universities. She has won some of the most prestigious literary awards: a Guggenheim Fellowship, a Straus Living Award, and the National Magazine Award for Fiction. Her work appears in several anthologies of highly regarded writing, as well as in two collections of her stories, *Taking Care* and *Escapes*.

Jeanne Wilmot (1950, United States) A former Manhattan attorney, Wilmot lives in Princeton, New Jersey. Her fiction, collected in *Dirt Angel*, has appeared in numerous magazines and has been included in O. Henry Awards compilations. She is also coauthor of *Tales from the Rain Forest: Myths and Legends from the Amazonian Indians of Brazil*, which won the Patterson Prize for Books for Young People.

Jeanette Winterson (1959, England) Born in Manchester, Winterson attended St. Catherine's College, Oxford. Her first novel, *Oranges Are Not the Only Fruit*, won the Whitbread Award, and *Sexing the Cherry* won the 1989 E. M. Forster Award. She is praised for her experimental style and provocative stories.

Tobias Wolff (1945, United States) Wolff teaches at Stanford University. In addition to being a finalist for the National Book Award, he has won the *Los Angeles Times* Book Award, the PEN/Faulkner Award, and the Rea Award for the Short Story. His stories are published in the collections *In the Garden of the North American Martyrs*, *Back in the World*, and *The Night in Question*.

Can Xue (1953, China) Honorary member of the International Writing Program at the University of Iowa, Xue lives in the People's Republic of China.

Her fiction has been published in France, Germany, Italy, Japan, China, and the United States. *Embroidered Shoes* is a collection of her short stories.

Banana Yoshimoto (1964, Japan) Yoshimoto's work is prized in her country and is well known worldwide. She has written two novels and the story collections *Lizard* and *Kitchen*. She lives in Tokyo.